Truly Madly Deeply

JENNIFER RUDY

This is a work of fiction. Names, characters, places, and incidents are either the product of the author's imagination or are used fictitiously. Any resemblance to actual persons, living or dead, events, or locales is entirely coincidental.

Copyright © 2023 by Jennifer Rudy

All rights reserved. No part of this book may be reproduced or used in any manner without written permission of the copyright owner except for the use of quotations in a book review.

First paperback edition June 2023

Cover design by Jennifer Rudy
Proofreading: Proof Corrections by Callie
Typesetting: Ines Book Formatter

ISBN 979-8-9883270-0-4 (paperback)
ISBN 979-8-9883270-1-1 (eBook)

Published by Jennifer Rudy Writing

To my Adam.

Contents

Freshman Year 1995–1996 1
    You Don't Know How It Feels 2
    Under the Bridge 26
    Bohemian Rhapsody 39
    Run-Around 55
    Losing My Religion 70
    Creep 86
    Runaway Train 112
    Tonight, Tonight 141
    Zombie 163
    The Freshmen 180

Sophomore Year 1996–1997 199
    Crash Into Me 200
    Regulate 218
    Wonderwall 243
    Don't Speak 260
    (I Can't Help) Falling in Love with You 277
    (Everything I Do) I Do It for You 305
    Truly Madly Deeply 341

Junior Year 1997–1998 361
    Crazy 362
    Wannabe 384
    All for You 405
    Killing Me Softly with His Song 437

As Long as You Love Me	461
Lightning Crashes	504
If You Could Only See	516
Closing Time	540
Senior Year 1998–1999	563
Kiss Me	564
I Love You Always Forever	583
Linger	604
Smells Like Teen Spirit	622
Iris	644
Champagne Supernova	666
How's It Going to Be	676
Foolish Games	702
Crush	722
Acknowledgments	733

FRESHMAN YEAR

1995-1996

Claire heaved a sigh as Tom Petty washed over her, blaring through the headphones attached to the Walkman in her back pocket. High school. Here she was. She wasn't sure how or when this had happened. But it had. She looked at the large building in front of her. New school. New people. New teachers. New everything. A slight butterfly escaped in the pit of her stomach at the possibilities . . . however nerve-racking this was . . . it was also a fresh start . . . new opportunities.

The harmonica seemed to play in tune to the wisps of her long brown hair dancing in the warm breeze, sticking to the deep burgundy lipstick she had put on this morning after leaving the house, knowing her father wouldn't approve. It was enough that he had let her leave with the new white crop top she had on. If she hadn't been wearing her high waisters to create barely a one-inch gap of exposed stomach, he definitely wouldn't have let her do that either. She had to admit to herself that she did feel a bit exposed and self-conscious. But this was high school. And she and Sam had vowed to try and get out of their comfort zones a little. She had made sure to bring her favorite flannel, currently tied around her waist, in the off chance she felt the need to cover up . . . a secret weapon.

She hiked up her backpack on her shoulder and stepped in time to the gentle drumming in her ears, pushing the doors open to those new opportunities. That first-day-of-school smell hit her, clean and fresh, the building having spent the whole summer being torn to its bones and put back together again. Claire looked around at the lobby that consumed the front of the school, with large glass windows letting in the early sun, upperclassmen sitting on the benches that ran along them. She couldn't help but notice how old some of them looked and how young she suddenly felt. Her eye was caught by a couple who sat straddling a bench across from each other, exchanging spit in a way that made Claire wonder whether they'd hit tonsils yet. The girl's black daisy-covered spaghetti-strapped dress layered over a white tee was being fondled by the hand of the dark-haired cutie, his other hand resting on her holey fishnet stockings. Claire felt a blush creep up her cheeks and quickly looked away, only to see what must be a duty teacher making her way to the latched couple.

She saw a sign pointing toward the gym that read Freshmen and quickly made her way through the double doors, pulling down her headphones to rest about her neck, Tom Petty silenced. She recognized many faces of students sitting in the bleachers, but only cared about one that sat halfway up waving at her excitedly. She couldn't help but smile. Sam. Her lifeline.

"Dude, where have you been?! I've been sitting here like a loser for like a half hour." Sam's voice hit Claire before she could even sit down.

"I misjudged my walk here. But I still have ten minutes to spare before the time we were given. Why are you flipping? We agreed on seven ten."

"And it's seven twenty," Sam snapped while chewing loudly on a piece of gum, her leg bouncing.

Claire knew Sam's anxiety all too well and couldn't help but smirk. "Okay. I'm sorry. I'm here now at least."

"Thank God. Okay, so while I was sitting here, I think I've already spotted three hunky boys who are from Saint Catherine's." Saint Catherine's was the Catholic school that didn't go beyond eighth grade, so all the students joined them at A. Thompson High come freshman year. Sam was quite excited for high school for the sheer reason that there would be new boys to gaze at because, besides Saint Catherine's, there was the other K–8 school that they joined with as well. Whether you were from Thompson or Thompson Falls was a big deal, and everyone took this identity very seriously. Though no outsider would ever truly be able to tell the difference, the towns being so interwoven, homegrown citizens did, and it definitely mattered. It made the joining of both schools interesting come high school, as, until that point, students were used to competing with each other from their eight years of elementary school.

"Oh my god, Sam." Claire rolled her eyes.

"What? How can you not be excited about cute Catholic boys?!" she asked, looking genuinely perplexed.

"How do you know they are even from Saint Catherine's? They could be from Thompson Elementary," Claire offered as she sifted through her bag to pull out her schedule.

"Oh, I can spot a cute innocent Catholic boy from a mile away," Sam said matter-of-factly, taking off the black beret-style hat she was wearing and nodding her head, her tight brown curls nodding along. Claire couldn't contain her smile.

"Ooh schedules! Let's compare again," said Sam, taking hers out from the front pocket of the jean overalls she was wearing. "What do we have together again?"

Claire chuckled. "Sam, we've been over this a thousand times already." They *had* too. Ever since they'd gotten their schedules in the mail, Sam had requested they look them over at least twice a week, and daily at first.

"Well, I want to make sure I know!" she said.

"Okay, okay. So today is a gold day . . . so we have period two, English together, and home ec at the end of the day."

Sam pouted. "Ugh . . . that's right. Why couldn't we have started on a blue day where we spend almost the whole day together?!"

"I know," Claire agreed. The only class they didn't share on blue days was last period when Claire had band. "But I'll see you second period, and I think we both have the same lunch, which is good," she added, looking at her schedule to double-check. "Yeah, lunch C! Plus the end of the day."

"Okay, true . . . it is *most* of the day, I suppose. I forgot about lunch," said Sam, but Claire still saw a hint of anxiety flash across her face.

"It'll be fine," she said. "Just think how much we'll have to catch up on on our walk home."

Sam smiled and let out a sigh. "You're right." She put on a determined expression and rattled off as if she were a self-help cassette: "We got this. New school, new us. Put ourselves out there. Make new friends. Meet boys. We got this."

Claire chuckled and turned her attention to the gym floor as their new principal took his place in front of the mic.

"Hello, new students of A. Thompson High!" Mr. Lewis had been a principal for nearing twenty years, and he had a great reputation among staff, students, and the community. Always fair, personable, and involved, it was nothing to see him at all the sporting events and arts programs, popping into teacher's classrooms, helping out in the cafeteria, or picking up something that spilled in the hall. Claire's older brother, who had just graduated last year, spoke very highly of him, which for Troy was saying something.

"I hope you all had wonderful summers and are ready for a fresh start as high school students. Here you will find many opportunities for you to step up and be your best selves. The staff here at ATH, myself included, is here for you. The only person standing in the way of success is you. So make a promise right now to do big things while here: absolute greatness. Let's get started on a good foot and make this year exactly that."

Claire noticed Sam nodding along with his words. He *was* quite the motivational speaker.

"Right now would typically be open campus for you, but we asked freshmen to meet here so we could get you set up with your homeroom teacher before the bell rings at seven forty. The bell to first period will also be held a little longer than usual to give your homeroom teacher time to assign your lockers, give you a little rundown, and answer any questions you may have. I promise you that the school is not very big and you will know your way around in a mere few days."

He paused to take out a piece of paper from his inside jacket pocket. "At the top of your schedules that you received this summer, your homeroom teacher should be listed. I will name them off one by one at which time they will step forward," he pointed to a row of teachers standing against the wall, "and you can come down and meet them. Once together, they will bring you to your homeroom classroom. If you do not have your schedule today, come see Mrs. Dennison, our lovely guidance counselor, and she will let you know where to go. Your homeroom teachers also have copies of your schedules if you need a new one. So, let's begin."

He began listing off teachers slowly as kids made their way down from the bleachers. Each homeroom only had about ten students in it, so in no time at all, Claire heard "Miss Phillips," and she grabbed her backpack. "See you second period, okay?"

Sam nodded, looking a little pale. "Second period!"

"Good luck," Claire said, and she descended the bleachers.

Claire joined the group of kids heading toward a petite auburn-haired teacher with large tortoise-shell glasses who was smiling brightly at them as they gathered. She wore a floral short-sleeved button-down dress that ended mid-shin and black slip-on sandals that had decent height to them. Claire wondered if Miss Phillips was trying to get all the height she could, working in a high school. Her deep red hair was long and swooped over to one side, bangs curled over her forehead, a scrunchy around her wrist. She was young and cute, and Claire already liked her.

"Okay! I think that is all of us! Follow me!" she said perkily. The group did as she said, heading out the double doors and to the right. Down a short ramp, they came to a stop outside a classroom, Miss Phillips standing ready to speak. Before she could, a bell sounded, signaling the rest of the school to head to homeroom.

"Here we are! I am the home ec teacher here, and so our homeroom is, well, in the home ec classroom! If you'll follow me in, please have a seat wherever you'd like."

Filing in, Claire was one of the first, and she took a seat at a middle table, a girl she didn't know following behind her. She watched as the rest of her homeroom trailed in, now able to better see who was in it. A few faces she recognized as kids she'd gone to school with and a few new faces, one of which was a boy Claire noted would pass the Sam cute test. He had short black hair, a jean jacket over a black T-shirt, and jeans. He looked a little tough to Claire, but his face was soft and smiling. She watched as the last few entered, and she felt herself groan.

Amber Clark walked in. And not just Amber Clark . . . but her two cronies, Lauren and Ashley, as well. How the hell had Claire ended up in a homeroom with these three? She couldn't help but roll her eyes as she watched Amber's long legs walk past her encased in thigh-high white stockings, which stopped six inches short of a plaid skirt that buttoned down the front. Tucked into it was a white V-neck short-sleeved blouse that showed off just enough to get attention. Her platinum blonde hair with all its volume was flipped to one side, framing her crimson lips and blue eyeshadow ever so perfectly. Style-wise she was the essence of cool and the muse to many a boy's dream. But Claire knew it all amounted to one thing—a bitch—and she'd been dealing with it since kindergarten.

"Okay, welcome, welcome," Miss Phillips sounded, and Claire came out of her depressed reverie. Hopefully, they wouldn't have any classes together. Homeroom was a mere fifteen minutes. She could handle this. "Before I give you a quick rundown, let's assign lockers so we can make sure we get that all squared away. Your lockers are right across from the classroom here, and though it's great they're in a quiet hall, we are also on the exact opposite end of pretty much the rest of the school, so you may find yourself wanting to travel with more than just one period's worth of stuff, unfortunately. As Mr. Lewis said, the school is not big, but planning accordingly will be key." She beamed at all of them. "Let's get to it. You will be sharing a locker with someone else. I have assigned all locker buddies, and for now, please don't ask to swap. Let's try this out! No better way to get to know someone new than to share a locker with them!"

Claire felt her stomach drop . . . Oh God . . . please don't let her locker buddy be Amber.

"When I call your names and your number, you may go find your locker, put your stuff away, grab what you need, and come right on back in here to have a seat. Okay . . . let's see. I have a Chris and Roy . . . you will be locker five six one." A boy with frosted tips got up, and Claire instantly knew this guy thought he was the shit, wearing baggy jeans, a long white T-shirt, and a sweatshirt tied around his waist that also looked like it was five times too big if he put it on. He stomped across the room with Timberland boots on, untied of course, tongues sticking out. His overall effect was that of zero care in the world. He was unfortunately followed by a boy who looked a bit terrified at the idea of sharing a locker with him.

"Heather and Jennifer . . . locker five six two," Miss Phillips went on. "Katie and Kristie . . . locker five six three. Lauren and Ashley . . . five six four." Claire allowed a maniacal laugh to play out in her head. Amber wouldn't like that her two lackeys got to share a locker together. But as Miss Phillips continued with another pair, she realized that she was getting to the end, and she and Amber were the only ones left.

"Claire and Amber . . . locker five six eight." Her voice rang in Claire's ears, and she couldn't believe her luck. Amber got up slowly from her chair, grabbed her bag, and stalked past Claire, but not before stopping to say with mock sincerity, "Well, won't this be such fun!" Claire rolled her eyes at her retreating back. Staring at the ceiling for a moment to heave a sigh, Claire dragged herself out to the hall.

Having been called last, there were students already trickling back in, and Miss Phillips stayed put at the front of the classroom, excitedly waiting for their return. Amber was taking her sweet time placing things in their shared locker. Claire watched her put some folders and notebooks on the top shelf along with some pencils. She then hung her bag on one of the hooks and took out a magnet mirror that she attached to the inside of the door. Checking herself over, she took out a tube of lipstick from the red designer clutch purse that was slung over her shoulder and began to reapply. Claire blew hair out of her face as she waited, arms crossed.

Amber finally turned just as the hall was clearing and shined an expression of fake surprise. "Oh! Are you waiting for me?" she said in her sweetest voice before dropping her tone to that of absolute disgust and blurting "Sorry" as she bumped past Claire.

Sighing under her breath, Claire quickly rushed to hang her own bag, throw a few things on the second shelf at the top, and take what she needed to start the day, trying to avoid being the last person back in class, which she failed at. Taking her seat, she saw Amber's cheap smile and glaring eyes watching her.

"Okay, great! So, just a few things to share. Again, I am Miss Phillips. This is my second year teaching, and as I said, I am the home ec teacher! I teach cooking, sewing, interior design, babysitting/parenting, and managing money all in the basic home ec course, which you all have to take! I saw a handful of names on our roster that I know I will be seeing this semester! And the rest of you I'm sure I will be seeing soon. I do teach other classes that extend on those topics, so maybe I'll get to see more of you all as well as the years go on. Those count toward your elective credits and are totally fun. I also hope you'll find being in our homeroom pretty sweet because I often make use of our kitchen in the morning and offer breakfast to anyone who wants to come to homeroom early and cook! So if you're here and want something to do, come on down!" A few people gave looks of interest and excitement.

"The bell for homeroom rings at seven forty as you heard a little bit ago, and you are considered late after seven forty-five. The bell for period one rings at eight, although today it will ring at eight ten to give you all more time, and your schedule will tell you the rest. Does anyone need a new schedule?" She paused. One student raised his hand, and she pulled out a new schedule for him before carrying on. "Excellent. You have five minutes to transition between classes, and your classes are each eighty minutes. Any questions *about* your schedules?" She paused again and was still met with silence.

"Okay great!" she plowed on. "Last bell is at two and buses leave at two ten. You do not have to report back to homeroom at all. Each of your teachers will take attendance, so be sure you are attending and not late.

Some of your teachers will be a little more lax than others. Most teachers will let it go if you're just a hair late. And when I say a hair, I mean that they see you coming down the hall as the bell rings. However, don't test it, and get to class. If you're reported late, you get a slip. Three slips is a detention. Three detentions is an in-school suspension, so best not to try and push it."

They all nodded, and she asked again, "Are there any questions? Anyone want me to look at their schedules and let them know where they're going? You may want to figure out if you have any classes that are at the opposite end of the school so you can decide how best to plan out your day." A few hands went up at this. "Perfect, I'll come around to anyone who wants me to take a peek. The rest of you can just chill and chitchat." She flashed them one last smile and then got to work helping pull apart schedules. The class was silent at first, but a dull hum of talking gradually filled the room.

Claire sat silently, praying that Amber wouldn't cause her any problems this year. Maybe part of her and Sam's agreement to make some changes for high school should entail finally sticking up to Amber, who had made many moments of Claire's life hell throughout most of their elementary school career.

Funny thing was, when Claire and Amber were younger, they had been friends. They played together all through first, second, third, and even fourth grade, had sleepovers often, and were practically inseparable. They traded Barbies and loved having Skip It competitions. They sat in awe while watching *The Little Mermaid* for the first time and both had matching sheets with Ariel and friends plastered across them. But, in fourth grade, they were separated by class, and Sam Levinski moved to Thompson Falls Elementary. Claire and Sam became instant best friends, and from the moment Claire tried to get the three of them to play on the playground, Amber wanted nothing of it. It started slowly: Amber teasing Sam while they played, giving her the ugly character in their make-believe skits, or making small borderline comments about her clothes and curly hair. For a little while, Claire didn't pick up on it, just thinking it was all in good fun.

But by fifth grade, Claire and Sam had really gotten close, and they had their first sleepover at Claire's house. When Amber found out the following Monday, she was livid, and thus began her tyranny. She made jabs at Claire's early developing body, like Claire wasn't self-conscious of that enough as it was, and her acne, which wasn't really all that bad. She gave her the label of being a nerd for her love of reading and told the entire female population in their class when Claire started her period—a day Claire still cringed at.

As Amber herself blossomed in middle school, she began wearing more mature outfits and makeup, enjoying the attention she was getting from the boys, attention Claire felt was sickening. Claire knew Amber's homelife was rotten: a dad who was a rich asshole and never home, rumors of his many affairs reaching everyone in town, and a mother whose greatest ambition was being the perfect trophy wife for the husband who spent the least amount of time with her out of anybody. In no time, the attention Amber was getting attracted others to want to be her friend in the hopes of claiming some of the spotlight too. Enter Lauren and Ashley. Amber now had support in her vindictiveness and evil, which made her words all the more hurtful, as they were now agreed upon by others.

At some point in time, Amber called Claire's beautiful curves fat, and though she hated to admit it, she'd struggled to let that go ever since. If only Claire knew that when others saw her, they saw large brown eyes that sparkled when her face broke into a genuine smile or shone with innocence when she was lost in thought, full lips enveloping a mouth of straight white teeth (thanks to an early catch by an orthodontist), and a shape that was curvy and caught the attention. Claire had grown into a body that maybe wasn't on the cover of magazines, or the objective of all the Richard Simmons workout VHS tapes her mother had secretly stashed in the living room entertainment center, but it was a body that, even without her believing, was the envy of many. The best part was that Claire's personality matched her beauty. She was a strong-minded, smart, empathetic girl with a heart of gold who valued her independent nature. She loved getting lost in a good book, often thought philosophically, and above all, absolutely, positively loved music . . . all of it. She loved feeling and journeying in ways that only music could influence. Music moved her and gave her a high no drug could reach.

Claire was the whole package, and though her ability to be social masked it, she was still self-conscious at times: self-conscious of her looks, her smarts, her overall being—most often when she was around Amber, or girls like Amber—and it was all because of Amber. And she hated that she let her get to her the way she did. Years of torment will do that to someone. And why she had never stood up to her, when for the most part Claire had no issue with being outspoken, was because part of her also felt bad for Amber: her home-life, her clear need for acceptance and attention, her hatred for Sam and Claire (which most likely stemmed from a place of fear for the loss of a friend who was making a new one, something fourth-grade Claire hadn't understood), and her overall vibe of unhappiness and dejection that she gave off when she thought no one was looking.

It wasn't easy having a soft spot for your bully . . . in fact, it was probably the worst kind of bully to have. But even then, sometimes, one can only take so much, and Claire had been determined when she had agreed with Sam to change it up this year. She was ready to let herself go and shine. Find confidence. Find herself. She was ready, and if that meant releasing herself of Amber and her ridicule, then so be it.

Claire's fast-moving thoughts were rent by the sound of the bell for first period. She jumped at the sound, having lost herself. Getting up, she heard

Miss Phillips wish them all luck, and as she moved forward, she collided with the short-haired boy she'd noted on their arrival.

"Oh my god, I'm so sorry," Claire said.

"No problem at all," he responded. He held out a hand. "Mark Calloway."

Claire took it, a little surprised at being offered a hand. "Claire Hanover." He shook it firmly, and Claire connected it with his haircut and wondered if he was the son of military.

"I'll see you around," he said, and he left with the frosted-tipped Timberland boy, Chris, but not before he threw a smile her way when he looked back on his way out the door. Claire returned it, and though she didn't feel overly excited by it, she knew this would be front-page news to Sam.

Walking into geometry, Claire quickly made her way to a desk at the back of the room. Five rows of five table-and-chair connected desks lined the room, a few students already sitting in some, talking and catching up. Claire knew she would be in the class with mostly sophomores and other upperclassmen, but now that she was here, she was a little more nervous than she thought she'd be. She knew absolutely no one and was beginning to imagine having to work in partners or groups when more kids filtered in just as the bell rang, the teacher closely following, closing the door behind himself.

Claire watched as students made their way to their seats, trying to figure them out in the brief moments before the teacher spoke, doing exactly what she knew she shouldn't, making judgments instantly. A girl right up front was taking out her notebook and straightening her other items, settling in to watch the teacher. Claire assumed her to be the scholarly kind, maybe a teacher's pet. Another girl sat at the far end by the windows, books closed on her desk, facing sideways while filing her nails, noticeably chewing gum. Bitch. Others didn't stick out as much more than the average student. She did, however, notice one guy in the corner back-row seat who was sitting quietly with a notebook out but leaned back in his chair with arms crossed. Claire couldn't help but notice his chocolate-brown hair parted down the center, which he happened to run his hands through while she looked on. She wanted to observe more, but the teacher began talking.

"Hello all, welcome to geometry. I'm Mr. Stevenson, and this year we will be . . ." he droned on, not even once doing introductions, and Claire got the impression this was going to be one of those full lecture, take notes, and leave kind of classes . . . at least no partner or group work most likely.

Next was English with Sam and Claire's newly acquainted homeroom buddy, Mark. They sat at a table together, and class passed in introductions of everyone, a breakdown of the class, and the first book assignment, *Romeo and Juliet*. Study hall passed silently. Well, mostly silent. There was a small group of girls in the back who looked to be juniors or seniors who spent the whole time gabbing quietly. The study hall teacher, whose name was Mr. Jones, didn't seem to care what they did as long as he got to do his own work. One guy was sleeping, his Discman on his desk, headphones snug around his ear. Claire thought she could hear hip-hop beats but couldn't make out any more than that. She wondered how one could sleep to it.

Finally, it was home ec time. It being her homeroom, she was quite excited, as it was near her locker and would make for an easy escape on gold days. It was at the other end of the school from her study hall, and though A. Thompson High wasn't huge, as they had been told multiple times this morning, she was still one of the last to arrive at the room. She hurried in and instantly saw the excited wave of Sam directing her to the open seat next to her that she had clearly been saving. To her disdain, her lovely "friend" Amber was in this class along with her cronies, and they seemed to have taken over the table with Mark and his friend Chris. She was pleased to see Mark smile at her and give her a wave.

"Hello! So many familiar faces in this class. Welcome, welcome." Miss Phillips was just as sweet as she had been that morning, and, as was the norm, she went around and had them each introduce themselves by giving their name and favorite meal to eat, as their first unit would be cooking. Sam gave one of her grandmother's traditional Hispanic meals, and to Claire's surprise, others gave some pretty gourmet sounding meals too. *Shit*, she thought. Claire had nothing fancy to speak of, considering her mom made the same five or so meals each week, and when it was her dad's turn, frozen mac and cheese or French toast was what was for supper.

"I'm Claire Hanover," she said at her turn, and then hesitantly, "and I guess my favorite food would be pizza." It was definitely lame compared to others, but Miss Phillips didn't seem to care.

"Can't ever go wrong with pizza," she said with a smile, and as others nodded in agreement, Claire didn't feel like a loser anymore. They didn't get into cooking but went over the syllabus and rules of the kitchen area, and when the bell rang, Claire felt she'd had a successful first day of school. But, of course, when you feel like things are going well, they inevitably change course.

"Meet me out front when you're done getting your shit so we can leave together. I just have to get my bag. Be there in a jiffy. I cannot wait to hear how your day was!" Sam said excitedly, running off.

Claire nodded, walking the very short distance to her locker, only to see that most of her stuff was on the floor in front of it. Amber was placing new books she must have gotten from class today on the second shelf, gabbing with Lauren and Ashley.

"What the hell," Claire said, standing behind Amber, who turned, looked her up and down, and grinned.

"Language, Hanover," she said. "What seems to be the problem?"

Claire gestured to the floor.

"Oh... that." She exchanged looks with the two trolls that were sneering behind crossed arms. "You see, I need both shelves for my things, and your stuff was just in the way. So sorry," she added, though she obviously wasn't.

"So what am I supposed to do?" Claire asked, glaring.

Amber shrugged. "Figure it out, but I better not find any of my stuff moved, understood?" She slammed their locker shut and stalked off, the three of them snickering.

Claire groaned under her breath, throwing the locker open, grabbing her bag, and bending down to pick up her things, slamming it once again to join Sam, who had shown up, clearly too anxious to wait outside for her.

Outside, it was warm and the sunshine felt nice on her face. A light breeze ran through, and it carried with it a hint of fall weather, which tickled Claire's heart, making her feel a bit better.

"Okay, tell me everything," Sam said in between the smacking of gum. "Like, I know how English and home ec were, but what about first and third period? Your first period was your smart-math class, right? How terrifying was it? Were they all upperclassmen? Did you have to speak to any of them? I have one upperclassman boy in my math class. I think he is a junior. Maybe he failed it. I don't know. But he is totally dreamy. His name is Nate. And did you see that cute guy in English? Chad, I think is his name. Oh. My. God. So cute. Did you have anyone good in your study hall? What did you do with no homework?"

Claire stared at her.

"Well, come on!! Speak up!" she said exasperatedly.

"Oh, it's my turn to talk now?" Claire joked, elbowing Sam.

"Okay. Okay. Lips are zipped." She made the motion of zipping her lips and throwing away the key.

Claire laughed. "Well, math was fine. And it isn't a smart-math class, Sam. It is just the next class. You'll take it too. The teacher just talked the whole time, and I feel that is all he's ever going to do. So it should be easy enough . . . but probably boring. And I didn't do anything but start *Romeo and Juliet* in study hall. There wasn't anyone I knew in it, but the teacher seems pretty chill about what we do, so that should be pretty sweet. And that was about it. Nothing crazy."

Her response was followed by silence. Looking at Sam, she rolled her eyes. "You can unzip now."

Sam released a heavy breath, like she'd been holding it in the whole time, and went right back into her babble. "I can't believe you already started *Romeo and Juliet*. I am totally NOT looking forward to reading that. Who the hell understands Shakespeare anyway? I have study hall tomorrow, and hopefully it's as chill as yours. But what about boys? Any cute ones in your classes? And what are you going to do about Amber?" She asked the last question with a little more sensitivity.

"I didn't notice any cute boys per se," she said as the thought of the brown-haired boy from geometry flashed past unexpectedly. She wasn't going to share that observation. "I did think of you this morning when meeting a guy in my homeroom though. Mark. The guy in our English class who sat near us. And he was in home ec too."

"Oh, he is adorable!"

"And I actually like Shakespeare. We'll read it together, don't worry. And I have no idea." She ended with a sigh, realizing just how much the altercation with Amber bothered her. More for the injustice of it than anything, and even more so because she knew absolutely nothing had changed, and probably wouldn't. "Like, does she really think she can just kick someone out of her locker and have one to herself? Like, for real?"

"Yeah . . . total bitch," Sam responded. "What are you going to do tomorrow morning? Just put your stuff back in there?"

Claire shrugged. "Yeah, I guess so. I mean, what else can I do? Carry all my shit around with me all day?"

"Maybe you could tell your homeroom teacher? Which, by the way, you totally lucked out on. Miss Phillips is amazing and super nice. I have the old hag Mrs. Bramble—like, who the hell has the last name Bramble? She could barely see the list to do roll call and had to ask a student to read off the locker numbers. Like, seriously. Come on! Retire already."

Claire couldn't help but laugh. "Yeah, Miss Phillips is pretty cool. What does Mrs. Bramble teach?"

"Would you believe she teaches a typing class? That old crone teaches a typing class."

"Maybe she can see the screen better than paper?" Claire suggested.

"Maybe . . . so ridiculous though. Hey, tomorrow we see each other for most of the day! I'm dreading gym, but at least we have it together. Do you think we'll have Amber and her bimbos in our class? God, I hope not. I think my life would end right there on the spot . . . Not cool."

"Yeah, that would suck. Let's just hope not. I am not looking forward to—"

"WATCH IT!!!"

Claire turned just in time to see the front of a bike heading directly at them. Claire quickly pushed Sam aside and moved back herself to allow it to go between them but, in the process, lost her footing over the edge of the sidewalk and fell.

Tires sliding across gravel sounded as the bike came to a sudden halt, and Claire heard an audible "Shit!"

Before she could even begin to pick herself up, a hand appeared above her. "Are you okay?" She took it and allowed herself to be brought to her feet, quickly getting back on the sidewalk. Not that Thompson Falls was an overly busy town, but thankfully, no cars had been going by when she took the digger.

"Are you okay?" was repeated as she brushed off her hands, which had small dents in them from the roadside dirt.

"Yeah, no, totally. No biggie." She brushed her hair out of her face and looked up to see none other than the brown-haired boy from geometry. As if. She could see him much better now. He had the strangest color of eyes. Not quite hazel, almost gray . . . yes, that was it, gray eyes. His simple white T-shirt, jeans, and red flannel tied around his waist gave off the impression of cool. As did his longish, parted hair. But those gray eyes were beaming into her with concern from behind a pair of black thin-rimmed glasses that gave his edginess a slight hint of dorkiness. It was adorable and hot at the same time.

"Are you sure? I was messing with my Walkman and not paying attention. Before I knew it, you guys were in front of me."

"No. For real. Totally fine," she said, smiling. His face softened a bit and a slight awkward smirk could be seen.

"Okay. If you're sure." He brushed his hand through his hair.

"I am. Thanks for helping me up."

"Well, it's the least I could do . . . I almost wiped you guys out. And thank God there wasn't a car on the road. Again—sorry. I'm Adam by the way. Adam Miller."

"I'm Claire Hanover."

He gave a nod of acknowledgment, watching her, partially making sure she really looked okay and partially because he couldn't help but notice her mane of brown hair that was a little on the wild side and eyes of the same color, large and shining, crinkled into a sweet smile. Though he had no idea who she was, he couldn't help but see a genuineness when looking at her. She was humble and yet striking, carrying herself with an air of confidence and yet seeming shy. That smile was welcoming, and he found himself much more distracted than he had been with his Walkman.

"I'm Sam Levinski." Sam's voice broke in, and Adam and Claire looked at her, both surprised to find they had forgotten she was even there.

"Nice to meet you both," said Adam. "Well, I gotta be off. Sorry again." He paused and once more looked at Claire, who felt the faintest of blushes forming, though she wasn't sure why.

"I'll see ya." He gave a half wave as he walked backward toward his bike. Grabbing it, he put his headphones back on and took off, but not before he took a quick look back at them and waved again.

"Sorry I pushed you," Claire said to Sam.

"Are you kidding me? You saved my life!"

"I think that's a bit dramatic," said Claire, laughing a bit as she brushed her behind, and they continued to walk.

"Well, still . . . you did . . . But oh my god! What about *him*?! He is adorable!"

Claire rolled her eyes. "Is that all you think about?"

"I mean, come on! He is. You know it. I saw you look at him."

"Oh come off it! He almost killed me! I was happy to be alive."

"Oh, now who's being dramatic?"

Claire elbowed Sam. "He was actually in my geometry class this morning."

"Really?! You told me you didn't notice any cute boys! You obviously noticed that one."

"Sam, I just *noticed* the other kids in my class . . . and I did tell you I thought you'd like Mark."

"Okay, whatever. But he is cute. You have to agree to that."

Claire tried to hide her smile. "I'll give you that."

Sam squealed. "And he just rescued you from the street like Prince Charming."

This time Claire really laughed. "Are you kidding me? He *rescued* me? He's the reason I was in the road in the first place!"

"Girl, if you say so." Sam giggled.

They linked arms as they turned onto Claire's street, her two-storied, old farmhouse-style home recently painted a calm yellow was tucked away behind trees and shrubbery on the urban village street. Claire always loved that though the street was a neighborhood with houses all around, her house seemed to be in its own little world. Cornered on two roads, it had a fence that bordered the half-acre lot and was surrounded by an army of lilac trees, rose bushes, greenery, and one large willow whose branches hung down over the roof, yard, and even hit the faces of unsuspecting walkers on the sidewalk. It was almost easy to miss and was the kind of home that, unless you were looking for it, you probably did.

Walking up to the fence, Claire lifted the latch and walked in. The yard was often thrown into shade due to the overbearing trees. Everywhere you looked, you saw flower and vegetable gardens. Claire's mom made as much use of the lot as she could, and it was a maze of things growing. Claire loved it because, to look on, you'd swear it was wild. It reminded her so much of the garden of secrets that Mary Lennox found on the grounds of Archibald Craven's manor in the moor.

Sam closed the fence behind her, and they went inside to find Claire's brother, Troy, in his sweatpants, cut-off tank, and sweatband doing pull-ups in the doorway of the living room and dining room. They passed through the entryway, past him and the living room, and into the kitchen. Because it was an old home, it lacked the open concept of many modern-day houses and instead had what felt like fifteen rooms you had to travel through to get from one end of the house to the other. You practically walked into the foot of the main staircase when entering the home, but there was a second staircase that went from the kitchen at the end of the house to the upstairs room, which was Claire's.

At one time, someone had split the old home into two apartments, and when it had been converted back, they had kept the second staircase, which Claire loved, as it gave her direct access to the kitchen and all its snacks. It used to be Troy's room until he graduated high school and moved to a smaller room down the hall, giving Claire a chance to have the cool room and Troy a chance to decide that he'd rather move out. He was currently splitting shifts between the local video rental store and the music shop on Main Street right around the corner, not really having a set idea of what he wanted to do. It was a source of tension with their father, who felt Troy wasn't living up to his fullest potential. Claire kind of felt bad for him. They had a decent age gap, though nothing huge, and it had never interfered with their ability to fight or their love as siblings. Knowing Troy, Claire just felt he was a bit lost. School had been tough for him, and so it hadn't set him up with a lot of confidence. He also managed to always date the wrong girls. Troy was such a great guy but, sometimes, just a big lug.

"Hey, Mouse," he said, walking into the kitchen as Claire and Sam were taking inventory of food options. Troy had called her Mouse for as long as she could remember, it having stemmed from her being so small as a baby that their father had called her Pip-squeak. It had evolved over the years, and Mouse had just stuck.

"Hey, Troy," she responded.

"Mom wants you to make sure you remember to practice your piano today and to call and thank Aunt Trudy for the school clothes she sent," he said while taking off his sweaty shirt to put in the wash in the bathroom/laundry room off the kitchen.

Claire rolled her eyes. "Okay . . . Did you see what Aunt Trudy sent me for clothes? Hopefully, she isn't expecting any pictures of me wearing them," and then added, "Really? You have to undress in the kitchen?"

"Well, don't forget, or she'll have my hide," he said, ignoring her question. "Hey, Sam," he added, smiling at her.

"Hey, Troy," she responded in a higher pitched voice than normal.

"I'm going for a jog and then have to work at five. See you guys later."

Claire and Sam grabbed as many snacks as their arms could carry and went up the secret back staircase to Claire's room.

"Oh my god. Your brother is so hot," said Sam instantly.

"Ew, Sam, really? We've been over this."

"Sorry . . . but . . . he totally is.

"Blech," Claire responded.

"Is he still dating that chick from the D&G?" The D&G was their local convenience store.

"Lydia? I'm not sure. I try not to know Troy's dating life, to be honest. But I hope not. She was an absolute dud."

Claire sat cross-legged on her white-and-pink floral comforter. She still had the white wrought iron bed frame she'd had since she was five, the posts each having a gold-tip ball with roses on it, the iron curving in whimsy designs fit for a princess. Her shelves were lined with snow globes, piano recital awards, music boxes, and other knickknacks that she liked to collect. One large shelf on the opposite wall was devoted solely to books and was crammed to its breaking point in Tetris fashion.

Sam sat on the floor on one of two purple beanbags against the one open wall, which was covered from ceiling to floor with magazine clippings, posters, and ads that Claire had collected. The smiling faces of Michael J. Fox, Christian Slater, Judd Nelson, and Rob Lowe sparkled among album covers from Red Hot Chili Peppers, No Doubt, and Soul Asylum that she had pulled out of her cassette tapes, her more recent addition being the newer *Jagged Little Pill* by Alanis Morissette. Movie posters for *Beauty and the Beast*, *Dirty Dancing*, and *Friday the 13th*, which Troy had snagged from the movie rental store, were scattered about the collage.

"I can't believe we have our first day of high school under our belt!" Sam blurted out with excitement. "High school! As if!"

Claire smirked. She wouldn't admit it, but it did feel pretty good to have finally entered the walls of high school. Though she knew it was merely one year older than eighth grade, there was something that felt significant about being a high school student. And all things considered, it hadn't been too bad of a start. Take out Amber, and it had actually been pretty great. Her homeroom teacher was super nice, her classes so far seemed doable, and she had Sam in some of them. She'd gotten to all of them on time, navigating around the school just fine.

And there was that smile and wave she'd received from her new homeroom acquaintance, Mark, and, her thoughts skipped back to geometry class and the altercation on the way home, Adam. She felt so ridiculous, as ridiculous as Sam sounded to her when talking about boys, when sensing her body trill a little remembering his face when he had helped her up, his concern, his gray eyes, and hair that matched Shawn Hunter's famous do to perfection. She didn't even know him, had spent about 10.2 seconds with him, and yet there was something . . . something about him. If she mentioned this, Sam would never let her live it down, so, for now, it was her own secret, especially because Claire thought it was probably nothing anyway. But to Claire, between the two moments today, she knew exactly which one she preferred, even if it had entailed her almost getting run over by a bike.

Under the Bridge

"Okay, here we go. Day two! And I get to see you almost all day!" Sam was excitedly talking on their way to school. Sam's mom always brought her in on the first day, a tradition they'd had since she started kindergarten. So, today, Claire had her walking buddy, and she was happy for it. There was something about Sam's energy in the morning that brought her a sense of calm, even if Claire was the polar opposite, being more of a night owl herself. As it was, she'd stayed up way too late last night reading a book she'd read too many times already, whose binding was crumbling and which was currently tucked away in her backpack, as it was every day of her school career, a constant comfort for her. Typically, she wouldn't let it keep her up, but there was no way she could close the cover when Elizabeth Bennet was finally falling in love with the handsome Mr. Darcy. Enter sigh here.

She let Sam's jabbering wash over her as the morning air woke her with every step. In no time, the gold-and-sky-blue sign of A. Thompson High came into view, the shining knight that was their mascot gleaming beside it.

"Hey, Claire," broke into Claire's morning reverie, and she saw Mark walk by with Chris, giving her a smile. It was brief, but Sam didn't miss it.

"Oh my god! Claire, Mark just said hi to you!"

"I know that, Sam. Shush," said Claire, looking at the boys' retreating backs, making sure they didn't hear Sam.

"Why did he say hi to you? Is there something you're not telling me? Oh, that's so exciting!" she said in a furious whisper as they pushed through the front doors and headed to their lockers.

"I'm sure he's just being friendly," Claire said, trying to downplay Sam's overexcitement.

"Well, I'm counting that as something," Sam said. Claire rolled her eyes but smiled while doing so. Sam elbowed her. "Would you expect anything different from me?"

"No, I wouldn't," she answered with a cocked eyebrow. The bell overhead rang. "See you in first period!"

Sam nodded, and they parted ways to their lockers and homerooms. This moment had been a source of mild anxiety for Claire, as she wasn't sure what the whole locker situation was going to be. She was glad to see Amber wasn't there at least and had hopefully already gotten what she'd needed. Opening it up, she saw that both shelves were still taken. She decided that today she didn't want to deal with it. She had left her books and things from yesterday at home. She threw her sneakers into the bottom of the locker and left her gym clothes in her bag. She would grab them later before class, considering it was so close to her locker. Taking a folder and notebook for geography and science, she went to homeroom. She could feel Amber's glare follow her into the room, but she held her head high and took a seat, not making eye contact, looking forward to making this day Amber-free and even better than yesterday.

Geography and science went well. She and Sam both liked their science teacher, Mr. Gibbs, but didn't care for Mrs. Drew, mostly due to her talking really loud and slow, not hearing anything they said, and droning on about her shih tzu, Pookie. They shared lunch A this time, which felt so early to eat. Claire had learned from the first day that they had hot lunch from the cafeteria, a snack bar, and a salad bar as options. Her mom had given her ten bucks for the week for food. She had decided to utilize the salad bar the day before, and today she was eyeing the snack bar, which had hot pretzels rotating in a case, the large chunks of salt making her mouth water. Caving, she and Sam both treated themselves and enjoyed eating lunch on the lawn outside the cafeteria door. Gym followed, and thankfully, they were told not to change, as the gym teacher, Mr. Monroe, a very fit guy who spoke with the severity of an ex-marine, told them they were going to go over the procedures, rules, and what was to come for the semester. It ended with a brief walk around the school outside, which Claire enjoyed immensely, feeling that late summer air play with her hair, the smell of an approaching fall intoxicating.

It was finally time for the class Claire was most looking forward to: band. If Claire was confident about anything, it was her love of playing the piano. She poured her heart and soul into every single key she hit. She had a keyboard at home, which was her prized possession, but was looking forward to playing on a real piano, like she used to with Ms. Shelly at lessons. Claire felt she became a different person when playing, ignoring the world around her, getting lost in the sounds lifting her heart, and allowing the music to envelop her entire being. She was always a little nervous to play in front of others at first, but once her hands began to move, a breath she didn't realize she was holding would release, and it was like stepping into a warm bath. She became one with the instrument, melting, paying no attention to the movements her body made in response to the melodies and harmonies weaving together. Though she was excited for this opportunity, the elementary school level having never really challenged her much, she also knew it was a class of upperclassmen as well as freshmen, and so her nerves were a tad on edge.

But walking into the band room, Claire already felt more at ease than any of her other first-day classes. There was a cacophony of noise, mostly drumming, with a few blasts on a saxophone and some twiddling on a flute. But the best part was just how chill the room seemed to be. Students were clumped in different areas of the large and open space, some sitting on the floor, others standing around the piano, occasionally hitting a few keys. She received a smile and nod from two others as she made her way into the room. She instantly felt she belonged.

Making her way to the other side, she saw a familiar face. Amy Smith, a quiet and shy girl with whom Claire had gone to school since kindergarten, was standing off to the side. She had lank hair that she kept pushing behind her ears and an oversized purple cardigan buttoned up over a white T-shirt. She stood with her arms crossed. Claire got the impression of a terrified mouse trying to hide from a big, vicious cat. She crossed the rest of the room to give her a friend. Claire was definitely not the most confident person around, but Amy was almost cripplingly shy, and Claire had always felt for her.

"Hey, Amy! Did you have a good summer?" she asked. Claire thought she could see Amy's shoulders relax ever so slightly.

"Claire! Thank God you are doing band. I thought I was going to be all alone!" Claire smiled at her, hoping it didn't look sympathetic, and peered around the room, seeing a few kids they had done band with at their elementary school.

"I see Greg is here. And John. Oh, and Jessica. So we're not alone," Claire said reassuringly.

"I know, but no one who ever talked to me anyway," Amy replied nonchalantly.

Changing the subject, Claire repeated, "So, how was your summer?"

"It was okay. I spent a lot of time with my grandmother and got to spend a week in Texas with my aunt and uncle. How was yours?"

"That's cool. Mine was good. Spent a bunch of time with Sam at the beach and on the lake with my cousins who have a camp there."

"Awesome. That must be why you're so tan," Amy said.

"Uh, yeah, probably," said Claire, unsure of what to say to that. Claire always wanted to be nice but had forgotten how random Amy could be sometimes. She decided to occupy her time by looking around the room, her attention drawn to the rhythms coming from the drum set. Whoever it was was keeping up a fun upbeat tempo. She turned to the corner to see not only a nice red set, but none other than Adam, the brown-haired cutie who had nearly run her over, sitting behind it clearly lost in his sweet jams.

Claire couldn't contain the grin that spread across her face. This added a whole new layer to this mystery boy. Once again he had his cool guy vibe going with a white T-shirt and an open short-sleeved button-down plaid shirt. His eyes were closed behind those glasses, and his head was slightly banging to his drumming. She watched as he added some more complicated moves. A few people close by clapped. He smiled a glorious, wide smile, pointed at someone with his stick as he fell back into the even tempo he had started with, and then looked around. They made eye contact. Claire slightly blushed that he'd caught her watching. But she was silently excited at the look of happy surprise on his face and the smirk and head nod that he sent her way. Boy, did he have a nice smile. So subtle, cute, and genuine. She waved as he continued playing and was just getting the courage to walk closer to listen when she heard, "Alright, alright! Everyone, this way please!" shouted over the noise. The drumming ceased, the scattered chatting came to a halt, and everyone turned and moved toward the center of the room to stand in front of who Claire assumed was Mr. Johns, the band and chorus director.

"Perfect. Please have a seat on the floor, making a large circle." They followed directions, and Claire sat, mesh-nylon-covered legs out in front of her, Doc Martens crossed, leaning back on her hands. She rested her head on her left shoulder, her hair cascading all around her, tickling her bare arms that her short-sleeved burgundy dress didn't cover. Amy quickly grabbed the spot next to her. Mr. Johns sat right down on the floor with them.

"Hello, everyone. Welcome back to many of you. And a big ole welcome to the rest of you. I am Mr. Johns. I teach concert, jazz, and marching band, chorus, and our exclusive choral group, the Voices of Color, and am very excited to begin this year. We have a good number of new faces and even a new instrument that we've never had in our band before! Not played by a student anyway. But we'll get to that during introductions. So, a little bit about me. This is my twenty-eighth year teaching band and chorus, my tenth here at A. Thompson High. I have a wife and a beautiful daughter who is finishing up her college degree this year. I love music of all kinds, but I'm a particular fan of The Beatles. And I love riding my motorcycle. We will have a lot of fun in this room, only if we can also take our playing and practicing seriously." He looked around with a smile. "And that about sums it up."

Claire listened and got the vibe that Mr. Johns had once been a free-spirited hippie of sorts, and she liked that a lot about him. He spoke softly and calmly. He evoked a sense of chill.

"Now, normally we would have chairs set up in rows here and, of course, stands. However, each class I've had today has been more of an intro class, and we, of course, did not have time to really bust out the instruments. So for today, we sit on the floor. Before I go into the expectations of this class, let's go around and do *your* introductions. Please say your name, grade, the instrument you play, and your favorite musician or band. We'll start over here." He gestured to the girl to his right, whose name was Jill, was a junior, played the clarinet, and liked the Beastie Boys. They made their way around the circle, Mr. Johns adding in his own thoughts here and there or asking follow-up questions in such a friendly and genuinely interested manner.

Claire and Amy were halfway around the circle, and when it came to Claire, she said a little nervously, "Hi! I'm Claire Hanover. I'm a freshman. I play piano. And I love all kinds of music, so a favorite is hard. But I guess I'd say I really like the Red Hot Chili Peppers right now."

She felt her heart calm down once finished and felt a jolt in her stomach when she saw Adam nodding his approval of her band selection.

"Great! And Claire here is our new instrument! We haven't had someone in band playing piano in quite some time, and I'm super excited," Mr. Johns said to the group. And then to her, "So, Claire, you are going to be taking my place pretty much." He added a chuckle. "I am usually behind the piano for scales, tuning, and things of the like. I also play for the school plays, which maybe I can coax you into helping me out with, eh? I won't pressure you though." He threw her a wide friendly smile. "Welcome, Claire." She smiled and nodded back, and he adjusted his gaze to Amy. Claire could feel her seize up.

"Um . . . I'm Amy . . . Amy Smith. I'm a freshman. I play the flute . . . and . . ." She stopped, and Claire could feel the awkward tension permeating through every bit of her and instantly felt bad, taking on her embarrassment as her own, and hoped no one was staring rudely at her. Claire picked a spot on the carpet in front of her to stare at.

"Um . . ."

"You have a favorite artist or band?" Mr. Johns prompted politely, thinking that she had simply forgotten the last question.

Amy's face flushed. "Um . . ." If Claire dared to sneak a peek at her, she was certain she would see tears beginning to develop. Amy had clearly blanked out.

Mr. Johns quickly picked up on this. "You know, I have so many favorite artists that I often can't come up with a single one. I fall back on The Beatles every time. I'll let you think on it, and if you want to let us know, feel free to just jump in!" He gave her a warm smile and shifted to the next student. Claire was impressed with his interference but knew that this moment was probably something Amy would now think of for the rest of the day, and maybe even more days to come. She chanced a look at her while the next few kids went. Amy was staring at her lap, clearly trying to fight off her emotions.

Claire tuned back in when she heard a familiar voice. "I'm Adam Miller. I'm a sophomore. I play percussion, and I'm a fan of Tom Petty." *Nice*, Claire thought, *Tom Petty fan.*

"Yes, Mr. Miller," said Mr. Johns. "Good to have you back. Adam here is the go-to guy for pretty much anything in the classroom. A big help. Heck, he knows the place better than I do! And is our big drummer on campus, as he is the only percussionist who plays for us in the jazz band, marching band, and, of course, with us here in concert band." Adam shrugged off the compliment humbly, and the introductions continued.

At the end, Mr. Johns went through the expectations of band class, how they were graded, the number of performances they did, and his rules around practicing. It was mostly boring, but Claire appreciated the need for it and listened. When done, there were about five minutes of class to spare, and Mr. Johns released them. Claire was taken aback and had to adjust to the newfound independence of high school. Most kids took right off to get a head start on getting their things and heading to buses, cars, or their walks home.

Claire began to gather her things when she saw Amy sniff as she picked up her flute case. "Hey, Amy. No stress, okay? Everyone blanks out sometimes. It's no big deal."

"Easy for you to say. You always seem to know what to say. I never do. You would think I would be used to making a fool of myself by now."

Claire ached for her. "No. I don't always know what to say. But just own it, you know? Like I said, no biggie. You're good. And definitely not a fool."

She shrugged a thanks, but Claire knew she didn't buy it. "See ya, Claire."

Claire watched her go and, in her moment of concern, didn't hear her name being called.

"Claire?" It was Mr. Johns.

"Oh, sorry," she responded and walked toward him standing by the piano.

"Not at all. I know there isn't much time left, but I wanted to show you the piano and talk to you about a few things. I don't think we have time to hear you play, buses will be boarding in ten minutes, but—"

"I walk home." She smiled. "I can stay a little bit."

"Great!" Once again Claire appreciated his genuine nature. "This here is the piano, of course. So I'd like you to play the scales for warming up as well as the notes for tuning at the beginning of class. Is that something you feel comfortable doing?"

"Sure!" she said.

"Awesome. Now, do you have a piano at home for practicing?"

"I have a keyboard. Not a real piano though."

"That's fine. But if you ever want to stay after to practice on the real thing, you are welcome to, although you'll have to share the space with Mr. Miller over there, as he stays after a lot to bang around on the drums and pick up the room for me." He chuckled, and Claire noticed that Adam was in fact still in the band room, covering the timpani. He gave a two-fingered salute across the room. She smiled in return and then averted her attention back to Mr. Johns.

"Great. Thanks!"

"So how long have you been playing?" he asked.

"My grandmother used to teach me when I was small, but my parents put me in private lessons when I was five. I've been playing ever since."

"Awesome. That was going to be my next question. So you do private lessons?"

"I did. With Ms. Shelly over at Caroll's Music. Twice a week."

"I know Ms. Shelly. Perfect!" he said excitedly. "You have a moment to play us something?"

"Yeah. Sure," she said a little awkwardly. She saw Adam leaning on the timpani, now looking on. It made her a little nervous for whatever reason. She sat down and went to her favorite to play, one of the first she'd learned, "Somewhere Over the Rainbow." She could play this song with her eyes closed. It was a comfort piece that made her feel both happy and sad. She began to play, and that breath released. All she felt was the ever so slight vibrations of the piano beneath her hands floating gracefully across the keys, every single tone washing over her, and she was lost in it. She didn't see Mr. Johns's happy and impressed expression or Adam slowly moving toward the piano, grabbing a chair, flipping it around, and sitting in it backward, listening, resting his chin on his arms.

When finished, they all let the last note reach the furthest corners of the room. And then she heard some clapping, and it was coming from Adam. She beamed at him, surprised to see him so close.

"Excellent!" said Mr. Johns, joining in Adam's clapping. Claire smiled sheepishly. "Perfect. You have great form. I'm excited to have you in our band this year, young lady." And he really seemed to be.

"Thank you, Mr. Johns. I'm excited to be here."

"Well, with that, I won't keep you any longer. Just noticed the time. I myself have to scoot. Adam, as always, thanks for picking up. I'll see you both Friday." He grabbed his leather side sling bag and left, leaving Adam and Claire suddenly alone.

"You play great," Adam said as Claire picked up her bag from the floor by the piano.

"Thank you," was all she was able to say, his compliment having hit her somewhere around her navel.

They made their way out the door. "I really love that Hawaiian guy's version of that song. What's his name?"

"Iz! Me too!" Claire responded.

"Yeah, that's the guy." Adam smiled. Again . . . that smile. It was hard to not notice it. It was almost a smirk . . . almost something she would categorize as a shitty grin even. There was humor behind it, and yet humbleness, and definitely a genuine quality. It was an expression that Claire felt ran deep somehow, like he was making a personal connection with it. Maybe that's why she was so taken aback by him. It almost seemed intimate.

They went down the main hallway toward the front doors. "You'll like band. It's pretty chill and cool, and Mr. Johns picks pretty up-to-date pieces, which is always fun."

"Sweet. Yeah, he seems great." She didn't know what else to say. Quite frankly, she was surprised he was still talking to her.

"Hey, uh, sorry again for yesterday . . ." he trailed off sheepishly.

"Oh, when you almost ran me over?" she said in mock irritation.

His face snapped to look at her. His concerned expression was too much for her, and she gave a burst of laughter. "I'm kidding." She giggled. "It's fine. Really. No big deal."

He exhaled a relieved sigh. "You had me going there for a moment. But, really, I am sorry."

"Well, thank you. But I assure you it is okay." They walked onto the front path and he stopped, the bike rack behind him.

"Props for liking the Red Hot Chili Peppers. They're one of my favorites too," he said. " 'Under the Bridge' is, like, my jam. My favorite to play when I'm on my own . . . riding around at night or something." He flushed ever so slightly, clearly thinking that he may have said too much. But to Claire, he had said just the right thing. What an insight he had just leaked, and picturing him riding around at night, those dulcet tones his backdrop, the words of a loner splashing over him, was something she could feel, right in her soul.

"I feel that," she said, and his expression was of appreciation. "I also like Tom Petty. So good choice there as well."

"Yeah, he's definitely top-notch. What's your favorite song from him?"

She thought for a moment before raising her eyebrows and sighing. "Oh gosh, that's hard . . . but I guess I'd go with 'American Girl.' I relate to that one."

He beamed. "I love that one: a classic. His very first album too. Most people only know 'American Girl' from it, but I love a couple others myself."

"I'm not sure I've actually listened to the whole album, to be honest," she said.

"Well, we need to change that, don't we?" he responded. "I'll hook you up."

She grinned broadly. "Okay."

He ran his hand through his hair. "Well, I'll see you around, then. Nice meeting you again, and in a less stressful situation this time," he said.

"Yeah." She laughed lightheartedly. "You too." He waved and turned to unlock his bike. She watched him until she heard her name.

"Claire!" It was Sam. She was waiting for her on the short concrete wall that surrounded a small square-like area to the left of the school. Claire hustled off to meet her.

"I've been sitting here for, like, an hour."

"As if. It hasn't been that long."

"Well, close enough!" Sam squeaked, a hand on her hip, the other holding a book. Adam rode by on his bike, and they both went quiet and watched him ride off. Claire could almost hear that lonely guitar intro as he glided off slowly, headphones on his head . . . Such an interesting guy.

Sam's affect changed immediately. "So tell me what you were doing talking with him?!"

Claire jumped and then rolled her eyes. "Sam . . ." But within moments, she gave in and told Sam the entirety of the afternoon. And however minimal it really was, Claire couldn't ignore the slight flip in her stomach as she told it, not even minding Sam's overdramatic exclamation of it being the most exciting thing, like, ever.

Bohemian Rhapsody

A knock pounded at Claire's bedroom door as she contemplated the choker necklace she had just put on in her mirror. The loudness and intensity could only mean one thing: Troy.

He stuck his head in. "Hey, Mouse. It's raining. Mom asked me to take you to school. Leaving in ten minutes, so you better be downstairs and ready, especially if I have to stop and get Sam too."

"I'm ready now," she said, deciding to keep the choker. She grabbed her backpack and followed him downstairs. She was excited for today for two reasons. Number one, it was Friday, and by the end of the day today, she would have officially survived her first week of high school (even if it was just a four-day week). And number two, it was band day, and she couldn't help but be a bit thrilled at the possibility of seeing Adam again.

She had battled with herself when these feelings had popped up this morning. But ended by telling herself it was okay to be excited because she was definitely not admitting to having a crush, having only *really* talked to him once . . . There was nothing wrong with having met a new person whose company she seemed to enjoy, and she was merely interested to see if she would continue to enjoy it by spending more time with said person. Totally reasonable. Plus he had waved to her in geometry yesterday morning, and she felt he had looked pretty happy to see her there. He had even come up to her after to tell her he hadn't realized she was in his class and that next time they should sit together because he sucked at geometry and could use a buddy. So maybe she wasn't the only one? But he did use the word "buddy." Regardless, there was absolutely nothing wrong with simply wanting to see him again. And it had absolutely nothing to do with his cute, mysterious vibe or his smile either.

Running to the car, she quickly jumped in Troy's '84 Chevy Cavalier that, according to Troy, could only run when he was behind the wheel. But Claire knew perfectly well it was because it was a piece of shit. But it was forest green and Troy's baby. Metallica blasted from the tape player when he started her up, and Claire rolled her eyes. They put-putted out of the driveway to pick up Sam.

Turning down the radio, Troy said, "So how's high school going? What do you think of it?"

Claire pondered a moment and then shrugged. "Seems cool. I like most of my teachers, and I think I'll really enjoy band."

"You have Mrs. Drew this semester, right?"

She nodded. She had shown Troy her schedule first thing when she had gotten it in the mail over the summer so he could tell her who he knew or had had for teachers.

"She's nuts. But so easy to play. Just get her off topic, and she'll spend the whole class talking about anything from her dog to her late husband or even her most recent trip to the grocery store. No joke, Matt and I used to do it all the time and then just sit and shoot the shit in the back row."

"Such an inspiration you are, Troy," Claire said, but she was smirking. She loved her brother, more so since she'd gotten older. Well, she'd always loved him, but they hadn't always gotten along. As the years progressed and she'd spent more time with him, Claire had gotten to really know him, and the more she got to know him, the more she felt that Troy was just a product of a school system that hadn't played to his strengths, giving him the impression that he wasn't good enough, and so he had just given up. Their dad loved him so much that it pained him to see Troy so lost and, not really knowing how to handle it, just got harder and harder on him. But Troy was a softy, and Claire loved him for it.

"What can I say? I still passed geography with a shining C plus." He grinned, pulling into Sam's driveway. She was ready for them and quickly ran to the car.

"Thanks for picking me up," she said from the back seat. "Man, it's coming down out there."

"Yeah," said Troy. "Supposed to clear up by noon though, so you should be good to walk home. I don't work till three. I'll pay attention to it and pick you up if it changes."

"Word," said Claire, looking out her window at the cascading rain as they pulled into the front of the school.

"See ya," said Troy.

"Tootles," she returned, and she and Sam booked it inside. They walked to Claire's locker first so she could get her things and get away from any Amber issues that may be presented. They had established this yesterday. Their second gold day, they felt a little more confident having had the classes once already and decided that when they got to school with time to spare, they would quickly go to Claire's locker and then vacate the area and hang out by Sam's until the bell. This had two promising side effects. One was the obvious: they could better avoid Amber. The other was that Sam's hallway had long windows along it, each window having a built-in bench they could sit on and chill.

They got out of Claire's wing Amber-free and managed to snag a bench seat right near Sam's locker. Claire took it up while Sam emptied and gathered her stuff, talking a mile a minute. "I canNOT believe we've made it through our first week of high school. Well . . . almost made it through. But today is an easy day because we're together almost all day, so I know we'll get through it just fine, and then we'll have completed our first week of high school. Totally sick!"

Claire chuckled, and Sam continued. "But we also can't keep avoiding Amber," she said, closing her locker and squeezing in next to Claire. They sat opposite each other, knees bent, backs resting on the walls of the little window seat alcove.

Claire stared at a drop of rain sliding down the window, waiting for it to hit bottom or collide with another stream before answering. "I know . . . It's not that I want to avoid her. It's more like I just don't want to waste the energy on her at this point, ya know?"

"I guess," said Sam, smacking her gum, her bright-blue-shadowed eyes staring at Claire. "But the more you just let it go, the more she's just going to try and get away with it . . . and other things."

Claire nodded and blew air through her lips. That was too true and was already starting to happen. In home ec the day before, Miss Phillips had let them partner up with someone of their choice. Naturally, Sam and Claire stuck together, and Amber snagged Mark, while Lauren and Ashley were left to be a pair. When Miss Phillips sent them to get aprons, Amber purposely bumped Claire out of the way and grabbed the plain white apron Claire was clearly heading for, leaving Claire with the pink-and-white checkered one that had frilly lace around it. She wasn't against pink or lace . . . but looking like her grandmother in the midst of Amber, her cronies, Mark, and Chris wasn't really what she was aiming for.

And then when it was time to play a scavenger hunt game where Miss Phillips wanted them to identify items in the kitchen, Amber was very blatantly listening in on Claire and Sam and just copying whatever they said. And finally, whenever Mark even attempted to say hi to Claire or speak to her at all, Amber would call him over to her, remind him in a sickly sounding whimper that he was her partner, "silly," and glare at Claire like she'd asked the boy to come talk to her. Sam was right, if Claire didn't say anything to her, she was just going to keep taking.

"I'll say something at some point . . . I'll be mature and respectable with her, and maybe she'll back off," Claire offered.

Sam took one look at her, rolled her eyes, and said, "Ugh . . . gag me with a spoon. Like that'll ever work! Slap her in the face . . . Maybe when she can't cover up her red cheek with makeup, she'll quit pissing people off for no reason."

The bell rang at this closing statement, and Claire scooted off to homeroom, only to join back up with Sam for their two morning classes. Lunch passed with another pretzel session, and they spent gym taking turns doing fitness tests for Mr. Monroe as a starting point for their goals for the semester. This involved the stretch test, push-ups, sit-ups, pull-ups, and the dreaded ropes. Claire and Sam barely made it off the ground on the ropes at which point Mr. Monroe very loudly said, "Hanover! Levinski! I want to see you climb halfway up that rope by mid-semester!"

Changing out of their gym clothes after class and freshening up, Sam called him a slew of crude names at which Claire laughed and tried to convince her he was just doing his job.

"No. Grading tests is just doing your job, mopping floors is just doing your job, answering the phone is just doing your job. This? This is taking your job to a whole new level. He. Is. A. Nazi. I'm sure of it."

Claire laughed.

"Who the hell can climb those freakin' ropes to begin with?! Not your average person, I can tell you that. What are we? Some kind of *Planet of the Apes* gorilla? And has anyone ever once thought of what happens when you get to the top, and then, oh, I don't know, lose your strength? Fall?! Do you know how far of a fall that is? Like that stupid mat that's about as thick as a slice of cheese is going to stop you from breaking your neck. As if!" Claire let Sam rattle right on till the bell rang for fourth period. They separated, Claire quickly dumping her stuff off at the bottom of her locker before heading to the band room, having no time to grab her bag.

"Gather round, folks," she heard as she entered right on the late bell. Mr. Johns was standing up front, and the room had chairs scattered around but was mostly open again like it was on the first day. Everyone was grouping up, and Claire joined them. "Okay. So today is audition day! Meaning I will be taking you guys one by one to the back room to hear you play. You'll play some scales for me and a snippet of a song I have selected. This is merely for me to see where in the band you will be placed. We have first, second, and third chair for each instrument, and I need to put you all where you will best shine in this ensemble. So, those of you who have been here before know this means that you have some downtime today. Think of this as an extra study hall. When it isn't your turn, feel free to do some work, read a book, or just hang out with your friends. I don't really care as long as you are staying in the room and being somewhat quiet and mostly respectful. Any questions?"

No one did, so he continued. "Great! I will call you one at a time. If you'd like, feel free to warm up before your name is called. I will start in about five minutes. Please do not interrupt me for anything shy of an emergency. If you need to use the restroom, wait until we are transitioning auditions to ask. Got it?" They nodded.

"Excellent," he said, and he went about collecting his things. Everyone else dispersed to their own corners of the room, sitting down and chatting or, for some, getting started on work.

Mr. Johns stopped by Claire on his way to the back room. "Claire, how's it going?"

"Good!"

"Terrific. So, I obviously am not auditioning you today. I heard you Wednesday, and where you're the only one on piano, you and I will just work through pieces as the year progresses. That being said, feel free to use this time to play around on the piano and get a feel for it. Do whatever you'd like, okay?"

"Okay! Thanks," she said, and he took off, calling a student's name as he went.

Claire went over to the piano. She wasn't going to interrupt everyone's chatter or work by playing, but she sat nonetheless, admiring the beautiful color of the wood and shine of the keys. That was when she noticed it. Leaning where the music pages would have gone was a cassette. And taped to the top of it was a small ripped piece of notebook paper that read "Claire." Lifting it, she saw the long-blond-haired face of Tom Petty staring up at her with a subtle crooked grin. Claire couldn't help but smile down at it. She opened it to see a white cassette with sky-blue type. Looking up, her eyes went straight for the drum set where a pair of gray ones were beaming at her. She returned the smile, stood up, and made to walk over to go give her thanks when Amy stepped in.

"Claire! How's it going? How's your first week been?"

"Oh! Amy! Hi!" said Claire, taken aback. She threw Adam what she hoped was a shrug of apology and gave Amy her attention. "First week has been good! How about yours?"

45

Amy crossed her arms in a self-hug. Claire always wondered if she was just trying to make herself as small as possible. "It's been okay. I mean, I haven't made any new friends, which I was hoping to . . . but it's been okay."

"Oh, it's only the first week. Give it some time! Everyone's getting into the groove of things," said Claire, giving her a sincere smile.

"True," said Amy. "I was doing alright today until now. I didn't know we were going to be auditioning! I'm so nervous. And flutes are first. I'm sure he's going to call me any minute."

"I know you'll do great! You're an amazing flutist. Don't worry. And Mr. Johns seems pretty chill. Just tell him you're nervous, and I'm sure he'll understand."

"Yeah . . . I jus—" Amy began, but she stopped when Adam stood by her side.

Claire looked at him and, though they'd introduced themselves to the group on the first day, did a formal introduction. "Hey! Amy, this is Adam. Adam, this is Amy."

"Hey," he said, raising a hand in acknowledgment.

"Hi," she squealed. "Well, I'll see you around, Claire." And she walked off.

Adam looked troubled. "Sorry . . . I didn't mean to interrupt. Just thought I'd come say hi."

"No, you're fine. She's just . . . she's just kind of shy like that. No worries."

He nodded.

"Thanks for the cassette!" she said.

He grinned. "Totally. Like I said, you gotta hear it all."

"Looking forward to it," she responded. "I'll listen to it this weekend so I can get it back to you next band class."

"No, don't worry about it. Keep it," he said.

"Keep it?" she questioned. "What do you mean? Isn't it your favorite?"

"One of them, yes, but I've listened to it plenty. Not like I can't snag another one sometime. You have it."

She couldn't contain her smile, and he reciprocated. "Well, thank you. I'll think of *something* to pay you back."

He chuckled. "So you gonna play for us?" he asked, gesturing to the piano.

"Uh . . . no." She laughed awkwardly.

"Why not?" he asked, taking a seat and hitting a few random keys.

"No one wants to hear me play, and I don't even have music with me." She took a chance and sat next to him.

"You're telling me 'Somewhere Over the Rainbow' is the only song you know by heart? I find that hard to believe."

She blushed a little. "Well, no . . . but . . ."

He raised his eyebrows at her as Mr. Johns called Amy over to the back room.

"Oh come on," she responded to his look. "Everyone's got their own thing going on, and they look quite content. They don't want me to interrupt them."

He looked around at the group. Giving her a quick sideways glance, he took in a deep breath and then said loudly to the room, "Who wants to hear Claire play?"

Claire felt her cheeks burn this time. "What are you doing?" she said under her breath as people chimed in.

"Yeah!" said a girl sitting beneath the whiteboard next to another who was nodding.

"Yeah, man," said a guy who was wearing a khaki bucket hat and a button-down Hawaiian shirt over a white tee walking up to the piano. "Let's hear it."

Countless others threw out a "Yeah" or a "Sure" or otherwise nodded.

Claire heaved a sigh. "You are kidding me, right?" she said to Adam, who was still sitting on the bench with her.

"Nope. Let's go, Hanover." He smirked.

"Okay, okay, I guess I have one . . . I practiced it a million times for a whole year so I could play it for my brother as a birthday gift. I'll do that one."

"Sounds perfect." Adam grinned, and Claire got a boost of confidence from looking at it. He was sitting so close, and the scent of Cool Water cologne mixed with the laundry detergent of his three-buttoned, long-sleeved gray-blue shirt was lovely.

She took a deep breath. She had in fact practiced this song so much in the year leading up to Troy's last birthday: she and Ms. Shelly going over it endlessly in lessons and then on her own at home whenever Troy was out of the house. It was his favorite song. It was his favorite song because of his favorite movie: *Wayne's World*.

Her fingers landed, and she began the slow intro to "Bohemian Rhapsody," picturing the music video, four group members' faces top lit as they sang in beautiful harmony. Once again, the world fell away as she fell into the music. She had just gotten to the long note that rang out before Freddie Mercury would come in singing about a poor boy when someone cut in from the outside world.

"Whoa, whoa, hold the phone," said the bucket hat boy, who'd come to stand by the piano back to listen. Claire stopped playing. "Are you telling me you're about to drop 'Bohemian Rhapsody' on the piano?"

Claire shrugged. "Yeah."

"Dude, for real?"

She giggled. "Yes."

"You can't play 'Bohemian Rhapsody' and not sing along."

"Oh, I'm not singing," Claire said matter-of-factly.

"We all will!" he exclaimed. "Everyone knows 'Bohemian Rhapsody.' " And then he turned to the room. "Come on, we got this." Some people came closer to the piano; others stayed put but adjusted themselves to pay more attention.

Claire couldn't believe it. "Well, okay. I'll sing along with you guys. But when it gets to the crazy stuff, y'all are on your own."

"You got it, chiquita." He gave her a wink.

Though she wouldn't normally go for such an address, Claire couldn't help but feel it was so completely innocent that it made her laugh. "Okay, here we go." Once again, she took a deep breath. She felt Adam adjust on the bench next to her, and she chanced a look before playing. He was staring right at her, excitement on his face. She fell into the song once more, and this time heard the beginnings of a group of people singing who weren't sure if they wanted to at first. She sang along under her breath, mostly to keep her own tempo going as she hit the keys. What started off as nervous singing quickly turned to more voices joining in, some people adding dramatic hand movements, and by the time the tempo changed for the introduction of Freddie Mercury's solo, almost everyone was singing strong, Claire included.

Like always when she played, Claire forgot everything. She forgot where she was, she forgot who was with her, and she even stopped hearing anything but her piano and the feelings pouring out of her own heart. She didn't mean to do it . . . but Claire sang at the top of her lungs with everyone else as she belted from the bottommost pit of her stomach, banging the notes down on the piano. She didn't see Adam do it, but when she continued to belt the next line, she noticed one thing: everyone had stopped singing along with her. She continued singing and playing but looked around to see everyone gazing at her with mixed expressions of impression and awe. She made a face clearly questioning why no one was singing.

"Whoo!" said her encouraging new friend.

She finished the line from the verse, continuing to play the break, and shouted over the piano, "You're supposed to sing WITH me!"

Adam laughed and others smiled. Bucket hat boy shouted back, "No way! It's all you, Claire. Sing it!"

Claire felt a mixture of embarrassment and nerves, but it was outweighed by this new outpour of support and encouragement. She threw caution to the wind and did exactly as he said, feeling her body vibrate with either passion or nerves, or both, singing her heart out. And when that last word of the first part ended, the room yelped and applauded, and she couldn't hide the broad smile that followed as she carried on playing the next section of the song and yelled, "Okay, it's all you guys now!"

The group laughed their way through the harmonies of the classical-style middle, shouting "galileo" and "mamma mia" as needed, and when Claire got to the final rock-style ending of the song, several boys, Adam included, played air guitar and fake drums, making noises with their mouths to "sing" along with others who covered the words until it calmed down again to the familiar tones of the beginning.

"Back to you, Claire!" was shouted, and Claire felt no nerves as she finished the slow repetition of the song's ending.

When the last note came to a quiet end and Claire lifted her hands from the piano, the whole group stood in silent awe for a moment, clearly soaking up the epicness they had just encountered.

"Dude . . ." bucket hat boy said again. "That was the raddest thing I've ever done. That was fucking awesome!" Others whooped and clapped, smiling broadly.

"Language, Mr. Fitzpatrick," came the voice of Mr. Johns. Claire and Adam both whipped around quickly to see Amy looking a little confused and Mr. Johns who was, thankfully, grinning from ear to ear. "But . . . I don't think I could have said it better myself." Everyone laughed.

Mr. Johns rested a hand on Claire's shoulder. "That was quite impressive." And he left to call the next person, the group dispersing again but chatting excitedly now.

The Mr. Fitzpatrick turned to Claire. "Dude, that was seriously the coolest thing ever."

"This is Will, by the way," Adam interjected. "But all of us guys call him Fitz."

"Nice to meet you," said Claire. She and Adam were still sitting at the piano, Fitz leaning on it.

"How'd you learn to do that?! Righteous!" he asked in his slow surfer tone that made Claire chuckle.

"I practiced it for, like, a whole year for my brother. He loves it."

"That's some serious shit. Kudos, man."

"Thanks!"

He did a high five with Adam, mentioned seeing him later, and then walked off to sit with a girl he had been chatting with earlier.

Adam turned to Claire. "I have no words. That was incredible."

Claire felt that flip in her stomach again. "Thanks. I love playing piano."

"I can tell. You were really into it. It was super cool to watch."

She flushed a bit.

"Sorry I had everyone stop singing." He shrugged. "But I could hear you and I thought everyone else should too."

"Oooh, that was your doing," she said accusingly.

"Yeah . . . sorry," he said very unapologetically, which made Claire smile. "You should do chorus," he added.

"Oh . . . no. I don't typically sing. That was a special occasion. And you owe me for having me sing alone in front of everyone."

He laughed loudly at that one. "Okay, okay. I'll think of something to pay you back."

"Do you think Mr. Johns was angry we interrupted auditions?"

"Nah. Are you kidding? He's been waiting for something like that to happen in his classroom for years. Truly."

She laughed. "Hey. I can think of a way you can repay me," she said.

He raised his eyebrows in response.

"Play me something on the drums."

"Oh come on. Me playing on the drums isn't going to come anywhere close to that."

"Come off it! I've heard you play a couple times now, and it's totally cool."

"Nothing like you though. It's just rhythms and beats!" he said exasperatedly.

"Yeah, but rhythms and beats that I can't play and can't even begin to fathom how you do," she said. "Come on . . . you owe me."

He pretended to be flustered at first, but broke into a light laugh. "Oh alright."

They went over to the drum set. Claire stood near it as he sat down and started with a simple beat, adding more and more complexity and eventually going full force, banging on all of it, adding his own creations in between, and keeping a beat that people in the room couldn't help but tap along to as they worked or chatted. Claire watched him shake or bang his head along with the music or bite his bottom lip when it got particularly intense. It was most definitely totally cool to watch, as she had said, and she couldn't help but note that it was also incredibly hot. She blushed at her own thought process. God, what would Sam say if she heard that come from her? But there was no denying it. She could tell herself not to crush, which, to some extent, she *was* keeping under control, still not wanting to get ahead of herself, but, boy, was it hard when every moment with him thus far had seemed so fun and easy, and right now every part of her was really digging watching him.

BOHEMIAN RHAPSODY

Mr. Johns came out with five minutes of class to spare and thanked them for their patience, apologized for not getting through everyone, and said they'd wrap it up next week. The bell rang and everyone scurried off.

Adam began covering the drum set, and Claire offered to help pick up, which he gladly accepted.

"So you'll have to tell me what you think of the Tom Petty tape," he said to her as they stacked a few chairs that were hanging around.

"Yeah! Definitely. Which are your favorites?"

"Tough choice, but I like 'The Wild One,' 'Forever' and 'Mystery Man.'"

"I'll pay closest attention to those." She smiled.

"Sounds perfect," he returned.

When done, Claire didn't want to linger, so she excused herself. "Well, I don't want to keep Sam waiting too long. I'll see ya next week."

"Yeah. See you next week. Have a good weekend," he said a little half-heartedly, and she left to grab her stuff from her locker before meeting Sam outside. Adam sat for a second in the one chair left to stack.

Mr. Johns came out of the back room, having put everything back in order. "Mr. Miller, thank you once again," he said, hurrying past him and then, noticing his quiet demeanor, stopped to say, "Everything okay?"

"Wha—? Oh, yeah," said Adam, coming out of his reverie. "Yeah, no, everything's cool. Thanks." He stood up and went to stack the final chair. Truth was, he wasn't sure what he was feeling. Why was he bummed that Claire had just left? Why did he find himself excited when she came to class? He had even waved to her the day before at the start of geometry class in what he was sure was the goofiest looking way.

Why did he enjoy watching her so closely while she laughed and talked and especially when she played that piano? The large roundness of her eyes, her mane of deep brown hair that seemed to be . . . everywhere, her trill of a giggle, and the smile that twinkled to her eyes. She had an air of depth that made him think there was so much more to her than any other girl he'd ever met. She was passionate—that was the word—passionate about everything, it seemed. She was so different than—He shook his head. *Snap out of it,* he told himself. *She's just a girl and you had a little fun today. That's it.*

"Uh, Mr. Miller? Are you sure you're okay?"

Adam spun around. "Yeah, why?"

"You've been holding that chair for a few minutes now."

Adam looked down to see that the chair was in fact still in his hands. "Oh . . . right . . . uh—just trying to decide where to put it," he responded stupidly, adding it to the stack directly next to him.

"Yeah, I hear that can be a tough call sometimes," Mr. Johns said with a grin.

Adam shrugged. "See ya next week." And with a two-fingered salute, he left the classroom, Mr. Johns shaking his head as he went.

Run-Around

"Ugh . . . forget it . . . I'm never going to get through this," Sam groaned from her usual spot in Claire's room. "Let alone understand it. Maybe we can convince Troy to bring us to the mall later to hit up the bookstore for a CliffsNotes copy."

Claire rolled her eyes. A few weeks into high school and they were already being pounded with homework, the hardest for Sam being the reading of *Romeo and Juliet*. Claire and Sam had tried for a short while to read it aloud together, taking on different roles, but Sam had gotten so caught up in her horrible ability to even read it that she had decided to just try reading to herself again. While she did this, Claire was getting through her twenty math problems for geometry, even questions only, of course, the ability to check answers in the back of the book null and void. Add their science sheets they had to label and color, questions for geography they had to answer, the additional English work of writing a short essay discussing two Robert Frost poems, and Sam's math test coming up that Claire promised to help her study for . . . and it was clear why they were spending a lovely mid-morning fall day doing schoolwork.

"We could. I'm sure he wouldn't mind. He gets off from job one at eleven and doesn't have to go to job two till late afternoon."

"Thank God! I totally don't understand this schmuck. Why do we even have to read Shakespeare? What's the point?!"

"He's a part of literary history. Was a genius at puns, irony, and humor . . . Master of themes of love, death, revenge . . . Not to mention murder and mystery in many."

Sam stared at her with her mouth agape. "Seriously?"

"You asked!" Claire said, throwing a pillow at her.

"Yeah, but I didn't think I was going to get a legit answer, dork!" Sam said, batting the pillow away.

Claire chuckled. She had had enough of math problems and homework, and though she didn't really condone CliffsNotes, Claire couldn't help but be intrigued by the thought of getting out and walking the mall. It was a perfect day for grabbing a chai tea at her favorite cafe there and walking the shops to see the new fall fashions, and she would love to take her warm and cozy drink to the bookshop.

"Troy should be home soon. Let's do it. I could use a study break."

Sam squealed her excitement, loving everything to do with hitting up the mall. Moving to sit next to Claire, she went off: "Sweet! I have totally been eyeing a corduroy overall dress in the latest Delia's catalog, but . . . can't afford it, so I want to see if there's anything similar at Deb. Aaaand, Joey's birthday is coming up, so I want to see what's at KB Toys! Oh, and we can check out Claire's and—"

"Yes, Sam," Claire said, laughing lightly. "We'll check it all out. You act like you haven't been to the mall in forever!"

"Well, it has been forever!"

"Sam, you were just there last week with your mom."

"Yeah . . . forever."

Claire burst out a laugh. "If you say so. Okay, we have about thirty minutes before Troy gets home. Let's vow to do as much work as we can until that point."

Sam clapped her hands together. "Alrighty. Yes, let's get some more work done."

Claire pulled her geometry book to her and attempted to work on the pesky problem she was struggling with. She hid her smile from Sam as she recalled how, over the past few weeks, Adam had in fact sat next to her in class as he'd said he would since noticing her there. In fact, once, when they were given the last fifteen minutes of class to start on their assignment, he slid his desk closer to hers so they could work on it together. It was subtle and simple, and Claire knew it was really nothing, but she couldn't help but feel like it *was* something. But that was really the only time she saw him now. Band had become practicing the pieces for their first concert in December, and she sometimes hung out after to help him pick up at which time they would chitchat a bit, but Claire didn't want him to think she was lingering, so she didn't stay often.

Getting further into the school year also brought an increase of opportunity for the hurricane that was Amber. Most recently, Claire found her sneakers soaking wet at the bottom of the locker, which Amber claimed to know nothing about, even though Claire saw her empty water bottle. And there was the time Amber decided to put a lock on their locker and not let Claire in on it. For this one, Claire at least threatened to get the janitor to cut it off if she didn't get rid of it. And let's not forget to mention the time Claire found her gym clothes spread across the hallway . . . underwear, sports bra, and all.

Claire thought she knew why Amber was hitting an all-time low. Of course, one reason was that she was just a bitch. But another was that Claire was getting a lot of attention from a certain Mark Calloway lately.

Claire wasn't really asking for it. Mark was just a really friendly, talkative guy, and they happened to have those few classes together besides homeroom. Mark seemed to talk to Claire more and more, even leaving Amber mid-conversation at times to say hi to Claire when she walked into class. Mark had even joined Claire and Sam's table in English, which was making *Romeo and Juliet* a little more entertaining for Claire, both Sam and Mark having their issues. This contributed to Mark and Claire having that much more to talk about as well since Amber only had home ec with him, which Claire was a part of. Claire thought Mark was a nice guy and definitely cute, and she was enjoying his friendship, but she really enjoyed Amber's face whenever they were together, which was a definite added benefit.

Regardless of Amber, high school seemed to be treating Sam and Claire well enough, and being about a month into it now, the edge had worn off and it was feeling comfortable.

"Hey! Earth to Claire!" Sam's voice burst through her thoughts.

"Huh? Oh, sorry. What's up?"

"Where the hell were you?! Troy just got home. I just heard him come in," Sam said.

"Oh! Sweet. Let's go," Claire said, slamming her textbook closed, along with her trailing thoughts.

They headed down to the kitchen to see Troy head-deep in the fridge.

"Hey," Claire said, announcing their arrival. "Can you take Sam and me to the mall?"

He backed out of the fridge with a leftover chicken leg from last night's supper in his mouth and an armful of the necessary materials for sandwich making. Dumping it all on the counter and pulling out the chicken leg, he said, "I just walked through the door, Mouse."

"I know, but we want to go to the mall. Can you take us? After you eat?"

He sighed. "Yeah, I suppose so." He could never say no to her. "How long you think you'll be?"

"How long can you give us?"

He looked at the clock. "How about two hours?"

Claire looked at Sam, whose face must have translated something because Claire said, "Two and a half?"

Troy smirked. "Fine . . . two and half. You guys run a hard bargain."

"Thanks, Troy! We'll meet you outside," said Claire, already heading out of the kitchen.

"I still have to eat," he called after her.

"I've seen you eat, Troy. You'll be done in no time."

He rolled his eyes, though she didn't see it, Claire and Sam already getting shoes on and heading out the door.

"So what's at the mall that is so important anyway?" Troy asked, still munching on a chicken leg, as they made their way down the road.

"We just needed a study break," answered Claire. "Can you go *any* faster?"

"What's the rush?"

"No rush, Troy. It's just that we're being outstripped by pedestrians on the sidewalk."

Sam giggled in the back seat. Troy rapped the dashboard. "This ole girl will go as fast as I think she should go. And right now . . . that would be thirty miles an hour." Claire rolled her eyes. "Patience is a virtue, little sis," he added.

"I'll remind you of that when you're yelling at me through the bathroom door to hurry up in the shower so you can take a big—" Troy's hand landed across her mouth.

"That'll do," he said, lowering it and taking a quick peek at Sam in the rearview mirror. Claire was holding in her laughter as Troy increased the speed ever so slightly.

Soon enough they were saying goodbye to Troy and promising to be back at the same spot in two and a half hours. He "sped" off as they entered the mall. For a Saturday, it wasn't all that busy. Claire and Sam immediately went to Gloria's Cafe to get piping hot chais, then started making their way from store to store. The neon lighting, mixed with string bulbs, zig-zagged its way down the center strip, areas of benches and chairs set up here and there for shoppers to rest, or in many cases, for husbands to take naps, and the smell of the candy kiosk and the food court at the other end of the mall provided an intoxicating combination of sights and smells that only the mall could bring. It was bright, it was in your face, it was packed with everything you could need, and it didn't matter how many times they visited, there was always something exciting about it all.

"Ooh, check this out!" Sam said, holding up a burgundy velvet dress that had a mock turtleneck and cap sleeves.

"Love it," said Claire. "Although . . . velvet, for me, makes my hair look like I stuck my finger in a socket. But it would be adorable on you. Try it on!"

"My hair already looks like I stuck my finger in a socket, so that will work for me," Sam said, looking at the dress, her shoulder-length, intensely curly hair seeming to bounce with her gum-chewing. "I'll try it. Looks like it's on sale. I only have like fifty bucks left over from my summer babysitting stint, and I need that book, and I don't want to blow it all today."

"I'm impressed with you that you made it last this long." Claire laughed.

Sam smacked her on the arm. "Get out. I don't spend money that crazily!"

"I'm kidding, I'm kidding. Hey, what do you think of this?" Claire held up a few long-sleeved crop tops, one that had stripes of burnt orange, forest green, and brown, the other a deep maroon.

"Totally you, and perfect for fall!"

"Cool. I needed some new tops to wear with my jeans and overalls."

They headed to the changing rooms, gabbing till they both came out to show each other their outfits. "What do you think?" Sam asked, looking at herself in the mirror.

"I think you look like a ten-year-old boy wearing a dress, Levinski." Of course . . . Amber.

Claire turned to see Amber and her pig-faced twits looking on with clothes in their arms, clearly heading to the dressing rooms too. "What the hell is that supposed to mean?" Claire asked them, crossing her arms, partly to try and look intimidating, partly to hide what she was trying on, though she didn't know why. Instinct, she guessed.

"What I mean is, Levinski over here has the body shape of a boy. Have you even hit puberty yet?" She mockingly laughed, gaining additional guffaws from her cronies.

"Shut up," Claire responded, then she turned to Sam. "Come on, Sam. I'm not sure I want this stuff anymore now that I know what shops here."

With final glares at Amber and friends, they retreated to their stalls, changed, and left, hearing Amber admiring herself in the mirror on their way out, telling pretty much everyone in the store that she looked so incredible in whatever dress she had on and just had to have it. Sam looked back, but Claire pushed her on. She didn't have the heart to see Sam's expression at the sight of Amber parading around in the burgundy velvet dress.

Next was the music store, Claire's second favorite place after the bookshop. She rarely ever bought anything there, as Troy could get her better deals at the music store in town, but this place had more selection, plus the chance to sample music and, of course, see what was new. She thumbed through some of her favorite artists—No Doubt, Soul Asylum, 2Pac, Pearl Jam, Mariah Carey—and checked out the classics she and her dad always liked—The Beatles, The Who, The Temptations. The unmistakable guitar and harmonica entry of Blues Traveler's "Run-Around" played overhead, and Claire had a sudden idea while looking through the new release CDs.

Claire liked CDs and owned quite a few now, but she still loved her cassettes, especially where that was all she could play in the car, and the stereo system she had inherited from Troy only played those and records. Luckily, she had gotten a small boombox for her birthday a couple years ago and could listen to CDs, but it didn't have the same sound as Troy's equipment, so she mostly stuck to her cassettes still. And with the ever increasing popularity of CDs, cassette tapes were dirt cheap.

She had quite enjoyed receiving Tom Petty's, and it dawned on her now that to pay Adam back, she would give him one of her own favorites to share. She had so many, and he had parted with a special one for her . . . it only made sense. When she turned around to ask Sam if she thought that was a good idea, or if it was too forward, she noticed that Sam seemed off and not nearly as perky as Sam on chai tea should be. Claire knew exactly why too.

"Hey, don't let Amber get to you," she said.

Sam groaned. "I know . . . but I can't help it. She's right. I am built like a twelve-year-old boy. Even you have boobs and an ass."

"Excuse me!" Claire blushed, looking around. "Sam, who cares! You're adorable and gorgeous anyway. Amber is probably just jealous because even she can't hide everything. You're like the modern-day Twiggy! You have what models have! A runway star!"

"Except I'm five foot two," Sam interjected.

Claire sighed. "Look, Sam. Every body is different and every body is special. We all look at ourselves and see flaws. It's just what we do. Some kind of underwritten rule of being a girl, unfortunately. And some bitches, like Amber, like to point those things out to make themselves feel good. It gives them power . . . *if* we let it get to us. But the truth is, even the perfect body isn't that. There's no such thing, and there's no obtaining it. So we just have to learn to love those flaws instead."

"And how the hell do I do that?"

"Well, for example, I can't wear low-cut blouses like you can. You have this beautiful bone structure around your collar, and V-neck blouses look so elegant on you."

Sam stared at her for a moment, gum-chewing slowing, and finally said, "You really think so?"

"Of course I do!" Claire put her arm around her. "Let's go get some food. I'm starving."

Sam smiled. A true Sam smile. "Oh thank God! My stomach was making noises like a gremlin after midnight."

"Well, maybe I shouldn't feed you, then," Claire said with mock concern. They both broke into giggles and made their way to the food court.

The nice thing about comfort food is that it always has a way of obliterating discouraging thoughts. It also helps having encouraging friends.

Claire and Sam were slurping down milkshakes and sharing a large fry, playing their usual game of I spy: mall rat edition, when another familiar face showed up.

"I spy . . . a goth chick with nose and lip piercings," Sam said.

"Got her . . . over by the carousel," Claire noted.

"Yup. What a fun juxtaposition. And seriously, major props to those peeps. I could never get that many piercings. I'd flip. Not to mention my mom would disown me."

"True that. Okay. I spy . . . Mark Calloway," Claire said with surprise.

"That's not how the game works, Claire. You're supposed to—" Sam paused as Mark walked up to their table, followed by a reluctant Chris. "Oh! Mark," she added in a whisper.

"Hey," he said.

"Hi," Claire said and then elbowed Sam, who broke out of her trance and said hi as well.

"Can we sit?" he asked.

"Sure!" Claire said.

Mark sat down immediately, but Chris paused for a moment.

"I thought we were looking for the girls," he said to Mark.

Mark waved a hand. "We'll find them. It isn't a big mall. Plus, they're probably going to make their way this way anyway. You keep a lookout."

Chris shrugged and sat across from Sam, who looked even more nervous than before. Claire begged her through telepathy to calm down.

"Who are you here with?" Claire asked Mark.

"Well, Chris and I came together, but we met up with Amber, Lauren, and Ashley when we got here. They told us they were coming today, so we figured, why not meet up? We lost them when they went into some chick store."

Claire nodded. "Nice," she said simply, avoiding mentioning that they'd already run into the three witches, not wanting to dredge up the memory of a not-so-great visit.

"What are you guys here for? Just chilling?" he asked.

"Yeah. And Sam here decided she was going to break and get CliffsNotes for *Romeo and Juliet*," Claire said, elbowing Sam with a laugh. She hoped it would break Sam's little reverie by bringing her to a topic that she could discuss and reminding her of their shared fun in English class with Mark. It worked.

"Ugh . . . yes. I caved. I just can't do it," Sam piped in.

Mark grinned. "Not a bad idea, Levinski. I may have to borrow your copy when you're done, if you're cool with that."

Sam gave a broad smile. "Totally. I'll help any fellow slacker."

"I still can't believe we were given that poem essay on top of reading. They're trying to break us, and we're only a month in!"

"For real," Claire said.

"Hey, I hear the high school puts on a decent Halloween dance. You guys planning on going?"

Claire and Sam looked at each other. "We hadn't thought of it, but yeah, probably!" Claire responded. She had seen the flyer for that this past week. It was coming up soon, and she had meant to talk to Sam about it but forgot.

"Cool," Mark said.

Chris meanwhile was spending this whole time looking everywhere but at them, and when he suddenly stood up, Claire knew it was probably because the trio had showed up.

And sure enough . . . "There you guys are! We've been looking for you! We thought you were going to wait for us outside Deb," came Amber's trilling voice.

"I wanted to go look for you guys, but . . ." Chris's drawling voice said as he pointed toward the table they were at. Amber saw Claire and Sam, and the all too familiar look of a person who smelled something awful spread across her face.

"Oh, what a fun little party we're having here," she said, trying to act nice and sweet in front of Mark but fooling no one.

"Hey, Amber," Mark said, giving a half wave but not standing up. "Look who I ran into! We were just catching up a bit."

She smiled at them. It looked so painful. "Hello." Then she turned her attention back to Mark. "Are you guys ready to hit up the other stores?

Chris's brother will be here soon to take us to that movie. We don't want to be late."

"Right..." Mark said. Addressing Sam and Claire, he said, "Well, it was great to see you guys. I'll see you Monday. Unless... Do you guys want—"

"Mark! Come on!" Amber practically screeched.

"Enjoy," said Claire. She and Sam smiled and waved. He took the hint and left.

"Oh. My. God. He is so cute. And I think he's totally into you," Sam burst out when the motley crew was out of range.

"As if! Come on. He's just really nice, and we have a bunch of classes together. As do you," she pointed out to Sam.

"Yeah but he totally came over to talk to you. And he totally didn't want to leave when Amber showed up. And he was totally going to invite us to the movies!"

"And he *totally* did the same things to you."

"No. He was coming to talk to you, not me. His 'hey' was directed at you."

"Whatever."

"For real, dude. I think he likes you. As for his friend Chris? He can take a long walk off a short pier. Dude's a total asshole."

Claire snorted into her milkshake. "I'll definitely give you that one."

"God... they don't make rooms big enough for his ego. And his look? Ugh... gag me. He's clearly trying to be some cool guy but is, like, a frosted-tipped skinny kid who's paler than my aunt Muriel's ghost. Troy could knock him over with a look."

Claire lost it this time and broke into a fit of giggles. "Oh my god, Sam. Come on, let's get to the bookstore. We have just under an hour, and I know we're going to make a few stops along the way."

Sam nodded. After stopping at another clothing store where Sam gawked at a jean dress that was way over budget, the Disney Store (which they couldn't pass without perusing all the knickknacks and stuffed animals), and Claire's where they checked out all the earrings, chokers, scrunchies, and more, they finally made it to the bookstore. Claire heaved a deep sigh as she stepped through the dinging entryway. Oh, the smell of books. She regretted getting her cozy drink so early, or not coming here first, but carried on, falling into a comfortable stupor all the same.

"Where do you think the CliffsNotes live?" Sam butted in.

"I think they have their own section near the classics," Claire offered.

"Cool. I'm going to find what I need. Find me in the romance section after." And she took off.

Claire slowly made her way down the aisles of books, dragging her hand along the bindings. She stopped in the fiction section and started pulling down books one by one to read their backs and smell their pages. She took tabs on books she thought she'd want to read. She had a stack at home she had to make her way through before she could justify spending any of her allowance, but just being surrounded by them put her mind at peace. She could spend hours here, getting lost in all the possibilities. She moseyed her way around and eventually found Sam looking at Harlequin books per usual.

"Find your CliffsNotes?" Claire asked.

"Yeah . . . and this steamy number," she responded. Claire laughed. Sam opted to leave the hot read behind but purchased her cheat sheet, and they walked to meet Troy, who was already waiting.

Returning to Claire's house, they flopped down on her bed.

"I still think Mark likes you," Sam said, chomping away on a new piece of gum.

"Sam, can you for once not think about boys?" Claire said.

"How can I not? We're in high school, and a cute one just came to talk to us at the mall," Sam responded.

"Maybe he likes you. You guys do laugh an awful lot in English," Claire offered.

"Yeah, because we are equally horrible at understanding Shakespeare."

"And maybe that's something you can bond over. Especially when you have a book that he'll want to borrow now."

"Oh come off it, Claire. I'm not the girl boys crush on. I look like a ten-year-old boy, remember?"

Claire sat up and made to scold her, when she saw Sam was smiling, holding in a laugh.

"You suck," Claire said through a grin. "You better be kidd—"

Claire was cut off by her mom calling to her up the stairs. Opening her door, she shouted, "Yeah?"

"Phone's for you, hunny," she said. "Someone by the name of Adam Miller."

Claire's stomach dropped, and she stared at Sam, who was staring right back at her in shock.

"Claire?" came her mom's voice.

"Yeah, coming!" she called down, and then to Sam, "What does he want? What do I say?"

"How am I supposed to know!? Go get the phone, you idiot!" Sam squealed.

"But—"

"Claire?!"

"Go!"

"Come with me!"

"What?! Why? Just go get the damn phone! You guys have a cordless now, remember?"

"Right! The cordless!"

"Claire!!"

"Oh my god . . . GO!"

Claire ran back into her bedroom, throwing the door closed behind her, hand over the phone. "What do I say?!" she whispered to Sam.

"Gee, I don't know. Start with hello?" Sam said sarcastically.

Claire glared, took a deep breath, and put the phone to her ear. "Hello?"

"Hey! It's Adam. Adam Miller," came a sweet voice. Claire swore she could hear his smile over the line.

"Hi. Yeah, my mom said it was you. How's it going?" She gave an exasperated look to Sam, who just egged her on with a nod.

"Good. How about you?" he asked.

"Great! Sam and I went to the mall earlier and just got back actually," she offered.

"Nice. I hope you don't mind me calling your house. I looked you guys up in the phone book. Thankfully, there are only two Hanovers listed. I can tell you from personal experience that the other Hanovers do not have a Claire living there."

Claire laughed. "Good to know. I'm glad you found me. What's up?" She hoped she sounded happy to hear from him but not overly excited. She looked to Sam again for confirmation of how she was doing and received two thumbs up.

"Well, I was actually wondering if you'd gotten through the geometry work yet. I was trying to do everything last night but got stuck on a problem. Wasn't sure if you could help me. Totally cool if it's not a good time," he said.

"No! Of course! Let me grab my book." She waved Sam out of the way as she sat on her bed and opened her book to her unfinished homework. "Which question were you struggling with?"

"That last one with a million parts to it," he said. Claire looked. It was a question regarding a floor plan where you had to find the perimeter and area of the room and then the areas of different pieces of furniture. The final part was to fit all the furniture into the room.

"Ooh . . . that one is a doozy. But I think if you take it step-by-step, it's doable. I can do it with you on the phone now if you'd like. I haven't done it yet."

"Really? That'd be awesome! Thank you."

Claire smiled at the phone while Sam looked on encouragingly. She then grabbed her math folder, which had what she thought would make this problem easier to figure out. "Hey, do you happen to have graph paper at home? It may make this easier."

"Yeah, I think so. Let me check my dad's office. He has everything in there. Hang on a sec. I'll be right back." And he left.

Claire looked to Sam. "He's going to get some graph paper. How am I doing?"

"Killing it," she whispered and then covered her mouth to squeal.

"Good," Claire said, grinning broadly, and then, hearing a noise, mouthed, "He's back."

"Alright. Got some graph paper. I was right: my dad had plenty."

"Perfect. So the way I would go about this is to first recreate that floor plan on the graph paper, the squares each equaling one foot. That way when it comes time to try and put those furniture pieces in, we have some room to work."

"Okay, I got you. Drawing floor plan." Claire did the same.

"Done," he said.

"Me too. Okay, so make sure you label the sides with the lengths, and the first question is to solve for that missing side and then that weird part that juts out."

They continued going back and forth, solving the perimeter and areas of all the parts, then worked on fitting in the pieces.

"There! I think we got it," Claire exclaimed a little while later.

"I think so! Awesome teamwork," Adam responded.

"Definitely."

"Well, thanks again for taking my call. And for helping me. I would definitely have been stuck."

"Nah . . . you would have been good, I'm sure of it. You barely needed me."

"No, I definitely needed you. You made it seem easier than I thought it was, so, thanks. I get overwhelmed with math. Especially when questions have seventeen parts to them."

Claire chuckled. "I hear you there."

They paused.

"Well . . . thanks again, Claire," he said.

"Yeah. No problem. See you Monday?"

"You bet," Adam said hesitantly.

"Cool. Well . . . bye."

"Bye," he said and listened for the click signaling Claire had hung up. He ran his hand through his hair as he hung up his own phone on the wall in the kitchen. He folded his arms, leaned against the same wall, and thought for a moment. He had gone back and forth on whether to do what he had just done. He really had needed help with the math work, and he didn't really have anyone else he could call. Well . . . some of his friends probably could have helped. Plenty, actually. Was he looking for an excuse to call her? And if so, what did *that* mean?

He had definitely been nervous and excited to hear her pick up . . . but was that just general nerves and excitement? Or just like seeing a friend . . . of course it was just like seeing a friend. But . . . he definitely didn't feel like that when Jason called . . . that would be weird.

No. He had definitely just needed math help, and she had been the best one for the job . . . that was it. It had to be . . . because if it was more than that . . . he had a bigger problem on his hands.

"I can't believe you just got a call from a boy. A sophomore at that. Who is absolutely dreamy," Sam said as Claire hung up.

"Sam, he just needed math help. That's it."

"And he chose you of all people to look up in the phone book and call!! Oh. My. God. This is so exciting. We need a calendar so we can mark this occasion." She let out a squeal.

Claire couldn't contain her smile. "Sam, come on. For real. Let's not make something of nothing. He's a friend. A really nice friend."

"A really nice, cute friend you mean! Claire, come on." Sam arched an eyebrow.

"What?"

Sam put on a dramatic impersonation of Claire from earlier: "Come with me! I don't know what to say! I'm Claire Hanover, and I forgot my parents have a cordless phone!"

"Shut up. My parents literally just got the cordless phone like four months ago. And we still don't have one in the kitchen and office. It isn't completely out of the realm of possibility that I would forget that."

"Or," Sam said, giggling, "it's because you were nervous to talk to him, and that is a something, not a nothing."

"Alright, enough of this," said Claire. "Let's finish the work we didn't get to."

"Oooookay," Sam said, throwing herself down on the beanbag. "Romeo, Romeo . . . wherefore art thou Romeo . . . oh right, you're on the other end of the line and my dear friend doesn't realize it."

"Really?" Claire said with a cocked eyebrow.

"Okay. I'm done now," Sam said, letting out a burst of laughter.

The following Monday, Sam and Claire followed their normal morning routine, but on their way to Sam's locker, Claire parted for a brief trip to the band room.

"I'll meet you at your locker. Be right back," she said to Sam as she turned off. Walking in, she saw that Mr. Johns was the only one there, looking over what appeared to be music arrangements.

"Knock knock," she said.

He turned immediately and smiled at Claire. "Miss Hanover. So nice to see you this morning. What can I do for you?"

"I was wondering . . ." She was afraid this was going to sound incredibly stupid, but she didn't know how else to proceed. "Is Adam the only one who will be using the drum set today?"

He looked slightly taken aback but recovered quickly. "Yes, I believe so. He sees me twice today and should be the only one using it."

"Is it okay if I leave something on it for him?" she asked, hoping that cleared up her odd question a little bit.

"Sure. By all means."

"Great. Thanks." She returned his smile. Heading over to the drum set, she pulled out of her front overall pocket a cassette with a piece of paper taped to the front that said "Adam." After Sam had left Saturday, she'd gone through all her cassettes to figure out what the best choice would be to return his favor. It was harder than she'd thought to decide. Should she go with something edgy so he'd think she had an edgy side? Should she stay away from pop? Something deep so he would know she was a thinker? Or maybe old-school so he'd think she had an old soul?

Then she decided to scratch all that because it wasn't about making him think anything. He hadn't shared a Tom Petty tape because he'd wanted her to think something special about him. It had been because it meant something to him. Claire had a little bit of everything in her collection. Music held such an emotional connection for her, and to be honest, sometimes she did feel edgy, and at other times she felt like sitting quietly and just thinking, and sometimes she liked to sing along with Sam, holding hairbrushes, to the most upbeat and ridiculous tunes. But she did have favorites, and to replace his Tom Petty cassette, she'd decided to go with one of her best. One that she'd had for a long time, playing it often since she was small, thanks to her dad.

"Thanks again," she said as she headed out, the cassette left on the drum set stool.

"Anytime." Mr. Johns waved.

Another day of classes with Sam passed in its usual way. They handed in their geography and science homework they had completed over the weekend; got all their lovely new assignments; were told they would be using the microscopes soon, which Sam was excited about; ate on the lawn again because Claire insisted on soaking up the fall weather as much as possible, even though Sam claimed she was a popsicle; and suffered through floor hockey in gym with the hot-headed athletes in their class who missed the memo that it was phys ed and not the Stanley Cup. Finally, Claire was making her way into band class, although just in the nick of time, as Sam had gone on a tangent in the locker room about those Stanley Cup finalists, leaving her seconds to grab her stuff from her locker.

She walked through the door as the bell rang and immediately took her place at the piano as Mr. Johns started addressing the class. She couldn't help but find Adam across the room, who was clearly waiting for her to do just that. He gave her a small wave and a smile. She grinned her response and couldn't help but blush a bit. She was nervous at the idea that she had given him one of her cassettes. In fact, after she had done so that morning, she had almost turned right back around to take it back. It was kind of an intimate gesture—letting someone in on her musical joys and loves—but she reminded herself that she was simply paying him back for the one he had given her, and so she just lived with herself teetering between contentment and embarrassment all day.

She played the scales as the band followed along, then the notes for Adam to tune the timpani, and finally they started practicing their pieces, stopping here and there for Mr. Johns to butt in. When the bell rang and everyone left, Claire grabbed her bag and decided she was going to take off, suddenly not wanting to hear what Adam thought of the cassette tape she'd left. But . . .

"Claire!" his voice rang out to her as she was heading to the door. She stopped and turned.

"Hey," she managed. He walked over, and she felt a flush creep up her face. Why was this happening to her now?

"I thought you'd stick around today, maybe," he said a little awkwardly.

"Oh! Yeah, I can hang for a sec," she said.

"Well, you don't have to. I just . . ." Adam ran his hand through his hair. Claire's blush flushed furiously. Of course she would make this situation more awkward than it needed to be.

"Thank you," he blurted out. "For the tape. I like Gordon Lightfoot. My dad had a few of his records."

Claire felt her nerves calm a little. So he was thankful for the tape . . . he didn't think she was some stalker weirdo chick. Good. "You're welcome. I said I had to pay you back."

"Well, I can't think of a better way." He grinned.

"I hope you like it. *Sit Down Young Stranger* is my favorite album from him. Mostly because of 'If You Could Read My Mind,' but I also love 'Minstrel of the Dawn' and his version of 'Me and Bobby McGee.' I listened to that tape with my dad all the time."

"Cool! I can't wait to listen," Adam responded, touched by the sentimental value of this choice.

Claire smiled. "Enjoy. And remember it's pay-back for Tom Petty . . . so keep it."

Adam raised his eyebrows. "But—"

"Ah—nope. Them's the rules," she said. She felt her face growing hotter and decided she needed to leave before she embarrassed herself, not knowing why she was struggling so much. "I gotta go. But I'll see you around, Miller." She left before he could argue.

Adam watched her walk away, the part of him he'd been trying to ignore lately wishing she hadn't. He shook his head and rushed to pick up and head out himself before he got in trouble for being late yet again.

Claire couldn't hide her happiness when she met up with Sam, and rather than arguing with her about her overly excitable way of discussing boys, she told Sam about the tape exchange, although she still denied, even to herself to some extent, having a crush. She was too practical for that after all . . . sort of.

The next geometry class, Claire found Adam waiting for her, and she took her seat. "Hi! Well, didn't you get here early today," she said, pulling out her math homework and book.

"Yeah. Kind of just came straight here this morning," Adam said slowly, a quietness about him.

"Bring the homework?" Claire asked, not really registering his answer as she looked over her own.

"Yup. Got it right here," he responded, changing gears and giving her a smile.

They went over the answers as a class to self-correct, and when Adam and Claire got all the parts to the final question right, they instinctively high-fived, then chuckled. They then suffered through the lecture as Mr. Stevenson just did math problems on the overhead projector, half the time erasing everything to start the next problem before Claire could finish her notes, until the bell rang.

Claire and Adam parted ways in the hall, where she headed to English.

Mark was at their table when Claire entered the room, Sam rushing in right behind her.

"Oh my god, you'll never guess what happened in math class," Sam said as they went to join Mark.

Claire had a guess that it had to do with a boy, but she feigned innocence: "What would that be?"

"Okay, so I was sitting at my desk, kind of in the middle of the row, like, to the left of the class, and out of nowhere this guy named Logan decided to sit next to me today. He usually sits all the way to the right in the last seat of the row, and today he sat right next to me," she said in one long breath, and then, taking another large one, "And so I said hi and he said hi and I smiled at him and he smiled back and at one point during class he asked if I had a piece of gum and I did so I gave one to him. That's when I asked his name and he said it was Logan and I told him my name and then the teacher told us to stop talking," she ended, breathing heavily.

"And?" Claire asked.

"And? What and? That's it," Sam said, looking at her in awe.

"Oh! Of course it is. That's exciting, Sam," Claire said, trying to hold in her laugh, Mark, who was listening in, doing the same.

"Oh shut up! That's a big deal!"

"Yeah! Sharing a smile and gum is a very big deal," Claire said, chuckling. When Sam glared, she back-tracked. "Okay, look. I'm just kidding, Sam. I'm glad you talked to a guy today, and you did get his name, which is major, so kudos."

"Yes. Thank you. I did get his name. So, good on me. And next time when we're in class together, I can say, 'Hi, *Logan,*' and maybe we'll have more of a conversation."

"I'm sure that is exactly what will happen," Claire said. "Honest," she added when Sam's eyes squinted.

Mrs. Lebel started addressing the class, and their conversation ceased. They were to read the next ten pages of *Romeo and Juliet* as a small group and then discuss the questions that she handed to them. Luckily, Mrs. Lebel didn't rearrange groups, so Mark, Claire, and Sam got to work together.

Sam groaned. "At least we get to read it together."

"I didn't even read the homework," Mark piped in.

"Me neither. I did, however, read the CliffsNotes version I picked up," Sam added.

They both looked to Claire, who rolled her eyes and said, "Of course I read it."

"Care to help us make sense of it all?" Sam said, batting her eyes. "Pretty pretty please?"

"Oh fine . . . But you guys owe me, then," she returned, and she then went on to explain the previous reading assignment before proceeding to read the next pages aloud. They each took on a role or two and got through it, with Mark and Sam stumbling through many of the words, all three of them falling into giggles often.

"Okay, okay," Claire said as Sam snorted. "Mrs. Lebel is looking at us. We need to answer these questions now."

Claire didn't wait for the nomination to be the scribe of the group. She read the questions out loud, they discussed to the best of their ability, and Claire took notes.

"How much more of this book do we even have?" Sam asked, flipping through her copy.

"Enough," Mark replied.

"You guys are pathetic," Claire said with a smirk as the bell rang. Mrs. Lebel shouted over the shuffle to turn in their responses on the way out, and Claire said a quick goodbye to Sam as she did just that. Mark waited behind her and walked out with her.

"Hey, before you head off . . ." Mark said, leaning in close to her as students rushed past. "You know that Halloween dance the school is putting on? The weekend before Halloween?" Claire nodded. "Well, there is actually another party that night that's supposed to be dope. My cousin who's a junior told me about it. Some senior dude whose parents are away is throwing it. I've been invited through my cousin, and he said I could tell a few people. Chris is going. And I asked Amber, who I assume is bringing Lauren and Ashley. But . . . you want in?"

Claire didn't really know what to say. A party? At a senior's house? That screamed questionable. But being invited to a party was a pretty big deal.

"Well . . . I mean, are we *really* invited? I don't want to intrude," she said a little apprehensively.

"Yeah, man! I can invite whoever I want. My cousin just said to keep it small so the party doesn't get out of hand. So is that a yes?"

Claire bit her lip. "Can Sam come?"

"Uh . . ." he looked a little hesitant. "Uh . . . yeah. Sure!"

"Okay . . . then, yes."

He smiled. "Sweet. It's the big yellow house on Vining Street. The one on the corner that's set off a little bit from the other houses. Number twelve."

"Okay. Sounds good," she said, and they both hustled off to class with seconds to spare.

Claire took her spot in study hall next to the sleeping beauty with the Discman. She had actually tried doing this as often as she could because sometimes she could hear what he was playing, and she enjoyed listening right along with him. Many times it was hip-hop, which Claire enjoyed, but sometimes he would switch it up. Today was one of those days. When she sat, she couldn't quite make out what it was, but soon enough the song shifted, and she recognized the guitar and drum intro of a chill alt-rock song that she loved. *Nice choice, Discman Dude*, she thought.

She leaned back in her chair and found herself letting the lead singer's unique voice wash over her. She knew going to a party that a senior was throwing at a house with no parents was probably a dumb idea. She also knew that getting invited to a senior party with no parents was huge . . . like, reputation changing huge. Did this make her *cool*?

She also couldn't help but notice that Mark hadn't invited her and Sam when they had all been together and had seemed hesitant when she'd asked if Sam could join. Was this because he didn't want to overstep boundaries and invite too many people? Or was this because he didn't really want to invite Sam? They seemed to get along fine in class, and he talked nicely to her . . . but he did only talk to her when Claire was there. Was he just being nice? Mark himself seemed nice, of course. But his being friends with Chris kind of turned Claire off. Chris had proven himself to be nothing but a jerk so far. She couldn't shake the feeling that when they had all met at the mall, he hadn't wanted to sit with them not because he wanted to go find Amber and friends, but because he didn't want to be seen with her and Sam.

She slid down her chair and rested her head on the back of it, staring at the ceiling. A party. She would have to sneak out if she wanted to go to it. Her parents would never let her. She and Sam had agreed to live it up in high school. This was a chance to do that. They had vowed to take risks, put themselves out there a little more, spice things up. She still struggled with body image and her own self-consciousness at being most likely viewed by all as a nerd, so getting invited was a huge boost.

Overall, she felt that she was coming into her own a bit this year. Not that the attention from others, let alone boys, should determine her worth, but it *was* kind of nice to feel that Mark was interested in her, at least enjoyed her company and had thought to invite her to a party. And then there was Adam . . . Adam, who hadn't overtly expressed interest per se but at least seemed to enjoy her company as well. And they now had a "thing", with the whole tape exchange, if he made the next move and gave her another one, that is. Adam's smile, his genuine quality, the mysteriousness of him, his depth—it gave Claire much to think about, and she felt that maybe that was why she was so keen on him. Not a crush . . . but intrigue. Oh, who was she kidding. It was a crush, but she wasn't going to admit that, and she was smart enough to know to play it cool, safe, and slow. It could just be the idea of him and not *him*. She didn't know him all that well. But the moments they'd shared so far had been nice.

Back to the party: she would just have to talk to Sam and see what she thought. They were in this crazy ride of high school together after all. The final twangs played next to her, indicating the end of the song. She sat up, shaking off her thoughts, and got to work.

"A party! No way! Pinch me, I must be dreaming. You got us invited to a senior's party? How in the actual hell did you do that?" Sam was squealing in between just about every word as they walked their familiar path home.

"You are so flipping right now. Mark just mentioned it to me, and I told him yes. But seriously, Sam, we need to think this through."

Sam wasn't paying any attention and was instead talking in a pure state of euphoria. "Sam Levinski will be seen at a party . . . and not just any party . . . but a senior party. With seniors. Like, upperclassmen seniors. I can't even."

"Sam," Claire butted in to no avail.

"What will kids say on Monday?" She put on a mock cool-guy attitude and said, "Hey, Sam . . . cool party this weekend," as she made eyes and finger-gun pointed with a click of the mouth at an imaginary person.

"SAM!" Claire grabbed her arm, which finally gained her attention.

"What?!"

"Sam. We need to think this through. It is cool we were invited and everything, but we need to think. Our parents are never going to let us go to an unchaperoned party of a high school senior."

"Yeah . . . I know," Sam said as they continued walking.

"Which means we're going to have to sneak out," she said.

"Yes . . . I know."

"Does this mean nothing to you? I see this as a pretty major problem."

"Claire, come on. Didn't we promise we were going to go outside the box this year? We'll figure it out. So we sneak out to a party for one night. It isn't the end of the world."

Claire rolled her eyes. "Maybe not . . . it may also not be the safest thing either."

"Oh come on! There will be so many students there, and we'll stick close to Mark, Chris, and the gang . . . even if that means having to be near Amber and her bitches."

"Oh, so now we like them because we're going to a party? And you really think Amber and clan are going to watch out for us?" Claire asked snarkily.

"Okay, but we'll have each other. We won't leave each other's sides. Come on . . ."

Claire bit her bottom lip, thinking.

"Claire, you said it was on the end of Vining Street, right? That's, like, a five-minute walk from our houses. We'll be fine!"

Claire let out a burst of held-in air. "Okay, fine. But—"

"YES!" Sam squealed.

"BUT—we need to promise to come up with a plan. A foolproof plan."

"Of course!"

"Like, a plan on how we're going to sneak out and get back and what we're going to do when we're there."

"Yes, yes!"

"Like, a safety word and everything. And if one of us wants to leave, no arguing . . . we go."

"Yes, Claire! We will come up with all of it, okay? Now take a chill pill and just revel in the excitement with me!"

Claire smirked, Sam squealed, and they continued their walk, talking animatedly.

Creep

"Okay so we each sneak out of our rooms around eleven and meet up at the tree on the corner shortly after. If one of us isn't there by eleven fifteen, we bail and go back home." It was Friday after school. Claire was pacing in her room while Sam looked up at her from the floor, gum smacking. They had to sneak out individually rather than sleep over at someone's house to then sneak out. The reason being that Sam had a family get-together around dinner and had already been shot down from spending the night at Claire's. It wasn't what Claire wanted, but they had to make do.

"Right . . ." came Sam's bored input due to having gone over this several times by now.

"We walk to the party, and we agree to stick together no matter what. We go to the bathroom together, we walk around together, we don't lose each other at all. Just in case."

"Yes."

"Two-drink limit. No getting trashed, or we'll have a hard time sneaking back in. And it's our first party. We need to feel it out."

"Mmmhmmm."

"If one of us feels uncomfortable or ready to leave, we do so, no matter what." Claire stopped her pacing to look at Sam expectantly.

"Oh, sorry . . . Yes."

"We leave by three a.m." She continued pacing.

"Word."

"We call each other first thing the next morning to make sure we're good and that our parents didn't catch us," she finished.

"Yes . . . Are we done now? We've been over this like a million times already."

"I know, Sam, but I want to make sure we're doing this safely and together."

"You read too much, you know that?"

"What? What does that have to do with anything?"

"All those mysteries, crazy fantasy stories, horrors—it gets in your head and messes around, and so you overthink too much and get all these crazy worst-case scenarios. Hence your clear desire to make sure we don't end up murdered or something. There will be no Freddy Krueger or Jason. It's a high school party. We'll be fine!"

Claire rolled her eyes. "Okay, okay. Plan is in place. I'll stop."

"Good. Because now we need to pick out your outfit!" Sam got up and went to Claire's closet. Thumbing through everything in there, she started pulling things out.

"Oh . . . I was just going to wear something simple."

"Really? Come on. What about this?" She pulled out a short-sleeved black dress with small pink flowers. It was a V-neck with three buttons. "With your jean jacket and holey nylons? You'd look fiiine!"

"Why do I need to look fine? And that will be a freezing outfit to have on. It's late fall, remember?"

"What, are you going to hang out outside or something?"

"Well . . . no, but still. We have to walk. And I need to be able to climb down and back up the trellis. I can't do that in *that*."

"Hmmm . . . I forgot you were mountain climbing tonight." Sam's house was a ranch and so only had one floor. She continued to look through Claire's closet.

"I was actually thinking of maybe wearing this," Claire butted in and grabbed some folded laundry on top of the bureau. She showed Sam a black long-sleeved V-neck snap shirt, light-washed high-waisted jeans, and a long burnt-orange sweater.

"It's cool . . . but not sexy cool," Sam observed. "I do like the top though. Is that new? It will really show off your boobs."

Claire put her head in her hand. "I'm not looking to be sexy, Sam. I don't need to flaunt around like Amber, okay? This is comfortable, will be warm, and is still cool."

"Oh alright, I'll give it to you."

"So, what are you going to wear, then?"

"I think my overalls with my purple velvet crop top."

"And why were you giving me a hard time for dressing relaxed and not sexy?"

Sam shrugged. "Because I think you have the body for it! Plus, Mark likes you! And maybe you should spice it up!" Sam poked Claire's sides.

"Ugh . . . Sam, come on! You're redic!"

"I know." She gave a burst of laughter. "Oh I canNOT wait for this party. It's going to be awesome. What are you going to do with your hair? I was thinking of putting some gel in mine and just let it be big and curly. Maybe throw a hat on after. Or a big ole ponytail on top of my head!"

"Either one, I'd say. I'm just going to let my hair do what it does."

"Yeah, you can get away with that though. Your hair is like the perfect amount of straight and wavy. Mine's just . . . zing!"

Claire laughed. "It is perfect too. Plenty of volume!"

"Thanks." She looked at her watch. "Doh! I gotta go! I have to watch Joey while my mom goes birthday shopping for him. Which, by the way, I realized we never did when we went to the mall."

"Whoops! What are you going to do?"

"Just give her some money to get him something from me."

"Well, have fun with Joey! I can't believe he's turning five already."

"I know, right? As if! I'll call you later."

"Sounds good. And I'll see you tomorrow night," Claire added, and they did their five-step friendship handshake, internally screaming their excitement.

Lying on her bed, Claire stared at the ceiling, her glow-in-the-dark stars and moons covering it. She was excited now. Nervous still . . . but excited. They had a plan and they'd be together. It'd be fine and fun, and they'd be seen at a senior party. Nothing could possibly go wrong.

Claire opened her door to peek down the hall. Troy's room was closed, lights off, and her parent's room was closed as well, the dim gleam of a bedside lamp shining under the door. Her mom was most likely up reading but would soon fall asleep, if she hadn't already, book in hand per usual. Claire carefully closed her door. Grabbing her sweater, she looked at herself in the mirror one last time. Her makeup was subtle but there. She had colored in her eyebrows a little and had put on some foundation to even everything out, some hazelnut tinted eye shadow, some mascara, and her favorite deep burgundy lipstick. She flipped her hair over to add some volume, hit it with a little hairspray, and shrugged. This was as good as it was going to get, and if she was being totally honest with herself, she did feel pretty good about how it had turned out.

She scanned her room to see if there was anything she should stick in her pocket. She grabbed a ten-dollar bill, just in case, and her red Swiss Army knife . . . just in case. That was maybe a little over the top, but you never could be too careful. Pulling on her Doc Martens, she steadily slid the window open, followed by the screen. Taking one last glance around her room, she climbed onto the windowsill and then down the trellis, landing softly below. She took a deep breath and listened carefully for a moment, not really sure what she was expecting to hear, and when nothing came, she made her way to the tree.

"Oh thank God. There you are," came Sam's whispered trill. "I was getting nervous standing here. A squirrel that ran by very much sounded like a serial killer."

Claire chuckled under her breath. "We're good now. Let's go."

They started walking around the block, arm in arm.

"So no problems sneaking out?" Claire asked.

"None! Mom crashed on the couch by, like, nine. I got her to bed and was golden. Quick little jump out the window and I was gone!"

"Same . . . although climbing down the trellis wasn't as easy as I thought it was going to be, but I managed."

"You should have practiced."

"Oh and that wouldn't have looked suspicious to anyone," Claire said, eyebrows raised. It was chilly, a sense of eeriness with Halloween so close, breezes blowing through the trees gently, crisp and clean. They were trying to keep to the shadowy parts of the street, and, thankfully, all the houses seemed quiet. Only one car went by, which sent Sam into a frenzy, causing her to grab Claire and dodge behind a hedgerow in front of a well-manicured lawn.

"Honestly, Sam," Claire said, fixing her hair from the shrub's prying limbs.

"Sorry! It made me edgy. What if it was someone going to kill us! Or a cop! Or . . . or . . ." she trailed off, clearly unable to think of any other horrific thing the random drive-by car could be.

Claire rolled her eyes. "Come on, we're almost there."

They made a few more turns around the blocks and finally saw what had to be the party house ahead. It was set off of the neighborhood road, cornered on the curb. It had a long driveway that led up to a large three-floored house that had lights on behind every shaded window and what Claire thought was some fancy dance lighting coming through one on the first floor. She heaved a deep breath as they made their way up the driveway.

"Okay . . . stick to the plan," Claire said as they approached the stairs.

"Yeah, yeah . . . How do I look?" Sam asked, fluffing her ponytail and tightening her scrunchie. The drumming bass of music could be felt vibrating across the porch floor.

"Great!"

"Okay. Let's do this!" Sam squealed, and they knocked on the door.

No one answered it. They exchanged glances, shrugged, and let themselves in. As soon as the door swung open, the music of Dr. Dre smacked them in the face, as did the overlying noise of voices . . . a lot of voices.

"There are a lot more people here than I thought there was going to be," Claire said.

"What?!"

"I said," she raised her voice higher, just shy of yelling, "there are a lot of people here!"

"Yeah!!" Sam yelled back. Claire got the impression that this didn't bother her at all. Claire looked around and took in just how many upperclassmen were there. But as she scanned the crowd, she recognized a few people who were in her math class and then two who were in band. And, of course, she knew Mark, Chris, Amber, and friends, wherever they were. She breathed a little easier. She could do this.

"Let's go somewhere," she said to Sam. "I don't think we should just chill in front of the door all night." Sam nodded eagerly. They decided to go left, the right leading to what looked like the dance room, which they weren't quite ready for yet. They walked into a professional grade kitchen, at least that's what it seemed like to Claire, and there was an island covered in cups and alcohol, as was the entire countertop. People were standing around chatting. It was a little quieter here at least.

Claire leaned into Sam and whispered, "Should we grab a drink?"

"Yeah . . . good call." They stepped forward, looking over the sea of bottles ranging from vodkas to whiskeys to liqueurs.

"What do we do?" Sam said in a hushed voice.

"I don't know. I mean, you mix it with stuff obviously . . . but I don't know *what* stuff." Claire had only ever had sips of wine coolers and a small glass of white wine with her mom on holidays. She didn't know how to mix drinks.

"Maybe there's, like, cans of beer or something in the fridge," Claire offered. As if on cue, a girl with curly blonde hair, a mini-skirt, and boots walked over to the fridge and opened it, revealing rows and rows of beer. Claire and Sam nodded to each other and walked over to join the girl. When she was done, she stepped aside and left it open for them.

"Okay . . . so my dad always drinks Bud Light when he does drink . . . Maybe we can grab one of those?" Claire said, unsure.

"Yeah! That sounds good," Sam added. They each grabbed a blue can, and Sam closed the door.

Hearing the cracked sound of the beers opening, fizz slightly engulfing the top, they tapped the cans together, said "cheers" simultaneously, and took swigs. Their faces of disgust mirrored each other to a tee.

"Ugh . . . blech! Your dad drinks this shit?" Sam asked through coughs.

"Yeah . . . it must be an acquired taste," Claire said.

"I guess the hell so. Maybe he lost taste buds in the marines or something."

"Come on, let's walk around a bit," Claire said. "Just pretend to drink it or something."

"Oh, I'm not wasting it," Sam said. "I'm just going to torture myself till I can finish it and get something else."

"Well, remember our two-drink rule."

"Oh come on, Claire. As long as we don't get drunk drunk, let's just have whatever, okay? We'll be careful."

"Oh . . . alright," she said a little hesitantly. A buzz wouldn't hinder their ability to sneak back in anyway.

They found the dining room, which had a table full of students, some girls sitting on the laps of others, playing what looked like poker, smoke wafting up around the chandelier. From there they continued on to a dimly lit sitting room that they passed right on by due to Claire's quick peek showing nothing but couples scattered about locking lips. This all brought them right back to the large front living room where the music was booming and a familiar friend was a blessing to be seen.

"Claire! Sam!" came Mark's yell. He sashayed over, red Solo cup in hand. "You made it!"

"Yeah!" Claire shouted back. "Cool party! More people than I thought!"

"I know, right!? Totally rad. A shit ton of people showed up with so much booze in hand. I overheard my cousin and his friend, the one throwing the party, saying it's their goal to drink it all tonight!"

Claire laughed. "That's a lot of drinking."

"Hell yeah!" Mark responded, then, turning his attention, said, "Hey, Sam."

"Hi! Thanks for the invite!"

Mark nodded and then returned to Claire. "Amber, Lauren, and Ashley just went to get more drinks. You guys want to follow?"

"Sure," Claire answered, not really wanting to see them but figuring it was better than the two of them being left alone again. They went full circle and ended back in the kitchen.

"What you drinking?" Mark asked.

"Well, we grabbed these, but we're not really feeling it," Claire said, holding up her can.

"Let's mix you something up instead," Mark said with a smile.

"Oh, Marky Mark! Where's my next drink?! What are you going to mix up for me this time?" Amber's whine trilled over them. She stumbled over, Lauren and Ashley behind her. She had picture-perfect makeup and hair as usual, wearing the velvet dress from Deb, which, on her, showed off enough leg to hail a ride.

Claire peered at Sam, who had decided to take a large swig of her beer at that moment.

"I was actually going to make Claire here a drink," Mark said, ignoring the arm Amber threw around him.

She turned to Claire with mock surprise. "Hanover! How wonderful it is to see you." Then she saw Sam. "Levinski! You too! How . . . surprising. Glad you were able to snag invites, you two. Hey . . . hey, Levinski, what do you think of my dress? Isn't it cute? Hugs all my curves in just the right places. Don't you think?"

Sam just smiled ever so sweetly and said, "It's lovely, Amber. Like the skin of stuffed sausage."

Claire stared, but thankfully, Amber was clearly feeling her drinks because she said, "Oh you!" and giggled sickeningly. Sam downed the rest of her beer.

"Here we go," Mark butted in. "Malibu, some orange juice, and a splash of cranberry." He handed cups to both Claire and Sam.

"Thanks!" they answered in unison. Sam took a sip first while Claire snuck her half-drunk can onto the counter, hoping no one would notice her wasting it.

"This is delicious!" Sam said. "Oh my god, you would never know it was alcohol. Huge difference from that beer." She laughed. Mark smiled but addressed his next question to Claire.

"What do you think?" he asked.

Claire took a sip. It was quite good. And Sam was right: it didn't really taste like alcohol at all. "It's great!"

"Good. I'm glad you like it. All the chicks seem to dig it."

Claire smiled. Sam took another swig.

"I'm really glad you came, Claire," Mark said.

"Thanks for the invite," she returned.

"Hey, you guys," Amber broke in, throwing an arm around Mark again, leaning into the circle they had created. "Enough of this little powwow. Let's dance!"

Mark looked to Claire, who shrugged her okay.

"Alright, Amber, let's go," he said, like one giving in to a two-year-old. She grabbed his hand and led him back to the living room. Claire noticed on second viewing that all the furniture had been pushed to the side and stacked on top of each other to create the dance area. That must have been why it appeared so big. However, it was a pretty big room anyway. Claire noted that these people must be rich.

Amber brought Mark right to the center of the room where about ten or more others were dancing already. Claire and Sam joined as La Bouche's "Be My Lover" started. They jumped around and sang along. "Can't Touch This," "I Like to Move It," "Another Night," and a slew of other songs played before Amber grabbed Sam's wrist and shouted, "More drinks!" and took off. Claire and Mark followed, along with Lauren and Ashley.

"Let's just mix whatever," Amber was saying to a laughing Sam when Claire and the rest made their way in.

"Sam," Claire said with a meaningful look. Sam just waved her off as Amber filled two cups with what looked like mostly Malibu.

"Cheers, Levinski!" Amber shouted, and they both took swigs. "Come on! I love this song!" she shouted as "Whoomp! (There It Is)" sounded through the house, the volume having been turned up. Sam allowed herself to be led off by Amber, giving Claire a large smile on her way by, drink in hand. Claire watched her go.

"How about another?" Mark said.

She looked at her cup. "I think I'm good. I could go for, like, a wine cooler or something. Do they have those here?"

"Lightweight, are you?" Mark smirked.

"Yeah . . . I quit back when I was ten and am just easing my way back into drinking," she retorted. "Of course I'm a lightweight! It's not like I drink all that often!"

Mark chuckled. "Okay, okay. I'll give you that. Here." He retrieved a red wine cooler from a drawer in the fridge and handed it to her.

"Thanks." She looked over toward the living room with mild concern.

"Don't worry about Sam. She'll be fine. Just having fun."

"Yeah . . ." she said half-heartedly and then saw him looking at her. "Yeah, no, you're right. She'll be fine. So, this place . . ." she gestured to the house around her, "it's huge!"

"I know, right? The upstairs has like fifty rooms, I swear. And a full attic space! There's a pool table up there. You want to go check it out?"

Claire glanced again toward the living room where the music was thumping its way through the walls and hallways. Their rule of sticking together had clearly gone out the window, right along with the two-drink one.

"Sure," she said.

Mark led her up a carpeted staircase to a hallway that had nothing but doors on it: bedrooms, some of which had socks hanging on the doorknobs. Claire noted to leave this floor alone. One door was open, and it led to a second staircase, this one wooden. Climbing up it, they stepped up into an open space the same length and width as the whole house. At one end was a pool table where a few guys were playing. The other end had a TV set up with a Nintendo. A group of guys, whom Claire could only see the backs of, were playing Super Mario. Mark led her over to the pool table where they watched the end of a game, the loser paying his opponent twenty dollars as Mark claimed the table.

"You play?" Mark asked as he reset the pool table.

"Not really." She laughed. "I've played down at Ron's, but that's about it."

"Ah yes, Ron's. Who hasn't played on that table, right?"

"Yeah." She smiled.

He finished setting up the triangle and then handed her a cue.

"I'll break and we play?" he asked.

"Sure!" she replied.

He hit the triangle of pool balls dead-on, sinking a striped one as they spread across the table. "Alright, alright, alright. I'm stripes. You're solids."

"Sounds good!"

He sunk another ball before missing his third shot, and Claire attempted to hit the two, but missed.

"Close!" he said as he shot for another and missed.

"Close? Either you've had too much to drink or are blind. That was not close. You don't have to be nice to me, ya know," she retaliated with a smirk as she went for another hit and sunk it.

"Well, I guess not . . . Alright, fine. We play dirty. And you're going down." They took turns, bad-mouthing each other the entire time. Claire did better than she thought and was left with two balls, while Mark attempted to get the eight.

"OH! Winnah winnah chicken dinnah! In your face," he said as the eight ball rolled into the corner pocket he had called.

Claire laughed. "You win, Calloway. Until next time."

"That was a pretty close game. I'll give you that." He held out a hand to shake.

"Psych!" he said, taking his hand away.

"Jerk," Claire said, taking his cue stick and putting them both away, but she was laughing.

"You're the one who said not to be nice."

"And the opposite of that is being an ass?"

He laughed. "Okay, okay. Friends?" He held out his hand yet again. She pondered it for a second and then reached out and shook it.

"Let's go check on the others," Claire said, suddenly aware of how much time she had spent there, and wondered if Sam was looking for her.

"You got it," he said, leading the way back downstairs. Peeking in the kitchen, they didn't see them, and so they headed to the dance floor. Claire spotted Sam in the center of the room, dancing animatedly with Amber, Lauren, and Ashley. She made her way toward them, noticing how pink Sam's cheeks were and how sweaty she looked. As soon as she got to them, however, Amber yelled, "More drinks!" and snagged Sam once again, running right past Claire, grabbing Mark on her way as well. Claire stood for a moment as Lauren and Ashley gave identical bitch stares toward Amber.

Claire was with them: she didn't like it either. It made her uneasy. Why was Amber so keen on being with Sam? They had never ever been friends, not even a little bit.

"Hanover! I knew you wouldn't be far behind. What are you two? Attached at the hip?" Amber shouted. Sam laughed. A drunken and ridiculous laugh. Claire ignored the taunt and sidled up next to Sam.

"Hey, I think you should slow it down a little," Claire whispered in her ear.

"Wha?! No way," Sam said in a voice much louder than the conversation Claire was trying to have. It was also shaky, with the hint of a giggle behind every word. It wasn't slurred at least . . . not yet anyway. "I'm having so much fun . . . like, seriously, the best time."

Claire stared at her intently. "How much have you had?"

"Oh, I don't know . . . two, three . . . okay, four."

"For real?"

"Yeah!" Sam said with a laugh.

"Levinski, catch!" Amber shouted and threw a small plastic container with a lid at her. Sam caught it.

"What is it?" she asked.

"It's a Jell-O shot, silly!"

"Jell-O? Cool!"

"Sam, can we talk?" Claire asked, grabbing her arm.

Sam rolled her eyes. "Fine." They went over to the hall that led around to the poker room and makeout session where it was a hair quieter.

"What?" Sam asked.

"Sam . . . I just . . . I feel like . . . We're not following any rules!"

"Claire. Chill out! It's a safe party with a bunch of people from school."

"A lot of whom we don't know. And it doesn't strike you at all odd that Amber is suddenly your best friend?"

"Why should it? You don't think I'm cool enough to be friends with Amber?"

"No . . . Sam . . . that's not what I mean. But, Amber hates us, remember?!"

"Mostly you," Sam said. Claire felt her cheeks flush, her eyes flash. "Look, Claire. I want to be cool. I want to enjoy this party and drink and just have fun."

"When did getting shit-faced drunk and making a fool of yourself make you cool? You don't think Amber is trying to do that? Make you the drunken idiot of the party?"

Sam's face burned this time . . . beyond the touch of alcohol. Claire knew she'd insulted her. "Sam . . . I didn't mean you *are* the drun—look . . . I just—"

"No. I know exactly what's going on. You're pissed that Amber is being nice to me and not you, that I'm getting the cool attention, AND that I'm not following your stupid rules. Who even comes up with rules for a freakin' party!?"

Claire glared. "Someone who doesn't want herself or her friend to get trashed, sick, and then caught by their parents. That's who."

"Well, lighten up, Sandra Dee, because this chick wants to actually have fun, and you're not going to stop her."

"Sam . . ."

"Just go, Claire. If you're so concerned about me making a fool of myself and embarrassing you, just go." And she turned on her heels and walked back to the kitchen.

"Sam," Claire said to no avail. "Sam!"

"Hey," a quiet voice behind her made her jump. It was a guy she didn't know. He had spiked hair.

"Uh . . . hi," she said, stepping back from him.

"Sorry about your friend," he said slowly. His eyes were squinting, and he reeked of skunk. Claire knew what that meant.

"Uh, thanks . . ."

"You wanna come hang out?" He pointed at the darkened room down the hall.

"No thank you," she said and quickly made her way back to the kitchen area. Mark was talking to Chris, Sam and her new pals nowhere to be seen. She groaned and decided to get some fresh air, seeing Sam and Amber jumping around the living room, holding hands, while shout-singing to some kind of homemade DJ mix version of "Dancing Queen" on her way out. Claire's heart stung, as that song had been a favorite of her and Sam's since they were kids. She threw the door open and slammed it shut behind her.

Claire stepped onto the front porch and felt the welcoming, cool air hit her. If Sam didn't want her there, then who cared. She'd do what she wanted and see how great of a friend Amber was when Sam was trashed and needed to get home . . .

Her face was flushed, and she wasn't entirely sure if it was from the heat in the house, her anger with Sam, the bit of alcohol she had consumed, or all three. Someone had opened the windows in the living room, the music now dancing across the front yard, lights from the house flashing across the leaf-covered ground. The streetlights glowed warmly along the nestled street of houses that were all dark, their owners long gone to bed. Claire wondered for a moment if the party would draw attention. Though it wasn't super loud outside, she could definitely hear the music and feel the thumping of the bass. Maybe it dimmed as it traveled across the yard and through the hedges that lined the property. It was a decent sized yard. She shrugged it off.

Making to sit on the steps, she stopped midway, seeing the sight of a familiar face chilling down on the curb. Smiling ever so slightly, her stomach fluttering a tinge, she changed pace and walked down the front pathway instead.

"Hey, you," she said as she sat next to him, stretching her legs out in front of her in the street. The scent of Cool Water cologne drifted on the air ever so faintly. He turned and smiled. It was always so genuine. Thoughts of Sam were swept right away.

"Hey," said Adam Miller. He was holding a bottle of something she didn't recognize.

"What are you doing out here?" she asked.

"I could ask you the same question," he replied with a grin.

"Well . . ." Not wanting to go into the whole drama that was Sam, she said, "You could say the party wasn't what I expected—I'm not really impressed with how a certain someone is acting—and so I came outside to take a break."

"You could say the same thing for me," he said, held up the bottle in a salute, and took a swig. "Here, have some. Though, I warn you, it tastes like shit."

"What is it?" She chuckled, taking it from him.

"No friggin' clue," he responded, the pained look still on his face from his gulp.

She shrugged and took a swig. He was right. It tasted like shit. "Oh God . . . that's awful," she said through coughs.

"I warned you." He laughed, taking the bottle back from her.

"It tastes like gasoline or . . . I don't even know what," she said, still making a face. It burned in her mouth and throat and tingled on her lips.

"Gasoline works," he said, taking another swig and half laughing, half coughing. She couldn't help but laugh along.

"The last tape you gave me was good, by the way," said Claire.

He nodded. "Yeah, I really like that album from Dave Matthews Band. I mean, everyone knows the singles, but their other stuff is really good too."

Claire nodded, recalling last week when she had found the present on the piano bench and the thrill she felt that they did in fact have a "thing" now.

"Agreed. I enjoyed it. Thanks," she said.

"Of course." He went quiet, took another swig of the bottle, and handed it off, which Claire accepted and did the same. "I've really enjoyed the whole exchanging cassettes thing, by the way. It's been fun."

She smiled wide, a slight flip in her stomach. "Me too. It's an exciting surprise to get one, and I enjoy picking out the ones I want to inspire you with." She gave a burst of laughter at how silly the last part sounded. Her cheeks were definitely getting pink now, her face beginning to feel flushed.

He chuckled, took the bottle, and drank, returning it right after.

"I agree. It is a nice surprise. And I'm not sure my selections have been inspiring at all, but it *is* fun to pick out what to give you. Hopefully, they've been new to you."

She nodded through her disgusted swig. "Yes! That's the thing. I mean, they have hits that I know, of course, like you said, but all the ones you give me I listen all the way through and find music I didn't know I liked."

"Right on," he said. They traded the bottle back and forth for a few more rounds, sitting in silence. It wasn't an awkward silence though. Adam leaned back on his elbows, and Claire sat, feeling the breeze blow by off and on, the distant sound of it lifting leaves and playfully whisking them across the ground and road.

Adam broke the silence. "How are you liking your freshman year?"

She thought a moment. "It's good. I've had a few run-ins with the class bitch . . . I think Mr. Stevenson has a stick up his ass . . . and the lunch kind of sucks unless I get a hot pretzel . . . but other than that, it's been good."

Adam laughed loudly, handing off the bottle again. "Sounds like you're kicking off your high school career well. How'd you get on the class bitch's bad side?"

"Well, it's been a thing for a while. But this time . . . I put my stuff in our locker," she said casually. Adam raised an eyebrow of confusion and she giggled. But her giggling turned into a roar of laughter that she couldn't stop. Adam, moving to his side to face her, started to chuckle along too, more at her than what she had said. Tears began coming to her eyes, and at this point, they both lost it.

"I literally put my stuff in our assigned locker, which was apparently too much for her, and she threw it all on the floor and basically told me if I crossed her again, I was done for."

"What?! That's whack, dude," he said, grinning. "What did you do?"

Claire calmed down a little bit and wiped the tears from her eyes, her breathing coming in heavily, still occasionally chuckling. Clearly, she had needed to let this out for a while. "Oh, I put my stuff there anyway, and when she came at me the next day, I told her to suck it, and if she didn't want to share a locker with me, then she could find a different one to throw people's shit out of."

Adam lifted his eyebrows. "For real?"

"Yeah . . . in my dreams. I haven't done anything about it yet."

"Dude . . ."

"Yeah . . . and that's my freshman year so far," she said calmly to which Adam laughed, and they both got going again, swapping the bottle back and forth, both appreciating the company of the other.

The thumping music inside shifted, and Claire heard the familiar beginning to Radiohead's "Creep."

"Oh man, I love this song!" she said.

"Me too," Adam agreed. They sat in silence for a few moments, letting the rhythmic drumming and simple guitar notes wash over them, followed by Thom Yorke's unique, relaxed voice that in combination with the music almost sounded otherworldly, waiting for those random and yet perfectly timed guitar riffs to punch the music.

They both went silent, and the air between them felt thick with meaning. Like they were sharing something more than a simple moment outside a party. Songs like this—they tear into your soul and force you to face things that are tucked away in the deepest parts of your mind and, maybe even more so, your heart. If Adam was feeling the same way she was, it was more than just a simple moment. It was a trip . . . an experience. And it was deep.

The voice screamed across the yard a lonesome question of belonging.

Sitting up, Adam squinted ahead of him like he was trying to see something that wasn't actually there and wouldn't ever actually be there. Like trying to see into your own thoughts. Like if you look hard enough, the things that bother you, the weight on your shoulders, everything . . . will just appear in front of you, and you'll be able to sort it all out . . . make sense of it. But in reality, you'll sit there looking on forever, until that weight squashes you . . . to nothing. But songs like this, they make you do that. They make you feel.

"Deep shit, huh?" he said quietly.

And when Claire turned to him, she saw that he was staring right at her. The music was getting more intense as the f-bomb once again rent the air, and the line that yearned to be something special shattered the sadder depths of your soul. Claire stared back and was at a loss for words. They *were* sharing something bigger than a moment. They *were* feeling this song on a whole different level. Whatever reasons didn't matter. Her eyes bored into his, and she felt a flush that had nothing to do with the bottle they had finished. He leaned closer, the Cool Water making a return, but this time mixed with a hint of cheap wine.

She leaned in too, heart fluttering in her throat.

They were almost nose to nose, when suddenly Adam's eyes widened, looking beyond her.

"Shit!" he said heavily.

"What?!" she said, jumping.

"Cops!"

"Wha—?"

"Come on!" And, as if on cue with the music, he shouted, "RUN!"

He put his hand out for her to grab, which she did without hesitation, and they ran.

The song still ringing in their ears, he led her around the line of hedges, beyond the small grove of trees in the back, through a neighbor's yard and driveway, across another street, and into a deeper wood. Time almost seemed to slow down, the world around her moving slowly, Claire feeling her heart race, adrenaline coursing through her, and yet the trees whisked by, the echo of the music seeming to follow them.

They slowed down, their breathing heavy, and finally came to a stop. Claire couldn't help but start laughing through her gasps.

"Oh . . . my . . . god . . . I can't even believe that just happened," she managed to get out. "Like . . . oh my god. We just ran from the cops!"

Adam couldn't help but grin back at her, his own breathing coming hard.

"Like, for real! The cops! With blue lights and everything . . . and we totally just ran from them. Oh, shit . . . Sam . . ." She felt a little tipsy and giggly. "Where even are we?"

Through his smirk, he said, "Well, once we walk this way a bit, I'm sure you'll know where we are. Come on." He held out his hand again and Claire accepted. They walked for maybe five minutes and stopped when they came to a tall chain-link fence. Claire recognized the playground of her old elementary school on the other side.

"Ever climb a fence before?" he asked, yet another smirk spreading across his face.

"Uh, no . . . but hey, I already snuck out, drank illegally, and ran from the cops tonight. I might as well add climbing a fence onto school property too."

He laughed. "Just stick your toes in the holes and climb on up. When you get to the top, swing your legs over and climb back down. Easy enough."

"Yeah . . . easy for you to say. You apparently jump fences all the time." His smile seemed to be permanently stuck on his face in the amusement that was Claire.

"Come on. I'll go up with you."

Together, they climbed the fence. The top got a little tricky for Claire but she made it. He made it down the other side before her, having jumped midway, and waited at the bottom. As she made her way down, she had another spell of giggles. "I can't believe I'm doing this," she muttered to herself.

"You got it. Come on," he said, raising his arms in case she fell. But she made it and jumped down the rest of the way.

"Good job. Fence climbing: check," he said. She nodded and swayed a little. "Come on. Let's chill for a bit. Gotta sober you up before you go home. I take it you snuck out? Or are you supposed to be at a friend's house?"

"I snuck out," she said as he took her hand once again, and they headed to the swings.

They each took a swing, Adam sitting with one leg on each side, facing her, and Claire pushing off. There was something so freeing about revisiting the swings. The wind blowing through your hair, leaning back just far enough to see the world upside down behind you, stretching your legs out as far as they could go till it looked like you could tap dance on the stars. The rush felt good on her face and in her heart. Adam's eyes followed her from below, quiet and watchful.

She dragged her feet on the ground and slowed, coming to a stop to look at him. "What are you thinking?" she asked. She wasn't usually this forward—it must have come from the confidence that was alcohol . . . or maybe it was the comfort that was Adam.

He gave a small grin. "Nothing really. Just watching you swing." He pulled out a pack of cigarettes and a lighter from inside his jacket. Tapping the box on his palm, he took one out, placed it between his lips, and lit it after putting the box away.

She smiled. "You're an interesting guy, Adam Miller."

"Yeah? Why's that?"

"I don't know. You have this quiet, mysterious thing going on . . . like . . . a deep thinker. The quiet, contemplative type. Then this dorky, band geek persona. And an edgy cool guy, bad boy vibe," she said, squinting at him as though sizing him up.

"Can someone not be all three?"

"Of course they can. That's what makes you interesting."

He blew smoke away from her. "I see."

"You know those are bad for you, right?" she threw out.

"Yeah . . . I know," he said, flicking the end.

"Then why do you do it?" she asked, chuckling.

He shrugged. "Something to do, I guess."

She rolled her eyes and threw one of his own shitty grins back at him, which he laughed at. " I don't know. My dad smokes. My friends all smoke. I think most people do . . . I mean they wouldn't put ashtrays in cars if most of the population didn't smoke, right?"

"I guess . . . although I'm pretty sure that's being phased out," she said airily.

"I know . . . It's a lame reason . . . Maybe I'll quit someday. I don't smoke all the time. Kind of . . . like . . . at social gatherings and stuff," he said, taking another drag. "I was going to ask you if you wanted one, but I'm going to assume no."

"I'm good." She smiled. He pushed no further.

"I don't do it to be cool, you know . . . I snagged some from my ole man once. My friends thought it was badass. So we tried it. And it stuck."

"It's fine." She chuckled. "You don't have to explain yourself. No judging. You're good."

"I know . . . but . . ." He seemed like he was struggling to say what he was thinking.

Reading his mind, she said, "I don't think you're trying to put on a cool guy persona . . . Just like I don't think you're trying to appear fun and dorky or quiet and mysterious. That's why you're an interesting guy. You seem to genuinely be all those things, and I find that fascinating . . . and special."

She didn't know it, but at those words, Adam heard the faint sound of that song again . . . no one had ever called him special.

"So . . . tell me, Mr. Miller, what do you want to be when you grow up?" Claire's voice cut through.

Adam took a moment to collect his thoughts. "Well, I thought about the military. I may still—army—make my dad proud. Or maybe something with computers. I really like building computers and stuff. I think IT would be cool. I think it will really kick off. Seems to be changing so quickly lately."

"Tell me about it! I keep begging my dad for my own computer. All we have is the family computer downstairs whose screen has turned pink hued, and he can't figure out why. But IT would be cool! As would the military. Very admirable."

He grinned. "What about you? What does Miss Hanover want to be when she grows up?"

Claire thought about it . . . She knew what she *really* wanted to be. "Well, what I really want to be, I don't tell many people. Or any really."

"Now you have to tell." He put his cigarette out in the dirt.

"Okay . . . Don't tell anyone?"

"Scouts honor." He held up his two fingers.

"Alright . . . I really want to be a writer. I want to write books and get published and be an author. I want my words to bring joy to others."

"Why would you keep that a secret?" he asked seriously.

"I don't know . . . kind of like when people say they want to be an artist. Or an actor. I worry I'll hear 'You won't make money doing that' enough times that I'll convince myself I don't want to do it. Plus, it's something that is all mine, ya know? Writing is so personal and vulnerable, and I'm not ready to tell the world yet that it's my dream. Then it has to become a goal for people to gauge my success against . . . I want to keep it a dream for a little longer."

Adam let that soak in and then said, "I think that's quite admirable too. And you have my support. Hope I get a first copy."

She smiled broadly, and he returned it.

They sat in silence a bit longer until Adam broke it. "Claire, I haven't talked this much in a while. And I certainly haven't laughed like this in forever, and I just want to say thank you. You made a pretty shitty night pretty rad."

Claire beamed and maybe blushed a little. "Right back at you."

They shared a lingering moment, and then he said, "I suppose it's time to get you home. It's going to start getting light soon, and I think you'll want to get back before that."

She nodded and they both got off the swing, Adam picking up his squashed cigarette, throwing it over the fence as they left.

"So how did you get out?" Adam asked.

"I climbed out my window and down the trellis."

Adam paused. "You have a trellis by your window?"

"Yeeeah . . . Why?"

He shook his head and continued walking. "A bit cliche is all."

Claire shrugged. "What about you?" she asked.

"Out the front door. My parents don't really care."

Once out of the school's parking lot and drive, they walked a few blocks toward Claire's road. Turning onto it, they made it to her house. All the lights were still off. A good sign. They walked around the back to the trellis and Claire's partially open window.

"Okay, this is me," she whispered.

"No wonder you climbed the fence so well." He grinned.

She snickered. "Yeah, I guess so. Well . . . bye," she said hesitantly. "Thank you for walking me home . . . and for everything else tonight."

"No problem. Thank *you*," he said. They paused for a minute and looked at each other until Adam said, rather reluctantly while pointing up, "Be careful."

Claire nodded and turned to make her way up the trellis, Adam watching her the whole time, perchance looking at more than just her safe return to her room. Once in, Claire turned and waved out the window. Adam gave a two-fingered salute and a smirk. She closed the window, and he left into the night, wondering what the hell he was getting himself into.

Claire quickly changed into the pj's she'd left out for herself, knowing earlier that she would make far too much noise when she got home if she had to go through her drawers in the dark, and got into bed. She rolled onto her side, looking out her window to the night sky that was just beginning to show a hint of morning, and couldn't help but squeal into her pillow.

Runaway Train

The sun washed over Claire's face, warming it as it peeked out over the top of the blankets she was currently wrapped up tight in. The cold air was drifting in through the crack of the window that she had left slightly open. It was so cozy, and she wanted nothing of getting up. Her mind slowly drifted to the sounds of the morning, to the birds flying from tree to tree, to her stomach that was growling, to the headache she had that was mildly pounding . . . and then her eyes snapped open.

The party! The memories of the night flew through her mind like a flip book. Sneaking out, Amber and Sam, Sam getting drunk, Sam and her fighting, cops, Adam, the playground . . . She sat up fast, which didn't help her headache, and looked at the clock on her bedside table. It flashed 9:00. *Not too late*, she thought. She never really slept in, so doing so would gain questioning from her parents, most likely thinking she didn't feel well . . . but still, no questions was best.

She got up and threw on her baggy Harvard sweatshirt, her black stirrup leggings, and her slippers. She threw her hair up in a scrunchied ponytail and went downstairs. She would grab some cereal and act like nothing had happened. She was also not going to call or go see Sam. As her brain woke up, her irritation from the night before in regard to Sam ebbed back. Maybe her rules had been a bit extreme, but she'd caved on most of them. They had just been to help her feel like they had some control over the situation. And nothing at all had constituted Sam being friendly with Amber and telling her, Claire, to leave. She had been a friend looking out for her, and Sam had chosen booze and bitches instead. A part of her deep down, however, was a little worried.

She grabbed a bowl and a box of cereal and poured it in, followed by some milk. Her subconscious mind was going back and forth between being pissed and anxious while she ate.

Throwing her bowl in the sink, she was contemplating getting a head start on her homework, and maybe taking some Tylenol, when she heard her mom call her from the dining room. Her guilty conscience instantly went into defensive mode, getting a sickening feeling in her stomach, but she shook it off, knowing her mom could smell guilt from miles away.

"Yeah?" she called, walking in to see her mom sitting at the table, thumbing through the Sunday paper's store flyers, scissors in hand, ready to cut coupons.

"Good morning," she said, smiling up at her before returning to her weekly tradition.

"Morning!"

"How'd you sleep?" She licked a finger and flicked to the next page. Did she know something?

"Good. Just had some cereal. Was going to go upstairs and work on some homework."

"That's good," she responded nonchalantly. "Planning to see Sam today?"

"Um . . . no, I don't think so."

"Oh. You usually do homework together, so I wasn't sure."

Claire didn't know what to say to that. She waited in silence before awkwardly saying, "So I guess I'll just . . . go do my homework."

"I got an interesting phone call this morning."

Claire's eyes widened, her heart in her throat.

"Yeah?"

Her mother was no longer thumbing through flyers. She was in fact staring directly at Claire, her glasses now on the table.

"Sit down, Claire." Claire slowly lowered herself into the chair opposite her mother. "Your father and I received a phone call early this morning from Claudia Levinski."

"Oh? Wh-what did Ms. Levinski want?" Claire stuttered.

"Well . . . it seems as if she was called in the middle of the night by the Thompson Falls Police Department, telling her to go pick up her daughter, Samantha Levinski, who was caught intoxicated at an unattended party last night on Vining Street along with several other minors."

Claire felt her face go pale, her stomach now doing nothing . . . It felt empty, and yet she felt like throwing up the empty that was inside it.

"Do you know why she called *me* after getting her daughter through the proper paperwork and back home?"

Claire opened her mouth, but nothing came out. Her sweatshirt was starting to feel tight and hot, regardless of how baggy it was.

"It seems," she continued, leaning forward at the table now, "that after Joey was put back to bed, having been awoken by the commotion, and after having a conversation with Sam, who was in hysterics for quite a while, Ms. Levinski finally got it out of her that she was concerned, not just because she was caught and brought to the police station, but because a certain someone wasn't at the police station with her and was in fact nowhere to be found. You want to guess who that certain someone was?"

Claire gulped.

"You, Claire... Sam was concerned that she didn't see you at the police station and didn't know if you got home safely last night... or should I say early this morning. Now, why would Sam be concerned about your getting home safely when you surely were sound asleep in your bedroom last night?"

"Mom... I—I—"

"What were you thinking, Claire?!" The mysterious tone gone, Claire was almost relieved to hear her mother's anger coming through. "Sneaking out in the middle of the night? Drinking? An unattended party? I heard from Claudia that this house on Vining Street is home to a senior. A senior, Claire! Do you know how stupid that was?"

"Mom... No, it really was safe... honest!"

"Oh really... And you knew everyone there?"

"Well, no... but—"

"And you knew that everyone there was in fact a student at your school and no one was older? College kids who were looking for drunk girls to party with?"

"No... but, Mom. Sam and I had—"

"And you knew that none of the alcoholic beverages were laced or that illegal substances weren't on the premises?"

"No... bu—"

"Claire, enough." Her voice was sharp and cut the air like a knife. Claire silenced. "It just so happens that a couple of those picked up at that party were in fact twenty-one years old and are now being charged with supplying minors with alcohol. *And* marijuana was found on the premises. So this lucky senior boy who decided to throw a grand ole party has now gotten his own parents in a swell of trouble with the law as well, since the drugs were found in their home and nobody claimed ownership. Now, I want you to tell me how you learned of this party, how you and Sam decided to sneak out, what happened, and when and how you came back home." She stopped, and Claire swore she could see smoke coming from her nostrils. Her eyebrows were raised, her arms were crossed, and Claire knew not to test this.

She launched right into her story, telling everything: getting the invite, coming up with the plan and rules, sneaking out, and the party. She told her mom how she hadn't been comfortable after her and Sam's fight at which point Claire teared up a little, and how she had gone to get some fresh air, had seen a friend from band whom she'd sat with for the rest of the night until the cops had shown up, and then had run. She neglected to tell the part about hanging out in the playground for an hour or two, assuming her mom didn't know what time she'd come in anyway, only that she was in her bed by the time Ms. Levinski called.

"And then I came home."

"Who was this friend from band class?"

Claire didn't know why she was hesitant to say his name. Maybe because she didn't want her mom to get the wrong impression of Adam . . . like he was some bad influence. "He's just a friend."

"That's fine. But who is he?"

"His name is Adam, okay? He's really nice . . ." she trailed off.

"I assumed as much, since he helped you get home safely. Not that running from the cops is a good idea . . . but still. I appreciate that much at least."

Claire felt some relief, and warmth for her mom, even if she was in the worst trouble she'd ever been in before.

"So you only had a little bit to drink?" she asked.

Claire, again, neglected to tell her that she and Adam had finished off a bottle of cheap wine outside.

"Yes, I swear. I only had a wine cooler, half a beer, and some Malibu juice drink thing."

Claire's mother stared at her, but her face seemed to have softened. It seemed that her anger, like most parents', was riddled with fear more than anything, and now, knowing the full story that was previously a large unknown, she could see the situation for what it was.

"Claire, look . . . I know you're in high school and you're going to want to do things that seem cool and exciting. I would be lying if I told you I didn't do any of those things too. But it is because I *have* experienced them that I know some of the consequences that come from them. You could have been deeply hurt or scarred, Claire. And just the thought of what could have happened is worthy of keeping your father and I up for days . . . Weeks! Years! You know it's because we love you that we are concerned. Parties aren't a bad thing, but you can't be going to them unattended by adults and with a whole bunch of people you don't know. If you want to have friends over for some fun, let me know! We can stay upstairs, and Troy can watch over or . . . I don't know, but let's talk about it, okay? No more sneaking to parties."

Claire teared up even more and managed to nod.

"You are grounded for this," she added. Claire nodded her head again, knowing this was inevitable.

"But your grounding entails only this: you are to call this number and talk to a woman named Mrs. Lawrence. You will set up a time to go meet her. I will drop you off. I've known her for a long time. Everyone calls her Babs. She needs a friend, and I want you to spend your grounding time with her . . . give back and do some good." She handed Claire a scrap of paper with the name and number scrawled out on it.

Claire looked at her quizzically. "Oh, okay."

"Now go get that homework done." She got up, walked over to Claire, and pulled her into a tight embrace. "Your dad will come talk to you when he gets home. He went to pick up Troy at the mechanic's. He broke down again in that dang car." They both chuckled, and Claire ascended to her bedroom, throwing herself down on the bed.

She knew she shouldn't be mad at Sam since she had just been checking that Claire was okay, and since Claire's sentence wasn't all that bad, it shouldn't really matter, but the way Sam had practically ditched her for Amber and the fact that she was the only reason Claire had even gotten caught irritated her. She couldn't help but think that if Sam had just taken it slow with drinking, hadn't gotten caught up in the ridiculousness that was Amber, and the two of them had had the fun they had planned to have, then Sam wouldn't have gotten caught, and Claire wouldn't have gotten outed. The way she saw it, it all came down to Sam, and no matter how concerned she'd been for Claire early this morning, Claire was working herself up into a tizzy about it because Sam had also basically made Claire feel like a prude and boring just because she'd wanted to play it safe. Turns out, that was exactly what they should have been doing.

Claire grabbed a pillow, held it to her chest, and let out a long breath of air.

Her room was touched with the reds, oranges, and golds of the trees outside through the window that was still open, allowing the smells of earth, crunchy leaves, and bracing air to swirl around her room, playing with the edges of posters and the papers on her desk. Claire drifted off to sleep as her room, snug bed, heavy sweatshirt, and somewhat clean conscience snuggled around her.

"Claire!" her mother's voice broke into her sleep. "Claire!" It was getting louder as Claire blinked awake, her whole room filled with sunlight now. She must have dozed right to lunch.

"Claire." Her mom poked her head through the door. "I thought you were doing homework?"

"I—I fell asleep," Claire said, sitting up and stretching.

"Phone's for you," her mother said. "It's Sam."

She didn't feel particularly keen to talk to Sam at the moment.

Her mother handed over the phone. "Make sure you bring it back downstairs after so it can charge."

Claire nodded. She watched her mom close the door before putting the receiver to her ear.

"Hello?" she spoke half-heartedly.

"Hi," came Sam's dull voice. Claire definitely had the impression Sam was upset with her too . . . but what could *she* possibly be upset about? There was a pause while she thought of what to say. Sam was the one who had called her after all.

Claire landed on "What do you want?" not trying to sound rude per se, but those words strung together rarely come across as pleasant.

"Oh, I don't know, just thought, maybe, you'd like to know I'm okay? Pardon me for thinking my friend would care," came Sam's snarky response.

"What is that supposed to mean?!" Claire could feel her temper beginning to rise.

"That you ditched me last night, and I spent the night in the slammer! I thought maybe you'd want to know I made it home okay!" Sam's voice rose with each word.

"Come off it, Sam. You didn't spend the night there. It was probably an hour, if that. And if we're going to talk about who ditched who, I think we know exactly who that would be!!" Claire retorted, her own voice growing edgy as she got up to begin pacing her room.

"Oh yeah?! And who would that be, Claire? Because as far as I can tell, I'm the one who got picked up by the cops, and you're the one who left me alone to do so!"

"Are you freakin' kidding me? What do you call leaving me for Amber all night and telling me to go home?!"

"I never told you to go home!!"

"Oh really? You must have forgotten that in your drunken stupor! Yeah, you were eating out of the palm of Amber's hand all night like some sick puppy and told me to leave when I tried to talk to you about it! So, as far as I'm concerned, you're the one who ditched me! Oh! AND outed me to my parents!" She could blow steam at this point, she was so mad.

"Excuse me? Outed you? Oh, silly me for worrying that my friend was in a ditch somewhere or abducted or SOMETHING! So sorry I thought it was okay to risk you getting caught if it meant ensuring you were safe!"

"Ugh, Sam, don't you get it? None of this would have happened if we had just stuck to the plan that WE agreed on! Nobody would have gotten drunk, we would have still been together, and we probably could have gotten away safely and made it home uncaught. But YOU had to go try and be a cool girl and get trashed and be Amber's little bitch!"

Sam gasped on the other side of the line. "So it's all my fault, huh?"

"YES!" Claire shouted.

"Oh, whatever, Claire. I don't even know why I called. Sorry to have wasted your time!"

Click.

Claire stared at the phone in her hand in disbelief. Throwing it at the bed, she gave out a loud groan.

A soft knock came at her door. "Mouse? Can I come in?"

"Yeah," Claire said haphazardly, looking out the window.

Troy quietly entered, closed the door behind him with a soft click, and stood looking at her. "I heard you yelling."

"Yeah," Claire repeated, not turning around.

"Was that Sam on the phone?" he asked, lying belly down across the foot of her bed.

"Yup."

Troy didn't ask any further questions, just lay there till she finally dropped her crossed arms and plopped on the edge of her bed.

"I'm sure you know what happened?"

"Yeah. Mom told me this morning," he said.

"Well, Sam is blaming me for ditching her, which somehow turned into me also allowing her to get caught by the cops, when she's the one who got trashed with Amber, of all people, and told me to leave when I confronted her about it."

He let out a slow whistle. "That sucks, dude." He paused. "Amber . . . she's the one you guys are always bitching about, right? Been a thorn in your side for a while?"

"That's the one. And last night, you'd swear Sam and her were the best of buddies."

"Well . . . maybe Sam was just trying to fit in."

"That's exactly it. She was trying to be cool. And if she had followed all the rules that we'd discussed beforehand, none of this would have happened." She threw her hands up.

Troy pondered for a moment and then said, "Well . . . life doesn't always go to plan, Mouse. It isn't a mathematical equation. There are far more variables than there are constants."

Claire rolled her eyes. "Okay, Yoda."

"Naw, come on. For real. You're going to have to get used to things not being able to be planned and, instead, focus on just how to handle different situations, or you're going to set yourself up for a lot of letdowns. Sam acted the way many would."

"Well, as friends, we had agreed not to."

"Peer pressure is a real thing. It wouldn't be talked about or taught if only one in a hundred teens fell prey to it . . . Look," he sighed, seeing Claire's unconvinced expression, "Amber, regardless of being a bitch, is cool, right?"

"Yeah." Claire was picking at a loose thread in her comforter.

"And Sam is a freshman girl who wants to be seen as cool, right?"

"Yeah . . . but who doesn't?"

"Doesn't matter. She does, right?" Claire nodded.

"Sam saw an opportunity to maybe be seen that way. It didn't matter that it was Amber. What mattered was that someone who is established as *cool*"—he made air quotes when saying it—"showed her attention, and in that moment, Sam would do anything."

Claire shrugged.

"It doesn't make it right, Mouse. But it happens. You fell prey to peer pressure too."

Claire looked up at him in surprise. "How?!"

"Did you not sneak out in the middle of the night without telling Mom and Dad? Go to a party that you knew had booze and was unchaperoned? Drink a little?"

"Yeah, but I was safe about it and—"

"Ah ah ah . . . But why did you go?" He gave her a smirk.

She thought a moment, and when coming to the answer, she returned his smirk. "Okay, okay . . . Because I thought it would be *cool*."

"Because you wanted to fit in. I commend you for wanting to play it safe . . . really! And I'm by no means trying to tell you you did anything wrong at all. Hell, I've done my share of stupid shit, some I got caught for, and some Mom and Dad still don't know about."

Claire chuckled at that.

"But high school? It's tough enough. You don't want to go through it without a friend."

Claire understood. And as much as she hated to admit it, Troy was right. It was all a big ole mess that they'd both gotten themselves into for the desire to be cool, and it had simply blown up in their faces.

"Hey. I hear you're not grounded fully," Troy said, sitting up, switching gears.

"Yeah, I just have to call some lady and go hang out with her."

Troy gave a confused look but shook it off. "What do you say to hot apple cider and a donut at the bakery? My treat."

Claire brightened. The bakery was really called Main Street Sweets, and they sold hot and cold beverages along with so many delicious goodies. Mrs. Leonard ran it, and she had a soft spot for Claire, Claire having gone to daycare and all of school thus far with Mrs. Leonard's son, James.

"Yes!" Claire responded.

Troy and Claire walked down, scattering leaves with every step, sat in the warm cafe together, stopped in at the music store Troy worked at so he could grab his check that he never picked up on Thursday and talk to the new girl who had started working there, window shopped at some of the specialty boutique stores, and moseyed their way back home, but not before Claire could question Troy.

"Who's the new girl you're workin' with?" she asked with a smirk.

"Her name is Gwen," he said, giving her a side-glance.

"She's cute," Claire said.

"She's nice to look at, sure," he said, clearly trying to hold back his grin.

"She seems nice." Claire was watching Troy's facial expressions. Truth was, she'd watched them talk while thumbing through some CDs. Gwen had a very warm smile and a laugh that was kind, and Troy seemed quite invested.

"She is," he said, not making eye contact and looking straight ahead, hands tucked in the pockets of his bomber jacket.

"When did she start?"

"Few weeks ago."

"I like her," she decided.

"You don't even know her, Mouse."

"A girl always knows," she said, Troy smiling. "I take it Lydia is out?"

"Yeah. She's been out for a while now."

"Good. I mean . . . sorry."

"Nah. It's all good. It was never going to work out anyway."

They turned onto the path to their front yard. "Well, you deserve a good person, Troy," Claire said, almost surprised at herself.

He looked at her as he held the gate open, laughed, and then shoved her lightly as they went through the door. "Thanks, Mouse."

Claire passed the rest of the day working on homework, reading outside, watching some TV, and lying around. She didn't realize just how much she hung out with Sam on the weekend till there was no Sam to hang out with. At one point, her dad came in to talk to her. He sat on the edge of her bed, fixed her with a serious but loving stare, and said, "You know what you did was wrong and potentially dangerous, right?"

"Yes . . . I do," Claire said apologetically. "I'm sorry, Dad. I just wanted to have some fun and fit in a little. It was dumb."

"No. It wasn't dumb. Just maybe not the smartest choice." He smiled. "Better next time?"

"Yes." She smiled back.

"Good. Remember you can always talk to us, right? About anything?"

"I know." She nodded, and she did. Her parents had always been very open in that respect. She was fortunate.

"Alright." He held out his arms, and she gave him a hug. "Dinner at five tonight."

"You got it," she responded.

Before she knew it, she was getting ready for another Monday at school and happily getting into bed. Even with a nap, she was exhausted. Hopefully, things would work out with Sam tomorrow. Her conversation with Troy had helped, but she was still not quite at the point of being ready to just jump into an apology and work it all out. She'd needed this time today, and maybe tomorrow they could talk it through . . . Yes, talking it through tomorrow would certainly work.

But her first attempt to talk to Sam didn't come to fruition. When she woke up, it was pouring rain. Troy brought her to school, her mother informing them that Ms. Levinski had already called to say Sam didn't need a ride. Once at school, Claire spotted her at her locker and walked over, only to receive a glare and a slammed door as Sam walked away from her. Claire couldn't believe it and felt her cheeks burn hot as she went to her own locker. How could Sam still be so angry at her? And for what?! She threw her stuff in her locker, not even caring that she took over one of "Amber's" shelves and the entire bottom with her gym stuff.

When the bell rang, she gladly went to homeroom, ignoring everyone else there and dreading her day of classes since Sam was in almost all of them. Entering geography, she saw that Sam had already chosen a seat near others where a free one wasn't available, so Claire sat by herself. In English, she still sat with Sam and Mark, but thankfully, there wasn't any group work today and they could ignore each other in peace, Mark being slightly confused but taking the hint to leave them be and not ask what he was hoping to ask, which was if they had gotten in a lot of trouble with their parents, as he had. Claire actually noticed that Mark had a slight bruise around his eye . . . Had he gotten in a fight after she'd left the party?

When it came time for gym, Sam and Claire were paired up for bouncing the basketball back and forth to each other as they started practicing beginning tricks for dribbling, passing, and stealing the ball. They were left to their own devices once shown how to do each exercise. Sam and Claire started just bouncing the ball back and forth to practice passing. Sam threw one a little aggressively that hit Claire a bit hard when she caught it. She looked at Sam, who glared back. Claire threw it back just as hard.

The next throw was ever so much harder still, and Claire returned it. When the next one was shoved in a way that Claire had to scoop it to catch it, and it hit her chest with a thud, she'd had it.

"What the hell, Sam!"

"What?" she said innocently. Fortunately, the whistle blew, and they went to watch an example of a play in basketball that they were then going to try to repeat in groups. Sam and Claire were split up. They finished class taking turns shooting before the whistle blew again and they were dismissed to the locker room, where Sam pushed past Claire to grab her stuff from a locker after having changed. Claire slammed her own.

"Look, I'm sorry, okay? I'm sorry I came up with a whole set of rules to try and have control of an uncertain situation. I'm sorry I made you feel bad for not following them. I'm sorry I went outside. And I'm sorry you got caught and picked up by the cops, okay? I'm sorry. I was pissed that you were being all buddy-buddy with Amber. I was pissed that you were getting drunk, because it made me uncomfortable. I was pissed you told me to go. So I did. But I only went out on the porch for some air. I wasn't going to leave you there. But I saw Adam outside, so we got to talking, and then the cops showed up and we ran. We *had* agreed to not tell on each other if we got home safe and the other got caught. So I figured I was in the clear to run. I'm sorry, okay? Of course I felt horrible that you got picked up. Of course I was relieved to know you were okay. And of course I'm not mad that you called to check on me. I know you were just looking out for me. But I was pissed that none of it should have even happened in the first place."

The bell rang. "There! Is that what you want to hear? I've been trying to tell you that all day, but you've been acting like a child, so I couldn't. But there you go!"

Sam looked stunned. "Claire—I . . ."

"I have to go to band." And she left. She threw her stuff in her locker, not even caring to grab anything else, and went directly to band in a huff. Entering, she went straight for her bench and plopped down just as the late bell rang. She slowly started calming down as she played the scales and listened to Mr. Johns talk about the concert before beginning practice. She made eye contact with Adam, who, per usual, waved and smiled, and Claire felt her irritation with Sam slowly drift away, recalling their night together, a flip in her stomach reminding her how special it had been. When band was done, she was more than excited to go talk to him.

"Hey!" she said in what she hoped was a casual tone.

His grin spread across his face as he looked up from his drum set. "Hey! How's it going? You recoup from Saturday?"

"Yeah . . . well, sort of." She heaved a sigh. "I got outed . . ."

His grin faded. "Your parents found out? How?"

She groaned. "Sam. She got picked up, and when she didn't see me at the police station, she told her mom, who then called my parents to make sure I was okay."

He let out a low, slow whistle. "Well, damn . . . that sucks. I guess she was just looking out for you."

She bit her lip, thinking of the anger she'd had and her blowup in the locker room. Hearing Adam so nonchalantly express the obvious about Sam made her feel a little ridiculous at how over-the-top this whole situation had become.

Adam seemed to notice her moment of contemplation. "Everything okay?" he asked with concern.

She shook her head. "Yeah . . . no . . . sorry. It's just . . . I kind of got mad at Sam about it all, and, well, maybe I was a little harsh."

He shrugged. "It happens. Nothing talking to her won't fix, I'm sure."

She nodded as he picked up his backpack, having finished straightening out his space in the percussion section. They headed toward the door.

"Thanks again, by the way . . ." she said into the silence. "For, you know, helping me escape and all." They stopped in the entryway to the large band room. "I had a really good time and . . ." she trailed off, not knowing what to say. So much seemed to have passed between them at the party, Claire could still feel its tension as she stood there next to him.

Adam adjusted his backpack and suddenly had a determined look on his face. "Claire, I—" But what he was going to say, she didn't know.

"There you are!!!" came a shout from the door. A girl, clearly an upperclassman, was standing there, one hand on her hip, the other holding a book and a few folders. She had platinum blonde hair (clearly colored, in Claire's humble opinion), was very obviously chewing bubble gum, and was wearing an outfit that Claire would never feel comfortable donning . . . This girl was slim, straight, and slender. The kind of figure that when Claire saw it, it made her want to hug her curves even tighter in the hopes of appearing smaller. Her entire demeanor was that of piss and vinegar, and there was one thing for certain: Claire decided immediately that she didn't like her.

"Where have you been?" she spoke sternly, with such a tone that Claire had to question who this girl thought she was.

Claire was wondering who she was even talking to when she heard Adam stutter beside her. "H-hey, Rachel. I was just picking up before heading—"

"Clearly, you're avoiding me," she said as she walked toward them.

"No . . . no . . . Why would you thi—"

"I called you three times yesterday, and every time, your parents told me you were out and that you'd call when you came home, WHICH you never did. AND I didn't see you at all this morning before homeroom, AND I've been waiting outside like an idiot so I could finally catch you."

"Sorry . . . I—"

"Where were you at at that party on Saturday?!" She was getting more and more agitated as she spoke, a slight flush hitting her cheeks, her head getting in on the action her tone was dishing out.

"I went outside because—"

"You know where I was, Adam?" She glared, cutting him off. He shrugged his shoulders, clearly giving up on attempting to speak. "I'll tell you where I was. I was at the police station getting written up and having to wait for my dad to come get me!!!"

Adam stared back at her.

"Well?!"

"Oh, it's my turn now?" he said snarkily.

"How dare you! Do you realize what my dad did?"

"Rache . . . I—"

"He took the Benz, Adam! I have to drive the shit car that my stupid brother got just to mess around with while HE gets to drive MY Mercedes!"

"I'm sorry—"

"So where were you?!" This time she was huffing, and it was clearly Adam's turn to attempt to get her nostrils to stop flaring.

"I went outside because I was tired of watching you flirt with every other guy at the party." His temper was rising now as well.

"Excuse me?!"

"Yeah . . . you heard me."

"I wasn't flirting!"

"Okay, well, then clearly enjoying everyone else's company but mine. Rachel, I literally didn't know where you were half the time and ended up hanging out with people who aren't even my friends. I went to this party because you wanted me there and then you ditched me for most of it. Did you even notice I left?"

Rachel just glared.

Claire was trying to piece this all together. Was this girl his . . .

"So, while you were outside and the cops showed up, what did you do?" Rachel finally asked.

"What anyone would do, Rachel. I ran."

"And you didn't think 'Hey, maybe I should,' oh, I don't know, 'grab my girlfriend first'?!"

There it was. "You're girlfriend?" Claire blurted. Both Adam and Rachel looked at her. Adam looked apologetic and quite torn, while Rachel clearly only just noticed that Claire had been standing there the whole time, or at least cared to notice.

"Yeah. And who the hell are you?"

Claire felt her own emotions rising to her throat, but it wasn't anger. She felt her cheeks flush ever so slightly. "I-I'm—"

"I don't even care," Rachel cut in. "What are you doing here? We're kind of having a conversation."

"Rachel, come on," Adam interjected, but Rachel was just staring at Claire with her eyebrows raised.

"Yeah . . . no, I'm sorry," Claire said, coming to. "I was, um, I was just leaving."

Rachel nodded her annoyance and approval at this.

"Claire, wait . . ." Adam threw out timidly.

"No, it's fine. I was—"

"Bye," Rachel dismissed her.

Adam made to move past Rachel toward Claire as she backed out of the doorway, but the sight of her face . . .

"Bye, Adam," she said. And even she knew that the venom she placed behind those two little words was enough to stop him, and it made her feel all too good to see the look of hurt on his face. She turned and left.

She rushed to her locker, not wanting to linger one second in school. And naturally, Amber was there with Lauren and Ashley. Why had she not grabbed her stuff after gym and left already? She marched up to the locker, and upon reaching for it, Amber stepped in front of it.

"Excuse me," Claire said, anger behind each word, not making eye contact with her.

"Hanover, I've been waiting for you. We have a little problem it seems."

"Please move."

"It seems you think you have claim to *my* locker space . . . and I thought we were doing so well."

"Move."

"I took the liberty of moving it all for you," she said and took a step aside. Claire opened the locker to find all her papers out of their folders, and everything tossed at the bottom, some things ripped, books wide open with pages getting crumpled as they lay with her gym shoes. The pile tumbled out of the locker, much of it falling to the floor. It looked like the job of the Tasmanian Devil, and Claire could feel the edges of her eyes burn, her face redden, her jaws clench. She grabbed folders, papers, and whatever else was worth saving, flattening them all out in no particular order to shove in her bag along with the books, and threw it over her shoulder. She tossed her shoes into the plastic bag that her gym clothes were in and slammed the locker, a mess of scraps still left behind. When she turned to walk away, Amber and trolls stood in her way.

"I'm not in the mood, Amber."

"Well, I am, and I want to make sure we understand each other."

Claire finally made eye contact and stared into Amber's bright blue eyes with all the malice she could muster, tears clinging for dear life, Claire willing them not to fall.

"Do we understand that this locker is mine? And you keep your shitty stuff to yourself and out. Of. It."

Claire just continued to stare.

"Do we understand?"

Claire felt her body shake. Not today . . . she'd had enough today. "No, actually, I don't understand."

Amber looked taken aback. "Excuse me?"

"You know what? I've actually had just about enough of you."

"Wha—"

"That's right. I've had enough of you. You and your two lackies here who clearly don't have enough brains between them to know that they're following the lead of a stupid, arrogant, insensitive bitch."

Claire stepped forward and was face-to-face with Amber, who stood her ground, but whose facial expression had lost its nose-up attribute and instead looked a little intimidated.

"I'm tired of you bossing me around like you own the damn place. News flash: you don't. That locker is equally mine. And from here on out, I am going to put my stuff on that second shelf, and I will put my gym stuff on the bottom of the locker and hang my backpack on the hook, and I will not ever find my shit ripped, tossed around, in the hallway, or otherwise touched by you or anyone else's fake manicured hands again. If you want your own locker, then go find your fucking own. Do *we* understand?"

Amber didn't say anything. She looked to be in shock.

"This goes for all your other shenanigans too. Leave me the hell alone." Claire pushed past her and left, adrenaline pumping.

Storming out the front doors of the school, Claire's emotions were coursing through her, the tears no longer holding strong. It felt good to back-talk Amber, however wobbly her legs felt now . . . But the reality behind her being emotionally unstable to have even done such a thing hit her like a ton of bricks.

Adam . . . How embarrassing. How could he have a girlfriend?! HOW could he have had such conversations with her, get drunk with her, almost kiss her, and let her drone on about her wildest dreams of being a writer when he had a girlfriend? She was so stupid to think that he maybe liked her. How could she be so dumb? She had told herself to not fall for him. It was too soon and too early. She had probably read every single thing wrong. Had he even wanted to kiss her, or was that just her having a buzz amid a moment that was completely fabricated in her own head? Was this her own mind getting carried away? Of course it was. She stomped across the front school grounds. She had dreamt up that this cute, interesting, quiet sophomore boy was interested in her. Of course he had a perfectly beautiful girlfriend. Of course! Watching him and Rachel, whom she was certain was even older, in that moment had made her feel so small . . . so . . . so . . . so much like a dumb little freshman.

Lost in growing embarrassment and anger, Claire didn't hear her name being called multiple times, till finally it was shouted.

"CLAIRE!" It was Sam, jogging to catch up with her. She turned right back around, calling over her shoulder, "Not now, Sam, okay? I'm kind of dealing with something."

"I can tell." Sam was even with her now. "Hey, slow down . . . Hey!" She grabbed Claire's arm and made her stop to look at her. "What the hell happened to you?"

"So you're talking to me now?" Claire couldn't help herself.

Sam's face fell. "Look . . . I-I'm sorry. I totally get why you ditched me, okay? I would have ditched me too. I was a total jerk, and I'm sorry."

Claire's shoulders fell and her face softened, releasing a sigh, tears forming yet again. "I'm sorry, Sam. I should've stayed with you anyway . . . And I know you were just looking out for me by telling, and . . ." she dropped off, energy depleted. "No hard feelings?"

Sam smiled, an expression of slight pity at her friend's clearly exasperated look. "None." They linked arms and continued walking. "So, what's going on?" she asked quietly.

"Ugh." Claire paused, letting the emotional welt that had surfaced in her throat calm so she could talk. "Where do I even begin?" She relayed everything that had happened at the party, after the party, and just a few moments ago, minus her altercation with Amber. She was focused on Adam right now.

Sam listened with all the gum-chewing and "as ifs" needed for such a story and, in the end, stepped in on her friend's clear defeat. "I can't believe he led you on like that. Totally not your fault, Claire! I would have assumed he was digging me too. I mean, I thought he was diggin' you, and what a jerk for not telling you he had a girlfriend!"

Claire was glad to hear her friend empathize with her, and spilling all this was a relief in and of itself, but something about Sam's accusation didn't sit well with her. "Well . . . I don't know if I'd call him a jerk. I mean, he didn't kiss me and, in fact, didn't say anything that indicated he was free or that he even liked me. I think I'm so upset because . . . well . . . I'm mad at myself. I let my mind race and make assumptions and fall for him . . . When I think back on it, we were literally just hanging out outside and talking. And before that, doing things any friends would do. I made it out to be more than it was . . . even though I kept telling myself not to."

"Don't be so hard on yourself. Geesh!" consoled Sam. "Any girl would get wrapped up in the soft eyes and cute face of a boy. Especially after a few drinks and hanging out till all hours of the night. But he should have told you he had a girlfriend at some point. I'm still going to blame him, even if just a little bit."

"Okay . . . but I think I'm mostly just bummed out. Even though we didn't spend that much time together, or get to know each other really well, I couldn't help but have a crush . . . and I'm embarrassed at myself for it."

"Claire . . . we've never met Michael J. Fox or Christian Slater. Hell, we literally know nothing about them except their zodiac sign and whatever *Tiger Beat* decides to report. But we still have crushes. Crushes that we're not embarrassed to scream from the rooftops about!"

"Yeah, because we know we'll *never* meet them, Sam. They're fantasies."

"But still . . . if it's that easy to get a crush on someone you've never met, then there is nothing to be embarrassed about by falling for a guy you've spent time with, who likes music, and who's both adorable and sweet."

"I guess . . . I'm more embarrassed that deep down I convinced myself that he was also maybe feeling something too."

"And who the hell wouldn't? And him having a girlfriend doesn't mean he didn't."

Claire raised her eyebrows at Sam.

"What? It's true! Having a girlfriend doesn't mean that he doesn't still have feelings for you. From what you said, she sounds like a bitch."

"That's another thing that's annoying. She was a skinny, blonde, Amber-like . . . thing. Why is he with someone like her?"

"Maybe she isn't a bitch. Maybe she was just pissed like we were at each other and letting it out on him. Sounds like she's had a few days to let it build up."

"Yeah . . . maybe."

"You said she looked older?"

"Yeah. Like a junior or senior I'd say."

"Maybe he just went with an older chick because it was cool. Maybe he didn't know any better."

"Possibly. But seeing her makes me feel like there is noooo way he is interested in me. We couldn't be more opposite."

"Oh stop. Enough of this. That means nothing. I say, continue treating him like a friend, and enjoy your time with him because there is nothing illegal about that, and who knows what may come of it."

"I'm afraid that my reaction today clearly gave away that I was upset he had a girlfriend."

"So?"

"*So* . . . he's going to know I had a crush on him, and that's so not cool. How can I face him again and just . . . be friends?"

"I think it'll be more obvious that you had a crush if you ignore him now. Face it head-on like you would tell me. Show no weakness, and treat him like the same ole friend you have been. Play it off."

"I guess . . ." Claire kept noticing the use of the word "had." She definitely still had a crush. Which would make trying to act nonchalant and like casual friends harder. She could get over it though. Of course she could.

RUNAWAY TRAIN

Adam stood there, staring where Claire had just left, as Rachel's voice attacked him from every angle. The hurt in her face, those final words . . . He felt the pit of his stomach drop. He felt like running after her and apologizing even though she was probably halfway home by now. He'd had every intention of telling her he had a girlfriend, but no opportunity had ever seemed to present itself. If he'd told her, then she would have thought he was telling her because he felt like she was coming on to him. And he definitely didn't want that. He enjoyed her company so much and hadn't wanted to make it awkward. But he'd known something like this would happen.

If he was being honest with himself . . . he hadn't told her because he was trying to decide what to make of his own feelings. If things had kept going the way they were . . . he probably wouldn't have a girlfriend *to* tell her about. Claire had opened up a whole new world of possibilities to him: he'd never felt so comfortable with a girl as he had with Claire over the past couple months. In fact, realizing it had only been a couple months surprised him. He felt like he'd known her so much longer. But he and Rachel had been together for a little over a year, and until now, he had thought it was going well. They hung out from time to time—made out too—she had a car, he always had a date . . . but, lately, he'd been realizing just how superficial it all seemed. Claire had done that. Claire had shown him that what he liked about being with Rachel was the surface stuff. The typical girlfriend/boyfriend high school stuff. He never talked music with Rachel, or shared it. He never called Rachel up for homework help and got a compliment in the process. Claire made him feel more confident in himself. She taught him things without making him feel stupid. She had more passion and depth than anyone he knew, and she made him feel like it was okay to feel that way too. She made him feel . . . well . . . special.

But, being with someone for over a year, you don't just break up with them on the fly. And he did care for Rachel.

He'd been brooding over this since the day he'd run into Claire on the sidewalk and found her to be something . . . he didn't know what, but *something*. He'd never looked at someone and been taken so quickly by them. Of course he'd looked at magazines and movies and thought girls were hot, and he, of course, found Rachel attractive—very much so. But there had been something about Claire that day. Maybe it was the way she looked at him. She had large brown eyes that he recalled appeared shining, kind—like they saw into others' souls, not faces, if that made any sense at all. Her broad smile was so warm and welcoming . . . like home. Not fake or plastered on. He watched her sometimes—not in a Michael Myers kind of way—in band or math class, and he noticed she didn't flash that smile just any ole time. It was reserved, which made it that much more special that he'd seen it so many times. No, Claire was beyond just attractive . . . He wasn't sure there was a word for what she was. And he wasn't sure he even deserved her.

Lately, since Rachel had become a junior, things had started to change. Maybe she was feeling more established in school. Maybe the honeymoon phase of their relationship had just ended and this was how it always was, he being too much of a lovesick puppy to notice. But now, it seemed that being a lackey was all Adam was good for. She had a sweet car, but she made him drive her everywhere. He'd had his license since June. When he was younger, his family had moved a few times due to his father's military deployment. Because of this, he'd missed so much school that he'd had to repeat first grade. It made him older than his classmates and rather cool, as he was by far the first to have his permit and then license, in fact he was the only one in his class who did. But this seemed to be Rachel's go-ahead to have him cart her everywhere, even when it was to drop her off to see her friends at the mall. He hadn't realized how dumb it all seemed till recently . . . walking to her house just to drive her somewhere else. Until now, he'd thought it was an okay trade-off to get to drive a Mercedes . . . but it'd lost its appeal.

No, he'd definitely intended to talk to Claire but was tossing so much back and forth in his own mind that he just hadn't yet. And now she hated him . . . and regardless of how he maybe felt . . . that was certainly the last thing he wanted.

"Adam! Are you even listening to me?" Rachel's voice tapped back into his consciousness.

"Yeah . . . yeah," he said. "Of course. Look, I'm sorry, okay?"

"That's it? You're sorry?"

"What do you want me to say, Rachel?"

"Do you even care that I was at the police station? Do you even care that you, as my boyfriend, weren't there to help me?"

"Do you even care how I feel? There was a reason I was outside, Rache."

"Maybe you should just not be so needy? It was a party. It's called mingling."

Adam's face went rigid as he felt himself shutting down, knowing nothing he said would be heard right now anyway nor would he even be able to put it into words, what with where his own head was at. And he hated confrontation. "Okay. Fine. You're right. Are we done now?"

She looked him over. "Fine. Whatever. We're done. For now. I need you to take me to work anyway. But this isn't over."

They left the music room to head to the parking lot, Rachel still muttering under her breath about the party, Adam once again getting lost in the thoughts he'd been battling with for weeks. Starting up the car, he let her ranting continue but eventually turned the radio up to drown it all out. She shot venom at him but fell silent, arms crossed, staring out the window.

Adam let the music wash over him, watching the lines of the road go by, staring at nothing. He wished he could play this song on repeat, its melodramatic melody and words of a lost and troubled soul speaking to him. He made a mental note to check his cassettes for this album to hand off to a certain someone.

Tonight, Tonight

Claire walked into geometry, her anxiety giving her a lump in her throat and a nauseous feeling in the pit of her stomach. Entering, she saw that Adam was already seated, and he saw her walk in. He gave a half smile. Was that a good sign, or a bad one? She sat down at the desk next to him per usual and started taking out her books.

"Hey," he said.

"Hi," she tried to say pleasantly, but she feared it sounded too pleasant . . . fake. A brief silence followed.

"Claire, look . . . I—" he began.

She turned to him and cut him off. "No . . . it's fine. I'm sorry I seemed so upset with you. I was just surprised is all. No big deal."

His eyes narrowed. "I should have told you about Rachel. I'm sorry. I wasn't purposefully keeping it from you or anything. I just didn't know when a good time was and—"

"It's fine. Really. There was no reason for you *to* tell me about her, really. I mean . . . well . . . we haven't known each other long at all, so I shouldn't expect to know all that, right? So . . . it's . . . it's okay. I don't even know why I was so taken aback. It's fine. Really."

Adam looked slightly abashed, his expression almost folding in on itself. "Well . . . I want you to know—"

Mr. Stevenson cut him off by beginning class, which Claire, for once, was grateful to hear. Yet another lecture, Claire trying to focus, her and Adam not exchanging funny looks or whispers. At the end, she collected her things quickly, threw a rushed "see ya" his way, and headed out the door.

"Claire!" she heard him call and couldn't stop herself from slowing. "Claire!" it came again, and she stopped and turned to see him jogging down the hall to her.

"Hey . . . look, I—" His gray eyes were looking tortured, and she wished she knew why. Was it because he felt sorry for her? Knowing she was a silly little freshman girl who had a crush on him and he'd broken her heart. Ugh, she hoped it wasn't that. "Well . . . does it matter?" He said it quietly.

She looked at him confused. "Does what matter?"

He sighed, like this was difficult to say. "Does it matter?" He said it like it held meaning, and Claire still didn't understand. "Does it matter that I have a girlfriend?"

Claire didn't know what to say. Of course it *mattered* . . . to *her*. But she wasn't about to let him know that. "Oh . . . no . . . no, of course not. No biggie at all," she said nonchalantly.

He looked down a moment—a shadow seemed to fall across his face for a split second—before looking at her and nodding. "Okay. I just . . . Claire, look . . . Rachel and I—"

She wanted nothing to do with hearing this. She was embarrassed enough. "Adam, please. It's fine. You're allowed to have a girlfriend. I'm happy you do. She seems . . . lovely. I was just surprised I didn't know, but after thinking on it, I realized we haven't spent enough time together to warrant me even knowing that. It isn't like we're best buddies with years of history. We each have plenty of secrets, I'm sure of it. So, can we just drop this? Please? It doesn't matter. It's all good."

He let out a sigh, his expression still pained . . . He didn't know what to think. "No reason to tell" . . . "haven't even known each other long" . . . That was certainly not what he was expecting or what he wanted to hear. And to top it off, she didn't care; it hadn't mattered to her. He knew deep down that he was kind of hoping it did . . . that him having a girlfriend bothered her because that would mean that there was maybe something there, and the further into the conversation he got, the more he was seeing that that was exactly what he wanted. But he had misjudged her anger . . . She was just surprised . . . not hurt . . . It hadn't mattered. "Yeah . . . sure."

Claire could tell it wasn't where he wanted to land, but she was thankful he agreed. "Great. Now, let's not be late for class. See you at band tomorrow?"

"Yeah . . ."

"Cool. Bye." She made to leave.

"Wait . . ." He held her forearm ever so lightly, throwing caution to the wind. She looked down at it and felt her heart flutter, which she immediately hated herself for. "Can we . . . can we still exchange tapes? And hang out sometimes after band?"

Her eyes snapped to his, and she saw them begging. She knew this would mess with her psyche, but she couldn't deny that she was happy he did still want this much . . . "Of course," was all she said before she left for class.

She sat in English, distracted by her own thinking. Sam kept nudging her foot, but she finally just shook her head, indicating to leave her be. Study hall passed by in a blur of mindless thoughts, each one just as ridiculous as the last, and she ignored everyone in home ec, happily getting lost in their chocolate chip cookie recipes, and didn't even care that her and Sam's came in first, earning them each a free homework pass, to the disgruntlement of Amber. It wasn't until she had grabbed her things and met Sam outside to start walking home that she finally opened up to talk.

"Okay, you can't keep ignoring me all day," Sam said, walking in time with Claire when she got outside.

"I'm sorry. I'm not trying to. I just have a lot on my mind. Adam talked to me this morning in geometry."

"Oh?!" Sam said a little too excitedly. "What did he say?"

"Just apologized for not telling me about Rachel sooner," she said.

"That's it?" Sam asked, a little disappointed.

"Well, I didn't really let him say anything else. I didn't want to hear it. I was embarrassed enough as it was. The last thing I needed was to hear him tell me how bad he felt that he had given me the wrong impression and that he was sorry I had a crush on him . . ."

"I have a feeling that wasn't what he was going to say . . . but okay," Sam said, shaking her head.

"What do you think he was going to say?"

"I don't know. But I don't think he thinks you're silly or that he holds himself in such high regard that he would express feeling pity."

"This coming from the girl who yesterday was ready to blame him for everything and called him a jerk."

"You know how my emotions get sometimes! I think he's nicer than all that, is all. Maybe he felt genuinely bad that he'd hurt your feelings, and maybe he wasn't intending to hold anything back. Maybe he was actually interested in you! Working through something like that doesn't just happen overnight."

"No. I'm not going down that road. I told him today that there was no need for him to have even told me he had a girlfriend. We aren't best buddies and don't *need* to tell each other anything. I told him I don't know why

I acted the way I did, but it's all good and I'm not upset and I'm happy for him and that we can just drop the whole thing."

Sam looked at her in shock. "You said all that?"

"In one way or another . . . yeah . . . Why?"

"You don't think that was a little harsh? Saying you weren't best buddies and everything?"

"Why would it be? It's the truth! We've only known each other for a couple months or so and have never spent time out of school together or even out of class really. Well . . . except for the night of the party, but I'm not going there because that is what caused all this confusion. All we really do is talk music and math. We're friendly and have things in common, but that's all. No reason to have gone so deep as to discuss relationships. None. So it's done. It's dropped."

"Just like that?"

"Yeah . . . Well, he did ask if we could still hang out after band sometimes and if we could still swap cassettes. I told him sure . . . It's a *friend* thing to do, so why not. But that's it."

"Wait, wait, wait . . . hold the phone. Backing up . . . beep beep beep. He still wants to hang out with you and swap cassettes?"

"Yeeee-ah . . ."

"Which is pretty much what your relationship has been thus far."

"*Friend*ship, yes."

"So he basically doesn't want anything to change?"

"I guess not. Yeah."

Sam stared at her.

"What?!"

"Guy has a cute upperclassman girlfriend, has finally come clean about her to you, and still wants things between the two of you to go on as they have been?"

"Yeah . . . he seemed pretty nervous about it too . . . like he really didn't want me to say no. Probably because it was a pity move . . . He also wasn't happy with me asking him to drop the conversation. That's when he asked me that. But I just think he didn't want him having a girlfriend to change anything. Like, we can still hang out and be cool, you know? Because he asked me if him having a girlfriend mattered. Because we're *friends*."

"Mattered? How did he ask?" Sam's gum-chewing was becoming so extreme Claire thought her gum was going to pop right out of her mouth.

"What do you mean? He said, 'Does it matter?' I asked, 'Does what matter?' . . . and he said, 'Me having a girlfriend.' Just like I said."

Sam let out a groan and put her hands on her head. "Claire!"

"What?!"

"He totally likes you!"

"What?!? What do you mean?"

"Does it matter? Do you even pay attention to those romance books you read?" Sam practically squeaked out. "Claire, he wasn't asking if it mattered to ensure that you guys could just continue being friends . . . He was asking if it *mattered*."

Claire laughed. "You're just as bad as he is. That doesn't clear anything up."

"Ugh . . . You're killing me. Like, does it matter that he has a girlfriend. Like, does it bother you. Like, the do-you-like-me-and-don't-like-that-I-have-one kind of does it matter!!!"

"No . . . that's not what he meant. He asked if it mattered and then ensured we could still do the things we were doing. He wanted to make sure I was cool that he had a girlfriend."

"Claire . . . no . . . guys don't ask—"

Claire cut her off. She couldn't do this. Couldn't go down this rabbit hole. "No, Sam . . . Let's drop it. Please. He has a girlfriend. Her name is Rachel. Adam and I are just friends, and that's it. I'm over it. It is all good."

"Okay . . . fine," Sam said, for once actually dropping something, hearing the pained tone in her friend's voice. It was the hurt that made her stop. "So, I never asked: what is your penance for the party?"

"I have to go talk to some lady."

Sam stopped mid stride, mouth falling open. "Are you kidding me?"

Claire turned to her. "Yeah . . . pretty easy sentence."

Sam started walking again. "Dude, that's totally not fair! I have a month's worth of grounding. I can't go anywhere. Not the mall, not the arcade, not Main Street, not Ron's, nothing."

"Sorry, dude." Claire smirked and Sam elbowed her.

"Yeah, you look it. How the hell did you get off so easy?"

"Not sure. But I haven't been to the lady's house yet. Maybe she's a pro at torturing teens or something."

"Still . . . When do you go?"

"Tomorrow after school. I called her yesterday. My mom is bringing me."

"Wait! Tomorrow is Halloween! Please tell me you're not missing Halloween! My mom is giving me a one-night pass for it. And you HAVE to be there. I'd be alone otherwise!"

Claire chuckled. "Don't worry. My mom isn't that mean. I'll be done before then."

"Who even is she?"

"Mrs. Lawrence. But known as Babs, I guess."

"Never heard of her."

"Me neither. But she lives in that big white house on the hill in town. You know, the one off Main Street." Claire had been quite excited when learning this. She had always admired that house.

"That house has all the makings of a Stephen King novel," Sam interjected.

"Oh come on. I love it!"

"That doesn't surprise me one stitch."

Claire sat in the front seat next to her mother. "You're not going in with me?" she asked as she looked through the window at the old white house, the driveway a long upward slope, her mother and her sitting at the top of it.

"Nope. I will be back in one hour. This is *your* grounding, remember?"

"Okay, okay," she grumbled. "Let's just hope you're not leading me into the hands of some voodoo witch lady." She continued muttering under her breath as she got out of the car and closed the door on her mother's smiling face. The air was brisk. Halloween was tonight, and here she was, walking toward an old home with a witch's hat perched atop a cylinder of windows on its corner connected to a long porch that ran the rest of the length of the house, several wind chimes ringing ever so lightly. Claire shuddered, recalling Sam's comment of horror-worthy houses.

Today, school had been chaotic. Chaotic for teachers but fun for students. Nobody was focusing, and every teacher had given up. Some kids were even dressed up, and many thought playing tricks was the best way to get through the day. She saw so many kids in the office on her way out of school, but only a handful of the number that should have been in there. In geography, they completed a mapping worksheet that gave coordinates to plot to make a pumpkin. In science, they did a cool mixing experiment that was coined "making potions," and in PE, they got to play flashlight tag in a darkened gym. Mr. Johns played a video for them about the importance of music in horror films. It was quite interesting and offered Claire the chance to not have to mingle with Adam. She took off immediately after class to make her appointment with Mrs. Lawrence.

Standing on the old porch, she rang the doorbell. After a moment, she heard movement inside. The door opened to reveal a woman in her early seventies. She had salt-and-pepper hair, a small figure, and a warm smile.

"Mrs. Lawrence?" Claire asked.

"Hello, my dear!" she said, and any fear Claire may have had in regard to the old crazy lady on the hill vanished. "Come right on in! And please, call be Babs. No more of this Mrs. Lawrence rubbish." She gave Claire's mom a quick wave as she stepped aside to let Claire in.

Claire slipped off her shoes in the entryway that had wall-to-wall windows, almost more of a closed-in porch. It had rocking chairs and a small table with a candle and a few books. Claire imagined how nice the warm breezes must be through here on summer nights and then followed Babs through the door and into the living room. In the corner sat an old television box with rabbit ears atop, a record player, a couch, and a loveseat and chair set that matched in a burnt-orange color. The old pumpkin pinewood floors beneath her feet were smooth and well taken care of, partially covered by a worn antique rug in the center.

"I'm going to go check on the tea and cookies," Babs said, strolling toward a doorway to the left. Claire could make out a grand dining room table with a hutch full of fine china. She assumed the kitchen was through this room. "You go ahead and look around and make yourself right at home. Don't mind the dust! We'll take tea in the circular room in the front."

Claire nodded as she shuffled off, then let out a deep sigh. Only seeing this one room, she already knew she loved this house. It was just as she had thought it would be. Antiquated and full of knickknacks and old furniture and books. Claire loved seeing all the random built-in shelves here and there that were lined with reading material, a few figurines and globes thrown in between. She moved through the living room in the opposite direction of Babs, through the other entryway. Claire found a beautiful wooden staircase on her left, and to her right, the circular room. This faced the town of Thompson Falls. Claire could see over all the houses and Main Street shops. The steeple of the church seemed to be on eye level with her. What an impeccable view. Two wingback chairs sat in the circular windows, a small table between them. Claire decided this would definitely be her favorite spot because, not only did she feel like a bird in the clouds, but the room was filled with the most books. This was impressive, as the room was circular. The architecture of built-in shelves on a curved wall was impressive. There was even a rod that curved around the top, a ladder attached. Browsing the titles of books, she saw some of her favorites. She wanted nothing more than to climb the ladder and push off, just like Belle, as she excitedly spoke of all the exciting places to visit in the pages of books.

She intended to continue on to the next room, which seemed to lead back toward the dining room, when Babs showed up, a tray in hand carrying teacups, a teapot, and a plate of cookies.

"You like books?" Babs said as she set the tray down between the two chairs.

"I love them," Claire responded, taking up a chair, folding one leg beneath the other.

"Good. A person can never have enough books, and a person who reads has all the more adventures." She winked as she too took a seat. "These are some of my prized possessions. All my classics and old collectibles. I have another room upstairs that has nothing but books, but they're of the more common and modern nature."

"So cool. I would kill to have my own library. I have a bookshelf at home in my room packed solid, but it is nowhere near as impressive as this, of course."

"Well, I have had quite some time to collect." She chuckled. Claire noticed Babs's deep crow's-feet and laugh lines. They weren't what Claire would consider wrinkles. They were the lines of many happy memories, of good times, of loud laughs. They were pleasant and wise, and Claire felt comfort in them.

"Cream or sugar?" Babs asked.

"Just a little bit of sugar, thanks," Claire responded as Babs followed her request. The cookies smelled decadent, and Claire reached for one without even thinking. They were warm, the chocolate chips glistening with gooiness.

"So tell me about yourself, Claire Hanover."

Claire swallowed quickly and cupped her tea, settling into the chair's squishy back. "Um . . . well . . . I'm a freshman. I love to read, like I said. All kinds. But my favorite book is *Pride and Prejudice*," she started. "And I love music. Like . . . love it. All of it too. Big band. Doo-wop. Sixties rock. Rap . . . all of it. I play piano. It is probably the thing I'm most good at . . . and passionate about."

"Oh, the piano!" Babs exclaimed. "How lovely. I used to play too, but my arthritis is too bad. Mind you, I didn't play a lot or very well. My late husband, Gary, he got me a piano for our fifth anniversary. It's in the den over there." She gestured to the room Claire hadn't gotten to yet. "I was able to get a few songs to memory so I could play them for him. But over time it just collected dust. A thing for kids to bang around on. Maybe you can play for me."

Claire lit up. "I would love that! I have a keyboard at home but not the real thing."

"Well, if you feel up to it and want to practice, my door is always open, my dear," she said.

Claire's heart swelled. Babs reminded her so much of her grandmother, whom she missed often. Coming to play the piano for her seemed like a beautiful thing. "That sounds perfect."

"So, a freshman . . . I remember being a freshman. It was an awful long time ago, but I remember!" Babs said, taking a sip of tea.

Claire chuckled. "Where did you go to school?"

"Right here in Thompson Falls. We had our own high school then. We didn't mix with those Thompson kids." Babs gave a laugh. "Been living here my whole life. Met my Gary when we were just little things. Dated all through high school. Went to college, though my mamma thought I was crazy. Got my teaching degree. Gary and I got married. And I decided to go back to school. Guess I liked it too much. And got my degree to teach right there at the college."

"You were a professor?" Claire asked, stunned.

"Well, sort of. They didn't call me that. I taught some of the teaching courses to future teachers. I loved it."

"What did your husband do?"

"He was a union man. Worked at the shipyard nearby."

"Cool," Claire responded. The fact that she had worked at a college and her husband had been a ship builder seemed to account for the large house full of treasures. "Did you guys travel a lot? I saw a lot of cool knickknacks on the shelves on my way through."

"Oh yes," she responded. "Went all over. We loved to travel. After Danny, it was what kept us going."

"Danny?" Claire asked.

"Yes. Your mother never mentioned him?" Babs asked.

Claire thought. She didn't really know many of her mom's old acquaintances or friends. Other than Dora, who was still around and came to visit for a week every summer, and Louise, whom she talked to regularly on the phone. "No. I don't think so anyway."

"Well, it was a long time ago," Babs said consolingly.

Claire took a few more sips of tea as they sat in silence before saying tentatively, "So, who was Danny?"

Babs smiled. "Danny was my son."

"Oh." Claire nodded. She recognized the word "was" and wondered if Babs was going to continue, Claire not wanting to push.

"He was a bright boy. Light of our eye. Cutest little thing, though he got into everything." She chuckled. "Found him in the kitchen once with the flour tin completely spilled over. There was flour on the counter, the floor, oh my my . . . the kitchen was nothing but a big dust cloud of flour. Danny was covered, and all he said when I found him was, 'Look, I'm a ghost.' "

Claire smiled as Babs chuckled and then settled back into her story. "He and your mom went to school together all through elementary. Practically inseparable in the summers, those two."

"Really?" Claire said, trying to imagine her mom as a nine- or ten-year-old, riding a bike maybe or jumping rope and climbing trees. She had seen some photos but not many.

"Yup. They even went to a few dances together in middle school. As friends, of course."

Claire was astounded she'd never heard of this Danny friend. "No way!"

"Yes way!" Babs dished back with a grin.

"I can't even picture my mom at middle school dances. I've only ever seen her prom picture with my dad."

"She was always a pretty girl. A tomboy when they were little, and found flared hair and makeup come middle school. Always so sweet and gentle. Danny just loved her. As a friend. Like a sister. They looked out for each other."

"Wow . . . I had no idea. What happened?"

Babs sighed. "Well . . . in high school, Danny befriended a boy named Ted, who moved into Thompson Falls. Good kid, but a bit rough. Gary and I would invite him over for dinner all the time, try to get him out of his house. His dad drank a lot and threw him around a bit. He was always polite and appreciated it. I think he knew what we were up to." Babs took a long drink from her cup.

"But, one night in their junior year, the two of them decided to go to a party of a classmate. We knew about it and let him go. Times were different back then. Everyone knew everyone, and so we figured it'd be safe." She took another pause. Claire almost felt bad for asking. It seemed it was becoming a tough one for her to tell. "Well . . . a little too much was consumed that night . . . or smoked, for that matter. Danny and Ted walked home a little intoxicated . . . not paying much attention . . ."

Claire stared at her.

"From what Ted could remember, he said the car came out of nowhere . . . never saw Danny at all."

"Oh my." Claire gasped, not expecting the sudden ending. She knew something must have happened but . . . hit by a car?

"Yes . . ." Babs said. "Just goes to show how quick and unpredictable life can be. It was a simple party . . . and it was Danny's last night on earth."

Claire felt her throat tighten and her eyes burn. "I'm so sorry." She wondered if this was why her mom had never mentioned Danny. How traumatizing that must have been. No wonder she was so terrified of Claire going to that party. She suddenly felt extremely guilty. What if that had happened to Sam? Or her?

Claire decided to express this, as she could tell the guilt and discomfort was playing across her face based on Babs's expression. "I guess . . . that's probably why my mom was so upset at me the other day."

"And why would that be?" Babs asked, returning to comfortably drinking her tea, pushing back her grief that never really went away.

Claire heaved a sigh and grabbed a cookie. "I kind of snuck out and went to a party with my best friend, Sam. The cops showed up and everything. Sam got booked, and I made it home, but my mom found out, of course, and tweaked."

"Ah . . . hence this being your little stint of community service," Babs said with a wink.

Claire laughed hollowly. "Yeah. But I'll tell you what, Babs. I definitely would pick coming here any day over being grounded in my room or picking up trash on the side of the road."

Babs let out a burst of laughter. "Well, I am glad." She continued to laugh before calming to say, "You know, Claire . . . kids do things like go to parties and drink underage and sneak out all the time. And in many cases, their parents never find out, and the night becomes a thrilling story years later. In some cases, they do, however, and they, like your mom and dad, are flooded with images of what my Gary and I actually lived. I don't think us parents want you to not do those things . . . or, at the very least, we don't expect that you won't. But it doesn't hurt to be aware of the possible consequences to at least keep you on your toes, I guess."

Claire nodded and agreed. She even wondered if her mom's choice of punishment was made to not only give Babs a friend, and Claire some community service, but to somehow bring about a conversation about Danny.

"You'll make mistakes. We all did. But just . . . be careful," Babs said and then quickly moved on from the severity of the conversation to say, "Now, tell me . . . what made you want to sneak out to an underage drinking party anyway? Was it a boy?"

Claire blushed. "No . . . mostly because my friend wanted to because she knew it'd be cool . . . and, well, I guess I thought the same thing. But there was a boy there! He helped me escape the cops."

Babs laughed. "Oooo-wee! Now, that's a fun tale. Is he cute?"

Claire blushed, not sure why she had even mentioned this, but there was a fun ease about Babs. Claire chuckled nervously. "He is. But . . . he has a girlfriend."

"Well, that just brought me right down." Maybe Babs could hear the slight letdown in Claire's tone because she then said, "But I bet she isn't as smart and talented as you, now, is she? How about something on the piano?"

Claire smiled. "Definitely."

They moved through the entryway to the next room. It was a study. More books lined these walls but so did an entire *Britannica* set, a *Funk & Wagnalls* encyclopedia series, and many map books and gazetteers. Pictures were hung everywhere, mismatched frames allowing for just about every square inch of the room to be covered. The piano was a small chestnut upright with a stool. Claire took her seat while Babs sat in yet another wingback chair that stood near an antiquated desk.

"What would you like to hear?" she asked.

"Oh, anything at all," Babs responded from behind her.

Claire took a deep breath and decided on Debussy's "Clair de Lune." It was a favorite of hers and one her mom had hummed to her when she was little. It was where she had gotten her name. And so it was a must to learn when taking up piano. Babs breathed her own sigh as she closed her eyes and listened to Claire play. When done, she moved seamlessly into Chopin and then Mozart. She decided to end on a more modern piece she'd learned recently from Broadway. Babs gave a standing ovation when Claire lifted her hands off the keys and spun in her stool.

"I didn't know that piano could sound so good." Babs beamed broadly.

Claire smiled sheepishly. To take the attention off her, she gestured to the wall. "You have a lot of pictures in here. I love it."

"Yes. All family and friends. I have my great-grandparents up there, believe it or not. It's the portrait up top there."

Claire saw a gold, oval, ornate frame that had an aged painting of a severe looking woman and a straight-faced man.

"They didn't smile much back then," Babs added to Claire's chuckle.

Babs stood up and took down a thin-framed photo from atop the piano and held it out to Claire. "That is my Danny."

Claire was caught off guard and felt the tightness in her throat return. He was a teenager. It couldn't have been too long before he died. He had long sideburns and a shaggy hairdo that was combed over. He was wearing a suit and tie. School photo day. And he had a soft smile that reached his eyes.

"That was 1971," Babs said. "Danny had just turned sixteen."

So it *was* right before he'd died. His last school photo. That hit Claire right in the gut. She looked into the face of a boy whose life would soon after end. All his hopes and dreams, what he could have accomplished . . . it was all there in his shining face. She wondered what he liked to do, what he wanted to be . . . if he liked music. The sixties had some of the best. Her dad had so many records, eight-tracks, and cassettes of his favorites, and Claire knew every single one. She had grown up on it. It was something they shared. She could picture this young man doing the same. Listening to The Association or The Guess Who in his car . . . maybe singing along to The Mamas & the Papas.

"He was very handsome," she said quietly.

"Oh yes. Got it from his father," Babs said, smiling at the picture over Claire's shoulder.

"Did he like music?" she asked, deciding she needed to know this. She could tell so much about someone based on the music that drove their soul.

"Oh my word, did he ever." This got a laugh out of Babs. "That boy would blast that darn record player in the living room as loud as it could go, all the windows up. Used to yell at him all the time for it." Babs sighed.

"Which ones would he blast?"

"Oh, I still have his records in the other room. I don't know it off the top of my head, but I'll know it when I see it. Come on. I think your mom will be coming soon anyway."

They left the den through the opposite doorway and ended in the dining room as Claire had suspected. She could see two doors to the kitchen beyond, but they just went right around to the room Claire had first entered. Babs led her to the old player, the shelf behind it filled with records. Babs flipped through them. Claire could make out some Glenn Miller and Dean Martin along with a Patsy Cline. Claire wanted to get her hands on them to see each one but kept herself controlled.

"Aha!" Babs said, pulling one out. "This was the one. He would play this over and over again."

She handed it over. Claire smiled down at the debut album of Gary Puckett and the Union Gap. She couldn't hide her joy at seeing it, its authenticity and age. She and her dad loved Gary Puckett. They would play it in the car all the time, both of them belting "Young Girl," Claire having absolutely no idea what it was about. She could almost hear the song playing through the halls and rooms around her, Gary Puckett's large vocals raising goose bumps.

"Gary Puckett and the Union Gap! I love it!"

"You know these boys? They were way before your time." Babs chuckled.

"I do," Claire responded, looking over the album again. "A favorite of mine and my dad's."

"Well, I'll be." Babs grinned.

They both looked up at the sound of Claire's mom pulling up.

"Looks like our time is up," Babs said.

Claire was surprised at how disheartened she was to leave. She was having such a good time. "Thank you, Babs. This . . . this was a lot of fun."

Babs brushed her comment away as they walked to the door, and Claire put her shoes on. "You think *you* had fun? I haven't had such a blast in a long time. You made an aging gal feel young."

They walked down the front steps, and Claire's mom waved. "Hey, Babs. How are you?"

"Oh good, dear, good. How are you?" Babs called back.

"Same ole, same ole." She smiled.

Looking on at her mother's warm smile and crinkled eyes, Claire could suddenly picture her young and playing outside with Danny. She'd never thought of her mother like that before. Babs was right, she was a pretty girl.

Babs turned to Claire and said, "Well, Claire, don't be a stranger. It was lovely to meet you."

"You too." She then realized that she was still carrying the record album. "Oh! Here. Sorry. Wasn't paying attention." She held it out. "Um . . . your son had great taste."

Babs grabbed the album and looked it over before giving a side-glance and saying, "You know what? Keep it." And she held it back out to Claire.

Claire looked on in amazement. "What? No, I can't. It was his favorite!"

"And it doesn't get played. It's too much for me in this big ole house all by myself. Too many memories. He'd want it to be enjoyed. Especially by someone who loves music as much as he did."

Claire opened her mouth, but nothing came out. The lump in her throat stopped her words.

Babs patted her shoulder. "Enjoy it."

Claire gave her a hug and went to join her mom, but not before stopping at the bottom of the steps to ask, "Can I come visit again sometime?"

Babs looked surprised, but her face was full of sheer joy, a lump forming in her own throat. "I would love that."

Claire nodded and got in the car.

They had a short ride home—Claire could actually walk it but her mom had wanted to bring her since it was the first time Claire was meeting Babs.

"So, how'd it go? You have fun?"

"Yeah," Claire said, her thoughts elsewhere.

"Did you get an album?" her mom questioned.

"Yeah. A pretty special one too."

"Oh? Why's that?"

"It was Danny's . . . his favorite," Claire said. "How come you never told me about him?"

Her mom sighed, and Claire thought she saw a slightly pained expression flash across her face. "I have. Just maybe not in an obvious way."

"When?" Claire asked.

"I've told you about what my best friend and I did in summers before. How you and Sam reminded me of us. I just guess I never really named him or went into detail. It was a long time ago. We were kids. It was traumatic . . . It isn't exactly something you share over dinner to make light conversation."

"No . . . I guess not," Claire said. "How come I've never met Babs before?"

"Well, after Danny passed, I finished up high school, she and Mr. Lawrence went traveling, and I guess . . ." her tone shifted, and Claire thought she heard guilt in it. "I guess I just found I didn't have any reason to go there anymore. I went to college, and then your dad and I started our life together and . . . I don't know. Just drifted from my mind, I guess. Sometimes I feel things just go so fast that before you know it, you don't even realize how much time has passed since you've said hello to someone."

"Does Babs have anyone?" Claire butted in.

Her mom sighed again. "No, unfortunately. Her husband died fifteen years ago or so. She had a sister, I believe, who would visit, but she lives in another state and is either too old to travel now or has passed. She was older than Babs by a bit. She had siblings in between, but they're all gone too. They never had any kids besides Danny."

"I'm sorry . . ." Claire said quietly, "about Danny."

"Thanks, kiddo. Danny Lawrence was a great guy. Always smiling. Always joking. I still remember that night . . . My mom came into my room to tell me what had happened. It's still so vivid. I didn't think of it then, but I can't imagine what Babs and Mr. Lawrence went through. I can't imagine getting a phone call like that about you or Troy." Claire saw her mom shudder, and they fell into a silence.

"Is that why you sent me there? Instead of grounding me?"

Her mom looked at her as they pulled into the driveway, sizing her up. "Yes and no. I'm a fan of service rather than grounding. Especially with you, where I send you to your room and you just read and it's like I've done nothing." She smirked, putting the car in park but both of them staying in place. "I was hoping to give Babs a friend. I knew she had a piano. And thought maybe you'd want to visit again. Keep you out of trouble."

Claire chuckled.

"And I guessed she would eventually talk about Danny. Maybe. And if so, I hoped that perchance you would feel something for him and what happened . . . maybe understand where your dad and I are coming from when we want you to be safe and make smart choices."

They exchanged a meaningful look.

"Thank you," Claire said.

Her mother patted her knee, and they got out of the car. Walking to the door, Claire said, "I definitely want to visit more. Babs deserves to have company. And have someone make her house be filled with music again."

"So no costumes, right?" Sam was saying on the other side of the line. She had apparently called five times while Claire was visiting with Babs. Troy mentioned that several times when telling her.

"Yeah, no, I wasn't planning on dressing up. Like last year."

"Okay, that's fine. I just wanted to make sure. Are you, like, *dressing* up? Makeup and everything?"

"Um . . . well, I have some on already from school, so I'll probably touch it up, sure. Why?"

"Well, I want to make sure I'm on the same level as you, you know? We're in high school now! We're making a high school statement!"

"I guess so." Claire laughed, not really following.

"Claire! Our classmates will be out there! Walking around and stuff. We need to look cool!"

Claire rolled her eyes.

"I heard that!! I heard that eye roll!" she huffed. "Okay, so look cute. Got it. I gotta walk Joey around the neighborhood first, and then we can go back out to hit up Main Street, and hopefully people will be out by then."

"Sounds good. Meet at the tree after dinner?"

"You got it, dude!"

They hung up. When it came close to time, Claire did what she said she would. She touched up her makeup, reapplied her cranberry lipstick, and threw on her forest-green bulky sweater atop her jeans. Adding her brown jacket and Doc Martens at the door, she went out to meet Sam, many young children already out on the streets. All the houses, including her own, were decked out with skeletons, pumpkins, hay bales, fake cobwebs, and more. It was always a sight to see Thompson Falls at Halloween. She spotted Sam and Joey by the tree and went to meet them.

"Hey!" Claire said when she was in earshot. "Hey, Joey! Great costume!"

"I'm Chuckie from *Rugrats*!" he said excitedly.

"I can see that! You guys did a great job making the costume!" Claire laughed. It was handmade by Sam's mom: a felt Saturn glued to a blue shirt, zig-zags drawn on green shorts, and what looked like an old red wig that Ms. Levinski had cut herself, teased and sprayed.

They started walking around town. Joey was old enough that they just had to stand at the foot of the driveways and watch him go up. He knew how to say "trick or treat" and "thank you" without prompting and didn't run off and out of sight.

They walked and talked as Joey made his way to the houses. Sam's mom didn't want him going to too many, as there was no need for him to have that much candy. In Thompson Falls it was easy to fill your pillowcase sack in a mere half hour if you were fast enough. Sam and Claire had always dumped off their candy at home midway through the night and then gone out again for round two, leaving them with a year's worth of candy and plenty of cavities between them. Sam's mom had apparently thought better of this with Joey.

"Do you ever feel like . . . I don't know . . . like we're getting old?" Sam asked randomly as Joey went up to yet another house with a handful of other kids.

"Old?"

"Not old, I guess. Like, I know we're young . . . but, like . . . I don't know. I love being in high school, don't get me wrong, and being a teenager is the bomb . . . but do you ever sit back and realize that our childhood, like, our real childhood, is over?"

"I never really thought of it, I guess. I mean, sometimes I find it hard to believe we're in high school already. It seemed to go so fast. And the way this year already seems to be going, I can see why people say high school flies."

"Yeah! High school already. And soon it'll be college and then moving out and getting jobs and families and . . . It just seems to hit you, you know? It just comes out of nowhere. Like Halloween, for example. One year we're dressing up and trick or treating, and just like that, it's over! Gone. We didn't plan it. One year we went out not knowing it was the last time we would. If I had known, I probably would have picked a better costume."

Claire chuckled. Sam had a point. "Yeah . . . same with playing with Barbies and make-believe in the backyard, I guess."

"One day we did it . . . and one day we just didn't. It's weird, huh?"

"Totally."

"And, I mean, there's plenty of things we're doing now that I bet in ten years or even twenty we'll look back on and say the same exact thing."

"I guess that means maybe we need to live in the moment a bit, huh?"

"Guess so . . ." Sam's thoughts trailed off. "Anyhoo. How was your visit with that lady?"

"Good! Really good actually. She was wicked nice. She made tea and cookies, and I played her piano. It was a good time."

Sam cocked an eyebrow. "Seriously? Well, isn't that just a positively charming afternoon."

Claire elbowed her. "Come on."

"Come on?! Me, come on? Drinking tea and eating cookies is your mom's version of getting grounded?"

Claire chuckled and shrugged. "She wanted me to do a civic duty. Volunteer my time. Because simply grounding me does nothing, apparently." Sam nodded agreement. "I also think she was hoping Babs would do what she did, which was talk about her son, Danny."

"What about him?" Sam asked, watching Joey talk to a boy dressed as a Power Ranger.

"Well, he went to school with my mom, apparently. Best friends, in fact. When he was in high school, he and a friend went to a party, and on their walk home, he got hit by a car, and he died."

"Holy shit, dude. Definitely wasn't expecting that," Sam said, shocked. "That's too bad . . . So *that's* the reason your mom sent you there. To teach you a lesson about partying? What is she, a D.A.R.E. officer?"

Claire chuckled. "Right?! But no . . . Well, partly. Like I said, she wanted me to do something. Babs is lonely. So she wanted me to spend time with her. And to draw attention to, like, the fear she felt and why she was so mad . . . I don't know . . ."

"Joey! Let's go!" Sam shouted. They continued down the next block where Mr. Henderson, the owner of the corner store, and Mrs. Sampson, who was the librarian at the elementary school, lived. "Well, man . . . I'll tell you what. That will stick with you more than a month's worth of freaking grounding."

Claire laughed. "Yeah. She was really sweet and has nobody. Danny and her husband were all she had, and she's lost them both . . . I'm planning to visit again. Give her company."

"Let's do it!" Sam said.

"Really?"

"Yeah, why not? I could go for some tea and cookies with an old lady. I bet she's got some great stories. Oooo, and love advice."

Claire rolled her eyes. "Well, cool. I bet she'd love that."

They continued around the blocks, Sam keeping an eye on the time. They waved to old teachers or people they knew from town. There were many families out, some kids dressed as Barney, others as their favorite Disney characters. Claire saw a few other Power Rangers, some Ninja Turtles, and a really great clown. They waved and said hello to a few other kids they knew from school who were out with siblings as well. They were making their way back to Sam's house when Sam had a sudden gasp of excitement that made Claire jump.

"Oh. My. God. I totally forgot to tell you!" Sam practically shouted.

"Goodness, Sam. You scared the shit out of me. What the hell is it?"

"I can't believe I forgot to tell you this!"

"Sam!"

"Okay." She could hardly contain her excitement. "Okay . . . so. Today in school I heard from Heather who heard from Steve that Mark likes you!"

Claire let out a huge burst of laughter. "What?! You're kidding me, right?"

Sam didn't let Claire's laughter deter her. "I'm serious, dude!"

"Who even is Heather?" Claire asked exasperatedly.

"Heather Proctor. You remember her from elementary school. She's in my math class. I sit with her most of the time. But her cousin Steve is in Mark's math class and they were talking and he told Steve that he thinks he has a crush on a girl in his English class. When asking her further, she said she was someone he sits with and that he sees often because they're in homeroom!" She ended on a squeal. "That's totally you!"

"Why is Heather Proctor even talking to her cousin about Mark's love interests?"

"Well, honestly? I think she has a crush on Mark and wanted to know whatever she could find out about him from her cousin. She talked to me because she knew I was in his English class, and I think she was nosing to see if I knew who it could be."

Claire tried to follow the line of communication that had transpired to learn this information. "I see."

"What? That's it? Aren't you excited?"

"Sam! This has gone through, like, four people, five if you include me now. I'm not believing this or giving it any energy at this point."

"Oh come on!! It's practically from the source itself!"

"Are you serious?" She laughed, looking at Sam smacking her gum and blowing a bubble. "You're serious. Oh my god, you're serious right now."

"Can't you just enjoy something like this for once! A guy has a crush on you. Mark!"

"We think he does. *I'm* going to leave it be."

"Oh Claire," Sam said as they made it to Sam's walkway. Her mother came out onto the porch to collect Joey and waved to the girls.

"Hi, Ms. Levinski!" Claire shouted across the lawn.

"Don't forget your curfew, Samantha. You're still grounded. This is a one-night deal!"

"I know, Mom!" yelled Sam exasperatedly.

"Take care, Claire!" She smiled as she started listening to Joey excitedly talk about all the houses he'd hit and the candy he'd gotten, leading him through the front door.

"Honestly . . ." Sam said with frustration. But she quickly lost the irritation as they made their way to Main Street. Halloween was always the best night for Thompson Falls. Well, that and Christmas. The street was shut down for pedestrians, and all the stores would have some kind of free goody. Usually cider or candy. But Main Street Sweets had the best of them all. Many stores would have special deals and drawings as the evening went on. There was always music playing from the shop Troy worked at, and the Masonic lodge had a walk-through haunted house every year.

Claire remembered all of Troy's stories over the years and remembered how excited she was when she and Sam finally got to walk it on their own. It varied from year to year, but the town's goal was to have a place for older kids to go and hang out, have fun, and, of course, keep them out of trouble. Troy was working tonight, along with the new girl, and had dressed as Frankenstein's monster. This was a must stop for Sam because she had wanted a peek at Troy's new crush ever since Claire had told her about it a couple days ago.

"Okay, how do I look?"

Claire sighed. "You look fine, Sam. As always."

"Oh stop. I'm serious! This is our first time downtown for Halloween as high school students. This is a big deal!"

"Okay, okay. You look good. Honest." They pinky swore.

"Alright. Cool."

They passed Claire's house and continued on till they turned the corner onto a sight that Claire couldn't help but grin from ear to ear at. It always reminded her of a scene straight out of a Halloween movie. In fact, when *Hocus Pocus* had come out a couple years ago, Claire had fallen in love because the scenes of Salem reminded her so much of Thompson Falls, which, of course, made sense since it was New England after all. Music was coming from Troy's store, and someone had set up a fog machine.

"Where do we even go first?!" Sam asked excitedly. They heard some distant screams from the Masonic lodge.

"Let's get some cider first. My hands could use some warming up. And then maybe go see Troy?"

"Yes! Let's do that!"

They walked into the bake shop, and the smells of nutmeg, pumpkin, and cinnamon encircled their senses, making their mouths water. They chatted with Mrs. Leonard and got a free bag of sliced pumpkin bread out of it, then grabbed their two cups of free warm cider. The music store was currently blasting "Enter Sandman," Troy's choice most likely, through the fog that was pouring across the street from within. They entered and saw Troy leaning on the counter, talking to Gwen, who was behind the register. She was laughing, Troy clearly having said something to make her do so. Claire and Sam exchanged looks and headed over.

"Hey, Troy," Claire said. He saw her and immediately stood up off the counter and cleared his throat.

"Hey, Mouse," he said, regaining his chill self. "Having fun tonight? Hey, Sam."

Sam waved as Claire answered, "Yeah! We dropped Joey off and just got here."

"Cool. Well, we have a drawing out front for some free merch. Make sure you both enter!"

"Will do," Claire said, averting her eyes to Gwen and then back to Troy, hoping he'd get the hint.

"Oh! Yeah. Um . . . Gwen, this is my sister, Claire, and her friend Sam. This is Gwen."

Gwen smiled a braces-perfected smile, saying, "Hi! Nice to meet you both."

"Ditto! So what's it like working with my brother?" Claire couldn't resist. She saw Troy give her an exasperated look, but he managed to smirk it off when politely looking at Gwen for her answer.

"Oh, it's good fun! He always manages to make me laugh," she said with a light chuckle.

"Oh, he's funny alright. You should hear him—"

"Alright, that's enough mingling, Mouse. We're working, remember? And you have a whole street of fun to get to," Troy interrupted. Claire and Sam tried to hide their laughter. Claire was happy to see Gwen doing the same. "Let me just show you where to fill out that drawing."

They went back to the entrance where someone Claire knew to be named Randy was watching over a bucket and tickets.

"Are you *trying* to embarrass me?" he asked as Claire started filling out the back of a ticket.

"Maybe."

"Why in the hell are you trying to do that?"

"Because this is the first girl you've ever seemed to care *how* you appear to. I gotta get some kind of sister jab in there. Makes it authentic. Besides, I barely said anything. Chill out!"

"Well . . . still."

"Don't worry, big bro. I won't say anything she wouldn't already be able to tell by knowing you," she said, patting him on the shoulder, then placed her filled-out ticket in the bucket.

"Why do I feel like that's a taunt?"

"Take it how you want." Claire smiled.

"You knucklehead," Troy said, throwing his arm around her but saving her from the act of a noogie and marching her out into the street instead. "Now, get out of here, you two."

Claire laughed. "Bye, Troy."

"Hey," he called back. "Be safe."

"We will." Claire rolled her eyes.

Once out of earshot, Sam said, "Even dressed as Frankenstein . . . you're brother is—"

"Don't . . . don't tell me my brother is hot."

"Fine . . . Gwen is though. She's really rocking that short edgy blonde hair. A great smile. Great boobs. She seems sweet too."

"I'll let Troy know."

Sam elbowed her, sniggering. "Alright, now what?"

"Claire!" they heard yelled from behind. They turned to see a group of people they didn't quite recognize at first, for they were dressed as zombies. But upon further inspection, they saw that it was Mark, Chris, Amber, Lauren, Ashley, and another guy they didn't know, all of whom were making their way toward them.

"You guys look great!" Claire said as they neared.

"Where's your costume?" Mark asked. Claire couldn't help noticing the unhappy expressions coming from the golden trio behind him. Claire appreciated Mark's enthusiasm for dressing up still. In fact, she loved it. But she couldn't help but enjoy the fact that she wasn't dressed up, looking at an Amber with black-and-green smudged makeup on her face.

"Oh, we walked Sam's little brother around earlier and then came here. No costumes for us. But this is awesome," she said, gesturing to them.

"Yeah . . . well. Amber thought it'd be fun for us to dress up and match. So I came up with zombies, told Chris and Mike to as well, and then Lauren and Ashley came, and yeah!"

"Cool!" Claire responded, nodding to Mike as a quick hello. She had a feeling Amber's plan was not to have a whole group of zombies parading around but to have Mark to herself as a matching couple. And she would bet money her choice would not have been zombies either.

"Mark," Amber butted in in her drawling voice. "We're supposed to be going to the haunted house. Remember?"

"Yeah! You guys been yet?" he asked Sam and Claire.

"No," they said in unison.

"Well, come with us!" he said, much to the annoyance of Amber, which was spread clearly across her face.

"Mark, we were . . ." Amber began. "Well, we kind of had a thing going. You know, three and three?"

Claire thought she had an idea of what was going on. Amber was hoping for a triple date since she couldn't get Mark to herself. And though Claire's little blowup at Amber had solved their locker issue, and had kept Amber at bay, she knew it wouldn't last forever and wasn't sure how this would go over if Claire crashed her plans. But she couldn't help what Mark said.

"Yeah, well, now we're eight. That's still even. We're good! You guys want to come?"

"Sure!" Sam and Claire said together.

"Great!"

They made their way to the hall, Mark walking next to Claire and Sam, Lauren talking to Chris, Ashley walking near Mike, and Amber trailing behind, alone. Claire almost felt bad for her. But got over it quickly.

The line was short to get in. They could see strobe lights flashing in one of the windows, black lights, shouts, and laughter coming from all over. Claire was excited, although a little nervous. She didn't mind being scared or jumped, but she struggled with walking herself through haunted houses. She preferred haunted hay rides.

"You scared?" Mark asked.

"Oh no . . . I'm fine. I just may need someone to, you know, push me forward if I stop walking at some point."

Mark laughed. "I'll make sure you keep going."

The man at the door gave them the go-ahead and the eight of them entered. The rooms were themed, the first being clowns, which Claire thought was unfair to start with something so intense. She screamed, arm in arm with Sam, and laughed, and screamed again. Amber managed to grab Chris's other arm, and all of them made their way through in a huddle. At one point, Claire thought she felt Mark try to grab her hand, but she avoided it by reaching up to put her hair behind her ear as they went through a room that had fake bats coming from the ceiling and a guy jumping out dressed as Dracula. A chainsaw room, a dark room with nothing but glow paint to light the path of constant terrifying shrieks and ghost noises, a mummy who chased you throughout, and finally a room full of hay bales and a scarecrow that came off its pole. By the end of it, they were all pink cheeked, the cold air feeling refreshing on their faces as they exited the back of the building laughing hysterically.

"Oh. My. God. That was, like, so awesome! I think they really upped their game this year," Sam said.

"Totally. My heart's still in my throat though!" Claire responded. They all exchanged excited words.

Mark swung an arm around Claire's shoulder and asked playfully, "You going to make it?"

"Yes." Claire laughed. "I assure you."

"Mark! Let's go to Ron's next," Amber said. "They're supposed to be serving pizzas for half price! Maybe we can snag the pool table."

"Yeah, that sounds like fun! You guys want to hang out with us for the night?" he asked Claire. Amber shot daggers.

"Oh! Um . . . we were—" Claire was going to say they were going to walk the shops, knowing Sam couldn't stay out late due to being grounded. But at that moment, the next group came out the back door, almost running into them, and the leader of the pack of three was . . .

"Adam," Claire couldn't stop herself from blurting, or from very obviously shimmying out from under Mark's arm.

"Claire," he said surprised, the adrenaline from his adventure in the haunted house ebbing away to be replaced with a broad grin.

"Cool haunted house, huh?" she asked, smiling at him, nervously flipping her hair to the other side.

"Yeah, pretty sweet," he said. He was wearing a jean jacket over a gray hooded sweatshirt. He too ran his hand through his hair. "Uh . . . this is Fitz, you remember him from band."

" 'Bohemian Rhapsody' goddess! How's it going, man?" he said loudly in his surfer dude lag.

Claire laughed. "Well, thank you."

Adam smirked. "And this is Jason. Another friend of mine."

"Nice to meet you," she said. Jason had short black hair, a kind smile, baggy jeans, and a black sweatshirt.

"You too," he returned with a genuine smile and head nod.

"You, uh . . . all hanging out tonight?" Adam asked, looking at the group behind her.

"Oh! Yes, sorry. This is my friend Sam. And this is Mark, Chris, Mike, Amber, Lauren, and Ashley," she rambled off, pointing at each of them. "All friends from classes." Claire didn't know how else to group them together without being rude, so, for now, Amber would be considered a friend. Considering Adam and his friends were older, she was probably okay with it.

"Nice to meet you all," he said, giving a quick wave to them. Claire thought she saw him linger on Mark for a second, but she reminded herself that she was probably making it up. Why was she still trying to see things that weren't there with him? Though she did notice there was no Rachel.

"They were all just going to head to Ron's, but Sam and I were just going to walk the streets," Claire said. "What have you guys done so far?"

"Well, we don't have to go to Ron's right now," Mark butted in. Everyone looked at him. Amber rolled her eyes. She clearly had had enough of all of this.

"Mark! That's where we were supposed to go next. We wanted to play pool and get pizza. It's cold. Let's go."

"But . . . well . . ." Mark stammered

"Let's go!" Amber insisted.

"Yeah . . . yeah okay. Maybe we'll see you at Ron's?" Mark asked Claire.

"Maybe," she said. He nodded, and the group left, leaving her and Sam, who Fitz and Jason thankfully started chatting with.

"You don't want to go to Ron's with them?" Adam asked.

"Nah. Honestly, most of them are not even people I choose to hang out with. Mark invited us along when he saw us."

"Ah, I see," Adam said. "The blonde . . . is that *the* girl? Locker girl? Class bitch?"

"Class bitch." Claire nodded.

"I can tell," he responded with a chuckle. "So how's it going?"

"Good," she said.

"Good," he returned.

She paused a moment and then blurted, "I'm out of trouble with my parents for the party!"

"Yeah? Short sentence?" He smirked.

"I didn't actually have that big of a sentence. I spent some time with a lovely lady who needed a friend and got a really special album out of it. Vinyl."

"Yeah? Which album?" he asked, the two of them falling back into their normal level of ease.

"Gary Puckett and the Union Gap. Their first one."

"Nice! An oldie. My dad definitely liked them."

"Mine too. He had a cassette we listened to a lot. I actually considered that for your next one. But I have another in mind . . . I won't spoil it."

His smile spread wide across his face. "That's . . . that's great, Claire. I was hoping to find a tape soon," he said quietly.

"You thought I forgot, didn't you?" She smirked.

He grinned. "Well . . . more like I thought you didn't want to do it anymore."

Her heart fluttered. She lightly punched him in the shoulder. "I told you everything was fine."

"I know, I know . . ." He chuckled. He looked at her meaningfully, sighed, and said, "Claire . . . I, um . . . I—"

"Hey, man, we chilling out here all night, or are we checking out other stuff?" came Fitz's voice. "I'm cool either way, but if so, I may need a little something to kill some time, if you know what I mean," he said, making the motion of taking a drag. Sam giggled.

Adam looked down and shook his head.

Claire chuckled. "Sam and I should be going anyway. We have more to see, and she's still serving time without parole. I don't want her sentence lengthened."

"Gotcha," he said.

"Nice meeting you both! Well, meeting you, Jason. Nice seeing you again, Fitz," she said to the group.

"You've got my heart, Bohemian. That's going to be your new name," Fitz said, making a heart with his hands. Adam shook his head yet again and mouthed *I'm sorry.*

Claire laughed. "It's all yours, Fitz."

Sam waved to them all.

"It was great seeing you, Claire," Adam said quietly. "I look forward to that tape. And seeing you Monday." He seemed surprised at his own last words.

"You too," she returned. "See ya." She waved, and they left to continue their way on Main Street.

"Gah! That was so cool. All of it! Haunted house with the cool kids in our class. AND hanging out with upperclassmen guys?! How did that just happen to us?!"

Claire half-heartedly smiled, her mind elsewhere. The moon was high now, though not quite a half-moon. The air was making her nose red, and the whole street seemed to smell of cinnamon. Hay bales were scattered about, the fog machine was still going, and music now blasted The Cranberries. She and Sam popped into a few other stores, filling out more giveaway slips. They did another run through the haunted house, which brought Claire out of her reverie for a bit. But, though it was a perfect Halloween night, filled with all the airs of spooks and tricks, Claire wasn't upset when Sam mentioned that they should head back before her mom flipped.

They passed Claire's house first, so they parted ways there, Claire reminding Sam to call when she got home. She went inside, gave a quick overview of her evening to her parents, who were watching the classic *Halloween* on TV, answered Sam's call, and after eating some pieces of candy and watching Michael Myers get up from the floor yet again, she turned in.

Lying down after braiding her hair and putting on pj's, Claire couldn't help but think back to the things Sam had said earlier . . . about growing up and losing childhood . . . Mark supposedly liking her . . . and then bumping into Adam. His smile. The happiness he seemed to have when he saw her. The fact that Rachel wasn't there. His fun friends. Claire liked Mark and enjoyed his company, and she couldn't deny it made her a little excited that he may like her. But there seemed to be such an ease when talking to Adam and such a comfort even with his friends. It was no secret how Claire felt around the people Mark claimed as his inner circle. She didn't really know Mike, but he seemed okay. But Amber, Ashley, Lauren, and Chris were enough to make anyone gag.

Sam was right, she thought as she drifted off to sleep . . . growing up was weird and did seem to just happen. When *had* any of this happened? And how had it all happened in such a short span of time? She knew one thing: high school was definitely the roller coaster everyone said it was.

Fall faded slowly toward winter. Claire's fifteenth birthday in early November found Troy, Sam, Claire's parents, and Babs singing out of tune to her around a birthday cake that had music notes iced across it. Thanksgiving, Christmas, and ringing in the New Year were all filled with laughter, warmth, and good memory-making times. School seemed to double down on homework, and just like Sam and Claire had predicted, it was turning to spring before they knew it, and soon after, the air of summer was coming.

Over the past months, Claire had had her first concert in band, and then a second, had swapped several cassettes with Adam, and had fumbled through geometry problems with him as well. She hadn't yet seemed to completely lose the tingle in her stomach when she was around him, but seeing him and Rachel dancing at the school's Valentine's Day dance did a pretty good job at it. However, what replaced it was what she would bet money on as jealousy, and she wasn't sure if that was any better of a sign of moving on from her crush. She had at least decided to just enjoy the time she had with him and not worry about it.

By April break, something that had become quite clear, and something Sam couldn't stop talking about, was Mark's increasing drive to see Claire in the halls whenever he could, catch her at her locker after school, and invite her along to get-togethers at Ron's Pizzeria or the movies. Claire always dragged Sam with her when she did go, but it unfortunately meant she was seeing a lot more of Chris and, oftentimes, Amber, Lauren, and Ashley. Amber was back to her old bitchiness, although leaving the locker issues alone. She still tried desperately to gain Mark's attention, and because it was getting harder and harder, she shot daggers at Claire more and more often. She threw petty insults her way whenever she could, but Claire let them roll off. One thing high school seemed to have done was give her the ability to do a decent job at ignoring Amber. Part of her wanted to chalk it up to her maturity and independent nature, but she shamefully knew that a lot of it had to do with the confidence boost she got from being friends with Adam and many other upperclassmen due to band as well as the attention from Mark.

The last big event of the school year at A. Thompson High was the carnival. After prom and the seniors' final tests and classes and just before graduation, the school put on a carnival in the open field behind the building. It was small but a fan favorite of high school kids, who got in for free all weekend and got the day off of school on Friday to enjoy it, with staff monitoring. Come evening, it was open to the public through the weekend, and all proceeds went to the school's programs. It was planned annually for the weekend before graduation, which was always on a Monday, and the hype up for it was immense.

"I can't believe we're almost done with our freshman year! Like, totally rad. And this carnival? I have been waiting for this for forever."

Claire smiled over at Sam on her beanbag. "I'm pretty excited too."

"Are we still meeting Mark there?" Sam asked, flipping through the latest edition of *People* magazine, celebrity prom photos plastered across its cover. "I can't wait to go to prom," she added as an afterthought.

"I think so. I mean, I told him we may."

"Why are you so wishy-washy with him?" Sam asked suddenly.

"Wishy-washy? What do you mean?"

"You never seem to want to commit with him. It's always 'yeah, maybe,' or 'sure, we'll see.' I'm pretty sure the guy would have asked you out by now if he felt like you'd give him a solid yes. But, at this rate, you'd probably say, 'I don't know, let me check, and I'll get back to you.'"

Claire stared at her for a moment. Sam was right. Claire wasn't sure why she was always hesitant to do things with Mark. Well, she sort of knew but hated to admit it was because of a certain brown-haired cutie with gray eyes that she still saw every day of school. She pretended her crush wasn't there and tried to push it away, but it didn't work very well. Since Halloween, she and Mark had grown closer as friends and still had classes together second semester. She'd enjoyed his company over this school year, but there was something nagging at her when it came to the more overt attempts he'd made to get closer . . . and she always gave vague responses to his invites because she wanted to learn first who was going and ensure it wasn't a ploy to get her on a date. Today, he had asked if they could meet up for the carnival. He seemed to want it to just be with her, and it was the first time she'd felt sort of okay with it. So she said sure and that Sam would be there at which point he said he'd let everyone else know, but Claire knew that if he wanted to ride a ride together or walk off to play a game, just the two of them, she would be okay with it, and maybe even be excited about it.

"I don't know. I just don't like jumping into anything and am trying to feel the situation out, I guess."

"It's been, like, six months. You think way too much, dude." Sam rolled her eyes. "To think, you could have probably had a boyfriend this entire time, and you're just pushing him away."

"Why is it so impressive to have a boyfriend anyway?"

"Because! It makes you cool. And as a freshman, even cooler. Plus, just imagine Amber's face if you told her you guys were dating."

"I'm not going to date a guy just because it would piss Amber off."

"No . . . but it'd be a great side effect."

When Friday morning rolled around, Claire took an extra minute to select her outfit. It was supposed to be a warm June day, but not too hot. Claire decided on a floral short-sleeved dress that had buttons down the front, her Doc Martens, and a black choker necklace. She left her hair down but added some fluff to it by flipping it a few times and adding some hairspray. Lipstick, her favorite thumb ring, and a few bracelets, and she was ready. Her dad, having the day off, gave her a hug, a kiss on the head, and a twenty-dollar bill for food.

"Dad, all I have to worry about is food and maybe a few games. I don't need a twenty!"

"Well . . . there's usually some booths selling stuff. And maybe you can treat Sam to lunch too," he said, smiling. Claire knew that was the real reason. The Levinskis weren't poor per se, but Ms. Levinski was a single mom and a CNA. Overall, it didn't bring in a ton of money, and though Sam rarely complained about it, Claire knew that there were times when she felt it. Claire's family would be considered upper middle class, and though they weren't living like kings or anything, they were comfortable, and her parents often spared some extra money when it would help the group as a whole.

"Thanks, Dad," she said as she grabbed her small purse, slinging it across her body.

"You got it. Enjoy today. I used to love the school carnivals. I can't believe you're already going to your first one."

Claire rolled her eyes, but with kindness. "Bye, Dad." She chuckled.

"Love you," he called out.

"Love you more!"

She walked out to the porch and felt the warmth of the sun and a breeze blow through. She breathed in deep. She loved fall the most, but she enjoyed the beginning of all the seasons. There was something refreshing about the first warm day of spring, seeing the plants beginning to peek through the ground, the birds chirping in the trees. And something exciting when the trees were all full, with the bright colors of summer, the breezes becoming warmer, and the sun leaving marks on the skin. And nothing could beat the first crisp air of fall or that first snowfall of winter. Firsts. They were exciting. The seasons knew that.

She walked to Sam's house and knocked on the door. She could hear Sam's mom yelling to Joey to finish his snack and get off the Nintendo. Letting herself in, she spotted Sam coming down the hall from her bedroom, who added in her own, "Joey! Ma said to get off the game. Let's go!" as she threw on her shoes and quickly scooted Claire and herself out the door.

"Oh my god! Sorry about that. Joey is going through a phase. We recently got my cousin's Nintendo when he upgraded to the Super Nintendo, and Joey won't leave it alone. He was all butthurt this morning that he couldn't go to the carnival, so Mom let him play on it for a bit. Bad idea. She's got a shift and has to bring him to daycare till I get home and can walk him back." She sighed. Claire could see slight guilt flash across her face for leaving, and especially when this was a day she could have stayed home if needed. But Claire knew Ms. Levinski would never let her.

"Anyway . . . you look smokin'," Sam said.

Claire blushed a tad. "Oh stop," she teased. "I maybe did pay a little more attention this morning than usual though, so thank you."

"Yeah, I can tell!" Sam said to which Claire raised her eyebrows in mock surprise and offense. Sam laughed. "I just mean, I can see the extra detail. You look gorgeous," she added with exaggerated flair.

"Why, thank you, dahling." Claire chuckled.

"Man . . . how is it almost the end of our first year?! What a year, huh? It certainly flew. I mean, mostly with homework and tests and stupid gym games—oh, and that one detention I got for forgetting my homework three days in a row . . ."

"It certainly did," Claire pitched in.

"You . . . um, planning on talking to Mark at the carnival?" Sam asked a little tentatively.

"You afraid of me now?"

"Well, I just know the whole Mark thing has been somewhat sensitive!"

"Because you've been bringing it up for months! Every day of just about every week of every month since, like, Thanksgiving!"

"Okay, okay. So I've been a bit pushy. But it is only because I think you guys are cute, he clearly likes you, AND—"

"I could have a boyfriend, which would be cool . . . I know. We've had this conversation about . . . hmmm . . . forty times at least?"

"Alright," Sam said, smacking her gum. "Alright. All that aside, are you ready to maybe talk to him today? On your own?"

"I think so . . . yeah," Claire responded after thinking carefully.

Sam squealed. "Oh, I can't wait. Okay. The very second you want me to dash, you just say the word. Okay? You just give me a nod or say something, and I'll beat it like Michael Jackson. Got it?"

Claire laughed. "Don't worry. Let's not overthink this. Let's just play it cool and see what happens."

"You got it!" They walked up the front path to the school but took a right to head around to the back. They could already hear the noises coming from the carnival. It was basically a free day for students, unless you had work to make up. They could choose to go or not go and could show up and leave whenever they decided. She and Sam had agreed on 11:00, and that was what Mark was tracking too.

They entered and strolled past the booth that had the school secretary, Mrs. Poppish, in it, who just smiled and let them in. She had the memory of an elephant and knew everyone, so it was a perfect job for her to ensure only students got in. They walked in, and almost immediately, Claire heard her name and saw the clan walking their way. They had apparently been waiting. Amber was arm in arm with Chris, which Claire noted as an interesting development. Lauren and Ashley were boyless, and they looked bored stiff, arms crossed, with vacant expressions. Once again, Claire didn't understand the workings that were Mark and Chris, and especially the addition of the trio. She often wondered what they were all like when she wasn't there because she had to believe that only her and Sam's presence could cause Amber, Lauren, and Ashley to become so sour. She couldn't imagine why Mark and Chris, and sometimes Mike, who Claire had come to find was sweet and quiet, much different than Chris, would enjoy the girls' company if this was how they always acted.

"Hey, guys," Mark said to them.

"Hi. You all weren't waiting long, were you?"

"No, not at all," Mark answered quickly, but Claire saw Amber's attempt to jump in to answer first.

"No Mike today?" she asked.

"Oh, he's coming later, I think."

"Cool," Claire said. "Shall we?"

"Totally! After you," he responded, and they all made their way into the throng. There were quite a few students milling around, playing some of the games, getting food, or riding the rides.

"What shall we do first?" Mark asked. He was walking very close to Claire, and it seemed the two of them were in the lead.

"Well . . . I could do some rides! Before I eat something." She chuckled.

"That sounds good," he answered, and then to the group, "You guys want to do some rides?"

"Yeah, man," said Chris in his drawl.

"Uh . . . no," Amber butted in. "I'm not ruining my hair by going on one of those. I'll wait. Chris, you want to wait with me?" Claire swore she saw her bat her eyes, and she wanted to barf.

"Didn't you just hear me? I want to go on rides," Chris answered, Amber's face becoming pinched.

"Well, Lauren, Ashley, and I aren't going on rides, so you guys go," she said, annoyed. Claire noticed Lauren and Ashley exchange looks behind her.

"I'll go!" Sam offered. Chris looked at her and sized her up, which made Claire irritated. He shrugged as if to say *better than nothing*, which made Claire then want to slap him. Sam, however, didn't seem to notice, so Claire did nothing.

"Okay," Mark said. "Meet you guys around here after?" he asked Amber.

"I guess so," Amber said, throwing her hands up. The three of them marched off to what looked like a row of games that a bunch of kids were at.

"Alright! Which one first?" he asked.

Claire got excited. She loved rides. She looked around and saw the Tilt-A-Whirl, the slide, the Scrambler, a Ferris wheel, the one where you stand and it spins so fast you stick to the wall that Claire couldn't name, and a few others. The rides section wasn't huge, but to be able to ride them for free and as many times as they wanted made Claire almost squeal with delight like Sam usually did.

"Let's do the Scrambler! It's my favorite!" she said, trying to be calm. She felt like a six-year-old, too excited to contain her joy.

"You got it!" Mark said.

They climbed into the buckets, and Claire didn't mind when Mark put his arm around her. Sam got in one with Chris and looked like she would burst with thrills. Claire knew it had nothing to do with the ride but riding it with Chris. And not necessarily Chris, but a boy.

The ride started, and Claire felt the rush in her stomach as the grin spread across her face, the ride slowly gaining speed. They glided across the lawn slowly, her hair blowing in the breeze. As it got faster, she felt herself pressing against the inside of the bucket, Mark pressed up against her. And then all the nerves and exhilaration came out, and Claire threw her head back and started to laugh. It was a loud and trilling laugh that almost sang like her music. Mark started laughing too, and as fast as the ride was going, it seemed to simultaneously be in slow motion. There was nothing like this kind of amusement. It was freeing. Her hair went in every direction, and she could barely see for it.

When the ride slowed and came to a stop, she could feel the water in her eyes and on her cheeks. The six-year-old had been released, and she held nothing back in suggesting the next ride. They rode the Tilt-A-Whirl and then took sacks down the slide to race, Sam winning. They did the full loop of rides and then did them again. Mark always sat with Claire and, any chance he could, put his arm around her. He even held her hand when getting on and off rides, which Claire, though she didn't need it, thought was a sweet gesture and went with it. Finally, they decided they needed to take a break and find some food.

"Well, that was fun," Claire said, laughing slightly. "I'm starving now."

"What do you feel like eating?" Mark asked.

"Whatever! There isn't a bad choice when it comes to carnival food."

"This is true. Let's find Amber and take a walk through the stands."

Claire turned to Sam. "Want to share some fries?"

"Sure!" Sam said. They found Amber, Lauren, and Ashley sitting with a few other kids they recognized from their class. One was Logan, whom Sam knew from math class and was quite excited to see, and a girl named Sarah, a friend of Mike's, who had now shown up. They all agreed on getting food and took turns getting up while others held down the table. Soon enough, everyone had plates full of the greasiest and yummiest fries, chicken tenders, burgers, and Italian sausages around.

"After we eat, you want to try playing some games?" Mark asked Claire quietly. "You know, just us? If you want to."

There it is, Claire thought. She hesitated for a minute. "Sure." She smiled. He looked relieved and returned her smile. Claire figured it was the best time. Sam had some friends she knew, so Claire didn't feel too bad leaving her with Chris and the witches, even though Sam had already told her not to worry about it. Maybe she would stick with Logan, Mike, and Sarah.

When the fries were depleted, she turned to Sam and whispered, "He wants us to go play some games. Just us." Sam started to get giddy, but Claire squeezed her hand. "Keep it cool."

Sam nodded. "Cool. Yes. Okay. Have fun. Don't worry about me. I'll find you after."

"Okay," Claire said, and she stood up as Mark told the group they were going to check out the games, feeling a little nervous.

Mark grabbed her hand, and she allowed it. They walked over to the area that had a whole row of shooting, water gun racing, balloon popping, and ring tossing games. There were variants and others in between. "What game is your favorite?" he asked.

"Hmm . . . I always loved the water gun one," she responded.

"I love that one too! Wanna go?" he asked. "Maybe I can win you something."

"Or I can play against you and see who wins who something," she countered competitively.

"Game on," he said with a smile. They reached the game and each paid the one dollar to play. Others came and sat, and when enough people were ready, it started. Claire lined up the site on the water gun and pushed the trigger, not taking her eyes off the black target hole until she heard the bells and whistles going off. A guy next to her had won.

"Go again?" Mark said.

"You bet!" Claire responded. They played a few more rounds and had no luck at winning.

"Guess we both suck at this!" she said, laughing.

"Let's try one more," Mark answered, chuckling. "I can't lose *this* badly."

The seats filled up once again, though most people hadn't left. Claire heard the teacher, Mr. Jones, who was running the game say, "Next round, guys. We'll make room for two on the next round," as he started collecting everyone's dollar. One person got up and offered their seat instead, and when it was Claire's turn to pay up, she said, "They can take my seat as well. I've played plenty." He smiled and gestured to whoever was waiting to come sit. Claire turned to stand behind Mark and almost ran into said person.

"Well, hello there," he said, his gray eyes crinkling up into that familiar smile.

"Hey!" she said, her face glowing. "How—how's it going? Enjoying the carnival?"

"Yeah! Just got here a little bit ago."

"Nice! We've been here for a bit. Rode a bunch of rides. Had some food, and now we've been here trying to beat this game, with no luck."

Adam looked around and saw the "we" she was referring to. "Cool. Speaking of which . . . I should probably sit down. They're all staring at me."

"Whoops," she said, stepping aside.

"Thanks for letting me play. I could have waited," he said, taking his seat.

"Well, if I'd known it was you, I would have made you." She smirked as he returned the shitty grin.

"Mark, right?" Adam said, looking at Mark, taking a hold of the water gun.

"Yeah," Mark returned rather straight-laced. "Adam, right?"

"You got it."

The game began. Claire looked down the line and saw that Fitz was the other guy now playing. She hadn't needed to look, however, because at that moment Fitz yelled, "You're going down, Miller!" in his all too familiar voice.

"Fuck that!" Adam yelled back.

Claire gave a burst of a laugh as Mr. Jones said, "Language!"

"Sorry," Adam said. The water released, and a quiet tension filled the row, but only for a moment before the lights flashed and the winner was, once again, no one in their crew.

"Damn it," Mark said. Fitz came over and stood next to Claire.

"Alright, one more," Mark said to Claire, who gave the thumbs up and smiled.

"Hey, man, what next?" Fitz asked Adam, who looked contemplative.

"I'm going to try this one again," he responded.

"Alright, dude, let's see it!" Adam and Mark spun back around, waiting for the game to fill back up. Fitz turned to Claire and said, "So how's it going, Bohemian? When are you going to play us a righteous song again? I've been waiting this whole school year!"

"I know, I know. I'm sorry, Fitz." She chuckled.

"You're killing me. You know, you should totally try out for chorus next year. You got some mad chops."

Claire blushed. "Well, thank you, but I don't sing, really." The game had started again, Adam and Mark fighting hard to win.

"Duuuude, you should reconsider. For real," he said, elbowing her as they watched another person win. Both Adam and Mark swore, looked at each other, and handed off another dollar.

"Maybe I will, just for you, Fitz," she said, elbowing him back. For whatever reason, Fitz strongly reminded her of her brother, and she enjoyed the banter they had gained over the year from band class. They didn't get to interact that often, but whenever they did, it was entertaining.

"I'm holding you to that, Bohemian. Don't break my heart!" The game ended and both boys had lost yet again.

"I think you both should throw in the towel," she said.

"One more," they said in unison. Now Claire could hear the determination in their voices that she had missed earlier. The sideways glances they were giving each other . . . *Are they competing?* she thought and couldn't help but internally laugh. She decided to take matters into her own hands. She made eye contact with Mr. Jones and held up a dollar. When he took it, she pointed to herself and winked. He got the hint and winked back. Claire knew these games were rigged. Her father had told her that from his stint right after Troy was born when her parents were struggling with money and he had picked up a side job as a carny. They were built for people like Mark and Adam, and Mr. Jones wasn't sparing them. Maybe it was due to the competition between the game booths. The profits of each one went to a certain department's fundraiser at the school. From what she heard, it was a pretty big deal between the teachers who ran them.

She took her seat on the other side of Adam, who looked at her, Mark leaning over to see her too, and she waved at them both.

"Alright, here we go," Mr. Jones said, and the buzzer rang. Claire focused on the black target once again, and when the noises and lights indicating a winner went off, it was she who had won.

She blew at her finger gun and holstered it.

"Go, Bohemian!" Fitz said as he raised a hand for a high five.

"Thanks!" she said, returning it.

"Alright, young lady. What will it be? Two of these little stuffed bears, or one of these medium-sized ones? If you get the medium, you can play again and upgrade to a large."

"I'll take the two small ones, thanks." She smiled. She pointed to a blue one and a yellow one, which he handed off with a final wink.

"Alright, boys," she said, holding out the cheaply stuffed bears. "One for each of you."

Adam laughed, taking the blue one she handed him. "Why, thank you. That was some skill there. I'm honored." He bowed, and she curtseyed, giggling.

"And you," she said, handing the yellow one to Mark, who just shook his head, smirking.

"Well . . ." Adam said, his smile fading slightly. "We won't crash your party anymore. Enjoy the carnival, Claire . . . Mark." He nodded to the latter.

"Oh, you weren't crashing anything," Claire said and immediately regretted it, knowing how it would sound to Mark. "I mean, it was fun chilling for a bit. I'm glad we caught up. But, yeah, we'll see you guys around, I'm sure," she backtracked, standing next to Mark. She didn't want him to feel pushed away, but she was also struggling with this moment in front of Adam. God, why was this so hard?

Adam gave a sheepish smile and ran his hand through his hair.

"Yeah, dude," Fitz chimed in. "You should probably find Rachel anyway. She's probably pissed you ditched her for this long and don't even have something to show for it."

Adam shrugged it off. "I'm sure she's found plenty of things to keep her entertained."

"Well, you can give her the bear if you want. Say you won it. Just so you don't get in trouble." Claire chuckled, trying to lighten the air.

"Nah . . . I'm keeping this," he said with a meaningful look that she had to force herself to look away from.

"Well, we'll see you around," she said.

Mark waved at them as he grabbed Claire's hand, and she almost instinctively pulled it away but luckily caught herself.

They walked to the other games, Mark playing a few while Claire watched, and he finally got some of his charm back when he won a stuffed dog that he gave to Claire. They walked around the edge of the carnival, seeing the craft stands that were open. Claire spotted a cute yin-yang friendship necklace set that she picked up for herself and Sam. Mark continued to hold her hand, and when they passed a sweets stand, he grabbed her a cotton candy that they enjoyed pulling pieces off of, talking and laughing. They found their way back to Amber, Lauren, Ashley, Mike, and Chris. They told them that Logan, Sarah, and Sam were over by the rides, and though Mark seemed to want to stay with the group, he went with Claire to find Sam. Eventually, they all ended up as a large group again to finish off the afternoon riding the rides some more, Amber, Lauren, and Ashley watching.

When late afternoon hit, they made their way to the exit, and they all began walking home, people breaking off as they went separate ways. When it was just Mark, Claire, Sam, and Sarah left, Mark pulled Claire aside, the other two continuing to walk, but slowly.

"I have to wait here for my dad to pick me up," he said. They were out front of the D&G. Claire remembered that he wasn't from the village. It was crazy how after only a year, she already thought of her classmates as her classmates and had forgotten that some of them hadn't gone to school with her since elementary. She wasn't sure where Mark lived, but it was probably on the outskirts of Thompson if he had to get a ride. Adam, for example, wasn't from the village and hadn't gone to the village school like Claire had, but he lived just over the town line in Thompson, and so he knew many kids from both and had grown up in the area. Being older than Claire, she had just never interacted with him, until, of course, high school.

"Oh, right! I forgot." She paused. "Well . . . thanks for today. My stuffy is cute," she said, holding up the dog.

"Thank *you*," he said. "I had a really good time, Claire."

"Me too!"

"Like, a really good time. I hope that with summer we can maybe hang out some more? Chris doesn't live far from town, and I spend a lot of time there. We could meet up at Ron's or something. Whatever you want. I'd just like to hang out with you again."

"That'd be cool!" she said.

"Great! Um . . ." He looked around her at the girls and saw that they were a little ways ahead of them, still facing forward and walking slowly. He looked at her awkwardly, and then . . . he kissed her. It wasn't the super involved or intense kisses like those in her favorite movies. He was no Richard Gere or Patrick Swayze. But it was a kiss, and however quick it was, it was her first. And so the butterflies were there nonetheless, and she felt the beginnings of giddiness ebbing their way up. When he pulled away, he smiled down at her.

"Um . . ." she said, not knowing what to say. They both chuckled a little. "I'll see you next week," she managed. "Only a few days left."

"Yeah. Next week. And maybe I can get your number before that so I can call you this summer."

"Definitely," she said.

"Cool . . . Well, bye, Claire."

"See ya," she said, waving to him as she walked to where Sarah was saying her goodbyes. Claire and Sam continued, Claire feeling the excitable tension and enjoying making Sam live in it.

"BLAHGH! I can't take it anymore! What happened?! Oh my god, tell me everything. Where did you go? What happened at the carnival? What did he say? What did you say? And just now? Oh my god. Did I see him kiss you? Am I making that up?"

Claire smirked, and Sam yelled, "Claire! Talk to me!"

"Okay, okay. I was just enjoying that for a bit."

"You bitch," Sam said jokingly.

Claire laughed and told Sam everything. The game, Adam coming along, the rest of her and Mark's walk, what they talked about, and finally the kiss she had just encountered. As always, Sam was a great audience.

"Dude! You got your first kiss! And you managed to get it in freshman year still! God, I'm jealous! But super excited. But jealous! What did it feel like?"

"It was super quick. I was nervous. I'm not sure I felt much beyond that. I assume that's what a first kiss is like, right? Uncertain?"

"I wouldn't know, but it sounds right. So are you guys, like, a thing now?"

"He didn't ask me. And I'm okay with that for now. Just, you know, ease into it. He said he wanted to hang out this summer. So that's something, I guess."

"Oh my god. This is all so exciting. Way to cross that off the list!" Sam said as they came to her driveway. "I'd go to your house, but I need to get Joey and watch him for a bit so Mom can go grocery shopping after work. She's tired of bringing him with her. He wants all the junk, and she's sick of him running up to her with everything and anything, asking, 'Can we get this?'"

Claire sniggered. "No worries. Call me later?"

"Totes."

Claire continued on. It *had been* quite the first year of high school, she guessed. She met a cool older guy who was super into music, friendly, and cute. She got a major crush and, though she got let down, still managed to have a really good friendship with him, swapping cassettes and chill moments. She sneaked out to her first party, got drunk, and got caught. Had her first big fight with her best friend. Made up. Somewhat stood up to her bully. Did well in her classes. Got a new elderly friend whom she now visited once a week. Caught the attention of a cute boy in her class who also gave her her fist kiss. Maybe it *would* go somewhere.

And yet, she also couldn't deny the ease she felt with Adam yet again, how she couldn't stop her mind from mentally noting that Rachel wasn't with him, Fitz's comment ringing in her ears, *Rachel's going to be pissed*, and Adam's defeated shrug. She had given up on trying to make sense of that. She couldn't. She would just push it away like she was good at, and it would probably pop back up the next time they saw each other . . . But this time, she was going to try and push it away for good, and maybe give this Mark thing a chance.

Yeah . . . high school was a bit of a roller coaster, but overall, it was going well. The summer was just about here! She wondered what it would bring on its warm rays . . . the new school year, with Sam and Amber and Mark and everyone else . . . when they would no longer be the freshmen.

SOPHOMORE YEAR

1996-1997

Crash Into Me

The Summer Olympics were held in Atlanta, Georgia, and the Macarena was making its way into every dance club, radio station, and bedroom sing-a-long. *ER, Seinfeld,* and *Friends* were must-watch shows each week, everyone was anticipating the release of the Nintendo 64, Beanie Baby collecting was a must, and Claire was entering her sophomore year at A. Thompson High School. She and Sam were spending the last free days lying outside in Claire's yard on a blanket they had thrown down, the heat being too agonizing for them to do much of anything.

"Oh my god . . . I can't take it. I'm sweating through everything, and I'm not even doing anything," Sam whined, her eyes closed, her arm over her face to protect it from the sun.

"I know . . ." Claire mumbled. "My whole body is a swamp."

"I wish we could have been at the beach today," said Sam. They'd had plans but hadn't ended up being able to get a ride. "I can't wait for you to get your license."

"I've barely got my hours from my permit clocked yet," Claire said. She had waited till the summer class started to go for her permit and hadn't really felt much motivation to get on the road yet, mostly because her mom stressed her out, Troy's car was junk, and her dad had been given a promotion at work, which was great, but the transition had brought a lot of extra hours for him. If he wasn't at work, he was tired and wanting to just unwind, which Claire respected, and so didn't bother him with it.

"Well, you need to hurry up! You can go for your license in, like, a couple months! I can't even start driver's ed till November. Hopefully . . ." Sam's birthday was in September and so was young for their grade. There was a driver's ed class beginning in mid-September, but her mother had asked if she wouldn't mind waiting until the next round due to the class being too expensive for them.

"I know, I know . . ." Claire responded. They felt a slight breeze blow ever so lightly across them, and both sat in silence, enjoying the rare phenomenon. Claire started thinking back to the summer months. After school had let out, Sam and Claire had spent just about every day together. And Claire had gotten her first phone call from Mark shortly after . . .

"Hey," he had said.

"Hi! How's it going?!" Claire responded, hoping she sounded chill and placing a hand over Sam's mouth. Sam was more excited than she was, leaning in to share the receiver.

"Great! Look, a few of us are trying to get a group together to go hit up the beach next week. I'd love it if you could come. We can figure out rides and stuff. We're hoping for Monday but are going to wait to see the weather in the paper over the weekend."

Claire looked to Sam, who nodded. "Yeah! That'd be awesome! Can Sam come?" she asked.

He hesitated, and Claire noticed, hoping Sam didn't. "Yeah, sure."

"Sweet! Yeah, I guess just give me a call this weekend with the details."

"You got it. And . . . um, Claire?"

"Yeah?"

"I also happened to check the paper for the movie announcements, and, um, I saw that the theater brought back *Top Gun* for its ten-year anniversary. I wasn't sure if you wanted to go."

"Oh! That sounds fun. Who else is going?"

"Well . . . I was actually wondering if you, ah . . . well, if you'd want to go as a date."

She felt her heart leap to her throat. She wasn't sure how she felt about labeling something as a date. Sam covered her own mouth before making a noise, and Claire finally said, "Okay. Yes, that sounds fun."

Claire recalled how awkward she had felt that night. Mark had held her hand and then put his arm around her. They shared popcorn, and it was an overall good time, but she kept questioning herself throughout the duration of the date. She chalked it up to first dates being nerve-racking and hoped Mark didn't notice. About halfway through the movie, which Claire enjoyed quite a bit, *Top Gun* being a favorite of hers after watching it with Troy a hundred times, Mark leaned his head over, and when she looked at him to see what he wanted, he went in for a kiss. She allowed it, still feeling incredibly embarrassed but kissing him back. And that was how she stumbled into her first make-out session. It wasn't incredibly long, and it didn't leave her breathless, but it was a first, and she got through it. She remembered thinking that it hopefully got less awkward with time.

One of the interesting parts of her date was how it ended with them bumping into Adam and Fitz after the movie was done. They exchanged hellos and asked how each other's summers were. Apparently, the conversation became too ostracizing for Mark because he butted in with "Where's your girlfriend?" to Adam.

"She didn't want to come. She's not into *Top Gun*," he said, looking a little taken aback.

"Oh. That's too bad," was all Mark responded with. Claire tried to lighten the mood by asking Adam if he'd been getting much practice time on the drums in his garage. She found out then that he'd gotten a job in the mall at RadioShack, and after a few more minutes of basic chatter, they departed.

Fast-forward a month and a few hangouts later, and Claire found herself at Ron's with Sam, Mark, and the whole gang. They squeezed into a booth with three pizzas between them and a scattering of cups, each taking turns playing pool. Claire was having a good time beating Amber, the two of them ending up as opponents through the process of tournament rules, when Mark asked her if she wanted to step outside for some fresh air for a moment. She agreed and followed him out the front door where they stood on Main Street.

"Nice evening," Claire said. "I love how it stays light so long in the summers."

"Me too."

He then blurted, "Claire, would you go out with me?"

She was surprised and didn't speak immediately.

"I really like you and enjoy hanging out with you. And I'd like it if you would be my girlfriend," he added to her silence.

"I . . ." she stuttered. "I . . . yeah!"

"Really?"

"Yes!"

He hugged her and then kissed her before going back in, hands held, the universal sign to the rest of the group that they were official. Amber looked like someone had just put dog shit under her nose to sniff. Sam was beaming, and Claire felt excited and a little nervous. She liked Mark and enjoyed their moments together, and it had gotten less awkward since their first date.

They then spent the summer getting together when they could. Sometimes, it was a quick meetup in town when he was staying over at Chris's, and they took a small handful of beach trips. It almost always involved some good laughs and a kiss or two. Claire was content. It was easy and enjoyable.

But more recently, as school approached and the summer dwindled, she was starting to feel like maybe there was something she was missing. And Mark had called her a couple days before this humid and muggy one with Sam to tell her that he was looking forward to school so he could see her more often. She had agreed but couldn't help shake the feeling of slight dread when thinking what it would mean to have a boyfriend in school. Would there be an expectation to hold hands in the hall? Or see each other in between classes? She was enjoying Mark, but the thought of publicly displaying their relationship all around school made her a little uncomfortable. She didn't really know why, but it did.

Claire valued her independent nature but couldn't help but notice that the people-pleasing part of her struggled with setting boundaries, especially with people like Mark who were so sweet. As school drew closer and closer, her anxiety grew, and part of her almost didn't want to deal with it at all . . . just break it off . . . but she knew it was just from nerves and told herself to try and let it go and see where it all went.

"So, what big things are we going to accomplish this year?" Sam asked, trying to fan herself with her hand.

"I'm not sure."

"Well, it would be nice if we could get *me* a boyfriend," Sam said.

"How about Chris?" Claire giggled.

"Um, no . . . He's a total asshole."

"True that," Claire said.

"How *are* things with Mark, by the way?" Sam rolled onto her belly to look at Claire, who mimicked her action.

"Things are fine, I guess," Claire said, playing at a hole in the blanket.

"You guess? Come on! Spill! You talked all summer about him and suddenly stopped! What gives? You still like him, right?"

"Yeah, I like him . . ." she said slowly.

"That's it? That's all I get? Come on!" she said, attempting to poke and pinch Claire, who laughed and pushed her hand away.

"Okay, okay! I like him . . . I don't know. I did . . . and it was so much fun. But the further into the relationship we get, the more I'm starting to get this feeling that all we do is hang out, make out, and go home." She sighed. "I mean, it is more than that, of course . . . but I'm just not sure there is much to Mark that really goes deeper for me. I'm not sure we have a whole lot in common, to be honest. Now that we've hung out more and gotten past the sort of early excitable things, I just feel like something is missing. Or maybe we just haven't spent *enough* time together, and I haven't found that stuff yet, ya know?"

Sam nodded along, listening intently.

"But . . . it just feels awkward sometimes. Not awkward like fumbling while kissing or something, but like I'm just going along with it . . . like my mind isn't in it. Just not quite right, if that makes sense."

"I'm sure that's just because you haven't gotten used to having a boyfriend still. You're an overthinker, and I think it is going to take more than a few summer meetups to stop your mind from evaluating and calculating *everything*."

"Yeah, maybe . . . I find myself even questioning when we kiss. Like, at first it was exciting. Thrilling, even. But . . . lately, I find it's fallen flat a bit. Like it's just what we're supposed to do rather than it *feeling* like something." Claire didn't feel like she was doing a good job at all of explaining herself.

She felt cliche saying that she didn't feel a spark, but that was pretty much what it came down to.

"Well," Sam broke into her thoughts, "I think it's just time. Of course you're going to go through weirdo waves. It's still somewhat new. Maybe seeing him more often at school, you'll have more to talk about, and things will unfold," Sam offered.

"That's what I keep telling myself. But . . . then that brings up its own anxieties . . . I'm not sure how I feel about being a couple at school and the pressures of PDA and others. It's been nice this summer, just having him and not other influencers . . ." Claire knew Sam would understand she meant Amber, Chris, and the "cool" clique that Mark seemed to always want to impress. Something that bothered Claire.

Sam pondered for a moment. "I think it's too new and you don't have a lot to go by. You're still figuring it all out, and it is also a first for many things, so I think it's going to feel new for a while . . . I'm sure that's what it is."

"Or that I don't really like him and we're just better off as friends," Claire said darkly.

"No. It's definitely not that! You guys are so sweet together and so cute! It's your first boyfriend! Stop overthinking it."

"You're right . . . Just play it out, right?" Claire said, taking a deep breath and letting it out.

"Exactly. That's what our motto for this year will be. Play it out. Go with the flow. I do think it's interesting that, though we hate Amber and the other two, we kind of became part of their group because of Mark."

"I know, and I'm not a big fan of it."

"Yeah . . . but whatever. Who cares. We're part of the cool clique, and that's all that matters, right?"

"I don't know . . ."

"Oh come on!" Sam slapped her arm. "It's high school! Of course it matters, and it's cool."

"Well . . . regardless, I think this year will be interesting," Claire said.

"Definitely," Sam agreed. "Can't wait for it to begin.

Claire walked into homeroom on the bell and saw that the first "moment" with Mark was waiting for her in the form of him saving her a seat and throwing his arm around her when she sat down. She wasn't sure why, but she wasn't fond of it. Claire was never a fan of overt attention, which, in high school, something as simple as putting an arm around someone was overt attention, because it caught everyone's attention. And, to Claire at least, it more often than not seemed to be for the purpose of gaining attention . . . showboating . . . informing everyone that you were an item. She didn't feel that Mark was just using her or anything, but she couldn't help but feel that so much of the hand-holding and arm-wrapping was a high school way to show off that you had somebody. Your status quo. It reminded her of how Sam talked: how it was more important to just have a girlfriend or boyfriend, not necessarily whether or not you actually liked them. Dating seemed to give you some kind of a leg up on everyone else, and bragging about it or showing it off was key to high school success in the cool factor. Claire wasn't a fan, and though Mark was great and nice, she wasn't entirely sure that his arm around her shoulder wasn't exactly just that . . .

They chatted with Miss Phillips as they waited for the bell to ring. It was extended so freshmen could acclimate, just like it had been for Claire's class last year. When it did, Mark walked with her hand in hand till they had to split, Claire heading to math. She walked into her Algebra II class and had to push away the disappointed feeling she got when she didn't see her math buddy there. This year she had a female teacher, Mrs. Simpson. She didn't drone on in a monotonous drawl but instead was friendly and warm, expressing that they were going to do a lot of work with manipulatives, videos, group work, and more. Then she had biology with a Mr. Holden, who was young and seemed shy but sweet, followed by a study hall. Finally, the end of the day came, and she was making her way to band. She felt the excitement grow in the pit of her stomach and shamefully knew it wasn't simply due to her love of the class.

Entering, Mr. Johns greeted them and, like last year, had them sit in a circle for introductions. Claire saw Adam and pushed away the giddy whoop that came with it. They exchanged smiles and a wave. Claire also noted that Amy was no longer there, which made her feel a little bad. She hoped it wasn't due to anxiety around the class or anything more severe. She liked Amy. She felt a little guilty that maybe she should have done a bit more in band last year to be a friend.

Looking around, she saw there was a handful of new freshmen in the class. They went over the protocols and rules of class and were let go with five minutes to spare. Claire walked over to the piano where Mr. Johns was standing, talking to another student. As she sat on the bench, she saw the cassette tape sitting atop the keys. She grinned broadly and looked over to see Adam watching. It was a newer album from a band he'd picked before. She hadn't heard it in its entirety yet.

"Hey," Adam said, walking up to her.

"Thanks," she said, holding up the cassette. After her initial happiness at seeing it, another feeling crept in. Guilt. Would this be okay to still do with Adam when she had a boyfriend? Would Mark be okay with them swapping tapes? She shook it off. He'd have to be. Besides, Adam had a girlfriend and it didn't bother *her*. However, not much seemed to bother her, from what Claire could tell . . . unless it interfered with her own agenda.

"I love that album. My favorite from them to date. It came out earlier this year, and I got the CD right off. I know we haven't done a lot of new stuff, but I liked it a lot, so I got you the cassette," he said.

She couldn't help but return the smile. So genuine he was. "I love it. That was really sweet of you . . . ." She saw him instinctively run his hand through his hair. "So which songs are your favorite?" She looked down at the cover art: a blue-and-red evenly split backdrop with an abstract design in the center that Claire couldn't quite figure out. It was interesting to say the least. "Crash" was simply written on the bottom. The latest of the Dave Matthews Band.

The cassette tape exchange had turned into getting great insight into each other throughout the previous school year. Even if it was a song or album they both already knew, knowing the other held it in such high regard made them listen to it differently. It made them wonder what was special about it, what they liked about it, what made them revere it above others.

As if on impulse, he ran his hand through his hair again, which Claire had now come to associate with nervousness. She wondered what he could possibly be nervous about right now.

"I think you should listen to track number three. I like all the songs a lot. Like I said, one of my favorite albums to date. Every single one is amazing. But . . . um . . . that one seems special. Definitely a hit. So yeah, that one. I think you'll like it." He looked at her meaningfully.

"Okay." Claire smirked. She thought she saw Adam blush but wasn't sure if she was imagining it. "How's Rachel?"

"Oh . . . she's good. Same ole, same ole," he said. He seemed a little uncomfortable at the question.

"Nice. You guys have a good summer?" she asked.

"Yeah. It was nice bumping into you a couple times," he said.

"It was!" She grinned.

At that moment, Mr. Johns interrupted. "Claire! Glad you're still here. I was going to ask . . . Would you be interested in doing chorus this year? We could use an extra person! And would love to have someone on piano."

She laughed lightly. "I don't think so, Mr. Johns. I don't sing, especially in front of others. And I certainly don't think well enough for chorus."

He shook his head and made to speak, but Adam cut in. "That's not true. Your singing is the bomb, Claire."

"When did you hear me sing?" she said, a little thrown off by the compliment.

"Uh . . . Bohemian!!" he said, mocking Fitz.

"Oh, right," she said.

"That's what I was thinking of as well," Mr. Johns jumped in. "You had great control of your voice, and singing along with the piano is a talent we haven't had yet."

"Well, I'm flattered . . . but really, I don't sing in front of people. That was a fluke. I got . . . caught up in the moment," she fumbled.

"Well, I'd like you to consider it. I could put you in easily. You may have to give up a study hall, but it'd be worth it!"

"I don't know . . ."

"Come on, Claire!" Adam inputted. "You'd be great!"

"Did you guys plan this ambush?" she asked, somewhat joking. Adam flashed his shitty grin and Mr. Johns looked hopeful.

"Look, I appreciate it, I really do . . . but it's just not really my thing."

"I won't deny that bums me out," Mr. Johns responded with an understanding smile. "But I won't push. Maybe second semester? We're doing Broadway hits this go-around but have an oldies themed concert in the works for spring, a combination of the forties, fifties, and early sixties. Have a few details to work out with getting the sheet music . . . Maybe reconsider then?"

"I'll think on it," she said.

"Promise?"

"Promise."

"Okay. Then I won't bother you anymore. Have a good afternoon, you two."

Claire and Adam made their way to the lobby. Claire was happy that the summer hadn't changed their friendship in the slightest. A great first day back.

"Well, thanks again for the cassette. I look forward to listening."

"Yeah . . ." He ran a hand through his hair yet again. "Yeah. I hope you enjoy it all, and . . . um . . . I—"

"Claire!" Mark's voice rang across the lobby. Claire and Adam both looked to him as he made his way over.

"Hey, Mark."

"I was waiting for you by your locker."

"Sorry. I got held up in band with Mr. Johns."

"And him, I see," Mark said, looking at Adam, who was taken aback by the tone.

"Uh, yeah . . . Adam's in band too," Claire interjected. "I was just ready to leave though. You good to go?"

"Yeah," Mark responded, still looking uneasily at Adam.

"Cool. Sam's out front. Meet you out there? I gotta grab my bag. I didn't have time earlier."

"Sure," Mark said, giving a second look before leaving them.

After he went through the door, Claire turned to Adam and said, "Sorry about that. I probably should have told him I stay after band sometimes."

"Are you guys . . . a thing now?" Adam asked hesitantly.

"Um . . . yeah . . . yeah, I guess we are," she said, not sure why she was hesitant with telling him this. "I mean . . . yes. We started dating early summer."

"Cool," he said. "He seems nice. He likes *Top Gun*, so that's a plus," he said.

"Yeah," was all Claire could say.

"Well, I'm happy for you," he said, running his hand through his hair, looking a little uncomfortable.

"Thank you," Claire said. She was quickly becoming confused by the feelings that were creeping up right now.

"I don't think he likes me." Adam chuckled, lightening the mood.

"Oh, no. Of course he likes you," Claire said, not believing her own words, and judging by the cocked eyebrow Adam gave her, he didn't either.

"Well, I should probably go," she said, smiling.

"Yeah. See ya, Claire." He waved as she walked backward, briefly waving back before turning to get her things and heading out.

Catching up to Sam and Mark, they began their walk. "Sorry. I didn't mean to stay after today. Mr. Johns wanted to ask me about chorus. He wants me to join."

Sam was about to question what she had said when Mark interrupted.

"How often does Adam stay after band with you?" he asked, ignoring her news.

"He stays after to play the drums pretty much daily. But I don't always stay," she said and could see that Mark didn't like that response.

She grabbed his arm and stopped him from walking, giving the eye to Sam to keep going. "Look, Adam's just a friend, okay? He has a girlfriend—"

"Who's never around him," Mark butted in.

"He has a girlfriend," she repeated firmly. "She's just busy a lot. She's involved in school stuff and is a senior this year, so I'm sure it'll only get worse. And regardless, Adam and I are just friends. We both like music and talk about it after band sometimes while helping Mr. Johns put stuff away. No big deal. Okay?"

"So there's . . . there's nothing there?" he asked.

"No," she said. He nodded and they continued home, talking school, until he departed to go to Chris's house, a first-day-of-school norm.

Sam and Claire continued the rest of the way, catching each other up on their first day of classes, which they didn't share any of on blue days. They landed at Claire's house as always, grabbed snacks, and headed up to her room.

"You know," Sam said, crunching down on a handful of Bugles, "I think you dating Mark will keep Amber off our backs this year. She said nothing to me when I saw her in the hall today. I mean, she wasn't happy to see me, but she didn't say anything."

"That's something." Claire smiled.

"I know, right? What was up with Mark after school?"

"Oh, it was because I was a little late leaving band." She sighed. "And I guess he was waiting for me at my locker."

Sam looked over at her, now putting Bugles on each finger before eating them one by one. "That was it?"

"Yeah," Claire said, not making eye contact.

"He was upset that you were a little late to your locker? Control freak much?"

"Okay, it wasn't just that," Claire said, sighing. "I left band with Adam. I think he didn't like that."

"Of course he didn't! He's a cute junior who keeps popping up randomly, clearly has a relationship with you, and is a mystery to Mark and everyone else."

"What do you mean a mystery to everyone? And it's a *friend*ship."

"Yeah, yeah . . . But, like, he's that guy. You know? He smokes outside school every once in a while, has a car now I noticed, plays drums, loves music, and is super kind to everyone. He's like the edgy, mysterious, cute boy next door."

Claire thought back to her night with him at the playground when she had flat-out told him he was exactly what Sam had just described. It was the main reason she had crushed on him so much at that point. "I suppose so. But he's a friend, and Mark shouldn't worry about it."

"Shouldn't he?"

Claire raised an eyebrow.

"I think I saw you sneak a cassette in your pocket. Did Adam give you a new one?"

Claire rolled her eyes. "Never miss a beat, do you?"

"You know I don't, dude."

"Yes, he gave me a cassette. But we've been doing this off and on since the start of school last year, and it means nothing. We're friends exchanging music."

"Then why did you hide it?"

"Sam! I don't know! What's with the third degree? What are we on? *Jerry Springer?*"

"No, *Ricki Lake*. I like her show better." Claire looked at her with venom, and Sam rolled her eyes. "Just noticing is all."

"I hid it because it honestly surprised me that he wanted to keep it going into this year. And Mark was already in a tizzy, and I didn't want to see what that would do to him. So I just put it away. No big deal. Mark doesn't need to know about it anyway. If, for whatever reason, it came up, I'd be more than willing to tell him that a good friend shares cassettes with me. It wouldn't be weird if you and I did that. So it shouldn't be with Adam."

"Alright, alright. I'll back off. You're right," Sam said, throwing the bag of Bugles aside. "Thank God we spend all day together tomorrow. Who did you sit with at lunch?"

"With Sarah and Mike. She's in my study hall, and Mike has the same lunch too."

"Lucky! I sat by myself! I repeat: By. My. Self." She threw her arms up.

"No one was in lunch with you?"

"No one I talk to!" she squeaked, taking out a piece of gum from her bag.

"Well, you need to pick a familiar face and just sit there," Claire offered.

"Easy for you to say. You have people in lunch who like you. And you get along with everybody. Everyone likes you. Me? I'm like Edward Scissorhands or something."

Claire gave a burst of laughter. "Edward Scissorhands?"

"Yeah! No one wants to come near me. Like I'm going to attack them or something."

"Sam. That isn't true. You just need to swallow some fear and take a chance. Sit with some people. I guarantee they won't act like you're going to slice them. People respond to confidence. Even if you fake it."

"Yeah . . . I guess . . ." She pondered a moment and then added nonchalantly, "Logan is in my lunch."

"Oooooo, that's good! From math class last year, right? Sit with him!"

"You don't think that's too forward?"

"Not at all! It's B lunch, not a marriage proposal. Sit and just say that you were happy to see a familiar face!"

"Okay . . . Okay, I'll do it. Obviously not tomorrow, but Thursday! I'll do it."

Troy knocked on the door, or banged on it would be more accurate, and stuck his head in. "Hey, Sam, your mom just called. She wants you home."

Sam groaned. "Thanks, Troy," she responded, Troy nodding and going back downstairs. "I'll see you tomorrow. Meet up to walk in?"

"You know it!" Claire smiled, following Sam into the hall.

"Cool. I need to go shopping sometime too. My clothes all suck, I've decided," Sam said as they walked downstairs.

"Why have you decided that?" Claire chuckled.

"Did you see Amber today? She could easily replace Alicia Silverstone in that *Clueless* movie from last summer. No joke."

"Ugh, Sam . . . let's not compare ourselves to Amber, okay? Your clothes are great. You look fine . . . But I am always down for shopping, so we'll figure something out."

"Sweet. Well, see ya in the morning," Sam said. "Bye, Troy!" She smiled broadly over Claire's shoulder with a cutesy wave as Claire shoved her through and closed the door behind her.

"So, Mouse. How was your first day back?" Troy asked.

"It was good," Claire said, checking out the fridge again.

"When are you going to tell Mom and Dad you have a boyfriend?" he asked.

Had Claire been drinking, she would have choked. "Excuse me?"

"You heard me." Troy smirked.

"How did you know?"

"I'm your older brother. It's my job to know. Mark, right?"

"Troy . . ."

"Yeah?"

"Butt out," Claire said, grabbing an apple and going back to her room. She went to open the biology book she had gotten earlier, just to take a peek, but Adam's cassette tape caught her eye. Grabbing her boom box from the shelf, she placed it on her bed and put the tape in. Finishing her apple, she tossed it and took the pamphlet out of the case to follow along with the song titles. She recalled the one Adam mentioned and was intrigued to listen. She noted it was number three, lay back, and hit play to listen from the beginning.

She let the catchy guitar of the first track and the quick-paced intensity of the second track get her fingers tapping along, the vibe being intrinsic of the band. When the third song started, she closed her eyes and got ready to listen. She immediately liked the soft stringed entrance, giving an air of calm and lightness. She fell into it, and when the vocals were introduced, they mimicked the softness of the music . . . so perfect. The light snare drumming in the background was sweet, and the lyrics . . . The more she listened, the more she fell in love with it. It was romantic, sweet, almost blush worthy at times. Claire's eyes snapped open. Was he so awkward and nervous to share this one with her because . . . *No*, she thought . . . *no, he isn't literally trying to tell me anything* . . . She was overthinking it, looking for things that weren't there, again. No . . . no she wasn't looking. Why would she be looking? She was . . .

But it *was* a very intimate song. But it was also just a really good one. She loved its simplicity, the dragged-out way he sang the single word of its title. Maybe Adam was just nervous because of its romantic factor, not for anything else. But . . . he *was* willing to share that with her, willing to tell her how he felt about it . . . that he wanted her to listen. She played it again. It definitely struck her. The tune of the lyrics was unique and sucked her in, pushing up the goose bumps she felt on her arms. The more she listened, the more she couldn't help but live in the hope that maybe there was a reason he wanted her to listen to this one . . . which, she then realized, was kind of a problem . . .

She rewound and played it again.

A couple months into the school year, Claire had her new schedule down pat, she was on a roll with her homework, and she had fallen into an okay groove with having a boyfriend at school. Holding hands and hugging occasionally wasn't so bad. But what she did have was some underlying guilt around her possibly still having a crush on Adam. Since finding out she was with Mark, however, Adam seemed to have backed off a bit, not talking to her after band as much, going right into picking up instead, and certainly not being seen walking out of class with her. He must not have wanted to get her in trouble, feeling Mark's uncertainty. With band being the only class they had, she didn't see him as much as she had the previous year, and guilt yet again raged in her stomach when she realized that that kind of bummed her out. So when he stayed to chat with her one chilly day in early November after Mr. Johns had asked her to wait for him to come back from the office real quick, guilt or no guilt, it made her happy.

"How's the year going for you so far?" Adam said, flipping a chair backward and sitting, facing her at the piano. He had on a cream-colored long-sleeved shirt under an orange plaid button-down. Boots and jeans finished it off, and Claire took a moment to take it all in. The fall colors and his brown hair were a nice, comfortable combination, like drinking a mug of hot apple cider on the front porch of a Sunday morning.

"It's going well. Homework seems even more involved than last year. But overall, it's going good! How about yours?"

"It's decent. All anyone seems to talk about are the SATs and preparing for them. But, decent."

She smiled. "That's good."

"Rachel is super busy with college applications and all her class president stuff and who knows what else that she's driving herself crazy. I don't see her much. Unless she needs me." Claire could tell he had let that last part slip.

"That stinks," Claire said. "I'm sure it'll calm down come spring," she offered.

"Yeah . . . maybe." But he didn't think so. He was quite sure this was just how it always was and always would be: he had just never noticed it before. He had also been getting a sinking sensation that she was going to dump him anyway before heading to college. She hadn't said that much, but the vibe of their relationship had definitely gotten shaky since the new school year had started, and the end seemed inevitable, with her constantly pushing him away, using him, or in many cases, completely ignoring him.

"Hey, so what did you think of my last tape?" she asked. She had given him Tracy Chapman's album of the same name.

"I enjoyed it! Very different than what I usually listen to, but—"

What he was going to say, Claire would never know, for Mr. Johns entered in a rush, saying, "Sorry about that." He grabbed a chair and joined them. "Okay, Claire. I want to talk to you about that part in the classical piece you said you were struggling with."

"Oh! Right," she said. She had mentioned it at the end of their last band class. She pulled out the piece and indicated the specific stretch she was having a hard time getting her fingering right for. Mr. Johns played it roughly before getting it himself and then showing her, giving her pointers. Not long after, Claire had an idea of how it went, enough to practice and perfect at least.

"Thanks! I find I learn best when I hear something rather than just reading the notes." She smiled at Mr. Johns.

"As do many," he responded happily, getting his things together.

"I don't know how you do any of it," Adam piped in. Claire chuckled.

"Hey, I noticed you driving in this morning. Got your own car this year?" she asked excitedly. "How long have you had it?"

"Saved up for it earlier this year." He smirked. "It's a 1980 Saab, nine hundred turbo."

Claire nodded. "Cool . . . I have no idea what that means."

Adam laughed. "At least you're honest." They gave waves to Mr. Johns as he said goodbye to them.

"Now, if Sam were here, she'd know exactly what to say. Her grandfather used to be a car mechanic and always showed her everything and anything to do with cars. Goes right over my head. I know colors and types."

"Types?" he asked with a smirk and a cocked eyebrow.

"You know: car, van, truck, SUV . . ."

"Ah. Gotcha." He continued smiling at her.

"I blame my dad and brother. They take care of everything cars."

"That'll do it. Maybe I can show you some stuff on mine, then. You have to come check it out anyway."

She beamed. "Sure!"

"Cool. Hey, I've been meaning to ask, what did you think of the pep rally? I saw you got called down by that blonde for the Jell-O eating contest."

Claire groaned. The homecoming pep rally had been the month before, and Amber had indeed called Claire down to participate as a sophomore in the Jell-O eating contest. The cheerleaders were in charge of the assembly, and, naturally, Amber chose Claire for the grossest and messiest challenge. She kicked herself for not finding an excuse to leave when she noticed Amber's obnoxious looks while talking to her fellow cheerleaders earlier in the assembly because those looks were never a good sign.

When it came time, she was handed goggles by the principal, who was dressed as a knight in the spirit of their mascot, and sat down while Amber ever so kindly held her hands behind her back rather tightly, her cheerleading cronies handling the others. When the buzzer sounded, the bleachers erupted, and Claire did the only thing she could: she shoved her face in the Jell-O, thinking that, at the very least, if she was going to make a fool of herself, she might as well try to win. She came in a close second, earning the sophomores an extra seventy-five points toward the homecoming competition. They ended up getting second place after the seniors when it was all over.

"Oh my god, don't remind me. I swear I was cleaning Jell-O out of my nostrils for days. I looked like an idiot."

Adam gave a belly laugh. "I thought it was rad. You did a good job. And . . . you pulled off green Jell-O just fine."

Claire blushed and thought how stupid it was to be blushing at a compliment about looking good while Jell-O was smeared across her face. "Thanks. It was all in good fun, I guess. I know Amber did it on purpose."

"Well, you showed her. You came in second and were a hero."

Claire grinned.

"She's the locker girl, right? The zombie at Halloween? The one who's been giving you a hard time since last year?" he asked.

"Since my life started . . ."

He raised his eyebrows.

"Okay, a little dramatic. But we've been enemies since elementary school. Mostly her doing."

"Ah, yes. I remember that now. She always looks like she's got a rancid smell under her nose."

"That she does. I think it's stuck like that now." Claire laughed.

At that moment, Sam entered the room. "Oh good, you're still alive."

"Yeah, sorry. Got caught up talking." She stood up and slung her bag over her shoulder.

"Oh, by all means, continue," Sam said, gum smacking. "I just wanted to make sure you weren't stuck in a tuba or something."

Adam chuckled. "Claire tells me you know cars?" They all started to make their way out to the lobby and through the doors.

"Yeah. My grandfather used to bring me to the garage all the time so my mom could go to work. He'd tell me what he was doing every step of the way. I was the official timer for him when he would change tires. He was always fascinated with the pit crews in NASCAR."

"Nice. I was just telling Claire that I saved up and got a Saab earlier this year."

"Ooh. Fancy. What year?" she asked as they continued down the front path.

"Nineteen eighty," he responded. Claire couldn't help but smirk in the background.

"Nine hundred turbo?"

"Yeah," he said, impressed.

"Oh! That's sweet. I like Saabs. Good quality. But expensive to fix when they do need it. Specialty parts." He nodded agreement. "But super mileage, and you can literally run them into the ground."

REGULATE

"Totally. I'm happy with it. I'm hoping to keep it for a few years and trade it for something newer."

"Nice. Take good care of it and you'll get a decent trade-off." They had all come to a stop while Adam prepared to head to the parking lot and Sam and Claire down the street to walk home.

"I'd offer you a ride, but I have to get to work. I just realized I'm already pushing it. Maybe sometime soon?" They both nodded. "See you, Sam. Good talking to you."

"You too!" she said. Claire could hear her concealed squeal.

"And . . . uh. Bye, Claire," he said, and his gray eyes seemed to bore into her brown ones. How did he do that? It almost made her want to look away, like if she looked too long, he'd see right into her inner turmoil of guilt for even liking those gray eyes in the first place. She shook it away. Mark . . . she was with Mark. She liked Mark . . . and his eyes . . .

"Bye."

"What do you want to do?"

"I don't know!"

"You must want *something*."

"I haven't thought about it."

"What girl hasn't thought about her sweet sixteen?"

Claire's mom and Claire were discussing her upcoming birthday. In just one week Claire was going to be turning sixteen. She was more excited about the potential to be able to go for her license and get a job. There was just something fun sounding about being sixteen too. A party wasn't really her scene, and regardless of how much begging and convincing Sam tried to do, she just didn't want anything crazy.

"Throw her a drinking and make-out party."

"Troy!" Her mother stared him down.

"What? What else would a sixteen-year-old want?"

She tisked. "Aren't you late for work?"

Troy looked at the clock. "Shit!" He grabbed his coat off the back of the chair at the kitchen table they were currently sitting at and ran through the house.

"Language!!" their mother shouted at his retreating back. Claire rolled her eyes.

"Well, can you think of something please?"

"How about a birthday party here with the family like always? And Babs."

"Just the family? You don't want to rent a place or something?"

"Where would we be able to rent a place at this point? It's a week away."

"I don't know. We could think of something. You don't want to invite your friends?"

"What friends? I only have Sam."

"What about Amber and Mark and the kids you went to the carnival with and hung out with all summer?"

"I guess."

"Come on, Claire . . . You don't even want to invite your boyfriend?"

Claire looked at her, astonished.

"Troy told me months ago . . . And why didn't you, I might add? We could have had him over for Sunday dinner. Is he cute?"

"This is why I didn't tell you, Mom."

"Okay, okay . . . Well, still. Let's invite your friends."

"Just do whatever, okay?"

"You want me to surprise you?"

"That's it. Surprise me."

"You're sure?"

"Totally."

"Okay." She sounded unsure. "But you better not complain about anything I do, Miss Claire Marie."

"I won't!" Her mother cocked an eyebrow, making Claire tag on an "Honest!"

"Alright," her mother said with a sigh of knowing better.

"Oh, and don't forget to invite Babs . . . Speaking of which, I have to remind Sam we're due there this Wednesday for our tea visit."

"How has Babs been?"

"Good, I think. I love getting to practice on her piano, and she loves to listen. She tells us old stories of town too . . . Did you know she has all kinds of old scrapbooks and record books dating, like, a hundred years ago of Thompson Falls?"

"I bet those are fascinating to look through."

"They are. They were handed down, and she's since added to them."

"I bet you and Sam have brought a lot of life to her old house. And to her. I'm proud of you, kiddo."

"Moooom." Claire rolled her eyes.

"I'm sorry. Not cool to grace my child with niceties. My bad. That's what you guys say now, right? 'My bad?' "

"Mom, please stop," Claire said through a smirk. They both laughed.

The following week, Claire and Sam made the trek past Main Street, down a couple blocks, and up the massive hill that led to Babs's house. She was waiting with tea as always and today had scones.

"Oh my god," Sam said in ecstasy. "These are amazing, Babs. How do you make such amazing things?"

"I purchase them in town at the bakery."

Claire snorted into her tea.

"Oh come on, Babs. You didn't make these? You're killing me!" Sam said.

"Sorry, Samantha. I can pretend I did, if it would make you happy." She paused to think. "Let's see . . . It is an old recipe from my grandmother Lorraine, who immigrated here from England where her aunt was a housekeeper at Buckingham Palace itself and copied it down from an old book there, if you want to know. Dates back hundreds of years, and now I make them too."

Sam stared at her. "Do you even have a Grandmother Lorraine?"

"No . . ."

"Well . . . it is still a much better story." Sam settled back in her chair, teetering her teacup on the arm of it and sitting crisscross. Claire had enjoyed their visits with Babs immensely. Sam was with her for most Wednesday visits, and Claire went over often to practice in between. The piano was so much better than her keyboard. Babs had told them that her house had a revolving door and they could go over anytime they wanted. There had been a few rainy days over the summer where they had enjoyed going up to play cards. Her house, being so high on the hill, caught a lot of wind on muggy, humid days. There was nothing like drinking fresh squeezed lemonade on a summer night in an old house, with all the windows open, the sound of a storm crossing over. They had shared so many laughs, mostly due to the banter between Babs and Sam. Today was no exception.

"I wanted to show you a photo I found the other day while in my attic."

"I told you you shouldn't go up there when you're home alone. I could've helped!" Claire said.

"I know, but I needed something to do. Next time you come over in a storm, we'll all go explore the attic. How's that?"

"Sounds super cool to me. Like something straight out of *The Goonies*!" Sam said excitedly.

"The what, dear?"

"*The Goonies*! You know: kids find a map to One-Eyed Willy's buried treasure? Follow it underground, find the gold, save the town . . . No?"

"What is a goonie?"

"Oh gosh . . . We need to get that movie over here. I have the VHS. We'll hook you up."

"Now, if it's treasure movies you want, then you need to watch *Treasure Island*. With Robert Newton . . . and . . . little Bobby Driscoll!"

Sam looked at her before mouthing *Bobby Driscoll* to Claire with a raised eyebrow.

"How about that picture?" Claire interjected.

"Oh yes, the picture. Here it is." She pulled it out of the front pocket of the apron she had on and handed it to Claire. It was of a beautiful dark-haired girl with pouty lips, an hourglass figure, and what looked like a simple floral dress with three buttons down the front breast.

"Who is that?" Sam asked, looking over Claire's shoulder.

"That's me," Babs said simply.

"Wow, Babs. You were fine as all get out!" Sam said.

"Pardon me, dear?"

"You were fly," she said.

Babs stared at her in enjoyable confusion.

"Ugh . . . Um, let's see. A looker? A doll? Fetching?"

"You were gorgeous," Claire said.

"Oh, thank you, dear."

"That's what I said!"

"I don't know what jargon you were throwing." Babs laughed.

"Just trying to keep you on your toes, Babs."

"Oh, you're perfect at that, Samantha."

"What was I thinking?" Claire spoke in quiet shock.

"It's cool. Really. It's good. We'll have fun and it'll be good," Sam said, overcompensating so much that Claire knew she felt the same way as Claire.

"Sam . . . my mother rented a room and a lane at the bowling alley for my sixteenth birthday, and Amber, Lauren, Ashley, Mark, Mike, Sarah, and Chris are all here to witness it."

"It's fine! Bowling is cool."

"Yeah . . . but not for a birthday party for a sixteen-year-old, Sam! There is literally a seven-year-old in the room directly next to ours, and two lanes are taken up by the seniors club! Nothing in between."

"I know it looks bad, but honestly! We'll have fun. Plus it's getting later in the day. The seven-year-old's party will leave. Teens will come out. Babs and your parents will have a great time reminiscing in the room while we play, and we can just go in when we want snacks. And you have a cute older brother who is going to play, and that will only give you brownie points with the witches. There's the arcade too. Your parents said we could stay however long we want. Trust me. It will be fine."

Claire sighed, watching her mother standing by the counter while the others got bowling shoes so she could make sure the guy knew they were paid for. Claire let out a long slow breath.

"Okay. Own it, right?"

"Claire, seriously. It'll be fine. Your mom told me that we're going to do your cake and gifts early so Troy can bring Babs home whenever she gets tired and we can just chill. Troy is staying to take us home. Everyone else has rides. This could turn into a fun night with a clique of people we wouldn't otherwise be hanging out with.

"I'm surprised they all came, to be honest."

"Me too, but we won't go there. Come on, own it, birthday girl," Sam said as the group made their way to the room with their new bowling shoes.

Claire nodded and followed. "Please remind me to never agree to a surprise party again."

"You got it."

Entering the room, Claire put on her smile and saw the spread of snacks that was laid out. Mark and Chris were already digging in.

Claire's mom spoke over the chatter: "Food's out! Have at it. We're going to sing 'Happy Birthday' now and do the cake and gifts while we munch so that you guys can go have fun. The lane is yours till nine tonight, as is this room. Tokens for the arcade are over there," she finished, pointing over at a line of cups on the end of the table. "You're obviously free to get more if you brought your own money. I assume you arranged rides for nine, but Troy will be here and can do some runs to drop you off if you need it."

They all nodded, Mark giving a thumbs up. Amber, Lauren, and Ashley had taken a seat together and seemed to be in decent spirits and were chatting. Claire breathed a little. Maybe this would be okay. The initial shock had hit her hard, but now she saw the party next door was in fact collecting their stuff and leaving, the neon lights were coming on, the overhead ones were dimming, and the plan for the evening did seem pretty decent.

They sang "Happy Birthday" as Claire blew out the candles on her music-themed cake for the fifth year in a row. She opened the gifts she'd received. Sam wrote her a sweet message in her card and gave her the newest album from Oasis. Claire was excited because she already liked the few songs that had been released to radio since it had come out. Amber, Lauren, and Ashley gave her a gift together: some scrunchies and yin-yang earrings with a gift certificate to the mall. Troy's gift was huge and surprising. It was a new sound system for her room. It played records, CDs, cassettes, and the radio, with detachable speakers.

"Wow! Thanks, Troy!" She couldn't wait to try out the sound.

Her parents got her some piano books, some money, and a necklace that her mom explained had been given to her on her sixteenth. It was a silver locket with a single diamond on the front. It currently had pictures of a young version of her parents in it.

"I started dating your father around sixteen. A little after. You can take those out if you want, but I used to wear it all the time," she said, smiling. Claire thanked her, not wanting to say too much, as it was a sentimental gift, and she found it quite special—too special for words at the moment. She boxed it back up, knowing she wouldn't ever want to take the photos out. She loved it as is.

Babs gave her a check for $200, and Claire couldn't believe it. She stammered her thanks to which Babs just put a hand up and said, "You've earned it, girlie." Then it was time for Mark's gift, which Claire was a little nervous for. Would he go the mushy route? God, she hoped not, not in front of everyone at least. She opened the card first, which simply read, "Happy Birthday, Claire. I hope you have a great day. I'm so happy you're my girlfriend." Claire blushed a little at the corniness, hoping no one would notice, and proceeded to open the gift. There was a velvet pouch, and when she opened it, a silver charm bracelet slid out. It had one charm on it that was engraved with "Claire." It was simple and sweet, and Claire felt no embarrassment in showing it. Everyone oohed and aahed, and Claire put it on her wrist, saying thank you to everyone for the gifts and party. The group mowed down on some food before heading out to the lane that was theirs.

"So, how many are we?" Mark said, looking around, counting. "Looks like we're nine. We can play teams, but one group will be uneven."

"How about Claire's brother?" Amber said.

"You think he'd play?" Mark asked Claire.

"I'm sure of it. Let me go—"

"I'll go get him," Amber piped in with a simpering smile that made Claire sick, but she nodded as Amber took off, adjusting her hair as she went.

"Okay, so let's do me, Claire, Sam, Chris, Sarah?" Mark said, counting off five. "And Amber, Lauren, Ashley, Mike, Troy?"

"Sounds good to me," Claire said as they took their seats opposite each other on the benches, Mark checking out the scoreboard.

"We'll be team one and you guys team two," he said as he entered it.

"What did I miss?" Troy asked, coming over, with Amber and her googly eyes behind him.

"You're on team two with these guys," Mark said, pointing. "You too, Amber."

"Alriiight," Troy said, rubbing his hands together and taking a seat. "You're going down, little sis."

"Whatever you need to tell yourself, Troy. Aren't you the one who still uses bumpers?"

"No, I quit those last year," he said with a smirk. Amber laughed louder than the silly comment warranted. Troy gave her a polite smile and then looked to Mark, who was telling them they were good to start.

"What order do we want to play in?" he asked.

"Well, Claire should go first. She's the birthday girl," Sarah said.

"Yeah!" Sam piped in.

"Of course. So let's do Claire, me, Sarah, Chris, Sam? Boy, girl, boy, girl?" Mark said. They all nodded in agreement.

"That means you're up, Claire!"

The game ensued. Claire was no good at bowling, neither was Sam. But they had fun regardless. Mark was a good sport and attempted to give Claire some pointers at times to which the other team would shout "Cheating!" in good spirit. Chris was the only one who seemed annoyed that he was on a losing team. Troy, naturally, stole the show for multiple reasons. Every girl but Claire loved watching him bowl, and he was so good at it that their team was miles ahead with points. When they finished the round, they decided to start up another game before hitting up the arcade.

"If we're going to play again, can we switch up teams?" Chris asked with his drawling voice, the visor on his head upside down and to the side, which made Claire dislike him even more.

"Sure, we can switch it up," Mark said, ignoring Chris's clear desire to just not be on a team with Claire and Sam. "Let's do boys versus girls."

"The groups will be a little uneven," Claire said.

"That's okay. You guys will need it," Chris said rudely, changing spots to sit on the other side.

Troy gave him a look and said, "You gonna let him talk to you girls like that? You better whoop his ass."

"You know that means they'd whip your ass, too, right? We're on the same team?" Chris said snarkily.

"Yeah, and it'd be worth it," Troy responded to Chris's eye roll.

"Okay, girls up first," Mark said.

"You're going down, boys," Amber said, getting up and winking at Troy, who once again politely smiled, but afterward sent a look of confusion to Claire, who chuckled. They played, everyone having a pretty decent time sending insults to each other. Troy seemed to be purposefully losing by being a tool bag while playing.

"Guess I lost my lucky streak," he said to Chris's disgruntled expression.

Troy shrugged and plopped down on the bench, only to jump back up, his face breaking into a huge grin at the person who had just come in. It was Gwen. Chris sat up a little straighter when the bubbly personality and striking features walked toward them.

Claire was excited to see her and stood up to say as much. She had gotten to know Gwen a lot more since she and Troy had started officially dating after a Valentine's date in which Troy took her to dinner and tried his best to be debonair, according to Gwen. She came over for Sunday dinners often now, and Claire went to see her at the music store all the time. They talked artists and albums, and her inner personality matched her outward beauty: so kind and open with just an overall chill vibe.

Both Amber's and Chris's faces were priceless when Troy reached Gwen and they embraced, Troy giving her a quick peck. Normally, Claire would yell at them to get a room, but she was enjoying the reaction from this particular crowd. When they broke apart, they came to the group, holding hands.

Gwen instantly detached and went to Claire with a hug. "Sorry I'm late. I had to work. Here's your card. You can open it later though. I don't want to intrude on your game."

"You're not intruding," Chris said quickly to which Gwen smiled, but Claire caught the hint of awkwardness behind it.

"You're not," Claire said too. "Thanks so much for coming! I was hoping you'd make it!"

"Of course! Wouldn't miss your birthday for anything!" Gwen said with another side squeeze.

Troy piped up then and said, "Everyone, this is my girlfriend, Gwen. Gwen, these are Claire's friends from school. You know Sam, of course." He then went around the circle to say their names, giving Chris the name Slappy to his extreme irritation, blushing and quickly correcting him.

"Hi, everyone!" Gwen waved with a chuckle.

"How about you join us," Troy said. "Boys against girls. Think you can beat us?"

Gwen winked at Claire. "You bet we can. Make room, ladies." She took a seat. Claire seemed to warm up even more with the added confidence of Gwen. Whether bowling was lame or not, having an older brother and his cool girlfriend present trumped it completely. Claire scored her first ever strike. Sam even got a split. Gwen was amazing and got multiple strikes and, otherwise, all splits. The rest of the team did okay, though Amber's heart didn't seem to be in it anymore with Gwen present. She seemed to particularly not like her. Claire guessed it was either because she clearly had developed an unrealistic crush on Troy, or because she was no longer the "coolest" chick at the party, Gwen even getting attention from the other girls, who admired her maturity, occasional swearing, and fun banter. When the game was done, the girls had crushed the boys.

"Booyah!" Gwen said. "In your face!"

"Hey now," Troy said, feigning hurt, clutching his chest. "No need to be nasty. My poor broken heart." They all laughed as Gwen went over and hugged him.

"It's just because you had more players," Chris said.

"What happened to the girls needing it, Slappy?" Troy said, tapping Chris's visor so that it flipped off his head and fell to the floor.

They all went to snack, and Claire introduced Gwen to everyone in a much more personal way so they could mingle. Amber gave a half-hearted hello, and when Claire got to Mark, Gwen talked to him for a bit. Claire had told Gwen about Mark and even some of the feelings she had been dealing with. More recently, she had even told her about Adam and her possible crush that had maybe never really gone away. Gwen had had great advice, and Claire almost felt like she had a sister. So it was no surprise that now that Gwen could put a face to the name, she had questions. Many of them. Claire joined when the topic got around to music, Gwen asking what he liked to listen to.

"I like rap and R & B mostly," he responded. He seemed a little nervous talking to a college girl as pretty as Gwen, which made Claire snigger. She loved Gwen's confidence and ability to make others squirm without even trying.

"Nice. Like who?"

"Uh . . . Ice Cube . . . Cypress Hill, Snoop Dogg . . . Warren G," he stammered.

"Nice. I don't listen to it a lot myself. It makes me angry. So when I'm in an angry mood, I like to put it on and pretend I'm tough enough to do whatever it is I want to do to whoever made me angry." She laughed. "But there are definitely some good ones!"

"Yeah!" Mark said, listing off some of his favorites, ending with telling her the concert he'd gone to earlier that year.

"Nice," Gwen responded. "I love concerts! Of any kind." Troy walked over and placed an arm around Gwen, kissing the top of her head. Mark nodded and turned toward Claire, placing his own arm around her, which instantly made her blush. This was too much with Troy and Gwen here. She felt that Mark was clearly just trying to be in the same league. It was obvious . . . and awkward.

"How about the arcade?" she suggested, turning out from under his hold to look around at the others. Everyone agreed and grabbed a cup of tokens. This was Babs's cue to head out, so Claire said her goodbyes and thank-yous to Babs and her parents, as they had packed everything up and were taking Babs home before heading home themselves so Claire and her friends could continue the fun with Troy's supervision, Babs having lasted longer than everyone thought she would.

They all scattered once they hit the arcade, except Sam and Gwen, who stayed with Claire, Troy helping his parents load up the car.

"Feeling better about everything now?" Sam asked.

"Yeah. This has been surprisingly fun," Claire said.

"This is awesome, Claire! Bowling *and* arcade tokens?" Gwen smiled. "You're a lucky gal with a family like you've got."

"Yeah. I guess I am." She smiled to herself.

"My dad wasn't around for my sixteenth, and my mom was too drunk to remember," Gwen offered with a chuckle.

Claire and Sam were startled by the sudden heavy comment.

"Sorry," Gwen jumped in. "It feels an eternity ago now. I forget how intense I sound to others sometimes. It's all good. Mom's still a drunk, but we're cool."

"Well, sorry though. That must have felt crummy at the time."

"Thanks, Claire." She smiled. "It was. So, appreciate what you got here."

Claire nodded her understanding to Gwen's wink.

"So what are you taking classes for?" Sam asked, changing the subject.

"I want to be a nurse. My end goal is to work in nursing homes. You know, with the elderly. The only solid person in my life growing up was my grandmother, and she passed when I was fifteen. The nurses who took care of her were always so nice to let me stay well past visiting hours and come in early. I think they knew she was all I really had, and me for her. My mom certainly never visited. But anyway, I want to do that."

"That's awesome!" Sam responded. "My mom is a CNA."

"Thanks. That's great! Maybe we can chat sometime." She smiled at Sam. "Well, enough of this. I'm sorry. Totally bringing down your birthday with all my family drama and life endeavors. Let's play some games!" she said, giving Claire one of her one-armed hugs.

They played Skee-Ball and PAC-MAN. And eventually, Claire and Sam were on their own, Gwen having stopped at a shooting game where an old friend from school was. A few games later and a couple walks around the arcade, Sam and Claire came across Amber, Lauren, and Ashley watching a game at a distance, Claire catching Amber saying, "Why does he have to have a girlfriend? And why are they so cute? Like, it isn't fair. I want a boyfriend."

"Oh come off it, Amber. You really think you could get him? He's like five years older than us," a scoffing voice responded.

"Shut up, Ashley."

Claire and Sam exchanged looks and moved closer to see what they were looking at. Gwen was now playing the shooting game while Troy had his arms around her waist and his chin nestled on her shoulder, randomly kissing her neck so she would squeal and miss a shot. She was harassing him to stop, but it was clear that she had no issues with the fact that she'd maybe hit two ducks total.

Claire rolled her eyes. She loved her brother, and he and Gwen were definitely cute, but she didn't need her friends or herself watching their mushiness, let alone gawking and admiring it. Blech.

"Get a room!" Claire yelled, not sparing them this time.

Troy put his hands up like a civilian under arrest. "Okay, okay. Sorry, Mouse," he said with a grin. "I'll stop." He walked to another game, but not before he gave Gwen another smooch and squeezed her side.

Soon enough, the time came when rides were showing up. Amber, Lauren, and Ashley were picked up by Ashley's parents, and Sarah and Mike each by their own parent, which left Mark and Chris, who were getting picked up together by Chris's dad. Troy and Gwen hung out on the bench at their rented lane, talking to Sam. Chris was by the door, waiting to spot his dad, clearly ready to leave, and Mark was saying his final goodbyes to Claire. She made sure they did this in the now-empty room they had rented so Troy wouldn't see.

"I had a really good time. This was a lot of fun," Mark said. "Happy Birthday."

"Thank you. Me too!" she said. "And thanks for my charm bracelet. It was really sweet."

"You're welcome. I was going to get some charms, but I didn't know what you would like." Claire knew this was a simple offhand comment, but for whatever reason, it ever so slightly annoyed her. *Didn't know what she'd want?* Was Claire that big of a mystery to him? Music, the piano, reading, fall . . . He didn't know her well enough to be able to select an appropriate charm on a bracelet? Not that she needed anything more. The bracelet was plenty of a gift . . . Heck, getting anything was plenty! But . . . even Adam, whom she barely saw, would know something that Claire would like . . . She instantly felt her stomach drop at the fact that her thoughts had even gone there. She told her brain to stop it, that he meant well.

"The bracelet is perfect. Thank you," she said.

"Thanks for inviting me," he said, leaning toward her.

"Of course," she said, nerves beginning to settle in and make themselves at home. "But my mom planned it with Sam, so they're the ones who invited everyone." Why did she say that? Who cared who invited him.

"Did you not want me invited?" He half laughed.

She groaned on the inside. "No, no, of course I wanted you invited! I don't know why I said that."

He then closed the gap between them and kissed her. He placed his hands on her waist, Claire resting her hands on his shoulders. She felt his mood was more intense than usual and prayed to God it had nothing to do with him once again trying to up his game after witnessing her brother and Gwen.

And then it happened. The tongue. He ever so slightly introduced it, and Claire had no idea what to do or how to react. She fumbled her way through it and felt her face grow hotter than when she had drunk too much at that party last year. She broke it off soon after it started, stepping away from Mark, unable to make eye contact.

Mark looked a little embarrassed himself. "Too much?"

"Um, no. No, just, uh . . . took me by surprise is all," she managed to say.

"Sorry . . ." he said, his own cheeks blushing. "I just . . . I really like you, Claire."

Claire hated herself for thinking it, but she wondered if he really did or if it was just the excitement of doing all of this.

"I—I really like you too, Mark," she stuttered, her face not cooling down at all. She made to say more, but it stopped in her throat as Mark moved forward as if to kiss her again.

She was saved by Chris, who came into the room, saying, "Dude, let's go. My dad's here. He's waiting."

"Be right there," Mark said, and Chris left without even saying a word to Claire.

Mark looked back to her, gave her a tight hug, said, "Bye, Claire," and kissed her cheek. "Sorry again. Happy Birthday."

"It's cool." She smiled. "See ya." Claire released a held breath, blowing hair out of her face, and made to join the others.

But before she could, Sam came in. "You good?"

"Yeah," she said, losing her mojo and dropping down into a seat at the table, sighing.

"What's up?"

"Oh, I don't know . . . I just experienced my first French kiss, I suppose, and I did not handle it well."

"Whoa. Slow down, dude," Sam said, sitting next to her. "You got tongue?"

"Must you say it so blatantly?"

"What? 'French kiss' makes it classier?" Sam laughed.

"It sounds better at least."

"Oh, fine . . . But . . . So that's a yes?"

"Yeah . . ." Claire's cheeks flared up again.

"What did you do? How do you not handle tongue well? What, did you lick his face?"

"Sam . . ."

"Okay, I'm sorry. Spill it. What's going on?"

Claire sighed again as Troy and Gwen showed up to check on Claire too, having seen Mark and Chris leave. "I just think I'm confused on how I feel about Mark . . . Like, I like him and like hanging out with him, but when things get, you know, close—"

"I'm out," Troy butted in. "Catch you ladies out front when you're done."

Claire rolled her eyes but nodded before continuing. "When things get close, I just feel weird. Like I shouldn't be doing it. Like . . ."

"Like you're just going along?" Gwen offered, sitting on Claire's other side.

"Yeah . . . which annoys me, and then I'm hard on myself. But then I tell myself that this is what starting to date and all this stuff is. Like, I'll get used to it . . . I don't know."

"Claire, that's the definition of peer pressure. You're going along with something because you feel like, at this time in your life and age, you *should* be doing these things. But that's a lie. Truth is, there is no age for anything . . . well, other than, like, potty training and stuff."

Claire chuckled.

"Look," Gwen continued, "this stuff is hard to navigate, but there shouldn't be any overthinking with it. It should just feel right. No different than that moment when you knew your dad could let go of the bike and you'd be fine. Or when you get the sixth sense that something is safe or not safe, right or wrong. It could be that you do like Mark but aren't ready for maybe some of the things he's ready for. Or that you like Mark as a friend, and doing anything more feels awkward."

"How do I know which it is?"

"You don't, really . . . You need to feel it out and listen to your gut. What is it telling you?"

"It's telling me that I didn't like getting a tongue pushed down my throat," she responded.

"Oh, now who's being crass?" Sam said.

Gwen laughed. "Yup. Now you have to ask yourself if it was because it was sprung on you and the idea of doing it again maybe isn't as bad? Or because you didn't like it at all? Or because it was Mark doing it? And you may not have that answer right now."

Claire nodded her reply.

"Look, remember what I said before," Gwen said, standing up. "Learning is living. You can't overanalyze life, because, without the experience, you have no idea how any of it will honestly pan out or feel. So give yourself some grace, cut yourself some slack, and just enjoy it. And when something doesn't feel right, say it. If you like it, go for it."

Claire and Sam stood up too.

"Come on. Troy used the pay phone and called Ron's. It's still open. We're going to get some pizza. You two want to join?"

"Yeah!" Sam said.

Gwen smiled and left to join Troy.

Claire and Sam followed slowly behind.

"I like her. Even if she is dating your cute brother."

"Yeah, she's pretty awesome," Claire agreed.

"She's right, you know. Go with the flow. Feel it out. Remember our motto?"

"Yeah," Claire said, and then more confidently, "Yes. Exactly."

"Totally." They linked arms, followed Troy and Gwen to the junk machine out front, and put-putted off to Ron's, the radio ironically playing one of the songs Mark had mentioned earlier. Gwen blasted it, and the car vibrated with the bass as they all sang along, Claire feeling a release of tension, laughing at her brother knowing every word.

As the holidays approached, Thompson Falls turned into the perfect picturesque town, straight out of *It's a Wonderful Life*. Lights strung across Main Street, all the storefront windows with colorful Christmas displays, the snow-covered rooftops . . . You couldn't help but sing carols as you walked through, and that was exactly what Sam and Claire were doing one mid-December Saturday as they did some Christmas shopping before meeting up with Mark.

"What do you think of this?" Sam asked, holding up a sweater. "My mom likes red."

"I like it. Looks like something she would wear. She loves turtlenecks."

"True that."

They were in Carrie-Anne's, a small boutique and gift shop. Claire had found her mom's favorite perfume while Sam stunk up the place spraying Baby Soft one too many times. She had a gift for Troy on hold at the music store that Gwen was helping her keep from him, a gift card to their local hardware store for her dad, and she had already handmade her gift for Sam. They had agreed to do so every year. The only thing left was a gift for Mark.

"I don't know what to do . . . I don't want to give him something mushy because . . . well, I don't know . . . it just doesn't feel right," Claire said as she and Sam made their way to Ron's.

"Get him a sweatshirt or something. Everyone likes a good hoodie."

"That's actually not a bad idea," Claire responded, thinking. "He likes basketball. Maybe I can get him a Celtics sweatshirt or something."

"Brilliant," Sam said as the bell overhead rang their arrival. Everyone else was already there. Claire took off her scarf as she slid into the booth next to Mark, who already had Chris and Lauren on his other side, Amber Mike, Sarah, and Ashley sitting opposite. Sam grabbed a chair and stuck it on the end. Mark smiled when he saw Claire, but faltered when he spotted Sam.

"I didn't know you were coming, Sam," Mark said. "Good to see you."

Sam smiled. Claire heard Chris mutter, "When doesn't she come?" which was thankfully unheard by Sam, as the waitress appeared.

They ordered some sodas and three large pizzas, and the chatter began. Lately, Claire had felt that when this occurred, she didn't have much to say. She and Sam often sat in the presence of a group that continued to have many classes together, similar circles of friends, and a different taste for conversation. It almost always involved tearing someone apart or bitching about something, or both. Sarah and Mike were the only ones who didn't really participate in that aspect, but they did both have a similar schedule with the rest and therefore more to talk about. They were currently poking fun at the math teacher they all shared, saying he had never learned how to properly socialize and was the most awkward person on the face of the planet, and for once, Sam had something she could comment on.

"Mr. Buckingham?! Oh my god, he's the worst. Total weirdo," she interjected.

The group all looked down the table at her, and Amber raised her eyebrows while saying, "Yeah . . . we know," and sharing a sarcastic eye roll exchange with Chris. To Claire's dismay, Mark joined in on the collective chuckle that followed.

There was no covering that up, and though Sam just nodded and acted unperturbed, Claire was sure that it had hit right in the gut. An attempt to bring the conversation around to a topic she and Sam could feed into was halted with the arrival of the pizzas. Digging in, Claire noticed Sam not really eating.

"You feel okay?" she asked quietly while the rest continued with their cool-clique banter.

"Yeah, why?" Sam said.

"Because you took a piece of pizza and haven't taken a bite of it."

"Oh. I'm fine. I'm not really feeling pizza right now, I guess."

Claire gave her a questioning look.

"I'm fine."

After pizza was finished, Chris and Mike decided to play pool while Amber, Lauren, Ashley, and Sarah watched. Sam left to go to the bathroom, and as soon as she did, Mark put his arm around Claire and nuzzled his nose against her ear, kissing her cheek.

Claire smiled, the gesture sweet. However, Claire couldn't ignore the increasing heaviness in the pit of her stomach that came whenever she and Mark were together. Since her birthday, she had been trying to do what Gwen suggested: go with the flow and feel things out. The more she did this, the more she started to think that perchance her uneasiness with Mark at times was not due to being new to the dating world but, in fact, due to not being able to let go of the things that she continuously pushed aside, which led her to believe that maybe things weren't right—that she maybe wasn't feeling him. Currently, she was feeling that awkward tension with the group, and Sam . . . poor Sam.

"I should go see if Sam is okay," Claire said, shrugging out from Mark's arm.

"Why wouldn't she be?"

"I think Amber may have gotten to her is all."

"How so?" he asked with a slight edge to his voice that Claire couldn't help but pick up on.

"What do you mean, how so? You were there. Her response to Sam trying to add to your guys' conversation?"

"What about it?"

Claire was getting annoyed, maybe more than the situation warranted given everything else she'd been feeling. "Um . . . it was a little rude. Sam was just trying to join in, and Amber shut her down."

"I think that's a bit dramatic," Mark said.

"Excuse me?" Claire responded. "Dramatic? It was blatantly rude and would make anyone feel left out . . . Look, Sam could very well be taking a leak right now. But I just want to make sure."

"I think," Mark said, standing up next to her, "that you're just trying to avoid me."

Shit, Claire thought.

"Why would I be doing that?" she asked, trying to sound nonchalant.

"I don't know . . . but . . ." He sighed. "Whatever the reason, or whatever is going on, I feel has been going on for a little bit now."

"Everything is fine," Claire said, not even convincing herself. Mark raised an eyebrow. She sighed. "I just have had a lot on my mind lately. All this is so new to me. I'm not sure how I feel about certain things. I struggle with Amber and whatever all that is." She gestured to the group. "And . . . I guess I've just been feeling a little off about how fast things seem to be going . . ."

"Fast? Claire, all we've done is kiss."

Claire shrugged. "I know . . . I mean . . . I don't know. It's fine. I'm fine. I've just . . . I don't know. I'm sorry. Okay?" She really didn't want to have this conversation right now. She wasn't even sure she knew if she could anyway. She didn't even know what the hell she was feeling.

"Just spit it out, Claire," Mark said with yearning and concern in his voice. She felt bad. She knew that Mark was a sweet guy and that some of her issues were around his friends, which wasn't even fair to him per se . . . But she couldn't deny her own thoughts and feelings either. Things just didn't feel right. How could she put that into words? Hurt a nice guy's feelings over nothing but a whim.

She sighed. "Mark, the French kiss thing just surprised me, and I guess since we started dating, you've been kind of calling all the shots, and I've just been feeling my way through it all. And I'm just taking some time to, like, chill and just let my mind and heart catch up with what the rest of me has been following along with, okay? It isn't you . . ." She couldn't bring herself to finish that cliche line that she couldn't believe she had even started.

"Okay. Well, I get that. I'm sorry I threw something new at you. We don't have to do that yet. I just wanted to . . . you know, try it out. I don't want to make you uncomfortable, Claire. But it just seemed like the next thing and what everyone else does, so . . . yeah."

"No, yeah, I get it. It's cool," she said, ignoring her mind's race to pick apart everything he had just said as yet more proof as to why she felt this whole thing wasn't a good idea. *What everyone else does . . .*

"I'm going to go check on Sam now."

He nodded and she left.

Entering the bathroom, she found Sam looking in the mirror above the sink.

"Hey," Claire said.

"Ugh, Claire, I'm a total loser," she said, throwing a paper towel into the trash can.

"You are not." Claire sighed. "Amber is a bitch; you know that."

"Yeah, but that's just Amber. Everyone else at that table thought the same thing."

"No they didn't, Sam. They were talking about a teacher, and you literally said something that agreed with what they were saying. There is nothing about that that is weird, odd, or call for being a loser."

"Then why do I feel like I am?"

"Because one tiny group of people out of the entire population of our high school has decided they are cool and follow the lead of one blonde airheaded bimbo who enjoys calling the shots on who is cool and who isn't."

"So I *am* a loser."

Claire groaned. "No. I just mean that you feel that way because Amber made you feel that way in the moment. But she's just a bitch and it means nothing."

"Except, in this circle and this moment, Claire, it means everything."

Claire made to speak, but Sam cut her off. "No, Claire. Look . . . maybe in the grand scheme of things, sure, Amber is nothing and her words are worth shit. But in high school, what we're living *right now,* the universe has decided her words do matter. And if she talks to me like I'm a loser, even if I say something hella cool, then I am a loser. It's a game of poker. She holds the cards. And if we want to do anything 'cool,' we have to shift the status quo, which has nothing to do with being witty or even interesting."

"What does it have to do with, then?" Claire asked, a little annoyed. She hated when Sam talked this way, she hated that there was some sad truth to it, and she hated that Amber was at the source of it all.

"I'm not sure . . . You seem to know how to do it."

"What? What are you talking about?"

"You've shifted the status quo. You're invited to everything the cool kids are, you have a popular boyfriend, Amber actually seems to like you, or tolerate you at least. . . They've accepted you."

"I—well . . ." Claire didn't know what to say and was getting surprisingly upset about this conversation. "No . . . No, Sam, this is dumb. There is no status quo. Amber is a bitch, and I'm only invited because I'm dating Mark, so I'm nothing special. And I'm not even sure how much longer that will go on anyway, so who cares."

Sam looked at her in shock. "What do you mean?"

Claire huffed.

"You're going to break up?" Sam asked quietly.

"I don't know." She sighed. "I just don't feel like I'm into it anymore. I'm not sure I ever was. I think I was just curious about the idea of it all, but it's gone nowhere. Mark knows nothing about me, really, and only seems interested in making out and putting his tongue in my mouth, and we have to retreat to the bathroom of Ron's Pizzeria just to survive an outing with his friends."

They stared at each other before bursting out in laughter.

"Oh God . . ." Sam said. "We're pathetic. We are legit pathetic. Let's get back out there. Let's go be the losers of a cool group and own it."

"That's the spirit." Claire chuckled, the bathroom door slamming behind them, Sam leading the way to the pool table.

Claire was just about to enter the back room when she heard her name and turned to see a familiar face, Sam continuing on, having not heard.

His brown hair was already being brushed through by his nervous reaction of a hand. The long-sleeved, blue plaid, button-down shirt he had on brought the gray in his eyes out, his smile making them sparkle behind his glasses. She changed course and approached his table.

"Hi!" Claire said and couldn't hide the grin that spread wide across her face.

"Celebrating the start of break?" Adam asked.

"Yeah! Sam and everyone else are by the pool table."

"Nice!"

"What about you?" she asked, looking behind him at his table.

"Oh, yeah! Sorry. Uh, everyone this is Claire Hanover. She's a friend of mine. Claire, this is Lisa and Kelly, Rachel's friends, and you know Fitz, and Rachel." He seemed to falter a bit at the last person. Claire knew why. The last time she and Rachel had met was when Rachel had reamed Adam out about the party and had rudely dismissed Claire from her own band room.

"Bohemian!" Fitz shouted.

Claire saw Rachel's slight eye roll directed toward her two friends, who couldn't have been more like Rachel with their short dress and skirt and black tights and cute sweaters. Claire didn't know why this bothered her. It wasn't like Rachel was dressed provocatively or anything, not that that mattered anyway. She was cute and fashionable and everything. If she could put words to it, it would probably be that it just didn't match. Her preppy, attentive-to-her-image-to-a-tee vibe just didn't seem to match Adam's. That's what annoyed her, she concluded. The words finally came to her: it was fake and Adam was so . . . real.

"Hey, Fitz!" Claire said with a grin. "And hi!" she addressed Rachel and friends, who politely nodded but didn't give Claire any warmth to join them, not that she was expecting it . . . but still.

"I was just about to put some money in the jukebox. Ron upgraded!"

"No way!" she said, genuinely shocked. "Did he get rid of the old one?" she added with some concern, turning to look.

"I know, right?! No, he still has the old one. Don't worry. Doo-wop will still play through the joint on afternoons and slow days, I'm sure." He chuckled. "But he got a new CD version as well. It has newer stuff on it from what I heard. I haven't looked through it yet." He took a gander at the table and saw Rachel and her friends talking animatedly, Fitz having moseyed over to another table with people he must have known, although Claire wouldn't have put it past him to go talk to random strangers.

"You wanna walk with me?" he asked, turning back to her.

"Sure." She smiled.

"I'll be back," he said to Rachel. She waved her understanding.

"You know," Claire said as they walked over to the machine, which was propped up right next to the old one. It was an interesting juxtaposition. "You know you live in a small town when the headliner is that the local pizza place got a new jukebox."

Adam chuckled. "Yeah . . . But I think you and I are the only two who think this is headline news."

She sniggered. "Yeah, true."

"Okay," he said, looking through the clear front. "Let's see what we got."

He started to hit the buttons, flipping through dividers holding the CD covers. "We got some Michael Jackson . . . Madonna . . . ooh, some Johnny Cash."

"I just saw Nirvana!" Claire said, getting closer and pointing across him.

"Nice!" he said, Claire seeing his reflected smile in the jukebox. "Oh! There's Soul Asylum and Red Hot Chili Peppers."

"No way!" She moved in even closer to see.

"Tom Petty too!" he said. He could smell her shampoo. It smelled of honey and lavender.

"This is going to be sick!" Claire responded excitedly. "How will we pick?"

"I got one, I think," he said. "But I have to check, and you can't see what I pick."

"Okay, I'll turn around." She laughed.

While he sifted, Fitz made his way over. "Sup, you guys?"

"Adam's picking a song, and I'm not allowed to see what it is." Claire chuckled.

"Ah. My man over here always picks the best jams."

"He does have good taste," she said, sneaking a peek at him, his dimples outing the smile he was trying to hide.

"Certainly does. If only he always followed his gut with those good tastes . . ." He clapped Adam on the back. "Isn't that right, my man?"

"Beat it, Fitz," Adam said, squinting through the music still. Claire laughed.

"I'm bouncing out anyway. I was coming to say bye."

"So early?" Claire asked.

"Early!? It's past my bedtime. I gotta get my beauty sleep."

"More like go smoke the reefer," Adam muttered, not taking his eyes off the jukebox.

Claire snorted. "Bye, Fitz."

"See ya, Bohemian. Bye, home slice," he added to Adam.

When Fitz walked past Rachel's table, he bowed dramatically and said, "Good evening, m'ladies. Thank you for letting me spend this splendid time annoying you beautiful people." Rachel exchanged looks with her friends, and Fitz continued out, but not before shouting "Booyah!" as he banged the front door open.

Adam dropped his head, shaking it. "I'm sorry about him."

"Don't be. I think he's hilarious," Claire said. Adam looked at her with his X-ray-like stare for a moment before turning back to the jukebox.

"Are you done yet?!" she asked.

"Almost. Picking between three now."

"So how did you manage to be out with three girls this evening?"

Adam gave a hollow laugh. "Well, it was supposed to be just me and Rachel. We haven't done much of anything lately, and when we do, it's with a whole group of her friends, most of which are seniors, and though I know them all, it isn't the most date-worthy of a time. But, at the last minute, she told me Lisa and Kelly were coming, so I invited Fitz along." He ended with a sour tone, making Claire suspect that inviting Fitz was a purposeful move.

"Does Rachel not like Fitz?" she asked tentatively.

"She hates him," he responded simply. "Okay. Done."

Claire waited, listening for and eagerly anticipating the sound of the first note to a song that Adam had specially picked. She couldn't help but feel that it held some weight after his careful selection. Her ears picked up on a subtle acoustic guitar. She squinted at nothing in particular as she focused on hearing the song over the din of the restaurant. She knew that as soon as she picked it up, she would have no problem hearing it fully, her memory for music being able to compensate and help.

And then it clicked . . . the first line ringing out above the music . . . his simple voice rising above the crowd around her. She listened as the first verse moved to the second, and the entry of a cello was followed by drums and more guitar. The words speaking of a somewhat lost soul, yearning for saving, not being able to express what he truly feels. She suddenly felt a blush creep up her neck as she felt Adam's gaze on her. She knew the chorus that was coming. She knew he had picked this song for her alone. The beat and tone shifted, preparing for the heart-tugging chorus that was coming.

And then it did . . . and the music seemed to grow high above the chatter and noise. The clinking glasses, the laughter, the random shouts, the sound of the game of pool in the back room were gone . . . and Claire met those gray eyes, looking for an answer. What did this all mean? Her pounding heart. Her sweaty pits. His look. What did this song mean? Was it picked for a reason? For more than just a good song to listen to? Was there something in it for her to know? It played between their locked stare, the dragged out, repetitive words ringing in Claire's head.

Adam wanted to say so many things but knew he couldn't. Not here, not now, and he certainly didn't know when he even could. His brain was a mess of thoughts, each as confusing as the last. Music seemed to speak better than he ever could, and though he had taken forever in selecting a song—not because he had three, but because when he saw this one and immediately knew what it could do, he couldn't decide if he wanted to take that plunge yet—he was glad he had, as it spoke exactly what he was thinking. But, not coming from him, would Claire get it? Would she get that he thought she was it? The reason for his confusion? Maybe he could talk to her sometime, explain where he was at . . . He had never ever been so lost and confused before. And for some reason, he felt that if he could just express all of it, just say the words . . . Claire would have all the answers. She'd know what to say. She would somehow be able to fix it all.

"Claire . . . I . . ." he stammered. But those words . . . they just didn't come.

In the moment of silence that followed, the switch was hit, and the restaurant was back with all of its noises, as were two voices saying their names.

"Adam!" Rachel yelled, standing at their table, all girls wearing coats and irritated faces. "Come on! We're ready to go."

"Claire?" Mark said from the doorway to the back room, holding the cue he was using. "What's going on? Are you coming to play pool with the rest of us?"

They both looked to their callers and back at each other.

"I . . . um . . ." Adam said.

"Adam!" Rachel practically screeched.

"You better go before she busts a vessel," Claire said with a half smile, releasing a sigh, a breath she didn't realize she'd been holding. She then turned to Mark and said, "Yeah! Sorry, I'll be right there."

Mark didn't move.

"I'll see you after break," she said to Adam. "And . . . um . . . good pick. I love that song."

Adam blushed and felt empty at the same time. "Yeah . . . right. See you at school." He wasn't ready to leave, wasn't ready to say goodbye. He had come so close. But, as he looked around him at the busy diner and Rachel . . . he realized that it wasn't the time. And seeing Mark reminded him of his place. But . . . he hoped she understood . . . he hoped she understood the song. Something at least.

She waved reluctantly and turned away from him.

"What's going on?" Mark asked.

Claire took a deep breath to shake it all off. "Nothing. I bumped into Adam and his girlfriend. We were checking out the new jukebox. I—"

"Hey, Claire!"

She turned to see Adam by the door, shouting across the countless tables full of happy eaters. "Have a good Christmas!"

She smiled, though it was half-hearted, and yelled back, "You too!"

Mark waited, watching Adam exit and the door close behind him before saying, "You were checking out the jukebox?"

"Yeah, it's new. Has new stuff on it, and—" She heard the words of Adam's song choice once more over the noise.

"And what?" Mark said impatiently.

"Huh? Sorry. Um . . . and . . ." She had lost her train of thought.

"What has gotten into you?" Mark asked as those repetitive lines faded out. The end.

"Nothing. Sorry. Play pool?" She made to head toward the back room. She needed a distraction. Needed to get Mark off her case.

"What were you doing at the jukebox?" Mark asked, more serious, not moving.

"Looking at what was in it. It's new."

Mark looked questioningly at her. "Seeing what was new?"

"Yes," she said, getting flustered at the emotions she was trying so hard to balance. "It's a whole new box with all new music in it."

"So?"

"So?" Claire repeated. "So, music is kind of my thing. So, I was excited. Adam told me about it and so showed it to me. I was merely checking it out."

Mark's face fell from being disgruntled to looking concerned. "Of course. I know you like music. That's cool Ron got a new player . . . Look . . . that Adam guy just makes me . . . I don't know . . . I don't like it."

"What? Why?" Claire said a little more defensively than she meant to sound. She knew why, and it was her fault.

"I just . . . Claire, he's a guy and—"

"And a friend," Claire interrupted, trying to smile warmly to make him feel better. "Please . . . we were talking music and got caught up in a song. That's all it was. I'm here now. Let's play pool, okay?"

"So that's it? Just listening to music . . . Nothing more?"

"Yes," she said, the sense of guilt hitting her hard. She wasn't lying exactly. They had talked music and had gotten caught up in a song. The nothing more piece . . . she wasn't even sure of that answer herself, but was almost sure . . . quite sure . . . but not sure sure . . .

Mark grabbed her hand and walked to the pool table.

"Finally! We can finish the game," Chris droned. Chris, Mike, and Mark were teamed up against Sarah, Lauren, and Amber. Sam and Ashley were sitting on stools watching on. Mark kissed Claire before letting go of her hand. Claire sidled over to Sam.

"How'd it go?" Sam whispered.

"I'm more confused now than ever," Claire said.

"We'll talk after," Sam said.

Claire nodded, staring at the green felt of the pool table, the final balls of the game rolling across, but not seeing any of it. She didn't need the jukebox . . . her mind was replaying that song over and over in its own recesses.

The night at Ron's gave Claire a lot to think about over break. She, of course, told Sam everything, and Sam got lost in la-la land before settling down and telling Claire that Adam totally liked her, even though Claire persisted that he had a girlfriend of a few years now and that she didn't want to jump to conclusions. Claire's biggest issue was, regardless of Adam being anything, it wasn't fair that she was dragging Mark along when she clearly had thoughts elsewhere. Sam had an opinion on this too, which was to keep dating Mark until she'd sealed anything with Adam. Claire pointed out how dumb and insensitive that was to which Sam just shrugged and said, "Status quo, dude. Boyfriend equals cool," which earned her a pillow to the face.

Christmas was extra special this year, as Claire's mom had invited Babs over for the day. Troy picked her up in the morning. She attended Mass with them, then filled up on brunch and then a huge dinner, all while opening gifts and watching Christmas movies. Claire got to hear Christmas stories of old, and Babs got to have Christmas with family.

Sam and Claire had a sleepover a few days after Christmas for their own gift exchange. Sam had made Claire a collage of her favorite crushes to add to her wall, and Claire had made Sam a mixtape of their favorite friend songs. She was sure to put "Dancing Queen" on it. Shortly after that, Mark called her to ask if he could come over so they could exchange gifts as well. Instead, they met at the gazebo in the small town park that was somewhat between her house and Chris's. Mark loved his sweatshirt, and he gave Claire a matching scarf and glove set with a gift card to the bakery in town. It was her favorite spot for goodies, and she really appreciated Mark's attention to that.

"I'm glad you like the scarf. I wasn't sure, but I know you like purple, so it made me think of you," Mark said.

"No, it's great!" she said.

"And I remembered you saying you loved that baked goods shop. The donuts you brought me at school once were amazing."

She smiled. "It is my favorite. Thank you."

"Cool. Well, thanks for my sweatshirt," he said, leaning in for a kiss, which she accepted. Moments like this were so nice with Mark. He was sweet and she enjoyed him. These were the moments that made her feel better about continuing to see where things would go or if her feelings were scrambled up for nothing . . . With the absence of the gaggle of teenage hormones tagging along, it felt more real between them.

"Hey, so Amber is having a small party this weekend. It's kind of a holiday party, you know, between Christmas and New Year's. She wanted a New Year's party, but her parents are gone, and she's with her aunt. No gift exchanges or anything, just a get-together. You want to go?" Mark said.

"I'll have to ask my parents," she said. "Sounds fun though."

"Yeah! She's got a giant-ass TV and a Ping-Pong table. Her dad is loaded, so she's got all kinds of stuff down there."

"Cool," she responded, noting that Mark had apparently been in Amber's basement before. And Claire was all too familiar with Amber's house and lifestyle. Going back would be interesting. "So, I can invite Sam?"

Mark sighed. "Um . . . well . . . I don't know. It isn't my party, and, uh, I'm not sure if she has a limit on how many can be over or anything like that."

"Okay," she said. She totally understood, but the tone behind Mark's words didn't sit well with her.

"Sweet. Let me know what your parents say," he said before they walked together till their destinations caused them to separate, leaving on a final exchange of goodbyes.

Don't Speak

When asking, her parents gave their permission for Claire to attend the party, having known Amber's family and being reassured of the type of party it was. Claire felt awkward about telling Sam since she had been turned down to being invited so, to avoid hurting her feelings, decided not to. That Friday, she felt more nervous than she thought she would. She was already in an icky mood from having Sam over earlier and not telling her where she was going, and she still wasn't even sure if that was the right move. Sam would probably understand, but she had been so hard on herself lately after the night out at Ron's that Claire didn't want to add one more thing.

She put on a plaid skirt that she had bought while out with Sam a little while back and paired it with a white top, but decided against it. It wasn't really her style. She had bought the skirt thinking she'd try something new and more fashion-forward, but all she saw when she looked in the mirror was a preppy, fake, Amber wannabe. Instead, she put on a burgundy spaghetti-strapped velvet dress over a white blouse. She wore black nylons and her Doc Martens. It was dressy and yet chill. It was a somewhat holiday party after all. She looked herself over, thinking how much easier this would have been with Sam's input. Maybe everyone else would be in jeans . . .

She finished off her makeup and grabbed some bangles, Troy waiting for her downstairs to drop her off. It wasn't too far of a walk, but snow had fallen heavily in Thompson Falls, and so she was grateful for the ride.

"Stay clean, Mouse," he said to her eye roll and door slam.

Claire walked up the steps and knocked. Mrs. Clark answered. It was strange to see her at first, memories flooding forward.

"Claire! How wonderful it is to see you! It's been a while." She gave her a hug. "You have turned into such a beautiful young lady! How have you been?" she said as Claire entered.

"Thank you, Mrs. Clark. I've been well," she responded.

"Oh, that's so great. When Amber said you were invited, I was over the moon. It has been too long." Claire took in her large pearls, picture-perfect makeup, name-brand upscale clothing, and cheesy expression. Nothing had changed. Even the house, she noted as she scanned her surroundings, was spic and span with all the latest furniture and gadgets. Claire knew that Amber's dad made big money. But she also knew that her dad was rarely home, often out on business trips, and kept his wife at home to tend house and raise Amber, establishing her as the stereotypical naive trophy housewife. As a kid, she hadn't registered it at all. But as she had gotten older and reflected back on her times at the Clark residence, it had become all too clear why Amber was the way she was.

"How have all of you been?" Claire asked.

"Same as always." She chuckled. "Oh, you always were such a polite child." She smiled again. "Well, I won't keep you. You didn't come to see me! Everyone is downstairs. You remember where the basement is?"

"Yes. Thank you," Claire responded and made her way down the hall to the door that would lead her downstairs to the party. The basement had been remodeled since she'd last been there. It had a new TV by the looks of it that was currently hooked up to the Nintendo 64, which Mark, Chris, and Mike were playing. Claire assumed Amber had gotten the system for Christmas, as it was the hot ticket item, having only come out in early fall. Those playing it didn't even notice she'd arrived, but the three girls standing by the snacks placed along a buffet table certainly did, their faces, moments ago smiling and laughing, now morphed into that of scoffing, or in Amber's case, fake joy at the sight of Claire.

"Oh, Claire! I'm so glad you could make it!" she said loudly, directing her words up the stairs for her mom to hear, before turning to Claire with an expression that did not match in the slightest. She said quieter, "Hanover."

"Nice to see you too, Amber," Claire said with a sigh. She turned her attention to the boys on the couch as they played their way through Super Mario until Chris yelled "Fuck!" while Mark and Mike simultaneously grabbed their heads in frustration, the universal sights and sounds of game over.

"As if, dude! What the hell. This is crazy!" Mark said.

"Yeah . . . definitely not used to this one," Mike agreed.

Mark stood up and stretched, saying, "Time for some grub."

"I hope you guys aren't planning to play that *all* night," Amber said, annoyed.

"Nah, just most of it." Mark laughed, and then seeing her face said, "I'm kidding!"

He then saw Claire and quickly went over to her. "You made it! Why didn't you say something?" he said, grabbing her two hands in his, giving her a kiss. She blushed a bit and saw Amber roll her eyes over Mark's shoulder.

"I didn't want to break your focus!" she replied.

He chuckled. "It's pretty fun! You should try it."

"I'm not really good at video games. But I'll try at some point," she said. They scanned the snack table and joined in on the conversation and group that was happening around it, Claire once again feeling like a silent observer as they talked about classes she didn't have and things they had been doing over break. Claire realized just how often this group hung out. Varying configurations of them, but it sounded like they had all seen some of each other in one way or another multiple times over the holiday. This didn't bother her, as she probably would not have wanted to tag along whatsoever, but it did further deepen her feelings of not belonging, and definitely solidified the idea that she was only there because she was Mark's girlfriend rather than a genuine part of the group.

As the conversation carried on, eventually Claire took to looking around the basement. There was a foosball table, a pool table, and a Ping-Pong table scattered about, not to mention a setup for darts. A shelf in the corner held a massive stereo system with a mess of records, cassette tapes, and CDs. Claire was impressed with the collection and wondered whose it mostly was. The CD player was a six player and was currently off.

As if seeing Claire's averted attention, Amber said, "Shall we play some music and try some games?"

They all agreed. Mark grabbed Claire's hand, saying, "Want to play some pong?"

"Sure!" She smiled as the Beastie Boys played overhead.

She was horrible at Ping-Pong, but Mark didn't seem to care. The rest of the group had split up into teams to play pool.

"I'm glad you came," Mark said, setting up a serve.

"Me too," Claire said, returning it, happy it was just the two of them at the moment, as it was the only part that seemed comfortable. The nagging feeling of abandoning Sam and just the awkwardness she felt at being here was creeping constantly through her mind, so a mindless game with just Mark was perfect.

"Are you doing anything for New Year's?" Mark asked.

"Not really," she said. "My parents are going out to a lodge party for the Masons. Just going to be Troy, Gwen, and I, which means I'll probably be in my room so I don't have to see them."

Mark paused in thought for a moment and then said, "Sam isn't going over?"

"No. She is going with her family to a relative's house. They do every year. They have a big get-together because it's so hard to get everyone on Christmas. Her mom's family is huge."

"Cool," he said, again taking a pause in thought. "What if I came over to keep you company?"

"Oh!" Claire said, taken aback. She felt a blush creeping up. "Um . . . yeah. Let me talk to my parents. They won't usually let me have a boy over if they aren't home . . . but Troy will be . . . I'll see what they say," she added contemplatively.

"Sweet," he said with a grin. "I'll be at Chris's that night anyway. So I could always walk over."

"Okay." She smiled.

After failed attempts at Ping-Pong—turns out Mark wasn't that great either—they joined the group, who were settled back on the couch and beanbags that were scattered around the TV area to watch Mike and Chris play Mario again, Mark quickly joining, taking turns with Mike to play Chris.

"Tom is supposed to be coming later. Mike invited him," Amber said after a while, to the nods of Lauren and Ashley. "I'm surprised you didn't drag Levinski along, Claire. Do you two go anywhere without each other?"

"Oh, um," she said as Mark was aggressively beating the buttons on the controller in his drastic attempt to not die, but to no avail. "Mark told me the party was small, and he didn't want to invite others since it wasn't his house."

Amber snapped her eyes to Mark, who was just now tuning in, taking a break with the other two. At the look on his face, Amber's broke into a smile that resembled that of Jack Nicholson's Joker. "Oh? I told Mark he could invite whoever. I just needed a head count. I was actually assuming you all would make three. I had prepared myself for Levinski's tag along."

Claire looked at Mark, who shrugged sheepishly. She felt her face grow hot.

"Sounds like Marky Mark here didn't want Levinski to come," Amber said with a fake pout, Chris laughing stupidly. Claire glared at her for a moment and then looked back to Mark.

"Amber, stop," Mark said.

"I don't blame you, Mark. Who wants that annoying little thing flitting around anyway?" Amber said to more chuckling. "Oh my god! I'm Sam Levinski. I'm so excited about everything because I don't know what it means to be cool and I'm hanging out with the popular kids. Oh my god. Hanover is the best person in the whole wide world: I should kiss the ground she walks on," Amber trilled in a horrid imitation of Sam. Lauren and Ashley burst out in laughter. Mike looked uncomfortable, and Mark, to Claire's great dismay, smirked a little, until he saw Claire looking at him.

"Alright. That's enough," he said rather weakly.

"Don't forget the insane gum-chewing," Amber said, ignoring Mark. "And that wild curly hair."

Claire felt her body shaking.

"And that twelve-year-old boy's body."

Claire's cheeks were hot with anger, Amber's cackle crawling under her skin, Chris's dumb guffaws making her blood boil.

"She's up Hanover's ass all the time. How did you shake her to come here anyway?"

"Knock it off, Amber," Claire said, teeth gritted.

"Oh my . . ." she said with that same evil grin. "You didn't tell her, did you?" She let out a bark of a laugh. "My, my, what will she think when she finds out you came to a 'cool' party and left her behind?"

Claire felt sick in her stomach. Amber was twisting what was a move Claire had made to spare Sam into making it seem like Claire was the one leaving Sam out. And Claire wouldn't put it past Amber to tell Sam exactly that at school on Monday. "I didn't leave her behind. I was told she wasn't invited, so I didn't invite her."

"And you didn't tell her about it at all . . . Why keep it from her?"

Claire felt her anxiety join her frustration and anger.

"Didn't want to hurt her poor lame feelings?" Amber said with malice. "Maybe you're more like us than I thought."

Claire didn't know what to say and knew that if she spoke, it would be something she'd regret. The room suddenly felt small, and she wanted to be anywhere but there. She put on the fakest of smiles and said, "You know what? I need some air." And then to Amber's smug expression said, "And you can take that look off your face. It isn't flattering."

Claire went up the basement stairs and stormed straight out the front door to sit on the steps, thankful that Amber's mom was elsewhere in the house and didn't see her. It was quiet but for the music that she could vaguely hear coming through one of the thin basement windows near her seat on the steps. At some point, the CD changed, and she heard the repetitive guitar notes and the sultry voice of Gwen Stefani when Mark came outside.

"Hey," he said.

Claire didn't say anything.

Mark sat next to her on the stairs and elbowed her lightly. "I'm sorry about Amber."

Claire just made a face of acknowledgment but didn't address him.

"It was all in good fun . . . It didn't mean anything," he said, trying to put his arm around her, but she shrugged it off.

"I don't think it's really fun to insult a person behind their back, especially when that person's best friend is right there."

"I know . . . It was in bad taste."

"No, it was rude. She's a bitch. What do you see in that whole group anyway? Chris never speaks to me, and the three witches scowl and want nothing more than to be the most miserable people to be around. Mike is the only decent person down there. Gah, it's so annoying."

"Chris is just . . . I don't know . . . Chris. We've been friends since we were kids," he said.

"So tell him to cut the shit and try being a decent human being."

"Hey, he is my friend, you know," he said a little defensively.

"How does it feel?"

Mark let out a sigh. "Claire, look . . . it's just . . . well . . . Sam is great and all. But . . ."

"But what?" she said.

"I don't know . . ."

"Please do share, Mark, because from what I can tell, you thought Amber's comments were quite entertaining in there, and let's not forget that you lied to me and told me you *couldn't* invite Sam, not that you didn't *want* to."

"Well, I really didn't want to invite others along to a party that wasn't my own. Amber didn't specifically tell me who to invite. She just said I could bring whoever."

Claire laughed darkly. Of course she would word it that way because Amber would want nothing to do with Claire going, hating the fact that she was even dating Mark, so naturally wouldn't give Claire a specific invite. Again, it was only through Mark she was even there. "And you chose to not invite Sam even though it was a party, with a bunch of people, and she said to."

"Yes, okay? Is that what you want me to say? Yes. I didn't want Sam hanging around for once. And neither did anyone else."

Claire glared at him and then looked forward, jaw clenched.

"Is it such a bad thing to not want to invite Sam?"

"No, but lying to me about it . . . saying horrible things about her? Is. Not to mention that I agree to hang around with all your friends all the time. It isn't like you wanted to go on a date and I wanted to drag Sam along with us."

"Okay, fine. So I should have let you bring Sam along. Happy now? And that group in there isn't so bad. Cut them some slack." Claire raised an eyebrow at him. "Really! I have a fun time with them. They're just not always . . . I don't know . . ."

"Decent?"

He gave her a look. "No . . . aware of how they come across. And look . . . they just . . . well . . . Sam just isn't cool, I guess."

She raised her eyebrows once again. "Not cool?"

"You know what I mean. We just wanted a get-together without her for once."

"We?" she repeated.

"Yes, Claire. We. They aren't fans of her. I was tired of her. So *we* didn't want her here. But nobody specifically said that. I made the call. It was me. I'm the asshole. Happy now? What you wanted to hear?"

"If it's the truth, then yes. I want you to be honest with me!"

"Well, there you go."

"So you all don't like Sam, don't want her around because she isn't cool. Is that why you like hanging out with these assholes? Because they're *cool*? And where the hell does that leave me? Because if Sam isn't cool, I'm not cool."

"Can you stop calling them names? And you are cool, Claire. You're the only one who doesn't seem to think so."

"No . . . I'm only cool because I'm Mark Calloway's girlfriend. That's my status quo in this group." She recalled her and Sam's conversation in the bathroom of Ron's.

"That isn't true."

"Sure is . . . You think I would be invited here if it wasn't for you?"

He looked at her but said nothing.

"Exactly."

They sat in silence for a moment.

"They really aren't bad, Claire," Mark said into the quiet, his breath swirling in front of him. "Maybe you would be invited on your own if you actually gave them a chance. You and Amber have a history . . . Maybe you let that get in the way . . . cloud your judgment or something."

"Yeah, okay . . ." she said sarcastically. He had no idea. "Except they hate me. I'm the dork they have to tolerate."

Mark gave her a sideways glance, "Claire—"

"No," she said sternly, standing up from the porch. "No. I don't even care anymore. Sam is my best friend, and you all just threw her under the bus. Yourself included. You lied to me. Amber takes every chance she can to take diggers at me. I'm so tired of all this . . . all this . . . fakeness. I'm probably just a pawn to you anyway. Just a chance for you to show off that you have a girlfriend because that's 'cool.' " She placed air quotes around that final word, sick of hearing it spoken so often.

Mark stared at her. "Oh come on, Claire. That isn't even fair. You're more than just a girlfriend to me. You know that. I like you, or I wouldn't be with you . . . What is this all about?! What the hell has gotten into you?! So Amber was being Amber and said a bunch of stupid shit about Sam. You know most of it is just to get to you anyway!"

"And everyone else laughing along, including you? That's more than just Amber being Amber. Is that supposed to make me feel okay? Oh, let's just laugh and joke about a person who happens to be my friend, talk shit about everyone and anyone who isn't in the room with us, and friggin' compare notes on others' score on the loser-to-cool scale."

"Well, what are we supposed to do? Just stand around and stare at her?"

"YES!" she yelled. "You're being just as much of a jerk by feeding into it and playing along!"

"Okay, I'm sorry I didn't think to tell Amber off in front of everyone for making stupid comments," he retorted sarcastically.

"You know what? What even is the difference between Sam and I anyway? If Sam is such a bother to have around, then how the hell am I okay?"

"You're kidding, right?" he said, breathing heavily.

"No, enlighten me."

"Claire. People talk about you. *Guys* talk about you. Girls are envious. You have upperclassmen friends. You're pretty much a year ahead of us in classes. For Christ's sake, you're going to have your license before all of us. If anything, Amber treats you the way she does because she's jealous."

Claire let out a belly laugh. "Ha! That's funny. Lying to me about Sam is one thing . . . but that . . . that's rich."

"Come on, Claire."

"Tell me the honest truth. Why am I here tonight? Why am I around all of them at any given point? Huh?" She pointed at the house.

"Claire . . ."

"Tell me, Mark."

"Claire, stop."

"Tell me!"

"Because you're with me!" he burst out angrily. "They wouldn't invite you around otherwise. You're here because I bring you. They don't like you either."

There it was . . .

She glared, their argument ceasing. Mark knew he had said something wrong, and Claire knew she had pretty much forced him to get to that point, but he had no words to backtrack other than "Claire . . . I—"

"The only thing that makes me worth anything to all of them is that I'm *Mark's girlfriend*. Nothing more."

"No, Claire—"

"The only reason I'm allowed to be in their presence is because I'm *Mark's girlfriend*? Tell me, when you waited for me to get here tonight, were they all sighing and eye rolling that Mark had to go and invite his lame girlfriend to the party once again, like they do with Sam? And were you laughing right along with them?"

"No!" He stood up to face her. "Claire, come on. Just slow down."

"You know, the one thing about you that always struck me as odd and quite frankly a turn off was the fact that you were friends with them," Claire said, fueled up. "It never seemed to add up to me. But I figured you were the one I was dating, so whatever. You liked me, respected me, and that's all I should care about, right? But you lied to me about inviting my friend along and let a group of people put the same friend down. And not just tonight, but many times."

"I know. But—"

Claire shook her head for him to listen. "I only asked for Sam to come along because it was a party. I've never invited her to anything that was just the two of us. All you had to say was 'I'd rather go to this party with just you this time.' Or talk to me about how you were feeling about her, instead of letting me look like an idiot in front of everyone. And you *could* have said something down there. You didn't have to stand awkwardly, laughing along. You could have easily just told Amber to cool it. You're just as bad as all of them when you don't. You just hide it well behind a sweet-guy mask." She breathed heavily. "Now, I'm going back in to call Troy to come get me. I hope you enjoy your party with your *friends*."

"Claire . . . come on," he said, his tone a mixture of hurt and anger.

"No . . . just . . . just stop. Just . . . leave me be," she said. She was so angry at the whole situation. Angry about them putting Sam down, angry she hadn't told Sam about the party, angry at how uncomfortable and isolated she felt with all of them, angry at the feeling of embarrassment she now experienced, and angry at her own mixed emotions about Mark that she knew were probably the baseline for this entire argument. She knew he didn't deserve all this and that she was using the premise of Sam for so many more complicated issues right now, but she just couldn't think straight for even a moment to sort it all out.

"I'm going inside."

"Claire!" he said to her retreating back. She let herself into the kitchen and pulled the corded phone off its base. She hadn't realized how cold she was till she got inside and felt herself shivering from the change in temperature.

After a few rings, Troy, thankfully, was the one who picked up.

"Hey . . . can you come get me?"

"Sure! It's only nine though. Mom said you could stay till eleven," he said with a smile in his voice.

"I know . . ."

Troy's tone changed. "You got it. Be right there."

Hanging up, she went downstairs. They were standing in a group by the food, stopping their conversation when she came down. She was certain of what they had been talking about.

"Hey. My brother's on his way to get me. I'm going to head out," she said, mustering up as much airiness as she could. She hoped desperately they couldn't read through her and see the fight that she and Mark just had. "Thanks for inviting me, Amber. See you all at school." And she left, giving them no chance for a reply.

Mark was still sitting outside when she returned to wait for Troy.

"Claire . . . look . . . I'm sorry," he said.

"Me too . . . I was hoping this was going to be a fun night," she said, not really apologizing for anything she said. She just wanted to be alone.

Mark sighed. "I don't know what to say."

"I already told you. You don't have to say anything. I get it. I know where I stand."

"But that isn't what I meant . . . You got me all fired up. It isn't like that."

"But it is. Mark, it isn't anything against you. It's just how it is."

"No it isn't . . ."

"Mark, I appreciate you wanting to include me from day one. Really, I do. And since we started dating, even more so. I've always felt *cool* around you."

"Because you are, Claire. You're the only one who doesn't seem to see what everyone else sees. This group, Amber . . . it isn't because you aren't cool. She . . ."

Claire knew what he was trying to say. Amber was the reason Claire was looked down upon by the others. Outside of her little group, Claire didn't have any problems with feeling included. Sure, she wasn't the star cheerleader or the class president or even dating the quarterback, but she was liked and well treated. But Amber was the 'it' girl of her class, and so if she said something, it traveled.

"She . . . I don't know. But, I guess, Sam is just different, and because it seems she always has to come with you, I just wanted . . . I don't know . . . I don't make the rules of high school."

"No . . . but you don't have to follow them. And I don't want to be a part of any group that sees Sam as anything different than myself."

Mark let out a sigh, running his hands across his short hair. "Look, I'm sorry about all of this, okay? Please come back in and—"

"My brother is already on his way here. He'll be here any minute. Go back in and have a grand ole time."

"Claire . . ." A sadness had entered his voice.

She looked up at him. "Truly. Have some fun with your friends."

"What does this mean for us?" he asked.

"I don't know. But let's not worry about it tonight. We'll talk some other time, okay?"

He stared at her for a moment and then nodded. He wrapped his arms around her, Claire's still crossed, and kissed the top of her head. He went inside, the door softly closing behind him. Claire took a deep breath and released it into the night, her breath a mist. Headlights illuminating the yard announced the arrival of Troy, and she jumped in. Troy was quiet, which she appreciated. They traveled in silence, and when Claire started to get out of the car, Troy said, "Wait."

She sat back in her seat and looked at him, his Metallica cassette once again the backdrop of their car conversation.

"You okay, Mouse?"

She looked through the windshield, though not seeing anything in particular. "I think so." She paused, and then, "Would you date a girl who hated your friends, and whose friends hated you?"

"Well . . . that depends . . . Is she hot?" Troy grinned. Claire cocked an eyebrow. "What's this about, Mouse?"

"It's kind of a long story. But, bottom line, Mark hangs out with the cool clique at school, which has always annoyed me . . . They're jerks, and tonight they were bad-mouthing Sam, and I found out that Mark kind of lied to get me to not invite her. It was also made pretty clear that the only reason I'm even invited to their stuff is because of Mark . . . which I guess isn't a surprise, nor do I really want to be invited into their group . . . but . . . I don't know. It's all a mess."

Troy let out a low whistle. "Did you and Mark break up?"

"Not exactly. I said we should just talk later. I didn't want to deal with it. I'm not really sure how I feel."

"Well, Mouse . . . I can't really give you any answers. What you do with Mark is up to you. And I don't really want to know what you do with Mark. But what I can say is, though it's ideal to have your friend circles mix well, it doesn't always happen and doesn't mean you shouldn't be with that person."

"I guess . . ."

"But mutual respect and being able to talk about it is important . . . and worth considering as a deal breaker."

She nodded. "Thanks for listening, Troy . . . even if that was absolutely no help."

Troy shrugged with a smirk. "I try." They got out and headed up the driveway. "There's nothing else?" he asked, sensing there was.

Claire contemplated saying something, but just said, "No."

He nodded as they walked up the steps. "Oh," Troy said, recalling something as he reached for the door. "Am I correct in assuming you didn't tell Sam about this party tonight?"

Claire looked at him. "Yeah . . . Why?"

"Well, she called earlier, and Mom may have, kind of, asked her why she wasn't at Amber's party."

Claire groaned.

(I Can't Help) Falling in Love with You

Claire kicked herself for not telling Sam about the party. In retrospect, she realized how dumb it had been to keep it from her. She had just wanted to avoid the moment of telling Sam she wasn't invited altogether. And even now, as she paced in her room, repeatedly going through all the possible ways she *could* tell her, she had nothing. And she realized that Sam probably would have accepted it just fine, maybe even been excited to hear about it when she had gotten home. Claire did wonder at times, though, just how often Sam pretended she was excited—well, Claire knew she was excited—but how often there was an underlying feeling beneath the excitement that touched those deep-seated nerves of self-esteem. Sam put herself down at times, and she did it with such a grin and laugh that it could easily be seen as someone with high confidence who had learned how to laugh at themselves, but Claire knew her friend better than that. She was hard on herself, and Claire had only been trying to protect her from that. But, the way this had panned out . . . she groaned . . . this was way worse. Not only had Sam not been invited to a party, but her best friend had kept it from her, drawing more attention to the fact that she hadn't been.

She finished her pacing, took a deep breath, and called Sam's house.

"Hello?" It was Joey.

"Hey, Joey . . . Is Sam home?" He said nothing, and instead, Claire got to hear every step, some humming, and a door knock on his way to his sister. She heard Sam ask who it was, Joey respond, and the door slam before . . .

"Hello?"

"Hey . . . Sam . . . Look, I'm so sorry. I feel so stupid. I should have told you about the party. When Mark said it was a small group and not to invite others, I didn't want to hurt your feelings by telling you you weren't invited, but I know that was totally stupid because you totally would have understood. And the whole thing ended in a fight between Mark and I anyway, and now I don't know what we're doing and we're supposed to talk and . . . Yeah . . . That's it. I'm sorry. It was an asshole move to not tell you."

There was a pause and Claire waited, her heart beating in her throat, adrenaline causing her breath to shake and her pits to sweat.

"What do you mean you got in a fight? What do you mean you need to talk?! Are you going to break up? Are you thinking that? What happened?"

Claire froze in shock for a moment. Was Sam serious?

"Sam . . . I—What about the whole not telling you about the party thing?"

"Oh, don't worry about that. I understand why you didn't. Was *totally* a stupid move, but I understand. But whatever . . . What happened with Mark?"

Claire laughed out of relief. "I don't even know, dude," she said with more air in her tone than the situation lent itself to, her happiness that Sam wasn't mad with her superseding her upset with Mark. She then went on to tell Sam everything about the party, trying to tactfully skirt around the parts that may hurt Sam's feelings, saying, "And then Amber went off on a slew of insults about you and me, knowing it would get to me . . ." rather than telling her the specific details. She spared Sam the piece that involved Mark saying that Sam wasn't cool. Sam seemed to have listened attentively and, in true Sam fashion, read right between the lines of teenage gossip and angst.

"So basically, I'm lame, you're cool on your own, but more so because you're dating Mark, and I'm holding you back," Sam said nonchalantly.

"What? No!"

"Come on, Claire. It's fine."

"No, Sam, it isn't. I don't want to be part of any group that thinks my friends don't belong there. If I'm considered cool, then so are you. And if you're lame, I'm lame. And who even gives a rat's ass what cool is. It's dumb. Besides, we'll never be cool as long as Amber is considered cool."

"Thanks, Claire. Though I appreciate that, it really is okay."

"Well . . . still . . ." Claire said.

"So, what are you going to do about Mark?"

"No idea . . ."

"Well, he's just trying to fit in and follow high school norms. You can't hold that against him."

"Yeah I can," Claire said defiantly.

"Well, you shouldn't. If you still really like him, then just forget about it. He's trying at least."

"I guess," she responded dully.

"So, how *do* you feel about him?"

Claire sighed. She was a whole whirlwind of confused emotions in regard to Mark. She knew her shortness with him was in part due to actually being irritated and in part due to whether she actually liked him. The recent jukebox moment with Adam really shook her, as did seeing him at school every day prior to that. . . And, though she continuously told herself not to get wrapped up in it or assume anything, she at least couldn't deny that her mere friendship with him felt more genuine than anything between her and Mark seemed to.

"Want me to come over?"

"Yes please."

"Be right there."

"I say you give it one more go. Invite him over for New Year's and see how that feels. If you're still feeling like there's something missing, then call it off when school starts back up." Sam was painting her nails, cotton balls, polish colors, and nail files scattered about the floor around her. Claire had just finished telling Sam all the finer details of her thoughts and feelings. It felt good to get it off her chest, and for once Sam didn't turn it into some beauty parlor gossip sesh.

"Yeah, I guess you're right."

"I mean, this is obviously so much more than the friends he hangs out with and the stupid shit they say, Claire."

Claire just looked at her.

"I mean, I know you care about me, and the whole who's cool and who isn't thing has always annoyed you, but the real problem here is that you totally still have a major crush on Adam."

Claire made to butt in.

"Ah-ah . . . Let me finish. I'm not saying you need to do anything about it or even face it. You can deny it all you want and throw every damn excuse at yourself. The point is that you are feeling *something* in regard to Adam. *I* think it's a major crush, of course, but at the very least, it *is* a sense of what you clearly like and want in a boyfriend, and by comparison . . . well,

(I CAN'T HELP) FALLING IN LOVE WITH YOU

you're not feeling that with Mark," she finished off while dramatically ending a stroke of paint on her nail.

Claire watched, but wasn't looking. Sam's words sunk in, and as they bounced around the recesses of her mind, she realized just how spot-on Sam had been and, quite frankly, how relieved she felt. Until this moment, she kept thinking that if she wasn't liking Mark, it was because she was crushing on Adam, and when she didn't want to face that, she pushed that aside and went along with Mark again, telling herself it was just typical teen uncertainty. But Sam was right. Crush or no crush, Adam loved music and even shared an intimacy with her in regard to it. He was sweet and kind and didn't seem to care about social norms either. He didn't really fit in any group. He was just Adam . . . went to the beat of his own drum. And he had chill friends who were just as genuine. Regardless of any confusion of a crush, that was what she liked, and it was the exact thing she was struggling with when it came to Mark.

"Done!" Sam said, beginning to blow on her nails to dry them.

"Nice. Love the black," Claire said.

"Me too. A little edgy."

Claire nodded.

"So, you going to ask your parents about New Year's?"

"Yeah . . . I suppose so."

Her mom was standing at the kitchen counter cooking dinner when Claire entered, having just seen Sam off. Her deeply rich brown hair, the same color as Claire's, was tied back in a low ponytail at the nape of her neck, her floral dress paired with a cardigan, flowing long, just brushing the tops of her slippers. She was listening to "Walk Away Renee" by The Left Banke on the radio, singing along as she put together some kind of casserole.

"Mom?" Claire said, taking a seat at the small, scrubbed kitchen table.

"Mmm?"

"I know you and Dad are going out for New Year's and Gwen is coming to chill with Troy, but I . . . I was wondering . . ."

Her mother turned and looked at her, an eyebrow cocked.

"I was wondering . . . if maybe Mark could come over as well."

Her mom squinted her eyes as if to see whether Claire's words had any deeper meaning or intention.

Apparently, she didn't see anything because she said, "I suppose. I'll have to check with your father first. But I guess if Troy is here . . ."

"What about Troy?" Troy leaned on the kitchen doorway, and Claire rolled her eyes, her mother not seeing as she turned back to her cooking.

"Your sister wants to invite Mark over for New Year's. I have to talk to your dad, but I don't see why not. As long as you and Gwen stay here and monitor."

Troy's face lit up like a Christmas tree, grinning at Claire. "Sure, I'll *monitor.*"

"Ugh . . ." Claire grunted, shaking her head.

"I'll make sure Claire and Marky Mark don't get any smooching in under my watch." He laughed as Claire flipped him off behind their mother's back.

"Troy," their mom said with a tisk, turning around to see her two children acting perfectly angelic. She shook her head at him. "That isn't what I meant."

"But isn't it?" Troy said.

Their mom just rolled her own eyes. "Honestly."

(I CAN'T HELP) FALLING IN LOVE WITH YOU

"Don't worry, Mother," Troy said, standing suddenly erect and holding his hand in salute. "As long as I'm in charge, there shall be no hand-holding, touching, kissing, speaking, or otherwise underage fornicating under this roof."

"Troy!!"

Claire snorted, not able to help but laugh at the look on their mother's face, which quickly turned from venom to an unsuccessful attempt at hiding her own smirk as she whipped Troy with her kitchen towel. "That's enough out of you. And don't you dare say something like that to your father, or we'll be lucky if he lets Claire out of her room at all."

Claire went downstairs to get a snack off one of the many platters her mother had put together for their mini New Year's party. She had about twenty minutes until Mark came over, which meant Troy had about twenty minutes left of having alone time with Gwen, Claire having promised to leave the two of them alone until her guest arrived. She peeked into the living room and saw that they were taking full advantage of it, intertwined on the couch playing tonsil hockey, Claire pretending to vomit as she left the kitchen to head back to her lair.

A half hour later, she heard the knock at the door and jumped off her bed. Running down the main stairs, she yelled, "I got it!"

Before opening it, she checked on Troy and Gwen one more time and saw that they had separated, Gwen watching the entertainment on TV, Troy in the kitchen getting food.

"Hey!" she said, letting Mark in.

"Hello," he returned. He was wearing a turquoise-blue shirt unbuttoned over a black T-shirt and black jeans. Claire could smell a hint of cologne on him that reminded her of her dad's from Ralph Lauren. He gave her a hug and kissed her cheek, saying, "Happy New Year!"

"Yeah, happy New Year! We have food in the kitchen and are just chilling in the living room watching the show." Claire led him through to where Gwen was sitting.

"Hey, there! Mark, right?" Gwen said with a smile.

"Yeah, nice to see you again." He smirked. Claire noticed that his tone and walk seemed off, like he was going for a vibe . . . Maybe he was just nervous and awkward.

"Want a tour of the house?" she asked. It occurred to her that in the months they had dated, he had never been in her house. He had been to it, when his older cousin had picked her and Sam up to go to the beach a few times. But other than that, she had never gotten around to inviting him over for dinner, however often her mother persisted.

"Sure!"

She showed him through to the kitchen and dining room and her dad's office. Then up the stairs, pointing out whose room was whose and finally brought him into hers. He looked around, taking in the wall collage of magazine cutouts, posters, and album covers, her bookshelf crammed with books, and her cassette tape and CD collection. He then spotted the keyboard and said, "Cool. How long you been playing that? That's what you play in band, right?"

"Um . . . yeah. I mean, I play the piano, but that's what I practice on here. I've been playing since I was really young. Under five."

"No shit!"

"Yeah . . ." she said awkwardly.

He sat down on the edge of her bed. "Cool room."

"Thanks," she said apprehensively.

He leaned back on his elbow and said, "So how much of a chaperone is your big brother?"

Claire laughed out of nervousness. "A pretty big one."

"Maybe he'll lighten up as the evening progresses," Mark said with a smirk.

"Not so sure about that," she said hurriedly. "Hey, want some food? My mom put a bunch of stuff together!"

"Sure." They headed back downstairs, Troy giving Claire a quizzical look, which she shook off. They nibbled on food and chatted lightly, Troy trying to keep the conversation going with Mark while Gwen and Claire discussed the new stock at the music store. Eventually, Gwen suggested a card game to which they all agreed. Spreading out the food on the center of the dining room table, they played a game of Scat, which ended up being more fun than anticipated. Troy kept randomly throwing popcorn at everybody, and Claire was super appreciative of Gwen's easygoing nature and killer socializing abilities because she continuously kept the conversation going, often posing obscure would you rather questions or a discussion topic such as "If you could eat with any five people, dead or alive, who would they be?" to which they all enjoyed answering, and almost all ended in tear-worthy laughter.

Claire was surprised to see the time was nearing midnight when Troy said, "Well, I suppose we should go watch the tube. See what's going on." They settled into the living room, Troy cozying up to Gwen with his arm around her, kissing the top of her head. Claire and Mark had been sitting for no more than a few minutes when Mark mimicked Troy's motion, making Claire want to melt right into the fluffy couch cushions they sat upon.

It wasn't the act of having his arm around her per se: it was the fact that it seemed to be in imitation of Troy.

The ball was close to dropping. Troy handed around noisemakers and hats, and they all stood up to count down the final ten seconds.

"Three . . . two . . . one . . . Happy New Year!" they all shouted, roiling up their noisemakers. Troy grabbed Gwen around the middle and planted a big ole kiss on her. Mark looked at Claire and kissed her as well. She pulled away to ensure it was a brief one that lacked tongue.

"What do you say we go get some of those snacks picked up and put away," Gwen said, ushering a sideways glance at Claire.

"What? Party isn't over ye—" Troy began, but stopped abruptly when Gwen smacked him in the gut, and he followed her into the kitchen.

"Happy New Year," Mark said quieter to Claire and began kissing her once more. Claire returned the gesture at first, but quickly pulled away.

"What's wrong?" he asked, sounding mildly irritated.

"Nothing . . . I just . . . I don't know," Claire stammered.

"What is it? You've been acting off all night."

"No I haven't," she said, a bit upset with herself that she had let the confusion that was her brain show through.

"Yes you have. We've been having fun, but every time I try to kiss you or hug you or put my arm around you, you shake me off. We're having a New Year's party with your brother, who probably wants some alone time with his own girlfriend . . . at your house . . . with no parents."

"So," Claire said, not liking where this was going.

"So . . ." he said exasperatedly. "So we could be having a little fun too."

"Excuse me?" she said, taking a step back.

"Come on, Claire. Nothing crazy. I just mean . . . you know . . . some alone time . . . I don't know . . . something. Not you pushing me away every time I come near you anyway."

She sighed. "I'm sorry. I just . . . Look, we haven't even talked since Amber's party . . . I'm just not there, I guess."

"Then let's talk," he said, plopping down on the couch.

"Here? Now?"

"When else? It's obviously an issue."

Claire felt her heartbeat flutter, creeping its way up into her throat. "Okay."

Mark looked at her. Clearly she was supposed to start.

"Okay, well . . . I'm just not a fan of your friend group . . . I find them mean . . . and I didn't appreciate them blatantly putting down Sam at the party. And I especially didn't like you going along with it and expecting me to be okay with it . . . and you lied to me."

"I apologized for all that, Claire. I should have talked to you about Sam, okay? And I'm sorry for what Amber said, but I'm not going to jump down her throat every time she makes a stupid comment about someone. It's petty, sure . . . but harmless."

"Harmless until your support of her bitchiness leads to her acting on it by making those people's lives a living hell at school for no reason other than the simple fact that she's named them as her prey. I've been one of them, you know."

"But not anymore, and I have no control over Amber."

"Not anymore simply because I'm with you! And you do have control over what you egg on."

"So what do you want me to do? Be the guy in the group who's continually telling everyone to stop?"

"No."

"Stop hanging out with them altogether?"

"No, of course not . . ." she said, getting hot in the face.

"Invite Sam along to every single thing we do?"

"No . . . Mark. That's not the issue."

"Then what is?!" he half shouted, jumping up to his feet. "What is it?!"

"I don't think I like you anymore!" Claire blurted out. Mark looked stunned, Claire felt like the biggest jerk on the face of the earth, and Gwen stopped in her tracks to turn right around and head back into the kitchen.

"What?" he asked hollowly.

"I . . . I'm not sure how I feel anymore, Mark. You're an amazing guy, and one of my good friends. But . . . I just don't think I'm into this. Like, really into it. And you deserve someone who is. Sometimes I feel that our being together most often involves either making out or hanging out with a group of friends who have their eyes set on nothing but their social status, and it's just not me. I think you do like me, and I think we get along great. I do have fun with you . . . but I also think that our relationship as boyfriend and girlfriend is a label . . . It isn't . . . it doesn't feel . . . *real* . . ."

Mark let out a low whistle, slowly sitting back down yet again. "How long have you been feeling this way?"

"For a little bit . . ."

"How long?" he asked seriously.

"Oh, I don't know . . . a month or so?" she lied, plopping down beside him.

"Man . . . I feel like an idiot," he said, staring down at his hands.

"No. No, don't feel that way. Look, it's because you're such a wonderful guy and friend that I haven't said anything sooner. I thought I was going crazy! How could I be feeling this way with such a great catch?"

He laughed, but half-heartedly. "I'm sorry . . . I should have paid more attention. Checked in more, or tried to . . . I don't know . . ."

Claire shook her head. "It's fine. We were doing what high school kids are supposed to do. I'm just an oddball, I guess, who just wants more than that."

(I CAN'T HELP) FALLING IN LOVE WITH YOU

"No . . . you're genuine, Claire. Probably more mature than all the rest of us combined."

Claire had no response to that. They sat in silence for a little while, the mumble of the TV their backdrop.

"Well . . . I hope we can still be friends," he said. "We were before, and I don't want to lose that."

Claire thought her heart would burst. "Me neither, Mark. And I think our friendship feels as real as it gets. I would love that."

"Besides, who else would I call for Shakespeare help?" he joked, elbowing her lightly. Claire laughed, and they once again fell into a silent stupor, Mark looking more and more downhearted.

"Is it that Adam guy? The junior? From band?" he asked quietly, not making eye contact.

"What? No," she responded. He squinted at her with that same I-think-there-may-be-more look her mother gave her, but he didn't press it.

"I guess I should head out. It's late anyway and . . . well . . ." he said, the rest not needing to be expressed. They walked to the door, and before leaving, Mark wrapped Claire in a tight embrace. She hugged him back and felt tears welling up in her eyes. When they broke apart, she saw she was not alone, and Mark gave her chin a light tap with his knuckle, unable to say words. She closed the door lightly behind him but didn't move.

"Mouse?" came Troy's timid voice.

She looked at him, unable to hold the tears back anymore. And, like the wide receiver catches the football, Troy scooped her up into the kind of hug only a brother knows how to give, her tears dropping onto his gray Raiders sweatshirt.

Back to school meant facing the fact that Claire had had her first breakup. She had spent the couple of days following New Year's and the weekend working through her emotions, and doing some therapeutic shopping with Sam. After the initial blow, she found herself guiltily feeling a sense of relief mixed in with her sadness at ending things with Mark. His call on Saturday afternoon to tell her that he hoped she was doing okay and if they were cool for school Monday helped. It also reminded her of the part of Mark she liked, respected, and wanted to be friends with still. She had assured him of both and came to the conclusion that she had definitely made the right decision. Sam seemed to be mourning the loss of their group more than anything else, assuming they were done hanging out with the popular crew. But Claire attempted to soothe her overworking mind by telling her that they were still friends with Mike and Sarah, not to mention that Mark seemed adamant on them remaining friends. Sam didn't seem convinced, reminding Claire that he was adamant about remaining friends with Claire, not herself.

Come Monday, Claire felt content with the breakup and moving ahead but wasn't looking forward to coming into contact with Mark at school when Amber was around, which, of course, occurred first thing in the morning in homeroom. Claire walked through the door of the home ec room and immediately met Mark's gaze. He smiled sheepishly at her as Amber threw a vindictive grin, leaning closer to Mark. Claire had to chuckle at the ridiculous attempt to apparently make her jealous. She walked over to their table, which wiped the arrogance off Amber's face and replaced it with surprise.

"Hey," Mark said.

"Hi," she returned, sitting in her normal seat at their table. They mingled lightly, Chris and Mark eventually having their own conversation, Amber staring down Claire, who was ignoring her, reading her beloved copy of *Pride and Prejudice*. When the bell rang, she felt proud of her confidence in not letting the breakup or Amber get to her. The group may not be who she would choose to hang out with, but she did want to assure Mark that *they* were still friends, and that meant not being afraid to sit with him at school from time to time.

Her day was mediocre, a new semester of classes, although they hadn't changed all that much from the last, other than her study hall moving and her gaining a sewing and textiles class with Miss Phillips. Band was still at the end of the day and was, as always, the thing that got her through it, for a few reasons, of course. Mr. Johns was his usual cheerful self, giving them all a chance to share about their holidays if they wanted. Claire didn't, the end of her break kind of tainting the rest of it. He handed out new music, their last semester having culminated in the annual holiday concert. Per usual, they had a modern piece, a classical piece, and a marching piece, with more to follow as the semester progressed. They got into position and tried out their first dry run of the classical piece, which naturally sounded of sheer cacophonic noise. Mr. Johns, however, smiled down at them all as if he'd just heard the sweet sound of Beethoven's own symphony. When the bell rang, Claire was requested to hang back.

"Claire!" Mr. Johns said. "Good holiday?"

"Yeah, you could say that," she said as Adam came over and leaned on the piano. She had to admit she both loved and found it hilarious that he just assumed he was included in any after-school discussion Mr. Johns needed to have with her.

"Excellent . . . Say, I wanted to ask you if you'd thought about chorus at all. It is a new semester and a good time to join us," he said with hope in his tone.

"Oh gosh . . . I don't know, Mr. Johns . . ." She had known this was coming at some point.

"I'm not going to coerce, but I still think you'd be a brilliant asset to our choir."

"It's just not something I think I'd be comfortable with . . ."

"Come on, Claire," Adam said encouragingly.

"Tell you what," Mr. Johns said. "How about you join to get it on your schedule, and you just play piano accompaniment."

Claire thought for a moment. "What's the music look like?"

"Not sure how you feel about oldies, but we're putting on that classics themed show I mentioned in the fall. We're calling it a Blast from the Past. We've got our hands on some fun pieces that the chorus kids are pretty excited about . . . Frank Sinatra, Elvis, the Supremes, and whatnot."

Claire's heart fluttered, absolutely loving the idea of playing old-school music . . . Who wouldn't!

"Okay . . . I'm listening," she said, Adam's grin following.

"Well, first we look at your schedule to see if we can easily replace your study hall with chorus, and then you join us to play the songs on piano," he answered simply.

Claire stared at him a moment, contemplating whether that smile was masking the truth. "I know you're going to pester me to do more once I'm in."

Mr. Johns chuckled. "Okay, so maybe I'll ask you a few times here and there to see if you've changed your mind about singing. But I promise no pushing."

(I CAN'T HELP) FALLING IN LOVE WITH YOU

"Who do I ask about my schedule?"

"I'll take care of it. It does mean you'll lose your study hall, though."

Adam was watching them, his stare bopping back and forth between Claire and Mr. Johns like at a tennis match.

"I just play piano?"

"Just piano."

"What if they can't get my schedule to work?"

"We'll figure it out."

She looked to Adam, who gave her a supporting nod.

"Okay," she said, releasing a sigh.

"Great! I'll talk to the guidance office on my way out," he said, jumping up and getting his things together. "You'll love it, Claire."

Claire nodded, grabbing her own bag, Adam following suit. They followed Mr. Johns out of the room and toward the cold January air.

"You finally caved," Adam said with a knowing grin.

"Yeah, yeah," she said, trying to hold hers back.

"You'll be great."

"Thank you."

"I usually run the light and sound booth for the concerts and productions. Other than the band concerts, of course."

"Cool!" Claire added this to the many things she found interesting about Adam Miller.

"Yeah! The chorus concerts are always great. I'll be sure to give you your own spotlight," he said, elbowing her lightly.

"Um . . . no! No spotlights." She chuckled.

"Okay, okay. No spotlights. Even though you'd deserve one."

Oh, her heart.

They made it to where Sam was waiting. Adam said hi and asked how she was before heading off to his car, Claire having to listen to Sam ask her a million and one questions about her and Adam's five-minute conversation. Now that her breakup with Mark was official, and Sam was too smart to see through her friend's insistence that she still didn't have a crush, Sam wouldn't let any moment that involved Adam go, mostly just to tease her. Claire didn't mind so much, but she did think it fed into the crush she "didn't have" in an unhealthy way. Adam still had a girlfriend, and Claire was constantly questioning if she was just seeing and feeling things coming from him because it was what she was hopeful for.

The next band class, Claire stayed after yet again at the request of Mr. Johns and was informed that her schedule couldn't be moved in a way to allow for chorus. However, Mr. Johns's prep period was during her study hall, and he had been able to work it out with the principal and guidance office to have Claire do chorus as an independent study instead during that time.

Once that started, Claire found that it was a pretty sweet arrangement. She would go to the band room, practice for half the time, getting help when she needed it, and then spend the remainder working on assignments from her other classes while Mr. Johns worked on his planning. And the cherry on top? Adam had a study hall during that same period, and by getting a hall pass from Mr. Johns each morning to go to band for "extra practice" during it, he was able to join her. He would listen to her practice, occasionally seeing if he could help at all. And when she was done, they would work together on homework, Claire helping Adam out with his math, and Adam offering his assistance with her history, which, Claire learned, Adam loved and had a great memory for.

Sam was over the moon about this, and Claire couldn't help but be too, though she was trying to control this feeling, being well aware that Adam and Rachel were still a thing. However, it wasn't till a couple months into this special arrangement that Adam figured out she and Mark weren't.

(I CAN'T HELP) FALLING IN LOVE WITH YOU

They were lying on the floor, propped up on their elbows. Adam was working through one of his math problems when he casually asked, "So, are you and Mark going to that dance coming up? The fundraiser social thing?"

Claire was taken aback by the question and simply said, "What?"

"It kind of sounded lame, but the seniors are putting it on to get more money for their class trip. I would have to go anyway because of Rachel, but I'm actually DJing it."

"No way! I didn't know you did that!" she responded, distracted.

"Yeah." He chuckled. "I love that kind of stuff but could never do it before. The guy who usually does is a senior this year, so Rachel asked me so he could help out with the dance."

"That's so cool!"

"It's pretty sweet. I'm hoping that means they'll put me on the dances next year, now that he'll be gone. They hire out for prom, but all the smaller dances throughout the year are student led, as I'm sure you noticed, so yeah . . . I'm hoping I can do it."

"For sure. Do you have your own equipment? And, like, make your own mixtapes and stuff?"

"I use the school's equipment, but yeah, I make mix CDs so they can just play through."

"You have a DJ name?" She giggled.

"Um, no." He laughed.

"Oh come on. You can't DJ without a name." Claire tapped her chin with her pencil, contemplating. "What about Adam Mix-a-Lot? Or DJ Knight?"

Adam continued to chuckle. "Knight?"

"Yeah! Like our mascot," she responded, elbowing him.

"I don't think so." He grinned. This, all of this, was what made him enjoy Claire so much.

"Well, I'll think of something. And you better play some good stuff!" Claire joked.

"I'll do my best," he said, his grin crinkling those gray eyes and making Claire smile without even meaning to.

"So, are you and Mark going?" he asked again, trying to sound nonchalant.

"Oh . . . um . . . Mark and I kind of broke up," she said, looking down at her copy of *Hamlet* that she was working her way through.

Adam's head snapped up. "Oh! . . . Uh . . . I'm sorry, Claire," he said, looking at her strangely.

"It's okay. It was coming for a bit, I think. I'm cool with it."

"Well . . . I'm glad . . . that you're cool with it! Not that you broke up. I mean, I'm . . ." he stammered before saying, "I'm happy with whatever you're happy with."

She smiled. "Thank you."

Claire went back to her reading, but Adam was struggling to focus now. He wondered if the reason that Mark and Claire's breakup was "coming for a bit" had anything at all to do with the few moments that had occurred between himself and Claire . . . moments that seemed to mean something . . . something to him anyway. They had kept him up at night multiple times, a continuous stream of argumentative thoughts jumping from *She's totally feeling your vibes, you should break up with Rachel* to *You're being absolutely nuts and letting a few bad months with Rachel cloud your judgment* to *Be honest with yourself, stupid, it's been more than a few months* to *There is definitely something about Claire*. He couldn't help but wonder, or maybe rather hope, that those *somethings* were there for Claire too, and maybe, just maybe, they were part of why she was now sitting here with him, and Mark was out.

(I CAN'T HELP) FALLING IN LOVE WITH YOU

"You told me no pushing."

"I know, but I think you would be terrific."

"Do it, Claire!"

Adam, Mr. Johns, and Claire were sitting in an all too familiar powwow around the piano, and with the concert a month away, Mr. Johns was trying to get in one last attempt at convincing Claire to sing in the show.

"I know I told you I wouldn't pester, but I would love to have you sing. You have an excellent voice, Claire. And it seems that with the piano, you are a little more comfortable. You could sing with the piano!"

"No . . . no, no," she said.

"But, Claire," Adam butted in, "you did a great job with 'Bohemian Rhapsody,' and you totally had zero nerves."

"Yeah, but—"

"Come on." He smirked. Why did he have to smirk? That smirk should have a warning label, or be illegal.

"I'm not trying to push. But you have a talent. It deserves to be heard," Mr. Johns said.

Claire thought for a moment. She did love singing along with her piano, but she just never had the confidence, certainly not in front of people. She had felt it that day though, when she sang with the group . . . "Bohemian Rhapsody" . . . Her peers cheering her on had given her a boost. If she was behind the piano . . .

"I could play the piano? While I sang?"

"Absolutely," Mr. Johns said quickly.

She contemplated again. "I have a few conditions."

"Name them."

"Only one song. No pressuring me to do any more."

"If I get to pick your solo," Mr. Johns bargained.

"Only one solo," she said.

"Just the one," he responded.

She squinted her eyes, pausing for a while to enjoy watching them squirm. "Okay."

"Hot damn!" shouted Adam.

"Perfect." Mr. Johns's smile was the biggest she'd seen yet. "Excellent."

Claire didn't have long to wait to learn what her solo would be. She stayed after the very next day, Mr. Johns having asked Adam to stay as well.

"Okay. First off, Mr. Miller," Mr. Johns said to Adam, who was in his usual stance of leaning on the piano, "I know you've been running the light and sound booth; you good to go this semester as well?"

"Of course," Adam said.

"And Claire, I have your solo. I could have given it to you at your next practice time with me, but it's Friday, and I wanted to get it to you as soon as possible, as you don't have a whole lot of time to practice it. I thought you could look over it this weekend so we can get started on it in class Monday."

He handed her the sheet music. Opening it she saw it was "(I Can't Help) Falling in Love With You" by Elvis Presley. She couldn't help but be thrilled. Her grandmother had the biggest crush on Elvis, and Claire knew all his records. This one was a favorite. Looking it over, she had only one question.

"So, what is my solo?" she asked.

"Wherever the words are is your solo," Mr. Johns said, not making eye contact, collecting his things to head out.

She flipped through the song, seeing the entirety of the lyrics spread across the pages of notes. "Just about the whole song is on here," she said,

(I CAN'T HELP) FALLING IN LOVE WITH YOU

looking up at him. He was smirking, and she was not feeling it. "Wait . . . no . . . no, I'm not singing the whole thing."

"You said I could pick the solo. That's what I picked," Mr. Johns said.

"A solo is not an entire song!" she said. Adam was chuckling.

"Technically, it is. Now, the choir has been practicing this song, but there were no soloists. So they will be singing with you still, as backup. So, not totally alone."

"Mr. Johns!" she squealed. "You're missing the point here. I am not singing an entire song by myself."

"You won't be by yourself, Claire. You'll have the choir. You're just singing the melody, along with playing your piano, while they sing your harmony. Just like in class . . . a group."

She looked at him with eyebrows raised. "You are a sneaky, sneaky person, Mr. Johns."

"So you'll do it?"

"Do I have a choice?"

"You always have a choice, Claire."

She looked from Adam's encouraging face to Mr. Johns's hopeful one and sighed, throwing her hands up. "Alright. What is there to lose."

She spent the next weeks practicing constantly. She went to Babs's house almost every day so she could play the real piano and sing. She was still too embarrassed to sing at home with her parents and Troy hanging around to hear. Babs enjoyed it immensely and told her often that she had nothing to worry about. Babs was also prepared to go to the concert itself, counting down the days on her calendar with Xs.

The night before the show, they had a rehearsal, and Claire asked Mr. Johns if she could just play her piece for the choir to sing along to but not sing her part because she was so nervous and feared throwing up all over the keys. He said that was fine, as he had heard her sing some of it during practice a couple times. In fact, he and Adam were the only two at school who had heard snippets of her solo so far, her singing mere pieces of it once in a while during her practice with him. But still . . . Mr. Johns was putting a lot of faith in her skills, as he still hadn't heard the entirety of the song and wouldn't till the night of the show. Rehearsal was after school and involved the light and sound crew as well. Adam was there first thing after the bell to set up the mics and wiring and help bring out the risers for the singers. He also was in charge of rolling the piano to its position on the stage.

When Claire sat down to practice, she saw a cassette waiting for her in front of her music. It was an Oasis album. The Oasis album that held track number three . . . "Wonderwall." She smiled at the note attached that read, "You got this." She scanned for those gray eyes peering down at her from the booth in the back of the auditorium. They met, and she held up the cassette with a grin. He gave her his two-fingered salute, and she felt some confidence edge back into her system as Mr. Johns started arranging the choir singers. When it was time for the sound test, Mr. Johns went around tapping and speaking into the mics, giving Adam and his small crew out front either a thumbs up or down to indicate it needed to go louder or quieter.

"Mr. Miller, go ahead and play something on the sound system so I can walk around and hear how it sounds throughout the auditorium," Mr. Johns said, jumping down from the stage.

Claire was quite certain that by "play something," Mr. Johns did not mean Coolio's "Gangsta's Paradise," but that was what Adam chose regardless as Mr. Johns walked around the room. And everyone in the hall bobbed their heads to the string-heavy beats of the intro and sang along with every single word, the goons in the tech booth getting into it the most. Claire shook her head and laughed.

It was a testament to Mr. Johns's love of his students that he allowed them to get through most of the song before interrupting them and saying, "Thank you, Mr. Miller, for that marvelous song selection. Now . . ." and continuing on to direct the choir.

The following night, Claire's mother insisted on doing her hair. Claire gave in and was actually pleased with the outcome. It was loosely rolled up and pinned in the back, resembling a classic 1940s style, the front twisted and pinned just so. She wore her iconic deep red lipstick, filled in her eyebrows, and plumped up her eyelashes. When her parents dropped her at the entrance to the music room to go get their seats, Mr. Johns handed her the choir dress that all the girls would wear, the boys in tuxes. She had seen them hanging and was surprised at how excited and anxious receiving this piece of clothing made her feel. It was so official, so formal.

She went to the bathroom down the hall and changed into it. It was a floor-length satin dress in black. It had a slight V-neck and three-quarter-length sleeves, with a full bottom. Looking at herself in the mirror, her mother making her wear pearls tonight, she was embarrassed to admit that she felt . . . beautiful . . . classy.

She had brought authentic vintage heels in red, having borrowed them from Babs's closet, and squeezed her feet in them, the shoes being a hair too small, but she loved them and wanted to don them regardless. Walking back into the music room with her plastic bag of her change of clothes, she felt slightly exposed, even though she was wearing a black dress that covered her head to toe. She couldn't ever remember being this dolled up, and others' looks at her, however random and non-attention-giving they might have been, made her cheeks a little flushed. She dropped her stuff somewhere in the corner where she'd be able to locate it again and took a moment. She inhaled deeply, let it out, and threw her shoulders back, holding her head up. Turning, she saw none other than Adam walking toward her.

"You . . . you look . . ." he stammered. "You look very . . . uh . . . you look very . . . beautiful."

There was no denying or hiding this blush. Claire felt her face and neck flush warmly and even saw a slight pink tint enter Adam's cheeks as well.

"Thanks." She smiled.

"You, uh, you ready?" he asked, staring, and then, coming to his senses, "You ready for the show?"

"I think so, if these butterflies will calm down," she returned.

"You'll do great. I'm sure of it. Just focus on your piano, and everyone else will go away." Claire beamed. "I gotta go make sure the booth is ready, but was just coming to say, 'Break a leg!'"

She nodded as he took off, wearing all black, the word "crew" across the back of his shirt. Shortly after, she joined the group Mr. Johns was calling together to prepare to take the stage. Props and decorations had been hung and placed around. Claire liked the additions, seeing the hints to the night club vibe of the era . . . She took her spot at the piano and was pleased to see that the lights blinded her view of most of the audience. She knew her parents, Troy, Gwen, Babs, and Sam were somewhere out there and took a deep breath to get in the zone. Mr. Johns entered last, giving a welcome and an introduction to the program, and the concert began.

Claire played along to classics like "Fly Me to the Moon," "La Bamba," "Under the Boardwalk," and "Somewhere Beyond the Sea" mixed in with some later songs like "Never My Love" and "California Dreamin'." The choir did great, and the audience was enjoying the show immensely, tapping their feet or quietly singing along. As the last note sounded of "You Can't Hurry Love," Claire knew it was her turn next. Mr. Johns faced her, raising his hands to signal her start. The lights dimmed, and a spotlight turned on her. Its heat and intensity seemed to be coming directly from the gray eyes that were behind it.

She adjusted the mic and took a deep breath. She slightly adjusted herself on the seat and placed her hands, Adam's advice ringing in her mind. The audience was quiet, the room silencing with the dimming of the lights. She felt the keys fall beneath her graceful hits with the soft intro, the choir silent, waiting for her voice to start the song. It was hot up on the stage, but Claire felt her heart and body fill with the notes that were now releasing from her depths and the tones releasing from the piano. Her sultry voice moved smoothly through the song as the choir offered backup. She felt her confidence grow with every note, the room melting away, leaving just her, the piano, and the light that was shining for her. It was a magical and romantic song, and Claire poured all of her thoughts and emotions of late into it.

She lifted her hand slowly as the last note faded. The sound around her turned on as the applause shook her. She smiled at the audience, seeing them for the first time as the spotlight dimmed. She nodded to them in acceptance of their praise.

At the end of the show, the choir got a standing ovation, and when the lights turned on, Claire felt her nerves fall away and was happy Mr. Johns had encouraged and pushed her to this moment. She had found a new love: the stage.

Sam rushed it as Claire stepped down and gave her a hug. "Oh my god! You were totally amazing! Best one of the night! I had no idea! Why have you been keeping this from me for so long?!"

Claire giggled, releasing her relief, happy to hear her friend's compliment. Her parents, Troy, Gwen, and Babs followed behind, each giving her a hug and echoing each other's words of praise. After getting a few more shout-outs from others as they passed, she headed to change so they could get going.

"Claire!" Adam was running toward her. "You did it!!"

Her cheeks were hurting from all the smiling. "Yeah!"

"I know you said you didn't want a spotlight . . . but—"

"No. It's fine. It helped make the audience disappear." She chuckled.

"I wanted everyone to see you . . . see how great you are," he said quietly.

She blushed, realizing how often she did that around him and wondering if there was a way to control blushing, and looked to the floor, not having words.

"I won't keep you. Gotta go pick up. But, um . . . you were . . . you were great." He wanted to say that she was magnificent . . . gorgeous . . . talented . . . that he had stared at her the entire time, watching her hands roam the keys of the piano, watching her face as she passionately belted out the notes, eyes closed, lost in a world of music. He wanted to tell her that he was falling hard, but he didn't know what to do.

When May hit, all anyone could talk about was prom. Even freshmen and sophomores enjoyed discussing who was going with whom, regardless of the fact that they weren't allowed to attend unless invited by an upperclassman. One thing that was certain was that it was the goal of all students, maybe even especially underclassmen, to get asked to prom. Having a date for prom seemed to be the epitome of high school royalty, and it didn't go unnoticed by Sam.

"How cool would it be if we were asked to prom?!" she was saying as they walked home, the warm air carrying the scent of earth, mown grass, and just a hint of the coming summer. "I mean, I know it won't happen, but, like, how cool would it be? I can't wait for next year when we get to go!"

Claire just nodded in agreement.

"What's gotten into you today?" Sam asked.

"What?" Claire said sharply. "Nothing. I'm fine."

"Oh, now I know something is up. What is it?"

Claire sighed. "It's dumb."

"You know me better than that," Sam said, linking arms with her.

"Ugh . . . okay. I overheard Adam buying prom tickets from a senior in our band class . . ."

"Ah. I see."

"I don't know why it bothered me. I mean, I know Rachel is his girlfriend and a senior, so, naturally, they'd be going to prom . . . but I just hadn't thought of it, and I guess the idea of them going to prom just annoys me. I don't get why he likes her."

"Maybe he doesn't," Sam said.

"What do you mean? Of course he does. Why would he be with someone he doesn't like?"

"Maybe he's stuck . . . and he's a super nice guy and doesn't want to hurt Rachel in her senior year and right before her senior prom. I mean, how long did you stay with Mark even though you didn't like him anymore?"

Claire walked in silence, not wanting to put any more false hope in her mind than she already had. Their special study halls together, his warm words of praise and compliments, just him and being around him were all stirring in her thoughts enough as it was. She didn't need to question him and Rachel on top of it all and continue to further trick her brain into thinking she had a chance. She internally sighed. At least Sam was right about prom. They wouldn't be going, and so, at the very least, she wouldn't have to see Adam and Rachel lost in a magical dance.

Sam's assumption that they wouldn't get asked to prom was challenged a couple days later, however, when Mark sought Claire out at the end of the day. She and Sam were by her locker while Claire finished packing up when he asked for a word. Claire agreed, finished packing, and stepped aside to talk to him, Sam getting the hint to wait outside.

"What's up?" Claire said, throwing her bag over her shoulder.

"So, my older cousin . . . you know, the one who threw the party last year?"

"Yeah?" she asked, unsure where this was going.

"He got me a date for prom with a friend of his," he said. "Julie Herrick."

"Cool," Claire said, hoping Mark wasn't seeking her out just to tell her that he'd moved on, because that had already been made obvious with the two girlfriends he'd had since their breakup.

"Yeah . . . but, uh, he has another friend, Rick, who is in need of a date too. You met him once when we all went to the beach last summer."

"Ooookay," Claire said with a raised eyebrow. She remembered him. Tall, handsome, dark hair.

Mark sighed. "Claire, do you want to go to prom with him? I told him I'd ask you to see if you were interested."

This was not what Clare was expecting at all. "Oh! Um . . . he wants to go with me?"

"Well, pretty much everyone by now, juniors and seniors anyway, are already going and have dates. I told him I'd check with my sophomore friends, so this is me checking."

"Why me?"

"Well, because you're my friend, you're nice, you're easygoing, and he remembered you specifically from the beach."

"Ah . . . I see."

"Look, I figured it'd be fun. We wouldn't otherwise be able to go, so why not?"

"Well . . . sure, I guess," she agreed. "Will we be going as a group? I'm not sure I want to go to prom with someone I barely know on my own."

"Yeah, no, of course! I'll be there with my date, and I think another couple too."

Claire thought a moment again. "Can I get back to you? I'm not sure my folks will even let me."

"Yeah, sure. Let me know tomorrow in homeroom?"

She nodded.

"Awesome! I'll let him know. He already has tickets. So, once you decide, I'll give him your number to call and sort out details."

"Sounds good."

"Great! See ya, Claire!" he said, running off, leaving Claire a bit stunned.

As she suspected, Sam flipped when she told her, and she talked about it all the way back to Claire's house and the entire time Claire was trying to read *Animal Farm* in her bedroom.

"I just . . . I am totally speechless. Prom!! Oh my god! Of course you would get invited! We need to go dress shopping, like, ASAP. What color? What style? I am totally jealous, by the way."

"Sam, I haven't even asked my parents yet or told him yes. I'm not sure. It's just a dance, and I don't even—"

"Just a dance? You're going to prom with a SENIOR! Earth to Claire, do you have any idea how big of a deal this is? Damn, how does all this stuff happen to you?! Well, I mean, I know how . . . you're—"

"Sam, stop. I do not want to hear you list off all the reasons you think I'm amazing. You are too. So that's not it. I was honestly this guy's last possible resort because he couldn't get a date, and the only reason I was asked was because he knows Mark, who offered the position to me."

"He didn't offer it to Amber," Sam said stubbornly.

"Because Amber is already going with some junior that she coerced into taking her."

"Oh, right . . . that oaf from her math class who had to repeat geometry . . . twice."

"Exactly. See what people will do for popularity? It's apparently cooler to go to prom with an idiot than to not go at all. So dumb," Claire said.

"Says the girl with a date."

"Oh come on, Sam. Should I say no, then?"

"No! You're my one chance at even being somewhat popular!"

"Oh my god." Claire outwardly laughed. "You are seriously ridiculous."

Claire's dad was a little skeptical of letting her go to prom with a senior boy, but her mother talked him down, and Claire only had to agree to no parties after prom and to come straight home after the dance. He was also reassured to know that they were going as a group with Mark and his date. She told Mark the next day at school, and that weekend, Claire's mom took her and Sam dress shopping at the mall. Claire went home with a pale-pink spaghetti-strapped dress with a sweetheart bodice made all of flowy chiffon that landed just around her knees. It was elegant and simple and put her in mind of Baby's dress in the infamous finale of *Dirty Dancing*. Sam made her try on a zillion gowns before agreeing on this one, her mother determining that it was both beautiful and would pass the dad test.

Claire didn't want to deal with the over-the-top attention of getting her hair and makeup done, even though her mom offered to take her. So the night of prom found Claire and Sam in Claire's room, teasing, curling, and spraying her hair before pinning it up themselves, Claire's mother coming to the rescue when nothing was working. It ended up being an elegant pile of hair that looked natural and organic. Claire hated perfect curls hardened by too much hairspray. She went a little more dramatic with her makeup than usual, doing full foundation and eye color. She went for neutrals with a soft-pink lip.

Sam talked the entire time while Claire's thoughts traveled to what Rachel was going to wear, what it would feel like to see Rachel and Adam at prom, how Adam probably looked really cute in a tux, and how he had seemed a little off when Claire had excitedly told him she'd see him at prom as Rick's date. Sam stayed with her until the car pulled up and Mark, Rick, and Julie came inside. Her mother was all ready, a camera loaded with a fresh roll of film, and took pictures of the four of them and then each pair. Sam wished her luck as she left, new pink corsage on her wrist, Claire's mother taking Sam home shortly after.

Prom was held in the gym of the school; the theme this year was "Masquerade Ball". There were colorful streamers and balloons everywhere, eye masks on wooden sticks as a favor. Mark and Rick found an open table and were joined shortly after by one of Rick's friends and his date, Jenny, who Claire recognized as a chorus member. They mingled, Claire feeling a little awkward, not really knowing any of them all that well, except for Mark. She had talked to Rick a few times on the phone about prom plans. They had discussed the color of her dress so he could match her flowers and his tie and times for picking her up and whatnot. He had been polite and had asked her what she was into, and they had talked briefly about that. It wasn't nearly enough to get to know someone, but Claire was going to experience prom, so that was exciting.

The food was put out and they all ate. Julie was really sweet, as was Jenny, and Claire started to warm up when they talked about the chorus concert, finding something they had in common. When the dancing picked up, Claire and Rick joined everyone else on the floor, and Claire let the music settle her nerves and whisk her away. Rick twirled her around and danced really close, and though it was the first time she'd danced like that with a guy, Claire rolled with it, this being prom and music being her muse.

At one point in the night, Rick led her off the dance floor to the punch, pouring them each a cup and adding something from a hidden flask to his.

"I'm having a great time!" Rick yelled over the music.

"Me too!" she returned, pretending not to notice.

"You look real fly tonight," he shouted.

Claire blushed. "Um . . . thanks!"

"Thanks for coming with me," he said, taking another sip of punch.

"Thanks for asking!" She realized after she said it that he hadn't really, Mark had . . . oh well.

Mark and Julie joined them, and Rick added a splash of booze to Mark's punch as well. Claire didn't really care but was at least hoping they were smart about it when it came time to drive home. Rick's friend and Jenny were nowhere to be found, which Mark commented on.

"Oh, you know where they are," Rick said with a wink. Mark just laughed and nodded. They snacked some more and then went back on the dance floor. The first slow dance played, and Rick held Claire tight. Over his shoulder, Claire got her first glimpse of Rachel and Adam. They were dancing nearby, and though held in a tight embrace, Rachel was chatting with the couple that was dancing next to them, the two girls sharing a laugh. It seemed natural and fine, but Claire couldn't help but notice that Adam looked irritated. And Claire had been right: he looked really cute in a tux. Rachel was a class act in a form-fitted red dress that was sleeveless, the neckline an illusion that subtly covered her cleavage and wrapped around her neck, showing off her perfect jawline. She had on black heels, and her blonde hair was piled up on top of her head, dark lipstick finishing off a look that was of top fashion trends for the prom season. Claire felt Rick's hand slowly lowering and was relieved when the song ended and they broke apart to make way for the upbeat moves.

As the night wore on, it was getting closer to the time when the prom king and queen would be named and the last dances of the evening would be had. Rick grabbed Claire's hand and said, "Want to go get some fresh air?"

Claire smiled and nodded. She was definitely hot and could use it.

They stepped out into the night through the doors that led to a small courtyard beside the school. Benches were there, with some raised flower beds, and a low-lying wall that encased it all from the hill above surrounded it. Claire walked slowly down the path, enjoying the coolness on her pink face and the smell of the lilies. She stopped when she felt Rick's hand grab hers. She turned to face him, smiling.

"I had a lot of fun tonight," he said.

"Me too," she replied. He started caressing her arm. Claire looked down at his touch and then up at him. He had a hazy expression on his face, and it made Claire uncomfortable. He took a step closer to her, still gently moving his hand up and down her arm. Her brain told her to step back, but her body froze.

"You know . . ." he began, "prom tradition states that the party goes on after the last dance."

Claire felt her heart begin to race and her mouth go dry. "Ex-excuse me?" she managed.

"Oh come on. You must have known that. All girls put out after prom." He gave a small chuckle as if he thought she was playing coy with him. Was this his idea of a pickup line? He moved his hand up to her face, brushing away a small piece of hair, then slowly making its way down her cheek, where he held it for a brief moment before sliding one finger down her neck and ending at the peak of her chest. Claire had a lump in her throat and could hear her own mind arguing with itself to make this stop before it got worse, but again, she was frozen.

"There's a party after prom. All the seniors are going, and as my date, that means you get to come too. There'll be drinks and more dancing, and you and I can find a cozy room all to ourselves." He placed his hands on her hips, pulled her close to him so they were touching, and leaned in for a kiss, his hand making its way to what Claire assumed would be her breast.

She smelled stale liquor and knew he had snuck a lot more booze than she had witnessed. Her heart was pumping madly, and just as his lips were about to touch hers, her body finally took in what her brain signals were sending. She leaned back and broke out of his arms.

His face looked shocked for a moment and then recovered. "Playing hard to get, are we?" His grin sickened Claire as he took a couple steps closer and pulled her toward him again, a little more aggressively this time. "No need for that." He held her arms at her side this time, which heightened Claire's anxiety, but she wiggled as he moved in for that kiss.

"Get off me!" she finally managed to say, trying to free herself, but he held on tighter. "You're hurting me!"

In her movements of backing up to get away from him, she found that she had backed right up to the low-lying wall. She could hear the music inside and could make out the party lights flashing on the front lawn in front of the school. If only they were over there instead, someone would see her struggling. She found herself pleading internally that someone would decide to come out for fresh air like they had.

"What the hell is your problem?" Rick said, panting slightly in the effort to hold her.

"I don't have a problem," she said, still struggling against his grasp.

"It's prom. And my senior one. It's a given . . . You wouldn't want to make my last year of high school a miss, would you?" he said, his breath caressing her ear, making her want to vomit.

Claire felt her face grow hot, anger and embarrassment taking over her stress. "Excuse me? I simply agreed to be your date to prom. That's it. It isn't my fault you couldn't get one and had to go with a sophomore. And now I can see why."

His face contorted, and Claire felt fear creep into her system.

"You bitch," he said, glaring at her, his hands holding on to her wrists, his body pinning her between himself and that damn wall. "You will go to that party with me, and we will have a good time, if you know what I mean, and that's all there is to it, you understand?" Then softer, almost a whisper, which churned in Claire's stomach, "I know you'll like it, so don't you worry your pretty little head. It will be the best night of your life. I promise." He paused as tears formed in Claire's eyes. Wrapping his arms around her and pinning her to him, he said, "I have an idea. Since you're so antsy, why don't we just get started here and show you that you have nothing to worry about."

He kissed her ear and slowly started to kiss down her neck. Claire's tears burned as they mixed with the mascara she had excitedly put on earlier. Now she cursed it. Her body was still frozen. She stared at the sky. It was so clear, the stars so bright. It seemed wrong that it should look so alluring . . . like it was telling her to give in and take this moment as a romantic one . . . a milestone in her life, for the stars would not shine so for anything but perfection. It mocked her. The last time she had seen the sky like this was the night at the playground with Adam as she had swung on the swing set, feeling elated, that beautiful, beautiful night so unlike this moment.

She blinked hard, those stinging tears falling down her cheeks now, leaving tracks, anger settling in once more, the sudden memory of the playground giving her a burst of adrenaline. Determined, she mustered what she had and started pushing and thrashing against him as much as she could. "Get. Off. Me!!" she screamed.

"What the fuck!" He struggled to grab at her arms again, having let go when he thought she had succumbed.

"Stop it! Stop it!" she repeated, muffled through his attempts to restrain her. She broke free and managed to get around him, but only for a moment. He grabbed her wrist again, clear vengeance on his face, Claire in absolute terror.

(EVERYTHING I DO) I DO IT FOR YOU

A voice shouted from behind them: "HEY!"

Rick turned to see who had yelled, and Claire grabbed her moment. Pulling in all her malice and fear and packing it into each finger as they gripped each other into a fist so tight she knew it was already leaving marks on her palm, she swung hard and hit Rick right on the upper brow, just missing his temple.

He didn't see it coming at all. He instantly dropped to his knees, holding the side of his face. He didn't bleed as Claire had hoped. She had watched enough boxing with her brother to know that the brow could bleed an awful lot. But it did look like he was a bit dazed, and judging by his verbiage and her now sore hand, it had hurt most definitely.

"You fucking bitch!" he gasped between moans, clutching his head. "You—you—"

Claire watched the person behind the "hey" run down the hill, scooch down, and clear the wall. When jumping down into the light, she saw that it was none other than the face she had seen moments ago in her mind's eye while envisioning the clear night sky and the type of moment that deserved it.

Adam looked pale, livid, and deeply concerned. "Are you okay?" he asked her, stepping between her and Rick.

"Yeah, I'm fine," she said. She felt goose bumps creep up her arms, and she began to shiver, pieces of her hair now falling loosely around her face. Without saying anything, Adam took off his tux coat and put it on her shoulders, then turned to Rick, who was still muttering under his breath but was back on his feet.

"I think you're done here," was all Adam said.

"Fuck you, man. I don't know why you're protecting her. Chick's a dyke. Doesn't want dick and punches like a dude."

315

Adam took a step toward him. "I said . . . I think you're done." His tone was so deep, quiet, and filled with loathing that even Claire was shocked to hear it.

Rick looked pissed, but he didn't say a word. He glared as he passed Claire and stormed back to the dance.

Adam didn't take his eyes off him till the door slammed behind him.

His shoulders relaxed a little as he turned to Claire. "Are you okay?" he asked, rubbing her arms absentmindedly to warm her up.

"I will be," she said as she sat down on the wall, massaging her hand.

"Shit, Claire . . . I-I'm so sorry that happened. Uh . . ." He ran his hand through his hair. He was at a loss. When he'd heard the scuffle, he hadn't even known it was Claire, just that something was clearly wrong. When he'd seen her, a deep hatred like he'd never felt had coursed through him. "Let me go tell someone. Are you okay here?"

"No!" she said louder than she'd intended. "Sorry . . . no. Don't tell anyone. It's fine. It's over." She hugged his jacket closer around her.

He came and sat next to her, resting his elbows on his knees and clasping his hands together. "Are you sure?"

"Yes," she said sternly. He looked at her a moment, sizing up the situation, questioning whether to adhere or to tell someone anyway. He chose to adhere.

"Thank you, by the way . . ." she said into the silence. "For taking care of Rick."

"I don't think you needed me. You were doing just fine on your own . . . That was quite the punch." He smirked, unable to contain himself.

She chuckled darkly. "Well, you distracted him, so thank you."

"I guess you could say we made a good team." Adam looked down at his hands and then added, "I'd be your wingman anytime."

Claire cocked an eyebrow at the quote and let out a laugh.

Adam laughed openly. "Bad timing?"

"No . . . somehow it seems just right," she added with a half-hearted giggle.

They sat in silence for a bit, Claire occasionally sniffling.

"So . . . we find ourselves outside of a party yet again," he said after some time.

She felt her body relax a bit, the shivering calming slightly, and she gave a hollow chuckle. "I guess we do. We need to stop meeting this way."

He grinned . . . that beautiful grin that reached his eyes and captivated her.

"What's your reason this time?" she asked.

His grin fell as quickly as it had come, and he gave a heavy sigh, running his hand through his hair. "Just the usual."

"Rachel doing her own thing again?" she asked and tried to hide the hopefulness in her voice.

"Yup . . . It isn't that I don't want her to have a good time and enjoy herself, you know? I don't need her to be attached to my hip or anything. But . . . I just feel like I fill a role for her . . . I'm her ride or her date, and that seems to be about it." He looked down at the ground. "It wasn't always like this. When we first started dating, it was fun and we had a good time. But the more I think of it lately, our relationship was never based on anything remotely deep . . . or *real*, I guess . . . I don't know . . . There's a lot to it . . ." he trailed off.

Claire felt that word hit home. *Real.* "Well, you guys are young. And were even younger then. Maybe it was just fun . . . but now it feels like it isn't growing with you."

He looked at her for a moment, and she thought at first that maybe she'd been too outspoken. But she read his eyes, and it seemed he appreciated her for something. Maybe it was for putting into words what he couldn't. Maybe it was just her willingness to listen and respond. Maybe it was both.

"I think that's exactly it . . . except I'm the only one who seems to want it to grow, and Rachel is content with just simply having a boyfriend . . . I think that's all I am and all it is. I could be any guy and it would suffice. Maybe I'm just now realizing it's always kind of been that way . . ." He hesitated before continuing. "It—it seems more recently . . . I've kind of, maybe, gotten to see what it would feel like to be with someone who likes me for me and . . . and, you know, is interested in me and wants more than just the surface stuff . . . I don't know . . . I've just been thinking a lot."

Claire nodded but completely missed his pitiful attempt to express that *she* was the reason for all these thoughts.

"Oh, young love." She sighed in an attempt to lighten the mood. "I suppose I should go use the pay phone to call my mom."

"You can't go yet."

"What else am I supposed to do?"

"Well, according to my watch, there is about five minutes till the end of the dance, which means the last song should be playing any second."

Claire looked at him quizzically, not understanding why that mattered. "Sure, but my date kind of is a douche."

As if on cue, they heard the jumbled noise that was the DJ most likely calling for the last dance followed by the unmistakable beginning to Bryan Adams.

"There it is . . . every time," said Adam with that grin again.

Claire laughed. "That is probably the cheesiest last song they could play."

Adam chuckled too, but then stood up. "Claire, would you do me the honor of dancing the last dance with me? However cheesy it may be."

Claire's smile vanished in her shock. "You want to dance? Shouldn't you go in to find Rachel?"

Adam shrugged. "I'm quite sure she's already found a partner . . . probably the prom king. So what do you say? Let's end this night on a high note as the two most pathetic partygoers in the history of parties."

"Speak for yourself." Claire laughed.

"Okay, this is true. I am definitely the only pathetic one this evening. I was just looking for company in my pity party." He held out his hand, which she accepted, placing her other on his shoulder, his right hand resting on her waist ever so gently. They swayed.

She snorted out a quick laugh. The adrenaline of the evening and now being this close to someone she liked, okay, really liked, mixed to create a euphoria much like the giggle fits she had experienced last year from drinking too much shitty alcohol. "Okay, considering my last party's events that I found myself outside for, I'll join your pity party. And tonight was definitely a pathetic and horrific version of a prom night, even if I wasn't the pathetic cause of it."

He gave her hand a double squeeze, ever so slightly, giving her silent recognition for bringing up what had happened earlier. Though she was laughing and feeling good-hearted at the moment, it warmed her heart to know he felt compelled to acknowledge that it was still a situation that wasn't laugh worthy or good-hearted, a situation that was deep and had no words. It told her that he cared, and it was so much better than hearing an apologetic expression of sympathy. It made her heart swell, and she slid her hand from resting atop his shoulder to snaking its way across the top of his back, resting at the nape of his neck. It brought her closer to him, her temple resting near his, his arm on her waist adjusting to holding her a little closer and tighter as they swayed to the rough voice belting out words of sacrificing love.

Claire couldn't help it. Tears appeared in her eyes, and she let them fall. Fucking Rick. Adam seemed to know, but didn't say a word. He just tightened his grip around her as if urging her to let it out. Her hand instinctively clutched his shirt to hold tight as she let the tears fall onto his shoulder. He adjusted their holding hands to cradle near his chest, and they danced in this tight embrace, slowly circling. Claire was grateful that the DJ allowed the song to play the extended verse that the radio usually cut off. By its end, she had calmed, the tears dry on her cheeks, leaving behind tracks in her makeup. And as she leaned back to look at Adam, to thank him, what Claire now felt was the same urgent intensity she had felt that night when "Creep" had flitted overhead and she had gotten lost in Adam's gray eyes . . . just before the cops had come and—

The side door of the school flew open with a bang. Claire hadn't realized it, but she and Adam had been lost in their dance with no music. The lights clearly back on inside, Bryan Adams silenced, and prom over. Adam and Claire jumped apart.

Rachel was standing there, the sound of people grabbing their things, talking, and pulling out chairs rent the air around her. Her face looked livid.

"What the hell," was all she managed to get out.

Adam took a step forward. "Rachel . . . I was going to come in to find you before—."

"No you weren't. Don't pretend," she said. "Once again I found myself alone at a party. No one to dance the last dance with. Do you know how humiliating that is?! Prom queen without a date? Did you even stay long enough to watch me be crowned?"

Adam had a much more determined look compared to the last time Claire had seen Rachel get this angry at him.

"That was actually about the time I left and went for a smoke. Though I doubt you recall where I was anytime before that because needing me then wasn't necessary. Apparently having a date is only when it is convenient for you."

(EVERYTHING I DO) I DO IT FOR YOU

Rachel fumed. "What is your problem?! You pissed I was crowned prom queen or something? That I danced with the prom king?"

"I don't have a problem, Rache. I have no issue with you being crowned prom queen and getting to dance with your prom king, hanging with your friends, or anything else . . . This actually has nothing to do with friggin' prom," he said with clear boiling anger behind each word. "What I have a problem *with* is you never really making the effort to include me in your conversations with others. Even your closest friends. The fact that I've only ever really been present and not a part of your group in all the time we've been dating is frustrating. All night tonight you barely spoke to me unless requesting a beverage or needing a slow dance. And only acting like a couple when we posed for a damn picture. It's a show."

He breathed heavily and continued. "This is nothing new. It's been going on for a while now and I'm tired. I'm tired of being your lackey, Rache. That's all I am to you. I'm barely even a boyfriend. I'm literally a stand-in. I could be anyone. Take you places, carry your things, be at your beck and call pretty much. It wasn't always like this, I don't think, but . . . well . . . I don't even feel like you take this seriously. If there is one thing I'm confident in is that once you graduate, I'll be a thing of the past just like this school and town. I was going to ride it out till the end of the year because it was your senior year and I do care about you. But all that does is hurt me. And so . . . I'm done . . . now."

He went quiet, looking a little shocked at where he had ended up himself, Claire's eyes growing wide.

Rachel's face glowed hot. "Are . . . are you breaking up with me? Right now? At prom??!"

"Technically, it is after prom . . . I gave you your prom date . . . Now I'm done."

"Are you kidding me?! After everything we've been through together? You're going to break up with me tonight of all nights?" Rahcel's voice was reaching a screech, but Claire saw a glossiness come over her eyes. She was clearly holding on to her heated momentum in order to squash the emotion that was playing inside.

Adam seemed to falter a little at these words. "I'm sorry, Rachel. I didn't plan this. But I'm just tired of getting hurt constantly, and I'm not getting into a car with you to go to some after-party just to be ignored again. I want you to be happy and have fun. You won't be either with me anymore . . . I should have done this a while ago."

A car squealed up the school's roundabout driveway and parked in front of the grounds where they were. A guy stuck his head out the passenger side.

"Rachel! Come on!" It was Rick. Claire couldn't help but glare.

Rachel seemed torn. "Can we just talk about this tomorrow?"

A flash of uncertainty whipped across his face, but his jaw set, and he said, "It's over now . . . I'm sorry, Rachel. Go to the party and have a ball. You won't even notice my absence, I'm sure. And I know I'll be easily replaced."

She stared at him for a moment as the car waiting honked its horn and Rick yelled, "Let's go!!" Claire could see that the car was packed with kids all laughing and talking over each other.

Claire saw a small glimpse of humanity in Rachel's face as she said, "I-I'm . . ." Her eyes were glossed.

Adam just put up his hand to silence her, knowing he didn't need to hear an apology, and, because it wasn't really in her nature to begin with, the gesture was enough. Rachel nodded, shook on her party face, and ran off to squish into the front seat with Rick. But she stopped at the door to look back at him one last time. Whatever look passed between them, Claire could feel the mutual respect and agreement in this next step for their relationship. Adam watched them leave before turning back around.

"I'm sorry," Claire said quietly.

He shrugged. "It needed to happen. I'll be fine."

Claire watched him. She knew he would be, but knew he wasn't right now. "It is okay to not be, you know . . ."

His soft smile showed the utmost appreciation, and she knew that words would fail him if he tried to speak.

"Well . . . I guess I should go use that pay phone now."

"Don't be silly," Adam said, happy for the distraction. "I can take you home."

"Are you sure?" she asked, somewhat relieved. She didn't really want to explain to her mom why her date had decided to leave her stranded.

He cocked an eyebrow. "Of course. You finally get to check out Sadie."

"Sadie?" Claire laughed.

"The Saab." He grinned. They walked to his car, his jacket now slung over his shoulder, Claire having ditched it earlier for their dance. They didn't really speak for the duration of their walk or the car ride to Claire's house. Words didn't need to be said. They had both had one hell of an evening, and the mutual silence was just as comforting as supportive words.

Adam threw his car into park on the side of the road in front of her house, and Claire unbuckled. "Thank you for dropping me off."

"No problem." He got out of the car when she did and walked with her toward her door, stopping at the bottom of the stairs as she went up, hands in his pocket.

Turning at the top, she said, "Well, good night."

"Night." He watched her go for the doorknob, his heart racing, and blurted, "Claire, wait."

She turned, her own heart beating at an alarming rate, and only raised her eyebrows in question.

He ran his hand through his hair and puffed out his cheeks, relieving a sigh, and said, "I'm going to give myself a few days to kind of . . . uh . . . deal with this whole Rachel thing . . . but, um . . ." He was shocking himself with his own nervousness. But her face was soft, and so he continued. "But after that, would you, maybe, want to catch up sometime? Like, outside of band class? Maybe at Ron's? Play some pool? Have some pizza? We have a great time at school, might as well try it out elsewhere. Sam can come, and I'll invite a couple of friends. Fitz and Jason. Something like that?" He held his breath for her response.

"Sounds absolutely perfect." Her smile was as wide as it could be, her eyes twinkling. It put him at ease, and he returned it.

"Awesome . . . I'll, um, I'll see you at school, then."

"Have a good night," she said to his two-fingered salute and went inside, unable to shake her grin no matter how hard she tried.

Claire kept the events of prom a secret from her parents. There was no escaping their noticing that someone different had dropped her off than had picked her up, her dad anxiously waiting at the window for her to arrive home. She explained it away by saying that her date had wanted to go out with the other seniors, and so she had gotten a ride with Adam, whom her mother remembered being the boy who had made sure she had gotten home safely from the party she had snuck out for and seemed appeased.

She called Sam immediately, Sam's mother having already been warned that the phone would ring late that night. Claire told her everything, struggling through what happened with Rick but excitedly telling her the details that involved Adam.

"Holy fuck, dude! Why didn't you let Adam tell a teacher?! Rick totally assaulted you! That asshole!"

"I just want to forget the whole thing. The last thing I need is for a big deal to be made. It's over. He was drinking . . . Otherwise he probably wouldn't have done it."

"So what! That's not an excuse!"

"Sam, just drop it. It's done."

There was silence, and Claire knew Sam wanted nothing to do with dropping it but thankfully did. "Okay . . . so Adam and Rachel?!" she squealed. "I can't even tell you how happy this makes me."

Claire grinned.

"And, I mean, oh my god. The last dance. Bryan Adams. Breaking up. Wanting to hang out at Ron's. I can't! This is totally freakin' amazing!"

"Sam, goodness, take a chill pill . . . You're gonna have a heart attack!"

"Well, it's just so exciting!"

And for once, Claire wanted to squeal right along with her.

The remainder of their conversation was mostly just Sam continuing to squeal about the night's events. But when they got off the phone, Claire crawled into bed, her hair combed out and makeup removed, and she felt her heart slowly grow heavy as she recalled the night, tears making their way to the surface . . . Damn Rick.

The walk to school the following Monday was a continuation of the phone call Sam and Claire had had after prom, Sam talking faster than her jaws could chew gum, Claire trying to think elsewhere, wanting to keep her emotions in check before getting too overly excited about Adam, or too upset about Rick. Entering the school, she went to her locker where a boy she only saw in her biology class and never talked to said, "Hey, Claire," as he walked by. She smiled but was too late to return the sentiment, having been so taken aback. She collected her things for class and met Sam at her locker per usual, but not before another guy whom she'd never seen before in her life said hi to her as well.

"Sup with you?" Sam said to Claire's look of confusion as she plopped down on the window seat by Sam's locker.

"I'm not sure. Two guys I've never talked to just said hi to me in the hall. Just . . . weird."

"That's weird because?" Sam asked, sitting next to her.

"Because I didn't know them, and that doesn't usually happen?" Claire said.

Sam shrugged. "Claire, you went to prom. People are going to notice you now. Hence why going to prom makes you cool."

Claire rolled her eyes as the bell rang. She and Sam had most of the day together, and throughout it, Claire endured no fewer than five more instances of random guys she'd never talked to before saying hi to her in the hall or waving at her or saying, "What's up, Claire?" Not to mention James, a kid in her and Sam's history class, acting really odd around her, trying to sit next to her and chat before class. Something was definitely up with this day, but every time she tried to express that to Sam, Sam seemed to think it was nothing and that Claire should just accept that she was now popular.

When it was time for her session with Mr. Johns, Claire was bummed and a little anxious that Adam didn't join her. It had happened a few times before when he'd needed to meet with another teacher or help out somewhere, but because *this* time followed their evening together at prom, she couldn't help but overthink the situation.

Packing up her stuff at her locker, ready to get the day over with, she listened to Sam talk animatedly about how she and Logan had chatted all through lunch because the two others who usually joined them were both absent. Claire made to leave, with Sam trailing behind, only to find her path blocked by Amber and the witches.

"What do you want, Amber?" Claire said dully.

"Claire Hanover . . . I had no idea," she said with a snotty grin that made Claire queasy.

"No idea about what?"

"You know," Amber said, looking to her two cronies for a shared laugh.

"No. I don't. But if you're just going to scoff and make faces at your two friends here, then you're wasting our time and need to move."

Amber's face turned to that of honest surprise before it became one that made Claire extremely nervous. "Oh my god, girls. She doesn't know."

"Know what, Amber?" she asked through gritted teeth.

"The whole school's talking about it, and you don't know?" She let out a bark of laughter.

Claire pushed past, knocking into both Amber and Ashley as she did so, Sam following right behind. She heard Amber mutter something and was quite sure she heard it but couldn't believe her ears.

"What did you call me?" Claire said, whipping around.

Amber stared at her with sheer evil. "What else would I call someone who slept with a guy she barely knew on prom night? . . . A. Slut."

Claire took a step toward her. "Excuse me?" she said, her voice shaking. "What are you talking about?"

"Only what the rest of the school is talking about from your dear friend Rick."

"Claire, come on," came Sam's timid voice.

"Yeah, listen to your boy sidekick, Hanover. Run along now," Amber said, flipping her hair before she and her gang turned and left.

Claire was shaking, and she felt her jaw clench tight.

"Claire, she's probably making it up," Sam said quietly.

"That explains all those guys saying hi to me today," Claire said, thinking aloud.

"Claire, come on. Let's just go."

"Those sick sons of bitches," Claire said under her breath, wanting to kick something.

"Claire!" Sam said, alarmed, grabbing Claire's arm and beginning to lead her out.

"I can't believe that asshole," Claire said. "How could he . . ." She felt her eyes begin to burn, and she suddenly walked with a quicker pace, Sam letting go of her. She wanted to get outside, away from the walls that were beginning to close in around her, far, far away . . .

She busted through the front doors, but the path outside was blocked by a large group of people standing around, trying to see over one another at something that was apparently going on in front of the entrance.

Claire forgot her anger for a moment as she and Sam joined the throng, elbowing their way to see what was going on. It wasn't till Claire saw the head of brown hair she knew oh so well, having seen a hand run through it enough times, that she elbowed herself the rest of the way so she was in front.

Adam had Rick in a headlock, his own left eye already swollen from having been hit, Rick's lip bleeding. "Tell them what really happened," came Adam's muffled voice as he held on to Rick. They struggled for a few moments before Rick shimmied his way out and then rammed into Adam's stomach, holding him around the middle in an attempt to push him over. Adam held his ground though and pushed back, trying to get swings in where he could.

"I already told everyone what really happened. It isn't my fault she's a slut," Rick said, separating from Adam and struggling to breathe.

(EVERYTHING I DO) I DO IT FOR YOU

Adam's face contorted, and he ran forward, ramming Rick against the wall of the school building, pinning his neck with his forearm. "Tell them what happened," he said in a voice that gave Claire goose bumps.

When Rick was silent, Adam applied more pressure.

"Okay, okay." Rick gasped. Adam let up. "She didn't sleep with me, okay? She didn't do anything." The crowd all shared whispers and looks with one another.

"What else?" Adam said, not breaking eye contact with Rick.

"What do you mean, what else?"

Adam pushed on him yet again.

"Okay! I tried . . . I tried to force her. But she . . . she . . ."

Adam pushed a final time. "She what?"

"She punched me," he said, straining and defeated. "She punched me, and it's where I got this black eye."

Claire hadn't noticed it before, being distracted by the fight and all, but Rick did have slight bruising around the eye she had hit. Totally worth the pain she had in her hand.

Adam let go, and Rick dropped to the ground slumped over. "Jesus, man."

"Don't ever spread rumors about Claire again, you understand me? Or anyone else, for that matter."

Rick leaned his head back, massaging his neck, breathing heavily. More than just his lip was bleeding, Claire now saw. His nose looked awfully swollen too. The crowd was dispersing, and Claire heard people muttering "Scumbag" or "What an asshole" as they did so. Claire was about to step forward to help Adam when a teacher showed up.

"What is going on here?!" Mr. Dennison came forward, looking from Adam to Rick. "Principal's office. Now." The boys both went, Mr. Dennison following behind.

329

Claire and Sam were the last students standing there, unable to believe what had just occurred.

"What a friggin' day," was all Sam said.

Claire tried to make it through the next school day without anxiously staring at the clock, counting down the minutes till band, but to no avail. She practically ran into the music room, feeling her stomach plummet when she didn't see who she was looking for. Rushing up to Mr. Johns before he started class, she said, "Mr. Johns. Where's Adam?"

Mr. Johns motioned her to step aside with him. "Uh . . . Mr. Miller was suspended yesterday for the rest of the week."

"Suspended?" Claire said weakly.

"Yes . . . He broke another student's nose, and said student's parents are not happy about it. Because it happened after school hours, they're even considering pressing charges."

"What?! They can do that?"

"I'm not sure that they will, as the student harmed Mr. Miller as well, but he is claiming self-defense, and Adam won't tell anyone why he went after this student in the first place."

Claire felt the color drain from her face.

"Um . . . Claire," Mr. Johns said even more quietly. "Kids talk, of course, and based on the rumors that have been circulating, am I correct in making the assumption that you may know why this has happened?"

Claire felt like she could puke. She nodded.

"I think it may be in Mr. Miller's best interest if you told someone. I'm not sure what's going on and certainly don't want to put myself in it, but

Mr. Miller is protecting something, and it's getting him in a lot of trouble . . . And I would bet money that of the two boys in that scuffle, he's not the one who should be."

Claire nodded and made her decision instantly. After band, she told Sam what was going on and went straight to the principal's office, asking the secretary if she could meet with him. She told him the whole story. However uncomfortable it was, she told the principal what Rick had said and done the night of prom and how Adam had come in to help her. She told him what Rick had said about her at school following prom and about the negative attention it had brought upon her. And she told him that she assumed Adam must have overheard Rick and, through a series of events she didn't know all of, had made him announce to the whole courtyard what had really happened by fighting with him.

The principal listened and, afterward, immediately asked Claire if she was okay. He also said that he would have to call her parents and let them know what was happening and what the school was going to do about it. She didn't like that last part at all but understood and didn't argue. He assured her that this was a serious matter and would be handled as such. She nodded and left his office, only to bump into Mr. Johns, who seemed to guess what she'd done, giving her a quick pat on the shoulder, and they parted ways.

A second later, Mr. Johns backtracked and called to her.

"Oh, Claire!"

"Yeah?" she said, turning to him.

"Um . . . if I remember correctly, Mr. Miller's father is ex-military and their household at times can be a little . . . strict, for lack of a better word. When there is a cause for discipline, anyway. I'm not sure what the principal said or what he is going to say to the families of those involved, but it may make a difference for Mr. Miller's sentence if you let his folks know that their son is not a street fighter. He'll still be suspended, as he did put hands on another student . . . but it may make it a little more understandable all around. Just a thought . . . Again, I do not pretend to know the full story here, and if that is too much, I hold no pressure on you . . . He lives on Cherry Street, I believe, right across from the old Baptist church that's now an antique store. Big white house with black shutters. Can't miss it. If it makes sense to, of course."

She nodded.

"That must be it."

"What if it's not?"

"Then they'll just think you're crazy, tell you you're in the wrong place, and you leave."

"Oh, wait, that's his car. This must be it."

"Then go!"

"What if I'm interrupting supper, or it's too late?"

"Oh my god. It's, like, 6:45. I'm sure they've eaten, and if they're already in bed, then they're the lamest people I know. Now go!"

Claire was standing with Sam outside of the Millers' house. She'd just finished having a long conversation with her parents about what had happened. The principal had stayed true to his word and had called the house to tell them what was going on. It was a little more serious than Claire had thought, the principal talking pressing charges and things of the like. Her parents said they wouldn't and hoped Rick's parents weren't going to now, seeing that there was more to this story than just Adam randomly assaulting their son.

Afterward, her parents had sat her down to talk to her about why she hadn't shared all this when she'd gotten home from prom and the severity of the whole situation. She told them that she was embarrassed and just wanted to ignore and forget about it. She broke down. They comforted her and told her that she was brave for speaking up, and they were there for her no matter the situation. She appreciated it, took a few moments, and asked if she could follow Mr. Johns's suggestion. They agreed. So, here she was, with Sam, now incredibly nervous to do what she had moments ago felt determined to do.

"Just go. You can do it. You don't need to tell them what happened with Rick in detail. You just need to tell them that their son was a knight in shining armor, not a psychopath."

Claire walked forward, through the front yard, and up the stone pathway to the door. She turned once to see Sam standing on the sidewalk with thumbs up before knocking on the door. A medium-built man opened it, speaking to her through the screen of the storm door. He had brown hair like Adam, cut high and tight. He had on a simple white T-shirt with jeans and was staring at Claire, who gulped.

"Um . . . hi." She felt her voice shake. "You must be Mr. Miller. I'm um . . . a friend of Adam's at school, and I was wondering—"

"Adam's not seeing any visitors at the moment," he interrupted.

Claire took a deep breath and tried to evoke some confidence in her voice. "Yeah, I assumed as much. I was actually wondering if I could speak to you and Mrs. Miller if she's around. About what happened at school."

He seemed to size her up and then opened the door. She followed him inside to an old home similar to her own. All the rooms led into one another. They entered the kitchen where Adam's mother was. She was a petite woman, with short dark hair and olive skin. A woman who was very beautiful even with the hints of age around her eyes and mouth. Not that it mattered, but Claire noted that Adam's parents were a little older than her own. They must have had him later in life, although, she recalled, her parents had had Troy pretty young. The woman turned when they walked in, drying her hands on a towel, and broke into a warm smile resembling the one Claire loved so much.

"Well, hello. Who is this?" She had a slight accent that reminded Claire of her own grandmother's French one.

"Friend of Adam's. I'm sorry, I didn't catch your name," Mr. Miller said.

"Sorry, it's Claire. Claire Hanover."

"Nice to meet you, Claire Hanover. What brings you?" she asked.

"She wants to talk to us about what happened at school."

Adam's mother's face fell ever so slightly, but she said, "Oh! Well, let's go sit in the living room, then. I'll bring some lemonade. I just made it."

Claire settled into the chair that faced Adam's parents on a clawfoot couch, a tray of lemonade and glasses between them. Mrs. Miller poured them each one, and Claire took it gratefully, sipping before putting it down to talk. It was sweet and tart and absolutely delicious, but no matter how much she drank, her mouth was still dry as the Millers looked at her in anticipation.

"So, I just thought I should explain to you why Adam was in that fight at school."

They shifted a little, and Mr. Miller said, "He wouldn't tell us. Said it was just a fight."

Claire heaved a sigh. "At prom Saturday night, Adam stepped in on an . . . altercation I had with my prom date . . . Rick. Adam helped me shake him off . . . Well, today at school, Rick decided to spread some . . . uh . . . rumors about me and what happened. It got through the entire school and everyone thought I . . . I—"

"We understand, dear," Mrs. Miller said softly.

Claire nodded her appreciation. "After school, Adam must have overheard him talking about it, and he—well, I don't really know how it started—but by the time I got there, he made Rick tell the entire crowd the truth... So... you see, Adam was just, well, I guess you could say he was defending my honor." She paused, and then, "I'm so incredibly thankful, and though I didn't want anyone to get hurt... Rick deserved it."

Adam's parents exchanged a pitying look, and Claire looked down at her hands before going on. "I have since told the principal all this and so hope that Rick's parents won't press charges or anything. Hopefully... hopefully, it will just blow over. But I wanted you to know that your son is a good guy. I assume the school will call you at some point, but I know they wouldn't be able to tell you all this, so that's why I'm here."

She stopped and made eye contact again, knee bouncing. She wasn't really sure what to say from here.

"This took a lot of courage, dear," came Mrs. Miller's gentle voice.

"Yes. We appreciate you telling us," Mr. Miller added, and when Claire looked up, he had a concerned look on his face.

"I just... Adam is a really good friend, and I needed you both to know."

"Well, thank you. I think I speak for us both when I say it makes us feel a lot better about what happened... as far as Adam goes. I hope you're okay though," Mr. Miller said.

"I am. Thank you," Claire said, surprised by his concern, but grateful.

Mr. and Mrs. Miller smiled at her, and she reciprocated. And then Claire threw caution to the wind: "Is Adam home? Can I see him?"

Mrs. Miller nodded.

"Top of the stairs, take a left, last door," Mr. Miller said.

"Thank you. And thanks for the lemonade, Mrs. Miller. It was really good." Claire followed Mr. Miller's point and headed up the stairs, taking a left and going to the very end where a door stood slightly ajar. She knocked lightly and stuck her head in. Adam was lying on his bed, wearing gray sweatpants and an oversized white T-shirt (his suspension attire), and flipping mindlessly through a car magazine, the sounds of Red Hot Chili Peppers playing in the background. He dully said, "It's open," without looking up.

"I can see that," she said, standing in the doorway.

He jumped up at the sound of her voice, Claire seeing that his swollen eye was becoming a black one. "Claire! What are you doing here? I mean . . . it's good to see you. . . uh, hi."

She smirked. "Hi." She let herself in. "Sorry to surprise you. I came to talk to your parents."

"My parents?" he questioned, straightening up the bedding and magazines.

"Yeah . . . about the fight. I told them why you *really* went after Rick," she said. "I also told Mr. Lewis the truth. You're still suspended because . . . well . . . you broke a guy's nose, but he's hopeful that all charges and whatnot will go away once Rick's parents know what kind of a jerk he is."

Adam raised his eyebrows in mild shock. "You did all that?"

"Yeah." She shrugged. "Mr. Johns told me what was going on and that you weren't talking . . ."

"Well, you said at the dance you didn't want to tell anyone. And I was worried they were going to find you after and question you, and I just didn't want to put you through all that."

Claire's heart swelled. "Well, I appreciate it. But I'd much rather have your family and the school not think you're shooting to be the next Rocky Balboa, but that you're a pretty honorable guy."

He smiled sheepishly.

"So, your parents are nice," she said, walking around his room a little. He had an Aerosmith poster and a couple magazine pullouts of '60s and '70s muscle cars pinned to the wall. It was fairly neat, and nothing really stood out . . . simple. He had a bureau that looked like it had held something but had since been taken away. TV maybe? A hamper, a night stand, and a bench window seat, and that was about it.

"Yeah. My mom's nice. She's quiet. My dad's kind of a hard-ass, when he's around. He's at work or just busy most of the time, so he typically doesn't really know what I'm up to."

"Hence you being allowed to be out at all hours of the night, at parties, and smoke?" Claire said with a sly smile.

"Well, they don't know about the smoking part. It's not a whole lot either. But . . . yeah."

"They trust you."

"Yeah . . . I guess they do. Well, they did till today. I guess when the school calls to say your son got in a fight and they're pressing charges . . ." Adam shrugged off the rest.

"Well, hopefully, knowing the truth will change their mind," Claire offered, scanning his shelf of CDs and cassettes. She saw that all the ones she'd given him so far were in their own spot, separated from the rest, the notes still attached. This made her smile.

"So what *did* happen?" she asked, looking back to him.

He dropped down on the edge of his bed. "I started hearing rumors spreading around in the morning . . . a couple friends of Rachel's who hadn't heard of our breakup yet came up to me and were talking, knowing that I knew you, having met you at Ron's over break when we bumped into each other. I told them Rick was lying, but they didn't believe me, or didn't want to, as their version of events was far juicier. I used my study hall to talk to someone I knew was friends with Rick and got the story he was telling everyone. And then, when I left school, I happened to be behind Rick and a few of his buddies. I overheard him telling them all the gory details, and—I don't know—I just got really angry . . . went up to him, told him to tell them what really happened. When he told me to beat it, I started to say it myself, and he pushed me. At that point, I lost it and . . . well . . . you saw the rest pretty much."

Claire nodded. "How's your eye?"

"Meh . . . It's fine," he said.

"Well . . . make sure you ice it. And take some Tylenol or something till it's better."

He smiled at her, the bruise not taking away from it whatsoever. "Will do."

"How is the whole Rachel sitch?" she asked tentatively.

"Ah, it's fine. She came over Sunday."

"Oh?" Claire questioned.

"Yeah. We worked it all out."

Her shoulders fell. She tried to cover her disappointment. "Oh . . . So you're back together again?"

Adam quickly corrected. "No. Not at all. I just mean we talked. I told her how I had been feeling, and we properly ended things. I told her I was sorry for ruining her prom night, but I'd just had enough. She expressed her own feelings. We exchanged stuff back, and that was about it."

"Just like that?" Claire said, now trying to hide her relief as she sat down opposite him on the edge of his bed, hoping that was okay.

"Yeah . . . Crazy, huh? Three years just about . . ."

"I'm really sorry," she said, looking down at his blue-and-white-striped comforter.

"Don't be. Like I said, it was kind of a long time coming. Things hadn't been feeling right . . . She was using me, and she really didn't deny it."

"Were things ever . . . you know . . . not like that?"

Adam laughed hollowly. "I'm not so sure they were, to be honest. I was a freshman guy trying to make my way in high school. She was a cute blonde sophomore in my study hall. I talked to her, and when she showed me attention, I hung on to it. I think she liked me . . . and liked that I doted on her . . . She asked me to take her to homecoming when the guy she was with broke up with her, and I agreed. We started dating after that, and . . . I don't know . . . everything just kind of fell into place from there. I got my license my freshman year, drove her places, was her date for everything, and I was honestly totally cool with it for a bit, even if she did nag at me or get on my case about stuff. I had a cute girlfriend to have fun with who was also so busy with her own shit that I got to do my own too. Win-win, right?"

"But . . ." Claire said, hearing it coming.

"But it got old . . . after a bit. Although, I'm not even sure it would have if it hadn't been for—" He cut himself off.

"Hadn't been for what?" Claire asked, not understanding why he stopped.

"Uh—" he stammered. He started to panic a bit, not being prepared to say what it was he had started to say.

Claire raised an eyebrow, but Adam was interrupted from saying anything by a knock at the door.

They both looked up, Adam thankful for the distraction.

Sam stepped into the room, looking a little guilty and apologetic as she did so. "Sorry. I was just waiting outside for a while, and I didn't know what was going on. And I wanted to make sure Adam's parents weren't some psychopathic killers who had kidnapped you, and when I came to check, they just sent me up here."

Adam laughed. "You're fine. Come in."

Sam stepped further into the room.

"I suppose I *should* get going," Claire said, standing up, Adam following them to the door. Claire turned in the entryway, nearly bumping into him. "Um . . . thank you," she released. "I don't really know the words to express it, but thank you."

Adam's eyes bored into hers like they were so good at doing, making Claire feel exposed and yet deeply fallen. "You're welcome. I'd do it again in a heartbeat. It was worth the black eye."

She wasn't sure why, but she felt an emotional response forming at those words, her eyes stinging with the onset of tears, a lump in her throat leaving her unable to respond. Maybe it was the entirety of the day just now weighing down on her . . . the final release of anxiety that had been building up to come here this evening . . . just the whole situation with Rick in general . . . or . . . it was that those words echoed the tone of that cheesy last dance.

Truly Madly Deeply

Claire had barely made it through the door the following day when Troy yelled that the phone was for her.

Grabbing it, she asked, "Who is it?" to which Troy merely shrugged and said, "See for yourself."

Staring at his mischievous face, Claire said, "You're a weirdo," and held the phone to her ear.

"Hello?" she said.

"Hey!" she heard come over the line. Claire's heart instantly jumped to her throat, and she grabbed her bag off the floor and ran upstairs to her room.

"Adam! How's it going!?" she asked, closing her door behind her and plopping down on her bed, hoping he couldn't tell how winded she was.

"Going good. I thought I'd call and tell you that your visit yesterday got me my TV and Nintendo back in my room," he said. She could hear his smile.

"That's great! Glad I could be of service." She chuckled.

"Yeah. My days are a bit better now that I don't have to stare at the wall and slip slowly into madness."

Claire laughed. "Dramatic much?"

"Maybe a little . . . Hey . . . so my parents are shortening my sentence to Friday at three rather than the rest of eternity. Was wondering what you and Sam were doing after school Friday. Say, around six?"

"Oh! Um . . . I don't think anything. I'll have to check, but I think we're free!"

"Fitz and Jason are cool to hang out at Ron's for a bit and didn't know if you and Sam wanted to meet us there. I tried to get my buddy Nick to come along, but he can't."

"That sounds great!" she exclaimed, trying not to sound too excited.

"Awesome. So, how was school? How was band?"

Claire settled in, lying back on her pillows, ankles crossed, her arm behind her head. "Not too bad . . . That kid—um, Josh, I think it is?—still can't get that solo part on the marching piece. I actually think I saw Mr. Johns get mildly frustrated."

"No way," Adam said with a snigger. "Mark it in the calendar."

"I heard Rick had to go get his nose reset, and rumor has it that other girls have maybe experienced something of what I did and are making sure it is heard by all for when he comes back to school."

"Good . . . Asshole," Adam said darkly.

"So what have you been doing? Besides trying to beat Mario, of course."

"Other than work? Oh, you know . . . counting ceiling tiles and seeing how many Cheez-Its I can fit on the cat before it wakes up."

Claire burst out laughing. "We got to get you back to school."

"Tell me about it." There was a pause, though not an awkward one. "Well . . ." he said, "I guess I'll let you go. Hope you can come Friday."

"Me too. I'll let you know!"

"Sounds good . . . Bye."

She hung up the phone and stared at the ceiling for a bit before squealing and calling Sam.

She called Adam the next day when she got home to tell him that she and Sam were good to go for Friday evening. They then talked for almost a half hour about school and what had happened at it, Claire assuming that Adam just wanted to hear anything about the outside world beyond his room and work, which was in part true, aside from Adam also just liking to hear Claire's voice.

The week passed sluggishly in anticipation of their gathering. Sam went to Claire's after school so they could get ready, Claire actually wanting to put some intention behind her hair and outfit selection. She landed on one of her short-sleeved floral dresses, her choker and fat sandals as last touches. She fluffed up her hair and added her lipstick. Sam was perusing Claire's closet to see if there was anything she could change or add to her outfit, not liking what she was wearing.

"Sam, you look fine," Claire said. Sam's black overall dress layered over a multicolored striped shirt was cute and trendy. She was wearing Doc Martens and had her curly hair in two low buns at the back of her head.

"I look twelve, don't I?" Sam said, emerging from the closet.

"No, Sam . . . you look adorable. Let's add some fun makeup to top you off," Claire said.

Sam smiled. "Okay!"

They walked to Ron's around 6:00, Sam muttering the whole time about what to say and how they should act, a ball of nerves for herself as well as for Claire, who she felt wasn't taking this seriously enough.

"Okay, Sam, stop," Claire said, grabbing her elbow on the corner before turning onto Main Street. "Take a deep breath and chill!! Seriously. This is just us going to meet a few friends who happen to be boys. I'm trying not to freak out, and you're not helping!" she ended, with an edge in her voice. The truth was, she had become exceptionally nervous since leaving the house, and it had been annoying her since she'd started feeling it. She didn't usually get nervous like this, and Sam's constant babble was getting under her skin.

Sam took a deep breath. "Okay . . . okay, I'm sorry. It's all good. It's just Adam, who you've hung out with a gazillion times now, and Fitz, who is as chill as they come. We've met Jason only a couple times, but he was quiet and seemed übersweet. We got this."

"Thank you. We do," Claire said. They both took a deep breath and continued on.

When they walked into Ron's, the tables were already filled with people, many of whom were students they went to school with. It took Claire mere seconds to spot the glasses and gray eyes smiling at her through the back entryway to the pool room. Claire and Sam made their way there, waving at a couple people as they passed. Adam and his friends had claimed a large booth by the pool table, Fitz and Jason playing what already sounded like a hilarious game just from the few comments Claire heard upon entering.

"Dude, smoke another one, why don't you. I told you you're stripes," Jason said to Fitz.

"Damn . . . I worked so hard to get that one in too."

"I know it!"

Adam shook his head. "Hey! Ah, we got this table here. What do you want for drinks? I'll go let the counter know."

"Coke is fine," Claire said.

"Same!" Sam agreed.

"I put an order in for pepperoni and cheese. Are those fine? I can add a different one if not."

"No, that's good," Claire said, looking to Sam, who nodded. "Yeah, perfect."

"Great! I'll be right back."

"You hate Coke," Claire said under her breath when Adam left.

"I know. I panicked," Sam returned.

Fitz shouted across the pool table, "Bohemian! Good to see you!"

Claire smiled. "You too, Fitz. How's the game going?"

"Well, this guy over here keeps trying to mess with me by switching the balls around," he said, pointing toward Jason.

Jason threw his hands up. "You've got to be kidding me. You know what? Hit whatever ones you want to. Guy who sinks the most wins."

"Groovy," Fitz said.

Jason sighed. "So, how have you guys been?" he asked Claire and Sam politely as Fitz examined the table.

"Good. You?" Claire answered as Sam, yet again, nodded along.

"Going well. Anxious for summer. We got, what, two weeks left?"

"Sounds about right!" Claire said.

Adam returned and stood next to Claire.

"Sam here is into cars," he said to Jason. "Tell her what you just got."

Jason lit up. "A 1977 Chevy Camaro," he said with immense pride.

Sam looked at him in shock. "No freaking way."

Jason grinned, happy with Sam's reaction. "Yup."

"The Z28? How the hell did you get your hands on that?!"

"My uncle owns a car dealership, trades them all the time. Got his hands on this one a little while back. It was in rough shape. But he and I worked on it, and it's finally done. Picked it up yesterday."

"No shit. That's amazing. The second-gen Camaro is fly as hell. Detailing?" she asked.

"Not yet. It's just a burnt orange right now, but I want to save up to get it done in turquoise blue with some white stripes on the hood."

"Man . . ." Sam responded.

Jason nodded, pleased. Then, turning to Fitz and seeing he was still concentrating on his next move, he said, "You wanna go see it?"

"Yeah!" Sam said excitedly.

"Cool. It's just out here. We'll take the back door," he said, and then, pointing to Fitz, "This will take all night anyway."

Adam turned to Claire. "Want to see too?"

"Sure!"

They all checked it out while Fitz stayed at the pool table. Sam and Jason talked animatedly for a little bit before they all returned to find Fitz still staring at the table.

"Dude, would you hit the fucking ball already?" Jason said exasperatedly.

"Don't rush me," he said, leaning over and finally hitting a ball . . . and missing. "Damn."

Jason shook his head and went to take his turn.

The pizza arrived and they halted the game. Adam and Claire slid into one side of the booth and Sam and Jason the other, Fitz turning a chair backward and sitting on the end. Claire realized her nerves were long gone and was really happy to see Sam talking so comfortably with Jason, and, of course, Fitz, who talked to just about anyone, his easygoing personality a magnet for many.

They crammed their faces with pizza, Claire having no care in the world how she looked while doing so. Between the five of them, they finished off both pies and sat in a stupor as Fitz told them an extremely long story that ended in them all laughing so hard they were at risk of throwing up all the pizza they had consumed.

"Alright, Fitz, we still gotta finish that game," Jason said when the vibe calmed back down.

"Oh man . . . I don't know if I can play with such a full stomach."

"What does your stomach have to do with pool?" Adam asked.

"I can't focus when I'm this stuffed."

"Because you focus so hard otherwise," Jason butted in.

"I'll play," Sam interjected.

"Perfect. I could use someone who can tell the difference between solids and stripes," Jason said with an eye roll at Fitz.

They shimmied out, and Fitz turned his chair around to watch. "I'll be the commentator."

"Oh fuck, here we go," Jason said, setting up the table to start over.

"Jason Stevenson sets up the table for what is bound to be an epic game against the one and only Sam Levinski," Fitz said loudly, sporting his best announcer voice.

"Jesus Christ," Jason said. Sam giggled.

Adam leaned toward Claire in the booth. "Want to go pick some music on the jukebox?"

"Totally," she said, sliding out.

"Your turn this time," Adam said, putting money in the machine as Claire sifted through the titles. "You get five choices."

Claire selected songs she knew would be favorites for them both. They returned to the game to see that Fitz had turned the menu into a megaphone and was shouting the details of Jason and Sam's pool game.

"Levinski pockets yet another ball, the purple people eater, number four. This puts her miles ahead of Stevenson, the pool loser."

"Shut up, Fitz," Jason said, smirking, shooting, and getting one in.

"This just in, folks. Stevenson seems to maybe have a little talent after all! Sinking his fourth ball of the night. And the crowd goes wild!"

"Dude, shut him up," Jason said to Adam, who grinned. The night went on in this manner. Adam and Claire occasionally chatted about the songs Claire picked, sending them off on tangents about epic musicians and albums. Sam ended up beating Jason at pool and then went on to play

Fitz, who continued his commentating, referring to himself as the Great and Powerful Fitz. He lost as well, though it may have been due to Jason grabbing the end of his pool cue every now and then when he tried to shoot.

Before Claire knew it, it was already 10:45, and she and Sam were supposed to be back by 11:00.

"Well, I think we better get going," Claire said, genuinely sad to see the night end.

"Aw man!" Fitz said. They were back sitting around the table, talking at random about things like school, jobs, and cars. Claire expressed wanting to get a summer job, and Jason mentioned seeing a few places hiring in the mall when he was at work the night before, Adam nodding along, the both of them working at RadioShack.

"I know. We had a really good time. I wish we could stay," Claire said. "Hopefully, we can do it again?"

"Definitely," Adam said.

"Right on," Jason added.

"Anytime, Bohemian," Fitz said.

Adam scooted out of the booth so Claire could follow. "We're probably going to head out soon ourselves. The place probably won't be open much longer anyway."

Claire looked around and saw there were still quite a few people there. "I don't know. You could get a few more pool games out of it." Ron's didn't have a definitive closing time. He went by the crowd and called last call for drinks and pizzas when he felt it was dwindling.

"I'm not sure I can handle these two for much longer," Adam joked, gesturing to Jason and Fitz.

Sam scooted out, and Jason started showing her some of the pictures on the back wall that were historical shots from Ron's back in the '30s and '40s, talking about his connection to the family, giving Adam a sideways glance and a significant look to Fitz to join himself and Sam.

"I . . . um . . . I'm glad you had a good time tonight. I had the best," Adam said, instinctively running his hand through his hair.

"It was a lot of fun. Truly," Claire replied.

"Is it . . . is it okay if I call you sometime soon?"

"Of course! You don't need to ask me to do that." Claire smiled.

Adam chuckled nervously. "I just don't want to bug you."

"You could never bug me, Adam Miller," she said meaningfully.

"I . . . uh," Adam stammered, his hair being pushed back repeatedly at this point. "I . . . Cool. I will do that, then . . . soon," he said, chickening out of what he was trying to say.

"I like the brothel idea myself," came Fitz's voice.

Both Adam and Claire exchanged questioning looks before bursting into laughter.

"What the hell, Fitz," Adam said.

"What? This building has been many a things before it was Ron's Pizzeria. Jason was just teaching us about it."

Claire and Sam waved their goodbyes and left the restaurant to walk home. Neither of them talked for a while, both seeming to need time to let the evening soak in.

"Are you as excited about how that went as I am?" Sam asked, finally breaking the silence.

Claire grinned widely, and Sam squealed, linking arms with her, going off on a race of words explaining just how well, Claire only hearing half of it, her mind daydreaming of those gray eyes and crinkled smile.

The last couple weeks of school flew by in a haze of finals and catch-up work to try and get those last points in to pass, the excitement and anticipation of summer making doing those things all the more difficult. On the last day of school, Sam and Claire celebrated by getting ice cream with Troy and then renting a slew of movies to watch late into the night. They popped five bags of popcorn and immediately regretted it, seeing just how much popcorn that really ended up being. "Save it to make a garland for Christmas?" Sam suggested before they both fell into the kind of giggle fits that only two girls giddy on the air of summer break and a sugar rush can have.

Getting into their comfy clothes and throwing their hair up to do facials, they did their run of *Pretty Woman, Father of the Bride, Mrs. Doubtfire,* and *Sleepless in Seattle,* opting to watch on Claire's small TV so they could hang out in her room, Sam commenting on the cheesiness and unlikelihoods in each one, Claire rolling her eyes and throwing popcorn at her to shut up.

"But seriously! You *really* think a prostitute and a high-end rich dude would end up together and be happy? I mean, think about their personality differences!"

"Maybe they would balance each other out," Claire suggested.

"Always the optimist." Sam chuckled.

They crashed halfway through *Pretty in Pink*, the bowl of popcorn still between them as they sprawled on Claire's bed, Claire in the midst of a dream that she wouldn't remember when waking up only a short while after.

She tossed and turned as a tapping sound entered her thoughts, floated around, and then woke her, her subconscious mind finally realizing the noise wasn't coming from the dream. She sat up disorientated, listening.

Sam stirred in her sleep and mumbled, "What's going on?"

"Shh . . . Shut up a minute," Claire whispered, causing Sam to become more alert. The ticking noise sounded again, and it was coming from Claire's window. Sam and Claire exchanged looks. Claire slowly got up and walked over to the window, peeking through the curtain.

"Oh. My. God," Claire said.

"What?! Is it a killer? Oh my god, are they coming inside? Are they breaking in? We need to get Troy. I'll go," Sam said hurriedly.

"Sam, no, chill," Claire said, waving her down. "And you do not want to get Troy: he sleeps in his boxers."

"Well, I don't know. I could be okay with that," Sam muttered.

"Shush. It's Adam," Claire said.

"What?!" Sam launched herself off the bed and went to the window to hide behind the other curtain as the tapping noise came again.

"You moved way faster for this than when you thought there was a psychopath in the yard."

"This is way more exciting," Sam said with wide eyes.

"What do you think he wants?" Claire asked, a little nervous.

"Gee, I wonder . . . Open the freakin' window!" Sam said. Claire nodded.

She moved the curtains out of the way, pushed the window up higher, and opened the screen, sticking her head out.

"What are you doing here?" she whispered with a grin.

He smiled up at her. "Can you come out?"

She leaned back to look at Sam. "He wants me to go out."

"Then do it! I'll cover for you," Sam said.

Claire smirked and then stuck her head back out. "Be right down. Give me a minute."

She closed the curtains. "Okay . . . I gotta change."

She put on whatever Sam frantically threw her way in their haste to get Claire ready. It ended up being some jeans, a crop top, and a baggy sweater. "What about shoes?" Claire said anxiously.

"Where are they?"

"Down by the front door," Claire said.

"I'll be right back."

"What?! No! Sam! What if you wake somebody up?!"

"I'll just tell them I got lost and was sleepwalking."

Claire saw her disappear behind her door. She ran a brush through her hair and was happy they had done facials, her skin still slightly glowing. She threw on some mascara and clear gloss just in time for Sam to come back with her Doc Martens.

She slipped them on and grabbed a stick of gum. "Okay, how do I look?"

"Like someone who just woke up at two in the morning," Sam said.

Claire gave her a look.

"Kidding! You look fab. Now go!"

Claire went back to the window, turned herself around, and said, "Just lie under the covers, make a fake body for me, and my parents won't bug you," before making her climb down the trellis.

She jumped the last stretch, and Adam held his hand out. She took it with a grin and let him lead her. She had a feeling she knew where they were going, and her assumption was validated when he led her through the fence of the old school playground. He continued holding her hand until they were under a tree in the far back corner, which Adam was now behind, clearly retrieving something.

"Dug the player out of my ole man's garage," he said, coming back around, a silver two-cassette player in one hand and a cassette tape in the other. Claire noticed it looked like a mixtape, its cover white, with Adam's scrawled handwriting covering it.

Claire chuckled. "Nice. I think my dad has the same one in our garage." They took a seat, Adam leaning against the tree, and Claire, legs outstretched and crossed, facing him.

"So what's up?" she asked as he fumbled with the cassette.

"I couldn't sleep," he said, snapping the door closed and hitting play, "and figured you shouldn't be able to either."

She sniggered as the sound of Tom Petty washed over her. "I was actually up not *too* long before you came. Sam and I OD'd on root beer and popcorn and watched movies till we crashed."

"What movies did you watch?"

"Oh, some cheesy romances . . . *Pretty Woman, Sleepless in Seattle . . .*" she answered.

"Nice," he said.

"Yeah . . . I'm usually a night owl anyway though."

"Stay up watching movies often?" he asked.

"No. Usually keep myself up reading." She laughed.

He grinned. He liked this about her and could picture her lying on her stomach in bed, reading a book that she couldn't put down, maybe even getting giddy or sad or angry at parts. He didn't think she knew it, but Claire wore her emotions right on her face. There was no hiding them, and he imagined that watching her read would be entertaining. Much like watching her play piano. "What kind of books do you like to read?"

Her expression was that of mild embarrassment. "Oh, just about anything . . . But my secret drug is *Pride and Prejudice.*"

He laughed. "How many times have you read it?"

"Oh gosh, I have no idea . . . I think I've read it like three times every year for the past five!"

"Wow . . . What do you like so much about it?" he asked.

She thought a moment as the music shifted to the Red Hot Chili Peppers. "I think . . . I think it's the simple idea that people are not always what they seem . . . that sometimes our own shortcomings and self-conscious tendencies can portray us in a way that is actually damaging. But . . . when someone takes the time to better understand another, maybe they can see that that person is in fact trying really hard and has reasons for being the way they are . . . And that, sometimes, we can meet people in life who help us overcome those shortcomings and blossom into the wonderful person we were always meant to be. I think . . . when you meet someone who helps bring out the best in you—makes you *want* to be a better person—that is a beautiful thing. It's what speaks to me when I read *Pride and Prejudice* anyway, so I like it," she ended simply.

Adam seemed deep in thought while Claire sat in contented silence listening to the sounds around her.

"You think everyone gets the chance to meet someone who makes them want to be better? And help them find themselves?" he asked eventually.

"I think we meet many people throughout our existence who can do that. Like, that one best friend or . . . people like Babs, for example . . . We can find inspiration by surrounding ourselves with the beautiful souls who help us be . . . well . . . us. But I do believe everyone has that one soul mate in life out there—that one person who *really* completes us. And hopefully we're lucky enough to find them."

He stared at her for a moment, taking in her starlit eyes. "How do you think you know when you've met that person?"

She shrugged. "Sometimes, I don't think you know right away at all, and it just sort of gradually creeps up on you. Sometimes, I think you meet someone, and right away it's like you've known each other across galaxies of time. But, I think, in both instances, you feel it in your gut. They're the first person you want to tell a secret to . . . the one you don't mind telling

TRULY MADLY DEEPLY

your deepest desires to, the person who crosses your mind the most, the one you can do absolutely nothing with and feel at home . . . the person you are always happy for, and the person you truly couldn't imagine living a day without. That's how I think you'd know."

Adam nodded and didn't have much to say to that. The music and the warm air was making him relaxed, and his mind was enjoying listening to Claire's vision of love, because that's really what she was talking about, and he believed every single word. "Most people don't talk that way, you know."

"No . . ." she said. "But they should. It's how we feel."

"I like it," he responded.

They sat in silence, occasionally discussing school or summer plans, but mostly letting the music do the talking. Blues Traveler, Soul Asylum, and Dave Matthews Band all filled the night air. Eventually, Claire lay back and stared at the clear, beautiful June sky. Adam moved over and lay next to her, and suddenly it seemed like the music was coming from the stars themselves, engulfing them.

"What do you think the stars would say if they could talk?" Claire asked quietly.

Adam thought for a moment. "I think they'd tell people to get a move on." She looked at him quizzically.

He laughed. "Well, the stars are, like, light-years away and live for billions of years, right?"

"Yeah," Claire said, smiling up at them as she listened.

"Well, I think they live across space and time too, and so they see everything that has been and will be, maybe even play a part in the game plan . . . *I* think . . . if stars could talk?—they would be telling people everywhere to get a move on, to stop overthinking, to shoot for the stars . . . because they've been sitting for millions of years in anticipation for it to happen."

Claire lay in deep contemplation and awe of this thought process. When she spoke, she said, "Adam Miller . . . I didn't know you were so philosophical."

"Me neither," he responded. They both fell into a fit of giggles.

"Why do things seem so much funnier when you're lying on your back?" Claire asked through her laughter.

"No idea," he said, still chuckling.

They succumbed to silence once again, and Claire felt content and happy with the world. She also felt a bit of the tension and excitement coursing through her that comes with being in such close proximity to someone you feel so partial to—a "crush," Claire decided, not being quite the right word. They seemed to cover all the topics there were, scattered with bouts of silence.

"I guess I should get you home," Adam said after a while with a sigh.

"Yeah . . . I suppose."

He got up and helped Claire to her feet. They walked slowly to Claire's house, Claire wanting so badly to tell Adam all the thoughts that had been running through her mind for so long, but the words kept getting stuck somewhere in her throat. They made it to the trellis and paused before Claire finally said, "Well . . . good night. I hope you can get some sleep now."

"Thanks," he said, looking slightly pale and unfocused.

"Bye," she said, grabbing the trellis and making to climb up.

"Claire, wait," Adam blurted out. She stepped back down, looking at him, her nerves giving her goose bumps.

"Claire . . . I um . . ." He ran his hand through his hair and filled his cheeks with air before releasing it all slowly. He looked at her, and her sweet face of concern and support egged him on. "Claire . . . I . . . I've been wanting to tell you this for a while and just never had the guts to. The truth is, wanting to talk to you was what was keeping me up tonight. It has been for a while now . . . I wanted to at Ron's a few weeks back . . . I finally built up the courage and decided, before I lost it, to just come right over here and get you tonight. The point of me having you come out was so that I could tell you . . . tell you . . ."

"Tell me what?" Claire said. It was gentle and not at all containing any trace of the intense race her heart was beating, which she was quite proud of because it was quite a race.

Another run through his hair. "Claire, I'm sorry I led you on at that party last year, and I'm sorry I didn't tell you I had a girlfriend that night, and that you had to find out the way you did—"

"Adam, we talked about that a while ago. It's no—"

He butted in, "No, please, just . . . just hear me out. The truth is . . . I *was* leading you on that night . . . but not on purpose. You took me completely by surprise, Claire. We'd talked before, and I thought you were beautiful inside and out and a great friend with a sweet taste in music . . . but that night, you hit me like a . . . like a ton of bricks, and I didn't even realize what was happening."

He took a deep breath and plowed on. "Our conversation, the ease in which we talked, the fun we had sharing the booze, the adrenaline when running from the cops with you, hearing you laugh, talking about our future dreams, and sharing secrets . . . Claire, I'd never talked to anyone like that before in my life. I had certainly never talked to Rachel that way. So . . . don't you see? I *was* leading you on, Claire, because I was falling for you. Hard and fast. Like, really fast. And I didn't know what to do with it. It terrified me, actually. You completely confused me, and I've been pretty much confused ever since."

Claire's eyes grew round and big as he spoke, and he hoped that was a good sign. He quavered a bit, but he had told himself he was coming here to say all this, and so he was going to get it out. "I was seriously considering breaking up with Rachel that day when you found out about her. I hated how rude she was to you, and the hurt in your eyes when you left the room killed me. I paced all night that night, trying to tell myself that I was being ridiculous, that Rachel and I had been together too long to just throw that away over a low point in our relationship for a girl I hardly knew. And that part of my brain, that stupid, stupid part of my brain, won.

"I thought you hated me anyway. Then, with the start of the new school year, you were dating Mark, and I pushed any thoughts of you aside and just focused on Rachel and I . . . I figured you hadn't felt what I was feeling, and so I tried to let it go . . . but I couldn't, Claire. I couldn't. I still thought of you. My heart raced every time you walked into band, or when you came up to me to give me a cassette or to just talk. I especially had a difficult time watching you play piano or hearing you sing. I've never met anyone with such passion as you. It was so amazing to witness, and it hit every nerve in my body. I struggled to not blurt out how I was feeling right there and then. It was maddening. Because, the whole time, I didn't know what you were thinking, and I just kept convincing myself it was nothing.

"I was pumped when you broke up with Mark, the amount of which startled me. I took some time to think about it all, enjoying every second of our practice and study halls together. I had to be tactful and think of Rachel too. And then . . . at prom . . . I don't think I've ever wanted to do someone in as much as I did Rick . . . And everything in me just finally came to a head. I'd had enough. And I realized that whether you liked me or not, my relationship with Rachel was clearly not right . . .

"And so, I say all this to tell you . . . to tell you that I like you, Claire. So much. And I've liked you for a while. From the moment I almost ran you over in the street . . . the party, the playground, our last dance at prom . . . I've been holding it all back, and . . . and I just really like you." He ended, out of breath, not even realizing how shallow he had been breathing the entire time or how much he had just rattled off. Once he had started, there was no stopping, and now he stood, the silence terrifying him.

Claire stared at his face, which at this point looked both relieved and riddled with anxiety in anticipation for what she would say. Her heart was beating at an incredible rate, her face flushed. She felt that if she were to talk, she would cry or squeal or something absolutely ridiculous. So she did the only thing she could . . . something she'd secretly thought about doing many times.

She threw her arms around him and kissed him. He was shocked at first, but recovered quickly and kissed her back. His arms wrapped around her, feeling like a cozy afghan on a chilly fall night. He tasted of mint and just a hint of sweet tobacco. His lips were so soft and gentle. Claire felt her legs weaken, and she leaned back on the trellis, pulling him with her. She'd never felt this before. This was sheer ecstasy. This was every goose bump you would ever have appearing at once. This was the stars and the moon all mixed into one cocktail of magic. They kissed long and hard, with a passion Claire didn't think she possessed. Her heart was in her throat, and her breathing was coming harder and harder.

They pulled apart slowly, coming to rest their foreheads together, keeping their eyes closed, gasping ever so slightly. Neither of them spoke for seconds, minutes, or a whole decade, for all they knew. Claire was lost in euphoria. She could smell that crisp cologne. Adam was wrestling with his urges and desire to keep going, completely intoxicated by her surprise kiss, the sweet scent of her hair, and her innate passion, the same passion he'd seen her pour into her music and piano. Her passion was one of the reasons he liked her so much, and feeling it directed toward him was almost more than he could bear. The feeling of her in his arms, touching her back, and her hair tangling in his fingers was sheer bliss.

"Can I see you tomorrow?" he whispered, not breaking their stance, eyes still closed as they both soaked up the moment.

She felt his words brush against her face, sending a chill through her body. "Yeah," was all she managed.

Adam was the first to break away. "You should probably get back up to bed."

Claire nodded. It was the last thing she wanted to do though. Adam pulled her into a tight hug, and she nestled into his neck. "I'll call you, okay?" She felt his words vibrate against her. She nodded again, and after a moment, pulled away, grabbed his face in her hands, gave him a final kiss, and then ascended up the trellis. She looked down at him from her room, and he gave her that two-fingered salute she'd become accustomed to accompanied by the shittiest grin she'd ever seen. She laughed, quickly covering her mouth, realizing she was supposed to be sneaking in, gave a wave, watched him walk away, and crawled into bed, having no idea how she was ever going to get to sleep now, not that she needed to . . . because Sam was sitting up, anxiously awaiting a full report.

JUNIOR YEAR

1997-1998

"Okay . . . tell it to me again. Slower this time."

"I've told it to you a thousand times."

"I know, but I want to hear it again."

Sam and Claire were lying on Claire's bed, heads together, staring at the ceiling. Neither of them had slept after Claire had returned from her eventful evening with Adam, and they were now in a catatonic state, filled with exhaustion but still discussing everything that had occurred. They took a break at some point to eat their weight in cereal before returning to Claire's bed and becoming potatoes, dead to the world.

"When do you think he'll call?" Claire asked, ignoring Sam's request to repeat the story.

"I don't know. But I bet he's pacing his room wondering when the sweet spot to call *is*. You know, not wanting to sound desperate, but not wanting to push it so it seems like he doesn't care."

"I wish he just would. That sounds like an awful lot of thinking to just call someone."

"But that's what we teens do, Miss I'm-an-old-lady-in-a-young-person's-body."

Troy knocked and peeked his head into the room. "Hey, goobers. Sam has to go home."

Sam sighed.

"You want a ride?" he asked.

"Nah. Thanks, Troy."

Sam groaned as Troy closed the door. "Make sure you call me if Adam does call, and tell me what he says."

Claire gave the thumbs up in her exhaustion. She heard the click of her door, only to see it fly open once again.

"Jesus, Troy, you scared me," she said.

He leaned on the doorframe. "You look like you got hit by a bus."

"Yeah, well, you look like a dweeb. What's new."

Troy cocked an eyebrow.

"Sam and I just pulled an all-nighter is all. Watched movies and drank too much root beer."

"I see," Troy said, arms folded. "Or . . . you snuck out to meet that Adam kid and didn't come back in till four o'clock in the morning."

Claire started patting herself and looking down at the baggy sweatshirt she was wearing.

"What are you doing?" Troy asked, confused.

"Looking for the camera you apparently have attached to me."

"I heard you go down the trellis, Mouse. You're not the most graceful on that thing. Honestly. You'd be better off just taking the front door."

Claire threw herself back on her bed, having no energy to deal with Troy. Within moments of the door clicking closed once again, she fell asleep, only to be woken an hour later by her mother, phone in hand.

"Claire, hunny, the phone's for you," she said.

Claire's eyes snapped open. She quickly wiped the drool off her face and grabbed the phone, thankful that phones were for talking and not seeing. She waited for her mom to leave before saying, "Hello?"

"Hey."

Claire released the breath she didn't realize she'd been holding. "Hey." She smiled into the receiver.

"What are you up to?" Adam asked.

"Napping mostly." Claire chuckled.

"Whoa! Crazy girl," he joked.

"I know, right? But . . . a certain someone kept me out till all hours of the night, and I couldn't sleep when I got back in."

She loved that she could hear his smile. "I couldn't either. That's, um . . . kind of why I'm calling."

"Oh?" she asked, curious.

"I wanted to see you again and didn't know if you were free this afternoon. I just got off work."

Claire's face brightened. "Yeah! I'm totally free. I'd love to hang out!" She then thought of what Sam had said about the sweet spot of desperation and hoped she didn't sound like a lunatic.

"Great! I know it's past lunch, but I haven't eaten yet. What would you say to burgers and a round of mini golf at Sid's?"

"Sounds perfect."

"Pick you up in thirty minutes?"

"Yeah!"

"See you then."

They hung up. Claire sat in shock for a moment and then squealed before jumping up to get herself looking presentable, yelling to her mom to let her know what was going on. Thirty minutes later, Claire heard a knock on the front door as she looked over herself in the mirror. It was a warm day today, so she had on a basic white T-shirt and had put a scrunchy on her wrist in case she wanted to tie her hair back. She grabbed some cash that she had in her side table and stuck it in the back pocket of her jeans as she hurried down the stairs to the kitchen.

Adam was in the entryway, and her mom had beaten her to him.

"And how did the eye heal up?" she heard her ask.

Claire groaned as she looked for her Converse sneakers in the mud room that led to their side porch.

"Good! All cleared up now. It wasn't so bad," Adam said.

"Well . . . I'm glad. It was very nice of you to take Claire home that night. We thank you very much."

"Of course. No problem at all, Mrs. Hanover."

Claire frantically tried to find the missing right shoe.

"You're the one that plays the drums at the band concerts, right?"

"Yeah! That's me." Adam smiled.

"Very talented," Claire's mother said, returning the smile.

Claire finally put hands on both shoes and went through the living room to the front door.

"Ready!" she said.

"Well, you two have fun!" her mother said, Claire already opening the door to head out.

"Bye, Mom!" she said.

"Bye, Mrs. Hanover. Nice to meet you," Adam called over his shoulder as Claire led him out by the arm.

"Sorry about that." Claire sighed as they walked through the front gate.

"Not at all! Your mom is very nice. Offered me a cookie when I walked in. I told her I didn't want to spoil my lunch," he said, grinning.

Claire let go of him, shaking her head but smiling as they got to his car. She got in the passenger's side as he went around to the driver's, getting in and starting it up. The radio was blasting, but Adam turned it down.

"Sorry," he said sheepishly.

"Don't say sorry! Although, I hope you weren't rocking out to those auto parts commercials on your way here."

Adam laughed, putting the car into drive. "No. I promise. It was something much more worthy."

They turned off Main Street and onto the main route that would take them out to Sid's. Sid's was really called The Mini Swings Golf and BBQ, but absolutely no one in the area called it that. Sid had been the original owner and a personable guy in town back in the day. Though it had gone through many a different owners since, the locals still called it Sid's, and Sid's it would always be.

Claire adjusted the radio so she could hear it and started rolling through channels till she found something to stop on. Adam smirked at how comfortable she already seemed to be with him and being in his car. It was a simple act, but it said a lot to him. She stopped when she heard a commercial transition to the voice of Steven Tyler speaking the opening sultry lines of Aerosmith's "Crazy."

"Ah, I love this song!" Claire said, turning the radio up as high as she could bear and putting her window down, letting the wind of their speed blow her hair around as she sang along loudly, knowing that no one could hear her over the music. Adam hit the gas and they sped forward, Claire feeling the rev of the engine vibrate throughout the car and letting out a burst of laughter. Maybe it was the lack of sleep or the euphoria that was being with Adam Miller, but Claire felt light as a feather, like she could fly away. When the chorus came, Adam joined in, and they were both scream-singing along to the bluesy seductive song.

By the time they pulled into Sid's, they were both chuckling, having sung their way through multiple songs. Turning down the radio, Claire attempted to brush her hair with her fingers a little before getting out.

"I probably look crazy," she said as she got out of the car, looking into the window's reflection to check.

"You look beautiful," Adam said simply.

Claire blushed as she started walking across the dirt parking lot, but Adam grabbed her elbow before she could get far.

She turned and he pulled her to him. Placing his hands so they cradled her face, he kissed her. She brought her arms up to hold on to his and returned the gesture, her acceptance giving him permission to wrap his arms around her and kiss her harder. It was just as sweet and intoxicating as the night before. She hugged his waist and felt herself get lost in the warmth and comfort that was him.

When he pulled away, his grin spread wide across his face. Still embracing, he looked down at her and said, "I wanted to make sure I wasn't just dreaming last night up."

"And what conclusion did you come to?" Claire asked, a little hazy.

"Definitely not a dream. But sure does feel like one."

"Maybe I should pinch you." Claire chuckled.

He laughed, then kissed her on the nose, and they released their hold and walked toward the food stand, hands entwined. Claire couldn't put words to how right and comfortable everything about Adam felt. And how fast it had seemed to feel that way. It startled her at first, but she reminded herself that they *had* spent the last two years hanging out after school and during class and so had gotten past the whole getting-to-know-you phase. Not to mention their sharing of songs giving incredibly deep insight to each other. Claire decided to not even concern herself with it and just enjoy the feeling.

"Two cheeseburgers, a large fry, and two cokes," Adam said to the worker behind the counter, and they stepped aside to wait for the food.

"So, I know your mad skills on the piano. How are they at mini golf?" Adam asked.

"Not at all comparable." Claire chuckled. "And yours, drummer boy?"

He smirked. "Not going to lie, I'm not too bad at the ole mini golf."

"Well then, we shall have to see." Their food was called, and they found an open picnic table to sit at. They recognized a few people from school enjoying their own start to summer break, one of them being a fellow band member. Claire couldn't help but wonder what they thought of seeing her and Adam out together.

"So, are you going for your driver's license soon? You said you were waiting for summer, right?"

"Yeah! I have an appointment for next week. I slacked all winter and didn't get any practice driving in, but I'm good now."

"Awesome. How do you feel about it?"

"Pretty good," Claire said uncertainly, taking a bite of her burger.

"I'm sure you'll do great."

"Thanks."

"Any idea where you want to apply for a summer job?" he asked, reaching for fries.

"I would love to have a job on Main Street so I could just walk to work. I asked Gwen to see if the music store would hire me for anything."

"That would be an awesome gig for you!"

"I know, right? If not, I was going to go see if the bakery was hiring. Mrs. Leonard likes me, so maybe she'll hire me." She smiled.

"Hook me up with free donuts if you do?" Adam winked.

"You bet."

They finished eating and proceeded to the golf hut. Adam paid for their game, and they received their putters and picked their balls, Claire's pink and Adam's orange.

"Alright, let's see it," Claire said. "Master golfer Adam Miller."

Adam smirked. "But ladies are supposed to go first."

"Pfft . . . please."

He laughed, placed his ball, took a moment to set himself up, and hit it, getting a hole in one.

"Well, shit," Claire said. "Looks like I'm the Fitz in this scenario."

They both chuckled and their game ensued. Claire did better than she could have possibly hoped for but lost by a landslide to Adam. He offered pointers a couple times, helping her position her hands and feet, and it helped a tad. It was still to no avail. But playing the game was worth more than the points they earned combined, and when they returned their equipment and headed toward Adam's car, it was with an air of disappointment that the day was already ending. Adam pulled up to Claire's house, and she paused before getting out, partly to say goodbye and partly because she really didn't *want* to get out.

"Thanks for this. I had a really good time," she said.

"My pleasure. Me too," he responded, adjusting himself so he was facing Claire.

"I, um . . . . I hope we can hang out again soon?" she said.

"Yes!" Adam said quickly, and then rather sheepishly, "Sorry. Yeah. I would love to."

She smiled.

"Claire, I . . ." He sat back in his seat and stared through the windshield, gathering his thoughts for a moment. "Claire, I know I said a bunch of stuff last night. I hope I didn't overwhelm you with it all. It just sort of fell out. But it was all true, and I hope . . . I hope I got *something* across. I don't one hundred percent have words for it all, but I just want you to know that I feel so different when I'm around you. I've been thinking of you constantly since last night and wanted nothing more than to see you again as soon as I could." He faltered for a moment before continuing on. "I don't want to fuck this up. It's literally not been twenty-four hours, and the idea of that already scares the shit out of me. I don't want to rush this. Or put pressure on it. I just—I—"

Claire grabbed his chin in her hand and gave his cheeks a squeeze. "You have nothing to worry about. I agree. We take it slow."

He smiled through his somewhat squished face, making them both laugh. She released him and they leaned in, lips gently playing against each other. She definitely couldn't get enough of this. It made her stomach twirl with giddiness and her heart race with excitement. The radio played "Crash Into Me," and they simultaneously smiled through their kissing, the intensity building. Adam's hand reached up, lacing his fingers in her hair, and Claire found herself weakened, sighing against his soft mouth.

Once again, he broke them apart first, but this time with a face of absolute torment at having done so. He wouldn't tell Claire, but he was dealing with a struggle he'd never dealt with before, and he had to keep himself in check, her sigh throwing him off completely. He was telling her just as much as himself to take it slow because of this. She was quite literally driving him crazy, and he had absolutely no idea how to handle it.

"I think . . ." he said. "I think I should get you inside."

Claire nodded but not before she snuck another quick peck that made him grin.

They got out of the car, and he followed her up the path, stopping at the bottom of the stairs.

"Call me?" she said, hand on the doorknob.

CRAZY

"You bet." He saluted.

She smiled and went inside, closing the door softly behind her and sighing, leaning against it for a moment.

Adam slowly walked back to his car, making the decision to go to his favorite spot on the lake to have a smoke. He frequented it when he didn't feel like going home and didn't have anywhere else to be. It was a good place to collect his thoughts and be alone, which he really needed to do at the moment. He thought Claire Hanover had messed with his mind already just by being her. But now that all this was unfolding, he realized that she had barely scratched the surface of messing with his mind. Before, just the idea of her—her passion for music, her laughter and smile, her care, attention, and empathy to others, her smarts—had been enough to make him question his entire being and relationship with Rachel.

But now? Now he had the experience of kissing her, feeling her smooth lips on his. He knew what her hair felt like between his fingers. He could look into her eyes with deep passion and see it reflected back. He could call forth little nuances like her sticking her tongue out of the corner of her mouth while concentrating on hitting a golf ball, and missing, or how she couldn't stand commercials and constantly changed the station on the radio. Now he had all this to keep him up at night and consume his every thought. They were no longer daydreams but experiences that his mind could relive and struggle to turn off. He thought she'd made him fall hard before, but she'd somehow made him fall even harder, and those feelings were . . . a lot.

He made it to Thompson Point Lake, parked, and walked down the familiar path he'd worn down himself to an opening in the tree line where a part of the land jutted out and he could see the entirety of the water's edge of the small lake. Adam lit up a cigarette and sat there on the grass. The water was still, the trees reflected in it, the warm summer breeze lifting his hair ever so slightly. He thought about how he should take Claire here sometime to watch the sunset or maybe the sunrise, whichever she'd prefer. He made a mental note to ask her. He imagined sitting cozied up with a blanket, just she and him, and maybe some music. He smiled at the idea of it. He sighed. If he thought the lake was going to help calm the intense feelings he was having for Claire, he was absolutely wrong.

Claire went to her room to compose herself before heading down to dinner, which she was informed on her way through was only a half hour away. She paced her room, shaking her hands instinctively, trying to get the pent-up energy from the day to go away. She didn't know what to do with these feelings. Was this what it felt like to like someone? Like really like someone?

Troy butted his head in.

"Hey, Mouse," he said.

"Hey," she said, stopping her pacing and looking at him.

"Sam called a bunch of times while you were out," he said.

"Shit. Yeah I was supposed to tell her if Adam called and . . ." She trailed off, realizing Troy didn't need to know the intricacies of her and Sam's friendship and bizarre need to share every detail, or how much of a big deal Adam was.

"Also, you owe me," he added.

"Why? For taking Sam's calls? She always calls."

"Um, no. For distracting Mom from watering her plants in the front window so she wouldn't see you swapping spit with Adam."

Claire threw a pillow at him.

"What?! Just speaking the truth, little sis!" he said, closing the door on himself to stop the pillow from hitting him.

CRAZY

"Shut up, Troy," she shouted through the door.

He poked his head back in. "You really like him, don't you?"

She squinted at him, raising an eyebrow. "Yeah." She sighed. "Yeah, I do."

"Welcome to the Never-sleep-again-and-question-your-every-waking-hour club."

Claire sat. "Is this what it felt like when you started dating Gwen?"

"Like you could puke and shout for joy at the same time?" Troy came into her room.

"Yeah." She laughed lightly.

"Pretty much."

"Does it go away?"

"Hopefully not."

She looked at him quizzically.

"Come on, Mouse. That's the excitement! The thrill. That's how you know they're the perfect one. They make you feel like that every day for all time."

She smiled. "I guess that makes sense."

"But don't worry about that now. Just have fun. He seems like a nice guy. Maybe you, me, Gwen, and him can all go out sometime."

"I'd like that," she said, definitely wanting Gwen to meet Adam.

"Cool. Well, let me know." He made to leave. "Now call Sam before she freaks even more than she already has."

"You were supposed to call me! I've been sitting over here like a loser waiting for the phone to ring!"

"I know, I'm sorry. I fell asleep, and the next thing I knew, my mom was waking me up, he was on the phone, and I had thirty minutes to get ready!"

"Okay, okay. I'll let it pass this time. So what happened?!"

Claire relayed the afternoon's events after a rushed dinner. She told Sam of Adam picking her up and singing in the car, his surprise kiss in the parking lot, their game of golf, and their goodbye make-out session in the car. Sam squealed and laughed with giddiness the entire time, asked her to repeat it all over again, and then proceeded to ask more detailed questions.

"Like, what does it even feel like to French kiss someone?"

"Sam!" Claire blushed.

"What?! It's not like I know! How do you know what to do?"

Claire threw herself down on her bed. "Oh, I don't know. You just do it, I guess. Oh God, do you think I'm doing it wrong? I never thought about that."

"Um, no. You would not have that boy craving for more if you were bad at it."

Claire rolled her eyes.

"I heard that! I heard that eye roll."

"Well, you're saying ridiculous things," she said. "This isn't like how it was with Mark. It feels so . . . so comfortable and nice and sweet and not awkward in the slightest. Like, I just wanted more, and I wasn't thinking about where my hands were or my breath or if he was enjoying it or if it was what I was supposed to be doing. I don't know. I just . . ."

Sam sighed.

Claire laughed. "I don't know what I'm saying, I guess."

"This is all so adorable and amazing," Sam said excitedly. "When are you seeing him next?"

"I don't know. But I hope soon."

"Well, keep me posted. I have a family dinner thing tonight, but I'm free tomorrow. Let me know what you want to do!"

"Will do," Claire said before hanging up.

Claire found herself having a difficult time focusing on anything all night and all the next day. She kept thinking back to her night at the playground with Adam and now their first outing. She wasn't sure if she should call it a date yet. It felt like a date. Whenever she did think back, she would feel her heart flutter, her body get warm, and her stomach do a little somersault. She felt like she was going crazy. She found herself randomly smiling or laughing to release the pent-up giddiness.

That morning, Gwen had come over to pick up Troy to take him to work, his car being on the mend again. She sought Claire out when she was sitting on the couch trying to distract her mind.

"Hey you," Gwen said.

"Hey!" Claire said, turning the TV volume down. "What's up?"

"I talked to Martin, the shop owner? He says he doesn't have an opening, unfortunately. But I remembered what you said about the bakery. I went to school with Mrs. Leonard's oldest son. I told her you were looking, and she instantly got excited, having known you since you were small, according to her."

"Yeah! I go to school with her youngest son. We've been in the same class since, like, kindergarten."

"That's what she said! And she's all ready for you to go in and talk to her and fill out an application."

Claire sat up. "No way! Really?"

"Yes, ma'am!"

"Sweet! Thanks, Gwen!"

"No problem!" She then sat down next to Claire. "And, um, Troy tells me there is maybe a potential new guy?"

Claire couldn't stop the grin from spreading across her face.

"Ooh, girl," Gwen said. "He must be something special to deserve that look."

Claire chuckled. "He's pretty awesome."

"It's Adam, right? The one you've talked about before?"

"Yup. Adam Miller."

"Tell me more!" Gwen asked, settling back.

"He's really cute. Loves music. We've actually been doing this cassette exchange thing for the past two years. He plays drums. Is super sweet and thoughtful. He's kind of a dork with computers and stuff. Has fun friends. And is sometimes a loner, the deep thinker kind, who sometimes smokes."

"Damn," Gwen said, fanning herself.

Claire laughed. "We've been friends for a bit now through band and stuff. I kind of, maybe, have had a crush on him for, like, since I met him. And I guess he has too."

"Sounds perfect." Gwen smiled.

"Certainly feels that way," Claire said.

"Well, lap it up and enjoy every second of it," Gwen said. "And don't drive yourself too crazy."

Claire groaned. "Too late."

Gwen chuckled. "Hey, we've all been there. The start of a relationship is always hellish but worth every second of the anxiety-inducing madness." She patted Claire on the knee before getting up. "I gotta bounce, but I'll see you soon, I'm sure. Make sure you go talk to Mrs. Leonard as soon as possible."

"Sounds good! I'll go today. Give me something to do."

At 2:00, Claire walked down to the bakery. She was going to call Sam to see if she wanted to go, but for some reason, she wanted some alone time after all the recent excitement. She felt a walk to Main Street by herself would give her time to unwind and reflect. She had also decided she would call Adam after she got back to tell him about her job and maybe see how he felt about a double date with Troy and Gwen. She figured he shouldn't always be the one to initiate the phone calls.

Entering the bakery, the smell of blueberry with a lemony edge engulfed her senses, and she decided that working here would definitely have its perks. Mrs. Leonard was at the front, filling a glass case from behind the counter with fresh treats.

"Claire!" she said, looking up at the sound of the bell. "I was wondering when I'd see you. Come on in. Let me just finish putting these in, and we'll go in the back to talk."

"Sure thing!" Claire looked around and saw that the bakery had gone through a few changes since she'd last been in it, which, now that she thought of it, had been a surprisingly longer time than usual. She'd frequented the place all through fall and the holiday season, but she guessed it had dropped off come the wintery months, when she didn't feel like walking much, and the rainy times that kept her inside.

One wall where an empty counter had once stood, which had been mostly used for customers to take pause and mix their coffee, now had a rustic wooden shelving unit with antique crates holding what appeared to be pre-bundled specialty teas. The old bulky square tables that had been mismatched from a diner that had closed in town had been replaced by smaller ones with wrought iron chairs, two per table. The shop that had never been a place designed for people to come in and sit down, but more to pick up a coffee and a sweet treat and go, was now a great place to chill. Dried flowers hung from the ceiling, and the bay window in the front, which had always held a simple display, now had a bench seat in it, whose underneath was lined with books. A small sign read, "Take a book, leave a book."

Claire liked the changes. It felt homier and yet sophisticated, the kind of place she'd love to read in or bring her school work to. The possibility of working here seemed all the more exciting now.

"Alright, this way," came Mrs. Leonard's voice as she smiled over at her from behind the counter. Claire followed, and the smell only intensified as she went through the kitchen to a back office.

"Okay, so Gwen mentioned you wanted a job? She's so sweet. Went to school with my Rodney."

"Yeah, Gwen's great! She's dating my brother. And, yes, I'm looking for a job to work this summer and then to hopefully keep when school starts if it can work around my schedule."

"Well, I would love to have you work here. I'm actually losing a girl, Janie, who's heading off to college this fall. She's going across the country and has an apartment and new job all set up for the summer leading up to school! She leaves in two weeks. I was going to hold off on hiring to try and save some money. You may have noticed we did some revamping here. But it is too much for just me and the one other I have working here, so I decided to get someone now. Perfect timing!" She ended with a hearty laugh.

"I love the changes you made! It's so cozy."

"Thanks! It was my worker's ideas, actually—Carol. She said with the college nearby and more urban-style stuff popping up on Main Street, the place needed a cooler vibe. Whatever that means. I guess more like a coffee shop with specialty drinks and treats and occasional poetry nights. So we gave the place a quieter atmosphere with more places for people to come read or do work. We started doing teas and even have more flavors of coffee!"

"I love it! Very cool," Claire offered.

"Thanks, dear. So, what are you looking for in a job?"

"I'm looking for whatever I can get, really. I'll work anything for the summer, but once school starts, I will need to cut down to only, like, twenty hours a week. I was also hoping for something with somewhat of a concrete schedule but know that that doesn't always happen."

"I think that's doable. Carol is trained in the kitchen, and that's where I need a lot of the help, so I think I'll just train you on running the counter and storefront. Does that sound good?"

"Sounds great!" Claire beamed.

"Oh, wonderful. I can start you next Monday. Janie leaves us that following weekend, so that would give us a week of training and then some time to actually work together in case you have questions that come up."

"Okay! Monday works," Claire said.

"Perfect! Here is some paperwork you can take home and fill out. Bring it back to me by this Friday, and I'll get you all set up for payroll and everything."

"Will do!" Claire said, grabbing the packet. "Thank you so much, Mrs. Leonard."

"Oh, my pleasure. I'm glad it was you. My boys never want to work here. I'm happy to be able to have someone I know!"

Claire smiled and let herself out through the kitchen and out the front door. She breathed in that fresh scent of summer, feeling the sun's rays on her skin. She sighed and walked back home, her mother being the first to talk to her when she got there.

"Adam called," she said.

Claire felt the rush of adrenaline and excitement enter her stomach as she grabbed the cordless and went upstairs, dialing his number, ignoring her mother's comment of him seeming like a really nice boy.

His dad answered but quickly handed it off when she asked for him.

"Hi! My mom said you called," she said.

"Yeah. I just wanted to say hi, I guess," he said, a little embarrassed.

"I'm glad you did. I was actually going to call you myself when I got home this afternoon," she said, hoping to alleviate any anxiety he may have had at calling her too many times.

"Yeah?" he said. It had done the trick.

"Yeah! Guess where I went today?"

"Hmmm," Adam said. Claire could hear his calm tone even though she couldn't see that he had just lain back in bed, looking up at the ceiling with a grin. "Shopping with Sam?"

"That's a solid guess, but no." She chuckled. "I went to the bakery and nailed myself a job!"

"No way! That's awesome, Claire," he said. He sounded so genuine when he talked that Claire couldn't help but swell with pride. "When do you start?"

"Thanks! Next Monday," she said.

"I guess we need to squeeze in some fun, then, before we're both tied up with work. Do you know the hours you'll be working?"

She felt her heart skip at him wanting to ensure they saw each other more. "I'm not sure yet, but it sounded like she was going to be able to keep my schedule pretty consistent, so that should be easy to plan around."

"Yeah, that's always nice. I wish RadioShack was like that. My hours change constantly. And they're going up now that summer is here. Hopefully, our schedules don't clash too bad and we can still do some stuff. If you want to, of course. Maybe we can go to the beach, or just, you know, ride around. I know a lot of cool spots that aren't so overcrowded."

"Of course I do. And would love all of that."

"Obviously, Sam is invited. Would be fun to get a group to go to the beach."

"Definitely!" Claire said, having a difficult time concealing her excitement at all these plans.

"Well, I'm glad I called. This just made my entire day, Claire," he said. "I look forward to all of it."

"Me too. Maybe, if our schedules are a bit tight, I could visit you at RadioShack when Sam and I go to the mall?"

"Yeah! I'd love that." He couldn't contain the grin that spread across his face. Imagining Claire—beautiful, smart, sweet, and funny Claire—coming to see him at work, all his work buddies getting to meet her . . . made him more than happy.

"And you're always welcome at the bakery. I'll sneak you something sweet," she said with a smile.

Adam thought that her kiss was the only "something sweet" he'd like her to sneak but quickly shook his head and said, "You bet. Sounds like a good plan."

"Oh, um," Claire began, remembering something else. She hadn't expected to be nervous to ask Adam this, but now that she was, she realized how serious it may seem to ask a boy out on a double date, especially when the other couple included her brother. "I was wondering if you would be at all interested in maybe going out sometime with my brother and his girlfriend."

"Sure!" Adam responded. "That sounds cool. When?"

"When are you open?"

"Let me look." She heard rummaging around and then, "I'm free Friday night, actually. I get out at three."

"I'll check with Troy later and let you know!"

"Sweet," he said. Adam was a mixture of nerves and excitement at the fact that Claire even wanted him to meet her brother and the fact that he now had to *meet* Claire's older brother. He hoped Troy was just as easygoing as Claire, scared of horror stories he'd heard before of protective older brothers.

As if she sensed his anxiety, Claire said, "And Troy is pretty chill. He's kind of a big goober. Gwen keeps him in check."

"Can't wait to meet them."

There was a brief pause of silence, both of them refraining from saying what was on their mind, until Adam gave in. "I know I just saw you yesterday, but . . . I miss you."

Claire was stunned at the simple and yet incredibly deep words. "I . . . I miss you too."

They shared in the silence that followed, breathing it in and feeling its weight.

"Talk to you tomorrow?" Adam spoke quietly.

"Yes. Tomorrow." They hung up, and Claire didn't squeal or feel the need to pace and shake out her energy. She felt at ease, content. She felt incredibly happy. His telling her he missed her made her feel like everything had just become *more* somehow. She didn't know why, but she knew that she did miss him. One hundred percent. She had wanted to see him that day. Not to necessarily play golf or go to the beach or do anything at all. But just be with him. She realized that was the reason behind all her nerves and anxiety earlier. She wanted to hold his hand, feel his kiss, laugh together. Talk. She had been anxious out of an antsy desire to see him. It suddenly dawned on her that that had been the premise behind her crush on him from the get-go. Didn't she rush to band so she could see him, swap cassettes, and enjoy that hour they had together where they could spend time bonding over a joint passion? Didn't she go out of her way to stay after when he did so they could chat? Hadn't she been overwhelmed with joy when she had learned that he was going to share her study hall this past year and bummed at the times when he didn't show? She'd been enjoying his presence for two years, and now that it had been made perfectly clear that he had been too, and in fact missed her when he didn't get to, made her feel like this was big.

Later that evening she went and knocked on Troy's door, opening it on his pigsty of a room. Clothes littered the floor, and bikini clad girls littered the walls. Troy was lying on his bed, looking at a brochure that he quickly tucked away when she entered.

"What's up, Mouse?" he said.

"I just talked to Adam. He's free Friday night. You and Gwen around?"

"Oh! I think so. May have to be later though because I think I work till seven."

"That's fine. We could meet at Ron's after you get off?"

"Should be cool. I'll double-check with Gwen."

"Sweet," she said, pausing and looking around. "You ever going to learn how to pick up after yourself?"

"What? There's nothing wrong with this room."

"Ugh. You disgust me sometimes," she said, leaving his room, making a mental note to snoop out what that brochure was.

In a happy coincidence, Gwen ended up being available Friday too. But before that eventful night could arrive, Claire had to deal with an angry Sam. The day after Claire got her job at the bakery, Sam called her mid-morning.

"Dude. What the hell! I thought we were going to hang out yesterday!" Sam said after Troy had handed off the phone.

"Sorry, Sam. It just got busy. Gwen came over and told me to go talk to Mrs. Leonard about a possible job at the bakery. So I went and—"

"I could've walked down with you!" Sam interjected.

"I know. I guess I just wanted to do something on my own. It was a possible job interview. And I got the—"

"Well, why didn't you call me after?!" Sam butted in.

"Sam, I—" Claire started to get a little annoyed. "I don't know, okay? It just got away from me. I was feeling all weird and anxious most of the day, and I needed a distraction, which Gwen gave me, so I snatched it and went for a walk. Adam called later, and then I waited for Troy to get home so I could ask him about Friday night, and I don't know! I haven't slept much since you were here last, and so I've been just feeling off. It wasn't on purpose, okay? And, not that you care apparently, but I got the job at the bakery. I start next week."

There was a pause. "Of course I care. But I wish you would've called. I was waiting most of the day, bored out of my mind."

"You could have called *me*, you know!"

"I'm always the one that calls! You suddenly have a boyfriend, and now a job, and you can't be bothered to give me a ring?"

Claire groaned. "Sam! I don't have a boyfriend. Adam and I are just taking this slow and seeing what happens. It'd be nice if you actually listened to me! It was a stressful day, okay? I just needed some alone time to sort it all out."

"Oh, excuse me if I don't have sympathy for the girl who's getting swept off her feet, making out with a cute upperclassman who is head over heels for her, and whose anxiety is based on when he's going to call next, and who's *not* overthinking whether or not she's hideous because no boy seems to ever want to talk to *her* and wondering if *her* friend is just going to leave her in the dust!"

There was another pause. "Sam. It has literally been a day and a half since you were at my house. One complete day of not talking. That's it. I think you're being a bit dramatic. I'm not going to leave you in the dust. I'm *trying* to tell you what's been going on—"

"Dramatic?!" Sam half shouted. "Fine! So sorry for being so *dramatic*." The phone disconnected, and Claire stared at it in disbelief. But within minutes, it rang again.

"Hello?" Claire said tentatively.

"I'm sorry . . . I'm just—"

"Why don't you just come over," Claire said hurriedly. The phone clicked again, but this time Claire knew it was due to Sam dropping everything to head her way. In mere moments, Sam was bursting through her door.

"Geesh, what'd you do: run here?" Claire asked as Sam flew into her room like a windstorm and plopped down on her bed.

"Pretty much," she said between gasps. "And . . . I realized . . . I am really out of shape."

"Sam, I'm sorry I didn't call—"

"No, I'm being a jerk," Sam said. "I let my jealousy get in the way, and I got all crazy. My mom says I need anger management."

"Well, I should have called. I just—"

"You just needed some alone time with your thoughts. I get it," Sam said, though Claire had the sneaking suspicion that this was one of those times when Sam said what she knew she *should* say and express how she *should* feel even though she didn't necessarily feel that way.

"Yeah," Claire responded, not really sure what to say.

"So! Tell me what happened! What did Adam say last? What's going on Friday night? And, hello! A job?! When did this happen? I'm so out of the loop!"

Claire sighed, happy to hear Sam's usual tone of hysteria entering her speech. She told her about her and Adam's discussion of making plans for the summer: that he wanted to go to the beach with her and Sam and some others. She told her about double dating with Troy Friday, and Adam's enthusiasm at doing so, and finally relayed how Gwen had talked to the owner of the music shop and then Mrs. Leonard when that had been a no-go. "And I start next week! She's changed the place around, and it looks pretty cool in there now!"

"Holy cow! How has all this happened in, like, one day?!"

"No idea." Claire sighed.

"So a boyfriend and a job. Whoa, dude. This is big. You're, like, an adult. The boyfriend alone will definitely make you cool this school year! Hopefully, I will be too by association. And we'll be juniors. Officially upperclassmen. And you'll have a senior boyfriend. And we'll have spent the summer at the beach with his senior friends where others will see that we have senior friends. And you'll be a working girl. Hopefully, I will be too. Which is always seen as cool, being all responsible and shit. And—"

"Sam, stop." It came out more forcefully than she intended, but this banter was exactly the reason Claire had felt the need to walk to the bakery by herself the day before.

Sam looked at her, taken aback.

"I'm sorry. But can we not make everything a popularity contest? I don't have a boyfriend yet. It isn't official, like I said on the phone. But, even if I did, I'm tired of you making it out to seem that I only have one as a means of being popular, or in Adam's case, because he's a senior and it seems cool. Yes, it'll be fun to all go out, and, sure, others may see us and it may change their opinion in some way or another, but who cares! Who. Cares. I don't! Stop making everything about being cool or popular or being seen a certain way or . . . I don't know! Just let me have this! Let me have a potential boyfriend and a job without turning it into some souped-up high school version of it!" She ended, releasing a sigh, and felt a tad embarrassed at having blown up in that manner, especially toward Sam. Clearly, her emotions were shot, but it was also true.

"O-okay . . . yeah. Of course. I'm sorry."

Claire couldn't pinpoint where, but something in Sam's affect changed.

"Sam. I know where you're coming from. I really do. High school is tough enough as it is, and then there are all these social norms that we're supposed to live by, and finding our way through it all is hard. But . . . I guess I just don't care so much about all that and have no worry in the world whatsoever if I leave high school having never been thought of as popular. So I guess when I talk about Adam or what I'm doing, I hate that it gets held to that standard. It makes me feel like you think I think I'm cool as shit, and

I don't want anyone to think that about me. I also don't want anyone, even you, thinking that I base any of my choices on the level of popularity they will bring me. I'm sorry."

Sam sighed and flung herself down on her bed. "No, you're right, Claire. That's how it *should* be. I guess I just want to feel like *somebody*, and it just hasn't happened yet. And when I see you doing all these things, I just feel like I need to say it aloud so everyone knows that I know how monumental it is, and I guess if I put words to it, then no one will think I don't realize how lame I am. Like, you know, when you call yourself out on something before other people can, because what's worse than doing something dumb is other people thinking you did something dumb and that you don't know it."

Claire looked at Sam, who was staring at the ceiling, and a new emotion came to her that she'd never had for Sam before: pity. She gingerly sat down next to Sam and saw that tears were forming in her eyes.

"Sam, you're not lame."

"Yes, I am, Claire. How is it that you've had a boyfriend already and now some kind of made-for-Disney romance going on, and I've barely had a boy talk to me? Why? Why am I so different?"

"Logan talks to you often. And why does having a boy's attention determine whether you are lame or not?" Claire asked simply.

"Because it means you're envied by someone else—you're seen as beautiful by another's eyes. And that means you're something special. Which, apparently, I'm not."

Special.

"But, Sam, *I* think you're beautiful. Not to mention that the only person that matters in seeing you as beautiful is you. If you see yourself that way, then it'll shine through you to all others."

Sam cocked an eyebrow, blinking a few tears away. "That's a nice sentiment and all, but down here, on earth, in high school, it doesn't fly."

"Well, fine. Be miserable. But I'd much rather be alone with my books and a bunch of cats for the rest of my life than with a guy to simply be able to say I'm with a guy."

Sam continued staring at the ceiling.

"You know what you need to do?" Claire asked, getting up and going over to her shelf that held her boom box and music stash, having had enough.

"What?" Sam said, disinterested.

"You need to tell me what you want," Claire said with a smile, finding the CD she was looking for and placing it in the player.

"What??" Sam asked, confused.

"You need to tell me what you want," Claire repeated slowly, turning on the power and hitting play. "What you really, *really* want."

Claire turned the volume up as the Spice Girls rent the air, throwing herself on the bed next to Sam, singing along loudly in her ear, making her shout in surprise. Sam wanted nothing to do with it, so Claire then stood and began jumping and shouting the lyrics.

"Come on, Sam!" She giggled. "Don't leave me hanging!"

Sam finally broke into a grin and got up too, jumping along and eventually singing. Claire's hair fell loosely out of her ponytail as she and Sam traded off on lines, being each other's backup and repeatedly asking each other what they really wanted. They sang till they were crying through their laughter. When it came to Mel B's rap-like solo, Claire took lead while Sam danced along. They didn't even stop when Troy opened the door and leaned on its frame with a questioning look.

"Slam! Slam! Slam! Slam!" they yelled his way. When it ended, Claire jumped down onto the floor, breathing heavily, and turned the player off, thankful for this new edition to her music collection. Sam dropped onto the bed, and Claire was glad to see the genuine smile that was planted on her face. Her sing-off had worked.

"What's up, Troy?" Claire asked, her cheeks pink and her breathing still coming in slight gasps.

He smirked. "Uh, a Mr. Adam Miller is on the phone for you."

Sam sat bolt upright, and Claire's face fell to that of panic. "Wha—He's on the phone now?" she asked, seeing it in Troy's hand, very much open to the noise and sounds that had been filling the space just moments ago.

"I didn't want to interrupt your free concert here, so we waited."

"We?!—Troy!" Claire ran at him to grab the phone, but he held it over his head, which was much higher than Claire could ever hope to reach. She tried regardless.

So he could still be heard from the phone as Claire jumped on him to try and get it, Troy yelled, "Adam, I hope you didn't mind the Spice Girls. Not what I would have picked, but it wasn't a bad rendition if I do say so myself."

Claire groaned in anger. "You're. Such. A. Jerk!" she said, breathing heavily, staring him down, as Sam tried to hold in her giggles.

"Okay, okay, okay," Troy said, lowering the phone and putting it to his ear.

"Tro—"

"Ah—" Troy held up a hand. "Adam? Hey, yeah, I hope you enjoyed, and I'll see you Friday." He handed Claire the phone, which she swiped with a glare.

She went to the bed, sat next to Sam, took a deep breath, and then held the phone so they could both hear, Troy closing the door on his way out.

"Hey! Sorry about that!" Claire said.

"No sorrys at all," Adam said, and Claire could hear the laughter in his voice. "I quite enjoyed that." He had too. Claire was such a deep-thinking and passionate soul. To hear her singing along to the Spice Girls and clearly jumping up and down on the bed, based on their jagged singing, added yet another layer to her that made Adam's heart swell that she was someone he could say liked him. Like . . . like-liked him. He added it to the mental checklist he had of all the reasons he like-liked her too.

"Well, I'm glad we could be of some entertainment. But Troy is still a jerk."

Adam laughed. "We had a nice little conversation on his way to your room before he stopped and we took in the epicness that was occurring."

"Oh God. What did he say?"

"He told me he and Gwen were good for Friday night, which is why I was calling you, actually."

"Oh! Yeah, I was waiting to hear from Gwen before I let you know. That's great!"

"Yeah. He also mentioned that he worked till seven and we could meet up after?"

"Yeah. I was just thinking Ron's again. There's the diner too though, if we want."

"I'm up for whatever!" Adam said. "But I was thinking, since I get off at three and you don't start work till next week, that maybe we could walk down from your house a little early and check some stuff out."

"Sure! I'd like that! I actually have to stop at the bakery anyway to give her my paperwork. So that works out well."

"Great!" he said. "Also, my birthday is coming up. It's my eighteenth. My parents aren't doing anything, but I was wondering if you wanted to."

"Oh my gosh! How have I never thought to ask you your birthday?!" Claire said, feeling awful.

He chuckled. "Nah. I honestly don't really celebrate it. But it's the eighteenth of June."

"He's a Gemini," Sam whispered before Claire shushed her.

"And my eighteenth, so I figured why not. I'm not sure what the weather will look like, but whatever day you end up having off around that time, maybe we can do something. I was thinking it'd be a fun reason to pull off that beach day. Again, if the weather is good."

"Yeah! I will know my hours next week!"

"Cool. And tell Sam, if she isn't already listening." He chuckled.

Sam looked at her as if to say, *How did he know?* Claire giggled and shrugged.

"Well, I'll leave you two to your concert. Wish I was there. I'd hold my lighter up."

"Ha. Ha." Claire laughed. "Talk to you later?"

"You know it."

They hung up, and Sam instantly went into one of her spiraling spiels. "Dude. I'm pretty sure that Sagittariuses and Geminis are like a match made in heaven. No joke. That also explains why he's this cool, dorky, mysterious bad boy. He's the twins! He's everything. Oh, that's hot. I need to get my book so we can look up your signs for compatibility. Why have I not thought to do this before?!"

Claire shook her head and let her mumble, happy to have her old friend back.

"Thank you, Claire! This is perfect. I'll have you all ready to go on Monday!" Mrs. Leonard smiled from over the counter. "And who is this?" Mrs. Leonard asked in her jolly manner.

"Oh! This is Adam Miller. A friend from school," Claire responded. "Adam, this is Mrs. Leonard! The best baker in town."

"So I've heard. It's very nice to meet you," he said, giving one of those award winning grins.

"Oh, stop. I don't know about the best baker in town. But just for that," she paused, grabbed a bag from behind the counter, and began filling it with donuts, slices of bread, and a muffin, "here you both go! We're getting into the citrus and fruity flavors for summer. There's a strawberry muffin, some lemon bread, and a couple blueberry donuts."

"Thank you!! They smell amazing!" Claire said, peeking inside the bag and getting a whiff.

"Enjoy!"

They left the shop and moseyed over to the small park that was on the corner at the head of Main Street. Sitting down on a bench, the mid-June warmth caressed their faces as Claire dove in for a blueberry donut. She split it in half and held it up. "Want a bite? Because . . . you know, it's definitely all mine."

He smirked, his arms stretched out along the back of the bench, and then leaned forward to take a bite.

"Good, huh?" Claire asked, watching him chew through her small, round sunglasses, her hair tied back with a purple velvet scrunchie, a white short-sleeved crop top and faded jean overall shorts keeping her cool. She sat cross-legged on the bench, facing Adam, who was now adjusted to face her too.

"Delicious." He smiled.

She couldn't help but smile back, dropping the rest of the donut in the bag and brushing her hands of crumbs.

"I'm excited to start working and making some money!" she said, placing the bag of treats on the ground.

"I bet! Money is always good. Although, I'm going to miss seeing you as often as I could. Maybe I'll quit RadioShack so I can come bug you for sweets," he joked.

"Ha! You'd go nuts if you didn't work. But you come see me for sweets anytime." She smiled.

He brushed away a piece of hair that had blown across her face. His slightest touch gave her goose bumps. He leaned forward and placed a light kiss on her lips. "That's all I need for sweet treats."

Claire smiled, feeling the cry in her body for more. She shook it off. "So," she said, "we have a couple hours before we meet Troy and Gwen. What do you want to do?"

"Well," he said, "I want to get to know Claire Hanover even better."

"Okay." She giggled. "What do you want to know?"

Adam adjusted himself to get more comfortable on the bench. "Do you prefer sunrises or sunsets?"

"Um . . . that's tough. I would have to go with sunsets."

"What's your favorite flower?"

Claire thought a moment. "Peonies. I love their smell. They remind me of my grandmother."

Adam smiled. "What's your favorite TV show?"

"That's tough too. I like *Growing Pains*, *Boy Meets World*, and *X-Files*."

"Nice. I love *X-Files*," Adam added. "What's your favorite movie?"

"That's even harder!" Claire laughed. "I like too many."

"So it isn't *Top Gun*?"

Claire chuckled. "Are you going to leave me right on this bench if I say no?"

"Maybe," he said through a shitty grin. "Okay, so maybe a movie night, then. Let's see. What is your favorite color?"

"Super pale pink. I also love forest green."

"Food?"

"Tacos!" Claire said with relish.

"Favorite place to be," he asked.

Claire took pause. She knew that her favorite place would probably be anywhere with books or the outdoors during fall or the ocean. But, lately, it didn't really matter where she was if Adam was there. It made it the only place she wanted to be. "Well . . . I like book shops and the ocean. But, recently, I've found that the place I'm most anxious to be is with you." She ended simply and didn't make eye contact.

Her answer hit Adam in the gut, and he felt like he could soar. He could see she was a bit shy, having said what she did, but he one hundred percent agreed. It was what kept him up most nights. He thought he was going loony, going through bouts of anxiety and nerves, just wanting to see her again or talk to her. He'd never experienced it before, and she did it to him. Her saying this made him incredibly happy that he wasn't alone.

He stood up from the bench and held his hands out for her to take. She did so, looking slightly confused. He pulled her to him, draping her arms on his shoulders and placing his hands ever so gently on her sides, warm against her bare skin, her crop top having lifted.

It gave her a chill that she was quite okay with.

"Anywhere you are . . . I want to be," he said to her quietly.

She smiled knowingly, her heart swelling. Pushing her sunglasses up onto her head, she placed a hand at the nape of his neck and guided that adorable face, gray eyes, and soft lips to her, rising on tiptoes ever so slightly. Their lips brushed each other at first before falling closer and harder. All the flutters and chills came crashing forward, and Claire wondered whether this would happen every time, and then hoped it did.

Adam's hands left her waist as his arms wound their way around her, pulling her even closer. Adam couldn't help all the pleasant thoughts that swam forward as he held her so close, feeling her moist lips on his, their hearts beating in unison. To distract from the tension that was building, he squeezed Claire and lifted her off her feet to twirl her around. He felt her smile against him before she threw her head back and trilled a laugh that Adam felt in his soul. It brought him just as much joy as her kiss had.

Breaking apart, they smiled at each other, broad grins that solidified their intense feelings of happiness. He grabbed her hand, and they walked from their sunny spot in the park toward the shops of Main Street.

They hit up Ron's a little early to snag a decent table. They went with the one near the pool table in case anyone wanted to play. Adam grabbed himself and Claire Cokes before he slid into the booth next to her. They didn't have to wait too long before Troy and Gwen came through the door.

"Hey, Mouse!" Troy said, sitting down, Gwen following.

"Mouse?" Adam asked with a grin. "I didn't know that one."

"That's been Claire's nickname since she was a wee little one. Ever since—"

"Troy!" Claire said, half laughing.

"No! I wanna hear!" Adam said, giving her a light elbow nudge.

"Oh, fine."

"Anyway," Troy continued. "It isn't really an exciting story. But when Claire was born, she was super tiny, and my dad called her a pipsqueak. Pipsqueak turned to Mouse, and it stuck. It worked, too, because when she got older, she would creep around the house to read, and we'd flat-out lose her. Quiet as a mouse. So Mouse it is."

Adam beamed. "I like it." He did too. It gave a little insight into Troy and Claire's relationship as brother and sister, and once again, Adam could fully picture Claire sitting in a quiet corner surrounded by picture books, not hearing the sounds of her family calling for her, so engrossed in her stories. He had a feeling it wasn't too far off from what she still did now.

"Hey, how was work?" Claire asked, changing the subject.

"Not too bad. Had some weirdo come in asking where the adult material was. I pointed him to the curtain in the back. Then he comes out and proceeds to ask my opinion because he apparently couldn't pick between two."

"What?! You didn't tell me that!" Gwen said, chuckling. Adam and Claire laughed too.

"Oh! And, Adam, this is Gwen, though I'm sure you figured that out. And, Gwen, this is Adam. Troy you've talked to on the phone," Claire quickly added.

"Nice to meet you, Adam," Gwen said with a genuine smile.

"Likewise," he returned.

They discussed pizza options, and Troy went up to put the order in to save the waitress some time.

"So, Adam, you're a grade ahead of Claire, right?"

"Yeah," he said with a smile and nod.

"So a senior this fall!? That's exciting!"

"Yeah. I can't believe it, to tell you the truth."

"Doesn't it go so fast? Do you have plans yet for after school?"

Adam took a sip of Coke. "Um . . . well, I have an idea. I was thinking of taking a year off to work and then applying to schools for computer stuff."

"Wow! That's cool. I hear that's the business to get into for sure. I don't personally understand any of it." Gwen chuckled.

"Yeah! I'm hoping for it to take off too. The way things are going, I would think so. Claire said you're going to school for nursing?"

"Yes, sir. I'm full-time at the music shop for the summer. But classes start back up in the fall, and it'll be my last year!"

"That's great. Congrats."

Claire was happily listening along, glad that Adam and Gwen seemed to have an easy flow with conversation. Troy came back and changed the conversation from what they wanted to be when they grew up to who wanted to play pool. They agreed on a boys versus girls game, and when the boys snagged the win, Troy kept referring to Adam as his little buddy. They decided to play a second round, Adam and Claire against Troy and Gwen.

Claire noticed at one point that a table in the regular dining room was filled with Amber, Lauren, Ashley, Chris, and Mark and wondered if they would make their way to the back to play pool, and just as Claire was hoping they didn't notice her, the crew came strolling in to see if the table was open.

Amber gave her a snotty look, which Claire was used to, it having shown up more frequently since her and Mark's breakup. Seeing that she was with Troy and Adam, however, seemed to perk her up a bit.

"Claire! Hi!" she said, walking up to her with the most fake and insincere smile Claire had ever seen on a person.

"Hey, Amber," Claire said, and then looking beyond her, "Hey, everyone."

"How fun we should bump into you here," she said, though she was looking at Troy and Adam. "Hi, Troy!"

Troy gave an awkward wave.

"And you are?"

"Uh, Adam. Adam Miller," Adam said, taking Amber's outstretched hand to shake it.

"Oh, that's right! Silly me, we've met before," she simpered. Claire wanted to vomit.

"Hey, Claire," Mark said with a half wave.

God, she wanted to melt into the floor.

"How's it going?" she asked.

"Not too bad." He seemed to size Adam up and decided not to speak anymore.

"Well, we were playing a game," Claire said. "I'll see you guys around."

"Of course. Nice to see you again, Troy. And you too, Adam," Amber said with a look that was just missing a wink.

Claire felt her cheeks burn. It wasn't that she was jealous or thought that that kind of act would magically gain the affection of Adam. It was just that Amber thought it was okay to do it at all.

The group thought better of waiting around for the table, which Claire was extremely grateful for, and she, Adam, Troy, and Gwen got back into the rhythm of their own game, exchanging stories and jokes the entire time. When pizza came, they ate, and when they were done, they ordered an ice cream sundae with four spoons and enjoyed themselves. Claire was filled with joy at how easy it seemed, similar to her night out with Adam's friends. It was comfortable and nice.

"Well, I think we're going to head out," Troy said after a collective sigh of good times and good food having been had went around the table. "You guys are walking home, right?" Troy asked.

"Yeah," Claire said.

"Cool. This one's got an early morning tomorrow, and I have to bring her home," he said, gesturing to Gwen.

"I have a name," she said jokingly. Troy and Gwen slid out, and Adam followed, confusing Claire, as she had hoped they were going to stay a little longer. She had till 11:00, and it was only 10:15. But Adam's reasoning was made clear when he held out a hand for Troy.

"It was nice meeting you in person, even though our phone concert was pretty hard to beat," Adam said with a smile.

Troy grinned back, took his hand, and pulled Adam in for one of those quick, side, slap you on the back kind of hugs that guys do. "It was great to meet you too, man."

Gwen smiled at them both. "I'm a hugger, so excuse me," she said, grabbing a hug from Adam. "You guys have fun tonight. Claire, I'll see you tomorrow I'm sure."

"Yeah, bye, Mouse," Troy said with a wink and a wave.

"Bye, guys," she said, a little slowly. What had just happened? Had Troy and Adam's handshake meant something? It seemed so natural and yet like *something*. And Gwen too. *Were they giving approval?* she thought. Claire hadn't even thought of that or how this would be for Adam. To her it was just Troy and Gwen, but perchance this was more than that.

"Well, that was fun," Adam said.

"Totally," Claire said, snapping out of her reverie, deciding not to worry about it because, well, there wasn't really anything *to* worry about. If it meant something, then she got the vibe it was good, and if not, then who cared!

"I'm glad this worked out," Adam said.

"Me too." Claire beamed.

"Wanna play?" Adam pointed at the pool table.

"Sure!"

They went over and began, Claire realizing how competitive they really were, succumbing to banter and mild insults. Claire was proud to say she won, and Adam seemed genuinely surprised.

"No one ever beats me at pool," he said, laying his cue down on the table next to her discarded one. "You're pretty good, Hanover."

She grinned at his compliment and the use of her surname. She was leaning against the table, sitting ever so lightly on the edge, as he walked over to stand in front of her.

"What do I win?" she asked, and she couldn't help the playful tone that escaped.

He raised his eyebrows, and Claire smiled coyly.

"Well," he said. She looked over his cool gray eyes crinkled behind his glasses, his parted hair, his slight dimples from his grin. She allowed her teenage brain to exclaim, *He's so hot!*

"Well," he said again, running his hand through his hair, clearly debating on saying what he was about to say. "I can think of one thing."

She smiled broadly. He took that as approval and stepped forward, lacing his arms around her middle and pressing closer to her. He was nervous about the building tension from earlier. But, though they were the only ones in the back pool room of Ron's, they were still in a public vicinity, so he hoped that would help him keep himself focused.

She scooted back so she was sitting more on the pool table and wrapped her arms around him.

They skipped the light entry and went right in for the kind of kiss that gave Claire a flutter through her body. They're lips played against each other, occasionally parting to make way for even more. She recalled how turned off she had felt when Mark had attempted this kind of kiss and reflected on how incredibly much she loved it now.

He pulled away from her, placing his forehead against hers. She knew why he stopped. She'd felt it too. Claire felt that an entire range of emotions had opened and flooded through her body.

She let him rest there a moment before holding his face in her hands and giving him a final peck like she'd done before. It always seemed to lighten the intensity.

"I think it's time for us to call it a night. It's almost eleven," she said, still holding his face.

"Word," he said with a grin. She kissed him again, letting it linger for a moment, until she realized they weren't alone in the pool room. They both jumped as they noticed Mark standing there.

"Sorry," he said, a red blush creeping up his neck. "I was just checking on the pool table. I saw your brother leave, so I thought you did too. Not that you have to leave . . . or, like, I can't play if you're here or anything. I—um."

"It's open," Claire said with a smile, hopping down off the pool table.

"Ye-yeah. Cool. Uh, thanks," he said. "Have a good one."

Adam gave him a salute as Claire said, "See ya."

She let out a burst of laughter when she was sure Mark was gone, her giddiness at that intense kiss coupled with the awkwardness of the altercation. Adam joined, and for a moment, they just stood and let the giggles out before he threw his arm around her, kissed the top of her head, and led her out the back door.

They walked to Claire's house, hand in hand, talking animatedly about their potential beach trip, going for her license the next day, her new job, and more. When they reached her driveway, she saw his car parked on the side of the road and heaved a sigh.

"I suppose it's that time," she said.

"Yeah. I don't want you to be late getting in. I'll get in trouble." He chuckled. "I had an amazing time today. Hanging out and dinner. You're brother and Gwen are great, and I—I . . ."

"What is it?" she asked, sensing his nerves and encouraging him forward.

"I'm going to be blunt. It worked before. You drive me absolutely wild, and I often don't know what to do with it. What I do know is that I've never felt this way before, and so . . . I want to formally ask you to be my girlfriend. I know we said we would take things slow and not put pressure on things, but I think I'm passed that. I know I'm the one who mentioned it before but—"

"Yes," Claire butted in.

"Yes?" he asked.

"Yes. I don't care about taking things slow and labels and pressure. Whatever! I want to do what feels right when I feel it, and being Adam Miller's girlfriend does."

He broke into a wide grin as she threw her arms around him. He held her tight, and they swayed on the spot for a moment. He kissed her hard, but kept it short, not sure he could take any more at the moment. "Talk to you tomorrow?"

"Yes. Tomorrow," she said.

He didn't want to leave, but he did, holding her hand till the last moment.

Claire watched him get in his car and waved as he took off. Heading through the front gate and up the walkway, she froze when she saw someone sitting on the steps.

"Troy? What are you doing out here?"

"Hey, Mouse. Sit with me?" he asked.

She looked at him curiously and sat on the step next to him. "What's up?"

Troy sighed. "I wanted to talk to you about something."

"You're making me nervous," Claire said, feeling her throat go dry.

"Sorry. I . . . um . . . well, here," he said, handing her a pamphlet. It was the brochure she had seen him hide. She opened it warily and saw that it was full of recruiting information.

"What's this for?" she asked, hearing the nerves in her own voice.

"I've decided what I wanna be. Well, what I wanna do."

"Wha—? No. Troy, the military?" she said, hearing the panic in her voice. "But—but you'll be sent away. You'll have to go to boot camp and then be stationed who knows where. They'll send you overseas. To the Middle East or something. They'll take you away."

Troy didn't say anything.

"Troy!" She jumped up.

"I need to make something of myself, Mouse. Working at the music store, the rental joint, driving a shitty car—none of that is going to amount to anything. I need to be somebody. For me. For Gwen. For you!"

"For me?!" Claire said exasperatedly.

"Yes. I'm your big brother, and you deserve a better role model."

"Troy. You're the best role model!"

"Look. I've made my decision. I'm telling Mom and Dad tomorrow night, but I wanted you to know first."

"Have you told Gwen?" she asked.

"Yeah."

"How'd she take it?"

"Good. She just wants me to be happy. She is supportive and said she's already awaiting my return."

"That doesn't surprise me. Gwen would support you no matter what you did."

Claire stared at him. Stared at the eyes that were identical to her own. She saw his honesty, determination, and genuineness.

She slowly sat down. "You're not kidding."

"No."

She blew air through her lips. "Damn. I don't know what to say. I—" She felt tears well up in her eyes. "I don't want you to go."

He didn't have words either and instead just hugged her, and she him.

The following day, Claire took the test for her driver's license. Adam had called her that morning and wished her luck, which gave her an extra boost as her mom drove her to the local DMV. He had also told her to take a deep breath, take it nice and easy, and not to be too nervous, which was exactly what she did. And an hour later, she pulled back into the parking lot, her mom anxiously waiting outside for her return. Within moments, Claire was handed her temporary license, her mom taking several pictures before leaving. When she got home, the excitement of calling Sam and Adam wiped away all thoughts of Troy for a short period of time. It all came flooding back, however, when Troy popped into her room to give her a hug and congratulate her before offering up his clunker of a car while he was away. She laughed and said, "Yeah right," but when the door closed, the word "away" hit her deeply.

After dinner, her dad was telling a funny story from work, which got big laughs from her mom but received forced, quiet chuckles from both Troy and Claire, who felt the adrenaline of the conversation that was coming banging around in their stomachs, Claire's heart jumping up to her throat.

Her dad clearly picked up on their lack of humor and gave a questioning look to Troy, who put down his fork, dabbed his mouth with his cloth napkin, and heaved a sigh. Claire looked down at her lap after seeing her parents exchange a concerned look.

"Mom . . . Dad," Troy began. It wasn't normal to hear him speak so seriously, and Claire could even hear a hint of nerves hidden in the quaver of his voice, something that was certainly not a Troy norm.

"I—um—I have something I need to tell you," he said.

Claire's mom instinctively reached for her dad's hand that was set on the table.

"Ah," Troy was fumbling.

Claire wished she could help but knew this was his to tell.

"What is it, sweetheart?" her mother said softly with a hint of worry.

"Before I tell you, I want you both to know that I put a lot of thought into this. I really did. I—"

"Troy?" his father prodded when Troy went quiet again.

"I decided to enlist in the US Coast Guard. I've been working with a recruiter. I get sworn in next week."

Claire looked up to see her parents' stunned faces, her mom's eyes already glossy.

"Why didn't you tell us this earlier?" his father asked, not accusingly, just concerned.

"I wanted to wait till I was absolutely sure I was going to do it."

"What made you decide this?" his mother asked.

"Well, I've been thinking a lot about my future and know that working two part-time jobs isn't enough, and I want to do something with a little more purpose. So I revisited the military idea like dad had said in the past. I didn't think it was for me until I heard more about the coast guard. It seems more up my alley. I like boats and being on the water and like the idea of being more of, you know, the home front heroes, with border protection and rescue missions and whatnot. There are also a lot of bases near us that I'm hoping to eventually end up at. After talking to a recruiter, I was sold. They will even pay for me to go to school if I want to do something different when I get out. But I think I may want to make a career out of it." He ended with a shrug.

Claire's dad stood up suddenly and went around the table to Troy, who stood to accept the embrace that was being offered.

"I'm proud of you, Troy. I was proud of you anyway. But I'm proud of you."

"Thanks, Dad," Troy said.

Claire's mom, tears openly falling now, followed. "So proud, Troy. You'll do great things."

"Thanks, Mom."

Claire decided that this moment was best suited for Troy and their parents, so with a small wave and a wink from Troy as she stood up, she left the room, hearing her dad blow his nose and start asking Troy the logistics of when and where he would be getting sworn in and what the next steps were. She closed her bedroom door quietly behind her and sat heavily on the edge of her bed, looking down at her hands. She was proud of Troy, of course, and so happy that he seemed to have found his way. But suddenly, she started thinking of what it would be like to not have him down the hall or banging on her door or giving her shitty advice. She suddenly felt the pressure and anxiety at the idea that this may even be the end of their "normal" forever. Once in the coast guard, he would probably be living on base or on a ship, and when he got out or came home, he would probably look for his own place. She hadn't realized it till now, but Troy leaving in just a few weeks' time was bigger than just him joining the service. It was the end of an era, and Claire was feeling it in the tears she was holding back and the lump in her throat she was trying to swallow.

She wanted to tell Sam but knew right now wouldn't be a good time. She wouldn't be able to get it out, first of all. She also worried that Sam may not fully get the depth of it. Often skimming the surface, Claire felt that in this moment, Sam would be lost for words and maybe not even know *what* to say. She would probably resort to just telling her it was going to be okay and make some joke about Troy looking hot in a uniform. Claire laughed hollowly, knowing that was exactly how the conversation would go, and though she would welcome it greatly tomorrow perchance, right now, she needed someone else. Someone who would just listen or, quite frankly, let her do absolutely nothing at all.

Claire went to her parents' room to get the new cordless extension they had gotten a few months back. She dialed the number she had already come to memorize.

"Hello?" Adam's mother's voice rang.

"Hi, Mrs. Miller. I was wondering if Adam was available. It's Claire."

"Hello, Claire! I will call up to him now. One moment."

She waited until she heard the upstairs phone click on and Adam's distant voice saying, "Got it," to his mother and then, "Hey!" to her.

"Hey," she said. The lump in her throat was creeping up again. She willed herself to keep it at bay for just a moment.

"What's up?" Adam asked a little more seriously, hearing the edge in her voice.

"Um. Are you—are you around tonight? Like, late tonight?" She hoped he understood what she meant.

"Yeah, of course. What time your parents go to bed?" he asked with no hesitation.

"Usually by eleven or so."

"Okay. I'll come by around midnight. Should be in the clear then."

"Great. Thanks," she said quietly. His unquestioning manner and complete willingness to be there for her made the lump in her throat even harder to keep down.

"Anything—" he started and then, sensing her desire to not talk anymore, "I'll see you tonight, Claire."

"See you tonight," she said before hanging up.

She went back to her room, lay in her bed, closed her eyes, and took a deep breath, managing to calm her emotions just in time for Troy to come in, the conversation downstairs having ended.

"Hey, Mouse," he said, sitting on the end of her bed.

"How'd it go?" she asked.

"Good. They're both happy for me, and we got all the details squared away. I showed them the paperwork and messed up the date. I actually get sworn in in two weeks."

"Of course you did," she said with a smirk.

"You okay?" he asked.

"Don't ask me that," she said. Being proud and strong wouldn't happen if people went around asking her if she was okay.

"You know I won't be far, and I'll be home in between and everything," he said.

She nodded.

He thumped her feet. "Love you, Mouse."

"Love you too, dweeb," she said. He smirked, and she knew they were good right now. They would continue to go forward as Troy and Claire and would cross the path of mushiness when his departure was closer.

"I'm off to see Gwen."

"Enjoy."

He waggled his eyebrows. "I will."

Claire rolled her eyes, and they both laughed. "Say hi for me. I know I've said it before, but she really is great, Troy. I don't know what she's doing with you, but she's great."

"Thanks, Mouse."

Claire hung out with her parents for a bit, giving nods and a few words when they tried to talk to her about Troy. They seemed to get her vibe and let her be, enjoying watching *Jurassic Park*, which Troy had brought back from the rental store. She turned in early to read in the hopes her parents would do the same. Sure enough, she heard them head up around 11:00, and so she sat and waited to hear the welcome ticking noise on her window, which came promptly at midnight.

She grabbed a sweater, climbed down, remembering what Troy had said last time, and tried to do so more quietly. Jumping off at the bottom, Adam immediately grabbed her hand, and they were off to the playground, their familiar tree waiting for them in the dark beneath the summer night sky.

Sitting in their usual spots across from each other, cross-legged, Adam wasted no time in getting to the matter at hand. "So what's going on?" It was gentle, and Claire appreciated him knowing she probably wouldn't come up with it herself.

She sighed. "Troy," she started but stopped, feeling the tightness returning.

"Is he okay?" Adam asked, concerned.

"Yeah, no, he's fine. He just—he told me last night, after you left, that he's joining the coast guard. He gets sworn in in two weeks and then heads off to boot camp after that. He told my parents at dinner tonight." Now that she had started, she was able to fight past her shaking voice and plow through, spilling every thought that had occurred to her since Troy's announcement. "I'm really happy for him. Like, really. And proud. But it just came on so fast, and now I'm looking at the next two weeks as an hourglass, thinking that soon enough he'll be gone. And I'm just so used to Troy being around and just being . . . well . . . Troy. And I don't know what it's going to feel like without him. And then I just keep thinking that this is it! In just two weeks, I have to say goodbye to my brother and pretty much life as we've known it together for my whole life. And . . . and I'm trying to be happy and supportive for him, but it's just . . . it's just . . ." She couldn't fight anymore, and even though she wanted nothing to do with crying in front of Adam, she lost all steam and felt her eyes burn and her heartbeat excel.

"It's just hard," he finished for her.

"Yeah," she squeaked through the tears that now shamelessly fell.

"Claire?" Adam said after a moment, leaning forward and cupping her face in his hands, wiping away tears with his thumbs. "It's okay to not be okay."

That did it. She let out a cry, fully releasing the ball in her throat, and Adam undid his crossed legs, wrapped his arms around her shoulders, and pulled her to him, leaning back on the tree, cradling her, with his chin on her head. Claire allowed the tears to fall into his worn, blue, long-sleeved T-shirt. She felt his arms hold her tighter as she continued to feel all the confused and grief-stricken thoughts that had been looming since the night before. She felt Adam's kiss on the top of her head, and it released a sense of calm through her body.

She had no idea how long they sat like that. Adam never once spoke, just held her and allowed her to live in her emotions.

The night wore on, and Claire felt the tracks of her dried tears tight on her face as she pulled back from Adam. "Thank you," she said and hoped all the gratitude she was feeling was fully translated.

"You're welcome. But you don't have to say thank you. You can cry on me anytime." She smiled. "And, Claire. What your brother is doing is a good thing. I know you know that. But it is. It doesn't make it any easier.

But he'll learn so much and see so much and will be back before you know it. Your guys' life may change—it would have anyway—but he will always be your big brother. That will never change. May just look a little different. But you'll adapt, and with every new phase, it will only get better and better."

Claire felt her heart swell and her eyes tear up with appreciation at Adam's words. She leaned back into him and felt his warm embrace once again. The summer breeze blew past, the leaves in their tree rustling, and Claire felt she could stay like this all night.

Claire's first day of work went well. It was mostly video and on-the-job training. By the second day, she was cleaning the front of the store, keeping up with the coffees, and getting orders. By the middle of the week, she had learned the cash register and was now taking over the entire front counter, with one of the other girls shadowing. Both were really nice, and she was already feeling bummed that Janie would be leaving next week. While Claire was working, she was thinking of what she was going to get Adam for his birthday, which was also mid-week, and an idea occurred to her. It would take a lot of time and work, but she decided she would pull some late nights to get it done.

They had chatted on the phone, and she had told him that though she was working on his actual birthday, she was off on Friday. The weather looked great, and they agreed to do his birthday beach day then. She had a minor panic attack after realizing she needed a new bathing suit, but Sam came to the rescue, and Thursday night they went to the mall, Claire driving them for the first time. After multiple try-ons, Claire landed on a cute black one-piece that had high-cut legs and showed off her cleavage just a bit.

Claire couldn't help feeling a shot of confidence in it, though she would never openly admit it. She was a little worried about its level of appropriateness, but Sam reminded her she was sixteen and a half and deserved to show off her curves and a little skin, and for once, Claire agreed. Plus, it wasn't that bad, just different.

She tried to convince Sam to try on some suits as well, but she declined and said she still had hers from last year. Claire noted a hint of something in her tone but let it go when Sam started spewing all the latest fashion trends for bathing suits and how Claire's fit in perfectly because of those high-cut legs.

Sam spent the night, and they were both so excited for the next day, they could hardly sleep for it—Claire in anticipation of spending the day with Adam and getting to see the ocean for the first time this season, and Sam for spending the day with senior boys. They were also meeting a friend of Adam's they hadn't met yet, Nick, which had Sam really excited. Adam had mentioned him plenty, but their paths had just never crossed.

Waking up early, they took their time getting ready. Though Claire was a firm believer in no makeup for beach days, she couldn't help but add her signature lipstick, today in crimson. She had showered the night before, and her hair had been very generous to her come morning by drying in a slight wave rather than a frizzy mop. She never knew what to expect and thanked the heavens for this going right. She felt her adrenaline begin to race at the idea of smelling the ocean and feeling the salty water. She wore her oversized white T-shirt and packed a pair of shorts in her beach bag in case they stopped anywhere. Sunglasses, flip flops, a towel, and sunscreen were thrown in as well. The only thing left was a book to read. She was currently reading William Goldman's *The Princess Bride*, so she grabbed it along with *The Great Gatsby* and *Flowers in the Attic* on the off chance she read through its entirety and needed something else to read. This was beyond plausible, but Claire felt it was better to have too many books than none.

Sam turned back and forth in the mirror while Claire contemplated packing some snacks from the pantry downstairs, taking mental inventory of their options.

"I think there's a bag of Doritos and maybe some—"

"I look so dumb in a bathing suit," Sam interrupted.

Claire looked at her as Sam snapped the band on her bottoms. "What are you talking about? You look fine." She did too. She looked fun and sporty. Sam's suit was a red two-piece whose top was styled like a sports bra, the bottoms cut like shorts.

"No. I look like a—"

"Don't even say a twelve-year-old boy. I will strangle you. Sam, who cares if your chest is small. You have an athletic build, which is adorable. Your low curly pigtails are cute, and your sunglasses rival those of Jackie O. herself. You are rocking a two-piece bathing suit, for crying out loud. I can't do that. Stop overthinking. You look great. For real. Like Sporty Spice. Quite 'in' to be honest." Claire felt bad for being so quick with Sam at times, but the truth was that Claire really felt this way about Sam and got irritated at how negative she was about her own body. There were often times when Claire felt a pang of jealousy at Sam's thinness. Fashion trends were beginning to creep toward really toned stomachs and low jeans to show them off, and that made Claire feel the way Amber made her feel.

Sam smiled at her, and Claire felt it was actually quite genuine. "Thanks. I never thought of it as an athletic build before."

"Yeah! With the red, you could pass for an Olympian!"

Sam laughed. "Don't push it."

Claire smiled, and they went downstairs to raid the pantry, Sam throwing on a pair of jean shorts and a Def Leppard T-shirt and quickly stealing some of Claire's deeper lip color. Claire felt Sam was pulling off a very alt look, and it suited her. She hoped Sam felt the confidence that Claire was feeling for her.

Adam's car pulled up, Fitz getting out and waving to them as he climbed into the back seat. Claire guessed she was being given the front. Adam went around to the back to open the trunk, his swim shorts a teal blue with one leg covered in geometric and tribal-like shapes. He wore one of his traditional white T-shirts that she saw him in so often, and Claire couldn't help but think how cute he looked with his grin, crinkled eyes behind glasses, and that brown center-split hairdo she loved so much.

"Hey!" he said as they approached. "Hey, Sam!"

"Hi!" they said in unison.

"Is that all you guys have?" he asked, looking at their one beach bag each. They exchanged looks, and Claire said, "Uh, yeah. We're just going to the beach, right?"

"Well, yeah. I just thought—I guess I'm used to Rachel bringing half her house with her. I just assumed that was a girl thing."

Claire laughed. "No. Not us girls anyway."

"Sorry for assuming," he said with a smirk as Claire and Sam threw their bags in.

"Bohemian! Levinski!" Fitz shouted, his bucket-hat-clad head sticking out the back window.

Sam chuckled and went to join him in the back seat. Claire turned to Adam and threw her arms around him. "Happy Birthday!!" she sang.

"Thanks." Adam laughed, holding her.

She leaned back so she could look at him and his smile and wasted no time in giving him a kiss, which he accepted fully, squeezing her tightly. She kept it short for the sake of Sam and Fitz in the back seat and the fact that they were still out front of her house, even if her parents were at work.

"Best birthday gift yet," he said when they pulled apart. She gave him a smirk, and they got in the front seat.

The ride to the beach was just under an hour. Claire was always so grateful that they lived where they did. New England was beautiful with its perfect four seasons and expanses of forests and natural surroundings, but most importantly, because the coastline was so close. And their coastline was one of the prettiest, in Claire's humble opinion.

As they drove along the winding paths and coastal roads, Claire asked the group, "So who's getting in the water first?"

Adam laughed. "Not me, that's for sure."

"What?!?! You don't swim?"

"I swim, but not in the ocean."

"What?!? What do you do there, then?" Claire asked with both shock and humor.

Adam chuckled again. "Sit in the sand, get some sun, listen to music, walk the beach," he said.

"Well, yeah, I guess. But you *have* to swim. You have to get in the water. That's what you're supposed to do! That's why the ocean calls you to it. It wants you to swim." She giggled.

Adam looked at her with an expression that Claire couldn't quite pinpoint, but it looked almost like awe. "You like to swim in it, then, I assume."

"Duh!" she said with a smirk.

He grinned. "It's so cold though!"

"Yeah. That's why you just have to jump in. You can't go slow."

"I'd rather not die of hypothermia. Especially now! It's only late June! Not that it ever gets warm enough for me," he said exasperatedly.

"That's when it's the best!"

"Why is that?" he asked with a genuine tone of curiosity.

Claire thought a moment. "Because. It makes you feel alive."

Adam looked at her briefly. "How so?"

"Well, when the water is cold, and you jump in, it's like all your pores open up and your skin gets tingly, and the salt feels like magic, giving you vitality and life. And then, when you get out, the sand cakes on all your goose bumps and the rays of the sun warm you and you're just covered in the roots of earth. Salt, sand, and sun. I live for that feeling."

Adam was quiet a moment, taking in what she said. Claire was so different from others he'd met. It seemed that she surprised him every single day.

"How you speak," he said quietly, even though Fitz and Sam, who were having their own conversation anyway, couldn't hear them with all the windows down. "It's like nothing I've ever heard before. It's like you paint pictures with your words. It's—it's enthralling."

"That's a ten-dollar word," she said with a grin.

He chuckled. "I don't know what else to use. It's exactly what it is. You suck me into everything you say. It's an art form, and I wish I could see the world the way you do. I don't think I even knew people could. I could listen to you forever." His stomach jolted a little at his use of the word "forever," hoping she didn't take that as some major step he was trying to take. Although, in his current state of euphoria, there was a part of him that felt like that wasn't far from how he felt, which scared him.

Claire looked at him meaningfully and then said, "Well, according to my mom, I could talk for forever, so that works."

After giving a chuckle, Adam reached over and grabbed her hand to give it a squeeze. They exchanged understanding expressions, and he continued to drive.

She could smell the ocean, telling her they were close, the breeze from the open window already carrying with it the heavy air that wrapped itself around her every strand of hair, giving it an extra poof.

"Woo!" Fitz randomly screamed, making them all jump.

"Jesus, dude," Adam said as he parked.

"What? I'm excited!" he said in his chill tone.

During their ride, Adam had shared with them all that Jason and Nick were meeting them there and would probably already be set up. They had decided on a spot based on landmarks, and they wanted to get there early to secure it. Grabbing their things, they trekked their way to the spot that had been decided on.

Adam tried hard to quiet the thoughts that came to his mind as he watched Claire walk ahead of him with Sam, but it was hard. He couldn't believe how naturally beautiful she was. He hated to draw comparisons because he knew it wasn't healthy, but Rachel was all he knew for girlfriends, and he couldn't help it. She had always been so particular about her appearance and looks, dying her hair bleach blonde and wearing the best makeup and name-brand clothing. She was attached to her parents' money and all the fine things she could have. He had thought he liked that, thought it felt, for lack of a better word, cool to have a girlfriend who could sport the cover of a magazine and had everything.

But, since meeting Claire, from the first time he watched her play piano, she had done nothing but undo all of that. And he had come to realize that the reason he had never *really* been happy with Rachel was because it was fake. It was nothing. And Rachel and all that she was had slowly started to look ugly and wrong. It felt like he had been wearing clouded glasses that Claire had taken off bit by bit. She had this ability to see the truth. Genuineness. And it was so absolutely intoxicating to him. Her words, her thoughts, her passions. And now, as he followed her to the ocean, seeing the oversized shirt slip off her shoulder as she walked, talking animatedly to Sam, the bag she carried causing the shirt to hike up ever so slightly so that he saw her curves peeking out of her bathing suit with each step, her natural and wavy brown hair cascading down her back, the ocean breeze picking it up occasionally to playfully blow around her face, sticking to the lips that he always appreciated had a hint of color, he couldn't even put to words how much more Claire was compared to Rachel.

He got the vibe from her at times that she didn't see herself that way. That she saw herself as so-so. He caught little comments here and there that told him she wasn't quite as confident in her body as she was in her brain. But to him, they were equally stunning, and he hoped he was someone who made her feel beautiful, as beautiful as she was inside. As beautiful as she was to him. Because she was.

They found Jason and Nick, both sitting in beach chairs, shirts off, Ray-Bans on, baking in the sun.

"Hey, man," Jason said as Adam walked up.

"Yo," he said back, and then, "Hey, Nick, what's up? Long time no see." Nick stood and they exchanged a handshake and one-armed hug.

"Nothin' much, bro. Just enjoying this heat. Happy Birthday. Now you can legally buy smokes, lottery tickets, and porn."

Claire hid a chuckle as she saw Adam blush.

"Hey, dude," Jason said. "Ladies present."

Nick smirked and put a hand out. "So sorry. Where are my manners?"

"In the gutter with your mind," Adam said.

"Hey! I said I was sorry!" He laughed. "Nick Morelli."

Claire shook his hand. "Nice to meet you. I'm Claire Hanover, and this is my friend Sam Levinski."

Sam shook his hand as well.

"Nice to meet you both," he said, and then to Claire, "So you're the girl who managed to get my buddy over here to quit being a dumbass and ditch Rachel."

Claire raised an eyebrow and laughed. "Well, I don't know about that."

"Who invited *him*?" Adam said to Jason, setting up his own beach chair.

"Sorry, man," Jason said with a grin.

"No, no. *You* did." Nick continued, "I didn't think he'd ever get out from under Rachel's claws." He held up his hands like a bird's talons. "You must be something real special."

"She is," Adam interjected, with a hint of threat.

Claire smiled shyly at him.

"I'm glad you're here with us today, Claire Hanover," Nick said.

"Me too." She beamed.

Jason rolled his eyes. "Would you sit down, dork."

Claire and Sam set up their towels while Fitz sat in the sand next to them, no blanket or towel in sight, radio propped up, sliding through the stations till he found one that came through.

A moment that Claire hadn't thought would be one she would dread came when she wanted to take off her T-shirt. She suddenly felt a little awkward revealing her bathing suit in front of Adam and his friends. But she pushed it aside, giving herself her own advice to Sam from earlier, repeatedly telling herself to just have some confidence. She was beautiful just the way she was. They were sitting in chairs and chatting anyway, so she just went for it, pulling the T-shirt off over her head. She sat down on her towel and started excitedly talking with Sam about the water, not seeing Adam's stare through his sunglasses, his thoughts nowhere near what his friends were talking about.

Sam and Claire lay in the sun for a bit, enjoying Fitz's radio, currently playing Sister Hazel. When a set of commercials came on, Claire stood up with a surge of adrenaline at the prospect of getting in the water.

"Okay, who's going in with me?" she asked.

They all looked at her with grins, but not a single one offered to join.

"Oh, come on!!" She placed her hands on her hips. "You boys are a bunch of pansies."

"Them are fightin' words!" Nick said. "Okay, I'm in."

"It's so cold though," Jason said, chuckling.

"We'll make it a competition. I'll count us down, and anyone who runs in the water and goes completely under gets a prize."

Adam perked up, as did Fitz and Jason.

"What's the prize?" Adam asked.

Claire looked to the sky and then said, "I'll treat everyone to an ice cream on the way home."

"Oh, man, I'm in," Fitz said, standing up and ditching his Hawaiian shirt that had already been open.

"Okay. Let's do it. I refuse to be shown up by Fitz," Jason said.

"Alright!" Nick said.

Adam stood up. "This will be a first. But for you, I'll do it," and then more quietly for just Claire to hear, "Maybe I'll get to experience your sense of feeling alive."

Claire smiled at him and then whispered, "You won't regret it. And if you do it, I'll give *you* an extra prize."

Adam grinned broadly. "Now that's worth freezing my ass off for. Not that I don't appreciate the ice cream."

She laughed and gave him a peck on the cheek. Sam got up and joined the group. "Let's do this!" she said excitedly.

They walked down to the shoreline, Claire stopping a couple yards before the water, drawing a line in the sand with her foot.

"Okay. Here's the starting line. No feeling the water before. I'll count us down from three, and when I say *go*, we run in, no stopping, and go under!"

Nick started thumping his chest. "Okay. Okay, let's do this, like Sam said."

Jason, hands on hips swaying back and forth, let out a huge breath of air. "Shit, this is going to be rough. Okay."

Adam took off his T-shirt and threw it on the sand behind him. It quite literally meant nothing more than him preparing to get in the water, but it completely distracted Claire. He wasn't ripped or anything, but he had a healthy rugged look about him that Claire had always felt under his shirt when they hugged. His arms looked strong, and all she wanted to do was throw her own around him and feel him embrace her.

"Claire! We're ready!" Sam said.

"Yes! Sorry." She jumped. "Okay, everyone line up!"

"For ice cream!" Fitz shouted.

Claire laughed as she counted them down, seeing Adam's and Jason's looks of absolute doom. "Three . . . Two . . . One . . ." she shouted. "Go!" She ran forward and the rest followed suit. The water splashed around them. It was definitely cold, but it was exactly what Claire was expecting. Her breath caught as the water hit her stomach then chest before she dove in and felt the harsh temperature hit her face. Her skin broke into goose bumps as she popped back up, feeling the salty freshness cover her, the sun warm on her face.

"Woo!" Jason shouted as he, too, jumped up out of the water and immediately headed back toward the shoreline. "I did it, and now I'm out!" He laughed.

"Dude, did you not take off your hat?" Nick asked Fitz, who was floating on his back, bucket hat floating beside him.

"Nah, man. It'll dry."

Nick splashed him and then dipped down again himself. "I think I'm getting feeling back in my limbs. Slowly. It isn't too bad."

Sam, too, was floating about, chuckling at the boys' reactions.

Adam was waist-deep, shivering.

"You gotta stay in," Claire said, sniggering. "Otherwise, you won't get used to it."

His luscious hair was pushed back on his head as he grinned at her, dipping back down, breathing like a pregnant woman in Lamaze class. She went under again and swam in his direction, breaking through the surface right in front of him. He smiled.

Nick convinced Sam to swim down the shoreline a little ways where there were waves coming in so they could try and jump them or ride them in. Fitz was merrily floating around still, humming to himself, Jason sitting up on the sand watching them all.

"Come on," Claire said, swimming backward to where it was a little deeper. Adam followed. "You know how to float?"

"No, I sink," Adam said.

"That's because you don't breathe properly," she said. "You can't float if you don't trust the water."

He couldn't help but smile at everything she said. Her words were like magic to him: he got hooked on every one.

"Okay. So what do I do?"

"You have to lean back, stretch your body out, breathe deep and normal, and trust the ocean will hold you."

Adam did as she said, and a couple of failed attempts and laughs later, he closed his eyes, breathed deep, and truly let himself relax like Claire said. And he was floating. He felt the sun warm the exposed parts of his chest and his face. Claire did the same, closing her eyes to feel the small motions of the ocean. Adam looked up at the clear blue sky, not a cloud in sight, and couldn't think of a single birthday that had ever been this special.

He peeked over at Claire and saw her hair spread out around her, like a mermaid's, her chest breathing deep, peeking out of the water, her arms out wide. He couldn't help the spasm of heat that shuddered through his body and the sheer admiration for all that she was. She sensed him looking at her, and she trilled a laugh that sang to his heart. He released his floating pose and planted his feet on the sandy bottom of the ocean, still staying low so his shoulders were below the water.

Claire dropped under the water, and this time, when she came back up, she was right against him, putting her arms around his neck.

Feeling her against him, in the ocean, beneath the rays of the sun, was a moment that Adam would revisit in his every daydream. A moment that he would forever claim as the moment he realized what love was. He wrapped his arms around her, feeling her bare back beneath his hands. Kissing her in this moment was beyond anything it had been yet. She tasted of salt and smelled of sunshine. He felt he was holding some kind of mystical Siren in his arms, a beautiful creature that was so mesmerizing and so wonderfully different that she was inhuman to him. He kissed her hard and she him, playfully and deeply.

Claire laced her fingers in his wet hair, not sure what to make of the heightened hormones that seemed to be coursing through her. She tried to keep her mind straight, but quickly got lost in everything that was Adam. The feeling of his hands on her back, his arms tight around her, the water surrounding them, the sigh she heard escape him. She had been thinking this for a little while, but this very moment solidified that Claire had more than a crush on Adam. This was possibly more than just a like-like situation.

They pulled apart and placed their foreheads together, their breathing coming a little heavier, soaking up all the emotions they were both experiencing. Adam kissed her again, having not had enough, and they enjoyed each other for a little while more.

"I . . ." Adam said quietly. "I'm struggling a little bit right now."

Claire smiled, knowing exactly what he meant. "Me too."

"You are like nothing else I've ever come in contact with, Claire Hanover."

She chuckled. "I hope that's a good thing."

"Oh, absolutely. But it also terrifies me."

Again, Claire knew where he was coming from. She agreed. These emotions—they felt so mature. So much more than a couple teens should be able to hold, and yet, she knew what she was feeling. The idea that she could, and trying to keep herself in check, was scary and yet so incredibly exciting at the same time.

"If I could, I would stay in this ocean with you forever," Adam said. "This has already been the best birthday, and it's barely begun. You . . . you're . . . I . . ." he stuttered. He wanted to say it but stopped himself, not sure if it was too soon, if she would be ready to hear it.

"Me too," she said simply. He kissed her again, but they didn't get too far before they heard shouts of excitement.

In their lost moment together, the entire beach and all the people on it had disappeared. Now the noise seemed to turn back on, and they saw Nick, Fitz, and Sam swimming over some huge waves that had started up. They were laughing and screaming so loudly that Claire wondered how they had not heard it this whole time.

"Ooh! Let's go!" she said excitedly.

He grinned, and they swam down shore to join. The group of them spent what felt like hours jumping waves, riding waves in, or in some cases, getting completely taken out by waves. Jason laughed and enjoyed watching from the beach, sneakily smoking while listening to Fitz's radio. When they had tuckered themselves out, they returned to dry off, Adam laying a towel down on Claire's other side, holding her hand. He felt the salt dry on his skin and felt the sun warm him, and he knew what Claire meant when she had said "alive."

They snacked and chatted, and Claire didn't even realize that at some point, her self-consciousness had gone away. She openly joked with all of Adam's friends, taking a liking to the banter she could get into with Nick.

He was a little edgier than Jason, who was nothing but sweet toward her, and Fitz who was . . . Fitz. Nick had an insulting jokester way about him with a little bit of dark humor. Claire appreciated it and found it easy to dish right back what he put out, making Jason, Adam, and Fitz all laugh. Sam giggled along too, and Claire knew she had made a friend when Nick said with a smirk, "You're alright, Hanover."

"Not so bad yourself, Nicholas."

"Nobody calls me Nicholas," he retorted with a grin.

"Well, now I do," she said simply.

At one point Jason suggested walking down to the sandbar, which the tide had exposed. The guys all agreed with enthusiasm, but Claire and Sam opted to stay behind and let them roam. Adam kissed her on the cheek before they left, and Sam and Claire watched them till they couldn't see them anymore.

"So, Nick is cute," Sam said.

Claire chuckled. "Not too shabby at all."

"A dark-haired, blue-eyed cutie," Sam added. "Funny too."

"You got a crush?" Claire teased.

"Oh, please. If I did, it would be the equivalent of me crushing on the Backstreet Boys. It would never happen."

"Oh, come on! Why wouldn't it? And I have to say, those Backstreet Boys are pretty cute. I like the dark-haired one with the goatee."

"Kevin?! No, it's definitely Nick Carter," Sam said, and then excitedly, "Hey! They have the same name even."

Claire chuckled. Sam had clearly looked into the boy band more than Claire had thought. She initially wasn't feeling their vibe, more so because she had a soft spot for New Kids on the Block and felt like she was cheating by liking a new boy band. But she had to admit she had enjoyed their debut a little too much and had maybe convinced Gwen to get her their CD from the shop.

"So why do you think crushing on *this* Nick is out of reality?"

Sam sighed. "Because it is. He's hot. He's a senior. And I'm . . . me."

"And what the hell does that mean?"

"I'm a dweeb, Claire. I'm not the girl that gets the cute senior boy."

"Sam, that doesn't even make sense. If you like someone, you like them, and if they like you, then they like you and you go out. It's that simple. You are perfectly capable of attracting a cute senior boy, if that's who you like."

"Well, if you say so," she said with another sigh.

Claire didn't like this new thing Sam had going on. Sam had always been a bit hard on herself, letting out jokes that were a little self-deprecating, but she had never been so focused on this level of fitting in and dating guys and being found attractive by them. It was beginning to make Claire uncomfortable because she really didn't know what to say anymore. She saw Sam as this cute, funny, bundle of hilariousness, hence her wanting her as a best friend, and she couldn't fathom why Sam thought she was so unable to get a date or why she was so obsessed with it or why she thought Claire was so capable of it. That last part was what bugged Claire the most. It made her feel like she was doing something wrong for what had transpired with Adam or, at the very least, that it bothered Sam. Claire had even started holding back on sharing unless Sam asked, for fear of sounding like she was bragging. She didn't want Sam to think so poorly of herself.

"Let's go walk down to the fort," Claire said to break the tension. "Like we used to." The beach they were at was once a military fort, and parts had been left behind, making it a fun place to explore.

Adam, Jason, Nick, and Fitz walked the sandbar, pausing to sit on the large ocean rocks that were at the end of it.

"Okay, we're avoiding the obvious topic here," Nick said suddenly.

Adam looked at him, but the rest all looked at Adam.

"What?" he said.

"Oh, come off it, man. This is the first time we've all been together since you started dating Claire, and we've now all met her."

"Yeah?" Adam said questioningly but knew where this was going.

"Dude," Nick said. "Quit dicking around. You want our opinion, right?"

Adam laughed and ran his hand through his now dry hair. "Alright, alright. Opinion, yes. But approval, no. Just so we're clear."

Nick rolled his eyes. "Duh. We know you date whoever the hell you want."

"I just know how you are, fucktard," Adam retorted.

"I like Claire," Fitz said randomly.

They all looked at him.

"What?" he asked. "You want opinion. There it is. I like her. She's funny, nice, polite, and she seems to like me," he said, ticking it off on his fingers. "Or at least tolerates me, which is more than I can expect from anyone."

Jason nodded his head in agreement. "He's got a point there. She does handle Fitz well."

Adam shook his head with a laugh.

"Okay, okay. So she has impeccable patience," Nick said, taking out a cigarette from his pocket and lighting it up.

"I like her. She's definitely done a number on this one though," Jason said, pointing at Adam.

"What does that mean?" Nick asked. "I never see you guys at school anymore since I go to remedial classes. She doesn't boss him around like Rachel, does she?"

"Not at all. I just mean—the man has fallen hard," Jason said.

Nick blew smoke and said, "How hard?"

"Hard. Like doesn't-sleep-at-night-and-talks-about-her-constantly-at-work hard."

"I am right here, you know," Adam said, taking the cigarette from Nick and taking a puff before handing it off to Fitz.

"Okay. So tell us what you're thinking, then," Nick said.

Adam raised an eyebrow.

"I'm serious. No goofin'. How's it going?"

Adam took a deep breath. He was a little embarrassed to admit it, but he had to get it off his chest. "I think she drives me absolutely insane. Jason's right. I don't sleep. I just want to be with her, listening to her talk. She's such a deep thinker and has such a vision of the world that I've never heard before. She makes me feel special. Which Rachel never did. I struggle to focus on anything when I'm not around her. I don't eat well. I feel like I could throw up in excitement when I hear the phone ring, thinking it might be her. She's smart, talented, passionate, and absolutely beautiful."

Nick stared at him, eyebrows raised, the cigarette, which had made its way back to him, out. "Wow, you weren't kidding, Jason."

"I told you. He's got it bad. If I didn't know better, I'd say he was in love," Jason joked.

"He's been in love since he met her," Fitz piped in, lying on the small beach that surrounded their rock formation and staring at the sky.

Jason and Nick looked at him.

"He has. He hasn't been the same since he met Claire. He's been in love for two years, just about, and didn't know it."

"Are you high?" Nick asked.

"Is that even a question?" Jason said.

Nick shook his head. "Well." He lit the cigarette again and took a drag. "Her rack and ass had all of us looking, I'm pretty sure."

Adam punched him in the arm.

Nick laughed. "I'm kidding! Kidding! Okay, sorry. Joking aside. Adam," he put the cigarette out against the rock, "I think you have an absolutely ballin' girl, and you need to not fuck this up. She's funny, takes my stupid-ass jokes, brings out the best in you, and is in fact beautiful, as you said. For real. You're one lucky son of a bitch."

Adam smirked. "I think I may be in love. Which terrifies me. "

"Of course you are," Fitz threw out.

"Yeah, it's kind of obvious," Nick agreed while Jason nodded.

"I don't want to push it though. I don't want to scare her or move too fast. I mean, we're still in high school. And how do I even know what love is?"

"Dude, age doesn't mean anything. It is what it is," Jason said.

Adam nodded.

"Alright, enough of this," Nick said. "Guys, we're motherfucking seniors. What are we even doing with our lives?"

Meanwhile, Claire and Sam had made it to the fort, walked around the structure a while, and started the walk back to their spot, discussing what they were going to do this summer now that Claire had a license but also work and concerns for Troy, which Claire had told Sam about the morning after her night with Adam, Sam's response having been exactly how Claire had predicted it.

Walking along the shoreline so the water could splash on their feet, Claire's story of a customer she'd had to deal with at the bakery was interrupted by Sam's groan.

"Oh, what is she doing here?!"

Claire looked in the direction Sam was indicating and saw the blonde head and *Baywatch* worthy red bathing suit of Amber.

"Damn it. Maybe she won't see us," Claire said.

"We have to go right by her to get to our shit," Sam whined.

"Just don't make eye contact."

"Too late," Sam said. "She saw us."

Amber had in fact made a face of surprise and then of malice as she waved at them. They waved back and, of course, made their way to her, their towels so close and yet so far away.

"Hanover and Levinski. How great to see you here," Amber said mockingly. "We just got here ourselves." She indicated the group behind her, which, of course, consisted of Mark, Chris, Mike, Sarah, Lauren, and Ashley. Claire and Sam waved at them. It seemed lately that all their altercations with the group were really just altercations with Amber, her position being a clear barrier between them. Claire had the sneaking suspicion that this was on purpose. Of course Amber would be protective of her popular clique.

"Great to see you too. Hope you're enjoying your summer break," Claire said as Sam scowled.

"Oh, you know, trying to hang out together as much as we can!" she said with fake sincerity. She looked Claire up and down and said more quietly so the group, who had sort of started talking among themselves, wouldn't hear. "Nice bathing suit. Did it not come in a larger size?"

"Excuse me?" Claire said, not believing that Amber could hit so low so quickly.

"Oh, I just—well, I mean, you're kind of popping out here and there. But maybe that was the look you were going for. My bad."

"Look, if you called us over just to insult us, we'll see you later. And by *later*, I mean *never*," Claire said.

"Hanover, calm down. I wasn't trying to insult. Merely asking a question. I mean, you got the curves and the goods, why not show them all off?"

Claire felt her face grow hot and her shoulders and jaw tense, and like always, she found she couldn't move from that awful sneering face.

"Shut up, Amber."

"Too bad you couldn't trade some of your goods with Levinski over here. She could use some."

"You are such a—"

"What. What am I?" Amber asked. "Please do sha—"

Amber stopped. Claire wasn't sure why until she felt an arm wrap itself around her and a face nuzzle into her neck, planting a kiss that made Claire giggle. She looked over her shoulder to see Adam there.

"Not a problem here I hope?" Nick said, a cigarette in hand, his arm around Sam's shoulders, staring at Amber. The group behind her silenced.

"N-no," Amber stuttered.

"Oh, good! Amber, right?" Adam said.

"Um, yes," Amber said and then put on her Miss America smile. But Claire noticed that it was a bit faulty. "Adam, right?"

"Yes. Nice to see you again. This here is my buddy Nick," Adam said.

Nick blew smoke at Amber, who coughed and fanned it out of her face. "Uh, hi."

"Pleasure," he said. "We just got back from a little stroll down the beach and were looking for these two cuties. If you all don't mind, we're going to bring them back to our space over there, where there seems to be less of a stench."

"A stench?" Amber asked, a blush creeping up her neck.

"Well, I can only assume based on the pinch-nosed expression you were giving our girls over here because it certainly couldn't have been directed at them," Nick said, taking another drag.

"Oh. I, um . . ."

"Come, dear," Nick said to Sam as he led her away, Adam taking Claire's hand and giving Amber a two-finger salute before following.

Claire and Sam waited till they were back at their spot, rejoining Jason and Fitz, before bursting into laughter at the absolute stunned look on Amber's face.

"That was totally amazing," Sam said.

"I can't even. That was sick!" Claire said.

Adam laughed, lying next to her again. "Anytime. She's a bitch. I don't know why you guys even talk to her."

"Because she's been a pain in our sides since grade school, and she *wants* us to back down."

"Well, it isn't worth it," Adam said, placing a hand on her leg, which made goose bumps appear up Claire's arm that had nothing to do with being cold.

She looked at Nick, not really knowing how to thank him for coming to Sam's defense without saying it. But her look seemed to be enough. He winked at her and she beamed back.

The ride home was quiet. Everyone was beat from the day in the sun. They stopped off once, Jason and Nick following them, where Claire made true to her word and bought everyone ice cream, after which Fitz and Sam both fell asleep in the back seat, Claire nodding off in the front. When she leaned against the window and finally succumbed to her heavy eyelids and sunbathed body, Adam placed a hand on her thigh, his thumb moving ever so lightly. It was a simple gesture, but it made Claire's heart soar. She let the motion lull her to sleep, not waking till they pulled up to Fitz's house to drop him off and then finally ending outside Claire's. Sam grabbed her stuff, thanked Adam for a great day, and wished him a final Happy Birthday before heading home, where her plan was to shower and nap.

That plan sounded great to Claire too, but she had one more thing to do first.

"You got a minute?" she asked.

"Of course." He grinned.

She led him into her yard to a bench in the back that was secluded in the corner of her mom's flower garden. "I'll be right back," she said. "I have your birthday gift inside."

She went in and ran up to her room, yelling to her mom that she was back but that Adam was still outside. She felt her heart race with anxiety as she walked the gift that she had been working on all week out to him.

Sitting down on the bench, she said, "So, I racked my brain to decide what to give you that would be both meaningful and a gift you'd actually want." She felt her voice shake a little.

"Anything you could possibly give me would be something I'd want. And you didn't have to get me anything at all."

"Of course I did," she said with a smile. "So, I remembered back to our first playground visit and all the stuff we talked about. I told you that night that I wanted to be a writer. I've never told anyone that, really. And, well, I knew then that there was something special about you for me to spill that. So I decided on this. I'll let you open it."

He smiled at her, gave her a kiss, and then opened up the package that contained a composition notebook Claire had picked up in town the week before and contained . . .

"Writing? Is this your writing?" he asked, flipping through the pages and seeing what looked like full pages of Claire's neat scrawl, some drawings, some pictures, and more.

"Yeah. And, uh, don't read it now, please," she said, blushing. "Just read it later."

He closed the book slowly. "Are you sure?"

"Positive. Way too awkward to watch someone read my writing. So just read it at home." She chuckled.

"Can I talk to you about it after?" he asked genuinely.

She smiled. "Yes. I will say most are stories that may seem familiar to you. They're about you. And us." She blushed. "And I wrote down a few particular song lyrics here and there."

"Claire. I don't know what to say," he said, looking down at the book in his hands. It was covered in doodles, like the ones you would draw on a paper-bag book cover at school. Its title was the same as a song that was played often on the radio. A song about love and the depth of it.

"I don't think—I *know* I've never been given such a meaningful gift." He hadn't either. This was intimate. Thoughtful. She was allowing him into a vulnerable place of hers and trusted him with it.

Claire didn't have anything to say to that. "I also owe you your extra prize for going in the water."

"I think you gave that to me while we were swimming."

She giggled and blushed. "Well, then here is an extra birthday gift."

He placed the notebook carefully next to him and sidled over to be even closer to her. They joined lips, and Adam was reminded in fuller detail of their moment earlier and felt his body hunger for her. He ran his hand through her hair, stopping to cup her face as he kissed deeper. They were lost in each other, not knowing for how long.

Claire started to get goose bumps on her legs and shiver, as the evening was getting darker and her sun-kissed skin longed for heat.

He rubbed her arms and said, "I guess we need to call this a day."

"I hope it was a good birthday," she said, hugging him around the middle as he wrapped his arms around her, kissing the top of her head.

"I don't even have words for how good of a day this was. The beach, swimming, the sun, you, your gift."

"Happy Birthday," she said.

He squeezed her. He couldn't believe how lucky he was and how badly he wanted to say those three words to her.

Killing Me Softly with His Song

"I don't know," Claire said as she helped dry the dishes her mother handed her.

"Oh, Claire, come on. Why not?"

"It just seems cheesy."

"To invite your boyfriend to Sunday dinner?" she said, pausing her rinsing and staring at Claire.

"Yeah! It's so old-school. Like, 'Gee whiz, mister, want to come over for Sunday dinner?' " she said with an arm flair.

"Claire, hunny, I don't know what you're talking about. It's just dinner," she said, revisiting her washing.

"Okay, fine. I'll let him know he's invited."

"This Sunday is Troy's last family dinner before he goes. Gwen will be here, and we'd love to have Adam too. And any other Sunday for that matter."

"Okay."

"It's only a couple days away."

"I know," Claire said, wiping the dish she was given.

Her mother paused yet again.

"What?" Claire asked.

"Go invite the boy," she said.

"Right now?!"

"Yes!"

Claire mumbled her way to the phone. She really had no issue with inviting Adam to dinner but had been feeling a bit off about everything, as her mom constantly reminded everyone that it was Troy's last dinner. You'd swear he was a prisoner on death row, or Jesus, the rest of them his disciples coming together for the last supper.

She grabbed the phone and went to her room. Regardless of how she was feeling, hearing Adam's voice over the line perked her up and put a smile on her face.

"Hey you," he said.

"Hey," she said, lying back on her bed.

"I was just thinking of you, actually," he returned, also getting comfortable, the beige receiver to his corded phone wedged between his ear and shoulder, looking at the notebook Claire had made for him.

"Oh yeah?"

"Yes, ma'am. I just finished reading through your composition notebook," he said.

Claire felt her cheeks warm a little. "And?"

"And I love it."

"I'm glad," she said, feeling the mild embarrassment leave as quickly as it had come. "I enjoyed writing it."

"You're a great writer, Claire. And I love that these stories are all so special, of course."

"You're the best muse around," she said.

She heard his grin as he said, "Never thought I could be someone's muse."

"What? With your deep gray eyes, dreamy hairdo, and perfect smile? Come on."

Adam, who was glad she couldn't see him blush, chuckled. "Well, thank you. I hope I get to read more."

"I'd like that too." She beamed. "Just pretend you don't remember getting this so I can surprise you again around Christmastime."

"You got it."

"So, um. Apart from just enjoying talking to you, I did have a reason for calling."

"What's up?"

"Well, my family has always done Sunday dinners. Like, a sit-down meal. Sometimes Babs comes, and Sam has many times. And, well, my mom wanted me to let you know that you're invited to them." She finished in a rushed manner. "I totally understand if you can't or if that's, like, too much or if your family does Sunday dinners too or whatever. But I told her I—"

"I'd love to," he said simply.

Claire paused. "You would?"

"Yes," he said.

"Oh. Well, great!" she said excitedly. "I know this Sunday is only a couple days away, but you're welcome to this one. My mom said so specifically because it's Troy's last before he leaves." She faltered a little at the mention of Troy. "Gwen will be here as well. But I understand if it's too last minute."

"I'll be there. What time?"

"We usually eat around five. You're welcome to come earlier if you want," she said.

"Sounds good!"

"Cool, um, thank you."

"Of course," he said. "Not gonna lie, it makes me feel pretty special to be invited."

"Well, good, because you *are* special."

Adam paused for a moment, at a loss for words. "Thank you. See you Sunday?"

"Yes, sir. I miss you," she said, not really sure what she was trying to say. "I miss you" was accurate, as they hadn't seen a whole lot of each other since the beach trip because of work and Claire trying to hang out with Troy whenever she could. But it didn't seem to quite hit what she was feeling.

"I miss you too," he returned, feeling the heaviness of what he really wanted to say to her.

"See you Sunday," she said.

"Sure thing."

They hung up. Claire looked around her room and suddenly panicked, realizing Adam would be seeing it all in just two days.

Claire worked, had Sam help her clean her room, and saw a movie with Troy in the time leading up to Sunday dinner. At 3:00 there was a knock at the door, and Claire felt her heart flutter when she heard Adam's voice from her spot in the living room where she sat with Troy and Gwen. It was quickly followed by her mom's excited voice.

"Oh, you are just the sweetest thing," she said.

Claire exchanged a look with Troy as Adam and their mother came into the living room. She was holding a small bouquet of wildflowers, sniffing them and beaming.

"Look at these," she said to the three of them, Claire sitting up and smirking at Adam, who shrugged with a grin. "Aren't they just the prettiest things? I'm going to go put them in water. Thank you."

"You're welcome." Adam smiled. He sat down next to Claire, giving her a side hug and kissing her temple.

"Aren't you the dapper gentleman," she said.

"My mom wouldn't let me leave the house till I went out and put some together from her garden. Not that I didn't like the gesture myself."

Claire laughed.

"Hey, Troy," Adam said, looking over at Troy and Gwen. "Gwen."

"How's it going?" Troy asked good-naturedly, Gwen giving a small wave and smile.

"Not too bad. Congrats. All sworn in and everything, huh?"

"Yes, sir. Officially US Coast Guard owned."

"Nice. You leave Friday?" Adam asked.

"Yup. Early in the morning. Dad and I leave for the airport at six."

"Well, I'm sure there'll be time later, but I'll say good luck now."

"Thanks, man," Troy said with a meaningful nod.

They sat in silence for a moment before Claire said, "Want a tour of the house?"

"Yeah!" Adam answered.

They got up, Claire in the lead, and headed toward the entryway and back office space but didn't make it far before Troy called, "Oh, Claire, don't forget to leave your door open when you go upstairs."

Claire rolled her eyes as they heard Troy distinctly react to what must have been a hit from Gwen. Adam laughed. Claire made the loop from the living room through the entryway, office, dining room, and kitchen, which would lead right back to the living room, but Claire took her side staircase to go to her room.

"The upstairs was an apartment once, and my parents never took out the second staircase, so I have my own," she said as they went up and entered her room, leaving the door open but making no move to open the other door, which led to the hallway. It felt weird to have Adam in it but not the same kind of weird as when Mark had been there. She was more than excited to have Adam see her space and her things. And she knew he would be the perfect kind of gentleman, the kind that brings flowers to your mom. She also knew she wouldn't be completely against him being a little less of a gentleman, which she mentally kicked herself for for even thinking. It was really just a surreal experience to see her two worlds combine.

She watched him check out her books and smile at the stuffed nature of them taking up every possible square inch of the shelf they were on.

"That's all my music there," she said, pointing to the second shelf, which held her boom box, cassettes, and CDs as well as a hodgepodge of other stuff like her old piano ribbons, framed photos, and trinkets. "And that's my keyboard, obviously."

"So this is where the maestro practices," he said.

She chuckled. "Most of the time. Although I go to Babs's house at least once a week to get some practice in too. Which reminds me that you need to meet her. She's been nagging me on when I'm going to bring you to tea."

"Can't wait. She sounds like a great lady whenever you talk about her."

"She is. And she knows so much about town; she's fascinating to listen to. And she needs people in her life. She's lonely."

"Well then, we'll have to visit her soon," he said, feeling his heart swell at yet another reason why he liked Claire so much.

Claire smiled. "She'd be so excited."

Adam looked at Claire's wall papered with magazine cutouts and posters. Claire gave a half laugh as she realized how many of the cutouts were just cute celebrities and musicians she crushed on. "Sam puts a bunch of those up all the time." This was true but was not the only reason Christian Slater stared down at them from the wall in several places, or Christian Bale.

"Got a thing for Christians, huh?" he said with the shittiest of grins.

She felt herself blush slightly. "Yeah, well . . ."

"Good thing I'm Catholic," Adam said.

Claire gave a burst of laughter. "And, I mean, you got the hairdo going on too. Not to mention Mr. Slater's mischievous smile. So I think you're good," she added.

"Phew."

She went and sat on her bed, one leg draped over the side, grabbing a pillow to hold while he continued to check out her music collection.

"Now that we see each other more often, do we trade cassettes just during school time, or year-round?" He grinned.

"Ooh, good question. I say year-round, but no pressure. Just when one sticks out as a perfect pick that is absolutely necessary for the other to have."

"Sounds good to me," he said, sitting at the end of her bed, facing her.

"It's been a little bit, hasn't it?" she said. "Since your last one. Goo Goo Dolls! I'm slacking."

"Nah. Don't worry about it. One will randomly come to you, and it'll be perfect." He placed a hand on her knee, and she was quite happy to have it there.

"So how are you holding up?" he asked.

She sighed. "Okay. I think I'm just pushing it aside till Friday."

Adam nodded. "Jersey, right?"

"Yup. Boot camp in New Jersey, and then he'll get his orders from there. He's hoping he'll be sent to one of the bases nearby."

"Fingers crossed. Jersey isn't too far. But boot camp is boot camp, I guess," he offered.

"Yeah. I think that's why I'm doing better. Once I learned he's going to Jersey and that his odds of being stationed nearby are high, I felt a bit better. I think right now it's just the whole idea of everything changing that I'm struggling with."

"Completely understandable," he said, and then, "How's Sam?"

"She's good. I honestly don't see her nearly as much as I always have, which has been another tough adjustment. We still talk on the phone pretty much daily, but she started babysitting, and between that and my work and spending time with Troy and then seeing you whenever I can, we haven't had a lot of time together. After Troy heads out, I'm going to have her spend the night and hang out. I took Friday and Saturday off."

"That sounds like a good plan," Adam said, rubbing her knee. "I like Sam. You guys crack me up."

Claire smiled. "She's my bestest."

"Play me something?" he asked, pointing at the keyboard.

She grinned. "Sure."

She sat down at the wooden chair in front of her keyboard, not having a bench, with one leg beneath her, and thumbed through her favorite book of music, landing on a classic that had been remade the year before by Fugees, which Claire was quite a fan of. She remembered playing it for Babs not too long ago, who then had her play it three more times, having loved the song when it had been released in the early 1970s. She placed it atop the keyboard, not that she really needed it, almost knowing it by heart. Adam lay along the end of her bed, head leaning on his shoulder, watching her. She took her breath, relaxed, and started to play, hearing the words in her head. It was a soft sultry song, and so she played it in that manner, feeling the keys softly slip under her fingers from one note to the next, playing a song about the powerful, emotional movement that music brings to those who listen to it. She got lost in her music, and Adam got lost in her.

When she finished, she lifted her hands slowly off the keyboard and looked to Adam, who was beaming.

"Beautiful," he said. "Like you."

She blushed. "Why, thank you." She got up and went to join him, lying on her stomach in front of him.

"I love watching you play," he said quietly.

"Oh really," she said with a light laugh.

"Yeah," he said matter-of-factly. "I do."

"And why is that?"

"Because—" He thought for a moment. "Because you amaze me."

"Amaze you?!" She laughed for real this time. "Oh, come off it."

"No, really!" he said with a grin. "Claire, I've never met anyone so intense and emotional with their playing, and it's mesmerizing. I mean, I haven't met many pianists in my lifetime, but you've got to be the most enjoyable to watch. It's moving. You must feel it."

"I do," she said. "But so do you. When you play the drums. I see it."

He raised his eyebrows. "You watch me play drums?"

"Um, yeah! Duh!" she said. "The piano is always positioned sideways so I can see Mr. Johns, and I don't always have to look at my hands or notes, so when I don't . . ." She paused for dramatic effect. "I sneak a peek at the hot drummer in the back corner. And he is *always* lost in his rhythms and beats, and *I* find it mesmerizing."

Adam blushed this time, more than he ever had before, and laughed.

Claire laughed too and adjusted herself so she was also on her side, head perched on her hand.

"And while we're sharing, I don't think I've ever told you how much I enjoy your smile."

"My smile?" He grinned.

"Yes. It was one of the first things I noticed about you. I absolutely love it."

"And why's that?"

"Because it always seems to be there. And it is so variant. There's a smirk for when you're hiding something or know something. A shitty grin when you tease. A smile that you try desperately to hide when you're embarrassed, which usually causes a laugh to follow. And my favorite—a genuine beaming smile when you're happy."

Adam nodded and gave her a side-glance. "Well, you'll be happy to know that the reason I smile so much is because of you."

Claire leaned into him.

Before he accepted her advance, however, he whispered, "Should we open that door like Troy suggested?"

Claire smiled slyly. "No. I didn't hear my parents tell me to. Plus, that one is open, and I'm sure my mom heard me playing piano from the kitchen. She'll be content with that. We'll head down in a minute."

He gave her a wide smile and fully welcomed her move, having been longing for it for a while, their time apart being too often lately. They played lightly at first, small, short kisses. Claire felt adrenaline shoot through her as it did every time she felt Adam's soft touch. He pushed forward ever so slowly, never parting their locked lips. Claire followed, lying back, his arm that was supporting his head leaving to lie beneath hers, his other ever so lightly draping across her waist, his warm hand gingerly coming to rest on her hip, her exposed skin beneath her top feeling his warmth. They got lost in a moment once again, their embrace growing closer and tighter, both of them yearning for each other but knowing their limitations and surroundings.

They both smiled against each other, coming full circle to quick pecks, calming down the intensity of their make-out session.

"I will never ever tire of this," Claire said in a whisper with a small giggle.

"Me neither," he replied. He squinted at her seriously, made to say something, and then thought better of it. It wasn't time yet.

"I suppose we should go downstairs before someone comes looking for us."

"Probably. I don't want to get you in trouble, and I especially don't want to get myself thrown out before my first Sunday dinner."

She laughed. "Good call."

They got up, Claire running her fingers through her hair to make sure it didn't look at all disheveled, and they headed down the way they had come to join back up with Troy, Gwen, and now Claire's mom, her dad outside manning the grill, tonight being a hamburgers and hot dogs kind of night. They sat around and chatted for a bit before Claire's mom left to set the table, Gwen offering to help. To add to the hamburgers and hot dogs, Claire's mom had made macaroni salad and grilled potatoes with veggies. When it came time to sit around the table, their father offered grace and they dug in.

Adam, who had always had great but quiet meals with his parents, found the liveliness of the table entertaining, and he absolutely loved it. Even though there were only six of them, there somehow seemed to be several conversations happening at the same time, and Adam found himself just sitting back to enjoy it all.

At one point, when it lulled, Claire's mom decided to bring the conversation around to him.

"So, Adam, tell us about yourself. Your parents aren't from around here originally, are they? I didn't recognize the names."

"No," he said with a smile. "My dad is from out of state, and my mom is from Italy. She came here after they married."

"Oh, wow, isn't that fascinating. Claire never mentioned that."

Claire shrugged her apology. She had found that intriguing as well when she had asked Adam about his mom's slight accent but hadn't thought to run home and tell her parents.

"And you're a senior this coming year, right? That must be exciting. Any idea what you want to do?"

"Um, well, I think I want to go into computer sciences or IT or something like that," he said.

"Oh, wonderful. That's where it seems to be," she said.

He nodded.

"Any idea where you want to go to school?"

Claire rolled her eyes, and Troy grinned at her.

"Ah, well, I haven't made a clear plan yet. I was actually thinking I might take a year off—you know, to save some money for school—but was possibly considering trying to apply for MIT at some point. Or Wentworth."

"Wow, that's great! Boston. That's not too far at all. Like three hours or so, give or take traffic."

"Yeah, definitely not bad." He smiled. "But they're pretty competitive schools. And I'm not quite sure I have what it takes to get in. So I may think about just going to community college at first to get my core classes and then go from there. I'm not quite sure yet."

Claire gave his thigh a squeeze, hoping it translated to something along the lines of *I'm sorry for my intrusive mother.* They hadn't even talked about this stuff yet. Not that Adam talking to her about what he wanted to do was a requirement at all, but it dawned on Claire that at some point this would be a bridge they'd have to cross. She pushed it aside, reminding herself it was only July and they had the whole rest of summer and an entire school year ahead of them, not to mention they had really just started dating.

"Oh, I'm sure you could get in wherever you wanted to."

Adam grinned, appreciating her positive nature, so much like Claire's. "Thank you, Mrs. Hanover."

"So tell me—"

"Lynn," said Claire's father from across the table.

"What?"

"Let the boy eat," he said lightheartedly.

"Oh, I'm sorry," she said, patting Adam's hand while Troy chuckled and Claire laughed.

"Not at all. I understand I'm the new guy at the table," Adam returned.

"There, see? Thank you. I'm only trying to get to know him. That way, when he comes to future Sunday dinners, which I hope you will, I'll have something to check in about!"

"Alright. Alright," Claire's dad said. The conversations broke out again, and it remained a cacophony of talking, Adam's time mostly being taken by Claire's mom, until it was time to clear the table, which they all helped with, and Claire's mom brought out dessert—a blueberry cake topped with powdered sugar. She sliced the cake up as Claire's dad got them all glasses and popped some champagne, pouring some into each.

"Hope your parents don't mind," he said to Adam with a wink.

When done, he stood at his spot and said, "A toast. To Troy. May your boot camp experience bring you strength, integrity, and drive. And may you be blessed with safety and grace as you start this journey in the United States Coast Guard. We are going to miss you around here but are so incredibly proud of what you have chosen to do. We know you don't leave till Friday, but with all of us here tonight, your mother and I wanted to make sure your last Sunday dinner till your return was a good one. We wish you the best of luck and send you off with our love, support, and prayers. And will count down the days till we get to see you again. We love you. To Troy."

They all held up their glasses and repeated, "To Troy," before taking sips.

"Thanks, Dad. And to you all. Dinner was great, Mom. And I'm looking forward to this."

Claire didn't say anything, knowing she wouldn't make it through. She felt the warmth of the champagne in her belly and put aside her emotions to save them for Friday. Adam was overcome with a sense of gratitude toward Claire's family for wanting him there for this and including him in Troy's send-off. It was special and, in turn, made *him* feel special.

They enjoyed dessert immensely and, when done, fell into a food coma. Retiring to the living room, Claire's mom put coffee on, and they all lay around, Claire's dad in his lounge chair, nodding off, Troy, Gwen, and Claire's mom on the couch, and Adam and Claire on the love seat. A PBS special on The Mamas & the Papas was playing on the television, and Claire's mom hummed along as the rest succumbed to comfortable silence. Claire eventually laid her head on Adam's lap, and though surprised at first, he relaxed too and couldn't think of a time when he'd ever been made to feel so welcomed by another family. He scooched down so he could rest his head on the back of the couch and let "California Dreamin' " wash over him.

Friday came too soon for Claire's liking. She didn't sleep that much the night before, assumed Troy couldn't either, and visited him in his room. They stayed up talking until four in the morning, when they heard their parents get up and start getting ready for Troy's departure. Their mom made pancakes and bacon for breakfast, and they ate mostly in silence. Troy put his things in the car, not that he could bring much, and before they all knew it, it was time for him and their dad to hit the road. It was a moment that even the skies seemed to have prepared for. They were dark, with a heaviness in the air that called for summer rain. Maybe even a thunderstorm.

Gwen pulled into the driveway and entered the house as Troy started making his goodbyes. Claire waited as he hugged their mom first and exchanged some words before she went outside to stand by the car with their dad. He then turned to Gwen. Claire looked away while they hugged and exchanged their own goodbyes. Gwen started to sniffle, and Troy held on extra tight, whispering words of comfort to her. After a final kiss, it was Claire's turn. Gwen left to blow her nose in the bathroom.

"Okay, Mouse," he said with a heavy sigh.

Claire felt her eyes burn. "You do what you're told," she said. "And you be the best coast guardsman you can be so you can come back here in eight weeks a new and better Troy."

"Understood," he said with a smile.

"And you write to me. And Gwen. Even though you're horrible at it and can't spell worth shit."

"You know it," he said with a light laugh.

She paused as the burning got stronger and she couldn't hold back the tears that were determined to fall anymore. Troy wrapped her in a tight embrace and held her close.

"And you keep right on being you, Mouse. I'm proud of you. I don't say it enough."

"Because if you did, I'd think you'd gone crazy," Claire muffled into his arm.

"I love you, Mouse."

"I love you too, Troy."

He let go. Gwen came out of the bathroom. He gave a final wave and smirk and headed out the door. Gwen and Claire followed, stopping on the top step, Gwen's arm around Claire's shoulders. Claire watched as he hugged their mom one last time, got into the passenger seat, and closed the door, their dad hopping in to drive. The car backed out of the driveway, and they all watched it till it was no longer in sight.

"You girls going to be okay?" Claire's mom asked them, wiping tears from her eyes as she climbed the front steps.

As if her words were the open sesame to the floodgates of their combined emotions, Claire and Gwen both lost it. Claire's mom joined in their hug and added her own tears before saying, "I'll put on some tea. And let's make a second breakfast. We've earned it."

Claire and Gwen sat opposite on the couch, facing each other, both still in pj's, a cup of tea in their hands. Claire's mom was busy in the kitchen making everything she could possibly find, as this was her way of handling stress on any given day, let alone the one where she said goodbye to her only son as he began his journey as a soldier. They didn't talk much, but it felt good to have each other's company. In no time, plates laden with French toast, scrambled eggs, sausage, and fruit were delivered, and they were notified that cinnamon buns were currently baking in the oven.

They ate, and it seemed to help all three of them slowly come to terms with the change of the morning, and it gave them a boost of strength to be able to move forward. They were discussing how full they all were when the oven dinged for the cinnamon buns.

Gwen eventually left for work, and Sam came over for their sleepover. It was exactly what Claire needed to feel better. Sam had brought her favorite VHS movies and a slew of magazines for them to look through. Adam called at one point to ask how Claire was doing but didn't keep her long, knowing Sam was there and wanted them to have some time together. Claire planned to call him later the next day, but his calling started a whole discussion from Sam.

"You. Guys. Are. Adorable," she said, gum smacking. "I can't even tell you how much so."

Claire smirked. "He is a cutie. And I do really like him."

"Dude, he's hot. And duh! Of course you like him!"

"Sam," Claire began since Sam seemed to be in a chatty mood. She wasn't sure if sharing this would do more harm than good.

"What?" she asked with a slight edge in her voice.

"Do you think," she said tentatively but then threw caution to the wind, reminding herself that Sam was her best friend and this was something you discussed with your best friend. "Do you think it's possible to feel love at our age?"

Sam's eyebrows went up, her chewing ceased, and she stopped turning the magazine page mid-flip. "Oh. My. God!!!"

Claire rolled her eyes but grinned.

"Oh my god!! Oh my god. You love him, don't you?!" she asked, throwing her magazine aside.

"I don't know! We haven't been formally dating for a whole heck of a long time, so I don't want to push it, but—"

"But you've known him for going on three years and have had chemistry since day one: that counts for something."

"Well, true. But I don't know."

"Tell me everything," Sam said. "How long have you felt this way?"

"I've felt the same way about him since our night outside at that party freshman year. But I don't think I've really been able to label it—or try to label it anyway—as love till more recently."

Sam let out a loud squeal. "Have you told him?!"

"God no," Claire said.

"Why not?"

"Um, because he'd probably run away in the opposite direction! Sam, I'm not that crazy."

"How do you know he doesn't feel the same way?"

"I don't know. That's part of the dilemma, isn't it? If I say it and he doesn't, then there goes that. If I say it and he does, then great! But that's a terrifying risk to take."

"Aren't you the one who always says that what others think doesn't matter? That if you feel something, you just need to let yourself feel it and say it out loud? Or something like that?"

"Sounds like me," Claire said sheepishly.

"It definitely is." Sam took a moment to think. "Well, I guess I understand holding off a bit. How do you think you'll know when to tell him?"

"When I've decided if that is, in fact, what I'm feeling. Sam, I don't even know. I'm sixteen, for crying out loud. How do I know if this is legit and isn't just my stupid teenage hormones raging like lunatics? Love is a big deal. I can't just spew it out there."

"Okay, so what do you do?"

"I don't know. Feel it out, I guess."

Sam nodded. "To answer your question, I think we can totally feel love at our age. Isn't that what *Romeo and Juliet* is all about?"

"You mean you actually took something of that in?"

"Hey, I may have used CliffsNotes, and have continued to do so ever since, but I still took in a thing or two here and there."

They stared at each other before breaking into giggles.

KILLING ME SOFTLY WITH HIS SONG

The summer seemed to pass in a haze of working at the bakery, receiving and sending letters to Troy, seeing Adam as much as possible in between both of their crazy work schedules, and squeezing time with Sam in between that. Eating and sleeping filled in the rest of the time, and by the end of August, Claire hadn't done half the things she was hoping to, only seeing the beach a handful of times and not once going anywhere remotely entertaining.

There was the one day Claire and Adam managed to take a trip to the lake, just the two of them. It was the lake Adam frequented on his own. There was a long stretch of sand that families were set up on, but Adam took her down his trail in the woods that led to the smaller alcove near his spot, where they swam, hung out, and enjoyed their quiet little haven.

But now the start of a new school year was a mere week away, and Claire and Sam decided to take a drive to the mall to do some clothes shopping on a day that Claire had off. It was going to serve a dual purpose, as Claire was planning to pop into RadioShack to see Adam at work, having not physically seen him in a week, only talking on the phone when they'd gotten a few minutes.

"I don't know what look I want to go for," Sam said. "It's a new school year. I feel I should try something new, ya know? Fresh start."

Claire nodded along to "MMMBop" on the radio, wisps of hair blowing wildly around her. It was a muggy August day, and she was looking forward to the air-conditioned mall. Her white crop top was stuck to her back already, her high-waisted jean shorts not giving her much breathing room either. She had her hair piled up on her head with clips to keep it off her neck. Sam, who never seemed to break a sweat, had on a simple floral dress, Claire envying her lack of a chest and therefore lack of boob sweat.

They pulled into the mall and took deep sighs in unison as the sliding doors opened, the cold air enveloping them. Claire put her sunglasses atop her head, and they made their way to RadioShack first. She hadn't told Adam she was visiting and was hoping to surprise him. Walking into the store, they saw the latest cordless phone sets, answering machines, and cell phone accessories. In the back were the surround sound systems and radios. Music was thumping from one of them.

Claire spotted Adam right away. He had his back to her, and she snuck up behind him, laced her arms around his middle, and said, "Guess who?"

"Hey you. Better not let my girlfriend see you here," he said.

"Hey!" Claire said as he turned around with his shitty grin, wrapping his arms around her.

"I saw you in the mirror," he said, pointing over his shoulder at the mirrors along the ceiling that helped employees keep an eye on customers.

"Jerk," she said with a smirk.

"You think there could ever be anyone I would want more than you?" he said quietly.

"I mean, I am pretty amazing, so probably not." She laughed.

He grinned and went in for a kiss. It had been too long since he had tasted those sweet lips. She accepted excitedly, wishing they had the time and space for more.

"This was a happy surprise," Adam said, taking her hand and walking her to the counter where Sam was talking to Jason. "What are you guys doing here?"

"We decided to come do some school shopping. And, of course, couldn't do that without coming to see you two goons," she said.

KILLING ME SOFTLY WITH HIS SONG

"Well, welcome to our lair," Jason said, gesturing to the store. Another guy, whom Claire had never met before, came out from the back. He looked a little older than Adam and Jason, and Claire assumed he was the manager.

"Paul," Adam said. "This is my girlfriend, Claire, and her friend Sam. Ladies, this is Paul, our shift leader."

"Nice to meet you," he said, holding out a hand. "I've heard a lot about you."

"Hopefully all good," Claire said, shaking it.

"Most definitely." He smiled. He then turned to Jason to ask him about a delivery out back as a customer walked in.

"I guess I should let you get back to work," Claire said. "We'll stop back in on our way out."

"Sounds good," he returned, giving her a final kiss before walking over to give assistance, and Claire and Sam left the store. They hit up all their usual stops, Claire finding some fun pieces. Sam decided she was going to go for a slightly edgier look this year, buying some fun graphic tees that, according to her, she planned to wear with her plaid flannels. Claire, who was always partial to florals, bought a couple more dresses in patterns of the like, a new pair of jeans, and a few simple tops. They stopped and bought some fun earrings, a new choker for Claire, and a set of best friend necklaces for fun. Claire also bought a silver thumb ring she fell in love with and a few new scrunchies. They stopped at the photo booth kiosk like they did every time to take goofy pictures. Bath & Body Works, the music shop, the shoe store, and, of course, the bookshop were all perused before they stopped at the food court for a late lunch. They landed on good ole McDonald's, and Claire bought Adam a burger and fries to drop off on their way out.

Laden down with bags, they returned to RadioShack, where all three boys were helping customers. Adam waved to her with a slightly saddened expression. Claire went behind the counter, hoping she wouldn't get in trouble, grabbed a piece of scrap paper and a pen, wrote out "Enjoy! Talk to you soon! -Claire" with a heart, and left it with his food atop it. She blew him a kiss on her way out and was happy to see that handsome grin before she and Sam left.

"Dude, you're so lucky," Sam said randomly on their way home. "I'm just going to pray to the boyfriend gods that I get one this year. Like, for real."

"Oh, Sam. It'll definitely happen. I'm sure of it," Claire said. "And if it doesn't, who cares!"

"I care, Claire. Why don't you get that?" Sam said suddenly.

"I—I'm sorry," Claire said, quickly glancing her way. "I didn't mean—"

"Why do you always make it out like I'm crazy for wanting to have a boyfriend?!" Sam said, reaching hysterics.

"Sam, I don't think you're crazy. I just—"

"Every time I mention that I want a boyfriend or that I wish I had a figure or that I wish guys would actually pay attention to me or that I feel like I'm not worthy of attracting hotness, you always bring it back to how I just shouldn't care. I should just be me and not give a rat's ass. But I do! I do give a rat's ass! And telling me not to is like telling someone who's mad to just not be mad. It doesn't work that way, Claire."

"Sam, I—"

"And I'm not sure how much of you really *doesn't care* or if it's just the fact that you, oh I don't know, *have* a figure, *have* a boyfriend, actually *get* attention!"

"What is that supposed to mean?!"

"You know exactly what it means. It's easy peasy to tell others to not care when you're sitting on a wealth of greatness and popularity."

"What?! Popularity? Sam, have you ever stopped to think that maybe the reason I *have* a boyfriend is *because* I don't care? That the reason Adam

458

likes me is not because I have some stupid figure that you seem to think is something special or because I go out of my way to try and be cool and popular but because I was just being me and he likes *me*. I *don't* care, Sam. I don't. I didn't before I dated Adam, and I don't now. Popularity is just a—"

"Yeah, because before Adam, you were dating Mark."

"What!?"

"You don't care now because you have a boyfriend, and you didn't care before because you still had a boyfriend."

"Sam! Are you kidding me right now?!"

"And let's not forget that you got invited to prom your sophomore year!"

"Oh, and that turned out great!" Claire yelled.

"At least you were asked. You were a sophomore, and you went to prom with a senior!"

Claire gritted her teeth, her face reddening with anger.

"So, yeah, you don't get it. You tell me that I shouldn't care or that things shouldn't matter, but the truth is, it doesn't matter to you because you have it all. For us down on the bottom who are seen as übernerds and totally uncool and unpopular, it matters a whole hell of a lot."

"Okay. So the next time I get asked to prom by a goddamn disgusting asshole who assaults women, I'll send him your way because that's apparently better than nothing. Who knew!" Claire said with venom, slamming the button to turn the radio off as a commercial switched to "MMMBop."

"And they've been playing that friggin' song all damn summer!"

They sat in silence until they pulled into Claire's driveway.

"Claire. I'm—"

"I don't want to hear it," Claire said, slamming the door, still furious that Sam would even bring Rick up, and especially bring him up in a way that made it sound as though Claire should be grateful for even getting his attention.

"But, Claire," Sam said, sounding small, closing her own door.

"Seriously, Sam. Let's just call this a day, okay? I'll call you later."

Sam nodded, grabbed her bags from the back seat, and walked home while Claire stomped her way up the front steps, the screen door slamming behind her, having no intention of calling Sam anytime soon.

Over the next few days, Claire made no attempt to call Sam, who also left her be until the following Sunday when she called multiple times, which Claire ignored. Her mom wasn't happy about it, but she gave Sam whatever excuse Claire gave her—taking a nap, out for a walk, in the shower.

Claire was lying on her bed reading when a light knock came at the door, and Gwen stuck her head in. Claire smiled and sat up.

"Hey there," Gwen said. "Can I come in?"

"Yeah, of course," Claire said, gesturing to the end of her bed. "You startled me. I'm used to Troy doing that."

Gwen smiled. "I came to check in and see how you were doing."

"Not too bad," she responded. "How are you?"

"Hanging in there. Been enjoying Troy's letters. I feel so lost at times though, ya know?" Claire nodded her understanding. "I came to see if your mom needed anything, and she told me that Sam has called a bunch and you keep ignoring her."

Claire sighed. "Yeah."

"What's going on? I mean, you don't have to tell me, but—"

"It's dumb, really," Claire said, picking at a loose string in her comforter.

"Try me," Gwen said, getting more comfortable, leaning back against the bedpost.

"Well. I just feel . . ." Claire stammered. She didn't really know what to say. "I don't know."

"Start with what actually happened."

"So we went to the mall to do some school shopping. It was a lot of fun and everything. All normal. We stopped at RadioShack so I could see Adam because it had been like a week, with our work schedules not lining up and everything, and then we headed home. In the car she said something along the lines of how she hoped this year would be the year she'd get a boyfriend, and I told her I was sure of it and if not, then who cares! Because, you know, it doesn't really matter. And she tweaked."

"What did she tweak about?" Gwen asked, a little confused.

"That I always tell her she shouldn't worry about boyfriends or being popular. That when I do, it demeans *her* feelings of how important it all is. Like I'm lecturing because I know better. And that I don't *really* believe it; it's just easy for me to say because I have those things, but if I was 'like her,' I would think it mattered."

Gwen nodded, understanding.

"Which is stupid," Claire continued, "because I really *don't* care! And honestly, I am not popular by any meaning of the word. I'm so grateful I have Adam and really, really like him, but I like *him* and having him in my life, not simply the idea of having a boyfriend. I could give two shits about that. Like—"

"I gotchu," Gwen interjected. "Sam's more influenced by the idea of having a boyfriend and what it represents to her, not necessarily the real emotions that go along with it. At that point, it kind of demeans *your* feelings."

"Exactly! And I'm not like that, but she basically kept telling me that I really am and just say those things because I can."

"I see. Was there anything else?" Gwen asked, clearly assuming there was more to condone Claire ignoring Sam for days on end as well as the many unanswered phone calls.

Claire dropped her gaze. "Well . . . at one point, she told me that it was easy for me to say because I've already had two boyfriends and was asked to prom by a senior. Like I should be grateful to Rick," Claire ended darkly.

"Eeesh. Yeah, that's not cool," Gwen said. They sat in silence for a bit before she added tentatively, "You have every right to be mad, Claire, for sure. But you don't think Sam really meant that, do you?"

Claire heaved another sigh. "No. She tried to apologize, but I just didn't want to hear it. Any of it. I'm so tired of her need to make everything about popularity and focusing so much on having a boyfriend or having cool friends or talking me up in a way that makes me uncomfortable. I don't know."

"Sounds like you guys are just growing up. And, more importantly, your friendship is growing up. Which doesn't always happen gracefully."

Claire nodded.

"I think what Sam wants is maybe validation. That can be huge to people."

"Validation?" Claire asked.

"Yeah. I think she just wants you to validate that you understand how *she* feels about the whole social status of high school. Not to necessarily come to an agreement about it. As friends, we all have this instinct to fix and help. So, naturally, your gut response when she talks like that is to tell her that it doesn't matter anyway because, to *you*, it doesn't, and you don't want to see her thinking so low of herself. But maybe Sam just wants you to empathize with her. Validate that you hear her. Not fix it. Because maybe it sounds like you're trying to fix her, which implies she needs fixing."

Claire let Gwen's words soak in. They made absolute sense. But, boy, was that hard to do.

"Think on it, okay?" Gwen said, standing up. "You guys have been best friends for a while. Don't let something as idle and unimportant as high school get in the way of that."

Claire chuckled.

"Also, I was thinking. Maybe you and I could do something together sometime. Go to dinner or see a movie? We don't need Troy to hang out."

Claire beamed. "I'd love that."

"Great. We'll make a plan, then," Gwen said with a smile. "Catch ya later."

Claire waved and lay back again, Gwen having given her a lot to think about.

She gave it till that evening before finally calling Sam back.

"Thank God you called," Sam's voice squealed over the line. "I am so—"

"Sam," Claire said before Sam could get any further. "Can we just pretend this one didn't happen and move on?"

Claire really didn't want to revisit the Rick comment and was so used to Sam's apologies by now. She also felt that Gwen had a point, and so at this point, they were both in the wrong.

"I—yeah. Of course," Sam said.

"Let's just agree to both be sorry. I will try to be better about hearing you out rather than putting my two cents into everything."

"Oh, but, Claire, your two cents is—"

"No, Sam. Really."

"Okay," Sam said simply. They paused for a minute.

"So. Ready for school?" Claire threw out.

"Oh my god. I can't believe we're juniors, can you? I mean, everyone says this is the hardest year of our high school careers. Do you think that's true? I mean, we have SATs and stuff, but I don't know. Also, I am so totally bummed that we don't have lunch together either day this semester. How does that even happen?!?!"

Claire relaxed and let Sam's stream of consciousness wash over her, happy to have her back but feeling an edge in the back of her mind that things were still different. It was probably due to the fact that when two friends, especially best friends, just throw something under the carpet, it has a sneaky way of crawling back out.

The first day back didn't bring anything exciting in regard to classes, but Claire did enjoy that she got to see Adam off and on throughout the day in between them and even got to walk into band with him for last period. Claire made the sudden realization that she may even see him more now than she had all summer, which brought her a new sense of lightheartedness about being back at school. The usual routine of the first day of band class ensued, and when it was done, Adam and Claire stayed behind per usual, Claire twiddling a bit on the piano while Adam put away the few scattered chairs that had been taken out before sitting down next to her to listen.

She was just playing some random scales and looked to see him watching her with a grin. She stopped playing and turned to him, leaning in, Adam following, but quickly jumped back when they heard—

"Hanover. Miller." Mr. Johns returned to the room from using the photocopier. Claire began playing again out of nerves. "So nice to see you both. Did you guys have a good summer?" he asked with a wide smile.

"Yeah!" Claire answered, ceasing her playing once more, Adam nodding in agreement.

"That's great! Do anything exciting?" he asked as he packed his bag.

"Work," they said in unison.

"Well, someone's gotta, right?" Mr. Johns chuckled. Claire and Adam grabbed their own bags, not wanting to stay too long either, especially since Sam would be waiting outside soon. "And there seems to have been an evolution with you two since you were last in my class."

Claire blushed, and Adam ran his hand through his hair with a light laugh.

"I like it. You're good people," he said, still grinning.

"Thanks," they said together, releasing the awkwardness after seeing Mr. Johns's genuine nature.

They walked out together, Mr. Johns leaving them in the entryway to head down the hall that led to the back door and the teacher parking lot, Adam and Claire heading to meet Sam.

Adam drove them both to Claire's house. Sam went in while Claire said her goodbye to Adam, who had to go to work.

"Call you later?" he said, kissing her forehead, her nose, and then eventually her lips.

"Yes please," she said, returning his kiss.

In her room, she and Sam pigged out on DunkAroos and Doritos, going through the new textbooks they had accumulated and sharing their days, as they hadn't had any part of the day together.

"And I met a girl named Trina in my math class. She seems nice. She's new, so I offered to help her out a bit. She happened to be in my lunch too, so I had someone to sit with."

"Cool!" Claire answered. "Can't wait to meet her." Claire was happy that Sam had found a friend. She knew how much that would mean to her. "No Logan in lunch?"

"Actually, he *was* at lunch, and I swear at one point he was going to sit with me, but he turned and sat at another table by himself."

"You should have invited him over!" Claire said, astounded that Sam hadn't.

"Well, it seemed like meeting more than one person in a day might have been too much for Trina, so I didn't push it. Maybe next time."

Claire looked at Sam questioningly for a moment as she thumbed through her folders but decided not to persist. She was trying to lay off asking too many questions or letting her words take on an advice-giving tone in the hopes that Sam wouldn't think she was trying to fix everything. The result was that Claire felt like a fake friend who was just going along with everything Sam said. She didn't like it and it felt strange, but she had decided to give it a solid effort to see if it did anything.

"Do you think you'll be riding home with Adam often?" Sam asked, trying to sound nonchalant.

"I think it'll depend on work and stuff," Claire said. "But probably most days, yes. Except the days he has an earlier shift that he needs to get to and doesn't have time."

Sam nodded.

"Why?" Claire asked.

"Oh, just wondering. I don't want you guys to have to drag me around all the time. I like walking. I think I'll just walk home from now on," Sam said slowly.

"Oh—okay," Claire said. "I mean, it isn't an issue to drive you too. We aren't dragging you around. And you typically come here after school anyway."

"I know, but I like to walk, like I said. And I just don't want to intrude. Plus, there will probably be many days when you'll have to go straight to work too, right?"

"Yeah. But it's not like I wouldn't come home first. You could still get dropped here and then—"

"Yeah, see? So it would just be easier," Sam said, not making eye contact.

Claire paused before saying, "Okay. If you want. But anytime you want a ride, just let me know."

"Of course," Sam said, smiling at her. It didn't seem genuine at all.

"And the days I don't have to work, you can come with and hang out like usual, and when Adam has to leave quickly, we can walk together. I don't plan on having a car anytime soon. I'm saving, but it will take me a while." Claire half laughed.

"Right on," Sam said.

Claire stared at her again, though Sam wasn't looking at her. "Sam, is everythi—"

"Shoot! I just remembered I need to watch Joey for Mom. I'll talk to you later, okay?" Sam said, gathering her things and throwing them in her bag.

"Yeah, okay."

"See ya, Claire."

Claire sat in stunned silence.

AS LONG AS YOU LOVE ME

The next couple of weeks went by in a haze. Claire was feeling the struggle of going to school, working, and trying to squeeze in all her homework at the same time. The one thing she was counting down to was the end of Troy's eight weeks and his return home. It was a mere two weeks away now, and she couldn't wait. She had called Sam to see if she wanted to sleep over for it, as Troy was coming in late and she could use a friend to help distract her from her anxious excitement, but Sam had told her she had a babysitting gig that night and couldn't. Claire was bummed, especially because she and Sam hadn't seen a lot of each other lately due to all of the aforementioned drama, but babysitting was Sam's only source of money, and Claire knew she was saving up to pay for her own driver's ed course.

In the meantime, life continued to be hectic as Claire tried to find a balance to all the parts and pieces in her life. The piece she was finding the hardest to make work was her time with Adam. They had started to make a habit of playground visits in the night, where they spent half the time talking about school and work and catching each other up on all that was going on, the other half tightly wrapped in each other's arms. These nights were bliss, but they made for quite a long and tiresome day the day after.

One evening that Claire and Adam both finally had off, Claire scheduled dinner at Babs's house so Adam could finally meet her. Though it was only September, the evenings were already getting the cool crisp temperatures of fall, and Babs made them stew with homemade bread. She made Adam laugh with her stories of times gone by and blush every time she told him how handsome he was, and they both enjoyed a cup of tea while Claire played the piano for them. At the end of the night, the conversation came around to winter, and when Adam learned that she paid someone to come shovel her porch and walkway, Adam instantly told her not to and that he would come take care of it. He was quite fond of her already, and that made Claire's heart swell and her desire for him grow even further, if that was at all possible. He mentioned raking the leaves too and mowing the lawn come summer, and she was more than thrilled, promising him some sweet treats in return. It was a successful first meeting, and Adam would come to visit her often, sometimes with Claire and sometimes without.

The Friday before Troy's return, Adam had to leave school quickly to make his shift at work. Claire had taken it, as well as the rest of the weekend, off for Troy, so she caught up with Sam in the hall at the end of the day to tell her she could walk home with her.

"Oh," Sam said uncomfortably. "I-I've been walking home with Trina."

"Trina?" Claire asked. "The girl from your math class?"

"Yeah. She walks our way too."

"Oh. Well, cool!"

Sam looked at her for a moment. "You want to join us?" she asked slowly.

Claire was taken aback. "Uh. Well, yeah. I mean, if that's okay . . ." she trailed off.

"Yeah, no, of course," Sam said. "Meet you outside."

Claire felt unsure of the whole situation, kind of taken off guard that it seemed as though Sam hadn't been going to invite Claire at first. But she grabbed her bag anyway and met Sam, who was waiting out front near a girl with dyed black hair, dark lips, black JNCO jeans, and a nose ring whom Claire didn't know but assumed was also waiting for someone. The grunge/gothic vibe had really become popular as of late, but she still hadn't seen a lot of people don it. It wasn't for her, but some people really rocked it.

"Hey!" Claire said, walking up to Sam. "Where's Trina?"

"Uh, right here," the black-haired girl said in a low, drawling voice, turning toward her. Claire was most definitely stunned at first, this not being at all what she had expected, but recovered quickly.

"So sorry. Hi! I'm Claire Hanover. It's nice to meet you."

Trina looked at her outstretched hand, took it awkwardly, and let out a dark laugh. "Nice to meet you too, Claire Hanover. I'm Katrina Harrison."

Claire squinted at her, definitely getting the vibe that she was being mocked.

"Shall we?" Sam said, walking between them to begin their short trek home.

They began in silence, Claire noticing the sound of Trina's dragging feet on the sidewalk and secretly begging someone to say something so she wouldn't have to hear it. It was Trina who broke the quiet.

"I can't believe that asshole assigned us, like, seventeen pages of freaking math homework," she said in a monotonous drawl.

"Oh my god, I know," Sam agreed.

"So not doing it," Trina responded.

"Yeah. I'm probably going to throw some random answers down myself. At least make it look like I tried."

Claire made a face, not intending to, and it was caught quickly by Trina before she could retract it.

"Let me guess," she said to Sam, "straight A student?"

Sam didn't say anything but let out a small awkward chuckle.

Claire stared at Sam, who didn't look her way at all. "I'm actually not a straight A student."

"Ooh, what is it, then? As and Bs?"

Claire couldn't believe the gall of this girl and didn't give her the satisfaction of an answer, which only succeeded in backfiring.

"Exactly what I thought. Honor roll student, probably has a cute boyfriend, cute clothes, never does anything wrong. A practically perfect Mary freakin' Poppins. Am I right?"

Once again, Sam remained silent.

"I'm sorry, but is there something wrong?" Claire asked with a cold stare.

"Whoa, simmer down, tiger. Defensive much?"

"Well, I'd like to know why I'm being attacked."

"Trust me. This is not being attacked. Merely pointing out what I've noticed about you upon our first meeting."

"And is this how you typically acquaint yourself with people?" Claire asked, an edginess to her voice.

"Sometimes," Trina replied with a malicious grin, clearly enjoying the fact that she was working Claire up.

Claire gave her a look that clearly conveyed *What the fuck.*

"Oh my god," Trina drawled. "I'm sorry, okay? Geesh. Clearly, I hit a nerve. Must be so difficult to be so perfect."

Claire glared at her.

"Kidding! Kidding," Trina said, though Claire knew perfectly well that she wasn't, and her mounting anger at Sam's silence was boiling.

"So, Trina, where did you move here from?" Claire asked, attempting niceties.

"What's it to you?" Trina asked quickly.

"Nothing, really. Was just curious."

"Was just nosing. Or, better yet, trying to small-talk me and act like you care."

"And being nice by trying to have a conversation with you is bad because?"

"Just a waste of time. And fake."

"And who said I don't actually care?" Claire asked.

Trina gave a grunt that sounded like she highly doubted Claire had any ounce of care about her.

Claire fell silent, having no desire to attempt any more conversation with Trina. She fell into an internal conversation of why the hell Sam was friends with her mixed with what Trina had come from to make her have such thick walls up.

"Here's where I step off this fun train. Later, dudes," Trina said as they reached the start of Maple Street.

"See ya, Trina!" Sam said. "Call me."

Trina turned and walked backward, giving a thumbs up, "See you Saturday, right?"

Sam nodded.

Trina then said with the fakest of smiles and insincere excitement, "Nice meeting you, Claire Hanover! I just can't wait to see you again!"

Her enthusiasm left as soon as it had come, and she rolled her eyes before turning back around and continuing to walk home.

Claire stood in silence for a moment, watching her go, Sam starting to walk ahead.

"What the hell was that?" Claire asked, catching up.

"What the hell was what?" Sam asked hastily, not making eye contact.

"You know exactly what."

"I don't, Claire. Trina just has a dark sense of humor. No big deal."

"No big deal?" Claire said, astounded. "*That* was no big deal?"

"Yeah, Claire. It was."

"You have got to be kidding me! How are you friends with her?"

Sam stopped in her tracks and glared at Claire. "And what is that supposed to mean?"

"Sam, she's a bitch. She's worse than Amber, even."

Sam let out a high-pitched cackle. "Oh, as if! You just can't possibly fathom that I could have a friend other than Claire Hanover."

"Are you for real right now?" Claire said, heating up.

"Yeah. I am. I like Trina and she likes me. Did you think I was just going to sit around at home waiting anxiously for my friend to call me?"

"Sam, you know I've been working and trying to do schoolwork and—"

"And what, Claire? Say it!"

"And see Adam!!" Claire yelled.

"Yeah. I know! And in the meantime, toss your best friend of years aside like a rag doll."

"I have not! I have tried calling you for the past two weeks! You don't answer, or you blow me off!"

"How does it feel?!"

Claire let out a loud groan of annoyance.

"You know what, Claire? Enjoy your perfect little blissful world, okay?" Sam walked past her, bumping into her shoulder as she went. "Trina and I have real problems and help each other out with them. You just wouldn't get it."

Claire was astounded. She felt the stress of all that was going on in her life come forward and mix with the increasing sense of loss and grief that the situation was bringing. She shrieked after Sam, "Real problems?! I'll just let Troy know, then. That you don't give a shit that he's home. Shall I?"

Sam whipped around. "I never said that!" she said angrily.

"Yeah, well, you might as well have because, from what I can tell, you never had a babysitting gig this Saturday night, did you?"

Sam went silent.

"That's what I thought," Claire said with quiet loathing. "Enjoy hanging out with your *friend*."

Claire stormed past Sam this time, though she didn't bump into her. She mumbled the entire way into the house, up the stairs, and to her room, throwing her bag in the corner and falling onto her bed. She couldn't stop the tears that fell.

Adam surprised Claire by taking Saturday afternoon off and spending it with her at her house while she waited for Troy. She had called him the night before to vent about her and Sam's blowup, and he had felt so bad that he had talked to Jason about switching shifts and showed up at her bedroom door late that afternoon, having worked the morning.

She threw her arms around him and felt tears well up in her eyes but was able to stop them from falling. They didn't go unnoticed though.

"Thank you," she managed to say.

"Of course." He sat down on the edge of her bed and patted next to him, indicating for her to sit. He put his arms around her and rocked ever so slightly. "This is an exciting night. No tears."

Claire rested her head on his shoulder, tears clinging for dear life to her eyelids and lashes.

"Talk to me, Goose," he said.

Claire chuckled and sighed. "I think I'm just a ball of emotions. I'm excited to see Troy but, like, anxious at the same time. And the whole Sam thing. It's just a lot. And work and school and just trying to do everything and . . . I'll be okay."

"I know you will. You're tough," he said, kissing the top of her head. "But that's a lot. Have you tried calling Sam?"

"No. I don't even know what I'd say. She clearly wants nothing to do with me right now and sees me as the worst friend ever. But everything she's mad about, I can't help. I go to school. I go to work. I go to school. I go to work. And I try to see you anytime in between. I tried calling her before, but she never responded, so there's nothing I *can* do to fix this."

Adam sighed. "Well, as much as I hate to say it, maybe take me out of the picture and find a time that works for her. We can figure something out from there."

"No!" Claire said with a worried tone. "Are you kidding?! I need you. And we barely see each other as it is! When we do, it's mostly in the middle of the night at the playground. I can't replace that time with Sam anyway."

Adam nodded. He couldn't stop the belly flip he felt when she said the words "I need you." "I just wanted you to know that I'd understand."

"Thank you," she said with a smile, feeling better already just having him there, and cupped his face in her hands to kiss him. "I appreciate it."

They hung out in her room and watched *Dirty Dancing*, as it always made Claire feel better, and as the evening grew on, Claire started to feel nothing but excitement for Troy's return. Her mom ordered pizzas for dinner, and Gwen came over after work. Troy was due around 9:00 and it was nearing 10:00. They all sat in silent anticipation.

When the sound of car tires on gravel rent the air, Claire felt her heart race. Adam grinned at her and rubbed her back as car doors slammed. They all stood up when he entered the room, and Claire couldn't believe who she was looking at. Troy had always been on the muscular side but now appeared to be nothing but. He had lost a lot of weight and had gained muscle mass. His brown locks had been shaved down to almost nothing, a high-and-tight haircut. His face looked thinner, and he looked . . . like an adult. Claire didn't know how else to describe it. Troy had always had somewhat of a baby face about his whole person. Maybe it was just his childlike nature that made it feel that way, but he looked grown-up now. A man.

Gwen rushed him, threw her arms around him, and burst into tears. Claire saw Troy's own tears appear, which made her heart want to sing. "I missed you so much," she heard him say into Gwen's neck as he nuzzled it.

Claire's mom was already a mess, and when Troy went to her, she only became more so, rubbing his short hair and immediately telling him that he needed to eat.

"Adam," Troy said, putting out a hand and then pulling him into a one-arm hug.

"Welcome home," Adam said.

And then it was Claire's turn.

"Mouse," Troy said, opening his arms wide. It was all he needed to say. She jumped in them and felt him lift her slightly off the floor.

"Good to have you home, dweeb," she said, tears trailing down her cheeks.

"It's good to be home," he said to the room at large.

"Did you guys eat?" Claire's mom asked, going to her husband to give him a hug.

"Yes," he answered, returning the embrace. "Just at the good ole McDonald's."

"Oh, perfect. We have plenty of pizza left over if you're still hungry," she responded.

"I wouldn't say no to a drink too," he said.

Sitting in the living room together, Troy told them all about boot camp. They listened intently as he talked about what he'd had to do, the mess-up he'd made, which got lots of laughs, and the friends he'd made. He then told them that he had two weeks home and had been given his orders to be stationed at the port that was about an hour and a half away from them. Claire was beyond thrilled to hear this news and felt that nothing could make this night any better. Until something did.

Troy stood up and said, "You may have noticed that I was a little later this evening than I was supposed to be." They all exchanged looks. "Dad and I stopped off somewhere so I could pick something up that I ordered before I left." Claire felt her heart race, having no idea where this was going. "I thought long and hard about this, and my short time away has only solidified my feelings and intentions." Again, everyone looked at each other, each as confused as the next, besides Claire's father, of course, who was holding the best poker face known to man.

Troy sighed and turned to Gwen. He dropped to one knee, pulled something out of his pocket, and held it in front of her. Claire could see it twinkling from where she sat. "Gwen, will you marry me?"

Gwen looked shocked, but tears quickly filled her eyes as she nodded. Troy grinned wider than Claire had ever seen him grin before as he slipped the ring on her hand, and she stared at it with immense happiness before wrapping her arms around him and letting him lift her up and spin her around.

The room erupted as Claire's mom said, "Oh my god! A wedding!!" repeatedly, and they all rushed them with hugs and congratulations. Claire felt tears fall once again as she gave Gwen a hug and heard her say, "I've always wanted a sister!!"

"Welcome to the family," Claire's dad said, hugging Gwen. "You've got to be some special lady to keep this one in line."

Gwen laughed. "Thanks, Mr. Hanover."

"Hey," he said, pointing at her with a smile, "soon it'll be 'Dad.'"

After all the commotion died down, Troy said, "I know I just got home, but I think I'm going to go do my rounds and wake up the goon squad to give them the news." The goon squad being Troy's friends.

"And stop in to see Mom," Gwen added.

"Of course," Troy said, giving her a squeeze.

"Oh, yes, you must! Oh, how exciting! A wedding! Have fun you two!" Claire's mom said. "Oh my goodness, a wedding. John, we're going to have a wedding!"

Claire's dad smiled at her mother's excitement as she went into the kitchen to probably get some kind of celebratory treat.

Claire's dad settled into his rocking chair, nursing another drink.

"So, how long have you known?" Claire asked him with a grin.

Her mother brought in a bottle of champagne and some glasses. "I know they left, but exciting news calls for a toast, so we'll just have it for them."

Glasses were handed around while Claire's father responded to her question. "I knew back before he left. He talked to me about it. He said he felt just as certain about it as he did with his decision to join the service."

"You think he's really ready, John?" Claire's mother asked, drinking her champagne.

"I didn't." He chuckled. "But then I thought about our story. I shared it with him, and we talked, and I think he is. He's grown up a lot since he met Gwen."

"What is your story?" Adam asked, surprising himself.

Claire's mom jumped right in on answering. "Well, I'll spare you the details of all the beginning things, but when my Johnny decided to join the service, he was stationed overseas for a year after boot camp, and he tried to break up with me."

Adam chuckled at the coy look she gave her husband.

"I did not try to break up with you, Lynn. I merely told you I didn't want you to have to wait for me. I felt that was a lot to ask of someone. Though it killed me to say."

"Still is breaking up with me," she answered defiantly but with an air of lightheartedness. "I had stayed through boot camp, after all."

In the pause that followed, Adam asked, "So, what did you say to him, Mrs. Hanover."

Taking another sip of champagne, she said, "I think my exact words were, 'Are you stupid?' Is that right, John?"

"Yes, it is."

They all laughed.

"And so he made me a deal. He said, 'If you wait for me, I'll marry you when I get back,' and I did."

She ended so simply, and Adam couldn't help but feel the love that the two of them had. He saw the wedding picture on the mantle, their hair and attire a strong representation of the early 1970s. And he could picture the simple story they had just relayed. A soldier's goodbye. The letters sent back and forth. The exciting return and the prospect of their future.

"Troy will be fine," Claire's mother said, finishing her glass of champagne. "He may be an oaf sometimes, but he has a big heart and he loves Gwen. A mother knows. I knew it the moment I met her."

The house quieted down after all the excitement, and Claire had fallen into such a ball of happiness that she nearly forgot the time. "Oh my goodness. It's after midnight," she said suddenly, her dad already starting to nod off and her mom in the kitchen making tea. "You probably need to go home, don't you! I hope you're not in trouble."

Adam smiled. "Meh. My parents are good. They trust me. Plus, I'm eighteen now. Can do what I want." He laughed. "But I should probably go, yes. You must be drained."

Claire yawned her response.

Adam chuckled. "Alright. Let's do this." They got up, waking Claire's dad. Adam said his goodbyes to Claire's parents, and they walked outside to the front gate, where Adam turned, and Claire went in for a hug.

"Exciting night, huh?" Adam said.

"Oh my goodness. I don't even think I've taken it all in," Claire said honestly.

"It'll probably all hit you tomorrow. Good thing you took it off."

"Tell me about it. I hope you don't have to work too early tomorrow."

"Nah. Not till one."

"Oh good."

She looked up at him, enjoying his embrace as always, and went up on tiptoes to steal a kiss. He returned it, feeling his heart flutter as it always did around her. He never wanted to let go but found he had to. They shared one more smooch before he departed through the gate, Claire watching him till she couldn't see him anymore before heading inside and straight to bed.

Adam lay awake, thinking about the evening and all it contained, absolutely grateful for getting to be a part of Claire's life and family and witnessing such a big moment as a marriage proposal. He'd never thought of those things before, having no one around him really to make him think about those things before. And though he knew he was too young and not ready for such a major milestone, he couldn't help but imagine Claire's face looking as happy as Gwen's had tonight.

TRULY MADLY DEEPLY

November brought Claire's seventeenth birthday, which was just a simple cake after dinner with the family, Adam, Babs, and, of course, Sam. Claire definitely couldn't get around inviting her, not that she didn't not want to, but knew it was going to be an awkward moment, seeing that their relationship had been strained since the whole Trina debacle. Claire hadn't had a chance to walk home with them since, although that was more of a choice, and the few times they talked on the phone, it was forced. Claire had taken to riding to school with Adam as well, and so her time seeing Sam was practically nonexistent. Sam seemed to enjoy herself, though, but didn't stay late and didn't spend the night, not that Claire had asked her to.

Claire was struggling with how much to try when it came to Sam. She loved her, of course, and wanted to see her. But it seemed that she was getting more out of Trina right now. And though Claire did not approve of Trina's attitude and hoped that maybe she had just felt threatened by Claire that day and perchance she was better when she and Sam were alone, Claire thought that maybe it was for the best right now. She herself had been feeling the strain of their friendship. Maybe this time would be good for them. Adam reminded her off and on that she should maybe make a little effort, so that at the very least, Sam couldn't say she hadn't, and that perhaps, even more so, she needed it. But Claire's stubbornness got in the way, as did the lack of time, and so she didn't.

On the night of her party, around midnight, Claire heard the soft ticking sound on her window as it woke her out of her light sleep. She perked right up, waved out the window, grabbed her sweatshirt and Doc Martens, which she had learned to keep in her room now, and shimmied down the lattice.

"Here you go," Adam said, handing her a gift once settled at the playground. "Uh, don't mind the *Space Jam* wrapping paper. It was all we had at the house from my little cousin's birthday this summer."

Claire chuckled. "It's perfect."

She tore open the gift, and a stack of three composition notebooks tumbled out with a pack of gel pens. Claire smiled at the gift. She couldn't think of a more meaningful and thoughtful thing to receive.

"Thank you," she said.

"I was hoping you could continue writing those stories you started for me," he said with a grin.

"I would love to."

"And, because that would also kind of be a gift for myself, your real gift is on the first page," he said.

She looked at him questioningly and opened the composition notebook to see Adam's own writing on the first page:

Join me for the Thompson Community Little Theater's production of Rogers and Hammerstein's <u>Cinderella</u>? December 13th @ 7:00pm.

A ticket was taped to the page, and Claire stared at it in awe. To encourage and support her writing was a gift in and of itself, but to also think to take her on a date to see a play, a musical at that, made Claire feel like *she* was Cinderella.

"I thought we could dress up, get dinner, and, uh, see a show," he said to Claire's silence. "We have seats near the front. Center. A buddy of mine works the ticket booth there and hooked me up. . . . Do you like it?"

Claire looked at him. Her own Prince Charming. She beamed and threw her arms around him, which, taking him off guard, caused him to fall back onto the grass beneath their tree, Claire landing on top of him. "It is the best gift I could have ever asked for," she said.

"Yeah?" he said, draping his arms around her, having no intention of moving her off him.

"Yes," she whispered. "Not only do I get to enjoy a night of music and magic, but I get to spend the entire time with you. Which is the best gift you could ever give."

He looked at her meaningfully, trying to conjure the words to express just how much that meant to hear, but they wouldn't come. He flipped her onto her back while giving her a wide smile and pressed his lips to hers, their mouths playfully dancing against each other, words unneeded.

As the holidays approached, Claire took Adam's advice, slightly, and made an effort to reach out to Sam in the form of leaving a Christmas gift for her in her locker. It was a bag that contained scrunchies, lip glosses, gum, fun-colored nail polishes, and the latest editions of her three favorite pop culture magazines: *Teen Beat*, *People*, and *Bop*.

She got a call on the first day of Christmas break with a heartfelt thank-you from Sam, but their conversation didn't last long. Claire actually felt that it was her fault it didn't. She was trying so hard to be diplomatic about what she said, staying away from sharing anything that had to do with Adam on the off chance it would turn Sam off, which only caused her tone to sound forced, and she had the unfortunate sense that Sam felt it.

Troy was home for Christmas. He stayed in his old room, which hadn't been touched, as he was just living on base and didn't necessarily have a "permanent home," according to their mom, and Claire couldn't help but fully enjoy every minute of having things feel like they always used to. Gwen and Troy agreed on a two-year engagement, so wedding plans were definitely occurring but at a leisurely pace. Gwen was in her last year of nursing school and wanted to focus on that before really getting into the world of venues, cakes, dresses, and more. That didn't stop Claire's mom from bringing up ideas every time she was over.

Claire was shocked that her mother invited Adam over for Christmas dinner, thinking that would be a little too much, but she wouldn't hear of him not coming, and he happily accepted. Claire's family always went to visit her mom's side for an early lunch. Her dad's was small and out of state. They usually saw them on a different day after the holidays so they could travel without taking away from their own Christmases. This meant that they had their own family Christmas at dinnertime, besides the initial present opening and breakfast in the morning.

Adam showed up dressed in a red-plaid button-down shirt tucked into a pair of khakis, and Claire thought he looked absolutely adorable. Adam also thought Claire looked beautiful in the simple velvety green sleeved dress she wore. Having him in her home for Christmas felt like a big step, and she was happy at how comfortable it felt.

Before anyone knew it, it was the New Year, which Claire was happy to ring in with a real New Year's Eve kiss at Ron's Pizzeria where she and Adam enjoyed a night of food, pool, and music with Jason, Fitz, Nick, and a slew of other people they knew in some way or another from school. Some of those people were Amber and crew. Claire was surprised that Amber didn't try to come up to her once, and she even noticed it looked like she was only half-heartedly enjoying herself. Claire didn't waste too much time contemplating it, assuming it had to do with some missed try at having a date for the night. Mark came up to them to wish them a Happy New Year, and Claire was happy that it felt comfortable. It was Claire's first New Year's out, and it was perfect. Except for one thing. Though she was with family anyway, as was tradition, Claire still felt the heaviness at the absence of one person . . . Sam.

The New Year brought an additional stressor to juniors—SATs. Every teacher seemed to be bombarding them with study help, test-taking tips, and material to practice in preparation. Claire, being somewhat of a perfectionist and certainly having her mind set on going to college, was feeling the weight of this.

"What if I fail horribly and then I don't get into a good college and then I can't get a degree and then I just fail at life?" she said to Adam on the phone one night in late January surrounded by notes and reference books she'd gotten from school.

"Claire, calm down. The anxiety alone will be what makes you fail. You've got this. You're incredibly smart, have a good head on your shoulders, and as long as you get a good night's sleep, drink water, and take a deep breath, you'll do fine."

His words did have a way of calming her, but only slightly. "Yeah, but—"

"No," he cut her off. "No yeah-buts. You've got time before you sit the test. Four months. Take a little time each day to study and practice, and that's it. Don't overkill and don't overthink it."

Claire sighed. "Okay."

"Regardless, you'll be doing a lot better than our president right now," Adam said.

"Why's that?" Claire asked, looking over her corrected essays from English.

"Well, because he just publicly announced that he didn't sleep with that Monica Lewinsky chick. Now they're going to do some investigations, which could lead to impeachment," Adam said with a slight chuckle.

"Oh geesh," Claire said. "Yeah, I guess my night could be going a lot worse."

Adam laughed. "Have you heard from Sam lately?"

Claire sighed and took a break from shuffling through her papers. "No. But I did hear *about* her."

"About her?"

"Her mom called the house yesterday. I meant to tell you and forgot."

"What happened?" Adam asked, concerned.

"Well," Claire said with an edge to her voice, as it was still frustrating to her. "Sam apparently got caught smoking in the girl's room at school."

"What?!" Adam asked, shocked.

"Yeah. And guess who with?"

"Tri—" Adam began, but Claire cut him off.

"That's right! Miss I-hate-everybody-and-the-whole-wide-world Trina."

Adam let out a low whistle. "What did she want with your mom?"

"I guess to vent more than anything, but she also asked if I knew anything about it. Sam supposedly told her she wasn't the one smoking—that she was just holding Trina's cigarette while she used the bathroom. My mom told her that Sam and I hadn't been talking much lately with so much going on, and I think she mentioned Trina and how I didn't like her. I'm sure that went over great when Sam's mom talked to her about that part because I'm sure Sam hasn't told her much about Trina. Her mother would never let her hang out with her if she did. From the sounds of Trina anyway. I don't even really know her. Trina could be great," she ended snarkily.

"How has she been getting away with hanging out with her?" Adam asked.

"Well. Sam's mom does her best to take care of everything, but with Joey and everything, I think she often just assumes, or maybe hopes, Sam is all set."

Adam paused before saying, "Maybe you should give Sam a call."

"Why?" Claire asked, beginning her reviewing of notes again. She felt the pang of wanting to talk to Sam and missing her but just didn't know what to say.

"Because. Something tells me that the reason Sam's mom assumes and trusts Sam's doing okay is . . . well, is because she's usually with you."

"Well, now she's decided to be with Trina, so there's that," Claire said, knowing how stubborn she sounded. "Why can't I find my notes from *The Great Gatsby* symbolism lecture the other day?!"

Adam sighed. "Claire, take a deep breath, and take a break from the studying. Or I'll come over there myself and put it all away if I have to."

"That threat is not going to get me to take a break, now is it?" Claire said, smiling.

Adam grinned. "Well, I can try."

Claire slammed her books closed and shuffled all her papers together to fit into her folder. "No, you're right. Putting it away now."

"I do think you should talk to Sam," Adam said, revisiting the topic. "I think she needs you, Claire. I know it's hard, but you should try."

"I guess you're right. I'll try and catch her at school."

"Perfect," Adam said. "So, Valentine's Day is around the corner. Falls on a Saturday, and I just found out today that I got the gig! I'm going to DJ the school dance."

"That's great!" Claire said, throwing her stuff in her backpack and lying back in bed, covering herself with her blankets to get snuggled in. She could see snow falling softly outside her window.

"Yeah! I was hoping you'd still want to go with me. I mean, I'll be busy at times but would still love to have a few dances with you."

Claire smiled. "Even if I get one dance out of you, it'd be totally worth going still. I'll see if Sam is going. That will be my lead-in to talk to her. If she is, maybe she and I can hang out at it together."

"Good idea."

"I've been known to have them from time to time." She chuckled. "How did hanging out with Jason, Fitz, and Nick go the other night?"

"What?" Adam said suddenly.

"Hanging out with the guys?" Claire said uncertainly. "Did I mess that up? I thought you hung out the other night?"

"Ah, yes!" Adam said, recovering. "Yeah. It was cool."

"Good," Claire said, laughing lightly. "How are they?"

"Good," Adam said.

"Good."

"That reminds me. The senior variety show fundraiser is in March. I'm working the lights. You planning on going? You should!"

"What about Jason, Nick, and Fitz reminded you of the variety show?" Claire said, laughing harder this time. The variety show was an annual event at the school. Claire had only gone to one so far since being at the high school and had seen the one Troy was in his senior year. They were usually pretty entertaining and helped the senior class with their graduation trip. Essentially, students of the graduating class volunteered to put acts together. The night of the show, buckets for each act were put out, and after the show, audience members cast their vote by putting money in the bucket of the act they thought was the best. The act with the most money raised won a trophy. Most people brought enough to put money in different buckets, ranking the amount based on their first, second, and third choices. It was open to the community, and a lot of people in town would go, knowing it was the seniors' biggest fundraising event.

"Oh, um, nothing. Just thinking of how we're all seniors . . . and the talent show is a senior thing and all," Adam said slowly.

Claire wasn't really convinced but let it go. "Well, I'd love to go, although I'm not sure with whom if you're working the booth."

"Well, maybe Sam will want to go to that too."

"Maybe. I'll figure it out," she said, yawning, her eyes growing heavy.

"I guess it's time we hang it up, huh?" Adam said, also starting to feel the beginnings of exhaustion even though he loved their long conversations and hated when they ended. He'd never talked this much to anyone, and it was so easy with Claire.

"Yeah. I suppose. I'll see you tomorrow," Claire said.

"Yes. Definitely," Adam said. "I can't wait."

"Me too. Night, Adam."

"G'night Claire."

The next week at school, Claire sought out Sam to ask her about the Valentine's Day dance. To Claire's great surprise, Sam said she and Trina were planning to attend, and Claire asked if she could hang out with them while there, seeing that Adam would be working the event. Sam seemed okay with it, not thrilled but okay, and Claire felt like that had to count for something.

Sam and Claire shared a few phone calls between the time she asked and the night of the dance, and Claire felt that maybe they were finding some form of a groove with their friendship. It certainly wasn't what it was—the fight they had having never really been discussed—but it was a start. Claire felt that Sam was not herself, often sounding drained or tired, or maybe just disengaged, but having her on the phone and talking was more than she had gotten for quite some time, so she took it. She was feeling hopeful.

That was, until Friday morning before school. Claire had just finished putting on her coat and boots to go wait for Adam out front of her house when her mother stopped her.

"Claire," she said with alarm.

"What?!" Claire asked, jumping at her tone.

"Did you not tell Sam that Troy was engaged?"

"Oh, um, no, I guess I didn't." Claire thought back to that night, and it seemed eons ago already. It had been right in the midst of her and Sam's falling-out, and now that they had been starting to talk gradually, it hadn't even occurred to Claire to share. Not to mention that since they had started talking more, Claire had felt this insane desire to tiptoe around everything she did say, afraid she would upset Sam somehow. Trying to think that hard just to have a conversation would make anyone forget certain key details to share.

"Why not?!" her mother asked.

Claire shrugged, not really having a clear-cut answer. Her mother's raised eyebrows and hands-on-hips stance told Claire that that wasn't enough of an answer. "I don't know. We're having kind of a rough patch, I guess, and it just didn't occur to me to tell her."

"Well, Ms. Levinski just called to ask if I could help with Joey next week, and we got to talking, and she had no idea that Troy was engaged. I felt so horrible."

"Sorry, Mum," Claire said. She didn't have anything else to say.

"Claire, hunny, I'm not sure what's been going on with you and Sam, but you need to sort it out. You guys are best friends, and whatever silly thing has gotten in the way of that needs to be stopped. I mean, smoking in the bathroom and her new friend Trina? You need to say something. It isn't your place to make her change, but not talking to her about it isn't helping."

"I wish it was that easy."

"It is. You need to talk to her. Find out what's going on in that head of hers."

"Mom, I can't. Sam will just think it's another attempt at me trying to show my superiority or maturity or something. She'll think I'm trying to show her that I got shit figured out and she doesn't and then take offense at it and be hard on herself and hate me. It isn't that easy."

Claire's mom sighed. They heard a light knock on the door, and Adam poked his head in.

"Hey," Claire said, seeing him through the entryways of the kitchen and living room. "Be right there."

"Can you just try? I'm worried for the girl. And you too. I don't like seeing you girls like this."

"I'll try." Claire joined Adam, in his black wool coat and cute brown-plaid scarf, and headed for school.

If "trying" meant getting in yet another fight with Sam, then Claire tried her absolute hardest. When she joined Sam at her locker at the end of the day, it was to find a disgruntled Sam throwing her books in her bag and slamming the door in Claire's face.

"So Troy and Gwen are engaged," she said immediately.

"Yeah. Look, I'm sorry I didn't tell you. I—"

"Too busy swapping spit with the boyfriend, right? Or working your cute little job at the bakery? Or studying your smart little ass off for the SATs you know you're going to get a top score in?"

Claire felt her face flush. "Sorry I even attempted to come talk to you. My bad." And she turned on the spot and headed out the front doors where

Adam was waiting to bring her home. He didn't even attempt to ask her how her conversation went.

This all led to Claire heading to the dance Saturday night alone. Adam offered to pick her up, but she didn't feel much like hanging around while he set up, so she drove herself in her dad's car and walked in a fashionable forty-five minutes late. She wore a red short-sleeved baby doll dress with black tights and a short black heel. It was semiformal, so she added a little curl to her hair and a velvet black choker and attempted to vamp up her makeup a little.

She saw Sam and Trina, both in black, leaning up against one of the walls in the corner. Sam very clearly saw Claire and gave her a literal cold shoulder by turning to the side to talk to Trina. Claire felt a tinge of anger flare up but also a deep sense of sadness. She and Sam should be at this dance together. She and Sam should have gotten ready at her house, swapped clothes, discussed makeup, and driven here together. She realized that she was halfway through her junior year of high school, and Sam had barely played a part in it. This sudden emotion made Claire walk straight up to Sam and Trina. The act seemed to shock both of them.

"Hey, Sam. Hi, Trina," she said happily. "Nice to see you."

They both looked at her surprised but said hello in some form or another.

"Sam," she said after taking a deep breath and not caring that Trina was right there. "I'm sorry I didn't tell you about Troy and Gwen. It was in the midst of us arguing, and I know that isn't an excuse, but it slipped my mind. A lot of that seems to be happening lately. I'm sorry. I miss you and miss telling you everything and . . . I just miss you."

Sam's face softened, and Claire even thought she saw a hint of a glimmer in her eyes.

"I hope you and Trina have a fun time tonight. I really do. And maybe the three of us can get pizza or something sometime so I can get to know you better, Trina," she continued. "And, uh, Happy Valentine's Day."

Claire walked away and took a deep breath, feeling better. She was glad she had said it. And she didn't even need to hear a reply from Sam. It was off her chest and in Sam's court.

Claire made her way through the crowd, saying hi to people she met. She saw Adam's gang of friends hanging out near the speakers and went to join them, but not before she made eye contact with Adam. His grin spread wide when he spotted her, and he put down the CDs he was looking at and jumped off the stage. He took her hands in his and held them out at arm's length.

"You look stunning," he said. "Fly as all get-out."

She felt herself blush. "Thanks. You look quite cute yourself." He did too. He was wearing a black button-down shirt tucked into khakis and a bright-pink bow tie. His glasses and smile made him look like a handsome nerd. "Really cute."

He smirked and wound his arms around her waist, pulling her close and planting a kiss upon her lips. She smiled against him, putting her arms around his neck and kissing back.

"The guys are over there. Jason is the only one who brought a date. Her name's Melissa. Really sweet. You'll like her," he said when they pulled apart.

"Perfect. Dance the slow ones with me?"

"Wouldn't miss it for the world." He smiled. They kissed again, and she went to join the crew.

"Bohemian!" Fitz yelled, holding a punch and sloshing it all over the floor.

"Would you watch out?" Nick said to him as half the punch landed on his left shoe. "Jesus. Hey, Claire!" Nick put an arm around her shoulder. "You're my date tonight."

"You wish," she teased.

"Oh, my heart," Nick said with a wink and a grin.

"Oh fine. Except for the slow dances," she returned.

"You got it," he said, giving her a squeeze and letting go. "Where's Sam?"

"She's here with someone else."

"She's got a date?" Nick asked, looking around the crowd for her.

"No. She's here with another friend, I mean," Claire repeated.

"I was going to say. I want to meet him if so. Make sure he's decent."

Claire smiled, surprised at Nick's protective demeanor. She recalled how he had come to Sam's rescue at the beach. "Yeah?"

"Yeah. She's a nice girl. Deserves nice people," Nick said simply.

"I agree."

Jason interrupted by introducing Claire to Melissa. Adam was right: she was very sweet, and Claire took a liking to her immediately. They danced off and on as a group, laughing and enjoying their time. Claire was very glad she had come. And when it was time for the first slow dance, Adam surprised Claire by calling her up to the stage where she danced with him in front of the sea of couples, even though, to Claire, it felt like it was just the two of them.

Claire wasn't sure if her spiel to Sam at the dance had done anything, but she hoped it had and waited for Sam to respond. It didn't happen in time for the March variety show, and Adam informed Claire that his friends weren't attending. Claire wasn't sure she was going to go when Sarah approached her to ask if she wanted to join her instead. Mike was MCing the show—a junior typically did—and so Sarah was going along. Since she and Mike had been dating for a little over a year now, she wanted to go to support him, of course, but didn't want to sit with the crew alone. Sarah seemed more than thrilled that Claire agreed because the "crew" consisted of Amber, Lauren, Ashley, Mark, and Chris. Claire got the impression that Sarah wasn't overly in love with the fact that her and Mike's friendship with Mark meant constantly having to hang out with the rest. Claire had to laugh at how much she understood this.

Adam seemed quite excited that she was going to the show when she told him of her arrangement with Sarah, whom she'd be riding in with, and when Claire questioned his excitement with a laugh, he just shrugged, saying he was simply glad to have another opportunity to see her. She didn't quite buy it but had no reason to question it.

The night of the show, Sarah picked her up early, and they got front row seats so Sarah could cheer Mike on. He was a naturally funny guy with a dry sense of humor, and Claire had the feeling he'd be a great MC. They saved seats for the rest of the gang and, when they arrived, shared polite hellos with each other, though Claire still got her glare from Amber. Seemed like she was back to normal from New Year's.

At one point, before it got too close to starting time, Claire decided to walk back and quickly wish Adam good luck. On her way, she spotted Sam and Trina in the audience, which surprised her for some reason. She stopped, though, and said hello.

"Hey! I didn't know you guys were coming."

"It's a free country," Trina said in her lazy drawl.

"Uh, yes. Yes it is," Claire returned.

"Trina's friend is reciting some of her poems tonight," Sam said in explanation. It gave Claire some hope that she wasn't just being silent to Trina's rudeness.

"That's great! Well, enjoy," she said and left them.

Finding Adam, he gave her a smile, a kiss, and a hug before she wished him good luck and took her seat, and the show started.

It was a hoot. A couple seniors did a comedy sketch that was bordering on inappropriate but was an absolute riot. There were some instrumentals, dance routines, and other skill set talents like juggling, unicycling, and a pretty impressive magic act. Mike did a wonderful job MCing, adding in jokes from time to time and reminding the audience that all proceeds from donations and ticket sales went to the senior class and, of course, to keep in mind their favorites for the ultimate money-making part—the voting. What Claire wasn't expecting was to hear Mike say her name about three-quarters of the way through the show.

"This next act is dedicated to a Miss Claire Hanover. I've been told I'm not allowed to spotlight her because she doesn't like it, but she's the pretty brunette up front here." There was light laughter as Claire felt her face fall in shock, her cheeks instantly flushing beat red. "Without further ado, we have a nameless team of seniors here performing a lip-syncing skit. Let's make some noise!"

The crowd cheered as four figures took the floor and the instantly recognizable first notes of Backstreet Boys' "As Long As You Love Me" rent the air.

Claire's heart fluttered, and her stomach did a flip as the stage lights lit up the smiling face, crinkled gray eyes, and split brown hair of the guy she called hers.

"Oh. My. God," she said as the first lyrics were sung by Nick Carter and Adam mouthed along to them. They started in on a somewhat synchronized dance—the somewhat being that Fitz was in his own little world about two steps behind the others, which were Jason and Nick. The crowd went wild, and Claire was in a dazed combination of shock and utter enjoyment. People were catcalling and singing along; you'd swear an actual boy band had donned the stage. "I can't even believe this."

Sarah let out a burst of laughter. "Come on!" She stood up, dragging Claire up with her. The rest of their row followed, Amber rather reluctantly. Soon enough, each row behind them had stood, and the boys' skit had turned into a crowd affair. At one point, Adam came down to the edge of the stage and "sang" directly to Claire while the other three attempted to continue their simple dance moves, Nick playing with an A.J. inspired hat, Jason actually doing the moves that had clearly been practiced, and Fitz making everything up as he went.

Claire beamed up at Adam, and he winked at her. She felt like a fan girl getting a callout from her celebrity crush. When the music stopped, and they took their final pose, the cheers were the loudest, and Mike remarked how that could very well have earned the senior class their entire trip.

"I had no idea your boyfriend was such a ham!" Sarah exclaimed.

"I didn't really know either, to be honest! I mean, he loves music, plays drums, and likes to DJ, so I guess being in front of people isn't a big deal to him, but this!?! This was amazing."

" 'Amazing' isn't even enough of a word!" Sarah laughed. Mike moved on to introducing the next act, and Claire excused herself from Sarah to go catch up with her new favorite boy band, which had just exited the stage.

"Oh my god, you guys were unbelievable!!" Claire said, running up to them. She rushed Adam and he grinned, welcoming her with open arms and swinging her around. She moved on to give hugs to Jason, Nick, and Fitz too.

"Bohemian!"

"You know we would never have done that if it was for anyone but you," Nick said, accepting her hug.

"I absolutely loved it," she said. "And you guys were definitely the house favorite! I think you'll get a lot of donations for that performance."

"We better," Nick said with a smirk.

Claire turned back to Adam. "Was that really all for me?"

"It was," Adam said, his friends giving him a slap on the back and heading to the auditorium to have a seat and watch the rest of the show. "I know how much you secretly love those Backstreet Boys."

She laughed, holding his hands in hers. "Well, you were better than any Backstreet Boy. It was pretty epic. I didn't know you could be so outgoing."

It was his turn to laugh this time. "Well, I'm not. But we really wanted to help fundraise, and you've been so stressed this year with Troy leaving and coming back, Sam, work and school, and now SATs. I thought you could use some fun, and what's more fun than watching your boyfriend humiliate himself in front of the school and community for the purpose of raising some money?"

"You certainly did not humiliate yourself. If anything, you just gained yourself a following. You've never looked cuter." She tapped his nose. "But thank you."

He leaned in and kissed her, and she felt her heart flutter just as much as it had when she had seen him take the stage.

"I have to go help finish the show off in the booth. I know you came with Sarah, but come with me after the show?" he asked excitedly.

Claire kissed him in response. "She was part of getting me here, wasn't she?"

He flashed his shitty grin and made his way to the booth. There was no doubt who won the trophy. By a landslide, the boys were called up at the end of the night to claim their first place trophy for most money raised. The crowd gave them a huge round of applause.

Claire didn't see Sam and Trina on her way out and wondered if they had left early or were just really fast at getting out before everyone else. Trina's friend was the only one who had recited poetry, and Claire thought she had done a really good job. Her poems were a little dark but deep and powerful in nature. Claire appreciated art in all forms, and Trina's friend definitely had a gift. She was hoping to tell Trina so in an extra effort to be nice but instead just made her way to Adam. A few people she knew stopped her to tell her how great Adam had been, and when Adam finished cleaning up the sound booth and they were heading out hand in hand, more stopped to compliment him.

Getting out of the car at Claire's house, Claire said, "You know, I'm going to want to see your Backstreet Boys impersonation more often now. I'll want a repeat."

Adam chuckled, closing his door and joining her on the sidewalk. They were shielded by the massive willow tree on the corner of Claire's property, and he grabbed her around the middle and pulled her close to him.

"Claire," he said seriously.

"Yeah?" She cocked an eyebrow.

"I've been wanting to tell you this for some time and just didn't know the right moment. I didn't know how you'd take it, and I still don't, to be honest, but I can't carry on without telling you."

Claire felt the beating race of anxiety start in her chest and creep its way up into her throat. "Okay, what is it?" she said quietly, taking a step back.

Adam heaved a deep breath, and she heard the edge of nerves quake behind his words as he said, "I'm not sure if we're too young to feel love. Or to know what it is. But," he faltered a moment and plowed on, "but a very smart, talented, and beautiful person once told me that you feel it in your gut. That you know because they're the first person you want to tell a secret to, the one you don't mind telling your deepest desires to, the person who crosses your mind the most, the one you can do absolutely nothing with and feel at home, the person you are always happy for, and the person you truly couldn't imagine living a day without."

Hearing her own words recited to her, she could envision that first night she and Adam had spent at the playground as clear as day, and all the others since then. She couldn't believe that he remembered what she had said all that time ago. She felt her heart pitter-pattering at an alarming rate, though no longer laced with anxiety. She thought she knew what was coming and was struggling to contain the adrenaline and emotional buildup that was occurring inside her.

"Claire. That's you. That's how I feel about you. I feel it in my gut every single time I lay eyes on you. Quite literally. You are always on my mind; I want to spend every minute of every day with you. We're nearing a year together, and you still make me feel the exact same way I did when I would see you smile at me across the band room, barely knowing each other. Claire," he took a deep breath, "I love you. I love you so much. And you don't have to return it. I don't want to put pressure on you with this. But I had to tell you. I had to tell you how I felt because it was driving me crazy not to."

"I love you too," Claire whispered. She could barely speak for the sea of emotions that sat on her vocal chords, giving her a lump in her throat and causing tears to spring to her eyes.

Adam stepped forward and held her hands in his. "You do?" he asked quietly, placing his forehead against hers.

"I do. With all of my heart, I love you. I don't care if we're young. I stand by what I said. And I love you."

"You make me so incredibly happy," Adam said, and he wound his arms around her middle beneath her coat, kissing her with such passion and intensity that Claire felt the tears in her eyes escape as she held on to him tightly, winding one hand through his brown hair, releasing all that emotional buildup into her kiss. She felt his hands warm on her back and a wave of goose bumps spread across her body. She didn't think she could hold him any tighter, longing to be as close to him as possible. They stood there like that, lost in each other, for what seemed like an eternity and yet wasn't long enough when they pulled apart.

"I love you," he said again with a grin. "I'm going to enjoy saying that all the time now."

"I love you too." She smiled back.

"I'm not sure if I like saying it or hearing it better," he returned.

Claire giggled and gave him another kiss, wanting so much more, which Adam was able to read and needed to pause the evening; otherwise, he would lose his own willpower. "I think we should get you inside. I'm sure your mom is expecting you."

Claire nodded, knowing it was probably for the best, but not before stealing another peck. They walked together, Adam planning to go in to say hello.

Claire didn't realize how cold it had gotten outside till she felt the burst of warmth hit her face as she stepped into the entryway, Adam following, closing the door behind them.

"Hey, Mom!" Claire shouted, unwinding her scarf and hanging it on the hook with her coat. "Mom?" she said, walking through the living room toward the kitchen, Adam hanging his own coat and throwing a look of concern at the silent house. He entered the kitchen behind Claire to see her mom leaning forward on the kitchen counter, her back to them.

"Mom?" Claire said.

She turned, and both Claire and Adam felt the color drain from their faces.

Claire's mom was pale and looked like someone on the brink of a nervous breakdown.

"Oh, Claire," she said quietly. "Thank God you're back."

"Mom, what happened?" Claire said, fear and edge in her voice.

"Ms. Levinski called about ten minutes ago."

Claire just stared at her.

"It's Sam."

"Is she okay?" Claire said quickly, the worst running through her mind.

Her mom seemed to be trying to form the words. "She's in the hospital right now, and, um, she just got there. They don't know anything at this point..."

"What happened?" Claire asked through a clenched jaw.

Her mother looked at her, tears forming in her eyes, having a hard time coming up with what to say.

"What. Happened."

Her mom spoke in barely a whisper, like it would make what she said less heart-wrenching. "Attempted suicide."

Lightning Crashes

Claire's stomach plummeted, her head suddenly heavy, and she felt like she could faint. "Wha-what? What? How? When? What?" she sputtered, trying to stop the hyperventilation that was encroaching.

"Oh, hunny, I'm so sorry," her mother said quickly. Now that the initial news had been shared, she seemed to be springing back into mom mode. "It sounds like it was pills. I couldn't get much. Ms. Levinski was distraught on the phone."

"Pills?" Claire squeaked. "Tonight? Just now?" She thought about the talent show. She and Trina had been there. Then they had been gone. Had something happened to put Sam over the edge? Had Trina encouraged it? How had it gotten to this point?

She should have said more. Done more. Not just silently listen and be a fake friend and then not be a friend at all.

Claire's thoughts were a jumbled mess, and her anxiety and fear were getting deeper and deeper with every second. "We gotta go. We gotta go now."

"Yes. I'm waiting for your father to get home. He's on his way back from visiting Troy on base. I tried calling him there in hopes of catching him. I got a hold of Troy, but he said I just missed him. So he doesn't know yet. I just hope he doesn't take his time and stop anywhere." Her mother's face was lined with worry. "Once he's here, we'll go straight to the hospital. I told Claudia we'd take Joey home and watch him there. Joey doesn't need to hang out in a hospital all night or be a part of this."

Claire nodded but only half heard. "I gotta go though. I have to go now."

Her mom looked at her with absolute pity and sympathy. "I know, hunny. As soon as your dad gets here, we'll go. I don't want you driving like this."

"But—"

"I'll take her," Adam said to Claire's mom, joining in the conversation, feeling his own worry and concern. And then to Claire, "I'll take you."

"Okay, let's go," Claire said.

"Oh, be careful. Please," her mother said, talking more to Adam. "Emergency room at St. Mary's. We'll meet you there as soon as John gets back. Should be within the hour, I hope."

Adam nodded as he and Claire rushed to get their coats and boots back on. Claire practically ran to his car, though she felt she was moving in slow motion. The hospital was about a twenty-minute drive, and it couldn't go fast enough for Claire. They rode in silence until Adam said, "I know what you're thinking."

Claire didn't respond.

"This isn't your fault," he said sternly.

Claire felt her eyes burn. "How is it not?! I should have paid more attention. I should have said more. I shouldn't have cut back. It probably made her feel even more isolated. I should have validated her more, like Gwen said. I should have kicked Trina's ass. I should have been able to see this." She bounced her knee up and down and attempted to control her breathing.

"Claire, there is no way you could have seen this coming. You guys are in high school. Friendships change, and you were just trying to navigate your way through that to the best of your ability," Adam said. His tone wasn't harsh, but it was commanding. Claire hadn't heard this tone before. "You could not have predicted this."

"I should have though. I should have—"

"No," he said flatly. "No. Right now, you need to focus on calming yourself down. What-ifs are out the window. It's done, and nobody can do anything differently at this point. We move forward. We be there for Sam." He ended with such a final note that Claire didn't retaliate, and if she was being honest with herself, she knew he was right.

Adam placed a hand on her shaking leg. "She'll be okay."

Claire nodded, tears falling down her cheeks in quick succession. *Sam.*

They pulled up and parked, Claire practically running into the emergency room, Adam right behind.

"I-I'm here to see my friend. Sam," she blurted at the front desk employee.

"Okay. Are you family?" she asked.

"Wha? No. No, she's my friend. I need to see her now. Please!"

Adam stepped forward. "Please, ma'am. Her name is Samantha Levinski. Just came in a little bit ago by ambulance. We're friends of hers. Her mom is . . ." He looked to Claire to fill in the blank.

"Claudia!" Claire cried out.

"Claudia Levinski. Can you check with her? It's Adam Miller and Claire Hanover. I'm sure she'll let us back there when she knows who it is," Adam finished.

"Hold on a moment." The clerk left her seat and went through a door.

"What is she doing? Why can't we go back there?" Claire asked hysterically.

Adam put his hands on her shoulders. "They can't just let anyone in the ER. She's going to check with Sam's mom and I'm sure be right back, okay? It's okay." Adam saw the tears pool in Claire's eyes once again. He pulled her into a tight hug and held her close until the front desk worker came back. She motioned them forward, and they followed her through a few hallways until they came upon a small waiting room.

"Oh, Claire," Ms. Levinski said after looking up and seeing them enter. Joey was sitting in the corner coloring.

Claire met her outstretched arms and hugged her close. Having been friends for so long, Claire had come to see Sam's family as her own. She tried to send forth all her love and support through her hug.

"What happened?" Claire asked. Ms. Levinski's eyes watered as she dabbed her used tissue to her face. She glanced at Joey briefly.

"Well . . ." she said.

Adam stepped forward with a meaningful look to Sam's mom and then went over to him. "Hey, buddy. Joey, right?"

"Yeah," Joey said, not looking up from his coloring.

Adam dropped down to balance on the balls of his feet. "I'm Adam. I saw that there was a vending machine near the front entrance. I haven't eaten and could use a snack. Want to go for a walk with me?"

Joey looked at his mom, who smiled and nodded. "Sure!"

"Awesome!" Adam said, standing up and offering his hand. "It's your job to remember how we get there so we can get back because I'm awful at places like this," Adam said as he walked past Claire and Ms. Levinski and gave them a heartfelt smile.

"So, what happened?" Claire repeated once they left the room.

Ms. Levinski sat down and Claire followed. "She came home from the talent show early and went to her room." She sighed heavily, and tears welled up and started to fall. "On her way, I told her to take the garbage out for me. She said she'd do it in a minute, and I—I yelled at her that I needed it done now." She started to weep.

Claire put a hand on her knee.

"She just waved me off, and I was too exhausted to even argue. I went down the hall a little while later, and she wasn't in her room. I knocked on the bathroom door and called her name. It was locked. I banged on the door, but nothing. You know how old our house is. I was able to push my way in, and I found her on the floor unresponsive." She fell into shaking cries.

Claire felt the tears well up in her own eyes.

"I yelled down to Joey to call nine-one-one. I've trained him, ya know? It's just us, so I had to. I started CPR. She was breathing but shallowly, and I couldn't—I couldn't wake her." She took a moment to try and compose herself. "The EMTs showed up and took her in, and I followed with Joey, and now we're here. I haven't heard anything yet."

Claire felt her heart hammering. Not hearing anything yet was terrifying, and she was struggling with the deep nauseous feeling that was settling in her stomach.

"I was going to yell at her," Ms. Levinski burst out, shoulders shaking. "I've been so hard on her lately because things have been so difficult around the house. I was going to her room to yell at her about the stupid trash."

Claire blinked the tears that were clouding her vision and said, "Ms. Levinski, you were being a mom. And because you were being a mom, you found her sooner than later, and that could save her."

She nodded through her weeping.

Claire placed an arm around her, and the two of them cried together.

Adam and Joey returned, Joey running up to his mom to show her the pack of two Oreos he had gotten from the vending machine, clearly excited.

"I hope that's okay," Adam said sheepishly. "Pretty much everything was candy."

"It's perfect. Thank you," she said gratefully, drying her tears in front of Joey.

Claire and Adam went for a walk so she could tell Adam everything Ms. Levinski had told her. When they returned, they took a seat, Claire leaning on Adam's shoulder, sighing heavily, trying to distract her brain from thinking the worst.

When the doctor walked in, they all stood up simultaneously. He gave a quick glance at Claire and Adam to which Ms. Levinski said, "It's fine. They're family."

He nodded and proceeded to say, "Well, we've pumped Sam's stomach and have her going on oxygen and fluids. We have her stabilized. Her vitals are coming back to normal. She's sleeping now, but she should wake up in a few hours, I would say. When I say 'wake up,' I mean she may open her eyes and speak a little, but she will be very tired, and for that reason, she will probably be resting for a while. Her body needs it. We are going to admit her, of course, and keep her for monitoring. I suspect they will move her in an hour or so. Someone will come by to let you know."

"Can we see her?" Ms. Levinski asked.

"Yes. But I suggest only one to two people at a time. And try to just let her rest."

"Of course."

"If you have no further questions, I will bring you in. She's in the room right around the corner."

"Thank you," Ms. Levinski said.

At that moment, a nurse came in and asked if Mr. and Mrs. Hanover could come back.

Claire's parents came into the small waiting room, and Ms. Levinski was able to give them the good news.

"And it sounds like she's going to be okay," she finished.

"Oh, Claudia, that is so wonderful," Claire's mom said.

Joey was already sleeping on one of the long bench seats. Ms. Levinski picked him up and gave him a squeeze and a quiet reminder to behave for Mr. and Mrs. Hanover before handing him off to Claire's dad.

"Claire, hunny, just call Sam's house if you need me. How long are you going to stay?" she asked, giving Claire a hug.

"I don't know," Claire said.

She nodded as Claire's dad put an arm around Claire's shoulders and gave her a hug, kissing the top of her head. "She's going to be okay, kiddo. I'm sure of it."

Claire nodded, leaning into her dad, and gave Joey a light hug as well.

"What about your parents?" Claire's mother asked of Adam. "Do you want me to call them?"

"I saw a pay phone out front. I'll give them a ring," Adam said with a smile.

"Okay. Well, I left some blankets on the couch for you if you guys make it back there and you just want to crash."

"Thank you," Adam said, surprised.

"I just ask that you guys let us know when you're back. We're both going to bring Joey to his own room and settle him in. But your dad will be home eventually. So let one of us know."

"Okay," Claire said.

Claire's mom hugged her again and then Adam, whispering, "Thank you," to him.

Claire and Adam settled into seats as her parents left, Ms. Levinski having followed the doctor to see Sam.

"She's going to be okay," Adam said quietly.

Claire nodded, letting the emotion from that statement sink in. "Yeah."

"I'm going to go call my folks and let them know I won't be back tonight. You good?" he asked.

Claire simply nodded. She sat back and let her head rest on the wall behind her. She couldn't stop the ocean of thoughts that flooded through her mind. Memories of things that Sam had said or done over the past few years crept up to the forefront as Claire tried desperately to connect the dots to answer the question of why. She pulled apart all the things she had ever said to Sam, looking for a point where she could have said something better, something that would have altered the outcome. She knew Adam was right when he said that what was done was done, but Claire knew she was only at the beginning of this battle. Whether Sam was okay or not, she would have to work through these feelings of guilt. And though her fear for Sam being okay far outweighed her guilt, she couldn't help but recognize all that was to come and all that was to change.

When Adam returned, he brought hot chocolates.

"Where did you get these?" Claire asked, taking her small cup gratefully.

"I saw the coffee vending machine when I went with Joey to the other one. Turns out it does cappuccinos and hot chocolates too." He draped an arm around her and pulled her close, resting his chin on her head, saying, "Come here," as he did.

They waited in silence, drinking hot chocolate and listening for Ms. Levinski. When she came in, she looked tired, and her eyes were puffed, but she smiled at them.

"Go ahead and see her, Claire," she said. "You can go too. I'm going to call my parents to let them know."

Claire and Adam walked to the door she indicated, and Claire stepped in. Sam was sleeping peacefully, propped up slightly. She looked pale, her lips dry, but otherwise looked like she was simply dozing comfortably. The oxygen hose bothered Claire at first sight, reminding her of her grandmother toward the end of her life. Claire hated hospitals because of that. She sat tentatively in the seat that was next to the bed, Adam standing behind her, one hand on her shoulder.

"Oh, Sam," Claire said, voice shaking. "I'm so sorry. I'm so, so sorry. I should have been there for you. We know each other like the back of our hands, and somehow I missed this. I missed that you were hurting." She let the tears openly fall, making no attempt to stop them or wipe them away. She felt Adam's hand tighten on her shoulder. "I love you, Sam. You hang in there, and we'll get you through. We've gotten through everything before. I'm here." She reached over and grabbed Sam's hand, and Claire felt it move ever so lightly, an attempt at a squeeze back. Claire felt a tugging in her heart, and she didn't move for several moments.

"Claire. Claire, hunny," Ms. Levinski's voice washed over her, and Claire jumped up, startling Adam. "Sorry. They're moving Sam up to the fifth floor."

"Oh, okay," Claire said, coming out of her light slumber. Claire looked around at the dimly lit waiting room. They had swapped back with Ms. Levinski and had told her they'd wait with her at least until they moved Sam to a real room.

"I'm so thankful you kids came tonight. It did me a lot of good." Ms. Levinski smiled. "But go home and get some rest. I'm sure you'll want to come see her tomorrow. She may even be up. She opened her eyes a little bit ago but fell back asleep almost instantly. Tomorrow will be better, I'm sure of it."

Claire nodded as she and Adam stood up to give Ms. Levinski hugs. "Let me know if anything at all changes."

"I will. And drive safe, please. It's late."

They waved bye and left the hospital. Claire was so exhausted, she barely noticed the ride home, and when they got there, she plopped down on the couch. Adam went in the kitchen and put a kettle of water on the stove to make some tea. Not seeing her dad anywhere, Claire quickly called her mom to give her an update on Sam changing rooms and that she and Adam were at the house and fine. Her mother told her that her dad had fallen asleep on the couch there and to just get some rest.

"Thanks," Claire said when Adam handed her a mug. She cupped her hands around it and let it warm her insides, which had been chilled with anxiety and fear for hours. He sat next to her, Claire appreciating the quiet house compared to the never-ending noises of the hospital—the beeping, the hustling feet, the voices, her own maddening thoughts. She let the pounding of the silence enter her mind and brain, pushing away everything else till she was left with emptiness. She breathed in the steam of the tea, and a calm fell over her. Sam was going to be okay. It was going to be okay. She drank her tea quietly.

"Thank you," she said softly after a while.

"For what?" Adam whispered. His head was resting on the back of the couch, eyes closed, his stockinged feet on the coffee table in front of them, his tea already finished, placed on the end table next to the cordless phone that he must have snagged to have close by.

"All of this. Taking me down, staying, helping with Joey . . . just being here."

"Of course," he said simply. "And I always will be. I love you."

She placed her own tea down and snuggled into him, overwhelmed by warmth. She'd completely forgotten they had exchanged those three little words earlier. Well, last night now, as it was well after midnight and into early morning. It seemed like eons had passed. "I love you too."

He wrapped his arms around her and kissed the top of her head. She looked up at him and pressed her lips to his. They played against each other for a few moments before she said, "The talent show feels like forever ago at this point, but I am so much in love with that performance and kind of want you to sing to me again."

He laughed quietly, looking down at her. "Is that so?"

"Yeah." She chuckled.

"Yeah? You do remember I was lip-syncing, right?" He kissed her lightly.

"Yeah, but I think you can sing to me still."

"Okay." He grunted as he sat forward and grabbed a blanket off the pile of afghans and quilts Claire's mom had left out. "We need to get comfortable first though." He lay down along the couch, bringing Claire with him, draping the blanket over the two of them. Claire rested her head on his chest and cuddled up to him, letting her eyes finally relax.

"No Backstreet Boys though," he said with a light laugh.

"Okay." She smiled into his chest, which was rising and falling ever so slightly, lulling her. She felt a slight vibration as he started to sing a song just barely over a whisper. She didn't recognize it at first, only feeling it beneath her. But as she listened, she started to pick up on words and knew what it was. She nestled into him even further, if possible, feeling his breath with each word lightly blow over the top of her head, hearing them in his chest as though they were coming straight from her heart. In no time at all, she had drifted off to sleep, Adam not far behind, the words of his song, which he was absentmindedly singing, becoming more and more distanced from each other until they ceased.

Claire slowly woke, sunlight streaming through the bay window of her living room, warming her face. It was brighter than normal, the snow outside reflecting and glistening. She yawned and looked over to see Adam lying on his back, one arm up under his head, the other resting on his stomach. His glasses were on the end table, and Claire realized she'd never seen him without them. In the summer he wore sunglasses, and all other instances, his regular ones. It changed his face slightly. The glasses always gave him an extra layer of adorableness atop his attractive features. It was what Claire loved about him. It softened the cool guy vibe he had when he sometimes smoked or whenever he swore, which Claire noticed was often when his friends were around but not so much otherwise. It was all a part of what made him Adam and why Claire loved him. She thought that again . . . loved him. She loved him. Her bad boy, good-hearted, loveable geek. Now, as she watched him slowly breathe in and out, he looked different somehow. Still hot, no doubt. He was handsome. That's what it was. The glasses added adorable. Without them, it was deeper; he seemed older somehow—mature. And his looks were handsome. All Claire knew was that with or without them, she thought she had the best-looking guy in the whole wide world.

She yawned again and looked around. Suddenly, the night's events washed over her, and she felt wide awake. *Sam.*

As if on cue, the phone rang, causing Claire to jump. She reached over Adam and grabbed it off the end table.

"Hello?"

"Claire, hunny, it's Mom. I hope I didn't wake you. I wanted to let you sleep a little. Ms. Levinski called a bit ago. She said Sam was doing good! She woke up for a while this morning and is resting again. Her vitals all look good, and they will probably discharge her later this week, depending on when she can speak to psych and as long as her body is up to par after everything it's been through. They want to make sure she is sound. So you're welcome to go visit, as I'm sure you want to, and I'm sure Sam wants to see you. But no rush. Take your time. She's going to be okay."

Claire smiled wide. "Tha-that's great." She felt her eyes burn with tears of relief and joy.

"I'm still here with Joey. I told her that I'd feed him lunch and then bring him over after. Your father left a little bit ago to pick up some groceries and things to have here for when they return. I'm going to make them some meals to freeze. I also want him to shovel really well because they're calling for more snow later. So, hopefully, Adam can bring you there again today? I hate to put that on him. Not sure if he needs to work."

"Sounds good, Ma. I'll figure it out. He's still here. I'll keep you posted with everything. I assume you're just coming home after you drop off Joey?"

"Yes. I'll say hi to Sam and then come home this afternoon."

"Okay. Thanks, Mom," Claire said and hung up, hoping her mom had heard just how much she did appreciate her. Though they were two different situations, and, thankfully, Sam was okay, Claire thought she had felt a tiny hint of what her mother had gone through with her friend Danny. She breathed a sigh and felt Adam rustle beside her.

"Everything okay?" he asked through a yawn as he stretched.

"Yeah." She smiled at him. "Sam's awake, and it looks like she'll be coming home sometime this week."

"That's great," Adam said, propping himself up on an elbow, blinking in the sun as well.

"How'd you sleep?" Claire asked.

"Best sleep I ever got." He grinned at her.

She felt a blush creep up her neck ever so slightly. "My mom is still at Sam's house, and my dad is out running errands for her."

"What time do you want to go see Sam?" Adam asked. Claire appreciated that he didn't ask *if* she wanted to or wait till she had to ask him or tell her she was on her own altogether but, rather, simply assumed they were going and that they would be going together.

"I was thinking of taking a shower and freshening up a bit. And then eat something. I'm pretty starved."

Adam smiled and sat up. "Well, how about you go get ready; I'll run home and do the same and pick us up something to eat. Then we can head down."

"That sounds like a solid plan," Claire said.

"Sweet."

"You don't have to work today?" Claire asked.

"Not till later. But I'm going to call Jason anyway. I'm off tomorrow, so maybe he can switch with me so I can have today instead."

They stood up and embraced. Adam gave one of his head-top kisses that Claire loved so much and said, "You know, I have to admit, I'm pretty humbled by how much your parents trust me, letting me spend the night and all."

Claire chuckled. "Oh? Were you planning on trying something last night, Mr. Miller?"

Adam blushed furiously but laughed. "No, I just mean, your parents were more than willing to let me stay, and your dad was apparently unbothered. And I just—that makes me feel good. Your parents are good people, and I like that they think that way about me," he fumbled.

Claire went up on tiptoe and kissed him. "I'm just teasing. I like watching you squirm. And you're right. They do trust you. You're a great guy, Adam Miller. They have no reason not to."

Adam flashed a genuine smile, Claire's words meaning so much to him. "Catch you in a bit?" he said.

"You got it."

Claire washed up, staying a little longer than normal in the shower, letting the hot water encase her, beating down on her back, breathing in the steam. It was just what she needed. She towel dried her hair and blew the hair dryer over it to get most of the moisture out. Claire could never dry her hair completely without blowing a circuit and sweating profusely, which just defeated the purpose, so she more often than not opted to just dry the top to get some fluff and let the rest air dry. She threw on her stirrup leggings, some thick wool socks, and her oversized sweatshirt—a classic weekend look. She layered on some light pink gloss and went back downstairs. She only had to wait a short time before Adam was back with a box of donuts and a coffee for each of them from the bakery.

Seeing the pink box gave Claire a mild heart attack. "Oh my gosh! I totally forgot about work!"

Adam placed the coffees on the table. "It's okay, it's okay. Did you miss your shift today?"

"No. It isn't till three."

"Then you're fine. Call her up, tell her your situation, and call out."

"Okay. Yeah. Call out. Okay," Claire said, going over to the wall phone in the kitchen. "This is a legit reason to call out of work, right?"

"I would hope so," Adam said, sitting down at the small scrubbed table and taking a bite of a donut.

The phone rang and Mrs. Leonard answered. Claire explained the situation, and Mrs. Leonard was more than understanding, even asking if Claire wanted to pick up some goodies for everyone—on the house. Claire was warmed by her generosity and gave her a time that she'd be down to get them. She and Adam sat together at the little table and drank their coffees and ate donuts. It felt nice, like how a Sunday morning should be. Soon enough they were making their way to the bakery, picking up two boxes of a dozen donuts each and a carafe of coffee with cups, creamers, and sugars from Mrs. Leonard before then arriving at the hospital.

Claire had checked with her mom once more to get Sam's room number. Adam and she found it fairly easily, and when they walked in, Sam was sitting up and she gave Claire the biggest of smiles. There were no words to express the feeling that washed over her when seeing that smile. Claire rushed over and wrapped her arms around Sam, who returned the embrace. They held each other tight and both started to cry.

"I'm sorry," Sam said quietly.

Claire let her go and sat on the edge of the bed, holding Sam's hands. "Sorry? What do you mean you're sorry? I'm sorry."

Sam shook her head. "No, I am. For putting you through all this."

"Sam. No. Don't be sorry. For anything." Claire brushed a piece of hair out of Sam's face. "All that matters is that you're okay now, and we are going to move forward like Claire and Sam always have. No more of this bickering and arguing and not talking. We work through things now, and we talk no matter how awkward or hard or bad it may come out; we talk and we don't judge and we figure it out together."

Sam nodded through the tears that were streaming down her cheeks and threw her arms around Claire once more. "Yes. Yes," she said, withdrawing and holding out her pinky. "Pinky promise?"

Claire linked her pinky with Sam's. "Pinky promise." They pressed their foreheads together for a moment and giggled.

"I've missed you," Claire said.

"Oh my god, I've missed you too, Claire," Sam responded.

She leaned back on her pillows. "A counselor came by this morning. We talked for a while, and I think she's going to help me out a lot. I'm talking to her three times a week and have a number if I feel like I need her in between. I'll probably be seeing her for a while . . ." Sam trailed off, a little embarrassed.

"And there is nothing wrong with that. I'm happy for you. That's great, Sam."

Sam beamed. "It's so good to talk to you again. I'm sorry for all the shit things I said to you."

"Me too," Claire responded.

Sam looked up and only just noticed Adam sitting in the chair. "Oh my god, hi!"

"Hey, Sam." He grinned. "Looking good."

"Thanks." She smiled.

Claire and Adam stayed for a while. Adam left at one point to call his parents, but it was more to give Claire and Sam some alone time. He wandered around the hospital, stopping to see the newborns on the maternity ward and sitting in the quiet of the chapel before returning to find Claire lying across the end of Sam's bed and the two of them talking animatedly about what seemed to be everything that had transpired over the entire school year thus far. On his entrance, they quieted right down before bursting into giggles.

"That's not suspicious or anything," Adam said, smirking.

"Just girl talk," Claire said with a wink. They shared a glance, and Adam got the idea that Claire had been updating Sam on all the progressions of their relationship.

As the afternoon went on, more snow fell outside, the sun fading to dark gray clouds, and the doctor came in to talk to Ms. Levinski about the plan moving forward. They stepped out in the hall for it. If the girls had been privy to this conversation, they would have heard the doctor explain that as long as Ms. Levinski didn't think Sam was a danger to herself, she could be discharged in a couple days; that she needed to be on close watch for a while; that all pills needed to be locked up as well as any other items like knives or weaponry that were in the house; that he was writing her out of school for two weeks so she could really work with the counselor to get prepared for that transition; that he would talk to the guidance counselor at school about Sam's case, who would then share it with the teachers who worked directly with Sam so that there would be close eyes on her there as well; that it was common to see the upbeat turnaround Sam was showing right now in patients, and that the real struggle would come when routines and past stressors returned in her life for her to face again; and that Ms. Levinski and Sam's friends would be key components to her getting better. But the girls were not privy to this and were currently just enjoying feeling like things were somewhat back to normal and okay, even if they were in a hospital, and even if Sam had a long road ahead of her.

Late afternoon, Claire and Adam said their goodbyes. Instead of taking Claire home, Adam turned off to head to his secret spot by the lake. He thought she could use a calming moment before returning home to finish what bit of her Sunday she had left and preparing for being back at school the next day. She didn't question him when he changed direction and was happy to see the fresh snow and icy lake in front of her when they pulled off. She really did appreciate the beauty of every season. The fir trees were coated in the light fluffy snow that had fallen. The sun was hiding, the potential for more snow quite possible.

One of Claire's favorite things in the winter was crunching the first footsteps through a patch of white snow. She did so now as she walked toward the lake's edge, soaking in the tree line of white, listening to each and every step. Adam stepped down onto the lake and kicked around some snow to expose a small patch of ice. Claire followed, and the two of them enjoyed shuffling around on the slippery surface, Claire laughing as she fell flat on her bottom, the wet ice seeping through her thin leggings. Adam made to help her up but fell right down beside her. The laughter that escaped them was more than just enjoyment or humor; it was a release of the past twenty-four hours. Claire needed it, and though Sam wasn't Adam's best friend of years, he liked her a lot, and this ordeal was tough for him to play witness to, not to mention feeling so much for Claire's pain. So together they laughed till they cried, not caring about the cold or how soaked they would be when getting up or how absolutely ridiculous they looked and sounded.

Claire rolled on top of Adam, snow in her hair, and kissed him passionately. With the stress and anxiety significantly reduced, all she wanted was to be with him, feel him, and get that flutter and thrill that was him. He held her tight and gave in to her intensity, feeling heated regardless of all the cold, her hair cascading around him and tickling his face, smelling of spring flowers. She was a contrast to the season, a reminder to Adam of all the warmth and sunlight she brought to his every day.

She suddenly broke into a fit of giggles against him, Adam feeling her shaking.

"What is it?" He chuckled.

"You must be soaking wet. I'm sorry," she said, pushing herself off him and standing up, slipping the entire time, looking like Bambi on his first day of winter.

"It was worth it." He smirked, getting up. He took her hand, and they fumbled their way to the land's edge and walked back to the car, but not before Claire felt a whopping snowball hit her back. Turning, she saw Adam's shitty grin as he bent down to get more snow. She quickly did the same and chucked one at him that hit his shoulder. She ran to take cover behind his car as another flew past her. Shrieking with laughter, she threw a few more his way, one getting him in the face.

"Okay, I surrender," he said, laughing, pulling off his glasses and cleaning them of snow.

Claire came out from her hiding spot. "Are you okay?" she asked as he placed his glasses back on.

"Yes, of course." He smiled. "But I know what'd make me feel better."

"What's that?" she asked slyly.

"One more kiss," he said.

Claire delivered.

They returned to Claire's, Adam leaving her there to go home and change into warm clothes quickly but promising to return for Sunday dinner. Claire entered to see her mother pulling a roast out of the oven and Troy sitting at the small table talking to her.

"I didn't know you were home!" Claire exclaimed.

Troy smiled wide. "Hey, Mouse! Yeah, I had a couple days, so figured I'd come home for the night to see how you all were doing. How's Sam?"

Claire sat down across from him, taking an apple out of the center bowl and eating it.

"Claire, I literally just took dinner out," her mother said.

Claire shrugged and answered Troy: "She's going to be okay. She was doing really well this afternoon and should be getting home soon."

"That's great," Troy said meaningfully.

"How are you?!" she asked excitedly. It was nice to see him home. He had grown his hair out just a little bit so it wasn't so high and tight and had filled out just a tad, resembling a little more of Troy pre boot camp. But he hadn't lost the manly quality he had gained. Claire was starting to wonder if it wasn't the physical side of boot camp and more so the growing up that occurred while there.

"Doing good. Went out on a rescue mission a few days ago, which was exciting."

"Ooh tell me!" Claire said as their dad came through the door, having just finished helping the Levinski's once again with the snowfall. They paused Troy's story to hear what he had to say.

"Porch, stairs, and walkway are all done, and I called Dennis to go plow out the driveway, so he should be going there later. He said he'd go back if there is more snow before they return."

"Oh good," Claire's mom said. "Claudia called and said that they may even be home in just a couple days. Sam is doing really well."

"That is great. They'll be happy to be home, I'm sure," he said, going to her, giving her a kiss, and squeezing her side. "Dinner smells wonderful."

"Thanks! Just pulled it out," she returned.

He then clapped Troy on the back. "Good to see you, son."

"You too, Dad," Troy said, standing up and giving him a hug.

Everyone retreated to the dining room just as Adam came into the house, sitting around the warm and savory smelling roast, saying grace, and eating while Troy told them all about the successful rescue mission he'd gone on, their mother exclaiming words of concern the entire time.

When Claire went to bed that night, snuggled under her heavy, quilted comforter, pillows surrounding her, the snow beginning to fall once again, she thanked God for her friend Sam and prayed that things would only go up from there.

The following day, Claire rode in to school with Adam, not having Sam to walk with. It felt strange to be at school without her. Even through their off times, Claire at least still saw Sam and at least knew she was there. It somehow seemed different to be there without her at all. She wondered how Sam was doing with missing school and hoped it didn't bother her.

Adam and Claire separated at the bell to homeroom, and when Claire entered the home ec room, she saw Amber and gang sitting off to the side per usual, heads together, and when they glanced her way, she knew their gathering probably wasn't a good sign. She sat down, facing forward, and ignored it. Going through the motions of the day, she ended with band where she was able to release a lot of the tension she hadn't realized she'd still been holding on to into the piano.

"I'll meet you in the lobby," Adam said as the bell rang. "I forgot to get a book from my locker."

"Sounds good." She smiled as he brushed a kiss on her cheek.

Claire went and sat on the bench seats that ran along the front windows to wait, looking forward to getting home so she could call Sam. She was lost in thought when she heard her name.

"Oh, look, it's Hanover," came the snarky, vindictive tone of Amber Clark. Claire sighed her frustration at not making her escape in time, knowing that something had been up that morning. She just hoped it was due to something stupid, like her fly being down, and not—

"So where's Levinski?" she snarled.

"What's it to you?" Claire asked, standing up and adjusting her backpack.

Amber exchanged looks with her wingmen. "I noticed you two haven't been hanging together for a little while. Finally come to your senses and ditch her?"

"No," Claire said firmly.

"Hmmm. Not what I heard."

"Whatever you *heard*, Amber, I don't really care."

"Well, I *heard*," Amber plowed forward anyway, "that she decided to try and off herself."

Claire's stomach dropped to right around below her feet. She felt her blood boil. How the hell did Amber know? And what a bitch to speak in such a nasty way about something so sensitive. "How—" was all she got out.

"Oh, I have my ways. News travels fast in a small town. So it was an unsuccessful attempt, of course," Amber responded and then added an exaggerated, "thank *God*."

Claire was speechless.

"Tell me, did she do it because you ditched her for a guy?"

Claire glared at her.

"Was she feeling jealous that you had a cute boyfriend, and she hasn't even held the hand of a male besides her kid brother?" The three of them cackled.

Claire felt her face burn, adrenaline coursing through her, which she hadn't felt since that harrowing night of prom. "Shut up, Amber," Claire said through gritted teeth.

"Or what? You'll ditch me and leave me in a pit of despair so strong that I'll want to snuff it? As if! How could anyone put you so much on a pedestal?!

But tell me, how does it feel to be the worst best friend? Seems to be your thing, doesn't it? Be best buddies and then ditch them? Last time it was for a new friend. This time it was for a guy. Too bad I didn't like Levinski better, or I would have warned her."

Claire shook with fury. She wanted nothing more than to slap that porcelain skin and perfectly white, scoffing smile and make those vividly blue eyes cry with the pain she seared into those around her.

She lifted her hand and saw the fear flash across Amber's face. Claire was prepared to put all the power of every mean word she'd ever heard escape those crimson lips into the hand that was swinging forward. She didn't even care that there was a teacher nearby or that kids were staggering out. She wanted to make Amber hurt.

"Whoa!" came a voice, and Claire felt her arm be restrained as Amber threw her own up in front of her face, anticipating the hit.

"What are you doing?" Claire said angrily to Adam.

"Stopping you from making a mistake," Adam said under his breath. "She isn't worth it. She isn't worth any of this."

"Says you!"

Amber adjusted her hair and shirt, regaining her poise. "When you see Levinski, tell her hi from me," she said with mock sincerity.

Adam turned to her with absolute disgust on his face. "Just shut the fuck up."

Amber's face fell with not just shock at his words: Claire knew that hearing that from a senior guy was disheartening to her ego.

She looked at Amber with daggers as she left with Lauren and Ashley. But Claire was far from satisfied. When the door slammed behind them, she glared at Adam and stormed out after.

"Claire!" Adam followed. "Look, I'm sorry, but I didn't think you needed to add a school suspension to your resume."

"You should have let me smack her. You didn't hear what she said!!"

"And she totally would have deserved it," he said as they made their way to his car. "But it wouldn't have solved anything. You would have gotten suspended, and she would have won."

"Won how?! *She* would have had a nice big red mark across her nasty face!"

"Which would have eventually gone away, she would have played the victim, *and* she would have seen just how much she gets to you. You can't let her under your skin like that. You can't show her how much damage she does. It's what she wants."

Claire threw her bag in the back seat and slammed the door but didn't make any attempt to get in the front. "And what about Rick, huh? You got to smack him around! You let him get under your skin, but it didn't stop you from breaking his freakin' nose!"

"That was different." Adam sighed.

"How so?!" she shouted.

"Because he wasn't just being a dick and saying things that he knew would get to people. He attacked and assaulted you, Claire! Then he was bragging lies to everyone to make himself look better. And let's not forget that I did try and talk to him. He just didn't want to listen," he said heatedly.

"Sounds the same to me," Claire said stubbornly.

Adam sighed heavily, threw his hands up in the air, and then ran one through his hair, leaning against his car's hood. The act of this softened Claire just a bit.

"I just hate her so much. And I don't know how she found out about Sam. It pisses me off that she always seems to know everything and uses it all to be a major bitch."

"I know," Adam said, and he did understand. "I get it. And I know it isn't easy, and maybe impossible to do right now, but the best way to get back at people like her is to act like you literally couldn't care less. People like her have one weakness—feeling small. They live on big heads and people who walk behind them, kissing their feet and the ground they walk on. When someone doesn't do that, they mark them as their enemy and will do whatever it takes to keep them lower on the totem pole. Enter insulting you in any way they know will hurt you. Weigh you down and keep you at bay. Keep you from rising up past them."

Claire leaned against the hood of his car next to him, arms crossed, all energy she had moments ago drained. "You remember how you told me once that people don't talk the way I do sometimes?"

"Yeah," he said, looking at her questioningly.

"And I said they should because it's how they feel?"

"Yeah," he said, remembering their first playground night vividly, it being a memory he liked to go back to often.

"Well, that's how you sound."

He laughed. "Maybe you're rubbing off on me."

"Or you've just learned to speak how you feel," she responded.

Adam thought about that statement.

She smiled as he put an arm around her and squeezed.

"So did we just have our first fight?" she asked.

He grinned. "I think maybe. A small one."

"I'm still mad you stopped me from slapping her," she said.

"I know. You can be. But I'm still happy I did. Because, in the long run, I know you would have been mad that you did. You're above that."

She looked at him, but he continued to face forward, Claire soaking in his strong jawline and handsome profile. She threw her arms around his middle. Adam smiled and wrapped his arms around her, giving her a kiss atop her head. They stood like that till it became too cold, then they got in the car to drop Claire off before Adam went to work.

Claire called Sam before she also had to head to the bakery and told her about her day. She didn't tell her about the altercation with Amber because she wasn't sure how Sam would take that the whole school probably knew what had happened. It was a moment that gave Claire anxiety, as she really didn't know what to tell her and what not to tell her. She felt guilty about keeping anything from her but also didn't want to add more stress to her plate. It was confusing and gave her a heavy feeling in her stomach.

A few positives came from their conversation: Sam was coming home the next day, her counselor mentioned having Sam invite someone along to one of her weekly sessions, and Sam wanted to know if Claire would join her. Claire was more than happy to accept, giving her something to smile about on her way to work.

Claire enjoyed working at the bakery. When it was busy, she was able to see many people she knew from town, some whom she met through the bakery, them being regulars. She liked making people's coffees and handing off the warm, scrumptious-smelling treats. When it was quiet, like it was this evening, she loved the absentminded quality of cleaning the tables and sweeping the floors. It gave her a chance to think, and she had some of her best ideas and thoughts while doing this.

That night she came to a conclusion. She had been thinking about the day and how the news of what happened to Sam had traveled. It had puzzled her since Amber approached her, and now, as she worked extra hard on scraping a sticky something off a table, it dawned on her how this had to have happened. Trina. There was no other way. Sam must have told Trina. Claire felt her heartbeat quicken and instantly knew what she needed to do.

As soon as the last bell rang, Claire took off to Trina's locker and marched right up to her.

"Hey, it's Claire Hanover!" Trina said with a sneer and an eye roll.

Claire took a deep breath and said, "I need to talk to you."

"Whatever for?"

"Why did you tell the whole school about Sam's weekend?"

Trina glared at her and then slammed her locker door. "Please," she said with another eye roll and turned to walk away.

Claire was done taking her attitude. "Don't walk away from me," she said with the most authoritative tone she could muster.

Trina didn't have to listen to her, but something made her stop and turn to Claire with a look that was a combination of surprise, confusion, and irritation, if that was at all possible.

Claire stepped forward to close the space between them. "You don't have to like me, and I don't have to like you, but I'm willing to try if being Sam's friend is what you want. I'm Sam's friend too, and I'm not going away, so you're going to have to get used to me."

Trina eyed her, but Claire thought she softened a bit . . . maybe. Or it was wishful thinking.

"And if you're Sam's friend, I want to know why you told the school what happened."

Trina definitely softened. Her crossed arms fell, and her shoulders dropped slightly. The rough exterior left, and Claire saw perhaps the Trina that Sam did. "I didn't tell the whole school. I told one person, who I thought was my friend and would keep it a secret. Obviously, it was a bad judge of character."

Claire felt her own body relax just slightly. So Trina hadn't run around telling everyone about Sam.

Trina said quietly, "I just needed to tell someone. I felt—I felt like it was my fault and . . . I needed to tell someone."

Claire threw caution to the wind. "You could have talked to me."

Trina looked at her questioningly.

"Look, I get it. You've moved schools and have probably been duped one too many times. You have a protective wall up, and your first instinct is to push away before you can get hurt again. So you show your power and dominance. But I promise you I am not a bubbly bimbo who will be your friend one day and turn on you the next. I'm not fake. I hate high school drama. And I especially hate all concepts of fitting in for the sake of fitting in. So you can stop treating me like a valley girl with no brain. I felt a lot of guilt for what happened as well. We could have talked. We don't have to be best buds. But I will protect my friend. And if you're Sam's friend, then you're mine too whether you like it or not. And you need to tell her what happened."

Trina squinted at her, contemplating her words, and, to Claire's great surprise, said, "I'll call her later."

"Perfect," Claire said, and she walked past her but not before Trina called her name.

"Hanover. You're alright."

Claire smirked and said, "You're not too bad yourself," before leaving.

Once home, Sam spent the next couple weeks balancing her time between hanging out with Claire when she wasn't at work or school, meeting with her therapist, and chilling at home with her mom, who had come up with a plan with her on managing the house better so they could have more family time. Claire really enjoyed her trips to the counselor once a week and felt that their sessions brought so much to light about how Sam was feeling in regard to Adam, high school, and their friendship, and it even gave Claire a chance to talk about how she felt about it all in a safe environment. It was such a release to tell Sam that she loved her like a sister and just wanted what was best for her and truly believed she could get it. She told her how she felt about Trina, and they even processed what had happened at school so that Sam was prepared for her return. All in all, Claire felt it was just as much of a therapy session for her as it was for Sam, and she was truly grateful for that time spent. It helped Ms. Levinski out too, as Claire would bring Sam in, so she only had to have someone watch Joey once a week, and it was usually Claire's mom or Sam's grandmother.

When it was time for Sam to return to school, Claire was incredibly glad that it seemed like everyone, Amber included, knew the severity and heaviness of what had happened and didn't bother her about it. Sam and Trina still hung out in class and at lunch, but their friendship seemed to have taken a turn. With Sam not being on the outs with Claire, she found that she didn't care as much to spend so much time just complaining and bitching about others, and so, though she still enjoyed time with Trina—the parts of Trina that were real and deep—she had to take her in doses. Trina also seemed to find "her people," as Sam called it, by joining her poetry friend in an after-school writing group, which seemed to be a great place for her to relieve some of the clear hurt and anger she held on to. This gave Trina some brownie points in Claire's eyes, and she made it a point to try and bring up her own love of writing sometime if they were ever together again, though she didn't really see that happening. Trina was nice to her now at least, but Claire didn't think Trina would ever open up to fully accepting Claire, which she understood.

Claire and Adam also agreed that unless the weather was bad, or she had to get to work, she would walk to and from school with Sam, not only to check in on her but to get in some time together, considering Claire's schedule still consisted of work, homework, and school. Claire was annoyed at herself at first because she hadn't thought of that before, especially when Sam had even asked her if she was going to ride home with Adam every day. But she tried to remember Adam's words of not dwelling on the past and just moving forward to be there for Sam now, and this arrangement worked well for both of them. Trina sometimes joined them, and it was enjoyable.

Before Claire knew it, prom season was approaching, as were the SATs. One night in particular found her sitting on her bed studying with all of her work spread around her, with Sam on the floor doing the same.

"I don't even know what I'm supposed to be studying!" Sam said through quick-paced gum-chewing.

"I don't know," Claire whined. "I guess just anything. We know there's a math and reading section and then an essay. Just try to brush up on solving algebraic equations and memorizing geometric shapes and formulas. I have no idea what to study for reading. This book is full of practice questions, but they're all so specific that unless that is literally the question on the test, I have no idea how it will help." Claire groaned. She was starting to get really stressed about sitting the test and also about the idea that they were talking college, which also felt like talking about the rest of her life.

"I might just wing it," Sam said. "Like, I think I'm going to make it worse for myself if I keep doing this."

Claire nodded and slammed her book shut just as the phone downstairs rang, and she heard her mother approaching.

"Hey, girls. Hunny, the phone is for you. It's Adam," her mother said.

Claire took the phone, and per usual, Sam joined her on the bed, throwing a bunch of her notes and folders aside to listen in.

"Hi!" Claire said.

"Hey you," came his smiling voice.

"What's up?"

"Well. I know I won't see you for a few days because of work and whatnot and wanted to talk to you about prom quickly."

"Cool! You get a date yet?" she asked teasingly.

Adam chuckled. "Well, I'm hoping this really cute girl in my band class will go with me, but I haven't asked her yet."

Claire laughed. "She must be very cute to have caught your handsome eye."

"Oh, she is. Beautiful."

Claire beamed.

"So, Nick and Fitz are going stag, and Jason asked Melissa to go. I was hoping you'd be okay if we all went as a group. And we would love Sam to come with us. Nick and Fitz both asked if she was. I think they were hoping to have a fun dancing partner. If she doesn't have a date yet, of course."

Claire looked at Sam, who nodded excitedly. She seemed quite taken with Nick ever since Claire told her about his comment at the Valentine's Day dance when they spent an entire afternoon just lying on her bed and discussing all the events that had occurred while they had been on the outs. She also really enjoyed Fitz's company, and they got along beautifully, not that there was a living soul on this earth that Fitz couldn't get along with.

"She'd love that!"

"Awesome. They'll be excited. And going as a group?"

"Of course! The more the merrier. Sounds like fun. Plus, you're the senior! Whatever you want to do."

"Awesome. We're working on rides and whatnot. I think we'll end up at your house last for photos. I'll let you know. And make sure you tell me the color of your dress so I can try to match it somewhat. At least not clash with it. And for your corsage."

Claire smiled with excitement. "Will do. We're going dress shopping this weekend."

"I can't wait to see it. I know you'll be stunning no matter what."

"You're too sweet."

"It's the truth. Let me know the color Sam goes with too."

"Okay!"

Sam looked at her with glee.

"She's there, isn't she," Adam said with a light laugh.

"Yes." She and Sam giggled.

"Hi, Sam!" Adam said.

"Hey!"

"You guys studying?"

"Trying to."

"Well, just remember to not overdo it."

"Way ahead of you," Sam piped in.

"That's the spirit." Adam laughed. "I'll let you girls be. Talk to you tomorrow?"

"You know it!"

"Love you."

"I love you too," Claire responded, still enjoying every second of saying that, and hung up.

Sam let out a squeal. "Oh my god!! Prom!! And I have a date! Well, sort of."

"I think you do indefinitely," Claire said. "Sounds like you have two dates."

"Well, I'll take two sort of dates over nothing any day. Especially them. Nick is hot and Fitz is hilarious. They're a perfect combo."

Claire laughed.

"I missed hanging out with you all when I was being a major bitch and ignoring you."

"Sam, you weren't being a major bitch."

"Well, I was being difficult."

"So was I."

"That's fair."

They settled back into their studying.

The following Saturday, they sat the SATs. Sam slept over the night before, and Adam stopped in before work that morning to bring them each a coffee and donuts.

"You'll do fine. Deep breath and just do your best," he said to them both.

Claire realized she'd never asked him how he'd done on his SATs and so did.

He shrugged. "I did okay," he said. She didn't push, not that it mattered anyway. "But you'll do fantastic," he added, kissing her on the cheek and heading out.

Claire drove herself and Sam to the school where they got their instructions and room number. They were separated and agreed to meet out front when they were done. Claire was assigned to one of the health classrooms with about ten other students. They were spaced apart, and Claire took an available spot in the back. She pulled out her two number two pencils and listened to the instructor explain how to fill out bubbles, the rules, and so forth. When time started, she took a deep breath like Adam said and began.

It wasn't as bad as she thought. She knew many of them, some she sort of guessed on, and there were plenty she had no idea at all but picked a random answer for. She at least finished within the time limits and, when the final buzzer went off, felt fairly confident that she'd gotten at least a somewhat decent score. Claire was the first to arrive outside and only had to wait about ten minutes for Sam to show up.

"I am so glad that is freaking over," she said as she joined Claire and they headed home.

"Me too," Claire agreed.

"I think I guessed on, like, half. I spent so much time doing one math problem, and silly me was all excited to put my answer down, and it wasn't even one of the stupid options. I gave up at that point."

Claire chuckled. "Well, we can say we did it and survived, and we don't have to worry about our results till summer."

"Word," Sam said. "How do you think you did?"

"Okay. I think," she said. "Definitely plenty I didn't know, and I feel I overthought some of them, but overall I think I did okay."

"Sweet," Sam said with a smile. "You know what this means, right?"

"What?" Claire questioned, hitting the gas and driving down Main Street.

"We can now focus our attention on more important things."

"Like what?"

"Prom!" Sam squealed.

Closing Time

When Claire and Sam entered the mall, it was teaming with other girls looking for the exact same thing as them—a prom dress. Prom was a mere two weeks away, for A. Thompson High kids at least, and this seemed to be the day to shop. They recognized some from their own school, one being Sarah, with whom they chatted briefly, and others they assumed were from neighboring areas. Beginning their search, they started by going to all the possible stores that sold dresses to see what there was for options, naturally trying on a slew of ridiculous gowns for kicks. They ate lunch at the food court and then took their shopping seriously, resorting to the large department store that had the most selection.

"We should probably have done this before lunch rather than tooling around. I'm so bloated," Claire said over the dividing wall in the changing room.

"Tell me about it," Sam responded.

Claire tried on several dresses. A deep-purple satin dress, which she liked, a bejeweled peach number, and an elegant black dress that Sam told her made her look too old. Claire was a fan of most, but none made her feel quite like Cinderella as much as the shimmery frosty-blue one did. Almost a light silver, it had a sweetheart neckline with spaghetti straps and a chiffon bottom that flowed like an airy cloud. When she showed Sam, her face was priceless, and Claire knew it was the one.

Sam landed on a beautiful, simple deep-green dress that also had spaghetti straps but with a scoop neckline and a straight skirt. It was satin and shimmery, and Claire loved it on her, the scoop even giving her the illusion of a chest, which Sam noted was her favorite part.

They got sandal-style heels and stopped to get accessories. Claire wasn't sure how she wanted to do her hair, but Sam was set on getting it done at the salon, so when they returned home, Claire called and booked them appointments. Everything was set, and Claire couldn't contain the giddiness that had settled in her stomach. They squealed, laughed at absolutely nothing, and jumped around to some Brittney Spears to release the tension before calling Adam to inform him of their choices.

"Don't tell me too much!" he blurted out as Claire started describing her dress. "I want to be surprised."

Claire beamed. "Okay. Lips are sealed. But it is a really light blue. Like, how ice would be if it were a color. And Sam's is a really pretty deep green, like Christmas!"

"Awesome. I'll let Nick know! Can't wait!"

Claire found herself struggling with paying attention at school in the week leading up to prom. With the SATs behind her and prom so close, she fell into a stupor of daydreaming and slacking. She and Sam spent the Thursday evening before together, as it was one of Sam's session nights that Claire was invited to, and once the bell rang on Friday afternoon, Claire rushed out the door to meet Sam and Adam outside. Sam was spending the night so they could get up together and get ready, Claire having taken the weekend off. Adam dropped them off before going to work himself, only able to get Saturday off.

"EEEEE, I'm so excited!" Sam said when Claire entered her own bedroom, having taken a few minutes to say bye to Adam, knowing she wouldn't see him till he showed up looking dapper and prom ready the next night.

"Me too." Claire grinned, dropping her bag in the corner, having no intention of touching it again before school on Monday. She dropped on her bed, lying with her feet up against the wall at the head of it. Sam followed and lay opposite, her legs draped over the end, their heads side by side, staring at the ceiling. They fell into a tumbling of words, some pertaining to prom, others completely random, and didn't really stop till they took a break to eat dinner, and then again when they finally drifted off to sleep.

"Okay, how does it look?" Sam asked nervously across the salon. Sam was turned away from the mirror as the hairdresser went to grab a few more bobby pins, almost finished with Sam's do.

"I think it looks totally cool," Claire said, seeing the small sections of twisted hair that met in a bundle of curls atop Sam's head. Sam having naturally curly hair made the popular updo easy for the hairdresser, who had even straightened the top part of her hair so she could twist it properly with a little volume. It was a style seen on the cover of many magazines, and Claire knew that would be exactly what Sam wanted. "For real, dude. It looks sick!"

The stylist came back, put in the last bobby pins to secure the mound of curls, making Sam wince silently, and was finished. Turning the chair around, Sam looked in the mirror, and Claire was warmed to see her grin spread from ear to ear.

"Oh. My. God. I love it!" she exclaimed. "Like, totally what I wanted. I am pretty sure I have seen Jennifer Love Hewitt in this exact same style. No joke! It's the bomb."

Claire chuckled as her own hair continued to get teased, sprayed, and pulled. Claire preferred simple and natural. She had said she didn't want her hair up too high, as it gave her a headache, and didn't want it overly curled or plastered with hairspray when asked by the hairdresser, who had then opted to do an elegant twisted bun at the nape of her neck, teasing the top slightly to give volume as it was pulled back, leaving one strand to swoop down and fall on the side of her face. It was classy, clean, and sophisticated. Perfect.

Back at Claire's house, they hemmed and hawed over makeup ideas. Claire was going for a natural tone with browns and nudes. She did take Sam's idea to use her crimson lip color to bring a pop against the ice blue of her dress and her dark hair. Claire never turned down an opportunity to wear red lipstick. Sam went for browns and earthy colors to balance the green of her dress and her own rich dark hair. They ate light, not wanting to mess up their makeup, and when it was getting close to the group's arrival, they scurried upstairs to get dressed. Claire felt a ball of nerves and excitement and expressed this to Sam in case she was too.

"Oh my god, I know! It's the anticipation though. Once they're here and we get to prom, I have no doubt it'll just be rad!"

Claire smiled. Sam was right. The anticipation was the killer. She also remembered that she was going with Adam. Adam, whom she'd been dating now for almost a year. Adam, whom she'd been friends with for almost three. Adam, whom she felt knew everything about her and she him through their shared musical insights, long talks on the playground, and day-to-day time spent together. Adam, who had protected her at last year's prom, who kissed her so passionately and made her feel like the smartest, funniest, most beautiful girl in the world, who had been there for her and her best friend through a particularly scary time, who had danced with her in front of the school, and who had even dedicated a knockout talent show performance to her. He was the best, and she was going to prom on his arm, not as a date, but as a friend and partner. She loved him.

Claire did have a small feeling in the pit of her stomach that had started about a week ago and had grown steadily since. She tried to ignore it, especially tonight, but it was there, and she couldn't help it. It was sadness. Adam was a senior. This prom marked his senior prom and another checkbox on the events that led to graduation. Claire was beyond the moon happy for him as he took these big steps, but she couldn't help but feel sorrowful at the idea of an A. Thompson High without him in the halls. No smiling gray eyes beaming at her across the band room or from behind the lighting booth, watching her closely as she played piano at all the concerts. No surprise hallway hugs or the jolt in her stomach that came just from seeing him in the lobby at the end of the day. She even thought of missing Nick, who would often throw his arm around her shoulders during transitions in the hall to see how she was doing, or Fitz, who always shouted "Bohemian" every time he saw her, or Jason, sweet Jason, who smiled and waved.

She knew all this was inevitable. Additionally, she couldn't help the tinge of anxiety that crept in when she was really vulnerable, when her darker thoughts made her question if this would affect her and Adam's relationship. He would be a working adult, saving to go to school, and then she'd be graduating before they knew it, both of them heading off to college, and how would their relationship fare on the seas of being separated? In those moments, she would shake the thoughts away and remind herself that he had given her no indication whatsoever that their relationship would change because he wasn't at school anymore and was, in fact, for the time being, merely down the street at RadioShack. But it was a lot to think about and a lot to hold on to.

She knew the best person to talk to would be Adam, but finding the proper time to do that amid all this excitement was hard. She didn't want to feel like she was bringing anything down or taking away from it all. She knew he wouldn't think that way, but she did. Sometimes, Claire wished things didn't have to change so much and so dang fast.

"Claire," Sam's soft voice broke through, Sam looking at Claire with concern.

"Wha—oh, sorry!" Claire said, shaking those thoughts away once again.

"You okay?" Sam asked quietly.

"Yeah, why?"

"Well, you were kind of quiet, and your eyes were glossing over a little bit. I thought you were going to cry."

Claire heaved a sigh. "I'm just—it just feels like everything is changing. I can sense it. It's coming," Claire said in a small voice, unlike her.

Sam crouched down in her shimmery satin gown in front of Claire. "I know. But, speaking from personal experience, if you dwell on all the things that are changing or going to change, you miss out on what is happening now. At some point, you realize that you've spent all your time in a state of worry of what's to come, always looking forward, and not living in the present. Things will change. They always do. But take it day by day and enjoy it. Odds are, the anxiety you are feeling isn't even needed because things often have a way of coming together."

Claire nodded, appreciative of Sam's advice. Claire wondered if that was how Sam felt she'd lived the past couple years of high school, always worried about what was to come. If this feeling was how Sam felt all the time, Claire felt bad for not paying more attention to it. "You're right. Thank you."

Sam grinned. "Tonight will be a memory for a lifetime of recalling, so let's just let it roll and have some fun! Plus, I am starting to sound too much like a fortune cookie or Mr. Miyagi. Come on, I'm sure your mom wants pictures of us before the rest arrive."

Claire smiled and was happy to feel that she could release the growing tension, at least for tonight. She called down to her mom, and the two of them descended the stairs to clapping excitement. Claire's dad was there, smiling with a glint in his eye, as were Troy and Gwen, who catcalled and cheered.

Claire felt her face flush ever so slightly.

"Okay, you two, get in front of the mantle so I can take your picture," Claire's mom said. "I promised I'd get some developed for your mom, Sam."

They posed and grinned, taking a few fun shots inspired by *Charlie's Angels*.

"You girls look amazing, truly! Your dresses are gorgeous!" Gwen said, standing up and feeling the fabric of the gowns.

"Thanks!" Claire and Sam said in unison.

Troy stood up and went up to Claire. She waited for him to speak, not sure what was going to come out. "Claire," he said, "you look beautiful. You both do. I hope you have the best time tonight."

"Thanks, Troy," Claire said, giving him a big hug, touched by his words.

Claire's dad gave them hugs as well but seemed to be trying to keep himself together and so wasn't talking much.

Soon enough, they heard car doors slamming, and Adam was first to knock on the door and let himself in. He walked into the living room carrying a clear plastic box containing a corsage. He was wearing a basic black suit, a skinny black tie, and a simple ice-blue handkerchief tucked in the pocket of the jacket. It was just enough of a match.

Claire couldn't stop the smile that spread wide at the sight of him. He was debonair, he was handsome, he was adorable, he was all hers, and he was wearing an expression of absolute speechlessness at the sight of her. For a moment, the world stopped: Claire paid no attention to the others, who were following in behind, or her mother's excited gasps of awe at their suits and Melissa's dress.

Adam walked up to her, placed the corsage box down on the chair nearby, grabbed her two hands in his, and held them out so he could look at her. She looked down out of shyness.

"Claire," he said quietly while the others talked animatedly, "you look stunning." She blushed as he dropped one hand and twirled her around with the other. Now her Cinderella vision was complete. "Truly. I mean, you're always stunning, but . . . there aren't words. I'm by far the luckiest guy alive tonight."

Claire's cheeks flushed further. "Well, thank you. And you look exceptionally handsome."

He smirked at her and placed a soft kiss on her cheek, given that they were in a room of her family and their friends, although it wasn't missed by a smiling dad in the corner.

"Okay, everyone! Time for photos!"

Claire tuned into the hubbub of what was going on around her.

Melissa was in a dress of coral that matched Jason's tie and cummerbund. And—

"Oh my gosh, you two look adorable," Claire said at the sight of Nick and Fitz. They wore matching suits with green ties that perfectly coordinated with Sam's dress.

"Thanks. I think we clean up pretty nice myself," Nick said, holding on to the lapels of his jacket.

"Come on! Get together!" Claire's mom said, holding her hands up to indicate squishing in.

"We'll take some group shots, and then I want some of Adam and Claire and Sam and you two boys. Jason, did your mom get pictures of you two? I can take some if you like," she continued in one breath while holding up the camera and flashing photo after photo.

With pictures done, they said their goodbyes and headed to the cars. There were two. Adam was going to drive Claire, Nick, and Sam, while Fitz was going to ride with Jason and Melissa. It was a mere few minutes anyway. The night was warm for May, and Claire was happy she didn't need the small sweater she brought. Sam was glowing in the back seat, and Nick was already lighting up a cigar and blowing smoke out the open window.

"Fucking prom!!" he shouted to the pedestrians, followed by Sam's fit of giggles. Adam shook his head while Claire laughed. Getting out at the school, Nick put out his cigar on the pavement and left the rest of it atop the tire of the car for later.

Heading up the stairs, Adam lightly grabbed Claire's elbow, gesturing to the others to keep going. "We'll be right in."

Claire stepped down, smiling at him.

"I just want to say," he stammered, looking at her large round brown eyes, those red lips, her beautiful hair, "that you look stunning."

"You said that at the house, silly," she said with a smirk.

"I know, but, you do, and I wish I had more words. But that's what you do to me, Claire Hanover. You leave me speechless."

Claire smiled and blushed. "Well, thank you. I love you, Adam Miller."

"And I love you," he said, pulling her toward him and giving her a deep and passionate kiss.

They ascended the stairs, met the gang, and entered the "Midnight in Paris" themed prom.

Photos, food, tables with Eiffel Tower keychain favors, and a dance floor complete with lights and vibrating tunes engulfed them. Claire remembered this was Sam's first time at prom and so was thrilled to see her looking so in awe and happy. Nick pulled the chair out for her to sit, and he and Fitz took their places on either side of her like a couple of bodyguards. This seemed to thrill Sam, who gave Claire a look across the table that clearly said, *Not too shabby.*

Adam put an arm around the back of Claire's chair and they settled in.

"When do you think the food is going to come out? Like, the real food," Fitz asked. "All I see is chips and rabbit food."

"Rabbit food?" Nick asked, pouring himself some water from a pitcher on the table.

"Yeah, man," Fitz said, nodding. "A bunch of veggies and stuff."

"Those would be hors d'oeuvres, man," Nick responded. "Have some class."

The table chuckled.

"Speaking of hors d'oeuvres," Adam piped in, "did you tell everyone the good news?"

They all looked to Nick, who put his hands up and said, "Awe, come on. It isn't that big a deal."

"Come off it, man. Tell them!" Adam persisted.

"I may have maybe gotten accepted into the culinary arts program at the community college," he said nonchalantly.

Claire brightened. "Congratulations, Nick! That's awesome!"

"Congrats!" Sam added, which Melissa copied. Jason and Fitz seemed to already know this information, nodding along.

"Yeah, yeah, thanks. No big deal, like I said."

"Oh, come on! That's a really big deal!" Claire said. "Good for you!"

"Well, thank you," he said meaningfully, giving her a wink. "Now we just got to wait on this fellah." Nick pointed to Jason.

"Are you looking at the same school?" Sam asked.

"Yeah. I applied there and two others for culinary arts as well. I'm hoping for SMCC though. Still waiting to hear back." Jason smiled.

"Fingers crossed!" Claire said. "What about you, Fitz?"

"Oh, I think I'm going to just chill and work. I got this sweet gig set up for this summer working at a music store that sells instruments and shit. Will be pretty cool to just tool around on stuff all day."

Nick rolled his eyes in a playful manner. "Then there's this one over here. Slacker of the year," Nick joked, gesturing to Adam.

"Oh, shut up. I told you, I'm taking the year to work and save up. I'm still trying to decide anyway and don't want to waste my money if I'm not sold on what I want to do."

"If you say so," Nick said, but added, "I'm kidding!"

"What about you, Melissa?" Claire asked, ignoring Nick's teasing but giving him a sideways smirk in the process.

"I'm going to UMaine for a business degree." She smiled.

"That's great! I hear that's a really versatile degree to get," Claire said.

"Yeah! It'll be good for managerial work, and I can really take it where I want to. Always wanted to be an entrepreneur. Open my own business or something. I'm not sure!"

"Sounds great!"

"What do you girls want to do after school? Pretty soon you'll be seniors," Nick piped in.

Claire let Sam go first, not really sure what she was going to say.

"I think I want to go into social work, with kids," Sam said.

"Wow! That's cool," Jason chimed in.

"What about you, Claire?" Nick asked.

Claire felt Adam's hand give her leg a gentle squeeze.

"Um. Well, I haven't fully decided yet. I was thinking about teaching. I love school and learning and would love to do that. But . . ." she breathed deeply, "I also have a love of writing, and so I may look into creative writing programs."

"No shit," Nick said. "That's pretty cool. What do you like to write?"

Claire blushed. "Um, well, anything really. I just enjoy it. I like to write adventure fantasy-like stories and realistic fiction. It's just fun to put myself in someone else's shoes and tell a story. But I think my favorite things to write are spooky stories."

"Go, Bohemian," Fitz said.

"Pretty rad, dude," Nick said. "Next Stephen King! Whenever you write that *New York Times* bestseller, don't forget your pal Nick."

Claire laughed. She couldn't believe she'd just told a table of people one of her deepest secrets, and for them to accept it, and with that amount of support, was impeccably heartwarming.

They continued chitchatting till the food was finally put out, to the great excitement of Fitz. They ate and talked some more, and soon it was time to take to the dance floor. They stayed in a group for the most part, dancing to an array of songs. Fitz and Nick took turns twirling Sam around, and Claire and Sam particularly got into it when "Baby One More Time" played through the gymnasium. When the first slow dance played, Adam immediately pulled Claire into a tight embrace, and they rotated slowly, Claire holding on to Adam with all she had, never wanting to let him go. Their temples pressed together, they didn't speak and just let the music wash over them. Claire felt that twang of grief from earlier creep up again and tried to focus on the feeling of his hand entwined with hers, leading her, trying to stop her mind from dwelling.

Claire was shocked at how fast the time seemed to be going, though she knew that it had everything to do with having so much fun. They danced to almost every song, a couple times the boys retiring to the table while Sam and Claire stayed on the dance floor. Claire caught Adam watching her a couple of times, which made her both blush and feel like the only girl in the room. When they were all sitting back at the table, cooling off, drinking some water, and eating cake, Adam asked Claire if she wanted to step outside.

Claire welcomed the warm spring air as it splashed across her face when entering the benched area that she remembered all too clearly from last prom. She didn't think that memory would burst through like it did, but it did. She turned to see Adam watching her and instantly focused on him, her Prince Charming. He sat down on the half wall and tapped the spot next to him for her to sit. She did.

"I couldn't help but notice that something seems to be on your mind," he said. It was soft and welcoming.

Claire was stunned. How did he know? Had she let it show? "What do you mean?"

Adam smirked. "I have known you for a minute."

Claire chuckled lightly. "I'm sorry. I am having an incredible time tonight. I feel like Cinderella at the prince's ball."

"And you look it," he said, leaning into her to bump shoulders. "But?"

Claire looked at him, sizing him up. She didn't really want to have this conversation here, at prom. She didn't want to bring down this glorious evening for him. She was also a little upset with herself that she had let the emotions of those deep thoughts show.

As if reading her mind, Adam said, "Look, this has been an incredible night, like you said. And it will continue to be. Nothing will change that. And you haven't done anything to indicate otherwise. But I know you, Claire. I can see it in your eyes; I can feel it in the way you hold me when we dance. There is something."

Claire heaved a sigh. "I just . . . I just don't want to have this conversation here. I don't want to ruin anything. It's your senior prom! It's a big deal."

Adam smiled but it faltered. "Should I be worried?" he asked, concerned.

"No. No. Not at all."

Adam nodded. He stood up and held out his hand. "Dance with me?"

Claire accepted. "There isn't any dancing music though." All that was coming through from inside was some loud bass.

"That's okay," he said, lacing an arm around her middle and taking her hand in his. He moved from side to side, slowly dancing and turning on the spot. "Almost a year ago tonight," he started quietly, "I had one of the most amazing moments of my life. Forgetting everything else before it, of course. I got to dance with you for the very first time." He paused to lean back and look at her with a grin before returning to their close embrace.

"I remember feeling the anxiety bubble up when I impulsively asked you to dance. I remember the shock at having uttered those words and even more so at your acceptance. I remember feeling your hand in mine, soft and warm, the smell of your hair, just getting to hold you."

Claire smiled, knowing he could feel that she did.

"And since then, I have had the luck of getting to experience a slew of moments with you, each better than the last. I couldn't be happier, Claire. And I don't think I could love anyone or anything more. Happy prom."

Claire leaned back and gazed into his eyes, her own glossy from his words. They warmed her like hot cocoa on a cold day, giving her goose bumps. She had no idea how to follow that. So, much like the night he had confessed to liking her, she did the only thing that made sense. She let go of his hand, wrapped her arms around his neck, and kissed him. Their mouths played against each other, tongues quickly joining, and Claire felt the heat boil deep inside her. His arms were wrapped tight around her waist. She could feel one hand on her bare back, warm to the touch, issuing more goose bumps across her skin. She heard him groan slightly, and the two of them pressed themselves closer to each other, still not feeling close enough.

Adam pulled away, placing his forehead to hers, both of their breathing elevated, and closed his eyes. He was brought right back to their trip to the beach . . . when he had known for certain he had fallen in love. The rush of emotions that she brought on dizzied him, intoxicated him . . .

"We have to stop," he said with a slight laugh. "I'm not thinking straight."

He rested there for a moment before opening his eyes to find Claire looking at him with an expression he'd never seen on her before. An expression that both drove him wild and absolutely terrified him. An expression that she was quite clearly okay with not stopping . . . quite clearly okay with the things that come with not thinking straight. Thoughts of taking off flashed through his mind, his car a mere parking lot away, but he took her hand and placed a kiss atop it, then turned it palm up and kissed it again. It was a subtle move, but it made Claire's body burn.

"You know I love you, right?" he said.

Claire sighed. "Yes." The spark left, though her eyes were crinkled in a knowing smile. "I know."

"Good. Then you know it is because I love you that we need to stop." He brought her in close again.

"Yes," she said, resting her chin on his shoulder. He was right, she knew it, but, boy, was it ever difficult.

"So, you want to tell me what's on your mind?"

Claire thought a moment and then said quietly, "I'm afraid of the change I know is coming."

"Change?"

"You graduating," she said. And then, as if saying it had opened the floodgates, she carried on in one big onslaught of words. "Every event leading up to it is just one more reminder that I'm getting closer to the day that you won't be at school with me anymore. That we won't have band class together or walk down the halls together or . . ." she trailed off.

"Ah," Adam said, understanding. He too had his own feelings around this. He had thought of it more often recently. However, his thoughts seemed to be revolving around a slightly different angle. He would certainly miss seeing Claire every day of school, and though he trusted her and knew she loved him, the other guys at school not so much, and he couldn't escape the twinge of jealousy at the idea of what those guys may say or do knowing he wasn't on campus anymore. But the real thing he was beginning to worry about was something else, something he couldn't quite put into words yet. "Well, I will only be a small ways away at any given point. I can even still bring you to school and pick you up if my schedule allows it."

Claire smiled, pulled apart from him, and sat down in the same spot they had taken up before. Adam followed. "That does make me feel better. But I'm still going to miss you. I literally don't know an A. Thompson High without you. Quite literally from day one, you have brought some form of excitement or entertainment or happiness to my days at school. Dating or not dating doesn't matter. Since I talked to you on my very first day of freshman year, you have been a source of happiness in the midst of the day-to-day shuffle of school. But there isn't anything to be done or said about it. It's inevitable. I'm just going to have to get used to it, and that's hard. Change is hard." She ended by blowing the solitary ringlet out of her face.

Adam smiled. "It sure is. But you know what makes it easier?"

"What?"

"Having someone to go through the changes with. And you are a lucky person who has me, Sam, your brother, Gwen, Babs, your parents—all kinds of constants in a world of change."

She placed a hand on his knee, appreciative of his words. "You're right."

"I'm not dismissing it though. You're feelings are just. I, too, am going to miss seeing you every day tremendously and can't imagine all the guys that are going to come out of the woodwork to talk to you when they no longer see me around," Adam said, hinting at his own insecurities.

Claire grinned at him. "Oh? And who are these *guys* that are going to come out of the woodwork?"

He laughed lightly. "Any one of them. You're the prettiest, smartest, most talented girl in the whole school. They're going to come running to talk to you."

Claire burst out laughing. "Yeah, okay." When Adam didn't say anything, she said, "Well, if they do, I will just have to tell them that I'm not interested because *I* have the most handsomest, loving, sweetest bad boy in the world, and I am perfectly content with that."

Adam smirked.

They fell into a silence for a few moments, each letting those thoughts flow through their busy minds, neither of them expressing the thoughts that were deeper seated: the thoughts about the future and what it would bring or what it would do.

"Hey," Claire said suddenly, "this is prom. And this is exactly why I didn't want to talk about all this tonight! We're supposed to be dancing and having fun!"

Adam nodded. "You're one hundred percent right, my love. Let us go and finish off this prom with a bang." Adam held out his hand, which Claire took, beaming at his use of "my love."

They found Sam and the others quickly, Nick twirling Sam around, all of them singing. At one point, Claire noticed Amber sitting at a table with Chris, who was contentedly not dancing, slouched in a chair watching everyone else. Claire made a quick scan and found Mark dancing with a girl Claire recognized from her English class in a group with Mike, Sarah, Lauren, Ashley, and a couple others guys Claire didn't know. She laughed and pointed this out to Sam, who cackled. Clearly, Amber had picked the wrong date, though Claire wasn't sure why she didn't just ditch Chris and dance with the rest. They watched too long, and Amber's eyes found theirs. They quickly stopped laughing and gave little waves. She glared, arms crossed, with all the vengeance one could possibly put into an expression.

An eighth person joined their group toward the end of the night. Nick brought him over from the punch table.

"Hey, folks! This is Logan," he shouted over the music. "He's been a god in my study hall helping me with my homework this year. Pretty much owe him my college acceptance. Anyway, he says he knows some of you."

Sam smiled and waved, shouting, "Hi!" It was Logan: *the* Logan from her math classes, *the* Logan from her lunches, *the* Logan she had freaked out about freshman year for asking for a piece of gum.

He smiled at her. "Hey! You look great!"

"Thank you!" Sam beamed.

"He said he came stag, so I told him to hang out with us for a bit," Nick said with a quick wink toward Claire.

"Great! Nice to meet you," Adam said. The group all spoke likewise, and Logan joined for a bit, even dancing one slow dance with Sam. Claire could feel her excited energy.

As the night drew to a close, the all too familiar tones of that last song started, and Adam took Claire into an embrace, holding her hand close to his chest, his other wrapped tightly around her. Claire didn't mean to, but she got emotional. She remembered dancing to this song last time, how safe she had felt with him, how elated she had been to be so close. She thought of everything that had transpired since. Her heart was filled with ecstasy at how blessed she was. It combined with the grief she was feeling for the impending changes and mixed with an already defined sense of nostalgia for this school year and all that it had held.

Adam adjusted his head so he could look at her, and Claire could see his own eyes were glistening ever so slightly. He smiled at her, gave her a kiss, and they placed their foreheads together, closing their eyes to the world around them and allowing themselves to just be.

"William Fitzpatrick." Mr. Lewis's voice rang out across the gymnasium.

Claire and Sam shouted and clapped as Fitz received his diploma and walked across the stage, holding his fists up in the air in true Rocky fashion before descending the other side.

Students continued to be called up, Claire and Sam chatting in between. The gym was warm and packed, Troy, Gwen, and Claire's parents sitting on the bleacher behind them. The families of the seniors were in chairs on the floor, and Claire was excitedly anticipating seeing Adam walk across the stage. She used the program to fan herself as they hollered and clapped once again when Jason was called.

"I can't believe this is going to be us next year!" Sam said.

"I know! It's crazy. If this year goes as fast as the last three have, it'll be here before we know it!" Claire responded.

"Tell me about it," Sam returned, chewing animatedly on her gum.

"This place never changes," Troy said from behind them. "So, that room over there?" he said to Gwen. "Where the gym equipment is kept? That's where you'd take your girlfriend for a little smooching."

Gwen rolled her eyes. "So you never saw the inside of it, then?"

Claire snorted as Troy said an audible, "Hey!"

Claire knew where Adam was sitting and watched him as he rose with his row to make their way to the stage steps. She was so happy for him and, as silly as it sounded, exceptionally proud of him. She knew that he had struggled at times with school, the two of them having worked together often over the past few years, but he had done it and had managed graduation with a decent GPA. She let the last few years flash before her as the line of graduates got smaller, Adam getting closer to the stage. With this day here, and her senior year beginning soon, the conversations around the future and what they were going to do with it was near. Soon they would be expressing concerns and anxieties around where to go and what would happen with being separated. Solidifying plans. But for now, with the frenzy of graduation and the thrill of a whole summer ahead, Claire didn't bother with it. Not now.

"Adam Miller."

Claire and Sam jumped up, whirling their noisemakers. Troy made whooping noises and Claire hollered. They wanted to be the noisiest group there, and it worked. When he got to the end of the stage, he scanned the crowd and saw them. He flashed his award winning smile and blew a kiss. Claire beamed and sat down as Adam took his seat again, diploma in hand.

"That was so nice of him to throw me a kiss," Troy said.

"Shut up!" Claire smirked as Gwen elbowed Troy.

Once the names were done being called after two more rows went up, the principal had the seniors stand and face the audience. He informed them to move the tassel from right to left and said to the crowd, "I am happy to present to you the A. Thompson High School graduating class of 1998!"

Hats flew in the air as Claire and the rest of the gym jumped to their feet and applauded. There was a shuffle as the seniors hugged their friends, music rent the air, hats were located, and those looking on gradually made their way down the bleachers. Claire elbowed her way through the crowd and spotted Adam chatting with his parents, Fitz and Fitz's dad next to them. Sensing her, Adam looked to see her approaching. His grin spread, and Claire rushed him, jumping into his arms, him hugging her tight and swinging her on the spot.

"Congratulations!" she squealed.

"Thank you!" He laughed. His parents smiled on and then turned their attention to Claire's parents as they, Troy, Gwen, and Sam approached.

Adam kissed Claire quickly and said, "Thanks for the shouts!"

"You're welcome. We wanted to be the loudest!"

"I think you accomplished that." He chuckled.

"Well, you deserve it! We're so happy for you! A graduate!" she said animatedly.

"Hard to believe, huh?"

At that moment, Claire's mom burst through them to give Adam a hug, saying, "Oh, congratulations. John and I are so proud of you."

"Thanks, Mrs. Hanover." Adam smiled and then, shaking Claire's dad's hand, said, "Mr. Hanover."

"Congrats, kiddo," he returned and clapped him on the back.

"Adam!" Troy said, coming in for a shake and one of those side guy hugs he was so good at. "Congrats, man!"

"Congratulations, Adam!!" Gwen said, giving him a squeeze as well.

Sam followed, and Adam glowed with the affection from them all.

"Thank you all. And thank you for coming! This is great!"

"Well, of course!" Claire's mom exclaimed. "You didn't think we'd miss this, did you?!" She seemed almost appalled at the idea of it. She then turned to Adam's parents and said, "Do you want me to get some photos of the three of you?"

Claire rolled her eyes at how intrusive her mother could be at times, but Adam's parents gladly accepted, and the three of them went and stood in front of the stage next to the A. Thompson High gold-and-sky-blue knight-encrusted shield, Claire's mom squinting through the viewfinder and counting them down before snapping their picture. Then she asked if Adam's mom could take one of Adam with Claire's whole family, which she did. Next were photos of just Adam and Claire, and finally, after much coaxing from her mom, Claire rounded up Fitz, Jason, and Nick so her mom could take pictures of the boys and then with the addition of Sam and Claire.

"There!" Claire's mom exclaimed after the last photo was taken. "You have to have pictures!" she said in explanation to Adam's mom, who nodded politely with a smile.

"What time do the buses leave?" Claire asked Adam.

Project Grad was the same as all the classes before. The high school rented a ski resort in the mountains nearby that had a large pool, basketball hoops, and screens set up for movies among other fun things for the seniors to do and was more than happy to house Project Grad for all the neighboring towns since they didn't have much revenue outside of the winter months.

"I think in a half hour or so. My stuff is all in my locker," Adam said.

Claire grinned. "I hope you have a fabulous time!"

"I wish you could come with me," Adam said quietly, grabbing her hands in his.

"Nah. Enjoy your time with Fitz and Jason and Nick. You're seniors! Lap it up! Don't forget your yearbook so you can get signatures. Oh, and don't get caught smoking! I know Nick has some celebratory cigars up his sleeve. You're still A. Thompson High's responsibility till you get back, so you can still get in trouble! Mr. Lewis said so."

Adam chuckled. "I'll be careful."

Adam's parents and Claire's family said their goodbyes and left. Adam grabbed his bag, and Sam and Claire went out to meet the bus with him, the two of them planning to make the short walk home after. Sam wandered to sit on a bench while Claire said her goodbye, the bus already filling up with seniors.

"So how does it feel?" Claire asked.

"Not sure it's hit me yet but kind of feels like the end of an era."

Claire nodded. "I'm sure it does."

"You're still good to take me home tomorrow morning?"

"You know it." She grinned. He returned it and then pulled her into a tight embrace. They held each other close and, without even knowing it, closed a chapter and moved into a new one

SENIOR YEAR
1998-1999

"So, you feel ready?" Adam asked as he held Claire's hand in her lap, his other gently controlling the steering wheel of his car as he drove Claire to her last first day of school.

"Yeah! Feels weird though," she responded. "The last three years flew by. I'm sure this one will go by just as fast."

"They sure do."

"Thanks for driving me in." Claire smiled at him. He returned it, and Claire beamed. His look never stopped bringing her joy.

"Of course," he responded. "I'm more than happy to. I'm hoping my schedule will work out so that I can do it often. You sure Sam didn't want to come along though?"

"Nah. Her mom brings her to school on the first day every year. I'm sure she's a mess today."

"That's right; I forgot." They pulled up to the drop-off area in front of the school, and Adam pulled over to be somewhat out of the way. "It's going to be great. This will be a year full of fun and laughs and just a good ole time."

Claire smiled softly and sighed. "Yes. I am excited. I'm looking forward to being a senior. Lots of big things coming."

Adam nodded along. "For sure."

"It's still going to be weird without you though."

Adam grinned at her and gave her hand a squeeze. "I actually have something for you that may just help with that."

"Oh?" Claire smirked as he leaned into the back seat and grabbed his backpack, which he usually brought to work with snacks and his Discman and other things to help get him through the day.

"I didn't get around to handing these out in the spring. It isn't really my thing," he said as he unzipped the small front pouch and began rummaging around, squinting into its depths. "But I thought that maybe you would want one."

He found what he was looking for and threw his bag in the back seat, adjusting himself so he was facing Claire better. He handed her a small wallet photo of his senior picture. "You know, as a reminder in case you miss me."

Claire took the photo and looked down at his smiling face, his parted brown hair, and the plaid blue shirt she loved to see him in as he sat under a tree in the sunshine. Claire couldn't help but smile down at it. She hadn't seen this particular photo from his set. His parents had selected one to hang on their wall, and that was all she had gotten to admire of his senior photos. She didn't even know they had ordered wallets as well or she would have definitely made him give her one. "Oh, Adam. I love it. This is perfect." She leaned over and gave him a hug.

He broke into a wide grin. "Good. I'm glad."

"It's just what I needed. And there is no 'in case.' I will definitely miss you today."

He reached over and caressed her cheek before leaning in and giving her a loving kiss. "You should probably get in there. Sam is probably frantic, and you don't want to be late."

Claire kept her eyes closed to let the kiss linger for a moment before nodding in agreement. "I'll call you after school?"

"I don't get out till four thirty, so I'll call you when I get home," he said as he played with her hair.

"Okay. Sounds good." She opened the door.

"Good luck! I love you," Adam said.

Claire smiled. "I love you too," she said before shutting the door and taking her last first-day steps into A. Thompson High School.

Walking through the doors, she almost felt that her senses were on overdrive. Looking around, she was both seeing the school as she always had, and yet there already seemed to be a hint of age to it, like nostalgia. This was it. Her last year. Soon enough she'd be a visitor here, and at some point, she would walk through those doors and feel like a foreigner, someone whose mark on the place was long gone.

"Oh my god! There you are! I've been waiting for, like, forever."

"Sorry," Claire said, smiling at her best friend and all her ecstatic excitement, an everlasting joy to have in the morning. "I was saying goodbye to Adam."

"Yeah, no, of course," Sam said, chewing frantically on a piece of gum as they walked to Claire's locker, Sam having already dropped her bag off at her own. "So, guess who stopped me in the hall this morning when I was putting my stuff away."

Claire smirked, having an idea of who it was. "Who?"

"Logan!" Sam squealed. "Can you believe it?! He stopped to ask when I had math so we could check if we were in the same class!"

Claire's smirk widened as she hung her bag, noticing that Amber's stuff was already placed on her shelf, another year with her locker buddy. Maybe she would miss Amber after graduation. "And?"

Sam stared. "And what?"

"Do you have the same class together?"

"Oh!" Sam said loudly. "Yes, we do! I can't wait. It is going to be awesome. I have a good feeling about this year!"

"Me too," Claire said. Putting aside her feeling of loss at not seeing Adam or her other graduated friends in the halls, she was looking forward to this year. There was a ball of nerves and excitement rattling in her core at the idea of being a senior—the oldest in the school—which meant applying to colleges and hopefully getting accepted; easier class loads, so more fun; and all the senior shenanigans that went on. There was also the easygoing vibe that teachers seemed to have with seniors, knowing this was it and having known them for three years now. Then there were all the last concerts, dances, and prom, culminating in caps and gowns. It was definitely exciting and a little nerve-racking all at once. In a good way.

"Like, this is going to be our year. I think we've done good overall in high school. Well, compared to grade school anyway. We did good by our promise to put ourselves out there a little bit, I think. But this year, this is it! I'm not taking any shit from Amber, and I'm going to be more outgoing with Logan and any other boy who crosses my path. Maybe I'll even sign up to join a group or run for a class office!"

"I think that sounds like a great plan, Sam! I agree. This is our year. Who cares what we do. We'll be out of here in no time anyway." Claire slipped Adam's photo into the composition notebook she used to keep track of all of her assignments and schedules, slammed her locker, and exchanged a well-groomed five-step handshake with Sam.

"So how was your mom this morning?" Claire asked, leaning on her closed locker.

"Oh my god, don't even. She was an absolute hot mess."

Claire chuckled. "Of course she was! Would you have expected anything else?"

"No. But still. It's, like, my first day of school. No big deal. And she still has Joey."

"Oh, come on, Sam. You're her oldest and only girl."

"I know, I know. To be honest, if I think too hard on it, I'll be a mess too, so making fun of her for it works better."

The bell rang and they said their goodbyes, Claire heading into the home ec room across the hall.

"Hello, my beautiful senior friends," came Miss Phillips's trilling voice as her warm smile washed over all of them. "How have we already made it this far?! I can't even believe it. I hope you all had a great summer! Anyone want to share?"

A few people raised their hands and offered up a summer camping trip or family vacation to the ocean. Claire looked over at her fellow homeroom members, found Amber, and was surprised to see that she didn't want to brag about what was probably a wonderful summer of exotic and expensive travels but, rather, was sitting silently, staring off into nothing. Lauren, Chris, and Mark were next to her, but there was no Ashley anywhere. Claire wasn't sure if it was just her, but their group seemed to have lost some of its spark and energy. She wondered what had happened.

"So this year marks a big one for you all," Miss Phillips's voice broke back in. "And it is my job to make sure we get you through, which starts with an appointment with the guidance office. There they will talk to you about what you think you want to do, your options, and, if college is one of those, the how, when, and where you apply. They will be your best friends this year, so work well with them and reach out as often as you need. I have up here a schedule of appointment times for two weeks from now for you to sign up. Please do so this morning so that I can get this to them. You will be excused from class for your appointment, so, naturally, pick your least favorite class to sign up during. I will also photocopy this and hang it on the board in here so you don't forget to go. We have an extended bell today for freshmen, so," she placed the sheet on the front desk, "have at it."

There was a shuffle as people made their way to the front to sign their names in one of the offered time slots. Claire stayed seated and waited for everyone else to go, and, to her surprise, Mark sidled over to the open seat next to her in the meantime.

"Hey," he said, grinning her way.

"Hi," she responded. It seemed like eons since she had really talked to Mark, which was unfortunate, as they had been good friends, just not the best couple.

"How was your summer?"

"Pretty good," Claire responded. "Yours?"

"Not too bad," he said and stalled by looking around the room briefly. "So, seniors, huh? Pretty cool. This year will be sweet."

"Yeah! I'm looking forward to it," Claire said.

He nodded. "So, you and, uh, Adam still together?"

Claire looked at him skeptically for a moment and then said, "Yeah. Yeah, we are."

"Wow. Cool."

"You seem surprised?" Claire questioned.

"No! Not at all. It's just," he looked at her with a smirk.

"Just what?" Claire said, not returning the gesture.

"Well, I mean, most people break up after high school."

"Is that so? Do you have these statistics handy?"

"No." He chuckled. "It's just the norm. I mean, it's high school. You have fun while you're here, and then you go off to bigger and better things."

"So high school relationships are just for fun? And apparently there are bigger and better things out there than me?" Claire said snarkily.

"No. No, I'm sorry. That's not what I meant."

"Then explain," Claire said, enjoying watching him squirm.

"I didn't mean you weren't, you know, great and that there was someone better. I meant, you know, college and the real world as the bigger and better things."

"And people can't bring their high school relationships to college?"

Mark sighed. "I'm just going to stop."

"Good call." Claire nodded. She felt bad for his clear discomfort, so she offered, "Adam isn't in college right now. He's still in town working. He's taking a year off to figure things out and then plans to go, so I guess we'll see next year if we feel the need to move on to bigger and better things." She chuckled lightly, hoping Mark could tell she was joking.

Mark did laugh; however, he followed it with, "Well, we all know what that means."

"What?"

"Taking a year off," he sniggered.

"What does it mean?" Claire asked.

"Well, it usually means they never go," he responded, his smirk faltering a bit.

"Was it your intention to come over here to be a prick, Mark?" Claire asked.

Mark sighed again. "Yeah, I am being a major prick."

"Just a bit," Claire said but smiled.

"Look, I just wanted to come over and make friendly conversation. It didn't work well. I was hoping that you and I could maybe hang out more this year. I, uh, I got a little tired of the whole Amber clique. I even took a break from Chris this summer. Hung out with Mike a lot. You know, Mike and Sarah."

"Of course. I love Mike and Sarah."

Mark nodded. "Me too. I was thinking back to freshman year when we had English together and stuff. I always had a fun time with you."

"And Sam," Claire added with a smile.

"Yeah. And Sam. And, well, just wanted to say hey, and hope we can chill this year."

Claire nodded her head. "Sounds good. I'm sure I'll see you around," she said nonchalantly.

"For sure," he said.

"Speaking of your gang," Claire said, "where's Ashley?"

"Oh, she moved."

"Really?" Claire said, surprised. "Where?"

"St. Croix," Mark responded. St. Croix was a few towns over.

"Why?" Claire asked.

"To live with her dad," Mark answered.

"That's too bad. She couldn't stay for her last year here?"

"Yeah, I don't know the full story, but it sucks."

There was a brief pause, and then Claire said, "Is that why Amber's so sour over there?"

"It could be," Mark said. "But she also had an eventful summer."

"Oh?"

"Her parents got a divorce shortly after the end of the school year," he said quietly.

"No way!" Claire was shocked. She knew Amber's dad was always gone on business trips and her mother was as fake as they came, but she always thought that worked for them.

She leaned past Mark to sneak a look at Amber again, and a pang went through her. A pang of pity.

"Yeah," Mark said. "Well. It's good to see you, Claire. Better go sign up for one of those meetings. Hope to see you around."

Claire nodded as Mark got up and went to the front table. Claire sat back and thought about everything she had just heard. Mark needed some serious lessons in small talk. But Amber. She wondered if she should say something. They had been friends once upon a time. Slept over at each other's houses. Mrs. Clark had always liked Claire and had treated her well. But she wouldn't know what to say.

The bell rang, and Claire quickly added her name to a 10:00 opening before leaving for first period. As she did so, Amber pushed past her and threw an eye roll her way. Apparently, divorce didn't gain you any empathy or stop you from being a bitch. Maybe, Claire continued her train of thought on her journey to her class and right to her seat, maybe it even made it worse. She sighed, knowing that whatever Amber threw her way this year, she would more than likely do what she pretty much always did and take it.

When Claire hit last period, she felt a jolt in her stomach when she entered the band room and found that it was quiet. No drums, no Fitz talking loudly. She went to sit at the piano and looked around, recognizing the freshmen immediately, as they were standing quietly, scattered about and looking around with clear expressions of anxiety. She smiled to herself, wondering if she had looked the same way. She recalled her first day, and suddenly remembered Amy. Shy, quiet Amy. Claire felt her heart twinge as she remembered that Amy had dropped band sophomore year and had then gone to homeschooling shortly after. Claire had felt guilty then about it, wishing she had talked more to Amy. She still felt slightly guilty now. She hoped Amy was doing okay.

Mr. Johns came in shortly before the bell rang, and Claire felt his familiar, warm hand upon her shoulder as he said, "Claire Hanover! How was your summer?"

"It was good, Mr. Johns. Thank you!" she said, returning his ever true and broad grin.

"That's great," he responded. He paused before then saying, "Quieter around here without Mr. Miller, isn't it."

Claire gave a smile and light laugh. "Definitely."

"How is he doing? Did he head off to school this fall?"

"Um, no, he took the year off to sort out what he wanted to do and save up some money first. But he's doing great!"

"Wonderful. Smart idea. Tell him I said hello, would you?"

"Yeah! Of course."

"Fantastic. Looking forward to this year, Claire. Always great to see you."

He scurried off to drop some items off on his desk before joining the group together. Claire smiled at his kind words and couldn't help but reflect on just how much she appreciated Mr. Johns. The fact that he didn't question that Claire and Adam were still together and rather just went right into asking her about him meant a lot to her. She joined the group as they did the all too familiar introductions and basic band rundown, Claire's mind trailing off to the brown-haired cutie she couldn't wait to get home to talk to.

"Oh my god, so Logan sat next to me in math class just like we planned and we talked and it was amazing!" Sam excitedly squealed as they walked in the warm sunlight of early September.

"Sounds pretty promising," Claire said in a singsong voice.

Sam rolled her eyes. "No. Just friendly and fun! I don't want to get ahead of myself. Besides, if all it is is just a great friendship, then that's perfect too. Plenty of fish to meet."

"Agreed," Claire said with a smile and internally glowed at hearing words like that come from Sam.

"Plus, the best part was that I have Amber in that class, and she didn't have Lauren or Ashley or anyone, and she got to see me hanging out with Logan and a few others who I've had math classes with since freshman year! It felt so great."

Claire laughed. "That had to have been a good feeling. Speaking of her, though, turns out there *is* no Ashley this year."

"What?!" Sam asked, truly surprised.

"Yeah. She moved, I guess. And get this, Amber's parents got a divorce early summer, apparently."

"Holy shit! Where'd you learn all this?"

Claire reminded Sam that she had homeroom with Amber and had noticed Ashley's absence. She also relayed her and Mark's conversation in its entirety.

"What an asshole," Sam exclaimed when she was done. "And he was totally just trying to see if you were single and hit on you."

"I'm not sure about that, but he *was* being kind of a dick. But he is also still Mark and seemed somewhat genuine in trying to break away from the others. Maybe they rubbed off so much on him, he forgot how to be civil."

"They *would* be the group to decivilize humanity. I still think he was hopeful you were single and was thrown off to learn you weren't."

"Perchance."

"So did your homeroom teacher talk to you about meeting with the guidance office?" Sam asked.

"She did. I signed up for a random time. I wasn't even really paying attention."

"I signed up for the first thing in the morning. I didn't want to miss math with Logan and figured I'd remember it best if it was on my mind when I got to school. It seems so surreal, doesn't it? College? Plans after high school?!"

"For sure." Claire thought back to earlier in the summer when she had talked to Adam about all this: planning for college. Since he had already been through his senior year, she asked him question after question about the process. It was making her anxious at times, like taking the SATs. She couldn't help but notice that he seemed a little off when talking about it. His answers were short, and when she would ask him about the applying phase, he would get a little weird and remind her that he hadn't done that part since he took the year off.

Without meaning to, Claire apparently touched a nerve the last time they talked about it when she continued the conversation by giving him his own reminder that, though he hadn't officially applied, they must have talked about it still and that he *was* planning to do the same eventually. He shut down, and when Claire persisted, he told her not to worry about it.

They talked on the phone that night, after an afternoon of Claire pacing in her room wondering what was wrong and worrying about all the off-the-wall possibilities his attitude could mean. He apologized and just told her that he was happy for her and proud of her, knowing she would get into any college she wanted, and he was just doing a lot of thinking lately about college and if he'd even get into the one he wanted after waiting a year. He summed it up by saying he just had a lot on his mind but that everything was fine. Claire did what she always did and tried to boost him up by informing him that she was certain he could get into any school he wanted as well.

The conversation didn't really clear anything up, but it at least fixed their momentary silence, and life went on as normal. Since then, though, she hadn't brought much up in regard to college or plans after high school. She had to admit that part of her was nervous too. She was afraid of what it would mean. It seemed that everyone was suggesting to her that relationships end after high school. She was quite confident in her relationship, but with all these transitions, she couldn't help feeling a little concerned.

"I think I definitely want to stay close by and get my core classes done. Save my money at community college and then apply for school to go into social work. You still interested in creative writing?" Sam asked, though she knew the answer.

"Yeah!" Claire said, coming to from her thoughts. "I think so. I mean, I might minor in it somehow. I was thinking of how I can best utilize a degree and was thinking about the possibility of journalism or even getting into the editing and publishing world, you know? Either way, writing involved for sure."

"Cool. You think you want to stay close by? Or go away?" Sam asked this tentatively, it being a question that had also been asked earlier in the summer to which Claire didn't have a response, considering how far away from Thompson Falls she wanted to go was up in the air, the choice being somewhat dependent on something she didn't want to admit was a source of her confusion and anxiety.

"I don't know still," Claire said with a heavy sigh.

"What's got you tweaking about this?" Sam asked, seeing that Claire looked willing to talk.

Claire heaved yet another sigh. "I just—I don't know. I want to obviously go where I want to go, you know? Dad and I visited those campuses this summer that the school wouldn't go to last year on tours. The ones in Boston?" Claire began while Sam nodded.

She and her dad had taken a few days over the summer to visit a few campuses in Boston. It was a few hours' drive away, but Claire had fallen in love with one of them. It was a lot more expensive than the couple that were closer to home, one being a state college, and both of which would be sufficient choices. But the idea of living in the city and getting away from home for a few years was exciting. She loved her small town and knew she'd always find her way back, but college was a time for exploring. It seemed like a no-brainer.

Claire hated to admit the real reason she was confused. "But . . . well . . ." Claire had never told Sam about her and Adam's moment, preferring to live in hopeless anxiety rather than speaking.

"Spit it out! This has clearly been bothering you."

Claire raised her eyebrow at her.

"Come off it. I have known you for a bit. I know there is something tucked away in your brain that's causing a total combustion."

"That's going a bit far, don't you think?"

"Speak, Claire," Sam said plainly.

"Okay." Claire told her about the conversation she and Adam had had over the summer as they approached Claire's house, grabbed some snacks, and headed up to Claire's room. Claire had noticed how much food they seemed to have in the house ever since Troy was living mostly on base, and so their options were plentiful. Slumping on her bed as Sam took the beanbag, Claire continued.

"And I guess . . . I don't know. It just worries me. What if he's all weird because he doesn't want to make plans with me because he isn't sure he wants to be with me after high school? What if he doesn't want to go to college after all and just wants to work at RadioShack and date someone else when I go off to school?"

Sam let out a belly laugh, which, in this instance, made Claire feel better. "Claire, come on. Adam isn't waiting for you to walk across the podium at the end of the year just to dump you while you go off to college so he can stick around, and do what? Date another high school girl till *she* graduates? Eventually, that will become quite perverse and freakin' creepy. Maybe he is just worried about disappointing you. What if he truly thinks he won't get into a good college and that you'll think less of him. I mean, what if he does want to stay in town and work at RadioShack? Would you dump him because of that?"

Claire raised an eyebrow. "Of course not. But I would question his choice. If that's his dream job and truly where he wants to be and feels good about it, then of course it'd be okay. But, like, I know he wants more than that, and if the reason he doesn't try is because he just doesn't think he can, then he needs to talk about that."

"Does he know that? Because I know you, Claire. You are a driven, motivated, smart person who is going to do great and wonderful things. And you're so passionate, and sometimes when you talk in that way, it can be intimidating."

Claire looked at her in surprise.

"Don't have a cow. It isn't a bad thing." Sam adjusted herself and took out a piece of gum. "Look, I've had months' worth of therapy now, so I'm a pro. The problem is, when people like me, who have some areas of low confidence, meet people like you, who don't seem to bat an eye at anything, we tend to take your animated and motivated speech as a personal stab at how we aren't like that. Now, Adam always seems like a cool, calm, and collected type of dude, but you've said over the years he's asked for your help in different classes. Maybe it's an area of low self-esteem for him. And maybe he is afraid to apply or afraid of what you would say if he doesn't end up wanting to at all or doesn't get into the college he wants and you do."

Claire rotated to lie on her stomach, facing Sam.

"Furthermore. Maybe he doesn't want to make plans with you at this point because maybe he doesn't want to influence your college choice.

Because I can read between the lines here, little missy, and what has you concerned about choosing a college is what Adam thinks about it, isn't it?"

Claire took in everything Sam said and, at the end, almost felt a sense of relief because she hadn't wanted to admit exactly what Sam had just said.

"Yeah. Yeah, it is. But not to, like, make my decision for me. I just want to know that it matters to him."

"Matters how?"

"I don't know. I just want to talk about it."

"But then it's a joint decision, and where you go to school shouldn't be. You go where you want, girl."

Claire sighed. "I know. I know. I just . . . I don't know."

"Claire. Stop overthinking it. It's our first day of school, for crying out loud. Let's get through the first few months. We start applying after Christmas. Apply to whatever the hell schools you want to, and then when you start getting accepted, start the conversation. For now, stop worrying! Adam loves you. He isn't going anywhere."

Claire smiled. The rigid planner in her struggled with this direction, but she knew Sam was right. They were young, in high school, and only at the start of this pivotal year. She had time. Time to enjoy. Time to play. And, eventually, time to plan.

"Hey!" Sam said. "You know what you haven't done yet? Told me how dress shopping went a few weekends ago! Did you pick out your bridesmaid's dress?!"

Claire shook all her thoughts away, finding comfort in having time, and switched to excited mode. "I did! Gwen's going with this sagey-green color. We picked a spaghetti strap dress that is silk and straight lined. Super simple but elegant!"

"I can't wait. It is going to be so much fun! I can't wait to get my official invite!! I was so excited when Gwen said I was invited and being given a plus one! If things go well with Logan this year, I may totally invite him."

"That'd be fun! A good excuse to still see him after school!"

"I know!"

Troy and Gwen's wedding plans had gone through a slew of changes, Troy having been deployed at one point to aid in some conflict down south, them trying to find an apartment, and Gwen's increasingly heavy workload at the nursing home she now worked at, but they had finally decided on a July date, and Claire's mom couldn't be more excited, as the wedding was now less than a year away.

"Did they find a place yet?" Sam asked.

"Not yet. They've looked at a few, but Troy keeps turning them all down," Claire said with an eye roll.

"What doesn't he like about them?"

"Honestly? I think Troy is just ready for more. I think he wants to buy a house. I caught him at the computer the last week he was home looking up realtors in the area. I think he wants property, and I think he wants to surprise Gwen with it. He makes decent money with the coast guard, especially when he goes on those rescue missions and volunteers for extra shifts. I'm sure he can afford a house."

"Wow. Troy buying his own house."

"Right? My meathead of a brother is actually making something of himself," Claire joked.

"He is not a meathead," Sam argued.

"You just say that because you've had a crush on him since we've known each other."

Sam, slouching all the way down in the beanbag at this point, chomping away, staring up at Claire's wall of posters, which now had a lot more of

Leonardo DiCaprio and a few boy band members that Claire had shamelessly added, said, "Well, I mean, you can't blame me."

"Are you ever going to not gross me out with thinking my brother is cute?"

"Probably not." Sam sat up slightly, looking at the wall some more. "I don't know how you think JC is the cutest NSYNC member. It is totally Justin."

"Seriously? With the ramen bleached hair? No way," Claire retorted, taking out the notebooks and books from her backpack.

"Pfft. Get out. When he sings, he sings into your soul."

"So does JC."

"If you say so. Also, your choice in the Backstreet Boys: way off."

"You just like AJ because he's a bad boy." Claire smirked, looking over her schedule for the next day.

"Who doesn't like the bad boy, Miss I-was-obsessed-with-Christian-Slater-for-forever?"

"Christian was a different kind of bad boy. And I still love him."

"Mmmm-kay. So tell me why you like Kevin if you don't like AJ for being a bad boy."

Claire looked up at her wall. "I don't know. I think he's the quiet, thinking type. And he's cute."

"Hmm . . . Quiet, thinking type. I guess that makes sense for you. That fits. I'll give it to you."

Together, they looked over the work they had gotten that day, nothing crazy for the first day back, and talked about the classes they had together for the next day. Gwen stopped by at one point to talk to them, taking a seat on Claire's bed, helping herself to the box of Cheez-Its Claire had snagged, and answering Sam's millions of questions about the wedding planning.

By the time Sam left, it was around the time Adam was getting home from work, and he stayed true to his word by calling, but it was only to see if he could come over instead. He did, and Claire's mom was more than happy to feed him dinner with the rest of them.

Later that night, as Claire was preparing for bed and sifting through her school things for her aged copy of *Pride and Prejudice*, her notebook fell, and the picture Adam had given her floated out of it. Picking things up quickly, she made to stick it back in her notebook when she noticed it had writing on the back of it. Simple but perfect. "Love you, Adam."

A surprise in the form of an announcement from Mr. Johns came in early October. Claire and Sam were both settled into their school year as seniors, and Claire had managed to put her anxieties and worries behind as she enjoyed the homecoming dance, which Adam was allowed to go to with an approved note. She and Sam even attended the homecoming game, which Adam, Nick, Fitz, and Jason all crashed with a few other postgraduates. Claire had gotten used to the quiet band room, and on one particularly chilly day, she entered it for chorus to find a rather excited Mr. Johns motioning for her and the others to come gather around him.

"I have something exciting to share," he said, bouncing on the balls of his feet. "You know how we typically do a winter concert this time of year and nothing else?"

Everyone nodded. The band and chorus always each put on a concert that was a culminating event of their semester's work. It typically included a little bit of everything and ended with a few Christmas tunes.

"Well, I've been talking to Mr. Lewis, and he has agreed to let us put on a special Christmas fundraiser show! Tickets will be five dollars apiece, and all proceeds will support the arts programs here at A. Thompson High. This will be on a volunteer basis, and those who sign up will receive extra credit for chorus. I am hoping to get some band members involved too to help us out with music. And . . ." he stopped and looked at Claire, "I'm hoping, besides singing some numbers, you'll accompany on the piano for some!"

Claire smiled and nodded.

"Perfect! It will be a holiday special. Our regular concert for the semester will still go on; we just won't include any holiday music in it. Save those for the event!" He rubbed his hands together in eager anticipation. "I have a sheet here. You have a couple weeks to decide if you want to join in the fun. Should you decide you want to, simply write your name, and we'll figure out the songs and order and how many and whatnot after. This will be an after-school commitment, hence the extra credit."

Claire noticed that the group as a whole wasn't looking as overly enthused as Mr. Johns was, and once he said it would take time after school, they seemed to lose any fire they had. Claire was still excited though. For once, she didn't feel the extreme butterflies in her stomach at the idea of singing in front of a crowd, and putting on a Christmas show had such an old-school vibe that she was quite looking forward to it.

Mr. Johns seemed to be reading her mind. "The art department and drama club are going to help us decorate the stage for the show as well as put together some fun costumes. You know Mrs. Tuttle, the drama coach. She just loves the idea. We want it to have an Ed Sullivan, *American Bandstand* kind of vibe. Retro, you know? The show will run all weekend, and, like I said, the proceeds will help the entire art department, hence them all pitching in."

This was sounding more and more like a treat, and Claire was happy to see more faces lighting up at the idea of being able to wear costumes and the glamor of putting on this type of show, which was starting to sound more and more like a production.

"I'll be on the lookout for anyone in band or chorus who is interested in being the MC. It will be completely student run and put on. I'm hoping there will be a great turnout!"

There was mild chatter and excitement shared among them. Mr. Johns allowed it to continue, answering some questions here and there as he hung up the list, which Claire and three other girls signed up on by the end of their class, which eventually did get around to practicing.

When the bell rang, Claire hurried to grab her stuff so she could run to the bathroom before heading to her last class. The bumping and rushing of transitions led to her practically running into the bathroom nearest her English class so as to not be late and, in doing so, running right into Amber.

There was a moment when they stared at each other, Claire adjusting the strap of her messenger bag as she stared at Amber. She hadn't just run into Amber. She had run into an Amber who was applying makeup. Makeup to cover—

"What?!" Amber's voice cut through the air.

"I, uh, I need to use the bathroom," Claire blurted but came to her senses and added, "What happened to your eye?!"

"None of your business, loser." When Claire didn't move to a stall or to leave, Amber shouted, "Get out!"

"It's a public bathroom. I'm allowed to be here."

"Then do your stupid business and beat it."

"What happened to your eye?" Claire repeated. She could see the vague coloring of what was blatantly a black eye coming to fruition between the dabs of foundation. Amber's eyes themselves looked a little bloodshot as well, as though she had been crying. Maybe her makeup touch-up was for both reasons.

"What's it to you?"

"Did someone hit you? Someone here? Your boyfriend?"

Amber groaned. "Why do you even care, Hanover?"

"What happened? Or I go get the principal and guidance counselor and anyone else right now so *they* can figure it out."

Amber glared at her, but Claire saw the shoulder drop indicating Amber wasn't as angry as she was trying to make her believe.

"Fine. . . . If I tell you, will you get out?"

"After I pee, of course."

Amber rolled her eyes. "You're so annoying."

"So what happened?" Claire crossed her arms and leaned against the bathroom wall.

"My mom has been on a dating spree, and her latest guy was just being a jerk." Amber shrugged off.

"A dating spree?" Claire questioned.

"Yes. If you must know, my parents got a divorce at the beginning of summer," she answered with an edgy tone.

"Yeah . . . I heard."

Amber growled as she continued padding her eye with powder. "Why is everyone always in everyone else's business around here?"

Claire rolled her own eyes, thinking how rich it was to hear Amber say such a thing. "So what happened? He tripped and hit your eye? Come on."

Amber's lips pinched as she snapped the powder closed and chucked it in her makeup bag. She turned and looked at Claire, sizing her up.

"Look. My mom decided to kick my dad out for finally seeing what the rest of us already knew: that he was a cheating scumbag husband whose every business trip involved a series of side jobs including, but not limited to, hooking up with multiple women. So he took off to make California his permanent home, and my mom chose to go on a drinking and screwing any man who'll have her binge. They only come over once and are rarely still around by the time I wake up to get my morning OJ."

Claire raised her eyebrows as Amber continued her word vomit. "This time, they both had had too much to drink. I went downstairs to the basement to watch TV and get away from them, and when my mom crashed on the sofa, boyfriend number fifty-seven decided to come downstairs and join me."

She stopped here, Claire understanding that she had hit a wall, her emotions going from irritation to sheer anger and disgust.

Claire let her sit in the moment for a bit before whispering, "What did he do to you?"

Amber sighed. "He *tried* to get fresh with me," she said hollowly. "I kicked him in the balls. His drunken ass attempted to go after me, managed a decent hit, and then ran when I screamed."

"Holy shit. Did you tell your mom? Did you guys call the cops?"

Amber took a moment before saying, "My mom didn't even hear me scream. When I went up to wake her and tell her what happened, she was so toasted that she yelled at me for waking her up and for sending her boyfriend away. Can you believe that? Sending her boyfriend away."

Claire was at a loss for words. "I . . . I'm so—"

"Don't say you're sorry for me," Amber said, adding some mascara and eventually lip gloss.

"And you know what the bastard had the gall to say to me?!" she suddenly burst out, not even giving Claire a chance to respond. "He told me I asked for it. He told me I wouldn't waltz around the house in the clothes I wear if I wasn't looking for attention. If I wasn't trying to get his eye. He said he was only doing what he thought I wanted as he attempted to put his hand up my skirt."

Claire gulped.

"I don't know," Amber whispered, looking at her reflection. "Maybe he's right. Maybe I'm that screwed in the head. Always looking for attention no matter who it's from," she said quietly.

Claire snapped to. "No. Absolutely not. I don't care if you were walking around in a thong bikini. Nothing makes what he did okay. You did nothing wrong, Amber. He's the disgusting scumbag. You need to tell someone. You need to tell the principal or guidance counselor or someone—"

"No," Amber shot with venom. "No. It won't make a difference, and he's gone anyway. He won't be back."

"And you're confident that her next boyfriend won't do the same?"

Amber started throwing her stuff in her bag. "Look, no one needs to know. I don't even know why I told you. It doesn't matter. I turn eighteen in the spring, and as soon as I graduate, I'm going to go live with my dad in California. At least there I have a shot at being a model or something."

"Your dad?" Claire questioned.

"Yeah. Is that a problem? At least he's rich and takes care of me. What's it to me that he's a horny jackass."

Claire gulped again at Amber's crude words and thought for a quick moment how thankful she was to have the parents she did. "There's a lot of great schools out there. Maybe you could do that and really get away. From them both."

Amber scoffed. "Oh, please. Like I could get into a good school. No, I'll shoot for modeling or acting or something."

"You say that like it's an easy thing to do. Many models and actors have good educations, you know. You gotta fall back on something if it doesn't work out or when your career ends. I'm sure you can get into a school out there. Don't cut yourself so short! I mean, unless it's not your thing, but still. You shouldn't beat yourself down like—"

"Why are you even still talking to me? Why do you even care? I've been nothing but a bitch to you for years," Amber cut in.

Claire thought a moment. "Because I know you don't really mean it."

They stared at each other for a long moment. Claire broke it by saying, "Look, I need you to talk to your mom again. When she's sober. Tell her how you feel."

"Yeah? And what would that be?"

"I don't know. All of it. Tell her that her having all these guys over isn't healthy for her, and it certainly isn't healthy for you. That it's unsafe and makes you feel like you aren't good enough for her. Tell her she's still young and could do a lot, and losing your dad shouldn't stop that. That you're considering moving to your dad's because you feel tossed aside here. Tell her what really happened with that dude, and show her that black eye. Really show her. Be open and honest."

"You sound like a friggin' Hallmark card."

"Why does everyone say things like that?" Claire mumbled under her breath.

"What?" Amber asked with a cocked eyebrow.

"Nothing. Amber, please. Talk to her. Maybe it sounds cheesy. But tell her the truth. All of it."

Amber pursed her lips and stared at Claire. "Fine. I'll try. Are we done here?" She pushed past.

"I'll check back in, and if you haven't, I'll tell the guidance counselor. Or I'll tell your mom myself," Claire threatened over her shoulder, not turning to look at Amber.

Amber grumbled and shuffled out the door, but not before popping back in as Claire entered a stall, well aware of how late she now was for class, and saying, "This goes nowhere."

Claire nodded.

"And Hanover? This doesn't mean we're friends."

"I know." Though as Claire finished up in the bathroom and walked to class, she knew that it was different.

As the days drew on, Claire thought of Amber and couldn't help but notice how she didn't have any locker issues and had yet to be bumped into in the hallway. Even if they weren't friends again, it seemed that Claire's conversation had, at least, made Amber lay off. Claire wasn't sure how long that would last but, for the time being, was grateful. She also hoped Amber heeded her advice.

Claire would sneak a peek often to see if she spotted any new bruises or if Amber looked particularly down. Thankfully, she hadn't noticed anything since their conversation. As October got underway, Claire found herself staying after school to work with Mr. Johns on the planning for the Christmas show. It was a mere two months away, and at this point, only four people had signed up to sing in the show, and only three had signed up from band.

Claire was telling Adam about it one Saturday afternoon when he came over to hang out at Claire's, presently lying across her bed, propped up on one elbow, his head leaning on his shoulder. Claire noticed recently how much he had changed since she had first met him her freshman year. His face looked stronger and older, his jawline more profound. His chocolatey brown locks were still the same, however, and that smile never wavered as he watched Claire talk.

"So now it sounds like we're each going to have to sing at least three songs in order to fill the show, and Mr. Johns is actually all excited about it. He said he's going to make the program have our names headlining it like it's our show. And the drama department is all excited—well, Mrs. Tuttle is because she doesn't have to make as many costumes and so said she is going to make ours extra special. The art department is working on flyers to hang around town and posters to hang up in the school."

Adam's grin broadened, seeing Claire being so animated. "Sounds amazing. And I can't tell you how excited I am to watch you sing and play piano like you're the star of a show. And, of course, will be the prettiest and most talented one there."

Claire smirked. "Is that so?"

"Of course."

Claire leaned forward from her crisscrossed sitting position to give him a kiss, his light Cool Water scent playing at the tips of her senses.

"So what songs are you going to sing?" Adam asked with a grin.

"I'm not sure. Mr. Johns wants me to do 'White Christmas' with the piano. And then left the other two up to me."

"And you don't know which? Do you plan on singing all of your songs with the piano?"

"I don't know that either, but probably. My favorite is 'Have Yourself a Merry Little Christmas.' So I kind of want to do that one."

Adam smiled. "I didn't know that about you. Learn something new every day. You never cease to surprise."

Claire laughed. "What's your favorite Christmas song?"

"Baby, It's Cold Outside," he responded.

"Is that so? You like to hold women against their will?" Claire joked.

Adam chuckled. "No. But ever since knowing you, I've known what it feels like to know you need to end the night and not really want to."

Claire blushed slightly.

"So, it makes me think of you."

Claire beamed. "Because, usually, *I'm* the one telling you not to go," she trilled.

Adam laughed. "Yes. Precisely."

After a small pause during which Claire went back to looking through her math book, Adam said, "So when do I get to hear it?"

"Hear what?"

"Your favorite!"

Claire thought for a moment. "I actually have an idea."

"Oh yeah? What's that?"

"Why don't we pay Babs a visit. I can play you both a bunch and let you decide which songs I should do."

"I'd love to. And I bet Babs would love that too. Although, you're going to have to do more than just play it for us if we're going to help decide which you should sing."

Claire rolled her eyes. "Alright, alright. I'll play and sing for you both."

Claire called Babs the next day, and they scheduled an afternoon visit for the following Saturday, both Claire and Adam having early shifts at work. Entering her house always gave Claire an immediate sense of calm. The old furniture, the creaky floorboards, the ornate rugs aged with sunlight. Its walls were filled, as always, with photos and knickknacks, and all of its many rooms were so perfectly eclectic and yet classic. Claire and Sam had once taken a day to help her go through the upstairs. She couldn't do stairs so well over the past couple years, and she wanted it aired out. So they helped her get up there and propped her in a chair in each room they visited to open windows, dust, and sweep. While doing so, they found all kinds of treasures, old clothes, jewelry, trunks, etc. and got to hear a story for every single piece. Claire was shocked that the upstairs had five rooms and a bathroom. Though none overly huge, it was still a significant amount of space, and it only added to Claire's love of the antiquated home that sat on the hill, its views spanning the entire village below.

Today, when Adam and Claire visited, the house smelled of warm spices, and though Claire was there to practice Christmas songs, it gave her goose bumps of excitement for everything that was fall and Halloween.

Claire called out to Babs, who yelled from the kitchen to go ahead and make themselves at home in the parlor. Adam and Claire took off their shoes and moseyed through the living room, where Babs still had an ancient television set with rabbit ears and her record player in the corner, to the parlor, the round room where Sam and Claire had many tea parties.

Claire curled up in one of the wingback chairs while Adam sprawled on the love seat. Babs came in shortly after with her tray of tea and what looked like warm apple crisp. She set the tray down on the coffee table and smacked Adam's legs to make room to sit with him.

"Don't you know not to put your feet on the furniture?" she said as she started to pour the tea.

"My feet were hanging off." Adam grinned. Claire chuckled, knowing how much Adam enjoyed messing with her.

"What is my favorite couple up to today?"

Claire and Adam both accepted their cups of tea, Claire saying, "Well, we just wanted to come see you!"

"And," Adam interjected, "Claire here is going to be soloing in a Christmas show and wants to play some songs so we can decide which she's going to pick. Which, I might add, includes singing."

Claire rolled her eyes but smirked.

"Oh my goodness, how exciting! We need to move this party from the parlor to the den, then!"

"We can wait till after tea," Claire said. "How have you been, Babs?"

"Oh, can't complain. Enjoyed a nice afternoon at the bookstore the other day. Nothing like perusing books and drinking something warm this time of year."

Claire nodded, loving nothing more than to peruse books and drink something warm during the cozy vibes of fall.

"And I brought my car in to get an oil change."

"I told you to let me know when you needed that stuff done. I can do it," Adam piped in.

Babs tapped his knee. "I know. But it gets me out of the house. Plus, I like to give them boys down there a hard time."

They laughed as they enjoyed the rest of their tea and more simple chatter, Babs asking how school was going and how work was going for Adam. She asked about college at one point, and when Adam didn't really give a solid answer, she gave him a sideways glance but let it go. They eventually moved to the den where the piano stood, and Claire could feel her nerves ebbing up. Babs and Adam took spots in yet more wingback chairs while Claire took her spot at the piano.

"So, I'm not sure which ones I want to play—"

"And sing." Adam smiled.

"And sing," she added, giving him a look to which he only smiled broader. "But I guess I'll just try a bunch?"

"Sounds delightful," Babs said.

"Okay." Claire turned to the piano, her back to them, and tried to just pretend she was alone. She opened her music book and put it in front of her, placing her fingers upon the aged keys. She leaned into "White Christmas" to which Babs hummed along. She moved on to "The Christmas Song" and then "It's Beginning to Look a Lot Like Christmas" before turning to them to see what they thought so far.

"I think I don't know how to pick!" Babs said. "You have such a beautiful voice, my dear."

"Sings like an angel," Adam added, having gotten lost in everything that was watching Claire play and sing.

"I think you should sing your favorite," Adam said.

Claire gave him a smile, and, taking a deep breath, she began playing "Have Yourself a Merry Little Christmas." The song always had a beautiful and yet sad tone to it. She imagined Judy Garland herself singing it to the crying Margaret O'Brien. She thought of her Christmases past. Christmases as a kid with Troy. Her grandmother. Remembering the profound silence of midnight masses and the quiet of the first falling snow. She felt her vocal cords vibrate, and her body felt every note.

Adam had never given this particular Christmas song much thought, but listening to Claire sing and play it, he got an overwhelming sense of love and admiration for Claire as well as a sense of sorrow and loss. All his thoughts lately about college and what he wanted to do and not feeling good enough to get in and, in turn, good enough for Claire seemed to come crashing forward as he sat there, staring at nothing in particular and listening.

When the last note resonated, they all sat in it for a moment before Babs began clapping, her eyes glossy, images of her late husband and Danny flashing by.

"That one!" she said jovially. "That one is a must. It was absolutely beautiful."

Claire beamed. "Thanks. I do love it."

Adam shook his head and came to. "I quite agree."

He gazed into Claire's eyes the way she always loved. That look gave her the chills and made her feel at home at the same time. There was so much depth and meaning behind it, and Claire knew that Adam's love ran deep.

They were interrupted by Babs, who said, "Now your turn."

They both looked at her confused as to what she meant when they saw her looking at Adam.

"What?" He laughed. "My turn for what? I don't play piano."

"No, but I bet you can sing," Babs said.

"Babs, come on. No way," Adam said, his cheeks flushed.

Claire chuckled and said, "Yes, come on. You can sing for us."

"Don't you get started too," Adam said, to their laughter.

"Sing a duet. I want to hear you both," Babs said.

"We rocked 'Bohemian Rhapsody' pretty good," Claire said. "And you lip-synced the Backstreet Boys."

Adam looked at them both and then sighed. "Okay, okay. Just for you two though."

Babs and Claire exchanged winks as Adam sat down next to Claire on the piano bench.

"I have just the one," she said as she flipped through the book, found the page, and propped it back up on the piano.

Adam, seeing it, gave a knowing smile and kissed her cheek.

Claire began the opening lines of "Baby, It's Cold Outside." Adam spoke-sang along, and they had so much fun with it, giggling and laughing throughout.

When done, Babs gave an even louder clap and said, "You must do that one too!" They reminded her that Adam wasn't at the high school anymore, but it didn't stop her from encouraging him to sneak into it anyway because no one would mind once they heard what she just had.

Claire sang and played through most of her book, and they finished their visit back in the parlor, deciding which numbers Claire would sing and then talking about the upcoming Halloween holiday. When Adam and Claire left, it was with bloated bellies and full hearts.

Arriving back at Claire's house, they ascended the front steps, only for Claire to feel Adam's hand in hers, stopping her.

"Hey," he said as she turned to see what he wanted. "I love you."

Claire stared at him, recognizing the strange tone in his voice. It sounded like it was quavering. She stepped back down onto the front path, still holding his hand.

"I love you too," she said, questioning him with her eyes.

"I just . . . I had a nice time this afternoon, singing with you and listening to you, and I just wanted to tell you that I love you." He ran his hand through his hair, Claire picking up on the act as a sign of nerves. She hadn't seen that in a while.

"I had a good time too," she said slowly. "Is everything okay?"

Adam released a large breath. "Yes. Yes, everything is fine. I just . . . I love you."

"Are you feeling okay?" Claire smiled, ruffling his hair. It seemed to break whatever tension he was experiencing.

"Yes." He wrapped his arms around her. "In fact, I'm feeling great." He kissed her, Claire snaking her arms around his neck.

"What time are you expected home?" she asked against his lips.

"Twenty minutes ago," he responded. Adam's mom was putting on a dinner for some family friends who were in town.

Claire pulled away. "Then get out of here, goober."

He smiled and kissed her again. "Call you later?"

"But of course."

He pecked her cheek and took off, Claire watching him, contemplating what was going through his mind.

Halloween brought Adam and Claire to a house party at Nick's. Dressed up as Forrest and Jenny, they invited Sam along, dressed as Wednesday Addams, who invited Logan to join, who threw a last-minute costume together and went as a hobo. Together, along with Fitz, Jason, Melissa, and some other friends of Nick's, they enjoyed some dancing, games, and an overall good time. Sam spent the night at Claire's that night and relived her slow dance with Logan about twenty times before they fell asleep at three in the morning.

Soon enough, the leaves were all on the ground, dried and old, the weather colder, and Claire's eighteenth birthday came and went. Adam bought her his regular gift of a composition notebook, Claire having kept up with writing stories, poems, song lyrics, and more for him over the past year. He also gave her a special gift when they snuck out to meet under their tree the night of Claire's birthday party at her house. It made Claire cry. It was a light-yellow topaz ring, her birthstone. The ring was small, silver, and had a ring of tiny diamonds surrounding the topaz.

Adam blushed when she opened it and said, "It's small, but it's all I could, you know . . . it's all I could get. But I thought it was pretty. Like you."

Claire's tears clouded her eyes and she had no words for it.

Earlier, her mom couldn't stop talking about how her baby was eighteen. Babs told everyone the story of her eighteenth being the day she met her husband, and they had gotten married six months later, which gave Claire's dad a minor panic attack. Troy broke the moment by giving his gift of a cigar and lottery tickets, further informing Claire that he'd pay for and take her for her first tattoo, which gave their mom a minor panic attack.

Overall it was a good birthday, and Claire was immensely excited to proudly wear her ring.

November also brought on the final preparations for the big Christmas concert. It was occurring the second week of December, and Claire and the other singers were staying after school two to three times a week, rehearsals starting up after the Thanksgiving break. Besides the upcoming event, it was also time for college applications. The guidance office was going crazy with trying to get all the seniors in for meetings and getting the ball rolling with the first deadlines for applications coming up in January. All of this led to a stressed Claire pouring over applications after school on a Friday, happy for the distraction that came in the form of Sam bounding through the door and the phone ringing simultaneously, Adam on the other end.

"Hey," she said into the receiver as Sam made herself comfortable.

"Hey! Just got home from work," Adam said. "What are you up to?"

Claire threw herself back onto her pillows. It was a leggings and baggy sweatshirt kind of day. She released a groan. "Filling out college applications."

"Oh, right," Adam said. "I forgot you had mentioned needing to do that this weekend. How is it going?"

"Oh, fine. Just so much to write and so much repetition. My dad told me to fill out what I knew and he'd fill out the rest as far as what my parents make and stuff goes. So that's helpful at least."

"So which ones are you filling out? Did you decide?" Adam asked tentatively.

Claire and he had had a conversation a few days before about her different options. Adam had listened mostly, and when Claire asked if he thought those were good choices, he simply told her that they were great choices as long as they were places she'd want to go to and would make her happy. Two of them were in Boston, about three hours from home, one was close by, and one was on the other side of the country. She wasn't sure what she wanted him to say, but she had hoped for a little more discussion on his end. When it didn't come, she ended up saying she wasn't sure if she was going to apply to all of them or not but at least the one from Boston that she liked and the one close by.

Afterward, when she got home, her mom read her expression. Claire opened up, and her mom gave simple advice: "It doesn't hurt to apply to them all anyway. You aren't signing off on them. Why not see what your options would even be? It's just the applying phase; you're not deciding where you're going yet. Wait and see who accepts you."

Claire appreciated this advice, similar to Sam's at the start of the year, liking that it put off really making a decision for a bit. Claire had decided to go for all but one.

"Well, I'm applying to three of them. I figured I might as well see who will even accept me."

"Oh, Claire. I'm sure they'll all accept you. No doubt."

"That's nice of you, but we shall see." She smiled.

"So you're applying to the one in Arizona too?" he asked.

Claire sat up. "Um, yeah. Yeah, I am. Why?"

"Oh, just curious. I know you were up in the air about that one the most. Good! I'm happy for you."

She took a deep breath and said, "How do you feel about that? Me going to Arizona?"

Sam sat up straighter in the beanbag, eyes unfixed from her *People* magazine, watching Claire's body language.

"I think you'll do just fine in Arizona. Dry heat, a huge change, a chance to see a whole new part of the country," he said. He sounded excited, and yet Claire could hear a hint of something else.

"But how do you *feel* about it?" Claire asked.

"I'm not sure what you mean," he responded.

Claire paused, feeling her heart rate speed, knowing she was going down a path she probably shouldn't go down without more preparation and sleep, but the conversation had set her up, so she took it.

"How do you feel about me being all the way across the country? What do you think we—" Claire faltered. She wanted to say, "What would we do? Would you go with me? Would we do long distance for four years? Would it break us up?" But she knew that that entailed making major plans and decisions for the future, and so her own anxiety, fears, and not wanting to be the one who brought it up and scare him got in the way. "Just, how do you feel?"

"I *feel* like I want you to shoot for the moon. Follow your dreams. And whatever makes you happy will make me happy."

It was a finite answer. A very sweet and thoughtful one too, but finite and not open to further discussion. And as sweet and thoughtful as it was, it still wasn't what Claire wanted to hear.

"Thanks," she managed to say with a smile.

"You want to catch a movie later?" he asked.

"Sure. Check the paper and let me know. Sam's here. Cool if she joins?"

"But of course! I'll see if any of the guys want to as well."

"Sounds good," Claire said. "Talk to you later."

"Love you."

Claire returned the I love you and hung up. Releasing a loud groan, she plopped back down, arm draped across her face as Sam came to sit next to her.

"What did he say?" she asked.

"Just that he wants me to be happy and follow my dreams and that whatever makes me happy will make him happy," Claire muffled.

"Well, that's sweet," Sam said.

"Yeah." Claire removed her arm to look at Sam. "Sweet. And endearing. And nothing close to 'I would miss you like crazy, Claire, and want to go with you,' or 'Wish you'd be closer.' "

"But, Claire. What if he did say that? Would you take Arizona off the table?"

Claire thought for a moment. "No, but I think I would put more thought into it if I knew he wanted to, you know, make plans and stuff. I don't know."

"Claire, you know he would miss you, and I'm sure if he was honest he'd tell you he wished you'd be right close by."

"But I don't know that for sure, and that's the problem. He hasn't talked about applying for school himself. What if he wants to go to some other state? What if we end up states apart? Don't you think that's something you should at least talk over with your girlfriend or boyfriend? Something you should at least discuss and consider with each other?"

Sam shrugged. "Maybe he's waiting to see where you'll get accepted to. That's what I would do. Why have this heavy conversation if Arizona isn't even an option?"

"I guess," Claire said, appreciating this point of view. "Yeah. You're right. But what about him applying?"

"Have you asked him?"

"No. I thought that'd be something he'd offer up."

"Well, ask him. You've got a lot on your plate. Maybe he doesn't want to add to it. But, just chill, dude. This is college. Your career. The baseline for the rest of your life. It should be a decision you make for you, and then you talk to your boyfriend about what you guys are going to do about that decision after it's been made."

Claire stared at her for a moment and then smiled. "Thank you. I needed that."

Sam, who had ceased her gum-chewing, started up again and said, "So I heard mention of checking the paper. Are we going to a movie tonight?!"

Claire nodded and let Sam's drivel wash over her about the latest movies in the theater. Yet again, she placed her anxieties aside and reminded herself to just live in the moment. Applying wasn't making a decision. She had nothing to worry about . . . yet.

"Wait, this is what we're wearing?!" Claire exclaimed excitedly, looking at a fitted red-sequined dress that would probably hit just above the knee. It had sleeves and a slight V-neck. It was simple in form, but the red sequins made it fancy enough that Reba herself would don it.

"Yes, ma'am. Well, that's what *you're* wearing," Mrs. Tuttle said, staring at Claire through coke-bottle glasses. It was rehearsal day after school, and Claire caught her first glimpse of the stage setup and now her dress.

"I went to the thrift shop in town looking for red or green dresses to add some sequins or trim to. You know, to zhuzh it up. This one is yours. There is one other red and a couple greens, all with varying degrees of pizazz."

"I love it! This will be so much fun to wear!" Claire held it up in front of her.

"I knew you would," Mrs. Tuttle said. "What did you think of that stage my crew put together?"

"It's beautiful, Mrs. Tuttle." Claire had in fact been impressed with what they had come up with. The art department had painted a backdrop of a snowy outdoor scene with some snow-covered fir trees. They had placed the mobile backdrops mid-stage, with cutouts to look like windows of a house. With a Christmas tree, fake fireplace, and lights all over, the stage looked like someone's cozy living room amid the perfect winter storm.

"All the kids did such a great job," she mumbled as she went to snag another of the chorus members to give them their dress to try on.

Claire went to the bathroom to change. The purpose for tonight was to make sure the dress fit and didn't need adjusting. Mrs. Tuttle was a pro. The dress fit like a glove. She did a few twirls and giggled at herself and then made her way back to the band room, which was used as a backstage area during shows, as it was connected to the stage and auditorium.

"Fits perfect!" she said as a few others went off to do the same.

"Oh, it *is* perfect, my dear. Absolutely perfect," Mrs. Tuttle said, walking around Claire. "All the sequins are falling just right too. Okay! Go take it off before you do anything to it."

Claire did as she was told, admiring the other girls' dresses in the bathroom. One of the green ones was floor length and velvety. Mrs. Tuttle had attached white fluffy trim along the bottom and the cuffs of the sleeves. The other was a green knee-length A-line sleeveless dress with wide straps that Mrs. Tuttle had added gold trimming to every couple inches from the waist to the bottom. The final dress, which was red, was a shiny satin with cap sleeves and also knee length. Mrs. Tuttle must have decided the sheen would be enough in the stage lights and mercy added a belt that she had glued gold glitter to. Claire was very impressed with the simplicity of the work and yet how vastly different these dresses looked from the thrift store to now. She could envision them all together, and it was spectacular. Claire was getting more and more excited as the rehearsal progressed too. She daydreamed of how it would feel taking the stage the next night, as if she were in the grand finale scene of *White Christmas* with Bing, Rosemary, Danny, and Vera all donning those perfect red-and-white outfits.

While playing and singing, Mr. Johns helped the sound crew toy with the mic volumes as well as cut in to give some feedback to the singers. Nobody saw a brown-haired cutie with glasses sneak in and sit in the back of the auditorium. Claire sang her songs in between the other acts. She was beginning to feel a growing sense of anxiety mixed with excitement knowing that the show was only a day away. Mr. Johns decided to put her "Have Yourself a Merry Little Christmas" as the closing number, and when she practiced it for the crew and rehearsal cast, there was a definite hush that followed the last note. The night ended with Mr. Johns having them all join him on the stage where he gave them the rundown on time and all the last-minute touches, as this was it before the first show. Claire couldn't help but notice the little bounce in his step and the twinkle in his eye as he talked. She had to admit it; she was equally ecstatic.

While everyone was packing up, Claire felt arms wind their way around her waist from behind and a face nuzzle into her neck. She jumped and swiftly undid herself from the stranger, staring in absolute vengeance, absentmindedly holding up karate hands. A wide and familiar grin spread across the face of her supposed attacker.

"Remind me to never mess with you," Adam said through a chuckle.

"God, you scared the shit out of me!" Claire said, lightly punching Adam's arm but smiling. "What are you doing here?" She grabbed her coat off the music room floor and slung her bag over her shoulder as Adam put his arm around her to walk out.

"Just thought I'd come get a look at the sets and see how the new light and sound crew is."

"Oh yeah?" Claire smirked.

"Yup. They're awful. But you, my dear, are amazing as always." He kissed the top of her head as they crossed the parking lot.

"Oh, stop. Wait till you see what Mrs. Tuttle put together for costumes!" Claire said, separating as they approached Adam's car.

"That I really can't wait for," he said with a wink over the roof of the car before they both got in.

"What do you say to pizza at Ron's? The guys are all there, and I just so happened to call a Miss Levinski to see if she wanted to meet us there too."

"Is there a special occasion I missed?" Claire asked, excited for the sudden plans.

"Nah. Just know you could probably use a distraction tonight with your shows starting up tomorrow." Adam gave her a side smile that would have made her knees buckle if she weren't sitting down.

"Aren't I just the luckiest duck," she said.

"I think that's me," he said, placing a hand on her thigh.

Arriving at Ron's, they stopped by the jukebox as always and played some tunes before heading to the back where Claire heard—

"Bohemian!!"

Claire's face broke into a broad grin as she looked on at Fitz, Jason, Melissa, Sam, and Nick all sitting around the furthest booth, three large pizzas and cups of sodas already scattered among them.

"Hey!" Claire said, sliding in next to Sam, Adam right behind her. As always, Fitz took a chair and swung it around backward to fit on the end of the table.

"How did rehearsal go?!" Sam asked as Claire grabbed a slice and took a bite, washing it down with a soda nearby that was still full, assuming it wasn't anyone's yet.

"Good!" she said. "I think it's going to be a great show! The sets are insane, and the costumes Mrs. Tuttle made are sparkly and totally bomb."

Sam squealed.

"Can't wait to see it!" Nick said around Sam.

"S-see it?" Claire stuttered, looking around.

"Well, yeah, Bohemian. You think we're going to let you sing solo and put on a Christmas shindig without going to see you do it?" Fitz piped in.

"Wait, you're all coming?" Claire asked.

"Of course, silly!" Melissa said to Jason's nod. "The whole town's talking about it! We wouldn't miss it."

She looked back at Nick, who raised his shoulders. "I told you. We can't wait to see it!"

"Oh God," she said.

They all laughed.

"Come on!" Nick said. "We'll be on our best behavior and are honestly all for sure down with getting to hear the talents of Claire Hanover that our friend Adam over here has been raving about for years."

Claire turned a cocked eyebrow to Adam, who merely gave her his sly smile, which she still hadn't learned how to turn down.

"Well, what the hey," Claire said.

They all dug into pizzas and sodas, laughing at all the stories of ridiculous customers they had. Melissa talked to Sam and Claire about her first semester of courses in between the banter, and before Claire knew it, it was getting late and Adam was dropping off Sam and then Claire at home.

"You're going to do great tomorrow night," Adam said, cupping her cheek.

"Thanks. I'm starting to get a little nervous, but I'm excited."

"Sounds like a normal way to feel to me," he said with a comforting smile.

"You're picking up Babs, right? Mom and Dad know to save you two seats."

"You know it! She's my date."

Claire chuckled. "You are just too adorable, you know that? I love you."

Adam's face flashed so quickly, Claire thought she'd imagined it, but at her words, she was sure she saw the briefest moment of sorrow or worry or . . . she wasn't quite sure.

But she let it go when he said, "I love you more," and kissed her, allowing it to linger till it was high time Claire made her way inside.

The next day of school went by in a blur, as Claire had her mind only on the night's events and her first show. She was feeling the definite butterflies in her stomach as the afternoon progressed, and when the final bell rang and she headed to the music room to start helping Mr. Johns get ready, she wondered if she'd be able to walk onto the stage at all. Mr. Johns seemed to read this all over her face.

"Claire, you are going to be just fine. I wouldn't let you go out there if I thought you would make a fool of yourself."

Claire smiled, and his words did make her feel better. Mr. Johns was always encouraging her to do more and to get out there. Why would he do that if she sucked?

"Thanks! So what can I help with?" she asked.

"I appreciate you offering to stay after to prepare for tonight. I have the light crew here too, and between us and some art students, we'll be able to put all the finishing touches on. I have my wife bringing us some food later. Hope you like Chinese."

Claire did very much, and she helped run more wires, photocopy some directional signs to put outside the auditorium, move stage pieces around, and finish off some painting that hadn't gotten done yet. The concerts were always open to the public but were not generally attended by the public. It was mostly family and friends of students performing. This show, however, had been advertised at the town hall, Ron's, the bank, and most of the shops on Main Street, including the bakery. Claire got to hear customers discuss it at times, and if Mrs. Lawrence was around, she'd tell them that Claire was one of the headlining names on the poster. When they found out that the barista girl at their favorite coffee shop was in a show, they seemed more interested in attending, and so Claire was quite sure that if they did fill the auditorium, it would probably all be thanks to Mrs. Leonard.

Food arrived, and everyone took a break to eat together. Though the light crew wasn't Adam Miller, Claire did find them hilarious to chat with while they all picked at different buckets of lo mein or fried rice. When students who were in the show started arriving, Claire felt the pang of nerves return and questioned her choice of joining in on Chinese food.

In no time, Mrs. Tuttle was there with her two daughters, who were probably in their thirties or forties, telling everyone in the show to have a seat for hair and makeup. Cindy, the daughter who was assigned to Claire, was very nice and ended up curling Claire's hair and then combing the curls out so they would be natural looking and flowy. She then pinned one side up, giving Claire a retro era look, which was then completed with some stage makeup, winged eyelids, and red lipstick. When done, she was told to go get dressed and then to, in Mrs. Tuttle's words, put her bum in a seat and not move till the performance. As the other girls came in one by one, Mrs. Tuttle gawked at all of their completed ensembles and insisted her daughter take pictures of them.

Claire's heart began to pound when the lights dimmed and they were ushered into the side stage area by Mrs. Tuttle to await their cues to take the stage. There was a program there as well so they could keep track of the order, and Claire was definitely doing that. With each song sung along with Mr. Johns's accompaniment on piano, she was closer to going on. Her first performance was the fifth number, and when number four, Jill, came off the stage, Claire took the deepest breath she could muster. She heard her introduction, spoken by a junior named Ted, who was a drama guy who had signed up to MC. The program had him listed as playing Ed Sullivan, and he seemed to take this title very seriously, as Claire now noticed that he was definitely putting on his best voice and gestures to mimic the icon. And he was doing a pretty damn good job.

"Okay, folks, next up we have a very talented and lovely pianist and singer who is going to play for you tonight a grand performance of 'White Christmas.' Put your hands together for Claire Hanover."

Claire could hear the crowd's applause as well as the faint yell of "Bohemian" and a few whistles that she knew came from Nick. The stage lights hit her dress, and she felt like a disco ball, but a very festive and classy one. Oh, how great costumes were. In her mind, Claire felt like someone else, and that gave her confidence. In this outfit, she, too, was simply playing on stage. She smiled at everyone and did a brief wave and curtsy before taking her seat at the piano. First, a moment to adjust her music and feet, and then she took yet another deep breath, the spotlight beaming down on her, and she leaned into the intro of the classic winter tune. She was no Bing Crosby, but she and Mr. Johns had raised the song a few octaves while still working on Claire's voice to produce some deeper, more sultry tones with this one. It resulted in a very smooth and alluring sound that Claire had never used before but was impressed she could do.

Though she couldn't see him, or anyone for that matter with her mind and body completely in her music and her eyes blinded by the lights, Adam was completely and utterly in awe and fixed on Claire.

She had always been beautiful to him. He still recalled the first time he saw her after almost hitting her with his bike and how he had paused for a moment to stare. She had such large and deep brown eyes and hair to match, haphazardly everywhere and yet perfect at the same time. She had always been beautiful. But when she stepped onto the stage, red dress, sequins dancing in the lights, her confident and yet slightly nervous stature gesturing to the crowd, the red lips, the hair . . . Adam was beyond star struck, feeling as someone would feel when getting to see their favorite artist in the flesh for the first time. He had to remind himself several times that she was his. That the beautiful and sultry, young, talented woman was, in fact, Claire Hanover, a girl he had the privilege of knowing inside and out. Without knowing, he leaned forward in his second row seat in the auditorium—Fitz, the guys, and Sam on one side of him, Claire's family on the other—and just stared, soaking up every note, every piano chord, Claire, her piano, and the Christmas lights reflecting in his eyes.

After her hand paused over the piano, the last note reverberating, Claire stood up and bowed to tremendous applause, once again hearing, "Go, Bohemian!" shouted among a series of whistles that were coming from not only Nick now but Jason and Sam as well. She giggled and gave a wave before exiting the stage.

The rest of the show went off without a hitch, each performance a wonderful Christmas tribute, the commentary funny. People sang along with some, tapped their feet to others, and got lost in yuletide enjoyment. Claire's nerves had been washed away with the playing of her first song, making her second and third not just easy but so easy she was able to have a little fun with them too. Overall the show was an absolute hit and was only made better by the final number. Claire approached the mic, no piano to sit behind. It was the first time she'd ever sang solo, which, to her, was how it felt. Standing here, with no piano in front of her, she felt exposed. Her piano was her partner, and she and it had always done duets. With Mr. Johns in her place instead, she still had its voice at least, and the opening notes began.

She closed her eyes, pulled in the spirit of Judy herself, and broke into "Have Yourself a Merry Little Christmas."

A collective sigh seemed to wash over the audience. Adam sat back as the all too familiar emotional tug in his stomach reared its ugly head. It was just as beautiful as when he had first heard it at Babs's, which he recalled with a little pang. Adam thought of everything that was Claire. How she looked at him with genuineness and realness through their budding friendship and the turmoil of his own relationship at the time. Finally allowing his heart to go for what it yearned for, he had learned that he had met the single most amazing person on the planet. Her laugh, her smile, her passion, her smarts, her wisdom, empathy, care, and softness—it was all what made him utterly lost in her. It was also what made him more recently worried about just how much he did love her. Worried about all that was coming. Changes and bigger things . . . bigger things than him.

The clapping was astounding. The slap on the back of the head from Nick woke Adam up to the standing ovation that Claire and the other performers were receiving as they all took the stage together for a final bow. Adam jumped up and joined in the clapping.

"Dude, I knew you were in love with her, but, boy, you are gone," Nick said, laughing in between a few catcalls and whistles.

"I am," Adam admitted as Claire caught his eye and blew him a kiss.

"Boy, am I a lucky son of a bitch," Nick said.

"Why's that?" Adam chuckled.

"Who knew I would get to witness the greatest love story ever told," he said with the utmost of snark.

Adam rolled his eyes. "Shut up."

"No, really." Nick laughed. "Romeo and Juliet over here. I didn't know that stuff really existed."

"Mmhmm," Adam sounded.

"Cleopatra and Mark Antony," Nick said as the crowd started to shuffle to pick up their coats and make their way to the exits.

"Okay," Adam said.

"Jack and Rose. Zack and Kelly. Johnny and Baby—"

"Okay, I get it! I'm a pansy with a girlfriend, okay?" Adam laughed, stepping into the aisle to wait for Claire.

Nick laughed. "You really are, man. But I'll be honest, I'm a bit jealous."

Adam looked at him and they exchanged a quick smile.

"You okay?" Nick asked.

Adam blew air out, causing his hair to wave, and then looked around at Claire's parents and Troy and Gwen and Sam and the guys and then back at Nick.

"We'll talk about it," Nick said simply.

"Oh, there she is!" Claire's mom shouted as Claire came in from the hall where she was shaking hands with people as they left, collecting donations at the door. She bounded down the aisle and right into Adam's arms, who grinned and hugged her with the tightest embrace he had.

"You were unbelievable," he said into her ear.

"Thank you," she whispered back and then broke apart to move on to give everyone else hugs.

"Thank you all for coming," she said as she made her way to Nick and Fitz.

"Wouldn't miss it, Bohemian," Fitz said, giving her almost a headlock rather than a hug.

When Claire got a squeeze, an excited squeal, and a congratulations from Sam, she realized that someone was missing.

"Where's Babs? You were supposed to pick her up," Claire said, and to her horror, she saw everyone in the group shuffle and look from one to the other.

Adam exchanged a look with her mom, and before Claire could even repeat herself, though her heart was beginning to race so that talking may have been off the table, without puking anyway, Adam turned to her and said, "Claire. First of all, Babs is okay and is stable and doing well. But today she went to go to the kitchen and slipped and fell. She was thankfully close to the phone and was able to pull the cord to drop it to the floor and call nine-one-one. When the paramedics got there, she was unconscious, most likely due to the pain and strain. She bruised her hip and dislocated a shoulder. She's at the hospital right now but is feeling a lot better and will be fine. They're moving her to an elderly facility tomorrow to get physical therapy until they feel she is ready to be back home on her own. She may require some at-home assistance, but she will be okay."

"Have you—have you seen her?" Claire asked, voice shaking through tears that were beginning to form and cling to the edges of her eyelids.

"I have. The police officer on the scene couldn't find any obvious information for next of kin but saw my number taped to the fridge and called it. My parents called me at work, and I left right away. I stayed with her till they were able to get her back in her room after relocating her shoulder and giving her meds. She was conscious, and though tired, she managed to tell me that under absolutely no circumstances was I to tell you until after your show or she'd put a curse on me. She didn't want you worrying or missing it, and I didn't want to chance her cursing abilities."

"Can we go see her?" Claire asked, feeling her pulse calm. At least she was okay and stable and Adam had gotten to see her.

"I talked to the nurse on my way out earlier, and though visiting hours end at eight, she was leaving a note to have the night crew let you in for a little bit. Babs insisted."

"Oh, hunny, I'm so sorry," Claire's mom butted in. "But she is going to be all right, and Adam was with her most of the day."

Claire felt tears rising again as her mother hugged her.

"She's a tough broad, Mouse. She'll be fine," Troy added.

Claire nodded and said, "I'm going to go change, and then can we go?"

"Of course," Adam said.

"We'll meet you out front, dear," her mom said.

Claire frantically grabbed her things and ran to the bathroom. When she was back in the band room, she threw her coat on and heard Mr. Johns behind her.

"Miss Hanover. You were phenomenal tonight. I am very proud of all you have done here at A. Thompson High, and I'm going to really—" He stopped when she turned to look his way. "Is everything okay?"

"I'm sorry, Mr. Johns. I just found out that a dear friend of mine fell and hurt herself. She's at the hospital, and I'm going to go see her. She was supposed to come tonight and was looking forward to it and—" She heard her voice crack.

"Oh my. I'm sorry. Of course. Let me know if there is anything I can do."

"Thank you. I'll definitely be back tomorrow. I think she'd kill me if I missed my shows."

"Okay. Well, like I said, let me know if there is anything I can do."

"Thanks. I appreciate that," she said and left the room.

At the hospital, the nurses let Claire go right in, and she and Adam were able to sit for fifteen minutes with Babs, who managed to wake up enough to ask how her show went and to tell her she was sorry she missed it. Claire took no apologies and just told her to focus on getting better and that she'd be back to see her the next day. Babs squeezed her hand, and Claire, though happy to see her color looking good and her looking comfortable, felt hot tears track down her cheeks.

The ride home was quiet until Claire said, "I really hate hospitals."

Adam grabbed her hand and held it tight. "I know. I'm sorry."

"Thank you for being there for her," Claire said.

"Of course. I love the lady. I'm just glad she kept my number where I put it."

Claire smiled at him, and when she went to bed that night, she had barely closed her eyes before she was sound asleep, exhausted.

The next day, Adam and Claire visited Babs, who was sitting upright and much more alert than the night before. The three of them played a few rounds of Scat and Go Fish, and Babs let them eat off her tray for lunch, requesting more food when the nurse came back, claiming that she just had a major appetite. She asked for a play-by-play account of Claire's show and wished her all the luck in her second and final show that evening. Before leaving, Claire gave her the biggest hug and replaced the water in the flowers that she and Adam had brought as well as the ones Claire's mom and Sam had sent over. The heaviness of the realization of just how alone Babs was, apart from Claire and her little circle, weighed on Claire's heart and made her want to help and visit Babs even more than she already did.

"She's lucky to have you," Adam said quietly on their ride to Claire's so she could get ready to head back to school for her last two shows.

With the afternoon performance going off without a hitch, the final evening show seemed to bring, if possible, even more people into the auditorium. Mr. Johns told them he was expecting that, as word had probably gotten out about how spectacular the show was. Claire appreciated his zealousness and absolute confidence in their talent. The show went just as smoothly as the first one, and Claire's parents and Adam took up spots in the front row this time. At the end, they gave hugs and congratulations once again, and Claire was almost sad that it was done: all their hard work and all the anticipation, and in just two nights, the show was over. People couldn't have been more gracious with their compliments on their way out, and just as Claire was going to change, she saw Mrs. Tuttle and got an idea.

"Mrs. Tuttle!" Claire shouted at her back as she scooted up the hall toward the exit to the teacher parking lot. "Mrs. Tuttle!"

She turned and saw Claire. "Why, Miss Hanover. How can I help?"

Claire rushed up to her. "Mrs. Tuttle, if I'm really, really careful, could I borrow this dress for the night? I'll bring it back to you first thing Monday morning."

Mrs. Tuttle looked her up and down and seemed to contemplate for a moment before saying, "Oh, go ahead. I trust you. And you did such a beautiful job, you deserve it. We made a boatload on just these three shows, and I personally think we owe it all to you." She gave Claire a wink.

Claire blushed. "Well, I don't think it would have been nearly as magical without all the set decorations and costumes. Thank you!"

"Of course. I'll look for you first thing Monday morning," Mrs. Tuttle said before leaving.

Claire smiled and rushed back to get dressed and then to retrieve her stuff from the band room, where she found Adam talking to Mr. Johns. She wasn't sure what they were talking about, but whatever it was, she seemed to have interrupted it because they stopped talking to look at her, and Mr. Johns immediately changed the subject.

"Claire! Once again, you were phenomenal. I'm not sure of the exact number yet, but I know that between last night and today, the arts program raked in a pretty hefty pile of donations plus the initial ticket price. This was amazing, and I have a feeling that when I report on this on Monday to Mr. Lewis, he'll be sure to make this an annual event."

"That's great!" Claire said, looking at him and then to Adam, who seemed to shake off whatever emotion was on his face and broke into a broad grin.

"She's spectacular," Adam said.

"I quite agree," Mr. Johns said. "You know, Claire, you could have quite a future in music if you wanted it."

"Oh. I—I hadn't really thought of that," Claire stammered.

"Well, I'm certainly not trying to make you now. But it is a thought worth thinking sometime." He smiled.

Claire returned it and said, "I will. Thanks."

"Would you like me to take that?" he asked, gesturing to the show dress on Claire's arm.

"Um, Mrs. Tuttle said I could borrow it till Monday. I hope that's okay," she responded.

"Of course! Mrs. Tuttle's word is always the final word. Have at it!"

Claire beamed, and Adam joined her by the door.

"Thanks, Mr. Johns," Claire said suddenly. "For everything I owe a lot to you, and I don't think I've ever said that."

"I'm flattered. But you take full responsibility for the talented young woman you are."

"I may have had some talents up my sleeve, but you gave me the confidence to believe I really did. Thank you."

Mr. Johns had no words and merely pressed his hand to his heart in recognition of her kind ones.

Adam and Claire left and walked to Adam's car alongside Claire's parents walking to their own, saying goodbye even though they were going to the same place.

"So, I'm going to go out on a limb and guess you aren't borrowing that dress for my benefit, huh?" Adam asked with a shitty grin.

Claire rolled her eyes but chuckled all the same. "Sorry, Mr. Miller, but no."

"Damn," Adam sniggered.

"It does involve you, however. I want to bring the show to Babs. At least my parts of it anyway. She was up in the chair for a good part of the day, and I noticed the rehab facility had a piano in their common area."

"I think that is a fabulous idea."

The next day, Claire did her hair and makeup and carefully secured the dress in a bag. Adam picked her up just after breakfast, and they went to see Babs. At the counter, Adam asked if they could get a wheelchair to Babs's room, and in no time, Adam had rolled her out to the large room that held a TV, tables with puzzles, and a piano. During that process, Claire changed and was waiting for them at the piano.

"Oh, my dear, don't you look beautiful," Babs said. "Absolutely stunning."

"I thought I'd bring my show to you today!" Claire smiled.

A glossiness came over Babs's gray-blue eyes, and Claire's heart melted.

"Oh, absolutely," Babs said, adjusting herself in her chair to get comfortable.

Claire nodded and took to the piano. She ran through her own songs from the show but then played a plethora of other Christmas tunes. In no time, others were being wheeled in or coming forward with their walkers to listen. They joined along when she sang familiar tunes like "Jingle Bells" and "It's Beginning to Look a Lot Like Christmas." When she was finished, she got applause from all, and though it wasn't nearly as many as her school performances, the applause somehow seemed louder and filled Claire's heart more than any other. Babs had tears rolling down her cheeks and looked prouder than she'd ever looked before. Claire beamed.

"That was beautiful. And I think even better than the performances I missed because I got to listen to just you," Babs said, extending her arms, which Claire leaned over to accept.

"Thanks, Babs."

They mingled a little longer before Claire said, "Looks like it's just about time for lunch. Adam has to get to work, so we're going to head out. But you keep doing those exercises, Babs. I'm at the bakery every day after school this week, but I'll come over after I get off. Sounds like you'll be home in no time."

"They said possibly two weeks if my sessions keep going well. I told them they better not keep me for a day longer, or I'll break myself out," Babs said.

"Attagirl," Adam responded with a chuckle.

Arriving at Claire's, Adam got out to hug her goodbye.

"Hey, I gotta hit the road but was wondering if I could come over after work tonight. I wanted to talk to you about something."

Claire hated how quickly her heart rate sped up at the sound of needing to talk. "Of course. Everything okay?"

"Very much so. I just have an exciting opportunity for you that I wanted to discuss." He smiled and winked.

Claire waited rather impatiently for Adam to get off of work, which was around 6:00, and of course called Sam three times in the meantime to brainstorm what Adam could possibly have to talk to Claire about. However positive or exciting it may be, it still stressed Claire out to not know what it was. She informed her parents that Adam would be coming over to which her mom insisted on pushing Sunday dinner back so that Adam could eat with them, which meant that when he arrived, Claire had to wait even longer to hear this exciting opportunity of his.

"When Claire said you were coming over right from work, I just had to make sure you had something to eat, what with working a whole day and all," Claire's mom fussed.

"It was only four hours or so, a cover shift for someone. But I appreciate the meal all the same, Mrs. Hanover. Best cook around. Well, you and my mother," Adam said.

"Oh, go on."

Adam grinned, and they finished dinner, Claire being anxious to go upstairs after, only to have her mom come out with dessert and coffee.

"Claire, hunny, why are you so quiet tonight? It's Sunday dinner. Relax! You seem so tense," her mom said.

"I'm fine! Just not really hungry," Claire responded, trying to calm herself down and enjoy the lemon cake.

When they all finished dessert, Claire made to head upstairs, but her mom called from the kitchen, "Claire, can you give me a hand with these dishes?" Claire obeyed and left Adam to talk to her dad about the new train catalog he had gotten in the mail recently.

At long last, Adam and Claire were able to get away, Adam plopping down on her bed while she sat, grabbing a pillow to hold on to, and waited for him to speak.

"Dinner was good," he said.

"It was," Claire responded.

"You think your dad's going to buy another train for himself for Christmas?" Adam chuckled.

"Probably," Claire said.

"What did *you* ask for Chri—"

"Cut the small talk," Claire said to Adam's widening grin. "What did you want to tell me?! I'm dying over here."

"Okay, okay," he said, chuckling. "Nick's cousin's family owns a ski resort about three hours north of here. A few miles down the road from it is a lodge that they rent out to people, and they're letting Nick rent it for a weekend at a sick price. So he's invited all of us and a couple other friends from work. It's a Friday to Sunday. The last weekend before Christmas, and I am hoping that you'll be able to go."

Claire felt the squeal inside her trying to escape when she attempted to talk with a calm voice. The idea of going away for the weekend with Adam and a bunch of friends and no chaperones sounded too good to be true.

"Really?! That sounds amazing!"

"That's what I thought. Sam is, of course, invited, and if you or she, or even Nick, as he offered, can figure out a way to invite Logan, Nick said he's welcome. Or maybe she'll be excited to just hang out with all of us and meet Nick's work buddies."

"Oh my god, she is going to flip!" Claire said, quite excited to have her best friend along for the weekend too.

"So I guess the big question is if you think your parents will let you go," Adam said, bringing the mood down.

"Well, I mean, I'm eighteen now. They don't really have a choice," Claire said, her words not carrying the confidence to back them up.

"I'm not sure it works that way," Adam said. "You still live here and are still in school. I would tread carefully and not pull out the eighteen card."

"Alright, you're right. So how do I ask them?" Claire asked, a sudden rush of anxiety coming over her.

"Just tell them the truth. That a group of friends, most they've met, are going to a ski lodge for the weekend. There won't be any supervision, but we're all adults, or most of us anyway, and are looking to have a fun and responsible weekend of skiing and campfires. And you want to go. And Sam is invited."

Claire nodded slowly. "Okay . . ."

"No big deal," Adam said.

"So I'll go talk to them now," Claire said.

"Now? Not now!"

"Why?" Claire asked.

"I'm still here!"

"So."

"So what if they don't like the idea? I don't want to be here for that."

"You just said it wasn't a big deal!"

"Well, I lied," Adam said.

Claire threw her pillow at him. "Fine. I'll ask after you leave and let you know. That's, like, coming right up! I have to plan. So who's going?"

Adam started ticking the names off his fingers. "Nick, me, you, Fitz, Jason, Melissa, Sam, possibly Logan, and Nick's friends from work, Matt and Dave."

"Wow! Sounds like a blast!" Claire said.

"Yes," Adam said, sitting up and leaning close to her. "And I hope you can go."

"Me too." She smiled. She really did hope so too. This sounded like just the right distraction needed before the heaviness of what the second semester of her senior year would bring, with college letters coming in and big decisions needing to be made. She didn't know it, but Adam was thinking the exact same thing.

Adam leaned further and their lips met.

Claire made her way to the living room after Adam left to see what kind of space her parents were in. Her dad was still thumbing through his catalog, and her mom was flipping through channels.

"Hey," she said timidly, sitting down on the love seat.

"Hi, hunny. Adam gone home?" her mom asked.

"Yeah," Claire said, her mouth going dry.

"Such a sweet boy," her mom said absentmindedly, landing on the TV Guide and watching it slowly scroll through channels.

"Um," Claire said, "can I ask you guys something?"

At this, her dad looked over the top of his glasses, laying his catalog in his lap, her mom quickly looking at her.

"What's up?" her dad said.

"Well, you guys remember Nick, right? Adam's friend?"

"Of course. One of the boys who took Sam to prom, right? He was at your concert," her mom responded.

"Yeah, him. Well, his cousin's family owns a ski resort and a lodge nearby. They're letting Nick borrow it, and he's invited a bunch of us to go away for the weekend before Christmas. Friday to Sunday."

Her parents just looked at her.

"And I want to go," she added awkwardly.

"I assume there is no supervision?" her dad said.

"Correct," Claire said, a ball in her throat.

"And all these kids who are invited, they'll be older boys?"

"And girls. You guys have met most of them. Everyone who was at my concert . . . Jason, Melissa, and Fitz. Plus, Sam is invited and just a couple other friends of Nick's from work."

"Claire, hunny, you've never skied in your life," her mother broke in.

"I know. Neither has Sam. We're going to learn together," she said, though she hadn't talked to Sam at all.

"Well, we can't really tell you no. I mean, you're eighteen, and though your father and I are still in charge of your schooling, health, and well-being, this doesn't seem to interfere with any of those."

Claire looked to her father, who gave her a quizzical look. "Will there be drinking? Smoking? Drugs or any of that? That would interfere with your health and well-being."

"Honestly? I'm going to assume *someone* is going to have alcohol of some degree. Smoking is legal at eighteen. Definitely no drugs. And most importantly, *I* will not be smoking or drinking. I've been around it in the past and have been fine." Claire said, definitely sure she would probably have something to drink regardless. But she knew she would be responsible with it.

"Well, I don't see a problem with it," her mother said.

Her dad looked like he had something else to say but decided against it and said instead, "As long as you're smart and safe and feel comfortable going, not pressured."

Claire jumped up in excitement. "Thanks!!!" She gave them each a hug and raced upstairs to call Adam.

He must have been waiting for her to call, for the phone barely rang before she heard his voice over the line.

"They said I can go!" she blurted out.

As always she heard his broad grin as he said, "No way! Sweet!"

"I can't wait to tell Sam tomorrow after school!"

"This is going to be the best trip ever," Adam said, almost laughing with joy. "And will kick off your Christmas break. How perfect is that?"

"Perfect," Claire said.

"Shut up . . . shut up! And your parents are letting you go?!" Sam practically shouted as they walked home from school.

"Yes!" Claire squealed. "And we need to ask your mom as soon as possible."

"Oh my god. I need to go to this. How do I ask her to make her let me? I'm not eighteen yet! What if she doesn't let me because I'm the only one underage!"

"I'm sure if I've been allowed to go, you'll be. You just gotta ask."

Sam took a deep breath. "Okay. Just ask. Oh my god. I'll come over as soon as I find out," Sam said.

"I work till five, but anytime after!" Claire said, anxious to hopefully have much to celebrate at that time.

Claire's shift seemed to move as slow as the molasses in Mrs. Leonard's cookies, and when 5:00 hit, she rushed out the door and sped home.

When walking through the door, her mom said, "Hey, hunny. Sam's waiting for you." Claire dropped her bag in the doorway and rushed up the stairs two at a time, busting through her own bedroom door to see Sam sprawled on her bed, though quickly sitting up at the sight of Claire.

"And?" Claire said.

Sam's face broke into a wide smile.

"You can go?!" Claire asked.

Sam nodded before jumping up and squealing as they danced around in a circle for a moment of childlike joy.

"Oh my god, this is going to be so much fun," Sam said through incessant gum-chewing. "We need to go shopping. I need, like, a new coat and cute hat and mittens and cute boots."

Claire chuckled as Sam settled into her regular beanbag spot and Claire lay on her bed facing Sam. "Let's go this coming weekend. It's the only time we have, really."

"Okay, yes. What's your work schedule look like?"

"Pulling morning shifts. You?" Claire responded. Sam had gotten a job at the library putting books away and doing general housekeeping. She had been there for a few weeks now, and it offered more hours, so her schedule was a little tighter.

"Just Saturday, and I get out at three," Sam said.

"Perfect. We go at three on Saturday!" Claire said. "How has that been going anyway?"

"Great! I'm loving it! It's quiet, and I don't have to work with others or the public much."

"You think you'll be good to take next weekend?" Claire asked. She had thankfully been given the clear by Mrs. Leonard earlier that day.

"I think so. They're more concerned that the work gets done, and so as long as I leave it spick-and-span and ready to roll for Friday, they should be good. They're closed Sunday anyway, and I'm back in on Monday for a full day because of break. So really it's only Friday afternoon and Saturday I need to take."

"Excellent. Oh, I'm so excited about this," Claire said, voice quivering from holding down yet another squeal.

"Me too," Sam said. "I can barely contain it."

They had homework to work on, but neither of them were doing a very good job of accomplishing it. Claire put on the radio to try to distract them from their thoughts and attempt to refocus them, but it was no good.

"Hey," Sam said suddenly with a cautious tone.

"Mmm?" Claire said, looking up after having read the same lines in *Hamlet* for the fifth time.

Sam adjusted herself and said, "Have you and Adam . . . you know."

Claire felt herself blush. "Like I wouldn't tell you that."

"Well, I don't know. There was a whole school year where we barely talked, so I thought . . . maybe."

"I still would have told you."

"So I'm assuming you haven't."

Claire closed her book and gave Sam an appraising look. "No, we haven't."

Sam nodded, and then said, "Well, how do you feel about it?"

"Where is this coming from?" Claire said with a nervous laugh.

"Well, has it not occurred to you that you and Adam are going to be alone for a whole weekend with no adults for the first time ever? You don't think this may come up? Like, do you even know the sleeping arrangements? There's like ten or so of us going. How many rooms does this place have?"

Claire paused, taking in what Sam said. "I hadn't thought of it, no."

"Well, what if it does come up? How do you feel about it?"

Claire sat up slowly to buy herself some time before saying what she was thinking. "I—I don't know, I guess. I mean, there are times when we're together and things are getting really intense, and in those moments I think I'd be okay with it. Like, it feels right. He always stops it though. Sometimes I think if it was left up to me, it'd maybe happen. But after it's stopped, I feel like it was a good call and so wonder if maybe I'm not ready, you know?"

Sam nodded. "Sure. Like your body wants to get some but your head doesn't."

Claire rolled her eyes.

Sam laughed. "I'm kidding. I understand. You feel it and it feels right, but when you take time to think about it, you're maybe not sure."

"Yeah."

"I think," Sam said, "I think that that sounds exactly right. I think all this should be confusing."

Claire nodded. "The good thing is, I never feel pressured. So if it does happen, I know it would happen because I wanted it to and not because I'm trying to fit in or, like, doing it just to appease Adam."

"That is good." Sam smiled. "Have you guys talked about it? Do you know where he stands?"

"No, actually. We haven't." Claire realized that maybe they *should* have this conversation before heading off for a weekend together. There were going to be plenty of other people around, but Claire was also sure that the two of them finding alone time wouldn't be hard.

"Well, something to think about, I guess," Sam said nonchalantly, going back to not doing her math and reading *People* magazine. Claire was getting tired of having things to think about. To distract herself, she called Babs to ask how her day had gone since she hadn't been able to squeeze in a visit.

The rest of the week went by quickly. School was winding down due to break being only a week away, and between going to work afterward and then seeing Babs, it was Friday before Claire knew it, and she and Sam were snacking away on popcorn, discussing what they wanted to pick up at the mall the next day for their weekend trip.

"I bet they have some cute sweaters. I want a cute sweater and some comfy, warm wool socks to go with my boots," Claire said, legs propped on the wall, lying back on her bed, Sam next to her, the bowl of popcorn between them.

"You'd look adorable in that. Those nice thick ones like the people in the L.L.Bean catalog have. You're so lucky you have a pair of boots from them. My boots are so lame."

"Your boots are boots." Claire chuckled. "They're fine."

"Well, I want some L.L.Bean-catalog-worthy clothes too and a fun new hat."

"Sweet."

"So," Sam said, "are you going to talk to Adam?"

"I think so. He's coming over Sunday afternoon to hang out and have dinner. We both have the afternoon off. I think we may talk then because we won't have time otherwise before the trip."

"What are you going to say?!" Sam asked, not able to contain the excitement at such a juicy moment even though it was a rather serious thing.

"I don't know yet," Claire said, really having no idea.

"I'm sure it'll come to you," Sam said, slightly disappointed. "Hey, how's Babs? When is she coming home?"

"She's doing really well. They're releasing her Wednesday and have a nurse coming to work with her daily for a little while. You know, make sure she has what she needs, do some exercises, and whatnot."

"Oh, that's great. She's a tough lady," Sam said.

"For sure."

The next day, Claire drove them to the mall. Sam wanted to stop at every single clothing store and bought nothing until they had seen it all, claiming to need to know her options before making a decision. They stopped in between to have a snack at the food court, each getting a McDonald's sundae. Claire was just contemplating a sweater she had seen earlier, deciding to go back to get it when, lo and behold, Amber showed up. To Claire's surprise, Mark was with her and Lauren. No Chris. Their group had diminished and was definitely more subdued than normal while strutting around the mall.

"Look who's here," Claire said quietly to Sam, who looked over her shoulder rather obviously. She rolled her eyes when looking back to Claire.

"Oh joy. At least it isn't a gang of them. I thought Mark was trying to stay away from them?"

Claire shrugged. "I don't know. Maybe just Amber is fine."

"Pfft. She's the worst one."

Claire shrugged yet again, remembering her and Amber's bathroom conversation. She had been meaning to talk to Amber and follow up but hadn't had the moment to do so. Maybe everything going on was what made her more subdued. Maybe she had opened up to Mark.

"Shit. I think they saw us," Sam said suddenly.

Sure enough, Mark was making his way over with Amber and Lauren.

"Hey, Claire! Hey, Sam," he said, sitting down at their table, Amber and Lauren standing behind him.

"Feel free to pop a squat too," Claire said to them, gesturing to the empty chairs all around them.

Amber looked at her as though prepared to say something nasty but instead said, "Thanks, but we're good."

"Suit yourself," Claire said.

"What are you guys up to here?" Mark asked.

"Buying cute sweaters and snow gear for a weekend ski trip," Sam piped up.

Mark nodded and said, "Cool," but it caught Amber's attention more.

"Ski trip?" she asked.

"Yup," Sam said. "Claire and I are going up north for the weekend."

Amber looked from Sam to Claire, clearly deciding if it was cool to seem interested, but her curiosity got the better of her. "Up north? Who with, your parents?"

Claire butted in before Sam could, so as to save her from sounding too cocky. "With friends, actually. Adam's friend rented a lodge for the weekend and invited a bunch of us up," she said nonchalantly.

Amber looked at them both once again, then sneered and gave a shrug. "Cool."

"Sounds awesome!" Mark added. "How many of you are going? A weekend away with no parents? I mean, I know we're all seniors and turning eighteen and stuff, but damn, that's pretty cool. I'm jealous."

Claire chuckled. "There's like eight or nine of us or so."

"That's dope. You guys will have a killer time," Mark said.

Amber, clearly not enjoying the attention the conversation was getting, butted in to say, "Mark, we should probably get going. I gotta be back home in an hour, and Lauren and I still want to hit up Deb's."

"You guys go; I'll catch up with you," Mark said over his shoulder.

"We are actually finishing up here ourselves," Claire said, putting their trash together to prepare to toss it. "We have some shopping left to do."

"Oh, bummer. Well, it was nice bumping into you guys," Mark said. "See you, Claire."

He waved and walked off with the girls while Sam and Claire got rid of their trash.

"Oh my god, he is totally still into you," Sam said.

"What?! What are you talking about?" Claire said, truly surprised by Sam's observation.

"I just know. It's no biggie! But he totally came over to, once again, just talk to you, and he wanted to talk more. He probably wanted an invite to the ski trip."

"Of course he did. As did Amber and Lauren. But not because of me. It's because they see it as doing something cool."

"Because it is!" Sam squealed.

Claire laughed. "It is pretty cool. But we're going because we want to have some fun and it's our friends! Not to be cool," Claire reminded.

"No, of course," Sam said.

They fell into silence briefly before Claire said, "But it *was* pretty fun to see Amber's expression. Aaaand we are going away for a whole weekend with no parents and a bunch of guys!"

They both squealed and giggled, then continued on with their shopping, revisiting all the stores that Sam needed.

Sam spent the night but left early the next morning so Claire could go to work. A busy shift lent itself to a quick shift, and soon enough Claire was home, showered, and chilling in her room when Adam walked through her door.

"Hey you," he said, leaning over and giving her a kiss.

"Hey," she said. "How was work?"

"Not too shabby. Surprisingly busy," he answered, lying across the foot of her bed, propped on an elbow, wearing his glorious smile, as usual.

"Mine was too. Sunday mornings are usually busy," she returned. She was growing anxious, knowing that she wanted to talk to Adam about a subject that could very well be awkward, in fact, most likely would be.

"What are you reading?" he asked, noticing her propped open book.

"Oh, just *Hamlet*. I need to get through this act before tomorrow. I've definitely enjoyed other Shakespeare plays, but for some reason this one isn't doing it for me."

"Yeah, I definitely did not read any of the Shakespeare books in school. CliffsNotes all the way." He chuckled.

Claire rolled her eyes in a playful way. "Well, I wouldn't normally condone such things."

"That's because you're the smart one," he said.

"Is that so? Well, I don't think so. You're a smarty yourself."

"Yeah, okay," Adam said doubtfully and then changed the subject. "I'm getting pretty stoked for our trip."

Claire smiled but felt her stomach churn. "I actually wanted to talk to you about that."

Her tone had changed, and Adam had heard it. "Is everything okay? You can still go, right?"

"Yeah, no, I can still go. Wouldn't dream of missing it. I just—" she paused, feeling the stress getting stronger.

"What's up?" he asked tentatively, sitting up, crisscrossing his legs to sit facing her, concern edging over his face.

Claire made eye contact and felt a rush of comfort. It gave her the confidence she needed. She took a deep breath and said, "It's kind of awkward. I guess I'm struggling to find the words."

"You have nothing to feel awkward about, Claire. Try me." He gave an award winning grin.

"Okay. Well, I thought maybe because this is our first time being together . . . alone . . . overnight . . . that maybe we should talk about . . . well . . ."

Understanding dawned on Adam's face, and the tension he was holding calmed. "Ah, I got it," he said, taking one of her hands in his. "Let's talk."

She gave a small smile and released a light laugh of relief. "Okay. How does one start a conversation about this?"

He laughed too. "I'm not entirely sure myself."

Claire eyed him for a moment and then threw caution to the wind. "I guess I'll start by first asking something I've never thought to ask before."

"Which is?" Adam questioned.

"Did you and Rachel ever . . . you know?"

"No," he said blankly. "We didn't do anything more than what you and I have already done, and I'd even argue that you and I have done more because I am a lot more emotionally invested in you. I love you."

Claire blushed. "I love you too."

Adam looked at her expectantly. When Claire looked at him questioningly, he said, "And you and Mark?"

Claire actually let out a bark of laughter. "God no. No, we didn't. Not even close. Mark stuck his tongue in my mouth once, and I had about enough of that."

"Oh God," Adam said.

"I'm sorry," Claire said, still laughing. "But it's the truth."

Adam chuckled. Claire felt her moment of entertainment fall back to the reality of their conversation and said, "So . . . how *do* you feel about it?"

"Well, first I think I need to say that I certainly am not looking forward to this weekend because I am expecting anything of that nature. I have zero expectations of that and am not looking for it. I simply am overjoyed to just be spending a whole weekend with you. Between school and work and just everything else you've had on your plate, and then Babs . . . I am just excited to have a whole weekend of uninterrupted Claire time." He didn't add that he was also growing increasingly anxious for what was to come, that he was looking forward to just having quality time together before the plethora of potential change that was on the horizon hit. "I even made sure that there was a place for everyone at the lodge, including a bed and room for you and Sam to share."

Claire smiled. "I appreciate that. A lot."

"Of course." He paused before saying, "I will be honest and tell you it *has* crossed my mind . . . plenty."

"It has for me too," Claire said quietly. Adam looked at her and she continued. "There are times when we're together and I feel like if it did, I'd be okay with it. I have these moments where I just want to be so close to you and nothing seems close enough, and in those moments I think maybe that's what I want." She could feel her face burn at these words and couldn't believe she'd even voiced them but was happy she did, as they were being honest with each other, and she felt that having this conversation would do nothing if she didn't spill it all.

Adam sensed her vulnerability and shimmied closer to her. "I feel the same way, Claire. For sure."

Claire nodded. "And I also know that we're young and there are a lot of hormones and emotions at play, and I just want to be smart about it too, you know?"

"Absolutely." Adam nodded. They came to silence, which broke when Adam said, "Claire, I think as long as we know there is no pressure of any kind, that no one is counting on or expecting it, that we stay honest with each other in the moment and respect when one of us thinks it's going too fast or far, then we'll be doing good. You will never say anything that is too awkward or make me frustrated, or anything else for that matter, when it comes to this."

At his words, Claire felt a rush of gratitude. It sounded like a terrific plan, and she trusted him, which brought an overwhelming sense of comfort and peace. "I think that is perfect. And likewise," she said, throwing her arms around his neck, his own wrapping around her and holding her tight, his scent engulfing her.

"Okay. Okay, I think I got everything. Oh my god, what if I forgot something?"

"You'll be fine," Claire said to a frantic Sam as they piled a suitcase each and some extra bags by the front door. Adam would be picking them up along with Fitz. Due to the number of people going, they were taking multiple cars, Nick already on his way with Melissa and Jason, his two work friends meeting them at the lodge as well. Sam had contemplated asking Logan but decided it was a little too forward for her and wanted to just have some fun, knowing she would stress the entire time if he went. Plus, she was interested in getting to meet Nick's work buddies.

"You look adorable, by the way," Sam said with a sigh, looking at Claire.

Claire, who was wearing her new speckled gray sweater, jeans, wool socks, and boots, looked at her with a cocked eyebrow.

"No, really," Sam said. "This whole outdoorsy, cozy nature vibe works on you. I look like the lumberjack's daughter."

Claire rolled her eyes and laughed. Sam was wearing an off-white turtleneck under an opened baggy buffalo plaid flannel. Her high-waisted jeans and boots finished off the alt girl look she was so good at pulling off, and she would fit in just fine in the mountains. "Sam, you look perfect. Edgy and ski ready."

"You really think?" she asked, fluffing her head of curls that Claire always envied.

"I do," she replied with genuineness.

"Thanks, friend."

Claire heard a car pull up outside and felt her heart skip a beat. She yelled to her parents that Adam was here, and they came to stand on the porch while Adam and Fitz played *Tetris* with the luggage.

"Don't blame me: I only brought one bag," Fitz said.

"Why doesn't that surprise me?" Adam said through a groan as he shoved a suitcase into the back of the trunk. They managed, and when done, Adam went up to give Claire's mom a hug and her dad a handshake while Claire also gave hugs. A quick pee break later, they hit the road.

"Here we go," Adam said to the car as they pulled out of Claire's driveway.

"Righteous," Fitz said from the back seat with Sam.

"How far is this place again?" Claire asked.

"About three hours," Adam said. "I figured we could stop somewhere for lunch before we hit the lodge."

"Sounds great." She smiled.

Adam gave her a broad grin and took her hand in his.

The ride was smooth, alternating between cassette tapes that Adam had in his center console, many of which were cassettes Claire had given him over the years. Though both of them had mostly switched to CDs, they still entertained each other with random cassettes. It wasn't as frequent as it used to be but was still their thing, and Claire loved it. Most recently, she had snagged him a Nirvana tape that she knew he didn't have in cassette or CD form. It was one of her personal favorites, and per usual, they still requested specific songs for each other to listen to. This tradeoff was something Claire really appreciated in their relationship.

"You guys remember your bathing suits?" Adam asked.

"Yes!" Sam responded.

Adam had called Claire just the day before to let them know that the lodge had a hot tub outside, so naturally, Sam had panicked about her bathing suit not being cute enough, but with no time to shop had thankfully listened to Claire's reassurance that it was fine. Sam had come so far in her confidence and outgoingness that her sessions in therapy were down to only once a month and without Claire. Claire could still see snippets of the old Sam, such as the bathing suit debacle; however, Claire couldn't help but notice how quickly Sam could get out of her panicking, and often without Claire's help. She also seemed to just freak out about these things beforehand, but when actually going out and about was fine. It made Claire happy to see.

"Good," Adam said. "I'm super excited. Something about cold mountain air on your face while sitting in the heat sounds really nice."

"Agreed," Claire said. She was excited too. The closer they had gotten to this trip, the more thrilled she really had gotten about all the pockets of time she and Adam would have together. She couldn't help but feel that things had been a little off lately. She knew their love hadn't changed, but she had noticed that Adam seemed almost sad off and on, and he still didn't talk college plans or even talk to her about hers. She had scrapped the topic altogether due to just not wanting to dredge up an argument. She also sometimes went through bouts of fear for what that conversation might do. The unknown was a dark place. But she still hadn't heard from any colleges and wasn't expecting to till the new year and so was trying not to bother with it. She could tell that there was *something* that was nagging at Adam, but he wasn't telling yet.

"You good?" Adam asked.

Claire came out of her thoughts and shook them completely away. "Yes, fine," she said with authenticity. He kissed the back of her hand, and they drove on.

They stopped a few times for bathroom breaks, once at a McDonald's so the girls could use the facilities and they could all get food, and two times on the side of the road. They got lost at one point, so Claire looked over the MapQuest directions Adam had printed and figured out where they had gone wrong, and by early afternoon, they were rolling into a long dirt driveway that ended at a beautiful and large log cabin.

"Oh. My. God," Sam said beside Claire as they stepped out of the car.

"No kidding," Claire said, gawking at the beautiful structure and, even more beautiful, the line of high white-capped mountains that framed its background.

"This is amazing," Sam said. "Oh my gosh, I can't wait!"

They unloaded their things and went inside. Nick, Jason, and Melissa were there, and Nick shouted at the top of his lungs when they walked through the door.

"Isn't this place sick?" he said.

"Yeah, man," Adam responded.

"Duuuuuude," Fitz said. "Right on."

They were standing in the entryway to an open-concept layout, the kitchen with island and stools to their right, a dining room table to their left, and ahead of them, a large living room fit with three sofas and a huge coffee table. Claire couldn't decide whether the massive, gray, stone fireplace, whose chimney ran all the way up the cathedral ceiling, or the large mountain-facing windows that ran full length, giving an impeccable view of the snowy backyard that didn't seem to end, and the glorious mountain horizon stole the show.

"Can you imagine sunsets here?" Claire said, walking up to the windows and looking out. "And sunrises. Just beautiful."

"Jason and Melissa have the area up there," Nick said, pointing above them to an open loft with a railing. It ran along the whole side of the lodge atop the dining room and what Claire now saw were two bedrooms. "And I'm in this room." He pointed out the one on the left and then the other. "That one is available, and I'll show you the others."

They followed him past the kitchen to a hall with four doors that were all open. Claire could see one was a bathroom and the other three were bedrooms.

"They're pretty much all the same—the bedrooms. Full-size beds, homemade quilts, dresser. The loft is the only unique space. All the couches also pull out. This place could fit a shit ton of people in it if it needed to." Claire peeked in the bathroom, expecting to see something crazy but found it to be quite simple.

"Where's the hot tub?" Claire asked.

"Ah, itching for some hot tub time, huh?" Nick said with a waggle of his eyebrows.

"Shut up," Claire said to Adam's shitty grin.

"Kidding, kidding. It's on the side of the house. Double doors off the dining room go to a patio. Looks like it typically has furniture set out there during warmer weather, but it's all put away. Hot tub is running and ready though."

"Sweet," Claire said. "So it's just us and your two work friends?"

"Yup! Dave and Matt. Good guys. Matt turned twenty-one just last month, so guess what he was in charge of?"

Claire and Sam chuckled.

"And Dave is our age. Again. Nice guys. You'll like them. They're chill and get along with everyone," he added with a wink to Sam.

"Cool!" Claire said.

"So, we're good to take whatever rooms?" Adam butted in.

"Fo sho. Figured the girls here could have one, you could have the other, and I'll stick Fitz down here too. Dave and Matt can toss for the room next to mine and the couch."

"Right on," Adam said. They grabbed their bags from outside and unpacked. They took the two rooms at the end of the hall across from each other, and Fitz got the one across from the bathroom. By the time they'd settled in, the last two had arrived and with them a whole plethora of booze. They quickly dove in, and when everyone had a drink in hand, they cheered to a fun weekend ahead. Claire was excited. They were going to hang out and have drinks with close friends. They were going to ski, be outside, and enjoy the scenery. And she and Adam were going to have a chance to be alone. Really alone.

With a six disc CD player, surround sound speakers set up in the living room area, and an entire tower of CDs and drawers of cassettes, the lodge was bumping with tunes by dinnertime. Nick, who fashioned himself as world's best chef, laid out a smorgasbord of meats and cheeses and cut-up tomatoes, lettuce, and onions, and he opened some pickles for all of them to make their own sandwiches. A plethora of chip bags covered the island, and everyone was enjoying shouting over the music at each other and eating their way through it all.

"Those are some mad culinary skills right there," Claire said to Nick, teasing. "Putting out everything for us to make our own sandwiches."

"Ha. Ha. Very funny. You want to see some skills?" he challenged.

"Um, yeah," Claire said, grinning, twisting around in the stool at the counter.

"Okay, okay. Step right up. Here we have Chef Nick making an ultimate sandwich. No, no. THE ultimate sandwich," he said, putting on an accent that Claire couldn't name.

"First, we butter the bread, and we're going to lightly toast it on the stove top." Nick did this, and while they waited for the burner to warm up and the toast to cook, he explained what he was going to do with the rest.

"And now we assemble," he said when the bread was perfectly toasted. He layered meats and cheeses, salt and peppered a tomato to place atop with some lettuce, and then topped it with a smiley face of honey mustard. "And now dinner is served."

He handed the sandwich to a smiling Claire, who anxiously took a bite, Nick watching in exaggerated anticipation. She chewed slowly, acting as though every bite was being considered. "It's . . . delicious."

Nick shouted and threw his hands up. "Another score for the brilliant chef."

Nick's outburst drew Adam's attention away from Matt and Dave, with whom he was chatting, involving Sam so as to introduce them and give them something to carry on conversation with.

"What's going on in here? You got something to eat?" he asked Claire, kissing the top of her head.

"Oh, yes. I got a world-renowned sandwich specially made by Chef Nick."

"How lucky of you. Once in a lifetime experience right there," Adam said, taking a swig of beer.

"Right?" Nick agreed and then went to pick up where Adam left off, making sure Sam was comfortable. Fitz in the meantime was enjoying a smoke out back in his shorts and T-shirt in the snow.

"You good?" Adam asked. "Want another drink?"

"Sure." She smiled through a bite of sandwich. "I was drinking those pink wine cooler things."

Adam opened the fridge and got her another of the same. "Having fun?"

"Definitely," she said as he opened her drink. "Thank you for keeping Sam entertained and introducing her to Matt and Dave."

"Of course," he said with a grin.

"What's the plan for tomorrow?" Claire asked, continuing to eat her sandwich.

"The mountain has night skiing, so we were thinking of letting everyone sleep tomorrow morning, do lunch in town, and then hit the slopes."

"Sounds perfect!" Claire said, excited. "So, you going to show Sam and I how to ski, or are we on our own?"

"I will definitely give you some lessons. They have some bunny slopes too that you guys will be able to have some fun on."

"Awesome," she said. He leaned forward and kissed her. She was enjoying herself immensely. The chill atmosphere of drinking and hanging out with this crew was more fun than any party Claire had ever been to. She was starting to feel warm in the cheeks and happily content with the world. With the morning being low-key, she was excited to just have fun tonight.

"I think Nick wants to build a big fire out back. There's a nice pit and a bunch of wood stacked up."

"Sounds fun!" she said, and then, "I was kind of looking forward to trying out that hot tub."

Adam's eyebrows raised, but he caught himself and grinned. "Is that so? I think that can be arranged. How about we hit up the hot tub and join their campfire after. I'm sure they'll be out there all night. Nick brought his guitar, and we have nowhere to be."

"That sounds like a brilliant idea, Mr. Miller," Claire said with a giggle.

Adam broke into a wide smile. "Perfect."

"Hey, you two lovebirds, partying hard are we?" Nick butted in, and then to Adam, "Hey, you want to give me and Jason a hand with the pit? Time to take this party outside for some s'mores and music."

"Yeah, sure," Adam said, putting down his beer. "But Claire and I were going to try out the hot tub first. We'll meet you guys at the fire after."

Nick waggled his eyebrows. "Is that so."

"Shut up," Adam said.

Nick barked a laugh. "I'll go get Fitz to help. You two go ahead and get ready for that hot tub dip."

"You really want to start a fire with Fitz?" Adam cocked an eyebrow.

Nick contemplated. "Yeah, good point."

"I can come help. It's all good," Adam said. "I'll be right back," he said to Claire, kissing the top of her head again and rubbing her arm lightly.

Claire was finishing her sandwich when Sam came bounding up to her, all the guys having put on their snow gear to go outside, Melissa retiring to the loft to get her things.

"Oh. My. God," Sam said, jumping Claire to almost choking on her sandwich.

"Yes?" Claire questioned.

"Okay, so I am so happy I got to come this weekend," Sam said, getting a drink from the fridge. "Adam introduced me to Matt and Dave, and I cannot tell you how much I am digging Matt."

"Is that so?" Claire said with a grin.

"Oh my gosh, yes. He's the older one, the one that got the booze for tonight. He is currently studying criminal justice and eventually wants to be a detective! How hot is that?"

"Pretty hot," Claire said, laughing lightly. The wine was beginning to settle in the form of giggles.

"Right?! So, after Adam introduced us, he started talking about movies, I think because he knows I like movies, and right away Matt started talking about his favorite movies, and before we knew it, we were talking all about our favorites and how much we both love going *to* the movies and yeah! We are *really* hitting it off. Do you think twenty-one is too old? I mean, it's only like three and a half years older than me. Technically, if he had gone to our school, he would have been a senior when I was a freshman. Like, we could have met. What do you think?"

"I think age is but a number. He's not too old at all!" Claire responded, starting to put away the sandwich supplies that the boys had left out.

"Let me help," Sam said, covering the different platters with saran wrap while Claire attempted to fit it all back into the fridge.

"I mean, I'm not saying that I'm falling head over heels or anything," Sam continued. "But I think we *really* hit it off. Like *really*. He's super sweet, and he asked if I was going to join them at the campfire because he wanted to sit next to me!!"

Claire paused mid-stacking and looked at Sam. "Really?! That's something!"

Sam nodded vigorously. "Right?! He said he would help me learn how to ski tomorrow. So we'll both have instructors!"

"That's great! Sounds quite promising," Claire exclaimed, finishing her mission of filling the fridge. They got everything put away and the counters wiped down just in time for the boys to come back in to tell them the fire was roaring and ready.

"Sweet!" Sam said. "You ready?"

Claire shook her head. "Um, Adam and I are actually going to try out the hot tub first and then meet you guys out there!"

Sam gave Claire a sly look before saying, "Okay."

"Don't give me that look," Claire said under her breath.

"Have fun!" Sam called over her shoulder as she practically skipped to their shared bedroom to get her snow gear. Everyone grabbed a few drinks each and went outside bundled up in all their cold weather attire.

Adam looked to Claire. "Ready?! I'm excited to try that thing out too. It looked pretty big!"

"Yes! I'll be right back. Just gotta get my suit on."

She had brought her pink one-piece that was a little more modest than some of her others, knowing that she would possibly be using a hot tub with a bunch of people, many of them guys, and, though she was really close to all of Adam's friends, wanted to feel comfortable with it. Regardless of its modesty, Claire still felt pretty in it, the high-cut legs and V-neck just enough to add some flair. She grabbed a T-shirt to throw over and met Adam, who was already in his tropical swim shorts, grabbing them another round in the kitchen.

"Alright, let's get this party started," he said jokingly.

Claire took a wine cooler from him, and they made their way out the side door that led to a deck and the hot tub. Steam was pouring off the top, and the jets were already going. It was freezing cold, so they wasted no time in ridding themselves of their T-shirts and getting right in. The water engulfed Claire, giving her goose bumps all over. She sat so that jets were pulsing right into her lower back and the bottoms of her feet. Adam crawled in after her and released a sigh as he lowered himself in. The steam wrapped its way around her face and mixed with the frigid cold air, giving her a cleansing sensation. She couldn't help but think how glorious her skin would look after this. Adam sidled over and put his arm around her shoulders, kissing her temple.

"This is the life, huh?" he said, looking up at the sky.

Claire looked up too, resting her head on his arm. The sky was so clear and the night so dark; Claire had never seen so many stars in the sky before. With nothing to interfere with her sight and the sense of her body floating in the water, Claire almost felt as though she were flying through space.

"It's beautiful."

"Just like you," Adam whispered.

Claire smiled up at the sky. "You remember the last time I had rosy cheeks, was buzzed, and talked about the night sky to you."

"All too well."

"That party and running from the cops was a thrill I'd never experienced in my life." Claire laughed loudly.

Adam laughed too. "It was quite a rush."

"That night is one I'll always remember," she said.

"Me too. It was the night I fell in love," Adam said simply.

Claire thought a moment. The party, Sam and her fighting, she and Adam sharing some form of an out-of-body moment while listening to a song of such personal depth, the cops, the playground, sharing their secrets . . . Claire had had a crush on him already at that point, though she had been denying it at the time.

She smiled at the blessed expanse of heavens above them and said, "Me too."

"I always thought it was the day we went to the beach and kissed in the ocean, but I think it was that night. Although I was also quite blown away by your beauty the first day I saw you when almost running you over."

"Maybe it was all of them."

"All of them?"

"Maybe we fell in love each time. Maybe we just fall in love with each other over and over and over again," Claire contemplated.

"I think that's the truest statement you've ever said, Hanover."

"I feel that being out here, in the middle of nowhere, up in the mountains and trees and fresh air, staring into space makes you feel so, so small. And I think that people should feel that way more often," Claire said suddenly. "We get so caught up in life and everything else that we forget we are just beings here and have practically zero control, though we try to have it all. Being here, right now, in this moment, I can feel that. The world and universe are so big, and we're a mere spec. We can only live it as best we can. Be good."

Adam's silence told Claire that he, too, was thinking of what she said. Claire took a swig of her drink and giggled. "I think the wine is getting to my head."

Adam grinned. "Well, maybe all the best philosophers drank wine too because that was some pretty impressive shit."

Claire burst into laughter, Adam joining in. Adam could live inside her laugh. It stemmed from the gut and trilled from the heart. It was his favorite sound. He never ceased to be amazed that he had Claire, and that thought crossing his mind made him think of what he was trying to not think about.

"Claire," he said.

"Mmm?" Claire said, still lost in the skies.

"I—" he began but didn't know where to go. He wanted to tell her that he loved her more than words, that he wanted to be with her forever, that he wasn't sure if he could make it into a college, how that terrified him, that he was scared for her to leave town and meet new and impressive people, people who would show just how basic and small town he was, that he wasn't good enough, and that he was afraid to say all of this because he didn't want to have any influence on her decisions, because he wanted her to shoot for the moon that was above them, because he felt that Claire Hanover could move mountains like the ones that surrounded them, and because he didn't want to get in the way of that.

"You what?" she prompted.

"I . . . I love you," he said, chickening out.

She looked up at him, her body feeling limp and relaxed. "I love *you*."

He smiled and bent down to kiss her. When he went to pull away, her hand came up, running her fingers through his hair, pulling him to her again. Their lips locked, and all the thoughts Adam was having raced away as he tasted the hint of strawberry wine that clung to her lips. He set his beer down, hers already empty, and pulled her to him, allowing her playfulness to add to their kiss.

Claire felt her heart racing, and she swung herself around so that she was facing him, sitting on his lap and wrapping her legs around his middle. He smirked at her and she giggled, his arms wrapping around her, the feeling of his hands on her bare back sending shivers through her body. They kissed again and didn't stop, Claire pressing herself to him, feeling his bare chest rising and falling with every breath, his heart and hers pounding in unison.

From inside the house, they heard music begin to sound through all the speakers at top volume, someone deciding that Nick's poor guitar skills weren't enough for the campfire. Deep dulcet tones of a slow rock ballad played over them, and Claire felt herself getting whisked away by the euphoria that was Adam and this moment.

"Claire," Adam whispered, coming to rest his forehead against hers after several long moments.

"Adam," she returned, allowing a small laugh to escape.

Adam chuckled too. "I think you and I have had a bit to drink tonight."

"I think you're right," she responded.

He kissed her nose and her forehead and then pecked her lips once more.

"I think we should take it easy here; what say you?" he asked, cupping her face and looking into her large brown eyes that were crinkled into a smile.

"Yes. We probably should."

"Fire pit time?" he asked.

"My hands *are* a little pruny," she mused, showing him.

Adam kissed her fingertips. "Okay, up we go." He gave Claire a squeeze before she sidled off him, and they stood, immediately feeling their skin bump up from the cold air. Adam stepped out of the hot tub and offered his hand to Claire to help her out, both of them chattering as they wrapped towels around them, making a quick run to get inside, music blaring at them as they opened the door.

"Jesus!" Claire yelled, both of them laughing though not being able to hear each other.

Claire towel dried the tips of her hair that had gotten wet, threw on her long john pants, sweatpants, and two sweatshirts, and topped it off with a hat, mittens, jacket, and boots. Adam bundled up as well, and they quickly joined the others, closing the door on the screaming music, wondering who thought it would work, as it was pretty nonexistent by the time they got to the fire pit, which didn't matter, as Nick had the guitar out once more.

"Ah! Finally! Now I can have some beats," Nick shouted at them as they joined, fresh drinks in hand.

"What are we singing?" Adam asked, sitting in a chair next to Nick and tapping his knee for Claire to sit.

"Oh, just singing some Bob Marley right now: Fitz's request, of course," Nick responded.

Claire noticed that Sam was sitting next to Matt and they were talking animatedly.

"Of course," Adam said. "When did you pick up guitar anyway?"

"Two months ago, man. Where have you been?"

"Sorry I don't pay attention to your every whim," Adam mocked.

"Shut up."

"Play something for Claire to sing," Fitz said as he lay in the snow, a half-smoked joint hidden beside him.

"No, no, I'm good," Claire piped up.

"Even if she wanted to, Fitz, I literally picked this thing up two months ago. You really think I can just play whatever song you request?"

"You played Bob Marley."

"Yeah, because it's, like, an easy one to learn."

"Admit it, dude. You learned it just for me."

"Yes, Fitz. The first thing I thought of when deciding to try and learn guitar was, 'I wonder what song Fitz would want to hear; let's learn that one.' "

"Awe shucks, man, you're making me blush."

Claire chuckled at Nick's eye roll.

"Who needs another round?" Jason asked, standing up. "I need to relieve the cobra."

Everyone but Adam and Claire raised a hand, and Jason gave the thumbs up. "I make no promises on what I bring out."

Chatter broke out among the group. Claire talked to Dave for a while, learning that he was a shift manager at Nick's work and was working his way up to hopefully being manager someday. He had graduated the year before like the rest of the guys and had just signed the lease on a new apartment. Matt and Sam spent most of the time just talking to each other, and Claire made a mental note to ask about that when they went to bed later. Nick played "Take Me Home, Country Roads" five times, each time their singing growing louder and louder so that Claire was sure the mountains themselves were ringing with their off-key vocals.

"Okay, guys. I think we're turning in," Jason said a little while after Dave went to bed, he and Melissa both standing up.

Nick let out a catcall and whistle to which Jason flipped him off, Melissa rolling her eyes and saying good night to everyone.

Claire felt her own head getting heavy too, resting it on Adam's shoulder, his own resting against hers.

"I think I'm getting tired myself," Nick said quietly.

"Yeah," Adam responded. "I think this one's about to pass out."

Nick laughed. "Hit the bottle a little hard tonight, huh?"

Claire vaguely heard them but was too tired to pay much attention to what they were saying.

"I think she's good. Long ride, fresh air, hot tub, campfire . . . just content and happy."

"Best way to be when drinking. No fun getting sick," Nick said to Adam's nod. "How was the hot tub?"

Adam grinned and said, "Very nice."

"Aww yeah," Nick teased.

Adam rolled his eyes, trying not to move too much and disturb Claire. "No. It *was* very nice though. Cozy, warm, and just what the doctor ordered."

"I gotchu," Nick said, holding up his beer and taking a final swig. "Those two seem to be hitting it off," he said, gesturing to Sam and Matt.

"Yeah! Kudos to you," Adam said. "He's a good guy, right?"

"Of course," Nick said. "Sam's a good girl. I feel for her. Wouldn't dream of bringing someone along that was an asshole."

"Good."

They stared into the fire before Nick yelled, "Fitz?" to no answer.

He turned in his seat and repeated, "Fitz!" and heard a mumble. Nick got up to investigate and then said, "Dude's fucking sleeping in the snow."

"For real?" Adam chuckled.

"No joke. I'm going to throw a snowball at him."

Claire began to stir just as the sound of snow smacking a face sounded and an audible "Duuuuuude, where are we?" could be heard.

"Hey you," Adam whispered, looking down at her.

She smiled up at him and said, "Hey."

"Let's get inside," Adam said, kissing her nose.

"Dude, come one," Nick said. "We're all going in. Fire's going out. How are you not freezing your ass off?"

They all went in, Claire waking up from the cold air, disrobed from their snow gear, and in no time all plopped down on their beds in tired stupors ready for a long night's sleep, except for Claire and Sam, who huddled under the blankets to discuss all that had happened with hot tubs and campfires.

"But, like, how do I stop?"

"You can do a couple things, but the easiest way to learn to stop is to do the backward V."

"Backward V?"

"Yeah. You move your legs out to bring the front tips together. Like this." Matt showed Sam what he was talking about while Claire and Adam discussed tactics for making a wipeout less painful. Claire's biggest fear was just falling and tumbling down the mountain in skis and boots and busting her shins. She and Sam had both rented equipment, and she hadn't been expecting the boots to be so hard and stiff.

"Your boots will pop out of the skis if you fall good enough," Adam was telling her. "Trust me. It would be very difficult to fall on the bunny hill and bust yourself up too badly."

"Oh, 'too badly,' he says," Claire returned.

"You'll be fine. I promise."

Their morning had been a nice one of sleeping in, Nick waking up first and making everyone pancakes. They chilled, crammed into the hot tub for a bit, snacked on lunch, and then moseyed on up to the mountain, where the sun was shining and the snow, according to the guy who fitted Claire for her boots and skis, was perfect. All the others hit the slopes immediately while Matt and Adam stayed back to help Sam and Claire get used to their skis and teach them some basics before going downhill. At this point, the only thing left was to put their fears aside and try it firsthand. They headed to the chairlifts, and, after much laughing and screaming, Sam and Claire both managed to get on without issue.

"What happens when we get to the top?" Claire asked, snuggly sitting next to Adam, who had his arm around her and was enjoying the view.

"The hill will rise up to meet your skis, and the chair will be low enough that you'll just sort of glide off. Just have to remember to put your ski tips up."

"So, it won't push me? What if I fall?"

"You'll be fine and will easily be able to get out of the way." Adam smirked.

"This is stressing me out," Claire said. "But I'm having fun."

"Good. And once you do it, you'll be good. It's the unknown that's got you panicking. We'll get to the top, and you'll plop right off, get the feel for going downhill, and you'll love it. I'm sure of it." He kissed the side of her head.

"The view up here is pretty amazing," Claire said, looking around at the fir trees scattered in groups and covered in white fluff. It was like looking down at a Christmas village set.

"It is. This is actually one of my favorite parts of skiing. I love the chairlift. You get to chill, go for a ride, and feel like a bird looking down on the world."

Claire breathed a sigh, letting the image of being a bird flying on the breeze above the snow-covered mountains rest in her mind.

"Here we go," Adam said.

Claire got herself prepped and ready, Adam laughing silently. The mountain met their feet, and just like Adam said, they slid right off and over a little ways before it leveled off, Claire already using the V formation to stop herself from going any further. Sam and Matt managed to get off just as smoothly, and Adam led them all over to the bunny trail.

"Okay, you ladies ready?" Matt asked. "Just remember to use your skis, go slow, and have fun."

Claire and Sam stood side by side. They exchanged a look and a deep breath.

"This bunny hill looks steeper than it should to me. Does it to you?" Sam asked.

"Yeah. Yeah, it does," Claire said. It gradually sloped out in front of them, bending around trees and beyond, which they couldn't see. It didn't look *really* steep, but to go down it attached to what felt like two skinny pieces of wood strapped to their feet, it seemed steep. And right now, a little stupid. Adam and Matt stood on either side of them and started to glide down.

"Ready?" Claire asked.

"Ready," Sam returned. They nodded, knocked knuckles, and pushed forward. Claire couldn't help but giggle and smile through a mixture of nerves, giddiness, and excitement. They both enacted their V shape for most of the trip down, Adam and Matt gliding effortlessly across their paths, occasionally pulling off to the side to let them pass and then following behind them. What looked like a seven-year-old whizzed past them at one point, which made Claire laugh ridiculously loud.

"Oh God. We must look like the biggest losers on this mountain right now," she said loud enough for Matt and Adam to hear too. "Outstripped by children."

Sam started laughing too, and soon enough, they were both releasing the pent-up anxiety that had built in the form of unstoppable giggles. This led to Sam losing control, trying to grab Claire's arm, hitting poles, and both of them tumbling down. Claire felt one boot release from its ski, the other still attached, as she rolled a few turns down the hill, Sam, a mess of poles and skis, behind her. Claire rolled onto her back, spread-eagle, and expelled the biggest laugh yet. She felt the cold winter air enter her lungs with every deep breath and guffaw, Sam joining in too.

"I think you lost something," came Adam's voice as his silhouette blocked the sun above her, holding her ski in his hand, a broad grin across his face. She could hear Matt's laughter in the background.

"That was quite the wipeout, ladies," Matt said.

Adam helped Claire up, and Matt did likewise for Sam.

"Thanks! At least we're skilled at something," Sam said.

"You know what? I think we're good here," Claire said, still trying to catch her breath. "You two feel free to take off and get a few rounds in. I think Sam and I are going to be running at a snail's pace for a few trips."

"They definitely should call this a snail trail. Bunnies are fast, and it doesn't rhyme," Sam added.

"Snail trail. I like it; that's a good one," Claire said.

Adam shook his head, grinning. "You guys sure you're all set? I don't mind sticking around. It's entertaining, to say the least."

"No, no. You go get some skiing in, and we'll work on getting ourselves up to the level of at least getting down the hill without the breaks on."

Adam leaned forward and gave Claire a kiss. "Alright, but if you need us, wait by the chairlifts, and our paths will cross quickly enough."

"Sounds good," Claire responded. "You two be safe out there."

"Right on," Matt said with a laugh. They sped down the hill, Adam turning to get one more smile and to wink at Claire. She was impressed with his skill, cutting the corners and racing Matt. His smile never got old.

"Okay. We ready to try this again?" Sam asked.

"Yes. Let's do this. But let's try to stay to the side. I'm tired of twelve-year-olds glaring at us as they fly around."

They made it to the bottom at which point they participated in their five-step friendship handshake. They attempted the chairlift together and managed to get on all right but landed in a heap at the top of the hill. They were thankfully able to get out of the way quickly so as not to hold up the lift. Nick found them at one point and joined them on the bunny slope, giving them some more pointers, which Claire appreciated. The next trip on the lift, they decided to go separately, which went as smoothly as possible. Claire was getting the hang of the mountain path they repeatedly took and, after five trips, found herself actually allowing her skis to stay straight and gain speed. Sam, too, was getting more comfortable, and after their sixth attempt ended with zero falls or wipeouts and actually getting down quite quickly, they waited for Matt and Adam so as to show them how far they'd come.

Claire saw Adam whizzing down the hill and couldn't help but be amazed as he and what looked like Jason were racing, smiles wide, hitting small jumps and going so fast that it actually made Claire nervous. When they touched down at the bottom, Claire and Sam clapped.

"Wow. I'm impressed," Claire said as Adam drifted toward her, lightly bumping into her.

"Oh yeah?"

"Yeah, for real," she responded. "I didn't know you were a hotshot skier, Mr. Miller."

"Hotshot, huh? You think I'm hot?" He smirked.

"Uh, duh." She grinned.

"So how did it go?" Matt interrupted, asking Sam and Claire about their skiing.

"Well, we were waiting here for you both so we could show you," Sam said.

"Alright, let's do it," Matt said, giving Sam a look that Claire read loud and clear. Matt was quite certainly digging Sam.

They rode the chairlift in pairs again, going down the bunny slope together, the boys both very impressed with Sam's and Claire's progress. The whole group took a break and had an assortment of chicken nuggets, fries, and burgers in the lodge before hitting the slopes again. Sam and Claire ventured to the next difficulty up that was still considered an easy one but was different and so gave them a little bit of a challenge. They enjoyed it immensely, only tumbling a few times. As the evening progressed, and the lights came on, Claire felt an exhilaration at flying down the hills, darkness beyond the beams. After she and Sam did all three of the easy slopes a few times, they decided it was enough risk-taking for one day and simply enjoyed knowing the three slopes well enough to glide down them at top speed. Claire was thrilled with the whole experience, and skiing became top on her list to keep up with. Maybe she could cascade down those big hills with ease someday too.

The crew stopped one more time for hot cocoa and some sweets before taking on the mountain one last time. When they left, the stars were glistening, and they were all ready to warm up and have some drinks.

Back at their lodge, Nick passed around beers, and they all went to sit around the campfire again. Claire was peaceful and content, a day of fresh air feeling good in her soul.

"But I think I take the top for most wins today," Nick said to a conversation that all the guys were having, Melissa, Sam, and Claire discussing where Claire had gotten the new sweater she was wearing but tuning in at these words.

"No way, man. I beat you down that hill plenty of times," Jason said.

"Oh, come on. Not a chance," Nick retorted.

"Duuuudes . . . I totally killed the mountain more than any of you today," Fitz said from his spot on the ground in the semidarkness.

"Fitz, for real?" Nick laughed. "You tumbled down half the mountain each time."

"Got to the bottom the quickest though."

"No. You definitely didn't win."

"I know I'm out," Dave added. "I didn't even do the biggest slope there. That was more than I've ever done."

"Yeah, I'm with Dave here. I know I can't claim most badass skier of this crew. My vote's with Miller," Matt added.

They continued in this way, the girls losing interest, until Adam and Jason were standing up and preparing to go inside and Nick said, "Here we go!"

"What are you guys doing?" Claire asked with a chuckle.

"We're going to see who the badass skier is here," Nick answered. "Miller or Jason."

"And how do you determine that?" Claire mused.

"They're getting their skis and boots, and we're challenging them to an impossible skiing feat."

Claire squinted at him. "And what would that be?"

"Skiing off the roof."

"You're kidding me," Melissa said.

"Nope."

"They're going to ski off the roof?" Claire chuckled.

"Yes, ma'am. Here they come."

Claire rolled her eyes, and Melissa released a nervous laugh. "Are they serious? They're going to kill themselves."

Nick and Fitz built up the stack of wood so that it was higher on one side for Adam and Jason to climb up. Once they were both on the roof, the rest of the group below looking up, Nick threw their skis up to them.

"Okay," Nick yelled. "The winner is whoever can ski down the roof and stick the landing the furthest."

"Oh God," Melissa said.

"Ready. Set. Go!" Nick shouted into the night, his voice echoing behind them as everyone clapped and yelled.

Adam and Jason pushed forward, lifting their knees just at the perfect moment to attempt to get as much distance and air before both of them perfectly landed, the tips of Adam's skis a hair further than Jason's.

"And it's Miller for the win!" Nick rent the air yet again.

"Boom!" Adam said to Jason's laugh.

"Alright, fair and square," he responded.

Everyone was feeling the weight of the day, getting drowsy. Jason and Melissa turned in first, followed shortly by Fitz. Sam and Matt went to hang out in the living room, getting in on the fireplace and warmth after a day in the outdoors. When it was just Nick left with Adam and Claire, he made the decision to head inside himself, though not till they had had a plethora of conversation about anything and everything. Claire loved the ease with which she got along with Adam's friends and recently had even reflected on how quickly they had taken her in as their own, treating her like a friend too. She loved them all, and Nick in particular felt almost like a brother to her, maybe because he reminded her slightly of Troy. Either way, when the conversation died down, he turned in, leaving Adam and Claire to themselves. Claire joined Adam on his chair, and they sat in silence for a while, both soaking in the orange and red flames, the starry sky, the rising mountains around them, and the sudden realization that tomorrow they were heading back to reality.

When they were both feeling their eyes begin to droop, they too headed inside. They found Sam asleep on one couch, Matt on the other, Fitz curled up on the floor in front of the fire like a dog. Adam and Claire kissed good night before heading to bed, Claire putting on her stirrup leggings and baggy sweatshirt and cozying under the quilted comforter that was covered in cardinals and trees and other woodland critters.

She dozed for a while but then found herself awake and staring up at the ceiling, Sam still sleeping in the living room, the clock on the bedside table glowing, telling her it was two in the morning. She sat up, and without even knowing she'd made the decision, tiptoed across the hall, slowly turning the handle of Adam's door and standing in the entryway for a moment. He was sprawled on his back, one arm up around his head, the other resting on his chest. His mouth was slightly open, his glasses still on. He was wearing a gray sweatshirt and had clearly just dropped right into sleep. A radio was playing softly on the bureau, Claire remembering Adam had mentioned once that he couldn't sleep in silence. She lifted the blanket on his bed and shimmied in next to him, lifting his hand off his chest and laying her head upon it instead. Adam adjusted easily, wrapping his arm around her and pulling her to him.

"Everything okay?" he asked sleepily.

"It is now," she responded, hearing her voice vibrate in his chest, his heartbeat in her ears. She looked up, and as though he sensed it, he opened his eyes and saw the look in hers. Claire's own heart raced as she pulled herself higher up, allowing her hand to slowly play with his hair, making her way down his cheek and touching his lips.

"Claire . . ."

She leaned down and kissed him deeply, all her passion unleashing. His arms wrapped tightly around her as their tongues played, their breathing eventually getting heavier, coming up for air occasionally. Adam rolled

Claire onto her back, their lips never leaving each other. Claire took his hand in hers and slid it under her sweatshirt, his warm hand tingling against her bare skin. He moaned, and she felt it in her core.

"Claire," he whispered, looking deep into her eyes as though searching for an answer apart from just her words. "Are—are you sure?"

Claire heard the radio playing the same song that had blared through the house while they'd been in the hot tub the night before. She couldn't shake the pang of it being a sign, and the emotion of something feeling right had never felt more so. She nodded. And she was. She was utterly and unequivocally sure. And Adam could tell. He smiled sweetly and kissed her forehead . . . her nose . . . then her lips and neck.

The early beginnings of sunrise drifted across Claire's face through the thin curtains, morning birds already singing their tunes. She felt the weight of Adam's arm across her middle, holding her close to him, feeling his bare chest against her back. She shifted to face him, taking in his disheveled hair, his eyelashes, his mouth. Sensing her, his eyes opened, and a grin spread across his face.

"Good morning," he whispered.

"Morning." Claire smiled back.

"Sounds like some people are up out there," he said, hearing some clanging in the kitchen. "What time is it?"

"Early," Claire answered.

Adam stretched and then wrapped his arm around her, and they kissed. Claire recalled all that was last night and felt her body tingle with the thought of it.

Pulling apart, Adam looked at her in the way that made Claire feel he was looking into her soul and said, "And how are you feeling?"

Though an odd sounding question, Claire knew exactly what he meant. "I'm feeling good."

"Good." He smiled.

"What about you?"

"Never been better." He grinned, kissing her again. "Breakfast time?"

"Yes. Do you think anyone will notice?" Claire asked vaguely. The last thing she wanted was a series of whistles or jokes as she left Adam's room.

Adam chuckled. "Honestly? Whoever is out there will probably notice. However, they won't say anything. Promise."

"Okay." Claire laughed.

After getting her things on and hitting up the bathroom, she found Nick and Sam in the kitchen, Nick flipping pancakes and Sam at the stool.

"Morning!" Claire said.

"Morning," Nick half whispered back. "Just us up so far. Guess we're the early birds. We don't have to leave for a while, so I figured I'd let people sleep in a *little* bit. Pancakes?"

"Yes please," Claire said. "And coffee if you got it."

"But of course. You're in Chef Nick's kitchen now, remember?"

Claire smirked and made herself a cup while Adam came out to join them.

"Hey," Nick said.

Adam responded with a head nod. "We all that's up?"

"Yup. It is like six in the morning after all." Nick grinned.

"Is it really?" Adam said, looking out the big windows, seeing Fitz lying on the floor.

"Yes, sir."

Adam made himself a cup of coffee as well and snagged a pancake to eat dry while leaning against the sink. Claire had made a plate and was enjoying the warm and fluffy flapjacks, the syrup sweet and the butter melted.

"Sam and I were just talking about how we should make this place a yearly tradition," Nick said. "You know, regardless of where we all end up someday."

"That'd be pretty sick. You think your aunt and uncle would let you rent it out every year?" Adam asked in hushed tones.

"Yeah, I think so. Just have to pick a weekend that they aren't booked, you know, since they give it to me at a discount. All we have to do is leave the place the way we found it."

"Awesome. Yeah, it'd be pretty dope to come back here," Adam said with a grin.

Claire nodded her agreement, mouth full to the brim.

"So what has to be done today before we go?" Adam asked.

"Well, I was actually just making my second cup of coffee to prepare to go outside. The fire pit needs to be shoveled out and the chairs stacked against the house in case of wind. We also have some bottles to pick up. There's a bucket for recyclables. And we have to cut some wood to replace what we used up."

"Right on. Let's get to it," Adam said.

"You got it," Nick said.

Adam gave Claire a kiss atop the head before he and Nick threw their boots and jackets on and, coffee mugs in hand, went out to start doing some of the pickup. Sam watched them, and as soon as the door closed, she turned to Claire with wide eyes and a broad smile.

"Okay, you have some serious talking to do. What happened last night?"

"What do you mean?" Claire asked, eyes snapping up, trying to hold back the giddy smirk that was fighting its way up.

"Oh, shut up," Sam whispered fervently, moving closer to Claire. "You didn't sleep in our room last night. What happened?"

"I could say the same for you." Claire cocked an eyebrow.

"Oh, come off it. We were on separate couches, with Fitz on the floor. Literally were talking one minute and crashed the next. I woke up and went to bed around three, and a certain someone wasn't in our room. Now, I will ask again, what happened last night?!"

Claire stared at her a moment and then ever so slowly broke into a smirk, looking down at her empty plate.

"Oh. My. God!!!" Sam said.

"Shhhhh. Don't wake the house up."

"Oh my god!" she whispered. "Oh my god. For real? Does that smirk mean what I think it means?"

Claire nodded. "But don't make a big deal of it, okay?"

"Not make a big deal?! Claire, this *is* a big deal. I want all the details. Nothing is too small."

"Oh my god," Claire said, eyes rolling, feeling a blush creep up her neck. "Look, I'll answer all your questions, but let's wait till we're back home. There's too many people here and all literally right around us."

"Okay, okay, okay," Sam said. "I get that."

"And," Claire began, "it was a very, very wonderful moment."

Sam got the hint and chuckled. "Okay. I won't make a big cheesy deal out of it, I promise. But I do want to know everything. And . . . how are you feeling about it now? You good?"

Claire beamed with appreciation. "Thank you. And yes. Quite good."

A noise reminiscent of Frankenstein's monster waking to life came from behind them. They turned to see Fitz sitting up, yawning, and blinking in the bright sunlight.

"The great Fitz lives to see another day. Righteous."

Claire and Sam exchanged looks and broke into giggles.

After everyone woke up and had pancakes, Jason and Melissa did the dishes, Claire and Sam helped tidy up, and the rest went outside to finish up the woodcutting. They had a decent amount to replace. Soon enough, and to all of their dismay, they were hitting the road back to reality. Before leaving, Matt asked Adam if he could ride with them and switch with Fitz so he could talk to Sam some more. Adam and Fitz were more than willing to oblige, and so it was Matt and Sam in the back seat, Claire and Adam in front, as they rolled down the driveway. Claire looked in her side mirror at the mountains that seemed to touch the clouds, the lodge, and the vast blue sky and hoped that she'd get to see it again someday.

They passed the time in laughter and singing, Claire throwing her overtired and silly mood into her rendition of Janis Joplin's "Piece of My Heart" while Matt played air guitar and Adam banged around on the dash and steering wheel as the radio was blasted to full volume, Sam playing backup singer. They stopped to grab fast food for lunch and, when they were a half hour from home, fell mostly silent, the weekend and depression of returning settling in. Claire and Adam couldn't help but hide wide smiles, though, when Matt began to address Sam as they got close to Nick's house, where his car was.

"I, um. I just moved into my new place, so I don't have a phone set up yet. I was thinking of getting one of those TracFones, but the place does have a landline. Just gotta get a phone. When I do maybe I could give Nick my number to give to you?" Matt asked rather clumsily.

Sam smiled broadly. "Or I could just give you mine so you can call once that phone gets set up."

Matt returned the smile, saying, "That would be perfect."

When they got to Nick's, Sam scrawled her number out on a napkin and handed it off to Matt. They all said their goodbyes to Nick, Fitz, and Dave, Jason and Melissa having taken their own car and already heading home. Adam dropped Sam off first, Claire whispering an "I'll call you later," before then pulling into Claire's driveway. They both sat in silence for a moment, neither wanting to get out of the car, officially ending what was an amazing weekend.

"Claire. I feel it's important to say that—" Adam started, his cheeks tinting pink, "last night was perfect and quite honestly a moment I will keep forever. But I just want you to know that I still feel the same way I did before. No pressure. No stress. No expectations. And, well, you can talk to me about anything anytime."

Claire ran her fingers through his hair briefly and landed on his cheek, where she held his face for a moment. "Ditto."

He grinned, and they kissed, then got out of the car to greet Claire's excited parents and Troy, who wanted to hear all about the trip.

"Tell me everything. Like, everything."

Sam had bounded over after dinner, Claire's mom asking how they weren't tired of each other yet.

"Well, I don't know what you mean by everything."

"Okay, so how did it start? How did you end up in his room?"

Claire sighed, struggling. It wasn't like she didn't want to tell Sam everything, but actually putting this sort of thing into words was more difficult than she thought.

"We said good night after the bonfire. I woke up in the middle of the night and couldn't sleep and decided I wanted to be with him. So I did."

"That's it?"

"Yeah. Once I was there, I guess things just happened. I sort of knew it might when I went over. I think I was just . . . ready."

"Oh my god, oh my god, oh my god," Sam squealed. "Sorry. Trying not to make a fuss."

The two spent the rest of the evening and well into the night, as Sam was sleeping over to kick off vacation, talking about the weekend as a whole, Sam's excitement about Matt, and if Claire thought he'd call. Claire was happy to take the attention off her and was quite excited for Sam too. Matt seemed like a nice guy, mature, had a life plan, and seemed to really like Sam.

"What about Logan?" Claire asked as they huddled under the covers, still talking well after midnight though they were both exhausted from the trip and had to work the next day.

Sam sighed. "I don't know. I mean, I definitely was interested. But that level of interest and this level feel different somehow. Matt is so much more exciting, and I think we were able to talk so much more easily."

"Sounds like you really do like him." Claire grinned.

"No getting too ahead of ourselves though," Sam said. "We'll see if he calls."

"I have a feeling he will. He wouldn't have requested to ride home with you if he didn't mean something by it," Claire responded.

"Maybe," Sam said, then started giggling.

The week flew by between pulling full shifts at work, going for little rides here and there with Adam, and hitting up the movies or Ron's with the gang when it worked out. The end of the week brought Christmas, and Babs was brought over for the whole day. She was doing a lot better, though she still had a nurse going over daily. Claire and Adam also checked in on her often, and sometimes Sam and Claire went. Claire couldn't help but notice how the injury seemed to have set Babs back a bit. She was hoping that with more therapy she could gain her old strength back, but it was very obvious to Claire that it quite possibly may never come back. Babs's spirit and firecracker personality had not changed, however, and so spending time with her was just as much of a riot as it always was. Adam was going over daily on his own to salt and sand her porch, check her mail, and shovel any snow after storms.

When Claire invited her to Christmas day, they offered her a bed for Christmas Eve too, but she declined, saying she had spent Christmas Eve in her house for too many years to stop now. Claire had a feeling that she liked to listen to Christmas music and do some praying and talking—talking to the ghosts of those who had long passed through the halls around her. It seemed sad to Claire, but she could also see that however sad it may feel, it was necessary for Babs.

Christmas morning, Troy went and picked her up first thing. They had a big breakfast after opening gifts, and Claire left to have Christmas lunch with Adam and his parents, Troy doing the same with Gwen's. Babs took a nap while Claire's parents prepared for Christmas dinner.

By 3:00 everyone was back in the Hanover household, Adam and Gwen along too, and they kicked off the evening by playing a game of charades and opening stockings. They exchanged gifts with the newcomers before sitting down to have a full turkey dinner. Claire felt stuffed to the brim by the time dessert came around. So much delicious food and not enough places to put it all, but she still managed two helpings of her mom's German chocolate cake. When the night was over, Adam and Claire took Babs home and got her situated. When she was all set, Adam took a detour to his spot by the lake before taking Claire back home. They parked and sat in silence for a moment, the moon at a crescent, lightly glistening over the frozen water.

"I have something for you," Adam said after a moment.

Claire looked at him questioningly. He had given her her traditional gift of composition notebooks along with some pens and a few CDs that she'd been wanting. "You already gave me something, silly." She recalled the last time he had given her something special when it was just the two of them, and it had been her ring.

"I know. But I have something else." He pulled from his pocket something that was hidden within his hand. No box. Something small. He opened his hand in front of Claire, and lying across his palm was a small silver locket. Claire picked it up and opened it to see a picture of him inside.

"I know it's cheesy, but," he stumbled. "I just thought . . . I wanted to give you something to keep me close when you—when you leave for school. Wherever that may be. I also know you wear the one from your mom that your dad gave her. I figured you could have your own too. Of us."

"I—" Claire said, though she felt a drop in the pit of her stomach. Was this to remember him by? Was this a goodbye type of gift? She couldn't help but pick up on his word choice: "When *you* leave for school." Was he not going to school, then?

"It's beautiful."

Adam grinned. "Just like you. I'm glad you like it."

Claire smiled but couldn't help showing the weight of what she was thinking. It didn't escape Adam either.

"Everything okay?" he asked, his brow furrowing.

"Yeah, of course. It's Christmas!" Claire faked.

But Adam knew better and couldn't help but see that the necklace was still in her hand. "That doesn't fool me."

She looked at him and met his eyes. Those gray, deep eyes. So handsome and full of so much. She smiled sheepishly. "I just—I love it. It's beautiful. But I can't help but feel that it's a going away gift. And I guess we still haven't really talked about the going away piece and it sounds like I'm the only one going away apparently and so you've made a decision about not going away and that's just new to me and I don't know."

Adam sighed. "I'm sorry. I didn't mean it to come out that way. I just meant that, whatever happens, I wanted you to have something of me."

Claire chuckled. "That still sounds like a going away gift."

"I know. I'm sorry."

"No. Don't say sorry. Tell me what it is."

"I promise, it isn't a going away gift. Regardless of what happens, we may face time apart, and so I wanted you to have something for that."

Claire looked at him and decided she didn't want to have this conversation now. So switched gears. "Look at me. You gave me a lovely and special gift, and I'm bringing everything down."

"No," Adam butted in. "You are not bringing anything down." Adam knew, too, that her words of concern were well placed.

"Well." Claire put on a genuine smile this time. Maybe she was reading too much into this anyway. "Let's start over. Thank you, Adam Miller. This is beautiful." She put the locket around her neck, and she opened it once again, looking down to see the face she loved so much. "It's perfect."

They kissed, and the kissing led to more, and Claire snuck into the back seat, pulling Adam back to join her.

How's It Going to Be

Claire spent the week leading up to New Year's working every day and spending time with Adam and Sam, sometimes the gang as well. They had a particularly fun night at Ron's, where Matt joined in the fun to Sam's great pleasure. Claire enjoyed herself immensely but noticed that with every day closer to returning to school, she was getting a bigger and bigger ball in her stomach.

Walking to school on the first day back, she and Sam talked the whole way about how this was it—the home stretch. Claire found herself heavy, sighing often to release the stress that was slowly settling in her chest. She was anticipating hearing from colleges over the next couple months and knew that when it happened, she needed to make some major decisions, and those decisions would be based on some major conversations that she was nervous about having. All that put aside, the school days were fine, her work load being light and her classes fairly easy. Claire found she was enjoying herself in band and chorus, getting ready for their spring and, for Claire, final concert. She and Sam both worked most days after school, and Claire would visit Babs when she could as well.

The biggest surprise came a few weeks after the start of term when Sam and Claire were heading out the door and Amber called out to her.

"What does she want?" Sam asked with disgust.

"No idea," Claire said, rolling her eyes, walking toward her anyway. Amber was standing by herself, Lauren, Chris, and Mark off to the side, talking and so Sam too hung back.

"What?" she asked in a dull tone when meeting Amber.

Amber crossed her arms, the permanent scowl on her face a sight to behold. "I wanted to tell you that I talked to my mom."

Claire was surprised by this statement and waited for Amber to continue.

"She seemed upset at first, but I did what you said. I was honest and told her how I was feeling and about wanting to go to my dad's. She eventually listened, and, well, she felt bad. She's since tried slowing down on the drinking and, at the very least, has not had any men over at all. And—" Amber looked down at the ground. "She put us both in counseling. I think it's really working for her. And me, I guess." She ended so quietly that Claire barely heard it.

"Amber, that's great," Claire said, quietly as well.

"Yeah, well. I just thought I'd tell you. And . . . well . . . thanks."

Claire couldn't believe her ears. "Yeah. Of course. And I really am happy for you, Amber. You know I never wanted to not be your friend."

Amber stared at her, and Claire saw a flash of what she could only hope was warmth toward her. It went away quickly, but Claire saw it nonetheless.

Amber quickly switched gears and said, "I also told the guys that I was planning to tell you that you are crowding our locker and to butt out, so if you could act pissed at me when you walk away, that'd be great. And I know you and Levinski are, like, best friends and all, but if you haven't already told her about all this, could you not?"

Claire wanted to say that the two of them could have been best friends all these years too if she hadn't gotten so jealous of *Levinski*, but it wasn't the time or place, and quite frankly, everything about Amber and her situation spoke a lot as to why Amber had made that choice all those years ago. "I haven't and I won't."

They each nodded before Claire put on a scowl, rolled her eyes, turned on her heel, and stormed toward Sam, quickly telling Sam that Amber was a bitch and it was more locker drama before continuing to act angry for a little ways down the road in case anyone was still watching. Claire held true to her word and never told Sam what had happened.

"So, has Adam talked at all about applying for schools?" Sam asked as they reached Claire's house.

Claire sighed. "Nope. I feel bad asking because I don't want to put pressure on him, but it's getting really late to apply for this fall's semester, and . . . well, it'd be nice to know what he wants to do, ya know? To, I don't know, plan stuff."

"I hear you. Have you even tried to bring it up?"

"No. But I think it's time to." Claire sighed once again, grabbing food and walking up to her room. "I just wish things could stay the same. I'm so excited for college and getting out on my own. I just wish this was coming with less stress right now."

"What are you so worried about?" Sam asked, plopping down in her usual spot.

"What it's going to do to our relationship," Claire said without even thinking, sitting on her bed. Once it was said, though, she knew how right it was.

"What, like break you up?" Sam asked, surprised.

Claire shrugged. "Yeah. I guess."

"Claire. No way," Sam said. "You guys are, like, meant to be. Why do you think something like college would do that?"

"It does that to a lot of people, Sam. What if it just complicates things so much that we fall apart? I don't think he would just randomly dump me before I leave, but what if the stress of long distance just becomes too much? I'm a planner. I want to know these things. I want to know where he wants to go and what he wants to do. And what it all means for us."

"You do realize what that means, right? What you're asking of him?"

Claire looked at Sam quizzically.

"You are essentially asking him to tell you if he wants to be with you forever. Like marriage and life ever after. I know that sounds like a great thing to know and hear, but that is an exceptionally big thing to ask of someone. Especially at our age."

"Goodness, Sam. I'm not asking about marriage!" Claire squeaked.

"Aren't you though? In a way? You want him to plan a future with you. You want him to tell you if he's going to follow you across the country, and what? Move in with you? Live together? Or if he'll go to college too so you can make plans on what you're going to do about it?"

Claire thought about what Sam said and tried to put her feelings into clearer words. "I just want to know what's going on in his mind. I can tell he's holding something back and I don't know what it is and that bothers me. I'm not sure if he's holding back on his real plans for college or if he's holding back on his opinion of what I'm going to do. It seems like he's worried about something, which makes me worried, and I don't know what to do. Asking about applying to colleges seems like a sensitive subject to him, which I don't like, and it makes me feel like the plan I thought we were kind of going with isn't the plan at all, and I don't want the carpet pulled right from under my feet."

"But what do you honestly think is the worst case scenario here? You go to school far away, he stays in Thompson Falls, and what? He breaks up with you for someone close by? Because you know that wouldn't happen, no more than you would fall for another guy while away. It just wouldn't. You know that."

Claire looked down and felt tears burn in the corners of her eyes. "Maybe I don't want to go far away if he's going to stay in Thompson Falls. Maybe I want to stay here with him and go close by. If he's going to go to school, maybe I want to go near him. I don't want to be apart. Is that so bad?"

Sam understood. "Oh, Claire. No, it isn't." Sam left her spot to join Claire on the bed. She draped an arm around her. "I think we've all been so focused on telling you to go where you want to go and base it off nothing but your gut that nobody has thought about just how much you love this boy. And that gut might be with him."

Claire managed to say what was really bothering her about Adam's silence. "I just feel like I'm alone in feeling that way. That I'm the only one who wants to put us first, and that's a lot."

"All of this is a lot," Sam said. "College, leaving home, growing up, relationships, the future, being on our own, the unknown . . ."

Claire began to cry, tears silently streaming down her face. There was so much more she couldn't even put into words, and all she managed to do was lay her head in Sam's lap as Sam brushed stray strands of hair away from Claire's face, the two of them both feeling the weight of all that was to come.

Assemblies and spirit weeks were more fun as a senior. Mark and Claire chatted often in homeroom class, which brought Amber and the others over, and it seemed that the group could be a group again, except this time the tension wasn't there. Maybe it was because they were seniors and had realized how petty those things were, or because Amber and Claire had had a moment together that had brought them just a hair closer. But regardless, it felt good to have this for the last part of her high school career. Her teachers seemed more lax with all of them, and Claire had a few meetings with the guidance office in preparation for college planning. Claire and Adam squeezed in as much as they could, having many fun late nights by the lake in the back seat of his Saab. On one of those nights, Claire and Adam were sitting snuggled up, listening to Tom Petty, when Claire decided to push again.

"Can I ask you something?" she said tentatively.

He adjusted himself to be able to look down at her. "Of course. You don't have to ask."

Claire sat up so she could face him directly. "Well, I ask because this topic seems to be of a sour kind for you, and I just want to make sure."

Adam looked at her questioningly. "Okay. Well, you can always talk to me, Claire."

"Right. Well, I don't know how to ask without just flat-out asking, so that's what I'm going to do. Know that I ask only out of genuine care and curiosity, not judgment."

Adam felt his pulse quicken but nodded his understanding as he sat up to face her better.

"Have you applied to any colleges yet? Do you plan to? I know the deadline for a lot of schools is soon, for this fall admission anyway and you haven't talked to me about it at all and, well, I just feel that we always tell each other everything and I just don't know where you're at with this."

Adam's pulse quickened even more, and he felt his heart in his throat. He knew this was going to come up sooner or later and was stupidly just waiting until it did, but even now he didn't know what to say.

"Well," he started, but the words didn't come.

Claire waited, but then said, "Do you want to go to school?"

He sighed. "Yes, I do. I'm just . . . I'm not sure I'll get into the schools I was looking into and so was thinking that I should just apply to the local community college, but I don't know."

"What makes you think you won't get into the schools you want to? And what does it hurt to apply?"

Adam looked out the window. Truth is, he had applied to the schools. Both. He had applied to Wentworth and MIT. He knew those were up there and hard to get into. He knew he'd had decent grades and had done a lot at school to fill a resume for a computer degree, but still. They were hard. He hadn't told Claire for a few reasons. For one, he was nervous about them. He hadn't even told his friends. He had never had much confidence in himself when it came to school due to some really rough years when he was young. Sharing about applying to schools like MIT made him feel that people would immediately laugh, thinking he was way out of his league.

He knew Claire would never. He knew Claire would actually go the exact opposite way and have so much confidence in his getting in that his second reason for not telling her was the fear of admitting he didn't get in. He loved how positive and sure she was about his abilities. She made him feel so special. But that also made him feel like he'd be a major letdown if he failed. He knew this was all brought on by himself, but, again, it couldn't be helped.

One of the biggest reasons he hadn't told her was because, regardless of getting in or not, he saw in Claire's eyes a deep and mature love that scared him. He loved her just as much and just as deeply, but he feared, in fact felt he knew, Claire would base her college decision on him. She would go where he went, and he didn't want her to. He wanted her to make her decision solely on her because Claire was his everything. Claire deserved the world. And he didn't want to be what held her back. He couldn't be what held her back.

"It's fine; we can just talk about this later," Claire said.

Adam came to and saw that Claire looked quite emotional and embarrassed, starting to climb back into the front seat.

"Claire, wait. Wait." He grabbed her and gently pulled her back. "I'm sorry. It just isn't an easy answer."

"How?" Claire asked. "Don't you want to be together? Don't you want to figure this out?"

"Of course I want to be together," Adam said quietly.

"Well, then why can't you talk to me about this? Maybe we can make a plan that keeps us close to each other. Maybe this could all work out perfectly. Whether you want to stay here or go to school, maybe we can make something work. Don't you want at least an idea of what we're up against? Whether that's long distance or not? Or . . ." she trailed off.

There it was. The "we" in her statement was exactly what he feared. It was Claire offering to alter her path to possibly be near him. His own mind was such a mess that he couldn't possibly bring her along if he wasn't even sure what the hell he was doing.

Claire took his moment of thought as a cue that it wasn't a good sign. She threw the door open and got out.

"Claire! Wait," Adam said, throwing his own door open. "Where are you going?"

Claire started walking away. She was miles from home but couldn't help it. She needed to get out. Needed to breathe. Needed to let the tears fall, cold on her cheeks.

Adam caught up with her. "Claire, please."

"I don't want to talk anymore," she said.

"Claire, come on," Adam said. "Just stop. Please."

His tone crushed her, and she stopped.

"Thank you. Look, I love you. So incredibly much, okay? And that, as well as wanting to be together, is never a question. I can't imagine life without you."

Claire looked at him, her eyes still filled but trying desperately to not let the tears fall, her arms crossed tight around her like a protective barrier.

"You have to believe me about that at least," he said.

Claire didn't answer right away but kicked the ground a little before sighing. "I do believe you."

"My mind—it just has a lot going on in it right now, okay? I need you to trust me that I promise to talk to you about all of it when I have it sorted for myself."

Claire wanted to be stubborn and insist they talk now, but she knew that what he was asking wasn't a ridiculous request.

"Okay," she said finally.

Adam's shoulders dropped, a small ounce of relief coming to him. "And please, Claire, know that, regardless, I will never not want to be with you."

Though it wasn't a clear-cut plan, or any plan at all for that matter, the words were enough to warm Claire's heart and at least give her some sense of security in moving forward.

"But you better really mean that promise," she said.

"I do. Cross my heart," he said, making the hand motion.

Claire stared for a moment before dropping her arms in defeat and giving him a smile.

"Now, can we get back in the car? And let me drive you home? I'm afraid you'll still attempt to ditch me out here."

Claire rolled her eyes and chuckled. "Let's go."

Adam grinned, and they walked back hand in hand.

HOW'S IT GOING TO BE

As March approached, every day that passed, Claire checked the mail, or asked if anyone else had, filled with anxiety and excitement. And finally, at the end of the month, it happened.

Claire was sitting at the kitchen table, having a snack and reading the local section of the newspaper, when her dad came home from work. She heard him come in and kiss her mom on the cheek, and then they both entered the kitchen. Claire didn't look up until a letter fell down in front of her, covering the story of Thompson Falls trying to expand the library.

It was a white envelope addressed to her, with an officially labeled return address. It was the college in Arizona. Her first letter. She looked up at her parents, who were looking back with broad smiles that carried a hint of anxiety as well. Claire looked back down and picked up the envelope. She stood up and slowly opened it, pulling the folded packet from within. The guidance office had said that if it was thick, it was probably a good sign, seeing that it only takes one piece of paper to tell someone they didn't get in but a whole bunch to offer them a spot and a return packet to fill out.

She took a deep breath and unfolded the papers. She looked at her dad, who gave her a nod, before looking down at the first lines of the letter. Her eyes grew big as she read.

"Well?!" her mom burst out.

"I—I got in," Claire said simply.

"All right, Claire-a-belle!" her dad said. She hadn't heard that nickname in years. "Your first acceptance letter!" They both went around the table and looked over her shoulder to read the rest of the letter.

She was accepted into their English and writing program, and a packet with a return envelope was made available for Claire's response. She couldn't believe it. It was happening. She couldn't help but feel a pang in her heart regardless of the excitement playing in her belly. She called Sam immediately, and they shared in an excited squeal session. When she went to call Adam, she hesitated. Arizona . . . it was across the country. It wasn't like she was accepting it, but it was still exciting that she got in. It was now a contender and a possibility. Going cross-country did seem exciting after all.

"Hey," she said when Adam came on the phone.

"Hey! What's up?"

"I was wondering if you wanted to come over and hang out for a bit? I have some exciting news to tell you."

"Sure!" he said enthusiastically, though there was a hint of nerves, almost expecting what this exciting news was. "I have to help cover an evening shift, but I can come over for a little bit."

Claire was pacing in her room when she heard Adam talking to her mom downstairs before his footsteps made their way up and he walked into her room, broadly grinning regardless of the anxiety that was settling in his stomach.

"Hey!" he said, sitting down on her bed.

"Hi," Claire said, stopping her pacing but remaining standing by her desk where the letter gleamed up at her.

"For having some exciting news, you don't sound excited."

Claire looked at him and then placed a smile on her face. "Sorry. I'm just a little nervous about it all!"

"What's up?"

"Well. I got my first letter," she said tentatively.

"No way! And?" Adam asked, though he was quite sure what was coming.

Claire couldn't help but genuinely smile this time. "I got in!"

Adam jumped up and gave her a hug. "Congratulations, Claire. I had zero doubts. Which school is it?"

"The one in Arizona," she said, losing the gusto that had come so quickly.

Adam pushed aside the drop that had just occurred in the pit of his stomach. "That's awesome!"

"Yeah? You think so?" Claire asked.

"Of course it is," Adam responded. "Why wouldn't it be? You want to get into the schools you applied to, don't you?" He chuckled lightly.

Claire laughed half-heartedly. "Yeah, no, of course I do. It's just—"

"What?" Adam persisted.

"Well, it's just so far away," she said, looking at him.

"Yeah. But think about how cool it will be to go across the country. Arizona is nothing like New England. You'll get to see so much and experience even more."

Claire nodded. She wasn't sure what she wanted to hear, but his enthusiasm for her being thousands of miles away wasn't doing it for her for some reason. "I still have two other schools to hear from, so we'll see what they say."

"I'm sure you'll get into those too," Adam reassured her.

"Deciding will be the big moment, huh?" Claire said, trying to hit upon the thing that was nagging at her most.

"Yeah, it will be. Lots to consider. But I know you'll be able to weigh the pros and cons and follow your heart for the best fit," he said, rubbing her shoulders and kissing her forehead.

Claire sighed. "Thanks," was all she managed to say. And for the first time ever, she felt an awkward tension in the air between them. She just wanted to shout at him to tell her he didn't want her to go all the way to Arizona. That it would devastate him. Or that he'd follow her. But she didn't want him to do that either if it wasn't where he wanted to be. She wanted him to tell her what he was thinking and what he wanted. But he had promised he would, and she had agreed. As the anxieties grew and the end of the school year drew closer, it was harder to keep those emotions down. And with moments like these, believing that they were going to be together forever felt a little unclear, and that terrified Claire.

"Well, I don't want you to be late for work," she said.

Adam felt the shift in her tone and knew he was the reason for it. "I don't work for a little bit. I can still hang out."

"I actually have some work to do. A lot of reading this year for English. I just wanted to share the good news in person."

"Yeah, of course," Adam said, hearing the dismissal. "I'm glad you did. I'll just head out and let you work."

"Thanks," Claire said, feeling torn between just wanting him to stay anyway and wanting to be alone.

"Yeah," he said with uncertainty. "Well, bye." He gave her a hug, and they shared a kiss before he left.

Claire slumped down and groaned once he was gone.

Claire loved the smell of spring. The trickling little streams that crept down every road, tumbling over rocks that had been kicked up by snowplows all winter. The birds sang, things began to bud, and even though life was getting more and more busy, with talk of graduation on the horizon, senior prom, and people making college decisions, Claire couldn't help but feel a sense of calm when taking a deep breath of the fresh air on her way to school.

HOW'S IT GOING TO BE

She and Sam walked through the doors and passed the new chart that had been posted outside the office. It showed seniors who had been accepted and the college they would be attending. It seemed that almost every day at least one new name was put up there. Claire had since been accepted to another of her three schools—the state school that was nearby.

She was super excited and was now anxiously awaiting news from the last one. The one in Boston. It was three hours away, making her college choice either next door, a decent drive, or across the country. She knew her decision was going to be based on money, the program itself, and the campus, but the location was the part that was bothering her, as it was the part that she wanted Adam's opinion on. She didn't want him to help her choose or anything, but she wanted to hear his thoughts. She wanted to know what they were going to do based on her choice, and that conversation wasn't happening.

When she had been accepted to her second school, she called him to tell him, and he showered her with the genuine happiness and congratulations that she appreciated, but the conversation once again ended there. She wondered if he noticed she had called him rather than having him come over in person. She hadn't done it on purpose, but in the moment didn't feel like having another moment like the first one. It gave her anxiety and fear of the future and their relationship, and that was something she couldn't handle at all amongst school, work, and everything else. She often wondered if she was distancing herself out of fear. And then that scared her too. She told herself that when she had an answer from the three schools, then she would face the music and have the conversation, so for now, she was lying low and playing it cool.

But that didn't last long. Claire got home from school on a warm day in April and checked the mail on her way inside. She was going to Ron's with Sam and Adam and the crew later, so she was going in to get ready.

TRULY MADLY DEEPLY

Shuffling through the envelopes, seeing bills and junk mail, she stopped on the top step at the sight of an official looking letter whose return address was labeled quite clearly in an embossed and printed emblem. The final school . . . Boston.

She ran inside and called out to the house, but nobody was home yet. She paced the kitchen, wondering if she should open it, but the thought of being alone when she learned she was either accepted or not was terrifying. Both Adam and Sam were working, and so instead, she ate a snack and tried to distract herself with homework and music in her room, to no avail. The moment she heard the door open and close, she rushed back downstairs to find her mom walking in with groceries. Claire helped her unload and put food away, and when her dad walked in, she couldn't contain it.

"Finally!" she burst out.

"Claire, hunny, what is it?" her mom asked, surprised at her outburst.

Claire pulled out the folded envelope from her sweatshirt pocket. She held it up, and her parents' eyes went round.

"Open it!" her mom said excitedly. "Oh, all of this is like Christmas coming over and over again every few weeks!"

Claire grinned and slowly opened the envelope. Like déjà vu, she pulled out the thick packet of paper, unfolded it carefully, and saw the first line shining up at her.

"I got in!" Claire said. "I got in!" She jumped up and shouted it. This school was her reach school, the one that was a private school and competitive and potentially out of her league, but she got in.

"Oh my gosh!!" her mom exclaimed, giving her a big hug.

"Congratulations," her father followed.

"I need to call everyone!" she said.

"We knew you could do it," her mom said. "Now to decide which one you want to go to."

Claire felt the balloon in her stomach pop. Yes. Now she had to decide which one she wanted to go to. It was finally that time. She couldn't put it off any longer.

She decided she was going to share the news at Ron's when Sam and Adam were both there with the rest of her friends. She was just as excited to know for sure what her options were as she was about actually getting into all of them. A toast, some pizza, and laughter was just what she needed. And perhaps after, she and Adam could talk. It had to happen.

Before Claire took off, Troy stopped by the house. This was always a pleasant surprise. But due to the decent drive from the base, it was always met with question when it wasn't a normal visit, like Sunday dinners. This time was no different.

"Troy!" their mother said excitedly, getting up to give him a hug. "What brings you here tonight?"

"I have some good news," he said, beaming.

They all perked up from their spots in the living room.

"I have officially purchased a home." They all stared in surprise. "Like a real house. I own land and a house. Just signed the papers."

"Oh my gosh, Troy!" their mother shouted. "Where?"

Troy's smile was plastered on his face. "About halfway from here to the port. In Lanchester. It's a small cape, three bedrooms, two baths, and about three acres. Gwen's commute to the nursing home will only be about forty-five minutes, which isn't much different than it is now, and there is even a really nice new facility close by that she may apply to. It's all done."

"When can we see it?" Claire asked excitedly.

"Sunday! I'll meet you guys there if you're around."

"Of course we are!"

Troy continued to talk to them about the house and all it had, at one point stopping mid-sentence to rush Claire with a congratulatory hug about the college news.

At 6:00 Claire left them to walk down to Ron's to meet everyone. She wondered if she should bring an umbrella, as rain was in the forecast, but rain never bothered her anyway. When she walked into Ron's and saw Adam, she beamed, not able to contain the flip she still felt every time she was with him. It was all the more reason why she was subconsciously distancing herself, her brain needing to protect itself from all the anxiety the conscious Claire was putting it through.

She slid into the booth next to Adam, and he draped an arm around her, kissing her.

"Feels like we never see each other anymore," he said quietly. "I love you."

She felt her heart break a little, though she couldn't pinpoint why. "I love you too."

Nick and Sam were already there, and the rest showed up shortly after. When they ordered pizzas and drinks to go around, Claire cleared her throat and said, "Alright, everyone, I have some news."

They all quickly stopped what they were doing and looked at Claire.

"Today I received my last letter. From Boston." She could feel Adam shift next to her. "And I have officially been accepted to all three of my schools!"

The shouting that ensued was huge. It made people in the other room look over. They clinked glasses, and Claire laughed, allowing herself to be excited about this.

"Go, Bohemian!" Fitz yelled.

The talking settled in volume but, of course, continued to revolve around college and Claire's options. Sam, who was sitting on her other side, gave her a hug and a squeal. And finally, Claire looked at Adam, who was smiling. His genuine, happy, beautiful smile. But tonight it didn't quite match his eyes like it usually did. His eyes said something else.

"I'm so proud of you," he said to Claire.

"Thank you. I hope you don't mind I told everyone at once. I knew you were working and the first time I'd get a chance to see you was here."

"Not at all," he said. "I'm happy. I love seeing you this excited."

Time spent with friends was entertaining and enjoyable as always. At one point, Claire couldn't help but look around as the noise rose around her. At Sam, giggling animatedly at Fitz's backward-hat-clad face telling one of his amusing stories. At Jason with his arm around Melissa, shaking his head at everything Fitz said. At Nick, who kept cutting into Fitz's story to tell what really happened, every third word a curse. At Adam, eyes crinkled as he laughed along with the rest. She didn't want to lose this. How could college compare? She was hit with a rush of sadness. Of nostalgia. Of heat. Her face felt warm. She felt like she was there but not, like she was someone else watching this night unfold.

"Are you okay?" she heard Adam whisper in her ear.

"Yeah, I—" She felt her heartbeat quicken, a flush pump through her body, almost feeling dizzy. "No. I think I need some fresh air."

Adam tapped Sam on the shoulder from behind Claire, and she scooted out, Claire following. Adam grabbed her hand and walked with her out the side door. Claire felt the cool air flow across her face and breathed in as deeply as she could, counting herself down. The light mist felt good. It grounded her. She stood like that for a few moments.

Adam's hand lightly brushed her arm, rubbing up and down. "You okay?" he asked after a little while.

"Yeah, I'm good."

"You sure?" he asked tentatively.

"Yeah," she said vaguely to his stare. She shook her head, already feeling her heartbeat lower to normal, the warmth subsiding. "Yes. I am fine," she said more firmly.

"Okay," Adam responded, though he still seemed unsure. "Claire—"

"We should get back inside. I don't want them to worry," Claire said with a smile.

Adam nodded, and back in they went. The evening didn't last much longer, and soon enough, Sam and Claire were walking home, Sam having come straight from the library, which was right on Main Street, and so Claire offered to join her.

"So, all three schools, huh?"

"Yeah," Claire responded.

"Any thoughts on them?" Sam questioned further.

"I actually haven't thought much. I was so focused on just hearing from them." Claire did have a feeling she knew which she was leaning toward, but she needed to have another conversation first.

"I bet!" Sam said. "I hope my letter comes soon. I only applied to the one, other than the community college, which I already know I'm in, so I'm kind of counting on it." She chuckled. Sam had been torn between going to college right off or taking a year and working like Adam had. She liked the idea of not having college debt right away and saving up money. Never having much of her own, it was appealing. So she applied to one school for social work and figured if she got in, then it was meant to be, and if not, she'd take core courses locally while working.

"I think you will," Claire said with a smile.

Sam could sense her friend's mindset, and they finished their walk in silence. When they got to Claire's house, Sam stopped before heading further to her own. "Are you talking to him soon?"

Claire sighed. "He's supposed to be coming over tomorrow anyway. I'm going to talk then."

Sam nodded. "Good luck."

The next day, it was pouring. Claire called Adam's house to make sure he was still coming over.

"Hey, Mrs. Miller, is Adam home?" Claire asked. She heard Adam's mom's sweet voice call up for him, the shuffle of the phone upstairs getting picked up, and then Adam's voice.

"Hey you," he said. "What's up?"

"Hey! You still plan on coming over?"

"Yeah! I just got to eat something real quick. I'm starving. Anxious to see me?"

"Always am," Claire said with a half laugh. "Just wanted to make sure."

"Well, my lady, I'll be over in twenty minutes or so."

"Okay, cool," Claire responded.

They hung up, and suddenly Claire felt her throat tighten, the butterflies in her stomach taking flight. She once again paced around her room, and when she heard him lightly knock on her door, she couldn't help but swallow a feeling of nausea.

"We meet again," Adam said, smiling and walking right in but quickly picking up on her nervous stance. "Everything okay?"

"Yeah. Um. We need to talk," she said. The words came out sounding more dire than she intended, but she was nervous.

Adam slowly sat on her bed. "Sure. Yeah, of course." He was kind of expecting this but certainly wasn't ready and was still hoping it wasn't what he thought.

Claire heaved a sigh, shook her hands in nervousness, and sat next to him. "So I got into Boston."

"Yes," Adam said. "A really great thing too." He smiled.

"Yeah, it is. Really great," she said, but her face fell.

"Then why do you seem like it isn't?"

"Well, because I want to talk about it with you and that seems to be a struggle and I don't know if I'm supposed to but I need to and I'm nervous."

Adam sighed sadly. "Claire, I'm sorry if I've added any more stress to you."

"You don't need to apologize. Look. I have three options: Arizona State, the university here, or Boston. I want to know what you think. I—I need to know what you think."

Adam paused for a long moment while Claire's heart was at risk of jumping right out of her chest.

"Claire, I want you to go to the school that you want to go to. I want you to follow whatever dream you have and not look back."

Claire looked at him and felt all the stress that she'd been carrying and holding flush forward. All the anxiety. The fears and worries. She could tell that her brain wasn't working properly anymore. She wanted answers. She wanted to figure things out. This was her future. She was a planner. This was whom she loved and who was supposed to love her in return, and she couldn't keep doing this circular-thinking game of uncertainty. "That's it?" she said rather aggressively.

"What do you want me to say?" Adam said.

"Well, I want you to say how you feel, but is that all you have to say? That you want me to follow my dreams and not look back?"

"Claire, I want you to make your own decision and go wherever you want to go."

"And that doesn't matter to you? Where I go doesn't matter at all?"

"Wha—? What do you mean?"

"I want to know what you think, Adam!"

"You want me to tell you where I think you should go to school?"

"Yes! I want to know what you think I should do! Where should I go! What matters to you!" Claire said loudly, losing her cool. Her heightened emotions in combination with her irritation and absolutely aggravating inner turmoil were making the thoughts in her own head all jumbled. Of course she didn't want him to tell her what she should do, but that wasn't coming to her mind at all in the moment. She wanted him to talk. To speak. She wanted to hear words of desire and need for her and to be with her.

"I won't do that. I'm not going to place that kind of pressure on myself or you. It's not my call. It's yours and yours alone. I just want you to be happy."

Claire stood up and walked toward her desk. Walking gave her something to do. "Well, thank you, oh gallant gentleman, but I think I can handle my happiness on my own."

Adam stood up too. "Okay, then what do you want my opinion for?" Adam felt his face flush. He was, with quite a bit of difficulty, trying to hold down his own fears and emotions. He knew exactly what Claire wanted to hear, but he refused to do that, to give that to her. He refused to let her base a decision that would affect the entire course of her life on him. It wasn't fair to either one of them.

He was scared. He had never felt good enough for Claire. *She* had never given him that impression; he had given it to himself. Since he'd met her, he'd found her perfect and could never believe that he was with her, that he was so lucky to have her. She was now accepted into some great schools, and he couldn't bear the idea that she was going to pick one based on little Thompson Falls Adam Miller. He had let his self-consciousness get in the way of his thinking and cloud his mind, bringing fear of other things too, like if she would meet people who were more on par with her in college. A guy who was well versed in literature and wrote well and was a perfect Mr. Darcy. So many fears that his mind shut down, which was never a good thing.

"If you can handle your own happiness, then you can handle your own decisions. What do I have to do with any of this?"

Claire couldn't believe he asked that. To her, he had everything to do with this. His saying that hurt. Big time.

"Because your opinion matters to me! And rather than being so caught up in my happiness, why not put that energy into your own happiness?!"

"What is that supposed to mean?"

"Why haven't you applied to schools? What are *your* plans? What are you and I or *we* doing, Adam!?!"

"Sorry that I don't have a 4.0 GPA that will get me into any school I want."

Claire's face contorted. "So it's my fault that I want to go to school and make something of myself?"

"Is going to school the only way someone can make something of themselves? News flash, Claire, I guess you're dating a screwup."

"I never said that!" she practically shouted.

"No, but you might as well have."

"Why are you being so difficult?! Clearly, you don't want to make plans with me. Because you don't seem to care where I go to school, or how far away I am. Apparently, you don't care at all." Claire breathed heavily, her face reddening, all reason gone.

"Claire," Adam said sternly, but Claire wasn't having it. She wanted to throw everything she thought she could right now. They were both shooting from the hip, lost in a world of emotions and fear.

"So what was I?! Huh?" Claire asked. "What was I to you? Just a high school fling? Someone who's around and easily accessible?! And now that I'm ready to take a HUGE step in my life, you're pulling back! Not wanting to actually take a serious step with me!"

"Claire, come on. I didn't sa—"

"You're not even taking yourself seriously! You could get into any college you want to, Adam. You are a well-rounded, smart, and savvy guy who either doesn't see that for himself or maybe doesn't even want it. But what do I know? You don't talk to me about it! Maybe I just wanted to know that my being across the friggin' country would mean something to you. Maybe be tough for you. Maybe even trigger you to come with me! But clearly I was wrong. Clearly, Claire Hanover isn't anywhere in Adam Miller's future plans! Because he has 'nothing to do with this' apparently!!" she shouted.

"Claire—"

"Just go!!" Her chest heaving, she felt the burning in her eyes and didn't want him to see it.

"Come on—"

"Go. I'm done. We're done. It's all done. All this. I should have known it was too good to be true. Happy now? You don't have to worry about me asking any questions or pushing or nagging about your plans. I'll make my own and not worry about anyone else but myself. Sounds like that's what you want."

"Claire." Adam's face had gone pale.

Claire felt the hot tears coming. She was angry, she was hurt, she was frustrated, she was scared, and she was just ready to have all this go away.

And to her very clouded mind, these mixed feelings were from Adam, so she was done with it all. It was just easier than dealing with it.

"Go," she shot with venom.

Claire's mom knocked lightly on her door and opened it. "Claire? Is everything okay? I heard yelling."

"Everything's fine. Adam was just leaving."

Adam looked at her in anguish, his own eyes glossy, but he turned on the spot, internally telling himself this was probably for the best. For Claire. She'd do and get better.

He said, "Bye, Mrs. Hanover," and left.

Claire's mom watched him leave in shock and then looked to Claire.

"Claire? What's going on?"

Claire threw her closet door open, grabbed her hooded sweatshirt, and pushed past her mom.

"Claire!" her mom yelled after her. And then, not knowing what else to say, added "Claire, it's raining out!"

Claire stepped outside into the warm spring rain. It was a light rain as she walked toward Sam's house, but by the time she reached the front path, it was pouring again. Claire welcomed it. It hit her face hard and camouflaged the tears that were flowing freely. Claire knocked on the door, and thankfully, Sam answered.

"Hey! What are you doing out in thi—" Sam stopped mid-question, taking in Claire's limp hair, red eyes, sopping wet clothes, and the rain falling all around her.

"Claire, what happ—"

"We broke up," Claire said simply, her voice cracking, her face contorting with the sobs that were coming.

"What? Oh my god! Uh, hang on, let me grab my coat."

Sam vanished for a moment and returned with a rain jacket.

"No, Sam, it's fine," Claire mumbled through more tears, not really knowing what she was saying. "It's pouring out and—"

"What, the rain is good enough for you but not for me?" she said, throwing the coat around her shoulders and closing the door behind them. "Come on. Let's walk."

Claire and Sam didn't speak their entire walk, which Claire appreciated. They simply walked. Claire didn't know for how long, but she knew at one point that it was getting late and her mom would worry.

Returning home, she walked into the house, clothes dripping with water. Her shoes squelched as she took them off, and she stood for a moment, not knowing what to do.

"Claire?" her dad said quietly, walking into the entryway.

Claire looked at her dad and saw on his face that he knew. That her mom had told him what she'd witnessed and that they'd put two and two together, and he knew. Claire's face screwed up as the tears fell and her breathing became sharp.

"Oh, Dad," was all she got out before her dad caught her in all her dankness and held her tight while she loudly sobbed into his chest.

Foolish Games

The following morning, Claire woke with swollen eyes and the briefest of moments in which she forgot why they were, until it all came crashing back: the opposite of the sweet relief when waking from a nightmare, when reality is the nightmare. She rolled over, and without even caring that it was mid-morning, that she wasn't at school, or that no one had come in to wake her, she closed her eyes and forced herself to go back to sleep, not wanting to see the sun shining or hear the birds singing, a combination that was nowhere near her current mood.

Around one in the afternoon her mom came up the stairs, lightly knocked, and entered after hearing a grunt that came from somewhere under the covers. She urged Claire to get up and go downstairs for something to eat, and Claire agreed but then did nothing. At three, her mom came in with a much more urgent tone. Claire got up and went downstairs to eat a bowl of cereal. When her mom tried to talk to her, she ignored her. She had no words. She didn't know what to say.

"Sam called," her mom said, and Claire heard the hope in her voice.

But Claire said the only thing she'd say all day, croaking slightly, "I don't want to see anyone."

The following day passed in a blur. Claire went to school, but she barely listened to her classes and needed several cues from Mr. Johns to play her part, barely feeling a thing while she did so. She didn't know it, but Mr. Johns cut class short by a few minutes for the sole purpose of checking in on her.

"Miss Hanover," he said as everyone shuffled to prepare for the final bell.

"Hi," she said.

He grabbed a chair and swung it around backward to straddle it, crossing his arms over its back, looking at her as she sat on the piano bench.

"I can't help but sense that something is wrong," he said quietly.

Claire heaved a sigh and felt the tightness in her chest, the pain swelling in her throat. She went to speak but stopped herself and ended with just a heavy sigh.

Mr. Johns, noting all of this, raised a concerned eyebrow and said, "It's okay to be upset."

Claire nodded.

"And it's okay to not want to talk."

Claire looked at him.

"But don't live in it too long. Let it out. It's toxic otherwise."

Claire looked down at her hands. The bell rang, and the chatter and noise heightened. It seemed like such a strange sound to Claire. It was happy with laughter, people with no cares, just content the day was done. Maybe going to Ron's after school or to a friend's house. It didn't fit. Mr. Johns didn't move from his spot.

Claire squeaked, "Adam . . . Adam and I . . ." She felt the tears well up in her eyes and willed them away. They clung but didn't fall, with her words now silent; otherwise, the floodgates would surely be opened.

"Ah," Mr. Johns said. They sat in silence. There were no words needed.

When Claire looked up, she said, "Thank you." She appreciated feeling that she could be in someone's presence and not have to speak her feelings.

"Anytime, Miss Hanover," he said hesitantly. They stood up, and he placed a light hand upon her shoulder. "Claire, sometimes things seem big and overwhelmingly suffocating, but these times in life are but a stepping stone in a larger picture. It isn't easy to see it that way in the moment, but remember that nothing is final. Especially in the realm of love. What will be will find its way. We just don't have the luxury of knowing what that is."

Claire looked at him and managed a nod. She threw her bag over her shoulder and made to leave.

"And, Claire," Mr. Johns said.

She turned to him in response.

"Please remember what I said. Take the time you need, but then let it out."

Claire turned and left.

As a couple days passed, Claire felt her hurt and pain toggle to anger and frustration. She was mad that Adam hadn't even tried to call after their blowout, mad at herself for wishing he had, and frustrated when the thought that she hadn't called him either crossed her mind. Then the hurt would come back when she realized that maybe he hadn't called because she was right and he didn't want to make plans with her, that her exploding at him had been a perfect out for him. Maybe he was out with the guys, having pizza and meeting someone new already. Then she would remember all their times together, the moments they shared, their deep connection, and the words he said, and she couldn't help but feel that there was no way, and that would lead her back to the tears because the heaviness that was not having him in her life anymore—not meeting up at the playground in the middle of the night, not sharing deep secrets, not feeling his hugs or the warmth of his kisses atop her head, not smelling his Cool Water scent—was unbearable.

Sam burst through her door at one point, Claire having not taken any of her calls. But Claire didn't want to talk and ignored Sam's pleas to just call him to sort it out. Sam stayed and flipped through her magazines while Claire tried to read, but they didn't speak.

The days passed, and Claire eventually made it to a place of functioning, able to chat at school and get her work done, but she was still quiet at home and didn't go out.

Sam tried many times. She was meeting up with Matt more and more lately and wanted Claire to join, but that level of social interaction was too much. She felt pangs in her heart off and on when she thought about what Adam was doing or how he was feeling. At times, this whole thing felt like absolute torture, and at others, it felt like a dream or a nightmare, and sometimes she just felt numb.

One thing that had to happen was Claire's choice for school.

"Claire?" her mom's soft voice came from the other side of the door accompanied by her light knock and the door creaking open. Claire was lying on her bed, facing the window, staring at the budding trees that were now opening, a sign of late April and the fullness of spring. "Claire, hunny." Her mom sat on the edge of her bed, and Claire felt the slight sag as she did.

"Mmm?" Claire said, not moving.

"Claire, dinner is ready. I'd like you to come down and eat," she said quietly.

"I'm not really hungry," Claire said, trying to be nonchalant.

She heard her mother sigh. "I'd like you to eat."

"I'll probably just have some cereal later."

"You've had cereal for almost every meal for two weeks."

Claire didn't respond. She was right.

"Claire." Her mother's voice sounded sad. Claire turned to look at her. "Talk to me."

Claire sighed and rolled over, continuing to lie down. Once again tears formed in her eyes, but this time, the lump in her throat stayed at bay. "I don't really know," she said quietly.

"Well, start with what happened, hunny."

"I told him that I got accepted to all three colleges. I wanted to know his thoughts. Where he was at with applying and . . . and he . . ." The lump was forming, but she swallowed, allowing silent tears to fall. "He didn't have anything to say, Mom. He practically told me to go to Arizona. He had nothing to say about applying for college himself. He just . . . I don't know. I wanted to make plans. I wanted to know that what I did meant something to him and that we were going to do whatever it took to make things work, and I guess he didn't. And if he had plans for college or not college, he wasn't sharing them with me. I just feel like things got serious, and I guess it was too serious for him. It wasn't for me. I thought we were there, and I think everything just blew up. The quiet, the overly zealous support of me going across the country, no straight answers, waiting for letters, school, senior year . . . it—" She felt her words get choked by the growing tightness.

"It became too much," her mother finished. Claire nodded. "Well, if it is bothering you this much, Claire, you should talk to him."

"I don't want to," Claire said. She wasn't even sure she knew why she didn't want to, but she thought it might be fear. Fear that the worst case scenario that was playing in her head was true. That she would learn he didn't want to make plans, didn't want to take this to the next level. That he was okay without her. Or that it would just end in another fight. She didn't think her heart could bear it.

"Well then, you need to pick yourself up and make some decisions," her mom said rather firmly, which Claire felt wasn't coming from a place of tough love but from feeling that Claire was making a poor choice in not talking to Adam and so was directing that into the next thing. "You have three schools to pick from, and you need to make your decision. They're waiting on your response."

Claire sighed. "I know."

Her mom patted her on the leg and stood up. "Claire, I love you. I hate to see you hurt. I know you don't want to, but I think you should call him." She left without giving Claire the chance to respond.

Claire rolled onto her back and wiped away the tears that had streamed down her cheeks. Prom was a few weeks away and her graduation just under two months, and yet she felt nothing about it. She was wrestling with annoyance at herself for being so emotionally drained and moved by all this, letting it get to her as much as it was. And then she reminded herself that she'd been in love with him. She was still in love with him. She was pretty sure she'd been in love with him since the day she met him. Four years ago just about. And right now she felt like she'd always be in love with him. This would never end. And even more, he was her best friend.

She threw a pillow over her face and gratefully drifted off to sleep. She never went down for dinner. Instead, she woke up in the middle of the night for a bowl of cereal and went back to bed.

Each day got better, but each day still brought a pang of pain whenever she recalled even the slightest memory or imagined calling him and what she'd say or, even more, what he'd say. But the longer she held it off, the more her mind seemed to settle in that evil space of stubbornness. He could always call her too. And the fear over why he wasn't was always there.

To get out of the house one day, she decided to walk to Babs's. It gave her a chance to feel the warmth of the sun and breathe the fresh air, and she knew that however she was feeling, Babs would offer something that no one else could. She was always filled with distractions, music, advice—everything. And Claire needed all of the above.

She knocked and let herself in simultaneously. Babs called to her from the den, and Claire went to the kitchen to put on tea and then joined her while it sat on the stove top.

"What a lovely surprise," Babs said, putting down her book and giving Claire a calculated look.

"Hey," Claire managed to say.

"Spill it," Babs said, hearing everything in that one word.

Claire sighed. "Adam and I—" She couldn't even bring herself to say the words.

"Oh, I know about that."

Claire looked at her genuinely surprised. "You—you know?"

"You think you're the only one who visits me?" Babs said with a serious expression, and Claire knew whom she meant.

"He's been here?" Claire said quietly.

"He has," Babs responded simply.

Claire opened her mouth and then closed it.

"I'll save you the questions. His business is his just like your business is yours."

Claire nodded, understanding. They sat in silence until the kettle whistled, then Claire prepared a tray and brought everything out to Babs, the both of them sitting in silence for a few more moments, grasping their teacups.

"So what about college? You got accepted to all of them," Babs said, setting down her cup.

Claire nodded.

"Where are you going?" Babs said.

Claire looked at her. "I don't know yet."

"You better figure it out, girlie. Aren't there deadlines for this stuff? You must have to tell them soon."

"Yeah, I do."

"What do you think?"

Claire shrugged.

Babs sighed. "Put aside everything. Your parents, Adam, Sam, money... everything. Just think of Claire and her ideal world. What do you *think*?"

Claire put her own cup down. "Well... I like the campuses at all three," she began and paused. "But the state one a few towns over is my least favorite. I think I would have a hard time justifying spending money on room and board if I lived so close, and I definitely want to get out of the house and see things, you know?"

"Mmhmm," Babs responded.

"And, well, that brings me to Arizona. Which would be for sure getting out of the house and seeing things, beautiful things! The idea of such a different climate and being on the other side of the country pretty much is exhilarating. But... I don't know, I also feel like it's *too* far. Like, I would want to come home and see my parents and Troy and Gwen and Sam, and, well, I don't want to have to spend money on plane tickets every time I want to go home or be stuck there because I can't afford to go home. That college, though it is a good school, is also the least known for what I'm going for."

"And Boston?"

"Boston was my reach school. The one I wasn't sure of whether or not I'd get in. And so getting in was super exciting. I love the campus, and I feel like the city life and area would be vastly different from Thompson Falls and yet only a few hours' drive away. So I would be far enough to be out on my own but close enough to go home when I wanted to. Their program is also really good, and—" Claire had a new idea come to mind, "it has a lot of opportunities for internships, as it's closest of the three to the hub of publishing houses and magazine or newspaper companies. New York is just another few hours from there, and Boston itself has a lot too."

Babs nodded. "Sounds like you may have already made up your mind. I can hear it in your voice."

Claire could hear it too. She was much more excited when talking about Boston compared to the other two, and now that she had spoken it all aloud, she realized that she'd had her heart set on Boston the entire time. Hadn't it even been the one she loved the most when visiting campuses with her dad? She'd just been so concerned with wondering what Adam would think or where her relationship would go depending on which school she picked that she hadn't really thought about picking at all. They had just been three vague schools in her mind until now, when she had put them all out in the open, giving words to each. Boston. She already felt a flutter at the idea of having picked her school.

Claire broke into a wide grin. "I think I have!"

Babs smiled too. "Good girl. Now, where is Miss Samantha going? I haven't seen her in a little while."

"She didn't get into the college she applied to. But she did get into the local community college. So she's going to go there to get her core classes done first while she works. She wants to work and save up for an apartment. She still wants to do social work, but she wasn't sure about taking time to save up, so this kind of lets her do both!"

"Now, that sounds progressive. Good for her. And I bet she'll be happy to know that you are only going to be three hours away rather than across the country."

Claire let out a laugh that was fully based on the relief of finally having made a solid decision for the first time in months. "Probably!"

They chatted some more, and Claire left feeling better than she had felt in a few weeks. There was a nagging in the back of her mind and in the pit of her heart at the idea of Adam, especially knowing that he'd gone to Babs and talked. But she knew where she was going to school. That was step one in the next phase of her life, and she had made that choice. It was uphill from here, or so she hoped.

That night, she sat down to Sunday dinner with her parents, Gwen, and Troy after a quick peek at their new house, and she announced this choice, to great excitement.

"I was hoping you'd pick that one, Claire-a-belle," her dad said while giving her a big hug. "I couldn't bear the thought of you all the way out in Arizona. But I would have supported you either way."

Her mother looked relieved as well, and their excitement only added to Claire feeling slightly better, at least better than the day before.

"Congrats, Mouse," Troy said, giving her a hug. "Proud of you."

When she called Sam after school and work the next day to come over when she had a chance so she could tell her some big news, Sam took no time in rushing over and bursting through the door.

"What's going on?!" Sam asked. "I have to watch Joey soon, but I couldn't handle not hearing whatever it is you have to tell me."

Claire beamed. "I have decided where I am going to school. Filled out the paperwork already and sent it in."

"Oh!" Sam said, sitting down. Her expression wasn't what Claire expected, and a twang of hurt hit her when she realized that Sam had probably been expecting Claire to tell her that she and Adam were back together again.

Sam, however, recovered quickly and excitedly asked, "Well?! Don't leave me hanging! Where are you going?!"

"I've decided," Claire began, "to go to—" She gave a dramatic pause. "Boston!"

"Yay!!" Sam said, throwing herself at Claire in a hug. "Oh, I'm so happy. I didn't know what I was going to do if you had said Arizona. I don't think I would have survived, like, for real."

Claire laughed. "Thanks. I'm excited and feel super relieved."

"I bet! And now we just have prom and graduation, and we're done, dude. Like, done with school. How totally bizarre."

Claire felt the balloon in her stomach deflate slightly at the mention of prom. Sam seemed to feel it.

"Still not interested in going?" she asked quietly.

Claire sighed. "I don't think so."

"Mark said he would be more than happy to go with you. Just as friends, of course," Sam said, her gum-chewing picking up.

Claire's balloon completely deflated now. She didn't want to go to prom, or even think about it. It was a reminder of everything else going on, and Claire was hoping to hold on to the euphoria of having picked a school for a little bit longer than this.

"That's nice of him, but I don't think I'll be going. At this rate, it's even too late to get a dress and everything. Prom's only a week or so away."

"Oh, come on. You can get a dress anytime. You can wear one you've already got. Nobody will know."

"I don't know. I don't want to commit. And I don't want to go with Mark." That just seemed like too much for her: going to her senior prom with an ex-boyfriend after what felt like the worst breakup imaginable. Claire also couldn't help but think about how Adam would feel if he caught wind of her running off to prom with said ex-boyfriend. She knew that shouldn't be any of her concern, but it was. And the fact that she cared should have been telling to her—another reason to get on the phone to call him—but she shoved it aside. "No. I don't want to go."

"Suit yourself." Sam sighed and stood up. "I gotta go watch Joey."

Claire looked at her, surprised. "You sound irritated."

Sam stopped at the door. "Claire." She paused before continuing. "Claire, I've seen a lot of couples. My parents before my dad split, other high school romances, your parents, Troy. One of the lovely side effects of having zero self-esteem and confidence is the high ability to observe every single detail about others. And what I saw of you and Adam compared to others? Well, you guys definitely fall in the your parents and Troy category. So I guess, to me, it just feels like letting one tough conversation get in the way is pretty stupid."

Claire looked at her in shock. This was the first time someone had said anything so bluntly. Everyone had been walking on eggshells. And now Claire suddenly felt a twang of embarrassment. "St-stupid?"

Sam's shoulders fell. "Look, Claire. I don't mean to sound harsh. I wasn't part of your argument. I don't know what was said. But I just can't believe that anything said was worth the two of you splitting. I mean, it's been a month, and you're still brooding. You're not the same. Your mom said you've been eating practically nothing, and the spark in your eyes is gone. You're functioning alright, but you aren't living. The process—grieving or whatever it is—I know takes time, and everyone is different. But, within that time span, you should see growth bit by bit, but with you, it's been a solid month of just being broken. It's your senior year. You have a lot coming up in the weeks ahead. And if you're too stubborn to call him or try and fix this, then to me, it's time you moved on. Clearly, you don't want to be with him, so why mope for so long?"

Claire's eyebrows rose, and she looked at Sam. "I do love him."

"Then fix this."

"Well, why hasn't he tried to fix it?"

"Who cares. What does that have to do with anything?"

"Um, a lot," Claire said, her voice rising. "What if this is exactly what he wants? An easy way out. Now he doesn't have to worry about making plans, or moving, or having a long-distance relationship. Maybe he's been wanting a way out for a while. That's why he was so quiet and uninvolved in any conversation that remotely came close to getting a bit more serious."

"And so you're going to just keep your mouth shut on the assumption that that's how he feels?"

"Well—"

"Even though you know how *you* feel and what *you* want. You're going to just let it all go on the whim that he is possibly happier without you."

"I—"

"And you *really* think, like *really, really* think that he is? After everything you've been through, everything you've done together, everything he's said? You *really* think that's how he feels?"

Claire had no words. Adam had always treated her with the utmost attention and love. She recalled their nights together, their ski trip, all they had given to each other. There had definitely been no indication in there that he really didn't want to be with her. Hadn't he even said he would never not want to be with her?

But his silence. His silence was deadly and, to Claire, spoke loudly.

"Claire, I can't tell you what to do. I wouldn't even if I could. But I stand by what I said. It seems pretty stupid to let him go over one argument. And if you're willing to, then you don't love him as much as I thought you did, and so you need to put on your big-girl panties and move on."

Claire felt tears well in her eyes. "What if I try and he turns me down?" she said softly. "I don't think I can take that, Sam."

Sam stared at her, comprehension dawning. She went and sat down next to Claire, who felt the tears fall silently and knew this was her true dilemma. Of course she loved him. Of course she wanted to run right over to his house and burst through his door and tell him how she really felt. That she was sorry. She had to admit that, with the stress of picking a school gone, she felt foolish at her outburst, and now she had also crossed a line into embarrassment. But his silence, his staying away, his not calling her had planted a seed of fear that had made it so that living in this in-between world—limbo—felt safer.

"Claire, I'm sorry," Sam said.

"No. No, you're right. I don't know what to do with all this."

"I wouldn't know either. It's a lot. But I would call him."

They sat in silence before Sam said, "Why don't you come to Ron's tonight? I'm meeting Matt there, and I'm pretty sure Nick and Fitz are going too. I was going to ask you later. I wasn't expecting to be here now."

"Thanks. I'll see how I feel," she said, knowing she wouldn't go, just the mention of hanging out with Nick and Fitz hitting her in the gut.

"Okay. I hope you do." Sam stood up to leave. "And, Claire, congratulations on Boston. I'm super happy for you. You going to be okay?"

Claire put a smile in her tear-streaked cheeks. "Yeah, I am. Go: you're going to be late."

Sam gave her one last look before closing the door softly and leaving.

Claire plopped back down and thought about everything Sam had just said. She did need to make a move. She had to either call him and face the music or move onward. She sighed and instead made the move to just stay put and try to forget it all.

Sam went to see Claire the Saturday after her night at Ron's to tell her all about hanging out with Matt. Claire listened politely and truly was excited to hear how much fun she'd had. Sounded like much of the gang was there too, and Claire couldn't help but feel a pang of jealousy at Sam hanging out with Nick and Jason and Fitz and Melissa without her. She also couldn't help but ask, "Was he there?" She knew Sam would know who "he" was.

"No," Sam said. "Nick said he invited him along, but he declined."

Claire nodded.

"How are you doing?" Sam asked quietly. Claire had a feeling that Sam felt bad for her harsh words from before and could assume Claire's mixed emotions about her hanging out with all of Adam's buddies, so her tone was that of timidity.

Claire shrugged. "Okay."

They sat in silence, Sam having no idea what more to say, Claire well aware of how difficult she was to be around lately.

Soon enough it was May, and all anyone could talk about at school was prom. Claire was doing her best to enjoy what was left of her senior year. She met up with Mark, Amber, and Lauren once at Ron's and was happy to catch up with Mark and even Amber. Claire assumed it had to do with the impending feelings of graduation hanging over all of their heads that they were able to have a good time. Nothing like trying to squeeze in amends for all the people whose lives you had made miserable for four years in the last month of school. Claire declined to go to Ron's with Sam and Matt and others, as it was too painful to face. She was doing okay, but hanging out with Nick, Fitz, and Jason again would only be a sour reminder of how things used to be, how things were, and what she was missing. She enjoyed hearing Sam's report back on them though, happy that things were going well for them.

Though she was remaining adamant about not going to prom, Claire still found herself at the mall one Saturday afternoon with Sam to shop for prom dresses.

"Come on, just try some on. Maybe you'll find one you like!" Sam said as she threw another dress over her arm for the fitting room.

"I told you. I'm not going," Claire said, giving Sam another to try on. "I have to work earlier that day anyway, and I'll be tired. And I just don't want to go."

"That's all you do is work. Work and school."

"Well, it makes me some money."

"I hope you take some time off so we can enjoy our summer together before you head out to school," Sam said with a hint of sadness in her tone.

"Of course," Claire responded, pushing aside her own emotions at the idea of leaving Thompson Falls behind to head to the city . . . leaving Sam.

"Mark is going with Amber and Lauren. They're going as a group, I heard. Why don't you do that? You guys can be like Charlie and his angels."

Claire laughed. "Um, no."

"But I want you there," Sam said, stopping in her tracks and looking at Claire with such an expression of sorrow that Claire was taken off guard.

"Wha-what?" Claire said.

"Claire, it's our senior prom. We've done everything together since we were small. Not going to our senior prom together is going to be totally wrong!"

Claire sighed. She did feel guilty about missing it. "I know. But I just think . . . I just don't feel like it."

"Can we at least get you a dress, and maybe you'll feel like it when it's here?"

"You'll have Logan! And Mark and his crew and everyone else too. You'll all have a blast." Logan had asked Sam, and she had agreed to go as friends. Matt was older, and Sam felt a little nervous about asking him to go, thinking he would feel too old to be going to a high school prom. When she told him about going with Logan, however, he seemed bummed out, and when Sam explained to him how she felt, he told her that he'd have been more than willing to hang out with a bunch of high school kids for the night if it meant getting to dance with her, which, of course, made Sam squeal and swoon. So, though she couldn't go back on her word with Logan, she made it very clear to him that they were going as friends and was pretty certain that Nick, Matt, and Fitz were now scheming on sneaking in and somehow crashing prom.

"But I don't care about all them. I care about having you there," Sam said.

Claire heaved a sigh. "I'll look for a dress. But I make zero promises."

"I can deal with that! Oh my god, yes! I can deal with that," Sam squealed.

Claire tried on some dresses to humor Sam, but none stood out. In the end, Sam landed on a form-fitting red satin dress with spaghetti straps and diamond studs here and there. It was stunning, and Claire absolutely loved her in it.

"Okay, we still have time to get you a dress. We'll go again and find you something!" Sam said as they walked out of the mall into the bright sun of late spring, a hint of summer in the air.

Going again translated to being at the mall the day of prom after Claire got out of work, with only hours to spare, Claire trying on dress after dress and not feeling a single one. Sam had already gotten her hair done at the salon there. Claire had resolved to maybe make an appearance just to make Sam happy, which Sam took to heart, giving Claire the feeling that she couldn't back out and disappoint her. She had already done so by not getting her hair and makeup done with her, claiming she would just do it at home should she decide to go.

After what felt like a hundred dresses, Claire could tell her heart just wasn't in it. She had a feeling her subconscious was just hating everything as an escape plan for tonight. No dress equaled no prom.

"Claire, this one is beautiful!" Sam practically shouted. It was a periwinkle-blue sweetheart-neckline dress with a taffeta bottom.

"I look like a cupcake," Claire said.

"You look like Cinderella!" Sam said. "You have to get it!"

"I don't know," Claire said, sashaying back and forth to see how it moved. "It's too big for me, I think. And I did the Cinderella look once already." Her heart broke a little at the memory of it.

"But it's the last one in the pile! It's by far the best one yet! You have to get it!"

"I—"

"Prom is tonight! Come on."

Claire felt a flush wash over her. Warm and clammy, she needed to get out of the dress. She needed air. "No, I—I don't like it."

"Claire—"

"Sam, no," Claire burst out. "I don't like it. I don't want to go to prom. I don't want to dance and have fun. I don't want any of this!"

Sam stared.

Claire felt hot tears prickle her eyes, and she wasn't even sure why. "I just want to go home." This was too much. She'd been doing so well, but it was too much. "I just want to go home."

Sam nodded and helped Claire out of the dress, leaving empty-handed. Sam stopped to use the pay phone quickly on the way out of the mall, Claire paying no attention, only having the one act of getting in the car on her mind.

They rode in silence to Sam's, where Claire dropped her off. They exchanged no words. Claire felt bad after, thinking that she probably should have said something along the lines of "have fun" or maybe offer to go over and take pictures when Logan showed up. She just couldn't.

Pulling into her driveway, she felt the need to just sit in her car for a while and forget that the rest of her senior class was getting ready for a magical night—that there would be pictures of tonight forever cherished by her classmates, which wouldn't have Claire Hanover in any of them. She couldn't help but feel a mixture of aching sadness and anger at the whole thing. She was angry at herself for her outburst and angry at still not having the mental ability to just put this behind her to enjoy prom, to enjoy anything. She groaned and got out of the car.

Walking inside, she went to the kitchen to grab whatever she could find for junk food, laying it all out on the table: ice cream, Reese's Pieces, DunkAroos, Doritos—all of it. Claire was just about to dig into the ice cream, throwing some chocolate syrup and a huge helping of whipped cream atop, when her mom walked into the kitchen.

"Claire! You're home!" she said, a little breathless as though she had jogged across the house to greet her. "How did finding a dress go?"

"It didn't," she grunted into her ice cream.

"Oh. Well, um." Her mother looked anxious.

"What's wrong?" Claire questioned her, taking another big bite.

"Well, are you going to sit here all night? Or are you going to go get ready for prom?"

Claire raised an eyebrow. "I told you, I didn't find a dress. I'm not going. Hence the smorgasbord of food here."

"Oh," her mom said, wringing her hands.

"Mom, what's with you?"

"There's something upstairs for you. I think you should go see," her mom said.

Claire raised both eyebrows this time. Did her mom get her a pity gift or something? "Okay. I'll go up as soon as I'm done eating. Thank you."

"I think you should go up now."

Claire gave her a quizzical look. "I just got ice cream. It'll melt."

"Oh, for goodness sake, Claire, go see what is in your room." Her mother's tone sounded frantic. "Please."

"Okay, okay," Claire said irritably, though at this point a little curious. She was grateful for whatever her mom had decided to give her but really just wanted to sit in her misery and eat her way through all the scrumptious calories, burying her emotions in every bite. She gave her mom one last glance before heading upstairs. She sighed, opening her door and automatically looking to her bed to see what was there waiting for her.

There was nothing. Movement by her bookshelf made her jump and then froze her in her tracks. Warm gray eyes looked at her with concern. A hand brushed through thick, center-split brown hair. The only thing missing was the award winning smile.

Adam.

Claire just stared, almost unsure if she was actually seeing him standing there or if she'd finally cracked, creating the mirage of him.

"Hey," Adam said. There was no sheepish gesture, no smirk. What there was was a solemn tone, clearly nervous of how Claire would take him being there.

"What are you doing here?" Claire said, not knowing what else to say. Seeing him brought forward so many emotions that she wasn't prepared to feel, and her gut instinct was to run, or in this case, push him right away.

"I'm sorry for surprising you, but I wanted . . . I needed to talk to you."

"About what?" Claire felt her brain working so hard that simple words were all she could muster, and at the same time, she had no idea what her brain was working hard to do.

Adam ran his hand through his hair once more and sighed. "I, um . . . God, I didn't think this was going to be so hard . . . I wanted to explain myself, Claire. I wanted to explain what happened. I owe you an explanation."

Hearing him say her name was jarring, and she paused there, which led to a moment of silence passing between them before she registered the rest of what he said. So he wanted to explain why he didn't want to make plans with her and why they had broken up. She didn't really want an explanation; she didn't want to revisit any of that hurt. This was starting to sound exactly like the fear she had relayed to Sam. He was here to confirm the exact thing that had broken her for the past month and then some.

Her brain began to work quicker in an effort to protect her heart. "An explanation? I don't really want to hear an explanation as to why all this went the way it did. I just want to leave it there and figure out how I'm supposed to move on, okay?"

Adam sighed. "No. I mean—"

"I don't think this is a good idea. I think you should go," Claire said.

"Claire, please. Just hear me out."

"No. I don't want to, Adam." She hoped he would find the sound of his name just as jarring. "I've been . . . this has been . . ." She felt tears begin to burn, and her momentum died as quickly as it had come.

"Claire, please."

Claire met his eyes and saw the pain she felt reflected in them. She folded her arms and kept quiet, a nonverbal sign for him to take his moment.

Adam walked toward her, though he stopped a few paces away still. His jaw set, he resolved to get out what he had come to say. If she declined him after that, he could at least say he tried.

"Claire, I made a mistake," he started. "I—I just . . ." He sighed and turned away from her, running a hand through his hair. He hadn't thought the sight of her was going to make this so hard. He could see the pain he had caused, and his anxiety was boiling at the fear of what would happen at the close of this conversation—what she would say. He blew a heavy breath of air and turned back to her. "Claire, I think I should start by saying you are the single most amazing person I have ever met. You are smart, talented, empathetic, strong-willed, and, of course, beautiful. Inside and out. From the moment we shared a dance to our first kiss and every moment since then, I have found myself often looking at you in awe and wondering how on earth a girl like you ended up with me. For a while, I just counted my blessings every night, and it made me the happiest guy on earth. And then—and then the conversation around college and where we were going started, and, Claire . . . I panicked."

Claire raised an eyebrow, not quite understanding.

"I suddenly started to feel that I wasn't sure if I would even get into a good college. My grades have always been okay, but I never really felt like I was good at the whole school thing. I took a year off because I wanted to make money and save up for school, but I also did it because I was scared, Claire. I was scared I wouldn't get in, that I wouldn't make it. I figured a year would give me some time, some money, some experience, and some maturity. When you started talking college, I realized that maybe I had ruined my chances because now I was a year out of school and maybe colleges wouldn't like that. I was scared, and now I had an even bigger reason to be scared."

"And what would that be?" Claire asked, her arms still crossed, listening but feeling the flutter in her stomach and the nausea of anxiety, still unsure of where he was going with this.

"You."

"Me? I scared you? How nice of me," Claire said, not able to help the snarky tone.

"Yes. You did," Adam said firmly to get her attention. "But it wasn't your fault. Don't you see, Claire? Here you were, this brilliant mind, looking to go to these fabulous schools, and here I was, a year out, unsure of what I could even do. I suddenly became very aware that I could never amount to the college guys that you were probably going to meet. Never amount to the kind of guy you deserved. I felt that the least I could do was support any and all thoughts you had so that you would go and live your life to its fullest, so that you could never grow to resent me or feel that you had been held back. That thought, of course, made me think that you would do just that: probably meet that smart college guy and forget about me and Thompson Falls altogether. So I started to distance myself, I guess. I didn't even realize I was. And I'm—Claire, I'm sorry. I should've just talked to you. I should have told you how I was feeling because the truth is . . . I didn't want you to go to Arizona, but I also didn't want to stop you. What I should have said was that I'd do anything in my power to figure out what we could do regardless of where you went. But I was lost in my own fears. In my own insecurities. In having any part in your decision. I love you, Claire. Forever. I want to make plans with you. I never want to be without you. We can make anything work. With all my heart I love you. To the moon, to the stars. This has been absolute hell."

"You got that right," Claire piped in, smiling through the tears that had formed and were falling freely as she listened to Adam's words and saw his own gloss over.

He chuckled. "And I just want it to end."

Claire wiped tears off her cheeks. "Me too, but I owe you some words too." Tears continuously fell at this point, and she didn't even try to stop them. "I'm sorry. I'm sorry if I ever made you feel that you weren't good enough for me."

"You didn't, Claire. It was my own—"

"Just, let me finish," she said. "What I should say is, I'm sorry for having never told you before just how much you inspire *me*."

He raised his eyebrows in surprise.

"Adam, I don't care that maybe you need a little extra time to finish a math problem or didn't get straight As in school. You'll probably never use it anyway. But watching you play the drums, control the entire light and tech room at school, build your own computer, fix your own car, cook! I mean, goodness, you have more skills than I could ever dream of. You took on a senior in a fist fight for the dignity of a girl you weren't even dating. You lip-synced to a boy band in front of a plethora of people just for me. You're an impeccable friend to Nick and Fitz and Jason. You're thoughtful and deep thinking. You welcomed Babs right into your heart. You're badass talented on the slopes and have this high energy and zest for life, like skiing off rooftops and running from cops. I think I told you on the playground that first night we shared that you were this unique combination of a nerd meets a sweetie meets a bad boy, and I've never met anyone like you. That still stands and always will. So don't *you* see? You are the kind of person I want to amount to, the kind of person *I* want to be, Adam. That's why you can get into a good college. That's why I pushed and asked and prodded. That's why I have faith that Adam Miller can do whatever he puts *his* mind to. Because he *can* move mountains with the best of them. And . . . that's why I'm the luckiest girl who was in awe every day of the guy she could call hers."

Adam wiped his eyes, looking down, beyond touched by what she said. Having no words, he switched gears. "I, um . . . I heard through the grapevine that you picked Boston."

Claire nodded.

He reached into his pocket. "I may have taken your advice, however wrong I thought you were."

Claire looked at him quizzically.

"You did always believe in me, Claire, and though I didn't, I listened for once." He pulled out of his pocket a folded-up piece of paper.

"Here." He held it out to her.

She took it tentatively, not knowing what was going on. She opened it and saw that it was a letter addressed to a Mr. Adam Miller. It was an acceptance letter. It was an acceptance letter to Wentworth. Wentworth Institute of Technology, which was right in . . .

"Boston? You're—you're going to Boston?" Claire looked at him in amazement.

"I finally heard back a couple weeks ago. I already sent in my reply."

"You realize this is like ten minutes from me," Claire said.

Adam grinned. "I thought as much. I hope you don't mind."

Claire was in a state of euphoric shock. She finally managed to say, "Mind? Mind?! Oh my god!!" and threw herself at him, Adam laughing and swinging her around. Her heart was so full, she felt it could burst. She wanted to laugh and cry and kiss him and shout and every single possible thing she could do all at once. She wanted to yell from the rooftops. She felt tears cascade down her face, and when he pulled away, she saw his own. He grasped her face in his hands and kissed her so passionately, and Claire welcomed it with every part of her being. Finally. The number of times they had kissed was unknown, but Claire did know that none before this one had ever felt so good. Her heart was pounding out of her chest. The feel of him, his scent, his embrace, his warmth.

When they calmed, he placed his forehead to hers like they'd done so many times before, and Claire finally got to see that broad smile up close. It was enough to bring fresh tears to her eyes. Oh, how she'd missed that smile. And oh, how she never wanted to ever lose it again.

"So what's this I hear about you not going to prom?" Adam asked.

"Well, I was kind of in a state of distraught heartbreak."

A flash of guilt crossed Adam's face but was quickly replaced with a loving smile. He took Claire's hands in his and said, "Well. Would you be my date?"

Claire laughed. "What? You're not even allowed in without a signed form, and I don't have a dress or anything."

"Nick, Fitz, and Matt are taking care of the first part, and I have taken care of the second."

Claire cocked an eyebrow very high this time. "What do you mean?" she asked slowly.

Adam gestured to the door, and he led her downstairs, through the kitchen and to the living room, where Claire was shocked to see Babs sitting with her mom, sharing a pot of tea.

"Hi, Babs," she said uncertainly, looking at Adam's shitty grin. "Okay, what's going on?"

"I take it everything went well?" Babs said.

"Well?" Claire questioned but realized that Babs wasn't talking to her but to Adam.

"It did." He smiled. "Thanks for the advice."

"Okay, what's going on? For real," Claire said, though a small smile couldn't help but escape.

"Babs here was the reason I finally manned up to come talk to you. She convinced me to swallow my fear and to stop being a—what was it?"

"I think I just said an idiot," Babs returned.

Claire chuckled. "Well, thank you. I'm glad you did. But that doesn't really explain why . . ." She trailed off, not wanting to sound rude, but it didn't explain why Babs was sitting in her living room and what that had to do with prom.

"Well," Adam piped in, knowing Claire's question, "though I was terrified, I had faith and hope that if I could get out what I needed to say, we could talk and patch things up. To be honest, I don't know what I would have done if we didn't. I've been miserable, Claire. Anyway, I knew prom was tonight and heard you weren't going from Nick, and, well, I talked to Babs and your mom and came up with a plan. Sam was to try and take you shopping one more time, and when it was a no-go, she called your mom from the mall for plan B, which we already had in place: Babs. Your mom got her, and she hid in your dad's office while I went upstairs to your room."

Though this sounded fascinating, Claire was still unclear of what Babs's role was.

"Babs figured you were about the same size she was, and so our plan B was—"

Babs stood up and went to Claire's dad's chair, where she now saw a pile of what looked like trash bags on hangers. "I wore this one to my own senior prom," she said, holding up a peach-colored strapless dress with white petticoats that put Claire in mind of Lorraine's "Enchantment Under the Sea" dress in *Back to the Future*.

"This one I wore for my college graduation." She held up a teal dress with black polka dots. It had cap sleeves and was form fitting, the skirt ending around mid-calf.

"And I wore this one to my bridal shower." A purple dress with ruffled tulle and thin spaghetti straps.

Claire stared on in awe, her old soul brimming with excitement. "Really? You'd let me borrow one of these?"

"Of course! What am I going to do with them? Dance in my living room in my slippers? I am more than happy to see them step out for a night of dancing on the arm of a handsome man again."

Claire felt her eyes watering again. The entirety of this evening was beyond a fairy tale, Adam her Prince Charming and Babs her fairy godmother.

"Go try them on, hunny!" her mom chimed in. "Prom just got started. If you hurry, you won't lose much time."

Claire looked to Adam and then to Babs and her mom. "Thank you," was all she managed to say.

Claire ran up the stairs two at a time. Trying each dress on, she landed on the peach dress, the color reminding her of her own light-pink dress from her first prom when she and Adam danced under the stars, and the world was righted while in his arms. She curled her hair as quickly as she could, pinned up one side, and did her makeup. She put on a pair of black heels she had and flew downstairs to find Adam in a handsome brownish-gray suit.

"Don't you look dapper," Claire said, enjoying the retro vibes this was all giving off.

"Thanks. I borrowed it from my dad. Didn't have time to rent a tux."

"I like this even better," Claire said.

"Oh my goodness, you two just brought me right back to my prime," Babs said as they entered the living room. "Boy, did I know how to have fun with the best of them."

They took photos, and much like Cinderella's rush to the ball, they were off.

The school's music was blaring as they pulled in. Adam's plan of sneaking in entailed entering the school grounds, mingling briefly with students who were out there for some fresh air, Claire being a good sign that they were allowed to be there, until Nick and Fitz opened the doors when no teachers were near for them to nonchalantly go inside, not that Claire had to sneak in, but it was fun anyway. They quickly found Sam, who screamed so loud that Claire thought for sure it'd draw attention even over the loud music. Sam immediately went into questioning everything that had transpired and loving her "totally killer" dress. Claire explained as best she could over the noise but didn't really care anyway. All that mattered was that Adam was here, by her side, holding her hand. He was hers and she his and they were at prom and Claire and Sam could dance the night away for the last time as A. Thompson High students.

And when the night was wearing close to its end, Adam led Claire outside and laced his arms around her as they swayed on the spot.

"I can't tell you how unbelievable this night is," Adam said. "It feels like a dream."

"I agree," Claire said, arms around his shoulders.

"You look stunning, by the way. The 1950s look good on you."

"Why, thank you." Claire smiled.

Adam looked her over as though he were registering every strand of hair that was now falling loosely and every freckle. "Claire. I don't think I've ever felt the way I did these past weeks. It was misery. I'm now convinced that hell would just be an eternity without you."

"That bad, huh?"

"I was listening to country music," he replied.

"Oh God." Claire chuckled. "I ate nothing but cereal and slept more than the cat."

Adam laughed. "Can we promise to never do this to us again?"

"You have my word," Claire said.

Adam swung her around and dipped her. "I love you, Claire Hanover."

"I love you more, Adam Miller."

"Claire Hanover," Principal Lewis's voice rang out over the gym.

As Claire walked up the steps to the stage, screams and catcalls came from a section of the bleachers, a loud "Bohemian!" sounded above it all, and Claire was quite sure she heard "Go Mouse!" too. She looked down to the floor where her parents were sitting with Babs, Troy, Gwen, and Adam. She saw his smiling face and gave him a wink. Shaking Mr. Lewis's hand, she paused for a photo and took her diploma, walking the rest of the distance and taking her seat once more. Her heart was thumping, and she turned to look at Sam, who was in the row behind her, giving her a thumbs up, exchanging equally large grins. When Sam's turn came, Claire yelled the loudest, and when it was time to all stand, face the audience, and turn their tassels, Claire couldn't help but feel tears well in her eyes as she saw the faces of Amber, Mark, Chris, Lauren, Mike, Sarah, Trina . . . and so many others. How bittersweet. How crazy. How absolutely exciting. They had made it. Ahead of her she had a summer of fun, a wedding, leaving home, college in the city, and above all, doing it all with Adam. If it was possible to die of a heart swelled with happiness, Claire would have dropped right there.

"I present to you the class of 1999!" The crowd erupted, hats flew, and Claire and Sam ran to each other, grasping in a tight embrace.

"We did it! Holy shit, we did it. How did we get here? How are we graduates?!" Sam shouted.

"I have no freaking idea!" Claire laughed.

They pulled apart and did their signature five-step handshake.

"Friends till the end?" Sam said.

"Best friends," Claire responded.

Acknowledgments

I want to give a special thanks to all the members of the Totally '90s Research Project group who helped paint a well-rounded picture of life as a teen in the 1990s! Your fun answers, banter, and memories were a great help and influence to this 90s kid.

No writer would get anywhere without the support and motivation of others. Thank you, Heather Doran, for walking through this journey with me. Your thoughts, critiques, and corrections were always so helpful, and above all, your clear love for my work gave me the drive to keep going. You're an amazing friend and never cease to bring me such love and joy. Katie Caron, thank you for your love and support of my writing. You are the best sounding board, and I appreciate you always being willing to read my work even if reading maybe isn't necessarily your go-to. Your squeal of excitement at the sight of my finished product was the kind of shared enthusiasm only a sister could have. I love you. And thank you, Queen Bee Book Club, for being such a positive force, for encouraging me to continue my writing, and for always being willing to read and review.

And finally, to my Adam. The love of my life. The first three years of our marriage were quite the ride. Our marriage training wheels were ripped right off, and we jumped into the vows of sickness and health, richer or poorer, forever and always. Your strength and determination to battle the horrific villain of cancer is the most heroic thing I have ever witnessed. Your never-ending love for me and your ability to still flash your handsome smile my way, even on the hardest of days, is beyond words. Thank you for your constant support of my every whim. I owe this entire piece to you. I love you.

Made in the USA
Middletown, DE
06 August 2023